MW00831615

# THE
# DARK
# MIRROR

# THE
# DARK
# MIRROR

The Fifth Book in the
Bone Season Series

## SAMANTHA SHANNON

BLOOMSBURY PUBLISHING

NEW YORK · LONDON · OXFORD · NEW DELHI · SYDNEY

BLOOMSBURY PUBLISHING
Bloomsbury Publishing Inc.
1385 Broadway, New York, NY 10018, USA

BLOOMSBURY, BLOOMSBURY PUBLISHING, and the Diana logo are trademarks of
Bloomsbury Publishing Plc

First published in 2025 in Great Britain
First published in the United States 2025

Copyright © Samantha Shannon-Jones, 2025
Illustrations and maps © Emily Faccini, 2025

This is a work of fiction. Names and characters are the product of the author's imagination and
any resemblance to actual persons, living or dead, is entirely coincidental.

All rights reserved. No part of this publication may be: i) reproduced or transmitted in
any form, electronic or mechanical, including photocopying, recording or by means of
any information storage or retrieval system without prior permission in writing from the
publishers; or ii) used or reproduced in any way for the training, development or operation
of artificial intelligence (AI) technologies, including generative AI technologies.
The rights holders expressly reserve this publication from the text and data mining
exception as per Article 4(3) of the Digital Single Market Directive (EU) 2019/790

ISBN: HB: 978-1-63973-396-5; SIGNED EDITION: 978-1-63973-705-5;
BARNES & NOBLE SIGNED EDITION: 978-1-63973-697-3; BAM SIGNED EDITION: 978-1-63973-698-0;
INDIGO SIGNED EDITION: 978-1-63973-699-7; EBOOK: 978-1-63973-484-9

Library of Congress Cataloging-in-Publication Data is available.

2 4 6 8 10 9 7 5 3 1

Typeset by Integra Software Services Pvt. Ltd.
Printed and bound in the U.S.A.

To find out more about our authors and books visit www.bloomsbury.com
and sign up for our newsletters.

Bloomsbury books may be purchased for business or promotional use.
For information on bulk purchases please contact Macmillan Corporate and
Premium Sales Department at specialmarkets@macmillan.com.

*For those who feel adrift*

# Author's Note

In 2023, I made the decision to revise the first four books in the Bone Season series, creating the Author's Preferred Texts. While the changes haven't affected the overarching plot, there are some minor details in *The Dark Mirror* that may seem new or different if you haven't read the revisions. To make sure you can jump straight back into the story, I've listed these changes at www.samanthashannon.co.uk/more/revision-guide.

I hope you enjoy Paige's fifth adventure.

**Samantha Shannon, February 2025**

*Are mortal beings strong enough to ease the burden of your pain?*

– AESCHYLUS, *PROMETHEUS BOUND*,
TRANS. IAN JOHNSTON

# Contents

ITALY

Venice

Bologna

Orvieto

CORSICA

Rome

ADRIATIC SEA

Ischia    Naples    Matera

Capri

TYRRHENIAN SEA

SARDINIA

MEDITERRANEAN SEA

SICILY

TUNISIA

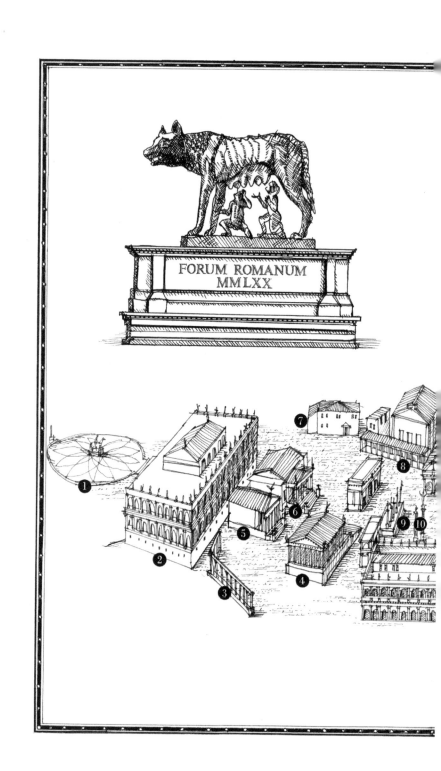

FORUM ROMANUM
MMLXX

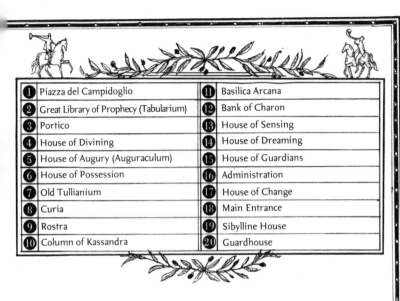

| | | | |
|---|---|---|---|
| ❶ | Piazza del Campidoglio | ⓫ | Basilica Arcana |
| ❷ | Great Library of Prophecy (Tabularium) | ⓬ | Bank of Charon |
| ❸ | Portico | ⓭ | House of Sensing |
| ❹ | House of Divining | ⓮ | House of Dreaming |
| ❺ | House of Augury (Auguraculum) | ⓯ | House of Guardians |
| ❻ | House of Possession | ⓰ | Administration |
| ❼ | Old Tullianum | ⓱ | House of Change |
| ❽ | Curia | ⓲ | Main Entrance |
| ❾ | Rostra | ⓳ | Sibylline House |
| ❿ | Column of Kassandra | ⓴ | Guardhouse |

PROPOSAL BY GIOSUÈ BARRACO, SAPIENZA UNIVERSITY OF ROME – TO BE COMPLETED BY 2070

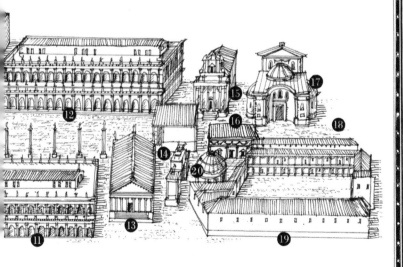

PART ONE

# UNDER THE HARROW

**Aduantas:** [Irish, noun] A feeling of fear or
solitude, brought on by unfamiliar surroundings.

I

# FORGOTTEN

Once, while it rained outside the den and the lamps burned low in Seven Dials, Nick had told me about a certain prison in Stockholm. Rosenkammaren, it was called – the Rose Chamber, the name a torture of its own. No roses could have grown down there, where sunlight never reached. Its prisoners were hung in chains and left to stand in icy water.

The night Nick found his sister dead in the forest, and devoted himself to destroying the anchor, he accepted the possibility that he could end up in that place. Sometimes he woke in a cold sweat, wondering if the æther had already condemned him to the Rose Chamber.

I've often wondered if my choices shaped my life, or if it was drawn before I existed, spun out for me like thread from a spindle. I've wondered if any of us have a fate; if the pattern and flow of time is ordained, or if we can force it to carve a new path. All voyants reckon with the idea. Some among us glimpse the future, and we like to believe that means we can stop it, but I suspect that degree of control is an illusion, and we have no more power than amaurotics. All we can hope for is a warning. A glimpse of time before it comes.

So we trust in the æther, or we try. As someone I love told me once, trust is never being sure if you should trust at all.

———

My dreamscape had changed. Gone was the field of flowers that had grown there since I was a child.

Now my safe place was a room in Paris, rendered skeletal.

There was the bed, the sheets turned down, lamps on either side. Some way from it, I lay in shadow. White flowers reached between the floorboards – my poppy anemones, still trying to grow, their petals bleached and translucent. Snow gathered around me, like dust on something left forgotten.

Beyond the distant windows, all I could make out was darkness. Night cupped the safe house in its hands. That was normal for a dreamscape; the pallor on its walls was not. Time and again I tried to rise, but an unseen weight pinned me in place, keeping me on the floor.

It might be for the best. Part of me wanted to get to the bed – surely it was soft and warm – but I sensed it would carry me farther away than I could stand to go. It would throw me to a world of teeth that wanted to rip me to shreds. As I slipped back into oblivion, I saw the blood that stained my spirit. Reph blood, human blood, all over my hands.

I slept for hours or weeks or years. Between my periods of absence, I thought I strayed towards the bed – thought I felt the sun, heard a voice – but I always ended up back on the floor, as if I had never moved. The flowers wove around my limbs, as if to hold and comfort me.

And then I stopped falling asleep. Now I was aware and cold, and I realised I had to get to the bed. My silver cord pulled me that way – a weak tug I had rarely felt when I was in my own dreamscape.

When I moved, the white flowers loosened their hold. I turned on to my front and crawled.

Another light trailed in my wake, faint and unresisting.

It was as if my limbs were stone. Each inch I gained left me exhausted, and the closer to the bed I moved, the worse my creeping fear that this was the wrong choice. The lamps had seemed dim and comforting from my place in the deep shadows, but now, as I approached, they shone too bright. No one could fall asleep with those lights flanking their bed. I feared what they might yet reveal, because something was different out there. I could sense it.

I grasped the sheets and hauled myself up. My arms gave way, and I crumpled back to the floor, almost surrendering. *You have risen from the ashes before,* the flowers said in a voice I remembered, a voice I both cherished and feared. And then I climbed, and I was there, curling up tight. *The only way to survive is to believe you always will.*

---

When I woke, I was on another bed. My head rested on a pillow, my hand on my ribs. I lay heavy and woollen for what felt like hours, my breathing slow.

This was not a dreamscape. No shadow pooled at its edges. Red sunlight passed through sheer curtains and glinted off a television on the wall. I sat up, rubbing coarse sleep from my eyes.

The room where I found myself was pristine, except for the unmade sheets on its twin beds. Beside a table, a chair was upholstered in beige leather, a coat thrown over its back. I braced myself with my good hand, listening to the quiet. A door slammed in the distance.

'Arcturus,' I said, unnerved.

No answer. I reached for the golden cord, but felt nothing. Not even a flicker of emotion in return.

*Are you there?*

Something was off about the room. The smoothness of the wooden floor, the straight clean lines of the furniture, the starched bedsheets – all of it spoke of regulation. This was a hotel – and no cheap dosshouse, at that – but it wasn't Anchotel, the only chain in Scion. Those rooms had scarlet runners and anchors stitched in gold on the pillows.

The last thing I recalled was the masquerade in Paris. Léandre in his lion mask, Le Vieux Orphelin at his side. My private conversation with Inquisitor Ménard. After that meeting, there was only fog, and now I was in a hotel with a headache. Even for me, this was bizarre.

'Arcturus,' I said again.

And then, with a sickening jolt, it came back to me.

Arcturus had returned to Nashira. He had been using me for information, all that time.

He was nowhere to be seen or sensed, which seemed to confirm the things I remembered. I forced myself to go over our confrontation in Paris. He intended to betray the clairvoyant syndicates to Scion. I had acted quickly to protect the Mime Order, but for all I knew, he might have beaten me to my allies. I might be the only survivor of a failed revolution.

Was that why I was here, alone?

With considerable effort, I roused my gift and focused on the æther, pain lancing my temples. There were thousands of dreamscapes in the vicinity, but none that I recognised. My legs shook as I rose, grasping the bedpost for support. Instead of my usual nightshirt, I was dressed in drawstring shorts and a white shirt with cap sleeves. My arms looked slimmer than before, the muscle less defined. How long had I been here?

Now my heart was pounding, my skin clammy. I walked to the window, my head swimming. The room overlooked a long street, where streetlamps were coming alive – and one glimpse of those streetlamps rocked the foundations of my world.

Their glow was amber.

Not blue.

All Scion citadels had blue streetlamps, supposedly to calm the population. Unless this was a city in Spain or Portugal, which had only recently fallen to the anchor, then this was not Scion. Somehow, I was in the free world.

The realisation broke me from my stupor. I stumbled to another door, which led to a bathroom, and tapped a pad to turn the lights on, revealing my startled reflection in the mirror.

I had dyed my hair for the masquerade. It was still brown, though a touch darker than I remembered. A fresh bruise stained my left cheekbone. I tasted a powdery bitterness, as if I had eaten flour. My left wrist, always troublesome, was throbbing. When I looked at it, I saw pink stripes – marks that could only have been left by fingers.

I rushed to the door, turned the deadbolt, and jammed one of the chairs under the handle.

Impaired recollection, nausea, unusual taste. Someone had been giving me white aster – an ethereal drug that caused amnesia – to meddle with my sense of time. There was no other logical explanation for why I hadn't a bull's notion of where I was or how I had got here.

This had to be something to do with the Domino Programme, the espionage network I had been working for in Paris. They used white aster on agents who wanted to leave, to erase their memory of its existence – but Ducos had told me I was classified as an associate, that I could keep my memories. I trusted her enough to think she would have kept her word.

It had been twelve years since I was last in the free world. I scoured the room for clues, finding no hint as to my location. When I saw a white mug on the table, I picked it up and turned it, revealing a smeared crescent of lipstick on its rim, a rich cherry I recognised.

Eléonore Cordier wore it.

Cordier had been the medical officer for my sub-network, Mannequin. Last I had seen her, she had drained the excess fluid off my lung, to give me some relief from the pneumonia that had plagued me for weeks. After that, she had vanished, apparently detained by Scion.

I soon found other traces of her. A dress I had seen her wearing in Paris. A comb with black hair in its teeth. A bottle of perfume – a blend of cypress and wild geranium, the label written in French.

Why I was sharing a room with her, I wasn't sure. But this might be my only chance to get away. I would have to go with my gut, and my gut was telling me to run.

In the bathroom, I forced myself to run the tap and splash my face with icy water. It shocked away the listless haze, even if it also left me shuddering. Next, I pulled open the wardrobe, finding three coats with a safe behind them. No luck with the master code that had sometimes worked in London, and trying to bounce it might draw attention.

There was a suitcase under the bed. I took out a cream jersey with a roll neck and yanked it over the shirt. A pair of dark twilled trousers were a perfect fit. So were the hiking boots in the wardrobe, and the woollen hat I placed over my hair. Finally, I swung on a fleece-lined jacket.

The fact that I had my own clothes was jarring. I seemed clean and fed, even if I had shed a little weight, but the bruises told a different story.

Supplies were my next concern. I took a canvas bag from the wardrobe, stuffed it with snacks and drinks from the minibar, and tightened the straps around my shoulders. No sign of a phone. Not that I would have been able to call anyone – all of my human allies used burners, and the Ranthen had never warmed to human technology. I searched the coats in the wardrobe and found a single banknote and a lighter, both of which I pocketed.

There were no weapons. I would have to rely on my wits. They had saved me before.

*Acting the part is half the trick, darling,* Jaxon had advised me once. *Behave as if you belong, and see who dares to question you.*

Jaxon might be a soulless bastard, but I could still use his lessons. I slipped out of the room, into a dark corridor, and walked until I saw an elevator. As I strode towards it, a display above the doors lit up. No sooner had I swerved into another corridor than the elevator pinged open and three people – two amaurotics, one voyant – had marched from inside.

'—room number did she say it was?'

'Fifteen.'

'Good. We do this carefully.' The voices sounded American. I flattened myself into a doorway. 'Scott, you get the personal effects. Torres, are you certain you don't need backup?'

'Not if she's sedated.'

'What if she isn't?'

'Guess we'll find out.'

Their footsteps were quiet. As soon as they were out of earshot, I ran to the elevator. Steeling my nerves, I hit the key for the ground floor and waited, sweat prickling under my shirt.

The elevator glided down. As soon as the doors opened, I knew I had made my first mistake of the evening.

A woman stood behind an illuminated desk. Twelve other people were stationed in the foyer, mostly built like houses. As I froze, the nearest saw me, his expression stiffening. I pounded the key for the highest floor.

'Ms Mahoney,' the stranger barked, running at me. 'Wait a moment—' The doors closed just in time, muffling the next command: 'Take the stairs! Do not let her leave!'

*What in the Scion Republic of Fuck is happening?*

I was not going anywhere with a group of armed strangers. When the elevator stopped, I rushed past an elderly woman and went for the nearest window, only for it to stick on a safety latch. Gritting my teeth, I detached a fire extinguisher from its bracket and punched it through the glass.

By the time my pursuers caught up, I was inching along a ledge, clinging to whatever fingerholds I could find. My hands were already starting to hurt, but if I could just get to the roof ...

A click stopped me dead. I locked eyes with the man from the foyer, now aiming a pistol at me from the window. He had olive skin and black hair, slicked back from his well-boned face.

'Easy,' he said. 'Stay where you are.' He reached into his jacket. 'Are you Paige Eva Mahoney?'

'Who's asking?'

'Steve Mun. Atlantic Intelligence Bureau.' He showed me a badge that probably meant something to someone, somewhere. 'I have orders to get you to safety, out of reach of Inquisitor Weaver.'

'I'm out of his reach now. And it might help me feel a touch safer if you lowered your gun, Steve.'

People on the street were staring up at us, keeping away from the broken glass. A woman held a silver phone up. Mun glanced at the crowd, his jaw clenching.

'All right.' He holstered the pistol. 'Take my hand, and we can talk.'

He held it out, showing a starched white cuff.

I did not believe for one moment that Steve Mun wanted a polite conversation. Craning my neck, I looked down the street, searching for a way out. I couldn't use my gift on him without losing control of my body, and the fall would break a few bones from this height.

The rumble of an engine drew my eye. I allowed myself a grim smile.

'If you think there's a safe place for me,' I said to Mun, 'you really don't know who I am.'

The amnesia had not stolen my training. As Mun made a grab for me, I launched myself back and landed on the lorry, the impact shuddering up through my knees to rattle my hips. The driver braked, but by the time he got out, I was on the ground and sprinting in the other direction, away from the three black cars outside the hotel.

I ran through the bustling streets of a city I had never seen, taunted by its amber streetlamps. Still no obvious clue where I was. I cleared some tramlines and skirted the edge of a shopping centre. Entering it might help me lose my pursuers, but there might be security cameras or guards. I kept going.

On the other side of the building, I found a row of bus stops, where people were stepping on to a coach. This was my chance. Holding my nerve, I slowed down and joined the back of the group.

'Hello,' I said to the driver, a grizzled amaurotic. 'Are there any seats available?'

He eyed me. 'You have a ticket?'

'No. Could I buy one?'

'Where are you going?'

'I'll … ride the whole way, if I could.' I offered the creased banknote. 'Is this enough?'

'No change.'

I nodded, and he took the only money I had. As the doors hissed shut and the coach pulled away from the curb, I sat at the back and glanced through the rear window, seeing one of the black cars speed past, none the wiser that their target had just slipped the net.

---

As the coach left the city, I scarfed down a chocolate bar from the hotel and managed a few swallows of water, keeping my hood up and my face turned away from the other passengers. It occurred to me that I should have looked harder at the banknote, which might have told me where I was. Now I had no money, and still no sense of where in the world I had woken up.

For the second time, I checked the golden cord. Even knowing Arcturus had betrayed me, it was disconcerting not to feel it answer to my touch.

I must have nodded off. Next thing I knew, the driver was clearing his throat above me, startling me awake.

'End of the line.'

With a nod, I sat up. It was unlike me to fall asleep in such a fraught situation. 'Thank you.'

I drew my bag on to my shoulder and stepped off the coach. At first glance, this seemed to be a smaller city than the last, though certainly a city, from the number of dreamscapes.

That escape had been lucky. From here on out, I had to be more careful, but it would be hard. I knew how to orient myself in Scion. I could work out where to go and who was probably safe to approach. In the free world, I was clueless. Worse still, I had no allies.

This felt like the longest day of my life, and I could only have been awake for a grand total of an hour.

The night was mild, almost warm. I passed some kind of bar, where people laughed and drank and ate beneath outdoor umbrellas. Across the street, a lone voyant sat on a bench, studying a phone. I paused, then kept walking.

Until I knew more about voyants in the free world, it might be wise to approach an amaurotic, someone unable to sense what I was. For all I knew, voyants here would hand me over to the authorities as quickly as anyone else. This man might not even know he was a binder. Had he ever learned why his skin itched? Had he asked his doctor time and time again, to no avail?

At least I had the tool I needed to perform an emergency invocation. I found a doorway, out of sight, where I sparked the lighter, creating a numen. The nearest spirits perked up.

'I call the itinerant dead of this place,' I whispered. A ghost detached itself from a house and drifted to me. 'I need to reach my friends. Can you take me to anyone who can help?'

The ghost rang with agreement. It must have spoken English while it had been embodied. I shadowed it to a row of pastel buildings in a square, lined up like cakes with fondant icing. Intricate white art decorated two of their façades, giving a false impression of chalk, until you saw the shadow and realised it was plaster. My guide slid through the door of a green building, and I followed.

Inside, people sat at round tables, working or talking over drinks, some with paperwork and books in front of them, or laptops illuminating their faces. Behind the bar, a lean amaurotic was concentrating on making a drink, dark curls falling over his forehead.

'Dobry wieczór,' he said, without looking up.

The ghost circled him twice. I gave it a nod of acknowledgement, and it disappeared through the wall.

'Hi,' I said to the bartender. 'Would you happen to speak any English or French?'

'English, yes.' He turned to face me, setting the glass on a wooden tray. 'What can I get you?'

'I was hoping you could tell me where I am. I think I got on the wrong bus.'

'It happens,' he said mildly. 'This is Legnica.'

'Right.' I was none the wiser. 'And where is that?'

He glanced at me over brow-line spectacles, taking in my bag and hiking boots. 'You are very lost,' he remarked. 'Legnica is west of Wrocław. Is that where you took the bus?'

'Yes,' I said, with all the unwarranted confidence in the world. At this point, I decided to sacrifice all subtlety: 'This is going to sound ridiculous, but what country are we in, please?'

'Are you joking?'

'Humour me.'

He raised an eyebrow. 'Poland,' he said, clearly expecting a punchline. 'In … Europe.'

All I could do, for a moment, was stare at him.

'Poland,' I repeated.

'Yes.' He drummed his fingers. 'From your expression, this is not where you are meant to be.'

For the life of me, I could not understand this. My knowledge of the free world was threadbare, stitched together from old maps and forbidden conversations, but I was certain Poland was nowhere near France. I could be hundreds of miles away from anyone I knew.

'One more question, if you'll indulge me,' I said to the bartender, who gave me a slow nod. 'Do you know anyone who tells fortunes, claims they can talk to spirits, that sort of thing?'

'Are you okay?'

I laughed. 'Absolutely fine.'

He eyed me, and I waited. There must have been a reason the ghost led me to him.

'Maybe,' he said. 'Kazik, my boyfriend.' The corner of his mouth twitched. 'But how do I know this is not a trick, and you are not a criminal, trying to rob the handsome bartender?'

'You don't think a criminal would have at least attempted to come up with a convincing story?'

'A good point.' He checked his watch. 'We are closing in half an hour. Can you wait?'

'If you could find me somewhere inconspicuous to sit.'

'Why, are you being chased?'

'Yes, actually.'

That got a chuckle out of him. 'And you say you are not a criminal.' (If only he knew.) 'Okay, sit around the corner, and I will bring you a drink. On the house,' he added, before I could turn out my pockets. 'You look like you need it.'

---

'I'm Tobiasz,' the bartender said, as we walked through the dark streets of Legnica. 'And you?'

'Cora,' I said. 'Thank you for helping me, Tobiasz.'

I wasn't sure why I gave that name. It had been a long time since I had last thought of my mother.

'Well, I had no other tourists to rescue tonight.' Tobiasz tucked his hands into his pockets. 'You are backpacking in Europe?'

'Yes.' It made for a good cover story. 'I got separated from my friends.'

'And where are you from?'

I tried to think of a safe answer. 'Iceland.' It was only one letter off. 'The capital of Iceland.'

'Reykjavík.' He looked impressed. 'I was never in Iceland.'

'Oh, it's great. Significant amounts of … ice.' I glanced over my shoulder. 'Are you from Legnica?'

'No, I am just coming south for university in Wrocław. I live here with Kazik in the summer. Which is where I am taking you now.'

'What do you study?'

'Art. I want to be a sculptor, like my grandmother,' Tobiasz said. 'Are you studying back in Iceland?'

I was almost lost for words. It was surreal to have a conversation this ordinary, without a single mention of Scion. It made me wonder what kind of life I would have led, had I remained outside it.

'I skipped university,' I eventually said. 'I'm in the demolition business.'

*Demolition of sensible plans, old palaces, and tyrannical regimes.*

As I kept pace, I checked the æther. The suits might have worked out where I had gone, from security footage. Tobiasz had been kind to help a complete stranger, but he was under the impression that I was a lost backpacker, not a fugitive from Scion. The last thing I wanted was to get anyone else caught up in the long trail of destruction my life had become.

We turned into an alley, where he unlocked a door. 'If you're going to rob me, this is your chance,' Tobiasz pointed out.

'Note that I've let it pass.'

He secured the gate behind us and tapped an intercom. When the door opened, he led me up a flight of stairs.

The apartment was neat, with a wooden floor and ivory walls. A whisperer in his early twenties sat at a breakfast bar, a laptop open in front of him, nodding along to soft music.

'Kazik.' Tobiasz grasped his shoulder. 'This is Cora. She thinks you can help her with something.'

'Okay.' Kazik kept looking at the screen. 'And is this why we are speaking English?'

I lowered my hood. When Kazik glanced up from his laptop, he went very still.

'Sorry to disturb you,' I said. 'I just need some information, and I'll be on my way.' As Kazik closed the laptop and breathed out, I stepped closer, scrutinising him. 'You're clairvoyant.'

'As you would call it,' he said. 'But we never thought you would visit us here, Underqueen.'

Now it was my turn to tense. Tobiasz looked between us.

'You know Cora?'

'We have not met.' Kazik glanced at him, a muscle flinching in his cheek. 'Underqueen, where did you come from?'

'Wrocław, I think,' I said. 'I woke up in a hotel, but I really have no idea why I'm here.'

'That makes all of us.'

'You didn't say this before,' Tobiasz said, frowning. 'You were in a hotel and don't remember why?' Shaking his head, he took a phone from his pocket. 'I do not like this. Someone could have been hurting you, like trafficking. I think we should call to the police, to—'

'No police,' Kazik and I shouted in unison.

'Okay, but please, someone tell me what's going on.'

'Cora, as you call her, is Paige Mahoney,' Kazik said. 'You remember I told you about her, Tobiasz. The one who is organising a resistance to Scion in London.'

Tobiasz knitted his brows. 'You mean the woman they're looking for,' he said. 'The fugitive?'

'I'm sorry I lied,' I said. 'I didn't know who I could trust with my real name.'

'You are … like Kazik, then,' Tobiasz said, a question in his tone. After a moment, I nodded, wondering how much Kazik had told him about clairvoyance. 'Then you are welcome.'

'Thank you. I need to contact the syndicates of London and Paris,' I said to Kazik. 'Are clairvoyants organised here?'

Kazik shook his head. 'Not so much in Legnica, but a number of jasnowidze – clairvoyants – were asked to keep watch for you in this region. There is also a reward for your capture and return to Scion.'

'Who told you to look out for me?'

'I think it is better that you don't know. I will send a message in the morning. You can stay here until then.'

'I appreciate that, but there are other people trying to find me. I don't want to put either of you in danger.'

'Who?'

'I don't know. They sounded American.'

'How can you not know who is following you, or how you got to Legnica?' Kazik said, exasperated. 'Do you even know how long you were gone?' Then he landed the blow: 'Six months, Underqueen. You disappeared for half a year.'

## 2

# THE SESTRA

I gazed at a water stain on the ceiling. Tobiasz had left me a bowl of homemade soup, which cooled while I lay on the couch, trying to accept the hole that had been ripped through my life.

Half a year, washed away in the blink of an eye. That alone would have been hard to stomach, but I had no sense of why or how it had happened. All the answers must be trapped in my locked memory.

I was getting a headache. Other than the chocolate, I might not have eaten for hours. I finally tried the soup, which Tobiasz had called *żurek* – a hearty concoction of sausage, bacon and potato, with an appetising tang to it. It took the edge off, allowing me to collect my thoughts.

I had clearly been given white aster. I had little practical knowledge of it, except that it induced some degree of amnesia. Jaxon had occasionally smoked it. He cut it with tobacco, which softened the memory loss, allowing him to write off the day without forgetting it altogether.

Eliza had been hooked on it at one point. To break free of the addiction, she had eventually run away from the dealers who had raised her, never attempting to recover her memories.

She had made me promise I would never touch aster – not even the blue or pink sorts, which weren't thought to be addictive. Surely I would never have taken it of my own free will.

A wolfish dog came to join me on the couch. Some animals were nervous around voyants, but she only looked curious.

'Hello.' I offered a hand. 'You won't stab me in the back, will you, girl?'

She licked my hand and lay beside me. I ruffled her fur, swallowing the lump in my throat.

Not since the torture chamber had I felt so weak, so violated, or so alone. I had to find a way to undo my amnesia.

*In theory, I could reverse the effects of white aster, though I have never attempted it*, Arcturus had told me. *Memory is complex. And fragile.*

He couldn't help me. He had used and deceived me for almost a year, then thrown me away.

Unless there was more to what I remembered.

Even as it happened, I had doubted his betrayal. Not until he made to strike me had I started to believe. It might be false hope, but perhaps there was a clue I could no longer remember. A piece that had been erased from the puzzle. Something that explained his actions.

If not, I would destroy him.

All day, my survival instinct had kept me on the move. Now a terrible weight filled my head. I pulled a blanket over myself and fell asleep, imagining a warm body shaped around mine, and a hand on my waist, holding me close.

———

'Underqueen.'

I woke with a start, reaching for a weapon. It took several cold moments to remember where I was.

Amber sunlight shone between the blinds, on to Kazik. None of that had been a vivid hallucination, then.

'Kazik,' I said. 'What time is it?'

'Noon. You slept for a long time.'

'Right.' I sat up, wincing at the pain in my wrist. 'Did you speak to whoever is looking for me?'

'Yes. Someone is coming here to collect you, to take you to the Sestra. She is a voyant from inside Scion.' He nudged the fridge shut. 'I will keep to my usual routine, to avoid suspicion if these Americans come here. We'll be at the coffeehouse if you need anything.'

'Okay.'

For the rest of the day, I dozed on the couch. Even when I had been racked with pneumonia, I had never felt an exhaustion this deep and relentless. Had six months not passed, I would have thought it was an aftermath of the fever I had barely survived in Paris.

At dusk, a car with tinted windows pulled up, and Kazik came back to see me off. 'This driver is working for the Sestra,' he told me. 'I hope that you can get in touch with the Mime Order.'

'I appreciate your help. Will you thank Tobiasz?'

Kazik nodded. 'Stop the anchor coming any farther, if you can. Do widzenia, Underqueen.'

The amaurotic driver opened one of the back doors. I got in and fastened my belt. Unless I was going to walk all the way to Paris, I would have to trust the spirit that had pointed me to Kazik and Tobiasz, and hope this Sestra had good intentions.

---

As night closed in, I was driven away from Legnica. Hard as I tried to stay awake, my eyelids weighed the world. By the time I pulled myself back to awareness, over an hour had passed, and it was too dark to see much of anything.

If the æther threw me a bone, the Sestra would get me back to Paris, so I could fortify my alliance with the French syndicate. As for the Mime Order, it had spent half a year without any word from its legitimate ruler. My subjects must think I had abandoned them, or that I was dead.

We drove for hours before the driver stopped the car and got out. I did the same, huddling into my jacket. He opened an iron gate and led me through a graveyard, which wrapped around a small church with dark roofs and spires. A few timid spirits brushed my aura, then darted away. When we reached a pair of doors, the driver tested one, and it creaked open.

'Go inside,' he told me, 'and you will find the Sestra.'

'Who is she?'

He returned to the car without answering. I faced the doors, steeling myself.

Inside the church, I glimpsed candlelight and followed it to a set of steps. I tried checking the æther, but my sixth sense felt as dull as the others, worn down by my fatigue.

As I descended, I kept my spirit ready, wishing I had other weapons. This seemed like the perfect spot for an ambush. Scion had outposts in the free world. For all I knew, the driver had delivered me to one.

At the bottom, I stopped, my breath coming in small white puffs.

At first, I thought it was carved marble that adorned the chamber ahead of me. It was only when I reached the showpiece – a chandelier – that I realised it was bone. There were bones tucked into recesses in the walls, stacked into grim pillars, strung like garlands across the ceiling. Even the chandelier was made out of dismantled skeletons, skulls blooming from petals of hipbone, bleached white. Appropriately, I sensed revenants: spirits that lingered with their remains, sometimes until their deaths were avenged, or their murders solved.

I stood beneath the chandelier and took in the macabre chamber, remembering the catacombs and quarries beneath Paris. We voyants did prefer to meet where death settled like silt.

A flame blazed to life on my left. A revenant, wreathed in fire. I took a step away, ready to attack the voyant I had failed to sense among the spirits. My sixth sense really was rusty.

'Who dares impersonate the Underqueen?' a voice said. 'Think before you answer. I find that I am in the mood to add your ribs to the décor.'

The voice was cold and wary, with a Bulgarian accent. When a tall woman came into the light, it took me a moment to recognise her with brown hair, which now skimmed her shoulders.

'Maria?'

The fire sputtered out.

'Paige.' A pair of stunned eyes reflected the candlelight. 'It's really you?'

There was a deep silence before the spirit backed off. Ognena Maria grinned and strode towards me, holding out her arms. I ran into them, and she bundled me into a tight hug.

'Damn you, Paige Mahoney, you bloody fool,' she exclaimed. 'We thought you'd been blown up.'

I could hardly speak for relief. 'You're the Sestra?'

'Sometimes, in these parts. Sorry for the smoke and mirrors,' Maria said. 'I was sure I was meeting an imposter.' She laughed when I buried my face in her shoulder. 'I really don't believe it. How the fuck did you get to Poland?'

'I couldn't tell you if you paid me.' I gripped her leather jacket. 'I'm just so glad I found you.'

'Are you alone?'

'Yes.'

'All right. We're not letting you disappear again.' Maria drew back and regarded me with concern. 'Oh, Paige, you look exhausted. Let's get you back to the living. I have a truck.'

'This isn't where you're based?'

'No, *this* is where I lure my enemies. Beautiful, don't you think?' she said, looking around. 'It's called the Sedlec Ossuary. Its care-takers are osteomancers – I persuaded them to cut me a key. Luckily for them, it's one of the very few buildings I could not bear to send up in flames.' She wrapped an arm around me and walked me back to the stairs. 'Domino has provided me with a lovely apartment in Prague. You can stay for as long as you need.'

'Prague?'

'Yes, sweet. You're in Czechia now.'

'But the car didn't stop. Wasn't there a border?'

'One can travel freely between some countries in Europe. Which is fortunate, for the likes of us.'

I nodded slowly. Over a decade trapped in Scion, and now I could apparently flit between countries without even showing a travel permit. The whole thing was too surreal to fathom.

Maria led me away from the church to an old petrol truck with faded red paint, parked on a nearby street. I climbed into the passenger seat, which was on the right side. They were always on the left in Scion.

'Maria,' I said, 'you should know there were Americans after me back there. I got away by the skin of my teeth.'

'Americans.' Her brow creased. 'Why on Earth should Americans be interested in you?'

'They said they worked for the Atlantic Intelligence Bureau.'

'That doesn't sound fake or sinister at all.' She blew out a breath. 'Shit. I'm shaking.'

'Why?'

'Because I came so close to not extending the search to Poland. I couldn't think of any reason you'd be there, but a friend vouched for a network in Silesia, so I made a snap decision.' She dug into her pocket. 'I suppose the æther was on our side. Who put us in touch?'

'Kazik. I didn't get his surname, but he and his partner let me stay in their apartment.'

'I'll make sure they're repaid for that.'

She turned the key, and the truck came to life with a rattle. A nearby window reflected its headlamps. And suddenly I was seeing Arcturus, pinning me with that soulless gaze.

*I decided to remain by your side. To learn every secret of every clair-voyant organisation, so that one day, we Rephaim could eradicate them all,* he had said. *You were thorough: London, Manchester, Edinburgh, Paris—*

'Wait,' I said. Maria braked. 'Maria, did the Mime Order follow my orders to move?'

'No, but—'

'Fuck. Was the shelter discovered?'

'Paige, listen to me. I know why you're afraid, but they were fine in April, when I last had word.'

Even with that reassurance, my stomach churned.

'April,' I said, softer. 'You're sure?'

'Yes.' Maria touched my elbow. 'I promise I'll tell you everything when we get to Prague, but it's a long story, and you've gone as pale as those skulls. You should get some rest.'

On any other night, I would have pushed her. But somewhere between the crypt and the truck, the tiredness had stolen back – a fatigue that ate into my joints and clouded my senses. The overpowering rush of fear had made it worse. All I could do was nod and recline the seat, so my body would stop aching. Surely I couldn't still have pneumonia after six months.

'Are you hungry?' Maria asked me.

'I could eat.'

'All right. I'll stop.'

She drove in silence for a while. Between dozes, all I could see ahead was road, lit by the long beam of the headlamps.

Next time I woke, Maria had pulled over at a fuel station. She filled the truck and went in to pay, returning with two cups of coffee and a brown paper bag, which she handed to me.

'Strange to meet outside.' She slotted her cup into a holder. 'Strange to *be* outside.'

'I'm not sure it's really sunk in.'

'Nor for me. I've been out of Scion for months, and I still find myself keeping watch for Vigiles.'

'I thought Domino sent you to Bulgaria?'

'I started there.' She fired up the engine. 'And now I'm here.'

I took a sandwich out of the paper bag. 'How did you know I was missing?'

'Nick. We met up in Copenhagen in June, and he asked me to put my contacts on the case. He was planning to return to Sweden, but he had managed to visit London, back in April.' She accelerated out of the fuel station. 'How long were you in Poland?'

'I don't remember.' My eyelids drooped. 'I don't … remember anything. Not since March.'

'Wait. The whole time you've been missing?'

I couldn't answer. My strange new dreamscape was calling me back.

———

Something made me stir. I tried to rise from my slumber, but the world felt so heavy. When I did manage to crack my eyes open, I realised I was in a bed.

Maria paced in the gloom with a phone. Even though she was close, her voice sounded distant, unintelligible. I lifted my head an inch off the pillow, drawing a tiny sound of exertion.

'Paige.' Maria was there at once. 'Paige, it's Maria. You're in Prague.' She brushed my hair off my clammy forehead. 'Did someone give you white aster?'

'Cordier.'

'Who?'

That was the last I heard. My dreamscape closed like a flytrap around me. I sank into the shadows of my dreamscape, where I lay among the blooms until voices woke me again.

'… waterboarded in London. I don't know how to get her to wake up, let alone drink.'

'You should have called sooner.' A new voice. 'She must have taken a great deal.'

'Paige has never touched drugs, to my knowledge.'

'Sometimes it only takes a bad day. Unless you think it was given to her by force?'

'That is exactly what I think, and when I find out who—'

'Shh.' The bed sank to my right. 'Paige.' My lashes fluttered, but everything was too blurred to see. 'Paige, my name is Verča, and I'm here to help. Can you hear me?'

'Mm.'

'Listen to me carefully. Do you remember when your birthday is?'

It was a long time before I could think of it.

'January,' I murmured. 'January … the fourteenth.'

A music box, a whistling bird.

'Very good.' The new voice grew louder. 'Paige, I really need you to stay awake, okay?'

'I hate seeing her like this,' Maria muttered. 'What is happening, Verča?'

'It's a whiteout. A severe overdose,' came the quiet reply. 'I have only seen this once before. We have to act quickly. If she slips any deeper into this state, she could lose all her memories.'

'You mean she'd forget who she is?'

'Yes, but she's fighting. We have time to stop it.' A warm hand touched my arm. 'The blue aster in my case. Bring it here.'

My awareness returned in small bursts. A rustle, and then the coarse snap of a lighter. I opened my eyes to see a swirl of bluish smoke, smelling of violets.

'Breathe in, Paige.'

Out of nowhere, a memory flashed, a shard of a mirror catching the sun: someone else, another woman, forcing white flowers up to my face. The scent of them, sickly sweet, on a cloth.

'No.' I tried to twist away. 'No—'

'Paige, it's all right.' Maria grasped my good wrist. 'You can trust us. You can trust Verča.'

I did trust that voice. Surely I could. But then Eléonore Cordier loomed, a shadow on the snow, promising me it was all for the good. She had lied. Still, I could hold out no more.

I breathed in.

———

By the time I woke, the world was golden. I blinked a few times, trying to remember where I was. An ache lingered in my temples. I lay on a low bed, my hair greasy, throat dry as sawdust.

Opposite me, large windows were cut into a sloping roof, soaking the floor in light. The same exhaustion clung to me, which seemed impossible. Satisfied that I was safe, I curled up in the sun-warmed sheets and closed my eyes, but thirst and discomfort kept me awake.

'Maria?'

She came in from another room, wearing combat boots and a sleeveless boiler suit of olive linen. A chunky leather belt cinched it at the waist.

'Finally.' With a broad smile, she sat beside me. 'How are you feeling?'

'Not great. Did I sleep for long?'

'Three days. Apparently, taking too much white aster causes an accumulation in your dreamscape. It eventually turns into something called a whiteout,' she said. 'If you stay in that state for too long, you forget who you are. You're out of danger, but you're going to be tired for a while, no matter how much you rest.'

'As if I wasn't tired enough.' I scraped grit from my eyes. 'I still can't remember anything since March.'

'We don't know a way to reverse such a significant degree of memory loss, but that doesn't mean there isn't one,' she said. I nodded as much as I could with a headache. 'You need a good breakfast. Do you want to shower first?'

'Is that a hint that I *should* shower?'

'I would advise it.' She ruffled my curls, then went to a wardrobe. 'Let me get you some clothes. Verča is about your height.'

'Who?'

'A local Domino recruiter, and a fixture of the voyant community of Prague. She works to ensure that relations with amaurotics remain open and amicable in Czechia.'

'So people know about us here.'

'To a degree. Not everyone takes us seriously, or even believes in us, but personally, I would rather be mocked and doubted than sent to the gallows,' Maria said. 'Verča is good with people. She even founded a group that intercedes on our behalf with the Mayor of Prague.'

'Any special reason her clothes are in your wardrobe?'

'From the sparkle in your eye, I think you may have guessed.'

I smiled. 'Since when?'

'A few weeks.' She unfolded a pair of dark trousers. 'But we've known each other for a long time – since the Balkan Incursion, in fact. I'm sure Verča will want to tell you the story.'

'I'm happy for you.'

'Thank you, sweet. I'm happy for me, too.'

I shifted my legs off the mattress and stood, waiting for another rush of dizziness to pass. Maria dug a collared white shirt from the wardrobe, along with a pair of socks and a jersey.

'So,' I said, 'are you Maria or Yoana here?'

'Maria is fine. I always liked it. My Domino name is Nina Aprilova, and Verča sometimes calls me Maruška, which is a Czech nickname for Maria.' She handed me the clothes. 'Help yourself to whatever you need from the bathroom. There's a spare toothbrush and a new comb in the top drawer. I'll go to the bakery while you're in there. We can talk over breakfast.'

---

Prague was one of the few cities whose criminals were ambitious enough to make the perilous journey to Scion. Over two years ago, I had met a Czech art dealer, who had bought a forgery from Eliza. I had done business with a handful of smugglers from other European cities, but their appearances had been few and far between.

And now here I was, walking in their world.

The apartment was all raw wood and brick walls, softened by throw cushions and worn leather furniture. A piano stood at one end of the main room. The Domino Programme housed its agents comfortably, presumably to make up for the constant risk of death.

In the bathroom, I peeled off my clothes and stood like a mannequin by the shower. I had hoped the white aster would have dulled my memories of the waterboard, but no such mercy.

*Filth*, whispered Suhail Chertan, or the likeness of him that lived in my head. *To think that you really believed he desired you.* My jaw rattled. *Imagine his disgust at the feel of your skin, the taste of death on your lips ...*

My heart was pounding. I reached out to turn a brass lever – slowly, so the water came out in a patter, not a flood.

In the torture chamber, the water had been foul. Here, it could be warm and clean and under my control. Little by little, I increased the pressure. Once the glass had steamed up, I stepped into the downpour, keeping my face out of the way. Soothing heat washed over my shoulders. I found a bottle of shower cream and covered myself in the scent of roses, working it up until it foamed.

As I scrubbed days of sleep off me, I remembered being naked in another room. I remembered the inviting warmth of sarx on my skin, the strong hands smoothing up my back. Before I could stop myself, I was picturing golden eyes, smouldering like coals in the dark. I was remembering the exact pattern of his scars, the contours of his body against mine.

It was an amaurotic notion that the heart was the seat of the self. The dreamscape was the home of the spirit – the heart was just a muscle, a clock – but my chest hurt when I thought of him.

My heart had beat like wings that night. He had shown me that my body was a gift, as much as my untethered spirit. Two days later, he had claimed it was all an act, to win my trust.

I stepped out of the shower and wrapped myself in a towel. Once I was dry and dressed, I locked gazes with my reflection. No one could ever know what I had done with him that night.

Just before I turned away, I noticed a few new scars on my face, small and faint, peppered across my brow and one cheek. From experience, I knew what they were – the marks left by exploding glass – but I had no explanation.

Maria waited on a terrace, where a pot of coffee gleamed, set out with chopped fruit, a jug of milk, and glazed pastries with honey and butter. The sun burned in a sky so blue it almost hurt. In London, it was rare for it to be quite this warm or bright in September.

Pink roses twined around the balustrade. I went to it and narrowed my eyes against the light. Beyond were the picturesque rooftops of Prague: cast iron and glass, green copper domes, spires needling up from a sea of cinnamon tiles, all giving way to hills in the distance.

'I've heard it called the Golden City,' Maria said. 'It's like something out of a fairy tale.'

'You could let yourself think Scion didn't exist here.'

'That's what I find so disturbing. I understand now why the free world has done so little to help us. If I close my eyes for long enough, I feel I could forget Scion was even real.'

She poured us both a coffee. When I sat in the other chair, she pushed the pastries towards me.

'This district is called Malá Strana,' she said, slicing into a loaf of crusty bread. 'I'd like to settle here once we've defeated Scion. I've never been somewhere that felt more like home.'

'It is beautiful.' I picked up a steaming cup. 'You wouldn't want to go back to Bulgaria, then.'

'I have nothing left there.' She stared into the distance. 'I found out that my father was detained for making alcohol, and died of a stroke in prison. He was the last of my family.'

'I'm sorry.'

'It's all right, sweet.'

From what little Maria had told me, her relationship with her father had been strained. She had only been able to live on her own terms after she marched to war against Scion.

'Tell me about Bulgaria,' I said. 'How did you end up here?'

Maria tucked her legs into her chair.

'As you will recall,' she said, 'Nick and I were forced to work for Domino to save your life. I was happy to do it, but I made it clear that I meant to return to London. Domino wanted me to carry out a single assignment, for which they believed I had relevant knowledge, in Scion East.'

Scion East was the collective name for the five Scion territories that lay east of France, including Cyprus, which functioned as a naval and air support base.

'The Third Inquisitorial Division usually guards that region,' Maria said, 'but many of its soldiers were transferred to the invasion force for Operation Madrigal, so the time was ripe for troublemaking. I was asked to liberate a Greek agent known as Kostas, who had valuable intelligence. He was in the Chakalnya, a fortress in the Balkan Mountains, where I was once imprisoned.

'I was authorised to recruit my own team of associates to help. I decided to go looking for the people I remembered from the Chakalnya, who knew its layout and workings,' she said. 'Many were dead, but I found three women – Nuray, Teodora and Carmen – who had survived their sentences. Together, we formed sub-network Plashilo and prepared to breach the prison. We were under strict instructions not to free anyone but Kostas.'

'I think I can see where this is going,' I said.

'Yes. We freed him,' she said, 'and then decided to celebrate by saving the rest of the prisoners.'

'And then you burned it down?'

'And then I burned it down.' She sipped her coffee. 'My supervisor blew a fuse. They were about to wipe my memories when a Czech organiser named Radomír intervened. He needed someone with my knowledge to teach agents how to infiltrate and survive Scion.'

'And you agreed?'

'I agreed to serve the rest of my fixed contract – another six months – on the condition that he put me back in touch with you and Nick, and that I could keep my memories. I arrived here in May to work as an instructor at the Libuše Institute of Prague, where Domino trains new recruits. Radomír, true to his word, arranged a meeting with Nick. He's also paying me, which is nice. I've saved most of the money to help the Mime Order.'

'So you're still an agent.'

'I am technically an associate, despite the salary. Too reckless and insubordinate to be an agent.' Maria propped her temple with her knuckles. 'Your turn. What's the last thing you remember?'

'A masquerade in Paris.' I tried the coffee. 'After that, there's nothing. It's like I fell asleep.'

'Could Ménard have been involved?'

'I did consider the idea, but I can't think of any reason he would have sent me to Poland.'

Maria reached for a pastry. 'Verča knows more than I do about white aster. One of her best friends was hooked on it,' she said. 'Assuming you didn't take it by choice—'

'I wouldn't have done that.'

'—then your captor must have drugged you multiple times over six months. One dose couldn't erase that much memory. Whatever they did, it seems to have left you with a kind of anterograde amnesia. Every memory since March is buried somewhere in your dreamscape.'

My upper arm gave a sudden ache, as if my body was recalling something I no longer could.

'Eléonore Cordier was the medical officer for my Domino sub-network. I'm certain she was involved,' I said. 'She's amaurotic, but she might know how to use ethereal drugs.'

'You think she betrayed Domino?'

'She might not even work for Domino. She's clearly mixed up with the suits who came after me in Wrocław.'

'I can't find any trace of this Atlantic Intelligence Bureau.' Maria dipped the pastry in her coffee. 'Do you remember the date of the masquerade?'

'March the seventh,' I said. Her expression changed. 'What?'

'There are no coincidences.' She chewed the inside of her cheek. 'On the seventh, there were simultaneous airstrikes against Paris and London. It seems the free world finally retaliated.'

I looked at her in disbelief. In two centuries, no one had dared to punish Scion for its aggression.

'You were in Paris when it happened. Nick and I feared the worst,' Maria said. 'It was the only obvious explanation for why you'd disappeared.'

Based on the timing, I must have been caught up in the destruction. I remembered none of it, but perhaps that was a mercy.

'Tell me we didn't lose anyone,' I said.

'I imagine there were a few Mime Order casualties on the surface, but most of your subjects survived in the deep-level shelter. They couldn't have been in a more perfect hideout.'

Our descent had seemed like a defeat at the time, but it might have saved hundreds of lives.

'I wonder if Cordier used the chaos to abduct you,' Maria said. 'Perhaps you were injured?'

'Maybe. I thought Scion had detained her. She vanished the same night—' I paused to steady my voice. 'The same night Warden was taken.'

'Nick told me what happened. He was there when the Mime Order received your warning. Nadine said Scion captured Warden, but when you ran to his rescue, he claimed he had been working for Nashira the whole time,' Maria said. I nodded. 'But she wasn't convinced.'

'What do you mean?'

'She didn't think Warden had really betrayed you.'

'Nadine barely knows Warden. How could she have been so sure?'

'Nick might be able to tell you more. I don't think anyone wanted to believe it,' Maria said. 'Warden and I talked a few times at the Mill. He didn't need to be civil, but he always was.'

Not just civil. He had spoken to humans from a place of genuine respect and interest, until the night that had nearly destroyed me.

'I understand the Ranthen were looking for him,' Maria said, 'but he disappeared into thin air, like you.'

'And no one's heard from him since?'

'Not as far as I know.' She held out a dish. 'Eat something, Paige. You look faint.'

I took a small pastry with cream.

'Scion didn't react to the airstrikes. Weaver made an ominous speech about the anchor biding its time, and so on,' Maria said, 'but Spain and Portugal have been keeping him busy, and the planes were unmarked, which gave everyone plausible deniability. A clever approach by the free world, I must say. You should also know that Scarlett Burnish has not been seen since April. Weaver claimed she had retired.'

That gave me a chill. My unexpected saviour, who had been a spy for years.

'The voice of Scion,' I said. 'She's not even thirty. Is anyone buying retirement?'

'They have to buy it,' Maria pointed out. 'There's more, I'm afraid. In early June, Norway declared its intention to join the Republic of Scion. Now Inquisitor Linda Groven rules from the Scion Citadel of Oslo.'

I took a moment to digest it. Thirteen countries under the anchor, and far more in its shadow.

'Nick told me Norway had always stood firm,' I said. 'Why the sudden change of heart?'

'We don't know. It shocked everyone.'

'Sounds like we need to ramp up the resistance. Do you have any more news from the Mime Order?'

'Only what Nick reported. After you vanished, the Spiritus Club upheld Eliza and Nick as your legitimate successors, but Nick is still under contract with Domino, so he's been stuck in Sweden for months. For all intents and purposes, that has left Eliza as Underqueen.'

'Is she all right with that?'

'Nick said she was managing, but she wasn't prepared for that degree of responsibility, and your subjects don't know her especially well. As such, a small number of detractors have been calling for another scrimmage ... or for the White Binder to be Underlord.'

'Jaxon worked for Scion. He sold and laundered voyants,' I bit out. 'How could he possibly rule the syndicate?'

'The Mime Order only had your word for that. Binder did win the scrimmage, before you turned on him. Some see him as the rightful Underlord, while others want to go back to the old ways. Now Senshield is gone, they don't see a pressing need to fight Scion.'

I sighed. 'Great.'

'They *are* criminals, sweet. You were always kicking against the current.' Maria topped up my coffee. 'Fortunately, Binder has not made any moves on London. Nobody has seen him.'

The Mime Order was ripe for the taking. If Jaxon hadn't gone for the throne, he could only be dead.

'Eliza will need support,' I said. 'I have to get back to London.'

'That may not be possible yet. Since you're alive, your contract with Domino probably stands. We agreed to work for a maximum term of a year,' Maria reminded me. 'You could vanish, of course, but Domino can get you back into Scion. You don't want to rely on smugglers, like I did. I was lucky to survive. And the crossing is much harder now.'

There was also the matter of the help Domino might be able to give the Mime Order, which Ducos had offered me in Paris, as an associate of the network. Whether the deal remained on the table was another matter.

*If you can provide me with proof that your organisation is ready to fight, you will receive financial support.*

'Eliza wanted to prove herself,' Maria said. 'Let her wear the Rose Crown until January, when you and I can return to London. I'm confident she can rise to this challenge.'

*I started off in the pits of the syndicate. I know how tough you have to be.* Now it was Eliza's voice that came back to me, laced with resolve. *Don't underestimate me.*

'You could be right,' I conceded. 'Eliza needs room to grow beyond the Seven Seals, without me or Jaxon.'

'And you need to trust your own people,' Maria said. 'Eliza can unite the Mime Order. In the meantime, perhaps you and I can use the opportunity to do some good from the outside.'

'I'm listening.'

'I've been summoned to a secret meeting at headquarters. Command only invites agents and associates there for matters of the greatest importance and urgency. It must pertain to what Scion is doing next.' Maria raised her dark eyebrows. 'How would you feel about coming with me?'

# 3

## A WORLD INVERTED

Prague shone like a trove of bronze at the golden hour. It was a dreamscape breathed to life, ornamented and worked like filigree, its plasterwork as lovely as piping on a cake. Even the doors were exquisite. I could imagine stepping through one and finding myself in the Netherworld.

No one took any notice of me here, on these streets. The idea that there was a life beyond Scion, a world not warped around the concept of unnaturalness – that idea had been so far away, for so long, that I had almost forgotten it. It had been twelve years and a lifetime.

The trees were on the turn, their leaves tawny and falling. While sunlight coppered the city, Maria and I walked along the River Vltava, waiting for the clocks to strike. She had arranged for me to liaise with her supervisor, Radomír Doleček.

There were no transmission screens in Prague. Their absence reminded me of Scarlett Burnish. Her decision to save me had cost her everything.

Verča would meet us after her shift and take us to Radomír. I needed a walk first, to shake off the fatigue. Maria had lent me a knitted cap to help conceal my face. I told her about my nine weeks in Paris, including my work for Domino.

My head rang with everything I had learned over the course of breakfast. The two airstrikes must have been a grave blow to Scion, but Norway joining the fold would have softened it. For every step we took towards unearthing the anchor, it only seemed to sink deeper.

The airstrikes explained the marks on my face, which I had found on my hands, too. If only other mysteries could be so quickly solved.

'It sounds like you did fine work for Domino,' Maria said, returning me to the present. 'Why were you demoted to a mere associate?'

'I burned down the Château de Versailles.'

'Very funny.' She looked at me through her oversized sunglasses. 'Wait. Are you joking?'

'I would never joke about the wanton destruction of imperial property.'

'Paige Mahoney.' Maria threw her head back and laughed. 'I always knew you would have made a brilliant Firebird, if I'd had my way. You're learning.'

'From the best,' I said. Across the street, an amaurotic was performing for a crowd, making a marionette play a miniature violin. 'I'm a fugitive. Am I all right to be outside?'

'On balance, yes. I had a look for you on Protean, and—'

'Protean?'

'It's like the Scionet, but open. Scion applied to Incrida – that is, the International Crime Database – to issue a red notice for you. It's a global request to law enforcement to locate and detain a fugitive. But the general public won't know anything about it. You'd have to go looking.'

'Do other countries have to act on the notice?'

'No, and the Czech government will not assist Scion. Of course, there is also the matter of the reward Scion is offering independently for your capture, to the tune of twenty million pounds.'

Twenty million pounds. It was such an obscene sum of money that I almost laughed.

'Wow. I'm tempted to hand *myself* over for that,' I said. 'It's absurd, for some girl off a dairy farm.'

'Some girl off a dairy farm who did more damage in a year than Scion could ever have predicted. You're lucky I hate the rich, or that bounty might tempt me to join them.' Maria took an electronic cigarette from behind her ear and gave it a twist, making the end glow blue. 'I think you're safe on the streets, but I recommend you keep a low profile, just in case.'

I nodded. The sunlight flickered and sparked on the Vltava, reminding me of the Thames.

'I'm guessing the Ranthen aren't too happy with my absence,' I said.

'When are the Ranthen ever happy?' Maria blew minty vapour from the corner of her mouth. 'Nick may know, if Radomír can put us back in touch.'

'Is it just Radomír we're meeting?'

'He's invited a courier named Yousry, though I'm not sure why. And Verča, of course. She assists Radomír.' A bell tolled in a nearby tower. 'Let's go and meet her, shall we?'

'You sound nervous.'

'Ah, you know how it is, introducing people from different parts of your life.'

I did know. It had been a strange experience when Arcturus Mesarthim met Nick Nygård.

Malá Strana was home to a number of manicured gardens, framed by ornamental trees. Their leaves were turning red and gold. In one garden, a woman crouched beside a rosebush with a set of clippers. She was about the same age as Maria, in her late thirties or early forties, wearing peg trousers and a green coat over a blouse.

Seeing us, she stood, a smile crinkling the corners of her dark eyes. Her thick hair was the brown of molasses and drawn into an elegant tuck, showing a pair of hoop earrings.

'Hello, you.'

'Hello.' Maria kissed her. 'Verča, meet Paige Mahoney. Paige, this is Veronika Norlenghi.'

'At last,' Verča said warmly. Freckles peppered her tanned olive skin, dusting her cheeks and neckline. 'Paige, welcome. I've heard so much about you. How are you feeling?'

'Better than I did,' I said. 'Thanks for helping me, Verča.'

'It was the least I could do, after everything you've done to prevent Scion moving any farther into Europe.' Verča took the measure of me. 'Have you remembered anything at all?'

'Not yet.'

'I am confident we can work on it.' She folded the roses into brown paper. 'Thank you for meeting me here. My friend had a surgery this week, so I thought I would collect these for him.'

'She says this like she doesn't spend most of every day helping people,' Maria said to me.

Verča gave her a soft look as she taped the paper. 'I understand this is your first time outside Scion in a decade, Paige,' she said. 'Prague is the perfect city to reacquaint yourself with the world.'

'You must love it here,' I said. 'It's beautiful.'

'Yes, it is. I'm glad to be back. I was born in Prague, but I lived for many years in Italy.'

I nodded at the flowers. 'Are these just a gift, or does your friend need them as numa?'

'Numa?'

'I don't know the Czech word,' Maria mused. 'You know, love, like my fire.'

'Oh, yes. Juraj uses flowers for divination. I persuaded the mayor to set this garden aside for that purpose,' Verča said. 'Now anyone with that gift can apply for a key and take flowers.'

The idea that a local authority would accommodate voyants – give something to us for nothing, to help us connect with the æther – left me speechless. I had woken to a world inverted.

'They don't use the Seven Orders here,' Maria said to me. 'Or anywhere beyond Scion, really.'

'Fortunately.' Verča made a sound of disapproval. 'That pamphlet was translated into Czech, but it's considered an academic curiosity, at best. Most of us just call ourselves *jasnovidci*, and don't bother so much with the small categories. Maru, would you carry these?' she said to Maria, holding out the bunch of roses. 'I'll drive them to Juraj after dinner.'

'Where is dinner?' Maria asked her. 'Překousnout?'

'Yes. A bar that Domino uses for meetings,' Verča told me. 'It's near Prague Castle.'

'Does Czechia have a monarchy?' I asked.

'Not any more, but we have leftovers. There is much here that you would not see in London.'

'Frank Weaver would pass out in Old Town,' Maria said with a chuckle.

'It would all be closed down under Scion,' Verča agreed. 'There is the Orloj, the astronomical clock, our reminder of the inevitability of death. The synagogues of Josefov, and Týn, the church in the Staromák – and of course, there are many, many absinthe shops.'

Even if Jaxon would be fuming over the lack of respect for *On the Merits of Unnaturalness*, he would be in his element here. A city of macabre clocks, where absinthe flowed on every street, would appeal to his particular tastes. As for Arcturus, he would spend months exploring this place, with its opera houses and art galleries, museums and pleasure gardens. Prague was a monument to human imagination, its cobbles steeped in centuries of talent. I could see him drinking it all in, walking through it at my side.

The thought of him weighted my chest again. The golden cord refused to move.

Verča led us down a narrow street, where cakes were being dusted with sugar and snapped up by tourists. Most held their own cameras, or used their phones to take pictures. Another shock for the collection. No denizen was allowed a camera for personal use in Scion.

'Keep your head down,' Maria muttered. 'Scion may not be in Czechia, but if your face ends up on Protean, I'm sure they will find a way to come after you.'

I nodded, adjusting my cap.

We stopped at a sweetshop before Verča unlocked the door of an apricot building. From its interior courtyard, we followed her up a set of steps, into an apartment with painted ceilings and sash windows. Between the three of us, we got the roses into vases of water.

'There,' Verča said, placing one beside a pair of silver candle-sticks. 'Let me change, and we'll head to Překousnout. We have a great deal to discuss.'

---

Překousnout turned out to be a cellar bar in the castle district of Hradčany, tucked under a winding street that translated as Golden Lane. We went through a red door studded with iron, and I followed Verča down to the bar, where dripping candles and a roaring fire held off the shadows.

About twenty people had gathered in this hideaway, their voices piling like crushed velvet. Most of them were amaurotic, but a crystal ball shone on a mantelpiece. We sat at a table close to the fire, beneath a painting of a woman picking a pomegranate from a tree. At any other time, I would have relished the prospect of plotting revolution in a new theatre of war, far away from Scion, but for all I tried, I couldn't shake my stubborn thoughts of Arcturus. Nadine had no reason to stick her neck out for a Reph, but she had spoken up for him.

*Tell me where you are.*

'I will get us some drinks.' Verča let her wavy hair fall to her waist. 'Paige, what would you like?'

I looked at the menu, handwritten in Czech. 'I don't, um—'

'She'll have a beer,' Maria said, rescuing me. 'How about that chocolate one we tried?' Verča headed to the bar. 'She will insist at some point, sweet. Prague is famous for its beer.'

'Fine by me.' I glanced over my shoulder. 'You're sure it's safe to talk?'

'As safe as it can ever be. Everyone in this bar is connected to Domino. Though I know that doesn't make it fail proof.' She reached for a carafe of water. 'So what do you think of Verča?'

'I think she's lovely, and you're smitten.'

'Is it that obvious?'

'Yes. You could see that blush from Galway.'

'True.' Maria sent a dazed look after her. 'You know, she's fluent in seven languages. She's been an interior designer, a professional singer, a tour guide, and several other things, each more amazing than the last. Oh, and she had a supporting role in an award-winning Italian film. All this and she's not even forty. How I caught her interest is a mystery to me.'

'What do you mean?'

'She's just so *interesting*. You know when you meet people who lead the most fascinating lives, and yours seems to pale in comparison?'

'Right,' I said. 'This from the woman who fought in a war at fifteen, escaped from prison, hitchhiked across Europe, joined the criminal underworld of an empire created by giants from a dying realm, helped kick off a revolution, worked as a spy, and can read the future in fire.'

Maria opened her mouth, closed it, and tilted her head. 'I never thought of it that way.'

'Mimi.'

The voice came from a tiny slip of a woman. Her brown skin was bright from the heat, and a knitted hat slouched over long dark hair. She flashed a grin at Maria, who went to embrace her.

'Nuray,' Maria said warmly. 'Kak ya karash, priyatelko?'

'Biva.'

They went to the bar, speaking what I assumed was Bulgarian, leaving me with the other arrival. He was heavyset, with a curved nose and thinning black hair, oiled back from a brown face.

'Radomír Doleček,' he said. 'Do you remember your alias?'

'Flora Blake,' I said.

'Very good.' Radomír extended a large hand, which I shook. 'I am pleased to meet you. Nina tells me you woke up in Wrocław and remember nothing of how you got there.'

'Yes.'

'I assumed it was the amnesic procedure, but you do remember Domino.' He took off his coat. 'A troubling turn of events.'

'Story of my life, sadly.' I looked across the room, to where the other three were chatting as they waited for the drinks. 'You were the one who stopped it happening to Nina.'

'Yes. I saw that she could be a good instructor, even if she is too reckless for fieldwork.'

'What is it you do here?'

Radomír clasped his broad fingers on the table, showing a plain gold ring on his left hand.

'The Libuše Institute of Prague is the oldest Domino training facility, established almost thirty years ago,' he said.

'I hadn't realised Domino was that old.'

'It is, although it grew slowly. We have a wide network of recruiters, who find people with potential to go undercover in the Republic of Scion. Veronika is among my best.' He nodded to her. 'We assess their suitability and train them to survive. You would not have needed that, coming from inside the empire, but you should have been instructed in combat and sabotage. I understand this was not the case for either you or Nina.'

'I didn't even get an assessment, as far as I know,' I admitted. 'I think I was a special case.'

Somehow I doubted I would have passed. I had been fresh out of the torture chamber.

'It is dangerous for operatives to work without proper instruction and preparation. Command is taking too many shortcuts in recent months. Too many *special cases*,' Radomír said. 'This is why we are having problems. Scion is moving fast, so Domino does the same.'

'What are you grumbling at her, Rado?' Maria was back with three glasses of beer, each with a layer of foam on it. 'Don't mind him, Paige. He's softer than he looks.'

'You should not call her by that name,' Radomír warned. 'This bounty on her is no small temptation.' When Maria held out a glass, he made a dismissive gesture. 'Not tonight.'

'I tried.' Maria sat beside me. 'Where is Yousry?'

'On his way. He will eat before he arrives.'

'Excellent. More for us.' She passed me a beer. 'Here, sweet. Welcome to the free world.'

'Thanks.' I took a sip of the drink, which was so bitter I grimaced. 'This is vile.'

Maria grinned. 'I love it, myself, but it is an acquired taste.' I willed it sweeter and drank again. 'I'll get you some wine to wash it down. A nice Moravian red.'

Verča returned alone, while the other woman went to a different table. 'That was my old friend, Nuray Erçetin,' Maria told me. 'She helped with the raid on Chakalnya.'

'Scion identified Nuray during that raid. We extracted her immediately,' Radomír said. 'I am keeping a close watch on the others, to see if they will also need to be removed.'

'Domino hired us with full knowledge of what we faced in that prison,' Maria said. 'Did anyone really expect us to free one man and leave the rest to rot?'

'You should not have been put on that assignment in the first place.'

'Enough about work for the time being, please,' Verča said. 'We will eat and enjoy ourselves.' She held up her beer with a smile. 'Na zdraví, my friends.'

'Na zdraví,' Maria and Radomír said, and we clinked glasses. I braced myself and drank again.

Verča had ordered quite a feast to welcome me to Prague. Roast duck and pheasant, steak with a garlic marinade, tureens of mushroom soup, spiced beef sausages, fried cheese, shredded raw cabbage, chicken tossed in breadcrumbs, and a thick goat stew, followed by apricot dumplings and an entire honey cake topped with cream and chopped walnuts. I avoided the beef, as always, but soon cultivated a taste for everything else.

Radomír was a man of few words, but Maria and Verča were talkative enough for all of us. They discussed a band that had toured in the city, a ballet they had seen. Verča had a knack for storytelling. She described the local spirits, like the poltergeist of Černín Palace, and the shade of a thief whose shrivelled arm hung in a church in the Old Town.

I was content to listen while I chipped away at the food and beer. By the time I reached the foamy dregs at the bottom of the glass, it tasted better, which probably meant I was drunk.

'Well done,' Maria said, patting me on the back. 'Let me get you that wine I promised.'

'Are you sure?'

'Of course – it's our treat. Verča and I will split it.' She rose, taking the glass with her. 'Or perhaps Radomír will peel open the mighty Domino wallet, if we can get him drunk enough.'

Radomír sipped from his glass of water. 'I need a clear head.'

'In your entire life, have you ever had fun?'

'I am too busy. And I do not need drink to have fun,' he said. 'But yes, I will pay for this.'

'Good man.'

Someone had started to sing along to a cello. Once Maria had gone, Verča sidled into the space she had left. 'Do you want anything else, Paige?'

'Oh, no, I'm stuffed,' I said truthfully. 'Thank you.'

'You liked the beer?'

'Delicious.' Before she could offer me another, I said, 'Radomír says you're a recruiter.'

'Yes. I am also an administrator and translator at the Libuše Institute,' Verča said. 'I wanted to be an intelligence agent, but Domino doesn't often send clairvoyants into Scion – we would be in constant danger of detection and execution. So I do what I can from outside.'

'Maria mentioned you met a long time ago.'

'Twenty years.' She sipped her beer. 'It is quite a story. I decided to go travelling before university, with two friends and my sister, Debora. We were two weeks into our gap year when the anchor invaded Greece. Scion had never attacked a country, so this was a great shock.'

'Not too great,' Radomír said. 'You must have been too young or distracted to notice the speculation.'

'Perhaps. Despite the danger, we were determined to achieve our goal of visiting every country in free Europe,' Verča said. 'Our trip was meant to end in Kazanlŭk in Bulgaria. After a few months, we decided it was safe – that Scion only wanted Greece – and went to see the Rose Valley. A few days after we arrived, Scion crossed the border.'

Radomír shook his head.

'All flights were cancelled,' Verča went on. 'It was the end of our trip, so we had very little money. We hitchhiked and walked as far as Sofia before it ran out. A lot of people were stranded in the capital. Maria was handing out food to the outsiders. She saw my fear and made me laugh, even though we didn't speak each other's languages.' She finished her beer. 'Scion approached the city not long after our arrival. My sister is diabetic, and with medical supplies running low, she became unwell. With Scion on the way, Maria bribed a station guard to get us on the last train from Sofia, leaving her with nothing to exchange for her own safety.'

Maria had spent years in prison for that kindness.

'We reached Serbia just before Scion did,' Verča continued. 'Our parents met us in Belgrade, and we got Debora to a hospital in time. Maria saved her life.'

'And then you met her again here.'

'Eventually. After our escape, I moved to Italy to study, but I often wondered what had happened to the young fighter who helped us. When I returned to Prague, I applied for a job at the Libuše Institute, which I thought was a private museum. When I realised the truth, I asked to go into Scion East, to see if I could find Maria.'

'I denied this request, of course,' Radomír said.

'Yes. Fortunately, this year, Radomír brought Maria out himself.'

Maria chose that moment to come back. She handed me a glass of red wine.

'What solemn faces.' She had got herself a serving of absinthe. 'Did Radomír try to tell a joke?'

'Verča was telling us how you met,' I said.

'Ah, yes.' Maria planted a kiss on her temple. 'The æther was good, to bring us back together.'

Verča clasped her hand, giving her a tender smile.

'Now we have eaten, we must get to business,' Radomír said. 'Flora, please, tell me what you remember.'

I was starting to feel tired, but I recounted everything again, in as much detail as I had to Maria. When I was finished, Verča leaned into the candlelight.

'Flora needs protection, Radek. She could stay in Prague and do the training she should have received,' she said. 'We could keep her safe, as we do with other fugitives, like Nuray.'

Radomír sat in deep thought for a time.

'This abduction may not be an isolated incident,' he said at last. 'Domino has seen a number of security breaches in the last few months. I do not know what to make of these Americans.'

'I'm not absolutely sure they were American, but—'

'Regardless, it is imperative that you see Command. I informed them of your return this morning, and they have already requested your presence,' Radomír said. 'Your former supervisor classified you as missing in action, but Command can reactivate you as an associate.'

'Where is Command based?'

'For safety reasons, I will not tell you the exact location, but our headquarters are in Italy. Maria is already going there. I could arrange for you to travel together.'

I exchanged a glance with Maria. The secret meeting she had mentioned.

'That would be appreciated,' Maria said. 'I don't want to misplace Flora again.'

'Yousry will drive you. That's why I asked him to join us.' Radomír frowned. 'On that note, I will call him. He should not be so late.'

He stood and headed back upstairs.

'I worry about this meeting in Italy,' Verča said. 'Other than Radomír, no one from the Libuše Institute has ever been summoned to headquarters, to my knowledge.'

'If they're calling in a known arsonist like myself, things really must be desperate.' Maria speared a fork into the last dumpling. 'Don't lose sleep over it, love. I'll tell you everything.'

'You can't do that, zlato. Radomír has already been too generous, letting us stay together.'

I looked between them. 'Are relationships not allowed in Domino?'

'They are discouraged, in case of leaks. Whatever Command says to Maria, she will not be authorised to share it with anyone, even within Domino,' Verča said. 'Radek has been looking the other way, and we owe him for reuniting us. I would prefer not to abuse his trust.'

'All right.' Maria swallowed her mouthful. 'I don't like it, but I won't say a word. We'll be in good hands with Yousry,' she added to me. 'He was the one who brought me to Prague. It will be a long drive to Italy, but I'll ask him to give us coffee breaks.'

I nodded. My gaze caught on a rack of wine bottles, then drifted to the crackling fireplace.

*Part of me feared, before that night. That I was a fool for wanting to know you.* The words sent a long shiver down my back. *For seeing you in everything, everywhere I turned.*

The exhaustion was tiding back. I drained my glass, willing it to drown his voice, to wash away those memories with the rest.

Command might have some idea what had happened to Arcturus. In a matter of days, most of sub-network Mannequin had disappeared. Ducos had been our supervisor. She would have tried to track us all down, and reported her findings to the people at the top.

I might learn where he was. Or I might learn something I didn't want to know.

'Good evening, friends.'

Nuray Erçetin had come to our table, bringing a steaming cup with her. She had an aura that could have belonged to a soothsayer or augur – but perhaps I needed to stop thinking that way, in rigid orders. *On the Merits of Unnaturalness* had been my benchmark for too long.

'So you are the Underqueen,' Nuray said, interest in her green eyes. 'Maria speaks highly of you.'

'Nuray is from Türkiye,' Maria said, 'but she moved to Bulgaria when she was twelve.' Nuray sat at my side, flicking back her sleek hair. 'Have you had a good day?'

'It was fine. Rado has found a place for me to stay, so I went to see it.' Nuray set her drink on a coaster and lifted a satchel on to her lap. 'I also did the castings, as you asked.'

'Share them.'

I watched Nuray take out a few lumps of metal. 'What sort of clairvoyance do you have?'

'I melt tin and pour it into cold water, and the æther twists it into shapes. Sometimes I see or feel things,' Nuray said. 'Since the fumes are poisonous, lead gives the best outcomes – you die a little with each casting – but I prefer to use tin.'

'Cully has the same gift,' Maria told me, referring to her moll-isher. 'A few days before you arrived, I asked Nuray to work out if

I would see you again, through the æther. She kept getting a shape that resembled a human skull.'

'And you reunited with Paige in the Sedlec Ossuary.' Verča chuckled. 'Very good, Nuray.'

'I'm glad that was the outcome,' Nuray said. 'I assumed it meant that you were dead, Underqueen.'

Now I remembered. Jaxon called her art *molybdomancy*. Hot wax could be used in a similar way.

'Maria also requested that I scry for information about this secret meeting with Command.' Nuray showed us a knotted silver lump. 'If the shape isn't clear, I hold the casting up to the light and interpret the shadow.' She used the candle to do this, and we all looked at the wall. 'Here is what the æther gave me. A message for you, Maria.'

Maria squinted. 'What shape would you say it has taken?'

'To me, it resembles an animal of some kind. You see the ears and muzzle?'

'No, but my numen is fire, not metal.' Maria sighed. 'So the æther is being its usual clear and helpful self. Are we to be eaten by wolves, Nuray?'

'The æther does not think or speak like us,' Verča said. 'You know, the shape … reminds me of something. I'm sure it will come to me. Paige?'

I studied it. I thought I could see the animal, but that might be because Nuray had put that idea in my head.

'I'm not sure,' I said. 'It could be a wolf. Or a bear.'

'Maria was the querent,' Nuray said. 'She should understand.'

'I don't,' Maria said.

Nuray shrugged. 'Fragile castings tend to indicate unlikely or possible futures. This one is strong, so it points to an old truth, or a certainty. I also had a brief vision, which is unusual for me. A flash of yellow eyes, bright as flame. Perhaps that's what made me think of a wild animal.'

My chest tightened.

'Paige, could you hold on to it?' Maria said. 'Sadly, this outfit has no pockets.' I tucked the casting away, wondering what sort of tailor would forget about pockets. 'It may look like a wolf, but

Rephs also have yellow eyes. Could this somehow point to another invasion?'

I looked at Verča and Nuray, then at Maria, my brow furrowed.

'I told them about the creators of Scion. Off the record,' Maria said. 'They're handling it.'

'It's true that we have not had nervous breakdowns,' Nuray said, 'but give us time, my friend. We have not yet seen these beautiful giants.' She picked up her drink. 'I am still convinced this is something you dreamed up on too much absinthe, Mimi.'

'It was a shock,' Verča said, 'but I do believe it.' She glanced at Maria. 'I believe you.'

Maria was seeking my gaze, as if she was afraid she might have overstepped. I answered with a nod. It was her truth to share as much as it was mine.

Radomír returned at that moment, looking grim as a storm. 'Yousry is not answering.' He picked up his coat. 'We should leave now. I have informed the doorkeeper of a vulnerability.'

Maria stood. 'Are you saying he might have been detained?'

'I take no unnecessary risks. Veronika, Nuray, come back to the Institute with me. Nina, stay indoors with Flora and wait for me to send you a message, please.'

People were starting to leave the bar in an orderly fashion, some through an opening behind a rack of wine, which led into a stone tunnel. Verča nodded to Maria, then went down the passageway with Nuray. Maria threw back her entire glass of absinthe in one go.

'Don't worry,' she said, beckoning me. 'This way. We'll be fine.'

---

Maria led me away from the bar on foot. In the apartment, she turned on a lamp and shut the door behind us, hooking several chains across.

'Radomír is probably overreacting, but we'll let him do his checks.' She turned the deadlock. 'Yousry will show up.'

I tried to speak, but nothing came out. There was a lid across my throat, screwed tight, bottling the air in my chest.

49

'I'll make us a nice cup of tea. That's what we need,' Maria said, with conviction. 'You must be worn out after all that talking.' She made for the kitchen, then stopped. 'Paige?' When I didn't say a word, she came to my side. 'Paige, it's all right. You're safe here.'

'I can't breathe,' I whispered.

'Come and sit down.' Maria got me into a chair. 'Paige, tell me what's going on in your head.'

'It's ... too big. Too much.' I looked at her. 'Does Yousry know I'm in Prague?'

'No. Radomír prefers to do things in person.' She crouched in front of me and took me by the hands. 'You say it's too big. Do you mean here, in Prague?'

'The free world.' My chest heaved. 'I feel like I'm not really here. Like none of this is real.'

'This happened to me, too. As soon as I saw the yellow streetlamps, I started weeping like a child.'

'That's the first thing I noticed. The lights.'

'We lived for years in Scion. Of course it's overwhelming to be free of it.' With a joyless smile, she showed me her electronic cigarette. 'You can make these things glow any colour. I chose blue, because it reminded me of the lamps of London. It reminded me of home.'

I was shivering like I was out in a blizzard. London *was* home, even if it was the capital of Scion.

'We had a handle on things there, didn't we?' Maria said gently. 'We carved ourselves a place in that citadel. And suddenly we were flung back out here, adrift in open water.' A rueful grin. 'I know it's painfully ironic, but ... it's like we need an anchor, isn't it?'

An eruption of helpless laughter escaped me. I laughed until my ribs hurt and tears escaped down my cheeks.

'I know. I'm the sharpest wit in Europe.' Maria chuckled, then looked worried. 'Paige, you're having a panic attack, and you're drunk. Mirror me, if you can. Breathe in.'

*Breathe in.* Now I was back in Paris, yellow eyes before me. Yellow lights. *Breathe in, Paige.*

'Maria,' I said, my voice trembling, 'if he didn't betray me, then Nashira must have him. And he can't have betrayed me, because the Mime Order was safe in April. And I can't feel him.'

'Feel him?' Maria said. 'Paige, are you talking about Warden?'

I was in my own head now, deep in my fears. The more I thought about his betrayal, the less sense it made.

The betrayal had shaken me to the core. In the days that followed, I hadn't been able to think straight. But the idea that he could have played such a long game, moulding each lie to win my trust, was so hard to believe in hindsight. His interest in humankind had been real. He had learned to play the organ, kept books and a gramophone in Magdalen. He had not flirted with flesh-treachery, but committed to it, savoured it. Every moment of that night had felt true.

Surely there was no reason for him to go that far. Surely there was no reason for him to have been kind to Michael Wren or Fazal Osman or Gail Fisher, the other human residents of Magdalen. He had taken them all under his wing years before my arrival in Oxford.

Surely there was another explanation.

'He was my anchor,' I said in a whisper. Maria leaned closer to hear me. 'Like Verča is yours.'

Maria scrutinised my face. I saw the realisation flicker into her eyes.

'In … the same way?'

I closed my eyes, and nodded.

# 4

## YELLOW LIGHTS

Maria made me a mug of tea, but went for a whiskey herself. She nursed it as we sat on the balcony, watching Prague. Late in the evening, it glowed as if with many bonfires, lit by all its golden streetlamps; the light smeared and pulled by my exhaustion.

Now I was sobering up, my nerves were threadbare. Until now, only Nick and Ducos had been aware of my relationship with Arcturus. I had known Maria for more than three years, but we had only been friends for a few months, and this was a big secret to lay on her.

'That night in Candlewick,' Maria said slowly. 'I left my coat at the meeting. When I came back for it, you were alone with Warden, and you looked flustered. Like I'd disturbed you.'

'That was our closest shave.'

'I would have guessed at once if he was human, but I cast the possibility straight out of my head.' She looked at me in complete amazement. 'You and Warden. You and a Reph. You.'

'Not sure how I feel about how shocked you sound.'

'I don't mean it badly, sweet. You're just so serious and focused, especially since you became Underqueen, and you've never seemed interested in anyone. And Warden is—'

'Warden.'

'Yes.' She drank some whiskey. 'Warden.'

We sat in silence for a while, listening to a street performer.

'It's never really crossed my mind to think of Rephs that way,' Maria said. 'I will confess to a crush on Pleione, but she didn't seem to notice my attempts to flirt with her. Probably for the best, since I prefer my significant other to have more than one facial expression.'

'Fair enough.' I shot her a quizzical look. 'Why Pleione?'

Maria considered. 'Something about the way she sits, like every chair is both a lounger and her throne. It speaks to me. But I digress,' she said. 'How long was this going on?'

I sipped the tea, if only to steady my hands. Even now, revealing this felt like betraying Arcturus.

*A secret, held within, can become a poison.*

He had told me that himself. Perhaps I could take it as his blessing.

'It wasn't serious at first,' I eventually said. 'We had a moment, in Oxford. I thought I was about to die. I wanted to be held, and … he was there.' Maria nodded. 'We spent a few nights together in London. It helped me cope. I ended it before we left for Manchester.'

'You hid that very well. Why call it off?'

'Rephs are forbidden to touch humans. That's why they all wear gloves,' I said. 'I worried that Terebell would find out and stop financing the Mime Order.'

'I assumed they had poor circulation. What happens if they break this law?'

'They're ostracised. Warden would have had no one, not even me. They'd have made sure of it.'

'And I thought I played with fire.' Maria drank a little more. 'You claim it wasn't serious, but it must have been, for Warden to stake everything on it. For you to risk our funding.'

There was no judgement in her voice.

'It always … meant something to me,' I said, with difficulty. 'But we never put a name to it. I think I was afraid to do that.'

'Because you don't find this sort of thing easy,' Maria said. I shook my head. 'I have some experience of torture. Trusting anyone after that, especially with your body, is very hard.'

'I'm sorry.'

'It was a long time ago.'

But she knew. She remembered.

'We had another night in Paris. And then Scion captured him,' I said. 'I tracked him to the Île de la Citadelle. He told me it had all been a lie, right from the beginning, so he could mine me for information.'

I tried not to remember his eyes on that night, as cold as they had been when I first saw him.

'But you have doubts now,' Maria said.

'The more I think about it, the more it doesn't add up. If he'd told Nashira where the Mime Order was, she would have destroyed it by now.' My fingers tightened on the mug. 'Even at the time, I thought she was coercing him. But then he went to hit me, and—'

'He *hit* you?'

'No, he stopped himself. He said he didn't want to ... dirty his hand.'

'Oh, Paige.' Maria breathed out. 'All right. Let's think about this. If he didn't betray you, what happened?'

'He's either imprisoned or worse.' I pressed my temples. 'I should have tried harder to get him out. He would never have abandoned me.'

'But he did, sweet. None of us could reach you in the Archon,' Maria said. 'Trying to save you would have been collective suicide, and even Warden knew it.'

'You were with him while I was in there,' I said. 'Did he seem upset?'

'You know what they're like. So hard to read, but ... Paige, I think he was devastated.'

I swallowed.

'We stayed at the Mill while you were imprisoned,' she said. 'One night, I went up to the roof for a smoke and found Warden standing by the parapet, looking towards the Archon. The next day, he said he wanted to offer himself to Nashira in exchange for you. I discouraged him, since I knew you must have gone in for a reason. Warden saw the sense in that, but I don't think he slept at all while you were captive.'

Arcturus must have felt echoes of my fear through the cord. He had known what they were doing to me.

'We should consider the possibility that there is something else going on. Maybe something you've forgotten. Maybe something you haven't learned yet,' Maria said. 'Either way, Command may know something. Warden was classified as a Domino agent, wasn't he?'

'He was my auxiliary.' I was tired again. 'You can't tell anyone about this. Not even Verča.'

'I swear it on the æther. Does anyone else know?'

'Nick.'

'All right. It goes no further,' Maria said. 'Do you definitely want to come to Italy?'

'I've no choice. I need Domino.'

'You do have a choice. You're out of Scion. If you want to leave it all behind – the Mime Order, all of this – then fuck Domino and their contract, and fuck the meeting with Command. I'll help you disappear.'

'All our friends are still in there. You wouldn't think I was a coward?'

'Never. You destroyed Senshield,' she said. 'You've already given more than enough.'

I could see in her face that she really meant it.

'Give it some thought.' She rose. 'You have a few days to decide.'

She took my empty mug and made to leave the balcony.

'Maria,' I said, 'how did you get Verča out of Sofia?'

Maria stopped.

'You were fifteen,' I said. 'You couldn't have had much to barter.' She glanced at her right hand, which had rings on the thumb and all but one finger. 'You don't have to tell me.'

'No. You shared something with me.' She rested her other hand on the door. 'When my mother found out she was dying, she gave me an antique gold ring – an heirloom she had concealed from my father, passed down from our clairvoyant ancestor. She told me to sell it, so I could escape him.'

'What was her name?'

'Ekaterina.' Her voice was soft. 'I took the ring when I left home. It was all I had, apart from the gun they put in my hands. It was worth enough to give me a foothold, so I could begin to live as myself, as Yoana. But I found I wanted to keep it, because it was from her.

'Verča told you how we met. They needed the last train out of Sofia. By the time we got Debora to the station, it was about to leave. I gave the ring to one of the guards in exchange for letting them on to the train: Verča, Debora, Tanveer and Evženie.'

'You could have gone with them.'

'I won't pretend I didn't sometimes wish I had.' Her smile was bleak. 'I cried over that ring in my cell. But in the end, Mama gave me the means to save four lives, including that of the woman I was going to love. That was her gift to me. So I don't mourn the ring any more.'

It was probably the exhaustion (and the wine), but I welled up, feeling a surge of tenderness towards her.

'You're brilliant,' I said. 'And I'm proud to be your friend.'

'Please. We're supposed to be soulless criminals.' Maria slid the door open. 'Go on, get some sleep. I'll still be here and brilliant in the morning.'

---

I changed into a clean slip and brushed my teeth. By the time I padded back to the living room, Maria was sound asleep on the couch, a phone tucked under her hand. Careful not to wake her, I left the wolfish casting by the kettle, where she would find it in the morning.

Maria had stood by me when the syndicate had railed against my rule. She had come with me to find Senshield. I was sure she would keep my secret. For too long, I had doubted the wrong people. Arcturus might have suffered for that.

My memories of Paris rushed back. I remembered his eyes in the Sainte-Chapelle – flat and empty, just like they had always become when I possessed him. But that made no sense. Arcturus was no medium; he couldn't have been controlled by a spirit. Only by a dreamwalker.

I was too drunk and drowsy to unravel it. Heavy with forgotten time, I got into bed and curled around a pillow.

The moonlit tin-glazed Prague. I gazed at the stars, thinking of the vast world beneath them.

Maria was right. For now, I remained a ghost, presumed dead, still able to walk unseen. It would be easy to hide for the rest of this war, however long it lasted, so nothing could ever hurt me again.

I hadn't chosen this path. Scion had detained me, that fateful day in March. In Oxford, it had either been fronting a rebellion for Arcturus or being murdered by Nashira. Not much of a choice at all.

But I *had* chosen to fight Nashira at the Bicentenary. I had chosen to be Underqueen. I had chosen to resist Scion. For better or worse, I had chosen Black Moth. I had pursued and accepted the Rose Crown, and with it, a lifelong duty to London. I owed it to my subjects to reclaim my throne. Without it, I had no real power to my name. My words would not ring with the might of a citadel.

Without it, I would just be Paige.

The wine sent me to sleep. Deep in the night, Maria got up to use the bathroom, and I stirred, thinking I was in Paris. I reached across the bed and found nothing.

*If you can hear me, answer me. Even if it's only to say you hate me.* I willed him to answer. *Please just tell me you're alive.*

No answer.

It was like he had never existed at all.

———

It was a few days before we heard from Radomír. I slept for most of it. Maria would wake me for meals and short walks, but otherwise, she let me rest. While I was in my dreamscape, I tried to break the pallor off the walls, to no avail. It was set as deep as lichen.

On the fourth day, I forced myself through a cold shower. I still felt like shite, but at least I might be able to stay awake for longer than an hour. I dried my hair and dressed warmly.

Maria made us both lunch. As she finished serving it up, I gazed out of the window.

'Maria,' I said, 'can you show me how to get on to Protean?'

She brought a wooden platter of food to the table.

'Yes,' she said, 'but you need to brace yourself, Paige. The Scionet is a walled garden, curated by the Ministry of Principles. Protean is the opposite, vast and ungovernable. It can be useful, but I read too much, too quickly, and I sometimes wish I hadn't.'

'What did you read?'

'Over a decade of news. I missed a great deal while I was in Scion.' She sat opposite me. 'Tuck in.'

I helped myself to the cucumber salad and skewers of grilled lamb with yoghurt. As it turned out, Maria was both an excellent cook and a spice enthusiast. As I ate, I suddenly thought of the tasteless stew Arcturus had made in Paris, smiling before I could stop myself.

Maria noticed. 'Good?'

'It's great.' I cleared my throat. 'So you don't think I should look?'

'Not yet. There will be time to fill the gaps in your knowledge, and you should use all the tools at your disposal,' she said, 'but at present, I think you have more than enough on your plate.' She speared a slice of charred pepper. 'On that note, have you made a decision?'

'I have.'

She raised her eyebrows in question.

'I'm not abandoning the revolution. The fight against Scion is who I am now,' I said. 'I'll meet Command to ensure their support, and to see if they have any idea what happened to Warden. I'll fulfil my contract, then go back to London. I'll let the whole empire know I'm alive.'

'And there she is.' Maria smiled. 'It's good to have you back, Underqueen.'

Radomír summoned us the next day, right on schedule, to head to Italy. Maria went out early to buy me a set of clothes and a bag for the journey. I drank a coffee and ate breakfast before I dressed in the new sweater and trousers.

'Sorry,' I said to Maria. 'I'll owe you the money.'

'You'll do no such thing. Like I said, I've been saving my salary for the Mime Order.' Maria picked up an overstuffed day pack. 'I'm looking forward to a little break in Italy.'

'I can't imagine it will be much of a holiday.'

'Let me dream, please.' She opened the door for me. 'I requested a gun for you, but I suspect Radomír will have to decline. You'd need a licence, and you have no legal identity in Czechia. Domino has to abide by the law in the free world. Can you use your spirit?'

'If necessary.'

'Good.' She locked the door behind us. 'Let's get back to business, Underqueen.'

Malá Strana shone under the afternoon sun. I tried to soak up every fine detail, so the memory of it would keep me warm in Scion. We made our way across a grand bridge, where statues and lanterns rose on either side of the crowd.

Now Maria mentioned it, it was unsettling to not have a revolver at my side. There might not be Vigiles out here, but there were other dangers, like the bounty on my head.

The Libuše Institute was an impressive building on the Smetana Embankment, boasting a turret with a pointed spire. Its bricks might once have been red, but had faded to a rich pink, interspersed with sandstone. The words LIBUŠIN INSTITUT V PRAZE were carved above the iron door, which Maria approached. There was no indication of its purpose. Just another door that could lead anywhere.

'Domino personnel call it the Boneyard,' Maria said.

'Why?'

'It's a name for a stack of domino tiles, but I suspect gallows humour, too. Many agents who pass through these halls never return.' She tapped a code into the keypad. 'If headquarters were ever to fall, this place would take over. There's a third branch in Istanbul.'

'And we thought we were alone in London.'

'It will take many hands to uproot the anchor.'

She led me into a cool interior. The entrance hall had carved marble walls and a domed glass ceiling, all presided over by a statue of a woman on a throne.

'Libuše, who foresaw the creation of Prague,' Maria said. 'Domino is mostly amaurotic, but it's rather nice that they named this place after a voyant, even if they oppose Scion for reasons that go beyond our protection.'

'I can't get my head around this.'

'That our existence is legal here?'

'Yes.' I gazed up at Libuše. 'That there are places where we're respected, commemorated.'

'It has been a wholesome experience, after years of everyone wanting to kill us.'

On the other side of the vestibule, Verča was talking to a fellow voyant, a woman in her early thirties, with deep brown skin and dark braided hair. Both wore tailored suits. Seeing us, Verča touched her elbow and came over, her patent heels clicking across the floor.

'I thought I would come down to see you off,' she said. 'Radomír will be here soon.'

'He's coming now,' I said.

'How do you know?'

'I forgot to mention that Paige can tell exactly where you are at all times, provided you're within a mile of her,' Maria said. 'And that's the least of your privacy concerns.'

Verča smiled, folding her arms. 'You do have some interesting friends, Maru.'

'I've sensed auras like yours before, but neither of the voyants could explain their gift,' I said to her. 'Do you know what you are?'

'I have no idea. I see visions, like Libuše, but they come to me in flashes, so they rarely make any sense. They also give me the most terrible migraines.'

Maria grimaced. 'Three days of bed rest after the last one, wasn't it?'

'Yes, that was awful.' Verča looked curious. 'Where did you meet others with my aura, Paige?'

'One was in Paris, the other in London.'

'That is intriguing.'

Renelde would be with Le Vieux Orphelin in Paris. As for Danica, she had relocated to Scion Greece. I doubted I would ever see her again.

Radomír emerged from a doorway, wearing a heavy coat. 'Yousry finally called in,' he told us. 'He was in an accident on his way into Prague. A speeding car ran him off the road. That's why he didn't come to dinner.'

'Shit,' Maria said. 'Is he badly hurt?'

'He will be in hospital for some time. Another courier, Harald Lauring, is going to take you to Command. We'll meet him in Salzburg.'

'I've met Harald a few times,' Verča said. 'He came to deliver a message a couple of weeks ago.'

'Yes, he trained here. My car is outside.'

'Taking us to him yourself, Rado?' Maria said sweetly. 'It's almost as if you can't wait to see the back of me.'

Radomír waved off her comment on his way out.

'I'm happy I could meet you, Paige,' Verča said. 'I wish you luck in Scion.'

'Thanks. Stay safe, Verča.'

'And you.'

Leaving Maria to say her own goodbyes, I followed Radomír out of the building. He unlocked a silver car and opened the door for me, letting me climb into the back.

'Salzburg is four or five hours away, depending on traffic,' he said. 'You should be careful in Italy, with this red notice on Incrida. The Czech government will not help Scion, but Italy may be tempted by a bartering chip, with the nearby threat from Scion France.'

'Is there any way to get this notice removed?'

'Perhaps by disproving the charges.'

'Which are?'

'Murder, arson, and formation of a terrorist organisation. It frames you as a threat to the public.'

That was nothing new. Frank Weaver had spent months trying to convince people that I was dangerous.

'Maria requested a firearm for you,' Radomír said. 'I cannot grant this request until your status in the network is verified. You should enquire with Command.'

I nodded. Until then, I would have my spirit, at least.

Maria dumped her pack in the boot before joining me. As Radomír started the car and drove, I glanced at the spires of the Libuše Institute, hoping I would live to visit Prague again one day. Just as I was getting used to this place, I was hurtling somewhere else. Still, it was a comfort to be moving in the right direction, with someone I trusted.

It disturbed me to realise I was measuring my comfort level by how close I was to Scion, not how far away.

Radomír was a sensible driver, staying below the speed limit. Now and then, his earpiece lit up, and he spoke in soft Czech. At some point, I started to nod off, leaning on Maria.

'You asked about going back to Scion,' Radomír said to her. 'I discussed it with Yelyzaveta, and the choice is yours. You are welcome to return to the Libuše Institute once you have seen Command – but unless they have any work for you, you are free to go, if you prefer. I only urge you to exercise caution. Your luck may only last so long.'

'I don't know,' Maria said. 'So far, it's lasted me thirty-six years.'

'With that attitude, you will not see the next one.'

'Perhaps not. But that prospect is less frightening than you think, for those of us who know the secrets of the other side.'

———

I woke a while later, when Maria gave me a gentle shake. 'This is our stop,' she said. 'We're early, so Radomír says we can take a break. Do you want to stretch your legs?'

'No. I'll stay here,' I murmured. 'Still knackered.'

'Rest. You need it.'

She strode across the street to a supermarket, leaving me alone in the car. I peered out of the window, seeing golden lights in a public garden. It must be the middle of the night.

The virtual map on the dashboard showed that we were now in Austria. We had been heading west, towards the last place I had seen Arcturus. The cord still didn't stir.

Maria soon returned and sat beside me, handing me a paper bag. 'Hungry?'

'Thanks.'

'A pity we didn't stop in Vienna. Best coffeehouses in Europe, if I remember correctly,' she said. 'Then again, I may not. I was quite drunk in Vienna.'

'Oh?'

'I wanted to learn more about clairvoyance, and I'd heard that London was the place to do it. I found a smuggler who claimed he could get me into Scion,' she said. 'A Dutch voyant named Jorien was making the same journey. We had given most of our money to the smuggler, but we spent our last week in the free world together, having the cheapest fun we could. Anything we wouldn't be allowed to do in Scion.' She popped a can open. 'The smuggler abandoned us halfway, and Jorien was shot dead. I barely made it into France.'

'You really went through the wringer to get to London.'

'And now you know why I would prefer to avoid smugglers.'

We ate and drank in silence. I realised how little I was speaking at all of late, too confused or drained to follow conversations.

Once we had curbed our appetites, Maria got back out and switched on her electronic cigarette. I paced up and down the street, trying to stay awake.

When Radomír returned, a car was trailing him. It stopped on the other side of the street, and the window slid down, revealing a pale amaurotic in his forties. He wore a hardshell jacket over a fleece.

'Harald,' he said, giving me a nod. 'I will be taking you to Command. Hello again, Nina.'

Maria retrieved her bag. 'How are you, Harald?'

'Well enough. Sorry to hear about Yousry.'

'Yousry will be all right,' Radomír said. 'He has survived worse. I will visit him tomorrow.'

'Send him my best. Dovizhdane,' Maria said to him. 'Thank you, once again, for bringing me to Prague. I would never have reunited with Verča if you hadn't seen a spark in me.'

'Less of a spark than a furnace. Please try not to burn any bridges with Command.'

'We will do our best.'

A third car suddenly pulled up. Verča climbed out of the right side, a jersey thrown over her blouse and trousers.

'Wait.' Maria frowned. 'What's happening?'

'Sorry, Radek,' Verča said. 'We came as quickly as we could.'

She strode towards us with a holdall. Harald looked at Radomír. 'You didn't mention another passenger.'

'Command called my secretary just after we left,' Radomír said. 'They learned of an Italian employee at the Libuše Institute and asked if I could send Veronika along. I have no idea why.'

Harald nodded, but his mouth thinned. Verča opened the boot and tucked her bag into it.

'I missed you, too,' Maria said gravely.

'Stop it.'

'I will see you in a few days, Veronika,' Radomír said. 'Flora, Nina, I wish you the best for your onward journey.'

He returned to his car, while the one that had brought Verča flashed its headlamps and drove off. Harald watched us pile into the back seat.

'Put us out of our misery, Harald.' Maria put her seatbelt on. 'Where in Italy is headquarters?'

'I can't tell you,' Harald said.

'Even though we're going there?'

'If we are detained before our arrival, none of you must be able to disclose the location.'

'Is there a risk of that?' Verča said. 'I had no trouble when I last drove to Italy.'

'Things have changed since the fall of Spain and Portugal. Italy has tightened its security, with checkpoints and patrols along the border, keeping watch for Scion scouts,' Harald said. 'Given that a red notice has been issued against a member of our party, we should try to avoid official attention. I will take you on foot through the Alps.'

'On foot?' Maria said in exasperation. 'Harald, none of us are dressed for mountaineering.'

'It's hiking.'

'Says a man who clearly exercises.'

'You are all dressed warmly, and this method of entry is necessary, to protect Paige. A border patrol may choose to respect the red notice and take her into custody, so Italy can use her to bargain with Scion.' He glanced at me. 'You have become a person of great interest, Paige Mahoney.'

'I know,' I said. 'At this point, even I can't deny that I'm interesting.'

'Yes. Besides, I assume that you and Nina do not have passports, which Italy would expect.'

I shook my head. Scion had issued me with a white passport a decade ago, but it would have been destroyed.

'Fine. The mountains.' Maria looked weary. 'The things I do for you, Underqueen.'

I raised an eyebrow. 'Aren't you wanted by now, too?'

'Definitely in Scion, but I don't seem to have an international reputation just yet. Give me time.'

Harald drove in silence through the dark. At some point, I surfaced from yet another doze, feeling a tilt as we started to move uphill. Maria had wrapped her arm around me, so I could rest my head on her shoulder while I slept.

Verča was looking at her phone, her face lit by its glow. 'I'm glad I could come. You might need an interpreter, and Radomír has a few messages that ought to be delivered to Command in person,' she said. 'Strange that Domino suddenly wants Italian personnel to attend the meeting. At least you won't have to keep any secrets from me now.'

'True.' Maria glanced at her. 'You said the casting reminded you of something. Has it come back to you?'

'Yes, the Capitoline Wolf. It's a sculpture in Rome, showing Romulus and Remus, the founders of the city. They were sons of Rhea Silvia – a priestess of the goddess Vesta – and Mars, the god of war. But I don't know if the casting pointed to it, Maru. I was not the querent.'

'But you know the querent, and the querent knows you. The æther only sends messages we have the means to understand,' Maria said. 'In my case, you could be the means.'

'What do you think it would signify?'

'The god of war, a specific city, yellow eyes … I'm starting to wonder if Scion has set its sights on Italy.'

'I have been wondering the same.' Verča brushed a loose ripple of hair behind her ear. 'I feel as if I should warn my family, but I'll wait for the meeting. I don't want to frighten Debora.'

'The casting may not be as important as we think. For all we know, the wolf could simply have been a sign that we're going to Italy.'

'I hope so.' Verča hitched up a smile. 'I am glad I can show you my other home, in the meantime.'

'I can't wait to see it.'

They were quiet after that, allowing me to drift off again. As I sank into that leaden sleep, I could have sworn I heard other voices, speaking from a buried past.

# SNOW AND RUST

I woke in the absolute darkness of the Westminster Archon. Once again, my wrists were bound. I tried to flex a hand free, but nothing happened.

This time, the water didn't hit me from above. It wrapped and invaded my entire body, filling my throat, my chest, my stomach. I was trapped in the black depths, unable to move an inch. *He gave himself up for you,* Suhail whispered. He loomed from the shadows, eyes red and soulless. *The concubine is ours now, dreamwalker. He will be ours for as long as you live.*

'Paige?'

I blinked, and he melted away. A bead of sweat trickled from my hairline.

'Maria,' I said. 'Is that you?'

'Yes. Harald says we need to walk from here.' Her face slowly came into relief, brow lined in concern. 'Paige, you're very pale. Are you all right?'

'I'm fine. Just … forgot where I was.'

'I'll remind you next time.'

My eyes were dry as smoke. The illuminated clock on the dashboard told me it was just past six in the morning. When I listed out of the car, my boots sank into snow.

The faint blue light of dawn revealed the mountains around us. I drew my jacket closer, my shivers worsening.

The Alps were not the gentle hills that had surrounded my grandparents' farmhouse, or the Galtees, which had seemed impossibly tall when I was young. Untouched snow and evergreens covered their rugged slopes. I was so used to living in a citadel, I had fallen out of touch with this sort of natural beauty.

Mist feathered in my breath as the wind blew, leaving wisps of snow in my hair. The cold would keep me awake, though it didn't help my sudden chill, or the stiffness in my fingers. That had been the worst flashback in a while.

Harald had brought us to a sleepy village. He knocked on a door and spoke to a grey-haired woman, then came back to us.

'The villagers have not seen any patrols,' he said, 'but we should proceed with caution, in case of drones.'

'I'm not convinced I know what a drone is,' I said.

'It's a small uncrewed aircraft, often used for surveillance. Scion does deploy them for military purposes, but not in its citadels,' Harald said. A sheep bleated. 'If a drone detects us, it may draw the attention of a ground patrol, which I would prefer to avoid.'

My nod was terse. Admitting my lack of knowledge to Maria was one thing, but having to do it in front of the others filled me with a hot rush of shame. I wanted to blame Scion, but I could have taken more of an interest when traders came from elsewhere. I could have looked harder for knowledge – but Jaxon had wanted me wed to London, so London had become my world.

'I never went this way through the Alps,' Verča said. 'How long will it take?'

'Around six hours. A car will be waiting on the other side, so I can drive you to Command.' Harald took a huge rucksack from the passenger seat and hitched it on to his shoulders. 'Domino maintains a supply cabin in the pass. We'll rest there, then continue to the border.'

A path led out of the village. Harald stuck in a pair of earphones, pulled on a woollen hat, and set off. I glanced at the sky, searching for aircraft, before I followed.

For the first hour, I tried to savour the sights and sounds, without much luck. Walking left me with too much room for contemplation. With every step, I wondered if I was moving any closer to Arcturus. When I sent another nudge along the golden cord, nothing came back.

I didn't know what that meant. If Arcturus had been executed, surely the cord would have broken. If not, he was almost certainly with Nashira. She liked keeping her trophy close.

I had no idea where she would be. London had been her seat of power for some time, but the airstrikes would have rattled her, and Versailles and Oxford were both compromised.

Scion had been founded on the promise of security for those who submitted. The airstrikes would have destroyed that illusion overnight. Now even its founders were running out of safe places. I allowed myself some bitter satisfaction at that dose of poetic justice, even if it might not last. I was a fugitive with no home of my own, but if anything I had endured had made Nashira Sargas less comfortable, I could live with it.

The sun climbed into a clear sky. We climbed with it, past larch trees and piles of timber, following a distant line of pylons. Maria and Verča waited for me, but I soon fell behind, weighed down by the fatigue.

To conserve strength, I had tried to keep my attention off the æther, but Harald had mentioned the possibility of patrols, so I let my awareness widen. At once, I sensed them.

'Maria,' I called. She turned and came back towards me. 'There are dreamscapes about a quarter of a mile ahead of us. Feels like eight or nine humans, and three animals. Can you warn Harald?'

She cursed and broke into a jog. I trudged after her, watching as she and Harald talked beside a boulder.

'This may be a patrol with dogs,' Harald said when I caught up. 'They could have set up a checkpoint or blockade.' He scratched at a scar on his lip. 'We'll have to go around.'

Verča blew into her palms. 'And how long will *that* take?'

'It will extend our journey by several hours. We'll have to stay in the Alps tonight. Our supply cabin is small, but it will keep us warm.'

'Let's go, then.' Maria took a sweater from her pack. 'I refuse to come to blows with a dog.'

We retraced our steps to a fork in the path. The first time we had reached it, Harald had marched straight ahead. This time, he turned south, into a wild and sweeping valley, and took us along the remains of a trail, following a stream. It must have been an hour before we stopped beside a shallow pool, where Maria eased off her combat boots and washed blood from her heels.

'Harald,' Verča said, giving her a plaster, 'how much farther to this cabin?'

'And does it have food?' Maria asked.

'Tinned food. Nothing too appetising.' Harald checked his chunky watch. 'If we maintain this pace, we should reach the cabin by sunset. We'll sleep there and take the bridge at dawn.'

I rubbed my eyes. 'What bridge?'

'It crosses an artificial lake. Using it will allow us to bypass the blockade, if that is what it was.' He took a whey drink from his rucksack and tossed it to me. 'For energy. The next part is the last and hardest. We need to go over that ridge to reach the cabin.'

He nodded to the peaks that towered right above us. Maria followed his line of sight. 'I thought you said we wouldn't be mountaineering?' she said, horrified. 'Look at my feet.'

'Think of the view.' Harald offered her a can. 'Come along. No point in putting this off.'

Maria looked up at Verča. 'Glad you came?'

'Of course.'

The way up the ridge was narrow and steep. The four of us ascended without speaking, saving our breath. The only sound was the moan of the wind and the gravelly scuff of our shoes.

I had scaled cranes and skyscrapers, but mountains were a different matter, carved by wind and time. I had to stop every so often to let the ache burn through my body, like a flame along a match. At least I could breathe without coughing, which was more than I had been able to do in Paris.

The others attacked the ridge in their own ways. Verča assessed each slope carefully, while Maria moved in scrambling bursts and Harald went like well-oiled clockwork. Before long, thicker snow was crunching underfoot. I pushed through the discomfort.

All the while, I never looked up. Looking up would show me how much farther I had to climb. I couldn't do that. I could only keep going.

I only realised Harald had stopped when I walked into him. 'Sorry,' I said, sleeving cold sweat from my brow.

'No problem. Take a break,' he said. 'We're at the top.'

At last, I let my gaze wander. All I could see were mountains, rising from a thin layer of cloud in all directions. Far below, a lake spread north, shocking blue against the snow. Maria appeared at last, doubled over.

'Fucking mountains,' she wheezed out. 'Nothing but ... jumped-up hills.' She clutched her side. 'Taking up space for eons, being outrageously hard to climb.'

I gave her a hand. 'You all right there, champ?'

'No, I'm dying. Let me expire.'

'Didn't you walk across Europe to get to London?'

'When I was your age. Now I get backaches for no reason,' she said, puffing. 'Nothing like a surprise hike to show you how unfit you are. Why did I smoke all those years?'

'Extreme stress?'

'I could have taken up gardening.'

'Come a little higher,' Verča called, hair blowing in the wind. 'It's beautiful!'

'You work indoors,' Maria despaired. 'How are you fitter than a career criminal, a commander of rebels?'

'Radek makes sure we're ready for anything. Did you never use the gym at the Boneyard?'

'Absolutely not. I gave up on all exercise the moment I left Scion.'

She collapsed into the snow, grumbling in Bulgarian. I cracked open the shake and shielded my eyes from the sun, looking south. Tomorrow we would be in Italy.

Just as I was about to take a sip, I became aware that Harald was observing me. For no reason that I could explain, it raised the hairs on my nape. I pretended to drink, swallowing twice.

*You only had eyes for the king and queen*, Arcturus had warned me once, while we played chess. *Remember not to overlook the other pieces.* It might have done me good to listen every now and then.

The cabin was hidden some way off the trail. We pressed on with as much caution as we could muster in our state, boots slewing on loose chips of stone. Not stopping to rest would be dangerous soon. When Harald wasn't looking, I emptied the can into the snow.

Maria knelt to tie her bootlaces. I waited beside her.

'Do you trust Harald?'

She glanced at me. 'Why do you ask?'

'No particular reason.'

'I don't know him very well, but Radomír will have vetted him. Don't worry.'

Radomír did strike me as the sort of man who did his research. I brushed off the misgiving and followed the others.

It was dusk by the time we got to the cabin. From a distance, it must look like part of the mountain, weathered grey and tucked beneath an overhang. You would only find it if you knew where to look.

Nearby, a suspension bridge stretched across the valley, so thick with rust it looked as if it was made of copper. It was high enough above the lake that a fall would certainly be fatal.

'That looks stable,' Maria said drily.

'It was closed several years ago,' Harald said, 'but it will hold if we cross one by one. I've tested it.' He unlocked the cabin. 'Domino built this place years ago, for anyone who needed to lie low. We can't risk lighting a fire, but there should be blankets and heat packs.'

I stamped the snow from my boots. 'So Domino even has safe houses outside Scion?'

'There is nowhere on Earth the anchor can't reach.'

He said it nonchalantly, but the reminder was chilling. I took off my jacket and boots without comment.

The cabin was rudimentary, made up of three cramped rooms. Inside were pots and pans, firewood, other necessities for cooking without electricity. I sank to the floor, muscles fluttering in my legs.

Harald walked past me. I heard him talking amicably to Verča and Maria while they searched for food. Perhaps my instinct had been wrong. I was no longer confident in my own judgement.

'Paige.'

I looked up. Harald held out a fleece blanket, which I took.

'You should sleep with the others, for warmth.' He had dark circles under his eyes. 'I'll keep watch.'

'I can go first, if you like.'

'I insist. You look tired.'

Pressing the issue would look strange, and I was in desperate need of sleep. I went into the next room, where Verča was cocooned in a blanket, opening a pack of salted crackers.

'Maria says you're concerned about Harald,' she said, too soft for him to hear. 'I checked his record before I left. He trained at the Libuše Institute, went into Sweden, then started work as a courier for Command. A total of thirteen years with Domino.'

'It's fine,' I said. 'I just don't know him.'

'I understand.' She passed me a cracker. 'I spoke to my friend about your aster poisoning.'

'Is that what I have?'

'Yes. You are still on the brink of a whiteout. I suspect your captor was using some kind of stimulant to keep you awake, and when you escaped, the accumulation of white aster suddenly overwhelmed you. If your captor had given you any more, the whiteout could have been impossible to break, leading to complete memory loss.'

I snapped the cracker. 'Will the amnesia wear off?'

'Evženie told me the memories can return, but it takes a long time, even in mild cases. Apparently, recent events will come back to you first. I have a way to speed things up.'

'Really?'

'Well, I hope so. I used blue aster to stop the whiteout. Have you ever tried it before?'

'No. I promised a friend I'd never touch ethereal drugs.'

'The purple sort is dangerous, but blue and pink are not. In fact, they can be very useful.' She pulled her bag into her lap. 'Many people don't understand what each one does.'

'Go on.'

'Purple aster distorts the dreamscape. We can't usually change the way it looks, so this can be thrilling, but over time, it makes the user anxious and paranoid. White aster leaves a kind of dust on the dreamscape, which builds with prolonged use, burying memories, disturbing the spirit. That's why they're not just addictive, but harmful. It's also why you're so tired. Your spirit can't reach a deep state of rest with all that dust in its sanctuary.'

'What about pink and blue?'

'They strengthen the silver cord, with different results. Pink seems to improve the connection between the spirit and the body, which is why it is often used as an aphrodisiac.' She unzipped the bag. 'And blue improves the connection between the spirit and the dreamscape. This makes you feel safe and grounded, and can serve to clarify recent memories.'

'So you can use blue aster to counteract purple and white?'

'To some extent.' She handed me a small tin. 'I didn't want you to have to smoke, so I had the essence infused into patches. It should fortify your silver cord. If nothing else, you'll sleep better.'

'Thank you.' I tucked the tin away. 'I appreciate you looking into it.'

'You've been a good friend to Maria,' Verča said. 'That makes you my friend as well.'

Now I had stopped moving, I could no longer hold off the exhaustion. When Maria returned, I wrapped myself in the blanket, and the three of us lay close together. Within a minute, I was out cold.

I woke with a sudden and inexplicable sense of danger. Slowly, I opened my eyes to see Harald, his face illuminated by the green light from his watch, aiming a pistol at my face.

'Come with me,' Harald said. 'If you please, Underqueen.'

I had never been so angry to be right. I reined in my spirit, tasting blood. 'Who are you?'

'Someone whose instructions you must follow,' he said. I sat up. 'Don't try to use your spirit, or Nina and Veronika will die. I will shout the order before you have time to stop my tongue.'

Maria and Verča were a wall away. They must have got up in the night and been ambushed in the other room, or the disturbance would have woken me. Harald took a step back, levelling the pistol at my head.

'Please,' he said, 'put your jacket and boots on. And keep your hands where I can see them.'

My legs hurt from the climb. Once I had done as he said, he walked me at gunpoint to the next room, where six muscular strangers, all wearing ski masks, had restrained Verča and Maria.

'What the hell is this?' Maria said through gritted teeth. 'Harald?'

'I am taking Paige.'

'Over my dead body.'

'Stay calm, please, Nina. Nobody needs to get hurt.' Harald checked his watch. 'I'm sorry you and Veronika had to be involved, but now you are here, I may as well take you all to Scion. I doubt they will refuse two agents from a hostile organisation.'

I lifted my chin. 'You work for Scion, then?'

'In a manner of speaking. I've been searching for you since I lost track of Eléonore.'

It took a moment to sink in.

'Cordier,' I managed. 'You know her?'

'Not as well as I thought.' Harald kept his pistol trained on my face. 'I am not here to answer questions, Paige. All you need to know is that your escapade is over.'

'Scion is not going to give you that ludicrous reward,' Maria bit out. 'It's just a carrot for the asses. Are you an ass, Harald Lauring?'

'It's not about the money.' He lowered his voice. 'They have my family, Nina. Grapevine has my family.'

*Grapevine?*

75

'These two women are *my* family,' Maria said, her tone soft and dangerous. 'Hurt either of them and I will—'

'Harald,' Verča cut in, 'please, let's talk reasonably. Who or what is Grapevine?'

I had been about to ask the same question.

'It doesn't matter,' Harald said. 'They told me to deliver Paige to London.' He dug into his coat. 'As I said, nobody needs to get hurt. Just do exactly as I say.'

He took out a vial of murky fluid. When he removed the lid, I caught the rank smell of it and stiffened.

'Drink it all,' he said. 'Don't test our patience, Paige.'

'Paige, whatever it is, don't,' Verča whispered.

Her captor pressed their gun to the side of her head. Over the next few moments, I weighed the risks.

The vial was full of alysoplasm, which could be used to conceal any dreamscape. The ski masks must have drunk it to stop me sensing their approach, but they were likely amaurotic, immune to the worst effect of the drug. If I drained this vial, I would temporarily lose my ability to dreamwalk, and with it, our best hope of escape.

There might not be a choice. If I used my spirit now, at least one of them would shoot, and there could be more outside. I needed to buy time to hatch another plan.

'You certainly did your research,' I said to Harald, and raised the vial to him. 'Your health.'

I steeled myself and necked the contents.

'Thank you,' Harald said, sounding relieved. 'I want this to be bloodless.'

'If this Grapevine has anything to do with Scion, it won't be,' I said, swallowing the aftertaste. 'You'll be delivering me to my death.'

The foulness chilled my throat. The æther began to fade away, as it had when Ménard forced me to drink alysoplasm in Paris. A terrible sense of desolation stole through me, and then I was trapped in my body, unable to sense the realm beyond the locked cage of my flesh.

Harald stopped me from falling over. This had to be the worst thing a voyant could experience – the removal of the sixth sense, the shearing of the self.

'Paige, what is it?' Maria pulled against her captor. 'Harald, have you poisoned her?'

'She will be fine,' Harald said gruffly. 'It wears off.'

'You know what doesn't wear off?' Maria shot back. 'The stain of being a traitorous shit.'

Harald didn't answer, but a muscle started in his cheek.

'One more precaution, before we leave,' he muttered to himself, reaching into his coat again. 'To be certain.' Before I could so much as tense, two sharp points had touched my back, and a burning shock crackled through my middle, sending me to the floor in convulsions.

'Paige,' Verča gasped. 'Paige, are you all right?'

Tears leaked down my cheeks. All I could do was groan at the searing pain in my back.

'Can you leave her alone?' Maria said hotly. Harald hauled me to my feet. 'Harald!'

'I am making sure that Paige will comply,' he said, 'and that we draw no unwanted attention.'

As he wrenched me into a freezing night, I tried to get a handle on his masked associates, but with all of us on alysoplasm, I could only rely on my physical senses. The whole group was dressed in mountaineering gear, with no obvious insignia, and each of them held a sleek rifle.

'Harald,' Verča said, 'does Yousry know about this?'

Neither she nor Maria had been allowed to bring their coats. I had a feeling Harald didn't care if they survived the night.

'No. Yousry is clean,' he said. 'His only mistake was trusting me. He told me Radomír had asked him to take a person of interest to Command. I guessed it was Paige and arranged the accident, knowing Yousry would recommend me to replace him.'

'You contemptible—' Maria fumed. 'You could have killed the man!'

'This is the only way. Again, Nina, I am sorry.'

'You're terrible at being a traitor, Harald. At least commit to villainy and stop apologising.'

'I am doing this so I won't have to betray Domino any more than I already have. It will be over now,' he said, more to himself than us. 'When I deliver Paige.'

Of course. I was nothing but a parcel, to be passed around and traded. First Cordier and now this.

In that moment, I saw my life as a path drawn by others, from the day my father had put me on a plane to England. For twelve years, I had tried to claw back some control, only to end up here, on this cold mountain, at the mercy of strangers.

I refused to be taken back to Scion against my will. When I returned, it would be on my terms.

The group escorted us towards the bridge. It might be our one and only chance to tip the scales in our favour. I searched for anything I could exploit, my eyes straining against the dark.

Harald stopped, keeping a firm grip on my shoulder. One of his people approached the bridge first. As they put their weight on it, the cables gave a tortured creak that carried right the way across the valley.

'Harald, this is madness,' Verča said, staring at the decayed structure. 'You're going to kill us all.'

'We'll be fine. One at a time.'

Verča huffed. 'One death at a time?'

We waited for the bruiser to cross. Maria was shivering. Once the chirps and shudders had subsided, her captor jabbed her between the shoulders with his rifle.

'Touch me again,' she said, 'and I promise you, I will burn you alive.'

The next shove almost knocked her over. 'Enough,' Harald said, with a note of genuine anger in his voice. 'We agreed there would be no violence. No bloodshed.' He blotted sweat from his upper lip, pupils down to pinpricks. 'Nina, please. These people do not work for me.'

Maria ignored him. She hooked a thumb into her back pocket, where I could just see the lid of a lighter.

Harald had been so concerned with bridling my gift, he had forgotten to do the same to the others. Maria could use that lighter to ignite the few spirits in the area, but couldn't risk it yet, with rifles pointing at us. From the way Verča had described her clairvoyance, she wouldn't be able to help in a fight, but if I could get her away from the guns, Maria would be free to act.

I took stock of the bridge again, noting the ice and snowmelt. The stabilising cables looked weak, corroded. A few safety railings had rusted away.

Maria strode out in defiant silence. Once she had made it over, her guard went after her. As we waited for the bridge to stop trembling, I spied a glimmer of torchlight in the distance, on the far side of the lake.

'That was a real patrol we ran into earlier, then,' I said to Harald.

'Yes.' He let go of me. 'Go across, please, Paige. We don't want any more company.'

'The present company *is* scintillating.'

'Don't try anything, Underqueen,' came a muffled voice from under a ski mask. 'It can get much worse.'

I shook my head and stepped on to the bridge, conscious of the guns at my back. Glancing over my shoulder, I saw Harald standing behind Verča, big and muscular, almost a head and shoulders taller.

Steel and wood squeaked as I walked. An idea was coming together. By the time I was halfway across the bridge, the darkness had thickened, and my heart was hammering. This needed to look authentic. I was going to have to commit to the bit. As soon as I saw a gap in the railings, I fell hard beside it, hoping my scream was convincing.

Torchlight gleamed towards me from both sides of the bridge. I had already swung half my body over the edge, holding on tight to the railings.

'Someone help me up,' I called out, my voice laced with true fear. The bridge quaked as Harald started on to it. 'Not you, you hulking great idiot – you'll take us all down!'

He froze.

'Harald, I'm lightest,' Verča said, catching on. 'Let me go.'

'This had better not be a trick, Paige,' Harald barked at me.

'Does it look like a fucking trick?' I snarled back. 'You think I would risk my life for a trick?'

'Hold on, Paige.' Verča grasped the sides. 'Hold on.'

One of the railings was already starting to strain in my grasp. My left wrist throbbed, and my arms were tired out from the climb. I fought to keep my elbows on the walkway. I hadn't feared heights for years, but my hands sweated as I thought of the death that waited down there. The cold black lake would hit me like concrete, shattering my bones.

This might have been a bad idea.

As Verča approached, the railing snapped. Without hesitation, she dived for me, seizing my arm just in time. I clung to her with one hand and clawed for the walkway with the other.

'I've got you. Come on,' Verča urged. I hooked a knee on to the bridge. 'Paige, what were you thinking?'

'I had to separate you. We need—'

Fire erupted at the end of the bridge, followed by gunshots. Almost blind in the dark, without the æther to guide me, I scrambled to my feet and pushed Verča in front of me, shielding her.

Our footfalls made the bridge shudder. As Maria wielded flaming spirits on her side, one of the masked bruisers barrelled past Harald.

'Back off,' I shouted at them. 'Back off!'

Too late. With a *thwang*, a cable gave way, and the bridge swung loose with a screech of rusted steel. It careered to the right, pitching me with it. Verča made a desperate grab for a railing.

A strangled cry went up as our pursuer fell. Harald was bellowing for all he was worth, but I couldn't hear over the deafening shriek of metal, the wind, my laboured breathing.

We lunged forward, trying to both move and hold on, as the bridge started to list, tilting us towards the chasm. Verča let go of the railing to our left, only to stumble and slam into the other side. A metal rod broke under her weight, but the others held, stopping her from tumbling off the bridge altogether. A moment later, I lost my balance and joined her against the railings, teeth clenched. If the bridge leaned much farther, we would be hanging over the drop by our fingertips.

Now the whole thing was coming apart. With a twist that uprooted my stomach, it rolled left, dumping us back on the walkway. Before it could steal our footing again, we picked ourselves up and sprinted for the end. Verča made it, right as two more cables sprang free.

I was too far behind. Realising what was about to happen, I wrapped an arm and a leg around the railings – seconds before the wind ripped through my hair, and I was weightless, holding on to one half of a torn bridge.

When it struck the cliff face, I lost my grip. I plummeted for two heartbeats, and then I caught myself.

The shock washed off me. As I heaved for breath, the other section of the bridge gave a groan before it crashed into the lake. The explosion of water soaked me to the skin. Somehow I fought off the panic and held on, kicking for a foothold.

The ruin made an ominous sound. Blinking water off my lashes, I stared up twenty feet, craning my neck. My side was still attached to the cliff. I was going to have to scale this skeleton of a bridge like a ladder.

I reached up and gripped a railing.

Cramps shot through my hands. My wrist was on fire. As I shinned between handholds, losing strength for every gain, I remembered climbing a ladder in Paris, saving myself from death once more. I had been tired then, as I was now. So tired I could hardly see.

No matter how far I ran, I always seemed to end up like this, trying to stop the world shaking me off, into the æther. The temptation to let it loosened my fingers. The thought of Arcturus firmed them again. If I didn't do this, I would never know what had happened.

Just as I thought my wrist would fail me for the last time, I glimpsed Maria and Verča at the top, shouting my name. Their hands found mine, and together, they pulled me up. I collapsed into their arms, shaking all over, as the rest of the bridge left its moorings and fell.

'You,' Maria said hoarsely, 'are the luckiest woman alive.'

'I strongly disagree,' I croaked.

Two bodies were on fire nearby. I turned to face the cliff where Harald Lauring must still be.

'Do you think this changes anything for me?' His voice came from the darkness, carried by the wind. 'Yes, well done, you got away. Well done, Underqueen!' Maria drew us both closer. 'I cannot, will not, let my family die. So now I will have to betray all of Domino! I will have to hand *everyone* to her, to Grapevine. Don't you understand that I know everything about Command, as their courier – where they are, who they are?'

'No,' Verča breathed.

'And now I will have to kill you,' Harald roared, 'so you don't warn them!' Maria wiped blood from her chin, panting. 'I told you all what was at stake. You made me do this!'

Before any of us could move, bullets sparked off what remained of the bridge. The entire valley reflected the din as we hit the ground, Verča smothering a cry. With all my might, I tried to dreamwalk, but all I did was give myself a nosebleed and a blinding headache. Instead, I went for the corpses, their weapons. Harald might be shooting blind, but one stray bullet could still find us.

On our side, a clipped gunshot rang out.

When the echoes had faded, silence descended on the valley. I looked around to see a tall woman step into the firelight, dressed for the cold, a sniper rifle in her grasp. She took in the two bodies, then me.

'Well,' she said, 'I see you remain a force of infinite chaos, Flora Blake. I can't say I missed it.' She held out a gloved hand. 'But it's comforting to know some things don't change.'

'Ducos,' I said, with a laugh of relief.

My former Domino supervisor gave me a firm tug back to my feet. 'I am going to kill you,' Isaure Ducos said, her dark eyes reflecting the fire. 'Later.'

'Thank you. I mean, yes, fine.'

Maria suddenly hissed, making Ducos raise her rifle. 'Yoana,' Verča said, 'what is it?'

She fumbled a torch from the snow and shone it on Maria, revealing the hilt of a knife, protruding from her sleeve.

'Oh.' Maria let out a pained chuckle. 'I probably should have noticed that sooner.'

# 6

## CITY OF MASKS

The rest of the night was a merciless slog. The collapse of the bridge would have drawn every Italian drone and patrol in the area, which gave us a chance to get clear of the Alps without being detected. Verča supported Maria, while Ducos led us onward, keeping to cover as much as possible. Two burning spirits lit our way, sticking close to Maria.

Ducos refused to answer questions ('Just walk, please, Flora'), so I fell back to check on Maria, plodding over rocks and snow with a combat knife in her upper arm. I had draped my jacket over her shoulders to warm her.

'Hey,' I said. 'How are you holding up?'

'I've had worse.' She gave me a wan smile. 'You're usually the one with the dire injury.'

The smile didn't reach her eyes. She had ruled her section of London with an iron fist, but she had never relished bloodshed. Now she had been forced to kill two people in one night.

'I'll let you steal the spotlight just this once,' I said. 'Are you all right, Verča?'

'I'm fine, thanks to you,' Verča said. 'I can't believe you hung off the bridge, all to separate me from Harald.'

'Oh, Paige has done bolder things in her time. She possesses the loyalty of a beagle and the chaotic abandon of a headless chicken,' Maria said. 'It's a dangerous marriage.'

'You're a riot, Hazurova,' I said.

'I know.'

'Less talking,' Ducos called from some way ahead. 'More movement, please.'

Maria sent an exasperated look after her. 'Yes. Movement is easy.' She sucked in a deep breath before taking another step. 'How do you know this mysterious sharpshooter, Paige?'

'Ducos was my supervisor.'

'The one who kicked you out?'

'She's sound. Just takes a while to warm up to people. And doesn't like arson.'

'We'll get on like a house on fire, then.'

'Please.'

'She must have come looking for you, Paige,' Verča said. 'Domino supervisors often go to great lengths to find agents or associates who disappear.'

I looked after Ducos, wondering.

Morning soon lit the summits of the Alps. At last, we stepped over the brow of a hill to see a wide green valley, most of it still cast into the shadow of the mountains. This must be the end of the pass. Ducos looked through a pair of binoculars, hair ruffling in the wind.

'Please, terrifying saviour,' Maria said, 'tell me we've reached Italy.'

'Fortunately for you.' Ducos tucked the binoculars back into her body warmer. 'Let's keep moving.'

Verča looked with concern at Maria, who was pouring sweat. 'How much farther?'

'Half an hour.' Ducos nodded to where our path thinned into a steep trail, winding down the slopes like thread. 'I would let you rest, but we need to get clear of this pass as soon as possible, for reasons I presume are apparent.'

She started down the trail, her rifle protruding from its holster on her back. Maria nodded to Verča.

'Harald made you drink something,' Maria said to me as we pressed on. 'What was it?'

'It was alysoplasm. Buzzer blood,' I said. 'It cuts you off from the æther for a while.'

'Of course it does. There is no end to the misery.' She sighed. 'I really can't wait for today to be over.'

Pine trees flanked the lower stretches of the trail. As soon as we had that cover, I could breathe a little easier. Ducos and I had shoved two bodies into the lake, but it wouldn't be long until the patrols found Harald. His surviving associates would have alerted Grapevine.

I was already out of my depth out here. Two groups had come after me in the space of a week, and I'd never heard of either of them.

Ducos led us to a black vehicle in a car park for hikers. She unpacked some emergency medical supplies while Verča helped Maria into the back.

'Try not to let her fall asleep,' Ducos said. Maria was now almost white in the face, hair stuck to her brow. 'Lie her across the seats, and maintain pressure on either side of the knife. We'll need to keep her stable until we get to headquarters.'

———

Ducos did as much as she could for Maria, bandaging around the knife. Once the blade was secure and the wound padded, she drove out of the valley and on to a long motorway, which stretched beneath a sun-bleached sky. Verča applied pressure and fought to keep Maria awake, but despite her best efforts, Maria drifted into a fitful sleep.

'Don't panic,' Ducos said. 'There is no point in panicking.'

Verča nodded, swallowing. 'How long before we reach headquarters?'

'Three hours. She'll be fine,' Ducos said, seeing our faces. 'Keep her warm, and don't pull the knife out.'

'She isn't a fugitive in Italy,' I said. 'Can we not take her to a hospital?'

'I wouldn't risk it.'

Ducos drove over a river. Maria made a sound of discomfort, her eyes restless beneath their lids.

I watched the mountains from a safe distance. My body was cold and bruised from the hike. After a while, I nodded off, which was clearly going to be a regular occurrence for a while. It was only when Ducos opened her window that I woke to the sound of blustering wind. Now we were out of the Alps, she had taken off her bodywarmer and sweater.

The æther prickled at my perception, like sensation returning to a dead arm. I sat up.

'You had an eventful night,' Ducos said. 'What happened?'

'You first,' I said. 'Why aren't you in Paris?'

The wind blew her dark hair, showing a recent scar near her temple.

'After the airstrikes, I believed Stéphane and I were the only surviving members of Mannequin. We were pulled out of Scion, and the sub-network was classified as non-operational. Given my years of long service, I was promoted to Command, despite the loss of three agents,' she said. 'But I couldn't stop thinking about Paris. At first, I presumed it was your auxiliary who betrayed us, but your underworld contacts remained safe in their usual hideouts. Warden knew about those places. Why didn't he tell Scion?'

We had been thinking along the same lines.

'I began to suspect he wasn't the leak,' she said, 'but someone was. I started combing through every record, every detail, leaving no stone unturned. It wasn't until late August that I noticed a clue I had missed for months. Cordier had once requested a tracking unit to monitor an informant, which I had approved. I checked if the unit had ever been activated.'

'Had it?'

'A week before the airstrikes. After her sudden disappearance.' She changed lanes. 'I assembled a team to analyse its available data. It had been in several countries. I watched it move to Poland, and then to Czechia. It arrived there on the tenth of September.'

'It's ... in me?'

Ducos nodded. 'Cordier must have implanted it when she drained your lung in Paris. This abduction was plotted with care. Most likely, she betrayed your safe house to separate you from Warden.'

'Even before that, she gave him her number. I thought she was just flirting with him.'

'She was. We have a term for it, in the trade – honey trapping. It was one of her specialities. I imagine she wanted to get rid of him quietly, without any risk of endangering you. When that failed, she had no choice but to expose the safe house while you were gone, so Scion could deal with him.'

I had given her that opportunity. I had left, when Arcturus was tired and weak, to hammer out my differences with Léandre. Cordier must have been keeping watch on the apartment.

'No doubt she received a reward,' Ducos said. 'To fund whatever she was planning.'

Her tone was stiff. She and Cordier must have built a great deal of trust, working together in Scion.

'So you went to intercept the tracking unit,' I said. 'Did you know it was me at that point?'

'I was nearly certain. By then, Radomír Doleček had informed Command of your arrival,' Ducos said. 'I gave him orders to send you to Italy.' She stopped at a red light. 'I decided to await you on the other side of the Alps. All day, I kept an eye on the tracking unit. You took a long diversion from the path. When you stopped moving at dusk, I assumed that you were resting at the cabin, but my instincts told me to head in your direction in case you needed assistance. Around one in the morning, however, your signal vanished.'

Harald had either known or guessed. He had given me that shock to fry the tracking unit.

'Fortunately,' Ducos said, 'I was close enough to your location that I could still find you.' She tilted the mirror. 'I take it your companions are Nina Aprilova and Veronika Norlenghi.'

'Yes.'

'At least you all survived the night.' She kept driving. 'What happened to you after the airstrikes?'

'I don't know,' I said. 'Cordier gave me white aster.'

'As much as you remember, then.'

Fighting the urge to sleep again, I recounted what little I had. By the time I had finished, her grip on the wheel had tightened several times.

'Grapevine is a Scion espionage network,' she said. 'I'll need you to repeat all of this to Command.'

'I thought you were Command?'

'Command is made up of twelve individuals. Two of us are based in Italy. You'll be speaking to one of the founding members.' Ducos glanced at me. 'You look drained. Is it the aster?'

'I'm worried about Warden.'

'You're doubting his betrayal, too.'

'I need to be sure.'

'I did my best to locate everyone after the airstrikes, including Warden. There was no trace,' Ducos said, 'but Italy is where our intelligence pools. You may not find all the answers you need, but perhaps we can make a start.'

---

At some point, the mountains shallowed into hills, and then we were driving past olive groves, vineyards and cornfields, kissed by the golds of early autumn. Ducos passed me a pair of sunglasses from the glove compartment, and I leaned out of the window, wind roaring through my hair.

So far, Italy reminded me of the southern France I had once dreamed of visiting, the place in the glossy brochures. My father had brought them home for me sometimes, so I could imagine being elsewhere.

About an hour into the journey, Ducos parked in a garage and got out to make a call, while a man changed the registration plates. She checked on Maria, who was in and out of consciousness, but hadn't gone into shock. Soon we were on the road again, and I drifted back to sleep.

And then there was bright water on either side of us, sunlight rolling off its waves. I blinked against the glare.

'Venezia,' Verča murmured. 'Of course. Domino is a game, but also a kind of mask, for Carnevale.'

I worked the ache from my neck. 'We're in Venice?'

'Yes,' Ducos said. 'Welcome to the Floating City.'

At the end of the bridge, a guard motioned for Ducos to stop the car. She showed him a pass and spoke to him in Italian. After a few nods, he waved us through.

Ducos drove into the outskirts of Venice, under a brick archway and down a slope, to where three other vehicles sat in a courtyard, beneath a trellis dripping pink roses. A woman emerged to deal with the plates, while another hooked the car up to a charging station.

'Domino has dispatched a boat,' Ducos said. 'Stay with her,' she told Verča, who nodded. Maria looked worse than ever. 'Flora, come with me.'

I followed her back into the sun, to a row of roofed jetties marked TAXI, which prodded into a broad waterway.

'Stay alert,' Ducos advised me, standing at the end of one. 'Venice should be safe, but I'll get you a dissimulator. Scion is offering a reward for your capture.'

'I know. I thought you said I'd had my last dissimulator?'

'I can make an exception. Try not to lose or damage this one,' she said. 'In the meantime, keep the sunglasses.'

Of all the places I had visited so far, it was most surreal to be in Venice – a city held in high regard in the syndicate, whose traders I had met before. A city I had never imagined I would see.

'You're quiet. Unusual for you,' Ducos remarked. 'Though I'm pleased to hear you're not coughing any longer.' She folded her arms. 'It must be strange, to be out of Scion.'

'How long did you work there?'

'Fifteen years. I was older than you when I went in.'

'Since we're out of Scion, do I get to know your real name?'

'Ducos will suffice.'

A motorboat approached us. Three people hopped off it, then lifted Maria from the car and into its cabin. Once we were all on board, the skipper pulled away from the jetty.

The Grand Canal was creamy green, lined with buildings. Most of the façades were painted in shades of pink and peach, with glimpses of crimson or harvest gold. Some looked timeworn, if not derelict: paint cracking off stone, windows boarded, shutters loose and rotten. Somehow they enhanced the charm.

I should have been afraid on that boat. This city was floating on my worst fear, but I wanted to make use of my time here. I didn't want to break down every time I stepped outside. So I took measured breaths, and I searched for beauty. The way the water glittered where it broke, the sunlight dancing on the waves. As we moved along the Grand Canal, it became easier, as more wonders unfolded. Engoldened by the sun, Venice was as stunning as Prague.

Mooring posts rose from the canal, striped like candy canes. Our boat forged under bridges and past other vessels – rowboats, barges, a water ambulance – before drawing up by a wedding cake of a building, adorned with intricate rope-work. We stepped on to a shaded quay and into a courtyard with a floor covered in black and white tiles.

Ducos strode past an old well and across an alley, into the garden of the next building, where insects chirped in the trees. High above the alley, an enclosed bridge connected the buildings.

Inside, people crisscrossed a magnificent foyer. A grand staircase went up several floors, and sunlight poured through a mirrored glass ceiling.

This was the heart of Domino. If there was any whisper in the world of Arcturus, it would be here.

The people from the boat got a sweating Maria up the stairs. Verča went after them. I was about to follow when a bearded man emerged from an archway to the right, face set in determination. He wore a collared white shirt and beige trousers. Seeing me, he stopped.

Nine months had passed since our parting on the docks of Dover. Those months had changed him. Once a pale blond, his hair was now sandy brown, and his face and arms had tanned. If not for his dreamscape, I might have walked right past him in a crowd.

'Nick,' I whispered.

We both started to grin. A moment later, Nick Nygård ran to meet me and scooped me into a crushing embrace. I threw my arms around his neck.

90

'I knew you'd be here,' I said, my voice muffled. 'I knew it.'

'Paige.' He grasped the back of my head. 'I thought you were gone. I thought you died in Paris.'

I gripped him just as hard. Nick was here, and he was alive, and we were together, the way it was supposed to be. 'You grew a beard,' I said, with a weak laugh.

'Domino made me.'

It was only now I held my best friend that I understood how much I had missed him. When he put me down, he took my face between his hands.

'I can't believe you're alive,' he said hoarsely. 'I grieved you, Paige.' He traced the scars on my cheek. 'I need to help the others, but I'll take you for dinner. Will you be all right?'

'I'll be fine.'

Nick ran up the stairs. I watched him go, still with a fond smile on my face.

'Ducos,' I said, 'did you know Nick was here?'

'I thought you might enjoy the surprise,' she said.

'Who are you and what have you done with my supervisor?'

'You may find me less tense outside Scion.' Ducos started up the stairs, beckoning me to join her. 'To most of the city, these buildings are offices. To us, they form the Palazzo del Domino. It's supported by the Libuše Institute of Prague and the Yerebatan Institute of Istanbul. I told you that Domino was created after the Balkan Incursion, which is what I believed, but I learned otherwise when I joined Command.'

'So even you don't know everything.'

'I do now. Domino was founded here in 2015, but the network only grew after the Balkans, when Scion showed it had ambitions to conquer the world.'

Ducos led me up two flights of stairs, to a wide corridor with a polished floor and screened windows.

'This building is the Palazzo della Notte. This is where we provide refuge for agents at risk, like you,' she said. 'The other side is the Palazzo del Giorno, where you'll meet Command.'

My room was an elegant affair. The huge bed was upholstered in gold brocade, laden with pillows and silk cushions.

'This will be yours for as long as you're here.' Ducos handed me a key. 'Dinner is served in the bar from half past five, and breakfast from six in the morning. If you'd like a meal in your room at any time, call the concierge. You'll find a gym on this floor, and a library above.'

'When do I see Command?'

'I'll let you know. For now, get some rest. Oh, and if you could restrain yourself from destroying this building, I would be grateful,' she said crisply. 'I may not be your supervisor any longer, but as the person vouching for you, your actions do continue to reflect on me.'

She closed the door. I locked it and leaned against it, listening to the quiet in the room.

Another temporary home. A base while I explored my options.

Behind a sliding door, I found a bathroom with a clawfoot tub. I checked that I could feel the æther, sensing the many spirits of Venice. While the water ran, I undressed and sat on the bed, letting the air conditioning do its work. This was the sort of warmth that drew sweat even in the shade, in stillness. It worsened the unrelenting fatigue.

Hard to believe this was the fourth country I had entered in as many days. So much had happened to me in so little time. It had only been a year and a half since I had learned the truth behind Scion. Part of me had thrived in the fast lane, but I could tell that I was running on empty batteries, and I didn't know how to recharge any more.

Even in this balmy weather, I needed the bathwater hot enough to steam. Once I had soaked the ache from my body, I wrapped myself in a thick fluffy towel, my hair dripping. While I was in the tub, someone had left a set of pyjamas on the bed, along with the dissimulator, rolled small in its airtight tube. Once I had changed, I took the tin of blue aster from my jacket. I was losing my patience with being so tired.

The patches were small and round. Peeling the back off one, I smoothed it on to my upper arm and lay on the bed. No sooner had my head touched the pillow than I was asleep.

And when I woke up, I remembered.

*Get out of my way. You've been poisoning me.* My voice was shaking. *I know something is wrong.*

*Paige, you're in shock from the airstrikes.* Eléonore Cordier stood in front of me, her hands slightly raised, her expression calm. *I told you you'd have memory issues. I'm not the person you're—*

*Where is Warden?*

*We've been over this. Warden betrayed you.*

*He wouldn't. He would never do that.* An indescribable ache in my chest, strong enough that I could barely speak, slicking my cheeks with tears. *He's in pain. They're killing him. I have to find him, before—*

*You can't leave, Paige. You're in too much danger.*

But the door was right behind her, and I had done more reckless things. I made a break for it.

Cordier grabbed my left wrist, the bad one. The familiar pain shot along my arm, but it was a shadow of the crushing force in my chest, which radiated through the golden cord. I fought her tooth and nail. A criminal against a spy. All the while, she kept hold of my wrist.

*Get your fucking hands off me—*

*I'm sorry. I don't want to do this.* There was strained remorse in her voice. *I promise this is almost over.*

She twisted my wrist. In the blinding moment that followed, she plunged a syringe into my arm.

At any other time, the agony would have floored me, but no pain on Earth could stop me in that moment. Not when I needed to reach Arcturus; when I knew that failing him could be fatal. With my last ounce of strength, I took out the steak knife – the one I had concealed at dinner – and drove it into Cordier.

A scream rang in my ears. I sat up and removed the patch. It had left a round blue stain on my skin, like a bruise.

Arcturus had looked into my past in Oxford, but with such a soft touch that I hadn't realised it was happening for a long time. There was a reason his gift was called oneiromancy – he could unfold a memory like an amaurotic dream, to be forgotten by morning.

Blue aster was different. It had brought my memory back with a jolt. That confrontation had been locked away, and now it no longer was.

*Recent events will come back to you first.*

That memory must have been the night before I woke up, alone and disoriented, in Poland.

Cordier had managed to inject me before I stabbed her. The syringe must have contained my dose of white aster, resetting my clock to March. She had left the hotel, presumably to patch herself up. I had driven the blade into her right side, which meant I could have hit her liver, or a kidney – a critical injury, but if anyone could have survived, it was a medical officer.

That was how the deception had ended. I had felt something from Arcturus, strong enough to nearly derange me. I would have fought anyone to leave that room, to get to him.

I gave the cord a tentative pull, trying to understand why it wasn't moving. And then an older memory stirred.

I was four years old, living on my grandparents' farm in Ireland. While I was out playing, I had found a mouse at the back of the cowshed, limp and silent. I had picked it up with care and carried it to my grandfather, who seemed to be able to fix anything.

*Daideo, look, it's poorly.* I had stood on tiptoe to place it on his workbench. *Can you wake it up?*

With a kind smile, my grandfather had sat me on his knee and told me no one could. The mouse was dead, but it was at peace, and I wasn't to worry. Nothing could ever hurt it now.

I had been told my mother was dead, but I had never seen a body. I had no physical evidence of her existence – not one keepsake or photograph – and so I had imagined death as the sudden and total erasure of a person, leaving no trace but a story. But when I saw that mouse, I began to understand that something could be there, but also gone.

That was how the cord felt now.

A distraction came in the form of a knock. I went to the door. Nick stood outside, wearing a fresh shirt.

'Hey,' I said. 'How's the patient?'

'Sleeping off a cocktail of painkillers and antibiotics. She'll have a scar, but the knife missed her axillary nerve,' Nick said. 'I can't believe she managed to walk out of the Alps.'

'You know Maria. Tough as nails.' I stood aside. 'Come in.'

He did, closing the door behind him. 'Verča seems nice,' he said. 'She has the same kind of aura as Dani, doesn't she?'

'I think so.' I stepped behind the folding screen and changed into the linen shorts and blouse that had been left for me. 'I don't suppose you've heard from Dani?'

'Not a word. Verča said you ran into some trouble in the Alps,' he added. 'We'll talk about it, but you need dinner and a few new clothes first. Italy can get hot in September.'

'I noticed.' I put my boots on. 'Shopping and dinner in Venice. You'd think we were ordinary people.'

'Out here, I think we almost are.'

I went up to the mirror to put on my dissimulator. My features changed as it bonded with my skin, pinching and tucking until a different woman looked back, one who bore only a passing resemblance to me.

'Unsettling, aren't they?' Nick said. 'I've been lax with mine, since I'm not on Incrida.'

'Just me that got slapped with a red notice, then.'

'You were always the one Nashira wanted most. There is a reward for my capture, but only in Scion. And not for half as much.'

We went down the staircase and through a side door, back into the alley. Nick led me out to a wide paved street, where people flocked in and out of shops and browsed at stalls. A white sign read STRADA NOVA, while two yellow ones read ALLA FERROVIA and PER RIALTO.

'This is bizarre,' I said to Nick. 'This morning, I was freezing my face off in the Alps. Now I'm sweltering in Venice. At least my life is never dull.' He chuckled. 'Nice hair, by the way.'

'Thanks. Domino asked me to dye it.' He smoothed a hand over it. 'Just as I got my first greys.'

'Bit early, aren't you?'

'I was a child prodigy. I've always aged early. And you're responsible for at least half of my grey hairs.'

'Right, like working for Jax never turned your hair grey.'

'That's the other half.'

I smiled and put the sunglasses on. It felt good to have my best friend at my side again.

Despite it being late in the afternoon, the air was still thick and warm. I lingered by a shop with a rainbow of glass ornaments in the window, then followed Nick over a narrow canal. On the other side, a man paced back and forth on a rooftop, shouting at the top of his voice.

'Abbracciate Scion! Non temetelo,' he called. A few people laughed, while others ignored him. 'A Venezia dimorano forze soprannaturali. Solo l'àncora può salvarvi tutti. Quando arriva in Italia, accoglietelo a braccia aperte!'

'Va a remengo.' An elderly woman gesticulated in disgust. 'Ti xe drio dir monae!'

Nick ushered me on.

'He mentioned Scion,' I said. 'Why?'

'He's urging Italy to embrace Scion when it comes. Apparently the anchorites are spreading across Europe.' He steered me towards a shop. 'Here. This place should have something you like.'

Fashion was the least of my concerns, but Nick was right. Most of the clothes and shoes in the shop were the sort of thing I would choose in London – though I usually dressed for the cold, not the melting point of iron. I couldn't get used to being this warm in September.

Nick passed me a roll of banknotes and left me to it. When I emerged from the shop, I had three stuffed bags, which he insisted on taking. 'From what Verča told me, your arms won't cope with these for long,' he said, giving me a look. 'Did you hang off an old bridge?'

'I hung off an old and rusty bridge.'

'I'd scold you, but I did give you that particular itch. I only wish you'd make a normal entrance every once in a while.'

'You think I don't want the same?'

'Not sure.'

I sat down to exchange my boots for the sturdy wedge sandals I had chosen. Nick had instructed me to buy a sun hat, which I donned.

He took me to a pharmacy so I could buy and stock a washbag. As I browsed the shelves, I thought of my trusty old backpack, which contained almost everything I owned, including the gift Arcturus had fashioned me for my twentieth birthday. I had left it with the perdues in Paris.

My inheritance from my father was also in that backpack. An applewood box. Jaxon had stolen its contents, and now he could be anywhere, including the æther. I might never know what Colin had given me.

It was almost sunset by the time we got back to the Palazzo del Domino. Nick showed me into a magnificent bar, dominated by a huge carved fireplace (mercifully unlit), marble pillars, and a glistening chandelier. Like the rest of the building, it was air-conditioned. A few people sat at polished tables, eating or working on laptops.

We chose a spot behind a folding screen. I kept my dissimulator on. Once Nick had ordered our food and returned to his seat, he clasped his hands on the table.

'Okay,' he said. 'Tell me everything.'

# 7

## GRAPEVINE

'Does it make more sense for me to start, or you?' I said. 'Our stories are going to overlap at some point.'

'You go first,' Nick said. 'I imagine you have more ground to cover.'

A waitron brought us a bottle of ersatz wine, as close as we could get to mecks. Nick filled two glasses, and I began.

For Ducos, I had stuck to the points that would be of interest to her, but with Nick, I spared no detail. I started with the day Warden and I had arrived in Calais and went from there.

I was halfway through the story by the time our meals arrived. The sun had gone down while I talked, and more Domino personnel had come in for dinner, creating a background hum that made it difficult to catch individual conversations. A pianist had started to play, and his music drifted across the bar, so eavesdropping was harder still. Even inside its own headquarters, Domino was cautious.

Nick ate his cod as I described the escape from Versailles, including the silver-haired stranger who had saved me from the flood. The man I was convinced had been Jaxon.

'How could it have been him?' Nick asked me.

'A few days after our escape, we found the Rag and Bone Man dying in a sewer. He'd been disembowelled,' I said. 'He said himself that Jaxon was the one who did it.'

'Jax could have escaped another way. If he *was* the man who saved you, he must have had a dissimulator,' Nick said, 'and that makes no sense, because Domino asked you to assassinate him. However he got out of Versailles, I worry he has designs on London.'

'He'll have designs on London for ever.'

'True.' He drank some ersatz. 'So you left Versailles and then went straight to hunt the Rag and Bone Man?'

I lowered my gaze.

'No,' I said. 'Something else happened first.'

It took all my willpower to recount the next part, when Arcturus had been detained and I had gone rushing to his rescue. His claim that he had won my trust so he could betray me.

'I'm sorry,' Nick murmured. 'It must have been terrible to hear him say those things.'

I hadn't admitted that Arcturus and I had taken our physical intimacy a step farther, but Nick knew me well. He would be able to read between the lines.

'You sent a warning to London,' Nick said. 'I was there.'

'How?'

'My supervisor was someone from my past. He gave me a lot of freedom.'

'Who was it?'

'Max.'

I raised my eyebrows. 'Wait, *the* Max?'

'The very same.'

Max Thorsell had met Nick when he moved to Stockholm. Nick had been a boy from the coast, with a rare aura and none of the knowledge he needed to protect himself. Max had taught him to fight and climb, and initiated him into a voyant gang named the Hökar.

They might have been a perfect match, had Max not thrived on danger to the point that he would go out of his way to create it, often provoking Vigiles. When he was training Nick, he had once sabotaged their handholds, just to see how Nick dealt with falling. Nick had broken his ankle. He hadn't told me a great deal more, except that the relationship had ended when he moved to London.

'That's quite a coincidence,' I said.

'No, I don't think so. Max had been resisting Scion since he was thirteen. Domino snapped him up. We didn't get back together,' Nick said, anticipating my question. 'He wanted to, but he was never good for me. I became the medical officer of his sub-network, Docka.'

'I take it you had an alias.'

'Isak Törnqvist.' He sipped his drink again. 'In late January, we received orders to investigate a new Scion detention facility on Gotland. This site was code named Tuonela III.'

'That's the next Reph city. Nashira mentioned it when I was in Oxford.'

'I suspected as soon as I heard the name. Not that the others believed me. The intelligence pointed to a town called Visby,' he said, 'but when we arrived, the population was still in place. I didn't understand it at the time, but you said Tjäder had allied with Ménard.'

'She's refusing to host the Rephs,' I murmured. 'I wondered when she would move against them.'

'I think you're right. She's stalling,' Nick said. 'Max thought I'd lost my mind, of course. I'd told him the Rephs would be there, but there was nothing. I asked him if I could visit London for a couple of weeks, to clear my head. He agreed.'

'When was that?'

'February. A few days after I arrived, so did Nadine and Zeke, with your warning about Warden.'

'But the Mime Order didn't act on it?'

'No. Nadine told us you had a dangerous fever in Paris, and Warden was never anything but gentle with you, even when he clearly thought no one was watching. She felt certain that he must have been coerced.'

I was turning numb. Had everyone seen the truth except me?

'Maria might already have told you,' Nick said, 'but I need to explain. You instructed the Mime Order to move to the shadow houses. The buildings you concealed from the Ranthen.'

'An abandoned industrial complex in Bromley,' I said. 'I never even told Warden about it.'

I had made that decision in my early days as Underqueen, when Jaxon had filled me with doubts about the Ranthen. Even in Paris, as I gradually fell in love with Arcturus, I had chosen not to mention the shadow houses, just in case. Just to quieten my fear of betrayal.

'The Ranthen refused to believe he was a double agent,' Nick said. 'Instead of moving to the shadow houses, we stayed put in the underground shelter. It saved us from the airstrikes.'

'You were still in London then?'

'Yes. In the Beneath,' he said. 'The bombardment of Paris was much worse. London must have been a warning shot, but they hit Tower Bridge and destroyed the Eye. Even the Vigiles were shaken, in the aftermath. If that was a glimpse of the war ahead, I'm afraid of it.'

Nick rarely admitted to fear. It disturbed me. Even now, I saw him as our fixer, the strong and logical Red Vision.

'They all spoke for Warden,' I said quietly. 'I'm the one who's meant to be his friend. The one who's lived with him, who—' I shook my head. 'Nick, I think I left him to die.'

'You had the whole syndicate on your shoulders, Paige. Thousands of lives were at risk. What could you do but take him at his word?'

It took me a few moments to collect myself.

Nick did have a point. As Underqueen, my overriding duty was to protect the syndicate. I knew I had made the logical choice – to preserve my own life and raise the alarm – but if that night had been a test of my faith in Arcturus, I had failed. Even when I'd had a chance to think, I had let my pride and pain keep me from going back for him.

And now his trail was long since cold. I might never see him again.

'Paige, look at me,' Nick said, softer. I lifted my head. 'The Sargas understand exactly which buttons to press. You have to forgive yourself for responding. I know Warden will.'

'He isn't here to forgive me or not.' My voice shook. 'I've no idea where he is, Nick.'

He was spared from having to answer when Maria appeared. Her left arm was in a sling.

'I say this as a pyromancer,' she said. 'It may be too hot.'

'Maria.' Nick stood. 'You should be resting.'

'I was hungry,' she said. He drew another chair up for her. 'Do stop fussing, Nicklas.'

'It's my job to fuss.' He returned to his own seat. 'You were supposed to call the concierge for a meal.'

'Well, apologies for not knowing the school rules.' Maria sat down with a wince. 'And I desperately need a drink, for the agony.' She drank from his glass, then pulled a face. 'What in the name of the æther is this?'

'It's ersatz wine,' Nick said.

'What does that mean?'

'It means it isn't alcoholic.'

'I remind you that we are outside Scion, and no longer bound by the Inquisitorial prohibition. I am overdue a touch of lawful damage to my liver, and I'd like some authentic Italian wine.'

'I'll order some,' I said. 'Red or white?'

'Red. Thanks, sweet.'

Nick rubbed the bridge of his nose. 'Maria, you just woke up from an anaesthetic. I had to pull a knife out of your arm with pliers. I'd rather you avoided drinking after surgery.'

Maria sighed. 'Do the specific antibiotics I'm taking interact with alcohol?'

'No, but it can—'

'Then you can allow me one little tipple, Dr Nygård. There's no scimorphine out here.'

Leaving them to bicker, I ordered a bottle of wine and perched on a bar stool to wait. Even if Maria couldn't drink it, I might. I asked for a second glass, just in case.

Nick had no word of Arcturus. I had been a fool to hope.

*I know you didn't betray me.* I closed my eyes, concentrating on the golden cord. *Help me find you.*

'Flora.'

I glanced over my shoulder. Ducos had appeared to my left, wearing a fitted linen suit.

'You look preoccupied,' she said. 'Is everything all right?'

'Fine. Just thinking.'

'Don't tell me that. I'll worry.' She signalled to the bartender. 'My colleague in Command will see you tomorrow morning at nine. I've brought her abreast of the Alps incident, so you won't have to repeat yourself. I imagine you've spent most of this evening telling Dr Nygård.'

'Yes. Thanks.' My throat was sore from talking. 'Have you worked much with Nick?'

'Here and there. An exceptional addition to Domino,' Ducos said. (I could only dream of such praise.) 'Try not to be tired or hungover tomorrow.'

She stepped away before I could say another word, greeting another well-dressed woman in French. I accepted the bottle and glasses from the bartender and left Ducos to it.

'Nick,' I said, sitting back at our table, 'I think it's time you told us your side of things.'

'Yes, please.' Maria fanned herself with a menu. 'You went silent on me for two months.'

'I'm sorry,' Nick said, 'but I did have a reason.'

'Let's hear it.'

Nick had stayed in London until April. Once he was back in Sweden, Max had allowed him to pursue his own goals – one of which was to find his parents and uncle, who had been in hiding since November. By summer, Nick had tracked them down and moved them into nearby Denmark, where a Domino liaison had connected him to the Libuše Institute. Radomír had put him back in touch with Maria, who had met him at a hotel in Copenhagen.

'That was when I asked Maria to search for you,' Nick told me. 'I'd been having visions.'

'What sort of visions?'

'I saw you walking in the mist, with snow on your lashes and stars in your hair. I've never had a vision of a dead person,' he said. 'I knew we had to keep searching for you.'

'Is your family still in Denmark?'

'Domino interceded with the Icelandic government. Mamma was allowed to resume her citizenship, so they've moved to Bakkagerði. I'm glad they're finally out of danger.'

'That's great, Nick.'

'Yes,' Maria said. 'You did well to get them out.'

'It was only thanks to Max letting me use his Domino connections,' Nick said. 'I'll try to visit them before I go back into Scion. I've never met my Icelandic grandparents.'

'Your parents must be terrified for you,' I said. 'Didn't they want you to go with them?'

'Yes. They're afraid to lose their other child to Scion, but they understood why I wanted to stay.' He topped up his glass. 'I had orders to return to Sweden, to meet the rest of Docka in a forest called Kolmården. I got there late, only to find the safe house had been raided. Max was inside, bleeding out from a gunshot wound. He lived just long enough to tell me that Scion had been waiting, and the others had been taken to Rosenkammaren.'

Maria shook her head. 'Rosenkammaren?'

'A prison in Stockholm.' Nick put the bottle down. 'I've never known anyone to come out.'

'Shit. Any idea who betrayed you?'

'I have my suspicions. There was a Danish amaurotic called Sven, who doubled up as our courier and locksmith, specialising in infiltration – a lot of dangerous work. He'd been captured on assignment, but escaped. I wasn't sure his story added up, but Max liked him, so I kept my mouth shut. Now I wonder if he cut a deal with Scion.'

Maria gave me a weighty look, and I knew we were both thinking the same thing.

'Sven,' I said. 'Blond guy with a scar on his lip, big muscles, blue eyes?' Nick nodded. 'Maria, you'd better tell him. I don't think I can talk any more.'

She obliged. The blue aster had kept me awake for longer than usual, but clouds were gathering in my mind.

'Sven – Harald – is dead, then,' Nick said, when Maria was done. 'He must have got away with betraying us and been reassigned.' He shook his head. 'If he's gone, that means I'm out of immediate danger. I was ordered to lie low until the traitor had been identified and eliminated. Command needed a resident medic, so they offered me a position here. I was told not to contact anyone outside of headquarters. That's why you didn't hear from me, Maria.'

'I might forgive you,' Maria said. 'In time.' She adjusted her sling. 'So here we are, the three of us, reunited in the City of Masks. Nick, have you been called to this secret meeting?'

'Yes,' Nick said. 'Is that why you're both here?'

I nodded. 'I also need to find out if Command wants me to fulfil the rest of my contract. And ... to see if there are any leads on Arcturus.'

'You want to go looking for him.' Maria hesitated. 'Paige, it's been six months. Would Nashira not have executed him for what he's done?'

Nick glanced between us.

'Nashira doesn't like to execute Rephs,' I said. 'She prefers to ... make them see things her way. By any means necessary. And she has all the time in the world.'

'Well, if he *is* alive, he'll be in Scion.'

'Terebell was leading a search for him,' Nick said. 'We need to let her know that Paige survived, and to contact Eliza. I suggest we negotiate with Command to cut our contracts short and get back to London.'

'I will ask,' I said, 'but I need to keep Domino on side. In Paris, Ducos told me they might be willing to help finance the Mime Order. If we're going to take the rebellion to the next level, we need as much coin as we can get. I'll fulfil the rest of my contract if it helps us.'

'Paige, you need to be in London. You're Underqueen.'

'And you and Eliza are my mollishers. You have the right to hold the fort.' I reached for the wine. 'How did Terebell react to my warning about Arcturus?'

'I don't want to tell you.'

'I can take it.'

Nick sighed. 'She refused to entertain the possibility that Warden was a traitor. She also said it was no surprise you'd turned your back on him at the first opportunity. That she'd expected no less from someone groomed and trained by a turncoat like Jaxon,' he said. 'I argued with her about it. I'm sure they wilfully misunderstand humans.'

I tried not to let it get to me.

'I understand why she's angry,' I said. 'I seem to be the only one who doubted his loyalty.'

'It's complicated, Paige. You two had a rocky start,' Maria said. 'I like Warden, but let's not pretend he's perfect.' She switched on her cigarette. 'Except his jaw. I can't fault that.'

'I agree,' Nick said.

'So glad you share my appreciation for a fine mandible, Nicklas.'

'Not his—' Nick gave her a stern look. 'I mean that I agree with it being complicated. Paige, I know you forgave him for Oxford, but he used you once before. He admitted it to both of us. Of course you would have considered the idea that he could do it again.'

I thought back to that terrible night. Every word Arcturus had said had seemed designed to puncture our trust, hitting every weak point. He had called me by a number, not my name. He had reminded me of my insignificance, told me that touching me dirtied his hand. My natural instinct had been to slam up my defences and run for my life.

'I'll get us a coffee,' Nick said. 'It's great here.'

He went up to the bar.

'Thank you for today,' I said to Maria. 'I'd be with Scion by now if you hadn't used that lighter.'

'I meant what I said to Harald. You motley lot are the only family I have left,' Maria said. 'Don't let Terebell get under your skin. You don't need to justify yourself to her or anyone.'

She picked at our leftovers, letting me brood. Nick returned with a silver tray.

'Nicklas Nygård,' Maria said. 'Is that tiramisù I see with my own two eyes?'

'I have no idea.' Nick put it down. 'I just asked for whatever dessert they recommended.'

'Scion heathen.' Maria pushed it towards me. 'Paige, dig in. You'll love this.'

I took a tiny spoonful of the dessert. It was soft and creamy, and tasted like sweet coffee.

'Nick,' I said, 'Maria has told me all she knows, but what has the Mime Order been doing?'

'Eliza decided to prioritise training and recruitment for the next couple of years, to make sure we have the numbers and skills to confront Scion,' Nick said. 'By the time I left, she had sent fifteen envoys to other citadels in Britain, and organisations in Cardiff and Birmingham had expressed interest in joining forces. Things were tense after the airstrikes, but now we can get them word that you're alive. That should steady the boat for a while.'

'Training and recruitment.' I raised an eyebrow. 'That's all?'

'This is the thing about you, Paige,' Maria said. 'You get things done quickly, but it's only because you take the risks no one else considers.'

'That's a good thing, isn't it?'

'Do you feel good?'

'I'll let the bags under my eyes answer that.'

'There you have it.' She scooped up more of the dessert. 'This is a long game. Scion is old. The Mime Order is young. It might take us years to unearth the anchor.'

'Years in which more people die, more countries fall—'

'If we go too fast, we'll make mistakes, and we don't want that. We're up against a being who's been around for longer than all of us put together. Nashira doesn't rush, does she?'

I couldn't argue.

'I think we've covered everything,' Nick said. 'It's late. Let's reconvene in the morning.'

'Nick.' Maria pursed her lips. 'This is the free world. We have rooms in central Venice and all night long to hit the town. Do you really want to go to bed at half past nine?'

'After years of long shifts, living in daily fear of detection, an early night *is* hitting the town,' Nick said ruefully. 'You and Paige stay up, if you like. The bar is open until midnight.'

'No, now you've infected me with sense. I should rest the arm.'

'I'll admit the aster is getting to me,' I said.

'I'm just so relieved you're both alive and safe.' Nick reached across the table to grasp my hand. 'If Warden is alive, we'll do everything in our power to find him. I promise, Paige.'

'Promise.' Maria placed her good hand on the pile. 'Let's get your straight-faced sweetheart back.'

I pressed their hands with a small nod. I might still be adrift out here, but at least I was no longer alone.

---

In my room, I changed out of my clothes. I hung my new ones in the wardrobe before I dimmed the lamps and lay on the double bed, long past the point of exhaustion.

I thought I would fall asleep at once. Instead, I tossed and turned, unable to find a comfortable position. Even with the air conditioning, I was too warm. All I could think was that I was in a luxurious room, safe and fed and clothed, while Arcturus was nowhere to be found.

After a while, I got up and paced the room, trying to stop picturing him in a torture chamber. I relived every time I had touched him, every small tenderness, every stolen embrace, and the fear that he was gone for good – the fear I couldn't stop – grew stronger.

Terebell had been searching for him. She would not have given up. No matter how tense the reunion would be, I had to get in touch with her. The vaguest lead was better than nothing.

At two in the morning, I gave up on sleep. I found the gym, where I ran on a treadmill. Once my calves were on fire and I was dripping sweat, I picked up a pair of weights, frustrated by how little I could lift. I had to buckle down and get to work on rebuilding my strength.

By the time I got back to my room, I was physically and mentally spent. This time, I slept at once.

At daybreak, I woke in considerable discomfort, my muscles sore. Trying not to kick myself for going overboard, I swung my legs out of bed and prepared to face Command.

After my antics in Paris, I had to leave a spotless impression. I took a shower, put on my dissimulator, and made a concerted effort to tidy my curls. When Ducos knocked, I emerged from my room in a grey trouser suit, bought for the express purpose of seeing Command.

'Flora.' Ducos looked me up and down. 'Did you sleep?'

'Not much,' I said.

'Veronika says she gave you blue aster. I recommend you use it.'

'I will.' I locked the door. 'I don't suppose Domino knows a way to reverse the amnesia.'

'No. Its permanence is the point.'

'Naturally.' I fell into step beside her. 'Who's coming to the secret meeting?'

'A number of trusted individuals from inside and outside Scion.' She rounded a corner. 'I'm confident you can restrain your curiosity for another few days. Until then, concentrate on *this* meeting.'

She led me across the enclosed walkway. We took a flight of steps to a lower floor, where she knocked on a large wooden door. I followed her into a room with blue walls, screened against the sun.

A solitary figure in a navy shirt waited at the end of a table. She had a brown and angular face, framed by a cream headscarf. I thought she was probably in her seventies.

'Flora Blake,' she said. 'Do you like tea?'

The question was so unexpected, it took me a second to answer.

'I'm more of a coffee lover,' I said.

'With your lifestyle, I can't blame you. Help yourself.'

There was a sleek black machine in the corner. Its screen confronted me with unfamiliar words like *cappuccino* and *espresso* and *latte*. I picked one at random and hoped for the best.

'So,' I said to the stranger, 'you're Command, too?'

'Part of it, like Ducos. You may call me Pivot. I will continue to call you Flora, despite that identity being obsolete,' the woman said. 'I confess, I am fascinated to meet the agent who burned down the Château de Versailles. Should I be concerned for this building?'

'You're grand. I only burn down tyrants' palaces.'

'Very well.' Pivot watched me. 'I'm relieved to see you. Widow has told me everything she knows about your return, but I'd like to go over some details with you, if I may.'

'Widow?'

'My code name,' Ducos said.

'Ah.'

I brought the foamy coffee to the table, feeling as if I was at a job interview. Ducos remained standing.

'I understand an organisation tried to apprehend you in Poland,' Pivot said. 'Can you confirm its name?'

'The Atlantic Intelligence Bureau.'

'That organisation is, for all intents and purposes, a Panamerican equivalent of Domino, specialising in counterintelligence against Scion. Some refer to it colloquially as Tinman.'

'Why?'

'Lack of heart,' Ducos said. 'Tinman is known for being unscrupulous. Its agents will go to extreme lengths for information, have been known to spy on their allies, and rarely assist or cooperate with other agencies that oppose Scion.'

'We have occasionally liaised with them,' Pivot said, 'but we report to different political interests, and do not exchange intelligence. Did any of its agents identify by themselves by name?'

'Steve Mun,' I said. 'Any idea why they'd want me?'

'Our working theory is that Eléonore Cordier and Harald Lauring were both double agents in Domino, working for separate organisations. Lauring was passing information to Grapevine, while Cordier may have been involved with the Atlantic Intelligence Bureau.'

'So Grapevine and Tinman might have both wanted me for different reasons?'

'Perhaps. As I say, it's a theory. Veronika Norlenghi has agreed to fly back to Prague to retrieve our records on Lauring and Cordier, so my colleagues can investigate further.'

'You don't have the files here?'

'No, and we prefer not to keep electronic records of our agents, in case of leaks or intrusions. This means they can only be transferred by hand. We operate this way in Scion, too.'

'Harald claimed Grapevine had his family,' I said. 'Nick thinks he's the one who betrayed Docka.'

'Lauring came here for sanctuary after the collapse of Docka. He claimed to have used his skills as a locksmith to escape. The story appeared credible, so I reassigned him – a grave mistake on my part. He is at least the second agent to have been turned by Grapevine.'

'What do you know about it?'

'Grapevine is the network Scion uses to gather intelligence on the rest of the world.' Pivot assessed me with dark eyes. 'On that note, we are seeking information on a high-ranking individual known as the Suzerain. I understand that title means something to you.'

I wondered where she had heard it. Nick or Burnish, perhaps.

'This is where I believe you can be of enormous help to us,' Pivot said. 'You've met the Suzerain, which means that you have unparalleled knowledge of *Advena sapiens*, as we've named her species. Widow believes your auxiliary in Paris was one of them. Is that the case?'

More and more people were learning about the Rephs. The secret Scion had protected for two centuries was gradually seeping out of its grasp. It was exactly what I had wanted when I paid for *The Rephaite Revelation* to be distributed in London, but it gave me an odd feeling in my stomach – like I was standing on the edge of a cliff, staring into a chasm, with no idea what could be at the bottom. Once we took this plunge, there was no going back.

'Yes,' I said.

'Dr Nygård has explained how you first encountered them.' Pivot held my gaze. 'Flora, this is the most inflammatory and urgent intelligence Domino has ever received about the Republic of Scion. I have not yet conveyed it to the nations that fund this organisation.'

'Why not?'

'Lack of conclusive evidence,' she said. 'More importantly, I must consider the potential repercussions. Were this information to be widely known, it would change our world irrevocably.'

I thought back to the night I had learned the strange truth behind Scion. At first, the Rephs had seemed distant and terrifying. Some of them still felt that way.

But the more time I had spent around the Ranthen, the more I had grown used to them. Living in close quarters with Arcturus had only rubbed off more of their mystery. I had seen him making coffee in the mornings, leaving the bathroom with wet hair, reading books and watching films. I had slept in his arms. To me, he was half a step from human.

All this meant I had almost forgotten how stunning a revelation it was, that humans were not the only sentient beings on Earth. I had never reflected on how deep its implications went.

I was going to have to make a quick decision on how much to reveal. My instinct was to keep the Rephs under wraps, but I was getting the distinct impression that the horse had already bolted.

'I thought you were paid to share that sort of information,' I said, stalling for time. 'Isn't that the whole point of Domino?'

'I answer to the twenty-eight nations that fund and protect the Domino Programme,' Pivot said, 'but before I tell them about *Advena sapiens*, I need to be certain of exactly what I will be reporting.' She clasped her hands on the table. 'Can you help me, Flora?'

I raised my chin. 'Were any of those nations involved in the bombings of Paris and London?'

'I can't confirm or deny that. What I can tell you is that King Esteban of Spain had signed a secret treaty with three other monarchies, agreeing to a principle of collective defence. Any Scion attack on those countries would be answered with a joint retaliatory assault on London and Paris,' she said. 'After many years of watching Scion, the free world is beginning to react to its expansionism. This is why I must ensure that any intelligence we provide is watertight.'

My nod was stiff.

'Dr Nygård has told us about the two core factions, the Ranthen and the Sargas,' Pivot said. 'What do they want?'

I considered my next words carefully. If Pivot could be selective about sharing, I could do the same.

'The Ranthen have no particular grudge against humans,' I said (mostly true), 'but the Sargas family wants to control us – clairvoyants, particularly. They come from a realm called the Netherworld. A civil war broke out there, and the Sargas defeated the Ranthen. Not long after, they all left the Netherworld for Earth. That was two centuries ago.'

Pivot mulled all of this over with more poise than I had anticipated, but I could see the disquiet on her face. In the corner, Ducos was listening intently. She had seen Arcturus in Paris – spoken to him, worked alongside him – without ever comprehending what he was.

'Why did they leave?' Pivot asked at last.

'The Netherworld started to rot. It couldn't sustain them any longer. They're not sure why,' I said, 'but one side blamed the other, hence the civil war.'

'Is this Netherworld accessible to humans?'

'No,' I said. 'When they arrived here, the Sargas chose not to reveal themselves, because they didn't want humans to govern or subjugate them. They created Scion to ensure they could determine their own futures.'

'The fear is understandable, to a degree. We humans can scarcely get along with one other, let alone a different species.' She reached for a notepad. 'Why do they hunt clairvoyants?'

Now I had to tread with care.

'Not sure,' I said.

'What else can you tell us?'

Ducos came to sit beside me with a tiny cup of coffee. I took a sip of mine, gaining another moment to think.

Once, I would have been delighted to spill the Rephs' secrets to an espionage network. But telling Pivot what I knew would arm twenty-eight nations with the ability to harm the Ranthen as well.

There was also the fact that the Rephs relied on voyants to sustain themselves. If the amaurotics of the free world knew the whole story – that we were a lifeline to creatures that posed a serious threat to humankind – there was no guarantee that they would treat us any better than Scion did. For now, I would stick to a skeletal version of the truth.

'The Rephs have existed for a long time. They don't age,' I said. 'The same ones that arrived two centuries ago are still running Scion now. They're also stronger and faster than us.'

'Do they have any weaknesses?'

'Bullets slow them down,' I said. 'Other than that, I haven't found a way.'

'I see.'

I kept my expression clear, hoping she believed me.

'I understand your auxiliary was detained,' Pivot said.

'Yes,' I said. 'I don't suppose you have any leads?'

'I'm afraid not.'

I had known it was unlikely, but my chest tightened.

'As well as your intimate knowledge of *Advena sapiens*, you have insight into Scion operations – for example, you know Inquisitor Ménard and his spouse, Luce Ménard Frère,' Pivot said. 'We understand from your French allies that you brokered a truce. No executions or attacks on clairvoyants, in return for your allies leaving him alone for two years.'

'Ménard hasn't honoured it,' Ducos said. 'He never stopped the guillotines, but there may be a reason. Frère went missing exactly when you did.'

That raised the hairs on the back of my neck.

'She wasn't at the masquerade,' I said. 'I remember thinking that that was odd.'

'Ménard has claimed she's on an extended diplomatic trip to the newly established Scion Citadel of Lisbon, but there is no actual record or evidence of Frère having left France,' Ducos said. 'It is unprecedented for the Inquisitorial couple to be apart for this long.'

This did sound unusual.

'Frère was having an affair with a clairvoyant,' I said. Ducos gave me an incredulous look, which I pretended not to notice. 'Ménard could have found out and killed her, but there is another possibility. The Suzerain was suspicious of Ménard, with good reason. He found out about the Rephs' existence and resented it. He planned to turn the tables, get *her* under control. If she got wind of that, she could have taken Frère to ensure his obedience.'

There was a brief silence.

'You've given us a great deal to ponder. Perhaps we could continue this conversation after the meeting on Monday,' Pivot concluded. 'Is there anything you wish to ask me?'

'I wanted to discuss my obligations to Domino,' I said. 'I was told I had to work for you for up to a year, but then I was demoted, not to mention abducted by one of your own agents. Where do I stand now?'

'We would like you to continue your contract. As you know, we risked an agent of exceptional value to liberate you. This agent lost her own life as a direct result of saving yours.'

'Burnish.' I paused. 'She *is* dead, then?'

'Yes,' Pivot said. 'Our last remaining informant in the Archon confirmed that she was secretly executed for treason in May, when she was identified as the individual who freed you.'

'I'm sorry to hear that.'

'We all were. Alice Taylan – her real name – was our most success-ful and courageous operative. She was the first to warn us about *Advena sapiens*, even if she was never able to provide specifics,' she said. 'I need to ensure that her sacrifice was not in vain. Command has therefore agreed, almost unanimously, that we must hold you to the full year of your contract. I intend to reactivate your status as an intelligence agent.'

'Even though I burned down a palace?'

'You are clearly not suited to the sort of meticulous and cautious espionage that needs to be carried out within Scion itself,' she conceded, 'but times are changing, and so are needs. There is work to be done in the rest of the world. Your ability is unprecedented, and an asset to our organisation. We simply can't afford to waste a skill as valuable as yours.'

'My friends agreed to your deal under duress, with my life hanging in the balance,' I said coolly. 'I paid off my life debt by possessing Luce Ménard Frère without pay. Do you not think I've done enough?'

'Paige, I would not usually hold you to a contract made under significant pressure, but I have outlined my reasons. And I hope that it will be a mutually beneficial relationship.'

I clenched my jaw.

'You will be promoted,' Pivot said. 'In Scion, you were a deuce, the starting rank for an intelligence agent. As an ace – the advanced rank – you would be granted more control over your assignments, and greater freedom to carry out your own investigative work, without close supervision. We would also increase your salary by a significant margin.'

That did sound like a tempting deal. As much as I liked Ducos, I didn't like being managed.

And I still needed money.

'In Paris,' I said, 'Ducos said Domino might be able to support my organisation, the Mime Order, and its French allies. If I work for the full agreed year, will you honour that?'

'In part,' Pivot said. 'Widow has vouched for the Parisian network.'

Ducos nodded. 'The wheels are in motion. I've been able to establish a fragile line of communication with the Nouveau Régime, with Léandre Rath as my key contact.'

'England is a different matter. It's the well-defended heart of the empire,' Pivot said, 'and an island, which restricts our access. Before we can persuade our benefactors to support the Mime Order, I require proof that you still have personal influence over it. You have been away from London for almost ten months. I need reassurance that this is a resistance movement, not a criminal or terrorist enterprise.'

'It *is* a criminal enterprise under Inquisitorial law,' I said. 'All rebellion is a crime in Scion.'

'I refer to an enterprise that engages in criminal misconduct for sport or profit, rather than necessity.'

'I can't really prove that unless I go back. You have me in a bind,' I said, frustrated. 'Its interim leader is someone I trust. Can you put me in touch with her, so she can speak to you?'

'Audiovisual communication with Scion is difficult and danger-ous. As you know, the anchor goes to great lengths to keep its denizens from interacting with the outside world.'

'Then you could let Maria – Nina – go back to London in my stead, to get you assurances. Her supervisor said she's free to go, so long as you don't give her any more assignments.'

'That is a possibility. I will discuss it with Nina,' Pivot said. 'Until then, you can be assured of our support for the Nouveau Régime, provided you remain with us until January, at least. Does that sound fair?'

It didn't. Domino had coerced me into working for them, and it was maddening to be kept away from London. To not be able to search for Arcturus in Scion, where he might be imprisoned.

But Scarlett Burnish had given up her life for me. I owed her. And this was the price.

'January,' I said. 'Then we'll talk.'

'Very well. Any other questions?'

'One more,' I said. 'You asked me to assassinate the Grand Overseer. I believe he escaped Versailles by using a dissimulator. Are you aware of a link between him and Domino?'

'Certainly not.' Pivot frowned. 'This is very troubling. Are you certain, Flora?'

'Yes.'

'I will look into it as a matter of urgency. In the meantime, I hope you have a comfortable stay.'

'Thank you.'

Ducos left the room with me. As soon as the door shut behind us, I knew I was in for an earful.

'You withheld information,' Ducos said at once, like clockwork. 'An affair between a clairvoyant and Frère, and you didn't think to mention it to me?'

'I only had the voyant's word for it,' I pointed out. 'Wouldn't you have wanted proof?'

Ducos withdrew into a chilly silence. When we reached the landing below, I turned to face her.

'I need the financial support you offered,' I said. 'How can I prove the Mime Order is legitimate?'

'You'd ideally need a Domino supervisor to serve as an eyewitness to their activities, as I did for the Nouveau Régime. If we could facilitate a meeting with your interim, that would be helpful.'

'Eliza has met someone from Domino. An ally of Burnish,' I said, remembering. 'After I was detained, he got my friends out of Edinburgh. He could vouch for the Mime Order.'

'Any idea of his name?'

'Nick might know.'

'I'll enquire. If not, I will advocate for Command to allow Nina to leave,' she said. 'We can ensure she gets to London, accompanied by an eyewitness. I know it isn't ideal, but it's only a few months. You can make use of our resources, in the meantime.'

'Good. I need a gun and some decent knives,' I said. 'If anyone comes for that reward, I have to be able to defend myself.'

'I'll get them for you after the meeting.' Ducos folded her arms. 'Even if you are rash, it is becoming clear that we need you. It's possible that no one in the world knows more about *Advena sapiens* than you do, and Scion is casting its shadow farther than ever. We have to contain this war. You can help.'

After a moment, I nodded.

I belonged in London. My love for it was deep and furious as the Thames – but my reign as Underqueen had been one of the hardest trials of my life. Three months of sleepless apprehension, endangered by Senshield, stalked by Hildred Vance. Three months of waiting to be killed or overthrown. Three months of setbacks, ending in a torture chamber.

If I had to stay out here a little longer, to make the Rose Crown easier to wear, so be it.

'I'll do it for the Mime Order. I'm still its Underqueen,' I said. 'Am I free to go out?'

'Collect a new phone from the concierge first. Keep it on so I can stay in touch with you,' Ducos said. 'Our devices are very secure – you shouldn't need a burner, like you would in Scion – but you should avoid mentioning real names or sensitive information. We can't be too careful at the moment, even in the free world.'

'What do you mean?'

'You'll find out at the meeting on Monday. Until then,' she said, 'try to stay out of trouble.'

# 8

# THE DEAD OF NIGHT

The Palazzo della Notte had come to life in the time I had been with Pivot and Ducos. People strode between its rooms with brisk purpose, some murmuring in pairs or small groups in the corridors. These must be the organisers, responsible for issuing orders to the people in the field who risked their lives for information.

Anyone here could be working for Grapevine. Harald was dead, but there might be other traitors.

As I headed towards the concierge, I slowed, remembering something Arcturus had told me. To help root out the Mime Order, Nashira had summoned her heir, Vindemiatrix Sargas.

*Her principal duty for the last two centuries has been to monitor the free world.*

Perhaps Vindemiatrix Sargas was the one behind Grapevine, gathering intelligence for her family. She must have built a significant network of humans or Rephs to watch the free world for her – a network she might also deploy to infiltrate and damage Domino.

I picked up a phone before finding the others on a balcony. They were sitting in the shade of its awning, Nick leafing through a newspaper. It was hot enough to toast bread on the table.

'Paige,' Nick said, seeing me.

'Buongiorno, sweet.' Maria was eating a cooked breakfast. 'I hope you slept better than I did.'

'Once I'd had a midnight jog,' I said.

'What?'

'Nothing.' I sat down and shed my suit jacket. 'How's the arm?'

'Still wrapped in a nice layer of padding and painkillers.' She passed me a cup of coffee. 'I see you survived Command. I'm scheduled to see Pivot at noon. Is she terrifying?'

'Not at all.' I unfastened a few buttons on my blouse. 'She asked me about the Rephs.'

'Me, too. I told her as much as I could.' Nick looked at me over his sunglasses. 'She asked me if the Sargas ever meant to reveal their presence to the public. Do you know?'

'Warden said that was their aim, but only once they felt secure.'

'Yes, because a public declaration of their presence would cause mass hysteria,' Maria said. 'I can't imagine the religious fervour and doomsaying that would follow that announcement. It would be the breaking news that broke the world.' She let her head fall back. 'Still, too hot to think about that. I don't know how people in Italy get any work done.'

I helped myself to fruit and yoghurt. The platter came with an orange, a rare and expensive treat in Scion. I peeled it and breathed in its sweetness. France sent clementines to England, but I hadn't had a proper orange since I was a child. It tasted like sunlight and summer.

'Paige,' Nick said, 'did you ask Pivot about your contract?'

'They expect me to work until January, at least. Apparently I'm too useful to lose.'

'Pivot said the same to me. I feel like we're being punished for being good at our jobs.'

'They might be willing to let Maria go.'

'I resent your implication,' Maria said. 'I was exceptionally good at my job. It's hardly my fault if I'm also exceptionally good at burning things.'

'Radomír said you could leave,' I said, 'and the Mime Order respects you. I've made a case for you returning to London to support Eliza, possibly accompanied by a Domino agent, so they can see it's a legitimate resistance. Are you happy to do that?'

'Of course.'

'What about Verča?'

'I won't pretend it will be easy, but she always knew I wanted to return to Scion. You're Underqueen,' Maria said. 'If you want me to go now, I will.'

'Not now,' Nick said. 'You can't go back with your arm in that state, Maria.'

'Don't be ridiculous. You're the resident medic, aren't you?'

'Yes, and I can't clear you to make the Alpine crossing with that injury. If you start bleeding or get an infection, you won't just be a liability to yourself. You'll endanger your guide.'

'He's right, Maria. It would ruin the whole plan,' I said. 'Wait until you're healed.' She bit the inside of her cheek. 'In the meantime, I'll try to get a message to London.'

'Good. I want a welcome party.' Maria checked her phone. 'Verča just left for the airport, to get more information on Cordier and Lauring. Hopefully we can find out why you were abducted.'

I still couldn't believe the ease of travel here. In Scion, one had to request authorisation to leave a country months in advance.

'I see you got a phone.' Nick held out a hand for it. 'Let me put our numbers in.'

'Thanks.' I passed it to him. 'I need a walk. Want to come?'

'Well, I currently only have one patient,' he said, nodding to Maria, 'and she looks quite comfortable.'

'Perfectly. Bring me back a gelato, please,' Maria said. 'And a souvenir. When we return to the horrors of Scion, I'd like to remember that I once spent a beautiful weekend in Venice.'

---

Nick showed me the streets around the Palazzo del Domino first. Once I had them memorised, he took me to the Rialto Bridge and the district of San Marco, which housed some of the famous landmarks of Venice. We had a drink in a Baroque coffeehouse, then walked some way along the promenade by the lagoon, cooled by a breeze from the Adriatic Sea.

I couldn't get used to the Venetian waterways. Every so often, I would hear the swash of an oar, or the slap of a wave breaking on stone, and my body would bead into a cold sweat. Still, with Nick at my side and the sun burning down, I found I could stay in the present.

'I like coming down here at night,' Nick said. A seagull winged overhead as he spoke. 'Being able to go out after dark without any fear of Vigiles ... I'm going to find it hard to give that up when we go back.'

'I should take advantage while I'm here. Maybe we could run the slates.'

'I'd really like that.' He linked my arm. 'I still can't believe we're outside Scion, Paige.'

'I remember a time before Scion. It must be even stranger for you.'

Nick had been born under the anchor, in the Swedish village of Mölle. He had spent almost thirty years inside.

'The first weeks were hard,' he said. 'Do you miss London?'

'I do, though I miss Paris more. It let me breathe again.'

'How do you mean?'

'You know I was never meant to sit on a throne. In Paris, I had the same kind of freedom I did as a mollisher, and none of the scrutiny on an Underqueen.'

'And you had Warden.'

'Yes.' I cast my gaze towards the horizon. 'But I need the Rose Crown. I have to go back.'

'It will be easier now Senshield is gone, even with martial law. Eliza will have bolstered our numbers, and we'll have support from Domino. We'll cross the Alps together,' he said. 'We can liaise with the French syndicate, then go straight back to London.'

'Okay.' I looked up at him. 'Where did you get your hair dyed?'

'Domino has a cosmetician. He covers scars and tattoos, deals with hair, does enamelling, that sort of thing,' he said. 'You can make a booking with the concierge.'

'I might do that.' I brushed a loose curl back. 'Let's get Maria that gelato. Whatever a gelato is.'

It turned out to be something like ice cream. Nick bought us all a cone. I went for chocolate and tried to stop it dripping as we made our way back to the Palazzo del Domino. It reminded me painfully of a conversation I'd had with Liss and Julian, before the end of the Bone Season. We'd discussed what sort of ice cream we would eat when we got out.

*We'll savour the culinary delights of London, and then we'll save it from the Rephs.*

When we reached the Strada Nova, Nick stopped to buy a miniature gondola for Maria. All the way there, I had been evaluating the rooftops. It had been months since we had gone for a run. Venice would be perfect for it, with narrow gaps between many of its buildings.

By the time we returned to the Palazzo del Domino, Maria was dozing in the shade. I woke her so she could eat the gelato, then left to book an appointment with the cosmetician.

Once it was done, I almost went to my room. Using the time before the meeting to rest would be sensible. Instead, I explored the Palazzo del Domino. I visited the courtyards and the terrace, then wandered through the corridors. Finally, I came to a room with a plasterwork ceiling and books lining the walls, where several amaurotics were on computers.

'Excuse me,' I said quietly to a woman. She took out an earbud. 'Can anyone use these?'

'Yes, of course.'

'Thanks.'

I took a seat in front of one. Protean was already open, waiting for a query. Unlike the insular Scionet, this network was connected to the whole of the free world. Maria had warned me not to look too far, but I needed to blunt my curiosity. I tapped in *Scion latest news*.

The results numbered in the tens of millions.

Maria hadn't been joking. A curdling sensation filled my stomach, for no reason I could explain.

A few popular stories had been highlighted. I took a breath to steel myself, skimming the headlines and previews. The *New York Times* offered a long read on the situation in Spain and an opinion piece on why Norway had reneged on its historic opposition to Scion. *Candid*, an entertainment website, had summarised what Scion was and what it wanted – I could only assume its readers had been asleep their whole lives – while *Publishers' Review* was discussing a book deal for a Scion defector.

Each time I went to expand an article, I stopped. I couldn't even get used to there being more than one news source. In Scion, there was only the *Descendant*. I needed to narrow this down.

I typed *Paige Mahoney*.

My name clocked up hundreds of thousands of hits. There was speculation about who I was, and why Scion was offering so much money for my capture. I selected the first result, which took me to a virtual encyclopaedia called Omnia. The entry included a school photograph Scion must have provided to Incrida, which showed me at sixteen, with a face on me like I was chewing a thistle.

**Paige E. Mahoney** (born 14 January 2040) is an <u>individual with extrasensory perception</u> who was, and may remain, a career criminal in the <u>Republic of Scion</u>. She is a fugitive from Inquisitorial justice whom Scion classifies as a 'preternatural' (see <u>Inquisitorial law</u>) for reasons that remain unclear. Mahoney is believed to have been born in <u>Ireland</u> before its <u>annexation</u> by Scion. She came to global attention following her red notice listing on the <u>International Criminal Database</u>, uploaded on 3 January 2060 at the request of the <u>Republic of Scion England</u>.

Mahoney is a person of interest to multiple authorities. An anonymous <u>Gazebo</u> user reported a sighting in <u>Berlin</u> on 17 May 2060. Her current location remains unknown. As of September 2060, the Republic of Scion is offering an unprecedented reward of £20,000,000 for her capture and return.

I read the entry again. The entire time I had been in Paris, I had been wanted in the free world.

Scion had prematurely told its denizens that I was dead, only for me to slip the noose and vanish. It hadn't been able to broadcast my survival to its own denizens, but it had issued the red notice in case I should ever leave the empire. To make sure I had no safe place.

'There you are.'

I started. Ducos had appeared over my shoulder.

'Don't sneak up on a dreamwalker,' I warned her. 'If I jump out of my skin, I might end up in yours.'

'Perhaps you should pay more attention to your surroundings.' Ducos leaned in to see what I was reading. 'So you discovered Omnia. Searching for oneself is usually seen as the height of vanity, but I suppose it's understandable in your case. You are gaining a reputation.'

'Just what a spy needs.' I closed it. 'Do you have a minute?'

'I could spare one. We'll talk in the bar.'

Ducos led me downstairs. We sat in the corner of the bar, which was empty at this time of day.

'Pivot said audiovisual communication with Scion is dangerous,' I said, 'but what if I wanted to send a message to someone in London?'

'It would take a long time, and no small degree of risk,' Ducos said. 'What sort of message?'

'I want to tell the Mime Order I'm alive and contact the leader of the Ranthen. Terebell might have news about Warden.'

Ducos lit a cigarette. She still favoured the slender French ones she had smoked in Scion.

'I may as well tell you how it all works,' she said. 'For someone inside Scion France to contact the outside, the insider goes on foot to the border with a foreign phone. This allows them to connect to a Swiss or Italian network, and ensures Scion can't monitor the call or message. The point on the border with the highest chance of success, where the anchor has no permanent detectors or signal jammers, is in the French Alps.'

'And for us to contact them?'

'All messages and intelligence must be carried and exchanged by Domino couriers. Either they must cross the barrier, or entrust the message to an insider at the border.'

'There's a physical barrier across the entire border?'

'Most of it. It's known colloquially as the Fluke.'

'So either way, a courier would have to risk their neck.'

Ducos nodded. As I considered, a possibility occurred to me. Perhaps I could reach Terebell another way.

'Thanks. I'll get back to you.' I stood. 'Is there a cemetery in Venice?'

She raised an eyebrow. 'There are two,' she said. 'The old Jewish cemetery on the Lido, and the Isola di San Michele, which is in the Venetian Lagoon.'

'Have there been any recent burials?'

'Why could you possibly want to know?'

'In case you'd forgotten, I'm voyant. It's in my interest to know where the spirits are.'

'I saw a water hearse the day before I left for the Alps. The vaporetto goes to the Isola di San Michele from the Fondamenta Nove, but I recommend you ask Noemi, our gondoliera, to take you there in her taxi. She makes appointments in the bar from six until half past seven.' She checked her watch. 'I need to go. Is there anything else, Flora?'

'One more thing. Could you translate a message into Italian for me?'

'Why?'

'If I can't get a message to Terebell physically, I can try it through the æther.'

Ducos eyed me.

'I only have a conversational grasp of Italian, but I can ask one of my colleagues if it's something more complex,' she said. 'Send me the message. I'll have it translated within an hour.'

---

The heat and the long walk had worn me out. I took off my dissimulator and examined my own face in the mirror. My skin was almost as pale as the flower that was draining me, worsening my dark circles.

I sent Ducos the message I needed translating. Her reply came in moments.

Are you calling their leader here?

After a pause, I wrote back: By voyant means. If I can't get to her, maybe she can get to me.

I'll need to inform Pivot. Will she need assistance crossing the Fluke?

I doubt it, but one step at a time. The séance might not work. Can you send me the translation?

It arrived a few minutes later.

I found the tin of blue aster from Verča and pressed a patch on to my hip. A cold tingling came first, and then a sense of calm. I could feel my silver cord thickening, resisting the dust, so my spirit felt more rooted. No longer locked in a state of strained vigilance, my body folded on to the bed, and I closed my eyes, my breathing deep and slow.

When I woke, I felt restored, but my skin flamed, as if I was running a fever. According to the clock on the nightstand, I had been asleep for more than five hours. I hadn't remembered anything new.

The gondoliera would be in the bar by now. I slung my shoes back on, then applied my dissimulator.

It was time to take matters into my own hands, and use the gifts the æther had given me. There might be another way to contact Terebell – one that didn't involve sending a courier into danger. It had to be worth a try.

By the time I got downstairs, I was burning up. I went to the bartender, who grimaced when he saw me, though he covered it with a smile. I must look more of a wreck than I thought.

'Excuse me,' I said. 'Is the gondoliera here?'

He nodded to a woman sitting at a table. She was a stocky medium, with tight dark curls piled into a ponytail.

'Salve.' A dimple appeared in her cheek as she smiled. 'Posso aiutarla?'

'Good evening.' I dusted off my crisp English accent. 'Sorry, I don't speak Italian.'

'You want to book a trip?'

'If you could slot me in. I'd like to visit the Isola di San Michele, preferably when it's quiet.'

'It closes to visitors around four, but I imagine you could find a way inside.' Noemi flipped open a notebook. 'I trust you are not going to do anything illegal or disrespectful.'

'Of course not.'

People might not always believe in clairvoyance here, but it wasn't against the law, to my knowledge. What I was about to do would be a death sentence in Scion.

'It might be easiest if I stay overnight,' I said. 'Could you come back for me in the morning?'

'You would stay in a cemetery overnight?'

'I don't think the skeletons will attack me.'

Noemi chuckled. 'You are braver than most.' She tapped a pen on her notepad. 'I have a free slot this evening, if you want. It would be best if we go around dusk, so fewer people will see my boat approaching the island. Could you meet at the canal entrance at eight?'

'Sure.'

That gave me half an hour. As I rose, I heard two familiar voices. A moment later, Maria and Nick entered the bar. Maria took one look at me and bit down a grin.

'Go on,' I said. 'I could use a laugh myself.'

'Paige, you're as red as your aura.'

I looked down. My shoulders and upper arms were scarlet, and a lighter flush had spread across my chest. 'Great.' I sighed. 'Mind you, sunburn is the nicest problem I've had in a while.'

'You two grab us a table.' Nick shook his head. 'I'll get you some aftersun, Paige.'

'I'll have to skip dinner. I'm going out.'

'This late?'

I nodded. 'To the cemetery island. I'm going to try to send Terebell a message.'

Maria looked curious. 'Through the æther, you mean, like we did in London?'

'This is something more subtle. And experimental.'

'Let us come with you, then. Any sort of séance will need a group of us.'

'I appreciate the offer, but I need a psychopomp, specifically.'

'Those odd little spirits that lurk around hospitals?' she said, frowning. 'I've never known a voyant to get close to one. I don't think even Jaxon managed it.'

'That's why I need to go alone. They're skittish.'

'At least let me get you that aftersun,' Nick said. 'I'll be quick.'

'I can see you're going to insist.'

'Sit with me, in the meantime,' Maria said. 'I'll tell you about my chat with Pivot.'

Nick left, while Maria and I went to the internal courtyard. Maria lit the candle on our table, piquing the interest of a few ghosts.

'Pivot wanted my perspective on what happened in Bulgaria. Probably wondering why multiple agents are burning things down,' Maria said. 'To my surprise, she wasn't angry. She also explained why I was asked to save Kostas in the first place. Domino usually prohibits rescue attempts.'

I was very familiar with that rule.

'Kostas was the only survivor of a Greek sub-network,' she continued. 'Before he was captured, he was investigating a string of suspicious disappearances in Athens. The majority of missing people were voyants.'

'Another Reph city?'

'It seems possible, as I said to Pivot.'

'Nashira must have sped up her plans. I don't suppose your man caught wind of a code name for the prison?'

'I wasn't told, but this could be a lead, nonetheless. What if Warden is there?'

I considered it.

'Nashira wouldn't put him that far away. Not unless she's there as well, which I doubt,' I said. 'She'll want to stay as close as possible to London.' I shook my head. 'All that death and misery to get rid of Oxford and Versailles, and more prisons just spring up in their place.'

'I know. The good news is that Pivot cleared me to return to Scion once I'm healed,' Maria said. 'The next crossing is in November.'

'Let's hope Eliza can hold on that long.'

Nick returned with the aftersun and a shirt with long sleeves. At least the hat had protected my face. 'Keep your phone on,' he told me. 'I'll check in later.'

'Have a fascinating night.' Maria tossed me her lighter. 'Here. In case you need a numen.'

'Thanks.'

I collected my new satchel before I headed to the quay, where Noemi waited on the stern of a black gondola with pale accents. Now the sun had set, lamps were flickering to life across the city, gilding the water. Somehow I doubted the cemetery isle would have much light.

Noemi rowed a short way along the main canal, muscles working beneath her freckled brown skin. Curled up in the seat, I was too aware of the water lapping the sides of the gondola.

The boat slid between tall dwellings, past candlelit windows and colonnades. By the time Noemi stopped at a pier, the sky was deep blue, and all I could see was darkness below. There was a sharp edge to the breeze, making me grateful for the jacket I had packed. Noemi secured her gondola before we moved to a larger boat with the same colouring.

'This won't take long,' she told me. I nodded and ducked into the upholstered cabin.

Noemi steered the taxi across the lagoon, to a walled island. I stepped on to a jetty. As far as I could tell, only birds and insects lay ahead of me. And spirits. There were plenty of those.

'Be in this spot at sunrise. I'll meet you,' Noemi said. 'Call Widow if you need help.'

'Got it.'

As her taxi left, I took a torch from my satchel and switched it on, keeping its beam low to the ground, so it wouldn't be seen from afar. No voyant worth their salt would be afraid of burial grounds, but since my torture, I had lived with a fear of the dark.

It didn't take me long to find a way into the cemetery. I walked slowly, using my torch with more confidence now I was out of sight. The main danger would be poltergeists, and I sensed none. There were only revenants and wisps – and a single psychopomp, standing out like a shout among whispers. I could sense it, keen as a knife against my skin.

I passed walls of plaques, inscribed with names and dates, posies of flowers left between them. Tall evergreens guarded the memorials, tapering up to points. There were statues of angels with wide, feathered wings – not just remnants where they had been smashed off.

Most voyants spurned religion. We knew what came after death. But I had never been quite as uncharitable as Jaxon, who had sneered at the books and ritual objects collecting dust at the black market. I could understand why amaurotics clung to the hope of more. In any case, none of us knew what awaited us at the end of the æther, beyond the last light.

Still, I wasn't going to pray or kneel. I had seen enough to be fairly sure that only the dead would come when I called.

I followed my sixth sense to the psychopomp. Once, these spirits had acted as guides, shepherding the dead to the Netherworld. Even though they had lost that role, they sought out places where death was common – hospitals, execution grounds – or where spirits might stand guard over their own remains, like cemeteries and morgues. The Ranthen had given them a new purpose as messengers, but they were exceptionally shy around the living.

Arcturus had told me more in Paris, as I taught him the finer points of cooking one evening, while I was trying to heal. He had said the psychopomps lingered with the recent dead to comfort them, so they weren't alone and stranded when they first entered the æther.

*Psychopomps may fear the living, but they would be drawn to a spirit like yours.* I could almost hear his deep voice. *You can dislocate from your body, even leave it. To a psychopomp, that would act as a summons.*

*It would think I was dying?*

*And come to guide you. A dreamwalker can dwell among the dead, and persuade them she is one of them.*

It was a long shot. I could perform basic séances and invocations as a voyant, but sending messages through psychopomps was a Ranthen art, not meant for the likes of me. But if any of my allies knew where Arcturus was, it was Terebell Sheratan. I couldn't give up on him.

If I could pull this off, it would be faster and safer than sending a human courier to London. Assuming I didn't botch the whole thing and summon Nashira to Venice, of course.

When I was ready, I sat beside a row of headstones. I would use my spirit as bait, to hook a wary fish. First, I took out the lighter from Maria, brass engraved with roses. She had been good to entrust me with this; a lighter was about as close as a pyromancer got to a favoured numen. I flipped the lid, so a flame snapped up, and planted it in the ground. Once I had switched off my torch, I dislocated my spirit, letting myself drift.

Whenever I moved my spirit from the middle of my dreamscape, it sent ripples into the æther. I kept them as soft as I could. As soon as they touched the psychopomp, I had its attention. It clung to its instinct to guide the dead, even if there was nowhere to lead them. I shifted my spirit back into place, then dislocated again. A fish splashing in distress.

For a long time, I held very still, my neck and sitbones aching. Moving a muscle could break the trance. Even the gentle kick of my heart might frighten a psychopomp.

Hours might have passed – hours of patient fishing – before it brushed my aura. It had darted away several times, no doubt confused by what it was sensing – this woman who was both dead and alive.

Now it circled me, sending cool prickles along my skin. This might be the first time in history that a human had ever got so close to a psychopomp. Without a medium, spirits had limited ways to communicate, but it was clearly trying to reassure me, so I would follow.

*I can't follow yet*, I wanted to tell it. *I still have so much more to do.*

Time to take my chance, before the spirit realised it had been tricked. I glanced down at my phone, reading the message from Ducos. She had sent a few pointers on pronunciation.

Rephs spoke Glossolalia, the language of spirits. I couldn't. But the majority of spirits could understand mortal languages, especially if their deaths had been recent. In this cemetery, I was willing to bet that most of them had a strong grasp of Italian.

'Aiutami,' I said very softly.

*Help me.*

The psychopomp recoiled at once, but I had piqued its curiosity. I willed my body still and quiet. When I was sure it wouldn't bolt, I spoke again, hoping my pronunciation was passable.

'Cerco colui che si oppone al nemico.'

*I seek the one who stands against the enemy.*

Now my new friend was interested. It circled me again, as if it were paying close attention.

Arcturus had told me how best to speak to a psychopomp, in case I ever wanted to give it a try. It was wise to avoid names or places, or anything else that might be hard for a spirit to convey in Glossolalia. I hoped a Ranthen ally would understand *the enemy* as Nashira Sargas.

'Chiedo che venga qui,' I said, slow and clear.

*I ask her to come to this place.*

'Chiedo che venga qui il più in fretta possibile,' I continued. *I ask her to come as soon as she can.* 'Dille che è una mortale che la manda a chiamare.' *Tell her it is a mortal who calls her.* 'Riferiscile questo messaggio da parte mia. Ti ringrazio.' *Thank you for bearing this summons for me.* 'Please … tell Terebell I'm here.'

The psychopomp hesitated for a long moment. It had no eyes, no form, but somehow I knew it was looking at me.

And then it simply disappeared.

# 9

## VENTRILOQUIST

After the psychopomp left, I tucked myself behind a rusted metal gate to sleep, but curious spirits kept disturbing me, intrigued by a living woman in the cemetery. In the end, I chose a spot on the grass and lay there to stargaze, searching for the constellation that was known in the free world as Boötes. I found its brightest star, Arcturus. His namesake on Earth.

*Can you hear me?*

No reply.

*I'm going to find you. Just give me somewhere to start.*

The cord remained inert, like a dead limb. I fastened my jacket and leaned against the nearest tomb. If he was alive, I was going to kill him for worrying me.

Noemi returned at dawn. I climbed into her water taxi, stiff and tired. Once we reached the Palazzo del Domino, I closed the shutters in my room, stuck an aster patch on my arm, and messaged Nick to tell him I had made it back. After that, I was out like a snuffed candle.

The white aster lay as thick as ever on my dreamscape, making my spirit too uneasy to rest for long. At some point, I stirred awake, shivering and burning up. In my feverish confusion, I thought I was in Paris, lying beside Arcturus. I imagined him back into my arms, so I could almost feel the comforting warmth of his body on mine, encircling me. I touched myself where he had touched me, fingers tracing my hot skin.

Then I saw the line of yellow light across the ceiling, needling through a crack in the shutters. I sat up and groped for the lamp, not sure if my face was damp from sweat or tears.

*I want to spend my life with you. I want a future with you.*

Why had I never told him that before he was detained?

---

After that, it was a waiting game. I decided to ease back into the gym and get some rest. It was sleep that fed and fortified the dreamscape, keeping its defences strong. If mine thinned any farther, my ability to deflect spools in combat would suffer, and I couldn't afford that. If I did get a lead on Arcturus, I might well have to fight to free him.

On Saturday, I went to see the cosmetician, who had a hair salon in the Palazzo della Notte. I was starting to miss my natural blonde, but that was in all my official Scion photographs. Instead, I asked the cosmetician to lift the brown, so it was more of a honey gold.

On Sunday morning, I reported to the dentist, who pronounced that my teeth were in mint condition. She gave them a polish and sent me to the optometrist. My eyes were fine. After that, I had a few examinations and injections I had missed in Scion. Once I had done a smear and had my blood taken for testing, I visited Ducos and requested that a pocket was stitched into one of my new boots, so I could keep a knife there, the way I had in Scion.

For the rest of the weekend, I lay in bed, gazing at the wall. The longer I was alone, the more I thought of Arcturus.

*Where are you?*

The cord offered no answers. I burrowed into the pillows, trying to blot out the fear that it would never move again.

---

On Monday, a knock roused me at nine. If not for that, I might have spent the rest of the morning in bed, lapsing into hopelessness. When I opened the door, Nick held out an iced coffee.

'Verča is back.'

'Great.' I took the glass. 'Will I see you downstairs, then?'

'Take your time. The concierge said you hadn't called for any meals.'

'I'll have something today.'

'You look a little better,' Nick said. 'Did you get any sleep?'

'As much as I could.'

'Good. Pivot has asked me to remove the tracker Cordier put in,' he said. 'It's disabled, but better it's out. Come and see me in the medical room later.' I nodded. 'Your results are back. You have mild anaemia and a couple of vitamin deficiencies. You're also dehydrated.'

'I'm always dehydrated.'

'I suppose I can only blame Scion for that.' He folded his arms. 'At least your teeth are in good shape, against the odds. I can't believe Colin didn't let you see a dentist for twelve years.'

'He was probably afraid I'd be detected,' I said. 'I appreciate you caring, Nick.'

'Always.'

When he left, I folded back the wooden shutters, letting in the light of another golden day in Venice. I stood by the balcony for a long while, trying to snap out of my torpor.

The Isola di San Michele was close enough that I would sense Terebell if she arrived there. It was unsettling to not know whether or not she had received the message, or how long it would take. I distracted myself by showering, which always demanded my full attention.

Verča was in the bar with the others. I ordered breakfast and went to join them.

'You dyed your hair.' Verča smiled. 'I like it.'

'Thanks. I needed a change.' I had wrestled my curls into a low bun. 'Did you get the files?'

'Yes. Pivot gave me permission to show you.' She placed a hand on a dossier. 'This one belongs to the medical officer assigned to Mannequin as Eléonore Cordier.'

'I can't believe Domino has people carry files around,' Maria said. 'What happens if you drop them?'

'You don't.'

She opened the dossier and slid it towards me. The picture was of a woman in her twenties, with styled brown curls, high cheekbones, and green eyes. The lines of her face were familiar.

'She would have dyed her hair,' Verča said. 'And this photograph was taken seven years ago.'

Maria glanced at me. 'Is it her, Paige?'

I kept looking at the photograph, seeing more and more of Cordier.

'Yes,' I said. 'It's her.'

'Her real name is Aysel Ekren. A qualified paramedic, fluent in French, which she claimed to have learned from her Belgian father,' Verča said. 'She was signed up in Istanbul and sent to Prague for training. She wanted to work in London, but her skillset meant she was assigned to Paris, since Mannequin needed a medical officer. Her appeal was rejected.'

'Did you or Pivot notice anything amiss?'

'One thing.' She turned a couple of pages. 'This dossier includes transcripts from her linguistic proficiency tests. When I ran these past a Belgian colleague, he noticed two oddities. As it turns out, they are specific to Québécois.'

Maria raised her eyebrows. 'So she could be Canadian?'

'Yes, which would be unusual. Most agents come from countries that fund Domino, and Canada is not one of them. Aysel claimed she was born in Istanbul, studied in Ghent, and had never lived anywhere else. Domino is rigorous about background checks, to make sure there are no conflicting loyalties or undeclared motives, but the examiner failed to flag the discrepancy.'

'She could have bribed them to ignore it.'

'I would be surprised. Domino personnel are selected for their integrity.'

'Cordier is clearly an exception. So was Harald.' Nick glanced at her. 'This seems to indicate Cordier works for the Atlantic Intelligence Bureau. Could they have planted her in Domino?'

'Possibly, but why?' Verča was frowning. 'I'm certain they have their own spies in Scion.'

Maria shook her head. 'Did anything else strike you as suspicious, slunche?'

'No, but the person who originally recommended her to Domino has since dropped off the radar. We're trying to find him.' Verča closed the file. 'That's all we have at present. Once this is back in Prague, Radomír will go over every detail with a fine-tooth comb, with help from our colleagues in Istanbul. We'll get to the bottom of this, Paige.'

I nodded. 'What about Harald?'

'Harald Lauring was in his first year at the Boneyard when Aysel arrived. His story seems to match what he told you, Nick. He was Danish, headhunted by a recruiter in Helsingør. Aysel was a quick study, so the pair enrolled in combat training at the same time. Radomír says the pair became close. He suspects they were lovers at one point.'

'Radomír knew them both, then.'

'Yes. He was not the head of the Libuše Institute at that point, but when I enquired about Aysel Ekren, he remembered her. He said she was an exceptional recruit, and a very convincing liar.'

I supposed that should make me feel better.

'Harald was issued with a false name – Sven Holmgren – and sent to Sweden, around the same time Aysel went into France as Cordier,' Verča said. 'I can only assume they stayed in touch, and that Aysel went to Harald for help with whatever she was plotting.'

'But both of them wanted Paige,' Nick said. 'So they betrayed each other.'

I scrutinised the photograph. Harald looked similar, but the scar was missing from his mouth.

'It still feels to me that a piece is missing in all this,' Verča said. 'We know what Harald was doing, but why did Cordier want Paige?'

'Everyone wants me for something.' I rubbed my temple. 'Thank you for showing us these, Verča.'

'Of course. I'll take them back to Prague after the meeting.' She fastened the files into her briefcase. 'Sorry to leave so quickly, but I need to speak to Pivot. I'll see you all later.'

'I'll head off, too. I'm getting a migraine.' Nick kneaded the corner of his eye. 'Paige, I'll give you a scan this afternoon. Let's get that tracker out of you.'

———

To keep myself from sinking into dark thoughts, I went for a run along the Riva degli Schiavoni, savouring the sun on my skin, the fresh breeze on the waterfront. In broad daylight, surrounded by other people, I found I could bear the sight of the waves. Once I had showered and eaten a salad for lunch, I went up to see Nick, sensing that he was awake.

The medical room was as beautiful as the rest of the Palazzo della Notte, with a plush examination couch and two beds. When I arrived, Nick was sitting in front of a laptop, paler than usual.

'Nick,' I said from the doorway. 'Has it passed?'

'It's getting there.'

'Did you have a vision?'

'Not this time. Just pain.' He found a smile for me. 'Let's have a look for the tracker.'

He pointed me to a large scanner. I stood in front of it and lifted my arms. As soon as the image fed through to his laptop, Nick could see the tracking unit in my back, no larger than a nail head. Harald might have fried it, but I still wanted the bastard thing out of my body.

'How are your parents?' I asked Nick.

'I speak to them on the phone every few days. I'm worried Scion will go after Mamma.'

'Wasn't she one of their best engineers?'

'I think that's why the Icelandic government was so quick to restore her citizenship,' he admitted. 'Mamma had one of the highest intelligence quotients in Scion. She's a huge loss to them.'

'Now I see where you get it.'

'Oh, no. I pale in comparison to her.' He pulled on rubber gloves. 'They'll be all right. If they could hide out for months in Scion, they can be discreet in the free world.'

I felt the smallest pang of envy as he spoke. Nick had a family. As far as I knew, I no longer did.

The operation was short, only requiring a local anaesthetic. Once the tracker was out, Nick showed it to me. It had been placed just deep enough that no one could have seen or felt it under my skin. He cleaned and stitched and dressed the wound, and I drowsed in the medical room for the rest of the afternoon, wanting to be alert for the meeting.

I woke suddenly. Once again, I had a feeling of suffocation, of being surrounded and flooded by darkness. I blinked and looked around, finding Nick asleep on the examination couch. I left him to rest and returned to my room, where I ate dinner by myself.

By nine, the anaesthetic had worn off, leaving a twinge in my back. I changed into a white shirt and my grey suit, then pressed the dissimulator back on, making my face as tight as my burnt shoulders. I headed across the enclosed walkway to the Palazzo del Giorno, where Ducos waited at a door marked STANZA BLU. She showed me inside.

In the Blue Room, Pivot sat at the head of a walnut table, while a stranger, sitting in his shirtsleeves, was chewing his cheek like it was a tender cut of steak. Pivot gave me a nod.

The windows had been covered, so the only light came from a lamp on the table. I took a seat. One by one, more strangers came. The three voyants among them all clocked me at once. Even out here, my aura was interesting. At least my dissimulator kept me anonymous.

Ducos moved to stand in the corner, watching us all like a well-groomed hawk. Nick took the chair on my left, and I wordlessly poured him a glass of water. Verča and Maria were last to arrive, the former looking as careworn as Nick. Ducos locked the door behind them.

Altogether, there were seventeen of us. When Pivot stood, the stilted conversations died away. Ducos turned off the lamp and activated the large screen behind Pivot, which showed three white dots on a dark background.

'Welcome,' Pivot said. 'Thank you for answering the summons to this emergency meeting. The people in this room are the agents, associates and valued personnel who I believe are most likely to help us understand the latest Scion military plan, Operation Ventriloquist.'

I traded a glance with Maria. Her instinct had been right. Scion was plotting something big.

'While all Domino personnel are trusted to know the importance of discretion,' Pivot said, 'I cannot overemphasise the pressing need for silence in regard to this meeting, even among our own. For the sake of this organisation, no word is to go beyond the people in this room.'

Everyone nodded.

'As you all know,' Pivot said, 'the Domino Programme is financially supported by twenty-eight nations that oppose the Republic of Scion. In less than half a year, three of those nations have fallen to our enemy. A fourth loss may be imminent, and exceptionally dangerous.' She looked around the table. 'The fourth may be Italy.'

The silence that followed was deeper. Verča stared at her, as did several other people.

'To brief you,' Pivot said, 'I call on Aparna Wells, a former military clerk for the Republic of Scion England.'

A thin woman in her twenties stood up. Her dark hair was in a bun, strands framing a bespectacled face.

'Thank you,' she said. 'Until earlier this year, I worked for Patricia Okonma, who stepped in as Grand Commander when Hildred Vance was hospitalised in January.' She spoke with a pronounced Inquisitorial English accent, reminding me of my schoolteachers. 'With Vance out of action, Okonma was the one who implemented the majority of Operation Madrigal, the principal objective of which was the occupation of Spain and Portugal. This succeeded in February, when both countries issued their unconditional surrender.'

'Just to be clear,' Maria said, 'you worked for Scion as a spy?'

'Aparna is a confirmed defector. She is risking her life to assist us with the fight against Scion,' Pivot said. 'If she returned to England, she would certainly be executed for treason.'

'So long as she's clean.'

'I would not endanger any of you by not vetting our sources.'

'I worked for Scion, too,' Nick said, drawing looks. 'Can I ask why you defected, Aparna?'

'Scarlett Burnish. We were classmates at Ancroft,' Wells said. 'She recommended me for my first job in the Archon. At first, I was just pleased to have the work, and never considered the sort of violence I was helping to facilitate. I suppose I was indoctrinated.'

Burnish was the most famous graduate of Ancroft. The Schoolmistress had praised her nearly every day, and her portrait had been everywhere, serving as a shining example to us all.

'My role within the Archon gradually became more senior, until I rose to the position of military clerk. As such, I was privy to more sensitive information,' Wells said. 'After the success of the first stage of Operation Madrigal, there were airstrikes on Paris and London, which were assumed to be retaliatory. Okonma didn't seem deterred by the attacks, despite the perpetrators remaining unidentified.'

Nick slid me a glass of water. I forced myself to take a couple of sips.

'On the twentieth of March,' Wells continued, 'civilian military staff in London were summoned to Whitehall. We were surprised to see the Grand Commander, Hildred Vance.'

Maria closed her eyes.

Vance had been in a coma since I deactivated Senshield. The eruption of energy must have overwhelmed her amaurotic spirit. If she was back to work, everything was about to intensify.

'Vance was clearly in a frail condition,' Wells said, 'but had called us together to tell us about a new and secret Scion plan, which would supersede all future military campaigns. We were not informed of the specifics, but Vance said that Scion had come into possession of an asset – a weapon – of significant value, thanks to the Suzerain. This asset would remove the need for expensive invasions in Europe, and prevent any further attacks on our citadels. She claimed it would end any meaningful opposition to Scion; that all resistance now would be like fighting smoke. It would choke the life from all who dare to stand against the anchor, leaving no trace of its presence.'

'That sounds like a chemical or nuclear weapon,' someone muttered. 'Is that possible?'

'I doubt it,' Wells said. 'Scion has maintained a missile silo for many years as a deterrent, but there is no desire to use the nuclear arsenal. This acquisition was recent.' She adjusted her spectacles. 'Vance informed us that Operation Ventriloquist would target the Kingdom of Norway, which had long resisted pressure to convert, despite being pinned between Britain and Sweden.'

She delivered all of this levelly.

'A week after this address from Vance,' she said, 'Scarlett invited me to her penthouse. I was shocked by how unwell she looked. She told me that she was a double agent, and had been since we were at Ancroft.'

I tried to imagine Burnish at the school we had both attended. Already observing Scion, even as her teachers praised her as a model student.

'Scarlett claimed there was going to be a major leak in Scion, and told me to leave at once,' Wells said. 'As a military clerk, I had access to classified information on supplies and movements, which she advised me to share with Domino. She told me they could give me a new life outside Scion.'

'Burnish confessed all this to you,' Maria said, 'and you did as she asked. Just like that?'

'Scarlett was my closest friend. I trusted her. That aside, the longer I worked as a clerk, the more I had learned about the brutality that occurred during every Scion incursion. It didn't match the promise of safety. I had nothing to keep me in England, so I agreed to go.'

I had to wonder if Burnish had singled Wells out. If she had noticed a shrewd girl at Ancroft and planted her in the Archon, so Wells could one day become an informant.

'You say Burnish mentioned a leak,' Nick said. 'Did you have any idea what she meant?'

'No,' Wells said. 'I'm afraid I still don't.'

'Please allow Aparna to finish,' Pivot said. 'We have a great deal to cover.'

Wells gave her a nod.

'This was in late March. I stayed a few weeks longer, to gather a little more for Domino. We continued to pour supplies and soldiers into the second phase of Operation Madrigal, but as hard as I tried, I could obtain no specific information on Operation Ventriloquist. It was well above my security level,' she said. 'That is the last I saw of Scarlett.'

She returned to her seat.

'Thank you, Aparna.' Pivot nodded to a thickset blond man in a suit. 'I would now like you to hear from Johan Opseth. He was previously our doublet at the Norwegian royal court.'

'For the uninitiated,' Ducos said, 'a doublet is an individual who acts as an envoy for Domino in a benefactor country. This purpose is known to only one or two officials in the relevant government or court – typically the head of state and the Minister of Internal Security.'

Opseth stood. 'Linda Groven, the Prime Minister of Norway, was always opposed to Scion, even if she maintained a position of relative neutrality in public,' he said. 'Given our shared border with Sweden, official policy has always been to avoid openly provoking the anchor, but also do nothing to aid it, and Norway has long been a Domino backer. However, on the eleventh of June, it joined the Republic of Scion. As confirmed by Ms Wells, Norway was formally targeted by Operation Ventriloquist in March, so this change only took three months.'

The fatigue was stealing back. I drank some more water, trying to keep my wits about me.

'There are a few other interesting details. In early April, a popular Norwegian politician, Helen Githmark, was arrested and imprisoned for a hit and run,' Opseth said. 'This surprised her colleagues, as she had a spotless reputation. Over the next few weeks, other politicians and officials began to behave … uncharacteristically. Their stances towards Scion became noticeably warmer.'

I watched him, my heart thumping.

'There is a reinforced barrier called the Brystkasse along the whole of the border between Sweden and Norway,' Opseth said. 'Domino had informed me of increased Scion activity near the main gate.'

'I saw armoured vehicles heading west before I left,' Nick said. 'I reported it to my supervisor, who said Porträtt was investigating.'

'Yes,' a tall woman said. 'I was part of that sub-network. We had been monitoring the change around the Brystkasse on the Swedish side. I trust you were alerted in good time, Johan.'

'Yes. Your intelligence allowed me to move my associates to safety in advance,' Opseth said. 'I warned the Minister of Foreign Affairs. When nothing was done, I went to Queen Ingelin, who said Groven was refusing to see her. I assumed there would be an invasion, but a few days later, Groven announced a conversion to Scion, with her as Grand Inquisitor. The Brystkasse was opened from the Norwegian side shortly before the announcement, allowing Scion soldiers to cross the border unchallenged and subdue the population.'

Each of us had been given a notepad and pen. I jotted down a few points, my palms clammy.

'Queen Ingelin was told to abdicate or be executed,' Opseth said. 'She chose the former. I left Norway with her entourage.' He shook his head. 'I cannot explain how quickly these events unfolded, or the unnerving change in the Storting. One moment, the Norwegian parliament was full of strong-willed politicians, loyal to democracy. Within three months, they were jumping at shadows and pledging allegiance to Scion. It was as if they were being … haunted.'

Hearing an amaurotic say that word gave me a chill.

'Thank you,' Pivot said. Opseth sat down. 'And now for the third and final piece of the puzzle, which pertains to Italy. As we've heard, Norway was the first target of Operation Ventriloquist. In the weeks preceding the conversion, odd behaviour was noted in its most anti-Scion politicians. Now we are observing a similar pattern among Italian politicians, up to the highest level.'

Verča swallowed.

'As most of you will be aware, this country has both a President and a Prime Minister, respectively Beatrice Sala and Lorenzo Rinaldi,' Pivot said. 'Our doublet in Rome was recently approached by a whistle-blower. This source claims that Sala and Rinaldi have signed a secret treaty with Scion, giving two Italian islands to the anchor.'

Speculative murmurs went up all over the room.

Ducos tapped her data pad, and a map of Italy appeared. Pivot used a pointer to indicate three small islands.

'Capri and Ischia, part of the Campanian Archipelago in the Bay of Naples. The Italians among you will know that both were evacuated at the end of August, along with nearby Procida.'

'Rinaldi said the volcanic complex under Ischia was stirring,' a man said. 'The bastard.'

'The press has been asking why it was necessary to evacuate Capri,' Ducos said, 'which is about thirty kilometres away from Ischia. Rinaldi has sent talking heads to explain that the government is simply being cautious. Ischia has not erupted since the Middle Ages, so they have no idea what to expect. We suspect at least one geologist was bribed.'

Pivot looked to the defector. 'Aparna, what do you make of this?'

'I fail to see what Scion would gain from possessing those islands,' Wells said. 'There have been some territorial disputes between France and Italy, but the Campanian Archipelago lies nowhere near French waters.'

I listened in silence. None of this was my area of expertise. I might style myself as a rebel commander, but I had no actual military training.

'So far, this development has stupefied everyone,' Pivot said, interlocking her fingers on the table. 'The general public has no idea these islands belong to the Republic of Scion.'

'Yes, because there would be a huge outcry from Italians, including this one. It implies that Italy is also about to convert,' Verča said, to mutters of agreement. 'Rinaldi is weak on Scion, but Sala—'

'Let us not rush to conclusions, Veronika,' Pivot said. 'Almost as soon as President Sala ratified the secret treaty, she cancelled all of her public engagements and disappeared. The official reason is illness. We have concerns that she is either in danger, or preparing to defect to the Republic of Scion, perhaps as Grand Inquisitor.'

'The second option is not possible,' Verča said firmly. 'Sala is a vocal and lifelong critic of Scion.'

One of the other Italians huffed. 'And have you never known a politician to lie?'

'But President Sala has been outspoken on the subject, even when it didn't serve her politically. A few years ago, she made such a combative speech about Scion that she was accused of overreach and threatened with impeachment. She would never give any ground.'

'I would have said the same of Groven,' Opseth said.

'Italy has been a high-priority target for decades,' Wells said. 'If Scion were to occupy it, the remaining free states in the western Balkans would be forced to capitulate, finding themselves virtually surrounded.'

'We are now in the unpleasant position of having to spy on one of our own benefactors,' Pivot said. 'Since it is possible that both leaders are compromised, we must do this with the greatest caution. We have a duty to protect our headquarters and this organisation, but also to protect our allies. It falls to the people in this room to understand what is happening and stop it.'

Nick cleared his throat. 'Do Rinaldi and Sala know where head-quarters is?'

'Sala is aware that Domino is based in Italy, but not where. Only the doublet knows that,' Pivot said. 'Rinaldi has no idea about Domino.'

'And the doublet stayed in Rome?'

'Yes, so as not to raise suspicions. He sent the whistle-blower to Venice in his stead.'

My gaze lingered on the map, measuring the distance between the islands and the mainland.

'We have three key questions to answer,' Pivot said. 'The first is why President Sala has disappeared, while Rinaldi continues to go about the daily business of government. The second is why Scion wanted these islands. The third is what sort of weapon Scion acquired to make Operation Ventriloquist possible, and how it works on politicians.'

The more I looked at those islands, the more I understood. The fine hairs on my arms rose.

'Perhaps this Operation Ventriloquist is simpler than it looks,' Maria said. 'Is it just good old-fashioned blackmail?'

'Norway had a strong democracy,' Opseth said. 'It is not so easy as blackmailing one person.'

'Domino has already taken steps to answer two of the questions,' Pivot said. 'Our operatives are searching for Sala. I also dispatched a team to investigate Capri and Ischia, to see if Scion has stationed troops or left supplies. They used propulsion vehicles to approach Capri underwater, endeavouring to avoid detection. They did not return. Neither did a second team. I prohibited any further attempts.'

Ducos brought up a new image of Italy, adjusted it to account for the darkness, and homed in on the right coordinates. Once Capri appeared, she made the image three-dimensional.

According to the onscreen data, Capri was about four miles long. Mountainous in the middle, scattered with small white buildings; it had previously had a population of seven thousand.

'Capri is closest to Naples,' Pivot said. 'So far, we have not made any attempts to reach Ischia. Before our investigation teams disappeared, they each reported a lack of light from both islands. The electricity appears to have been switched off.' She indicated the northern coast. 'Here is our point of interest. Early this month, a vessel approached Capri. Though unmarked and running dark, it was later identified as a *Dryden*-class patrol boat, used by Scion in the Mediterranean. It stopped at this spot, then left.'

'That port of call is right next to a sea cave, the Grotta Azzurra,' a man said. 'It could have been an access point for soldiers.'

'Yes,' Verča said. 'There are steps up the cliff from there.'

'It's notable that a Scion patrol ship was allowed to get close to Capri in the first place,' Ducos said. 'The navy would usually have intercepted it as soon as it entered Italian waters. Another sign that Italy is complicit.'

'Pivot,' I said, speaking up for the first time, 'do you know if the islands were given code names?'

She considered me with fresh interest.

'You have anticipated my final breadcrumb,' she said. 'Yes, they were. According to the treaty, Capri is to henceforth be known as Lugentes Campi, and Ischia as Orcus IV.'

That information was all I needed to know I was right.

The city in Sweden had been the third prison. Here, on the island of Ischia, was the foundation of the fourth.

'I think I know why Scion took the islands,' I said. 'Scion has a long history of building secret prisons to hold clairvoyants, isolating them from the so-called natural population. I've been in one myself, and seen another in France. There's always a harvest city nearby, where they can get hold of a lot of voyants. The sort of place where people can vanish.'

'Napoli.' Verča looked at the screen. 'The largest city in Italy.'

'If I'm right, it would mean every voyant there is at risk of being trafficked,' I said. 'When Scion took Oxford as a prison, they claimed it had burned down, which gave them an excuse to clear the city. That must be exactly what they've done with the volcano and Ischia.'

'Scion has never put one of these prisons on an island, to our knowledge,' Maria said. 'Then again, the definition of insanity is doing the same thing over and over again and expecting different results, isn't it?'

'There is precedent,' Nick said. 'My sub-network was sent to investigate a similar prison on the isle of Gotland.'

'It would be a logical development, strategically,' Wells agreed. 'Scarlett told me a little about Oxford. A black site, closed down last September. The prisoners escaped using the same train that was used to transport them there.' She looked at me, frowning slightly.

'Surrounding the next one with water would make it far harder to get in or out.'

It would also make it harder for me, specifically, to reach it. Nashira must suspect my fear of water.

'Maybe all this is a red herring,' a woman said. 'If we're looking at the islands, what are we *not* looking at?'

Wells nodded. 'Quite possible. Commander Vance is more than willing to make large, expensive gestures to achieve her purpose, even if that purpose is to capture just one person.'

Another silence rang.

'I have given you a great deal to digest,' Pivot said. 'Once again, I stress that all of it must remain between us.' Ducos switched off the screen. 'Inshallah, someone will be able to solve the mystery. I will summon you again in a few days, once you've had time to consider the facts, but come to me immediately with any urgent realisations.'

We all rose. I followed Nick from the Blue Room, and we crossed the walkway.

'Let's mull this over in the morning,' Nick said. 'You must be exhausted, Paige.'

'I'm fine. We should talk now.'

In the medical room, I shed my dissimulator and pinched some feeling back into my cheeks. Once Maria and Verča had joined us, Nick locked the door.

'I can't believe this,' Verča said. 'Italy, giving way to Scion without so much as a whimper.' She sank on to an examination couch, arms folded. 'I need to ... warn my family.'

'Take a moment,' Nick said. 'You've had a shock.'

'Verča.' Maria sat beside her. 'Are you all right, dusha?'

'No. I'm not sure if I'm more afraid or angry.' Verča raked a hand through her loose hair. 'Rinaldi has never taken a firm stance against Scion in public, except to shake his fist and offer platitudes, but Sala ... I'm convinced she doesn't want this. Perhaps she is in danger, as Command suspects.'

'How much power does she have?'

'The role of president used to be more ceremonial, but that has changed somewhat in recent years. Sala wields a significant degree of influence. She is the one who usually represents Italy abroad and deals with national defence and foreign affairs. She is also the head of the armed forces. I can see why Domino chose her as their point of contact.'

I went to the window and opened the shutters, needing fresh air. Ever since Pivot had broached the subject of the islands, I had been mentally elsewhere.

'We need to decide whether to risk staying in Italy any longer,' Nick said. 'If Scion does invade, we could be trapped here. Verča, I think you should leave as soon as possible.'

'Yes. I will visit my family in Trieste,' Verča said. 'I'll convince them to go to Prague.'

'And I'm leaving in November, as discussed,' Maria said. 'As for you two, Domino will probably send you abroad, regardless of what happens next.'

'I'm not going anywhere. Not yet,' I said quietly. 'Ischia is the location of the next voyant prison, or someone wants us to think it is. Wells was right. It does make sense as their next move. An island is much harder to breach or escape, and there's a big city nearby.'

'Orcus IV,' Maria said, musing. 'Does anyone know what that means?'

'Orcus was a Roman god of the underworld,' Verča said. 'The name was also used for his domain.'

'It's an homage to the Netherworld, like the other names,' I said. 'They're all realms of the dead in human stories.' Arcturus had told me that. 'What about Lugentes Campi?'

'That one sounds Latin.' Verča took out her phone. 'Let me have a look.'

'Maria, while you're here, I'm going to change your dressing.' Nick went to wash his hands. 'How's the pain?'

'I can barely feel it,' Maria said. 'Some days I simply forget I was stabbed.'

Nick sighed. 'You and Paige really are two of a kind.'

'Lugentes Campi means *Fields of Mourning*,' Verča said, reading off her phone. 'Omnia says it's mentioned by the Roman writer Virgil, who seems to have understood it as a part of the afterlife for those who died for love, where they relive their suffering for eternity.'

*Those who died for love.*

'Paige.' Nick noticed my expression. 'Come and sit down.'

'Yes, and don't look at my arm,' Maria said. Nick unwrapped it, revealing a livid red cut below her shoulder, puckered by dark stitches. 'I can see a plan taking form. What are you thinking?'

I closed my eyes. As soon as I voiced the possibility, I would start to invest time and hope in it.

'Warden could be on one of those islands,' I said. 'It would make sense for Nashira to imprison him in a Reph-controlled area, but … it's also a huge risk for her to build a prison off the shore of a country she doesn't control yet, let alone leave a valuable captive there.'

Verča looked up. 'Who is Warden?'

'He's part of the Ranthen, the faction of Rephs who don't want to kill us,' Maria said, wincing as Nick cleaned the wound. 'Actually, let me rephrase. The Ranthen are the faction of Rephs who *may* want to kill us, deep inside, but have not chosen to act on that desire.'

'Warden was my auxiliary in Paris,' I said. 'Scion detained him.' I took a calming breath. 'Capri is clearly not under threat from the volcano, and the populations of both islands will never be allowed to return. Thanks to Operation Ventriloquist, Nashira must be confident that Italy is about to convert, like Norway. She doesn't care how flimsy the façade is, because it only has to last so long.'

'I can't understand *how* they are doing this,' Verča said. 'What is this weapon Scion has?'

'I can't say I have any idea,' Maria said, keeping her eyes shut as Nick worked. 'But whatever is brewing, we need to stop Italy falling to Scion. It could tip the balance for them.'

I gazed back out of the window, watching the lamplight ripple on the dark water.

'I want to go to Naples and see the islands for myself,' I said. 'But first I'd like to speak to Terebell. Find out whether she knows anything more concrete about Warden.'

'Terebell is the leader of the Ranthen,' Maria said to Verča. 'And the co-ruler of the Mime Order.' Verča nodded. 'Did your message reach her, Paige?'

'I've no way of knowing. Even if it did, it could take her a while to get here,' I replied. 'It's not as if Rephs can fly. I'll give her a few days. Either way, I'm going to Naples.'

'Even though *two* specialist investigation teams have disappeared?'

'I'll wager none of them could sense the island from a distance,' I said. 'I can.'

'Then we'll need to talk to Command,' Nick said. 'Let's meet in the bar for lunch. We can let our thoughts steep, then formulate a plan.' He secured the new dressing. 'No matter how fast Scion moves, we can't rush into this.'

---

In my room, I sat alone, thinking of Ischia and Capri. One island to imprison voyants, and one – perhaps – to hold a traitor. Too subtle and poetic a brand of cruelty for Hildred Vance. She went for the throat, swift and efficient. This was a blade that aimed for the gut. A slow, torturous bleed.

It had to be Nashira, witness to our first embrace. The only person who had ever seen me kiss Arcturus. She had manipulated me before. Now I needed to think like my enemy.

Nashira knew I was willing to gamble on poor odds. She knew I had fallen for her trick in Paris, and that I might have realised it by now. By evoking the Lugentes Campi, she was not only rubbing my nose in my failure, but sneering at Arcturus for wasting his love on me.

In Paris, she had watched me plead with him, convinced he was betraying me. Time and again she had poisoned our trust.

It wasn't jealousy. Nashira was above such a petty emotion, and had never held a shred of affection for Arcturus, but our relationship had always threatened her beliefs. In her world, a Reph and a human could simply not feel the way we had for each other. She wanted to obliterate our bond to prove it had never been strong in the first place.

She wanted me consumed by guilt. She wanted me to charge to his rescue again. This time, I had learned from experience. I could see every pressure point she was touching. An island named for star-crossed love, surrounded by a fear Nashira had instilled in me.

Hildred Vance had a method. She worked out her opponents' weaknesses and exploited them. In Edinburgh, she had recreated the Dublin Incursion, knowing I had only just survived it as a child. She and Nashira could have designed this together.

Nashira must believe I was either long dead or in hiding. If it was the latter, she needed to force me out. Vance could have persuaded her that the best way of doing that was to send me running into the elaborate trap of Capri. That specific choice of island seemed deliberate, to draw media attention and make sure plenty of people were talking about it. Even with the threat of the eruption, there was no obvious reason it should have been evacuated.

I might find soldiers and tanks on its shore. The whole island could be sown with landmines. I might find Arcturus there, but only his severed head, left as a death blow to my sanity.

I could see it all from where I stood. Every cog and spring and lever, every move in a long game.

It felt like a trap.

It also felt like a test.

What if this time, she was expecting me *not* to rise to the bait, leaving Arcturus there for ever, abandoned by his faithless, mortal lover?

What if this wasn't just meant to torment me, but him?

All at once, the room was too stifling to bear. I needed to be outside. I dressed in a few swift movements and strode down the corridor, planning to jog a mile or two around the city. Before my torture, I had always thought most clearly on the roofs at night, under the stars, surrounded by the sounds of the citadel. I would try to tap into that state of mind again.

Before I could, a man blocked my path. One of the voyants from the emergency meeting – a medium, who had never spoken. I took up a defensive stance at once, but all he did was stand there. At the sight of his lax features and blank gaze, I realised he was possessed.

'I bear a message,' he ground out. 'For the dreamwalker.' I waited, heart thudding. 'Meet the one you summoned at the Certosa di Bologna, two days hence, when the sun is highest.'

He crumpled as the spirit let him go. I caught him before he could hit the floor.

'You're all right,' I murmured, while he coughed himself to tears. 'Come on. Let's get you to the medic.'

# 10

## REUNION

I took the medium to Nick. After that, I fell asleep, reassured by the knowledge that Terebell was coming.

It didn't last for long. I woke in a cage of cold skin, unable to move so much as a finger. I could only stare at the ceiling, feeling as if my blood had stopped flowing.

I don't know how long I lay there. At last, I managed to snap upright. Some instinct made me pull on the cord, the dead and heavy cord, more lead than gold.

'I'm here,' I whispered. 'What are you trying to tell me?'

I didn't know why I was talking out loud.

'Are you on Capri or Ischia?'

There was no answer. I held myself, taking deep breaths, waiting for the feeling of unease to pass.

It soon became apparent that I needed to shake it off with some force. Before the sun had risen, I was leaving the Palazzo del Domino, craving a run along the waterfront, where the streetlamps were aglow.

By the time I returned to my room, the sun was up, the streets burning. In the bar, I ordered an early lunch and chose a seat in the corner. When Nick joined me at noon, I looked up.

'How's the medium?'

'He has a sore throat and a headache, but he's stable. He doesn't remember what he said.' Nick held a glass of white ersatz. 'That was quite a way for Terebell to establish contact.'

'At least she got my message.'

'Let's hope she has good news about the Mime Order.' He sat down and rested his elbows on the table, steepling his fingers under his chin. 'Any more thoughts about Operation Ventriloquist?'

'Not yet.'

'And you still think Warden is on Capri?'

'Yes. That's the island named for love, and it's closer to shore, so it's more tempting.' I pushed my hair back. 'I think Warden is there as bait. I'm thinking about taking it.'

Nick waited for me to go on.

'I'm trying to learn from my mistakes. I know I can be impulsive and reckless, and I need to get a handle on it. If I don't play it safer, I'm going to get someone killed again, like I did in London,' I said. 'I know this is a trap. The water, the name – it's like Nashira is testing my nerve and my loyalty, asking me how far I'm willing to go to save him.'

'But you want to see for yourself.'

'I'm afraid that if I don't, he'll be stranded there for good. It would give Nashira such a kick to prove she'd finally broken us, to the point that I would ignore an obvious sign that he's there.'

'Reverse psychology. It's possible,' Nick said. 'If this *is* a trap for you, we've learned about it before Nashira is ready, which might work in our favour.' I nodded. 'What would Warden tell you to do?'

'Avoid the islands. Don't risk my life,' I said at once, 'but he's selfless to the point of absurdity. What he would tell me to do isn't necessarily the right thing to do.'

Nick considered for a while.

'Going there would be dangerous,' he said, 'but in our line of work, everything comes with risk. Sometimes that risk is justified. In this case, I think it is. First, because Scion doesn't know we're aware of the islands being annexed. And regardless of your personal feelings for Warden, saving him could be a smart move for Domino. He's been with the enemy for months, which means he'd be a valuable informant. He might even know something more about Operation Ventriloquist. You could use that to sell the idea to Command.'

'So if I can get them on board, you'd support me doing this?'

'Depending on the strength of our plan. We rushed into the ambush in Fulham,' Nick said, 'but Scion has only held these islands for a month. I doubt they've had time to fortify them.'

'That's what I was thinking. That patrol ship didn't stop there for long,' I said. 'They won't have had a chance to unload much security or surveillance equipment, but they must be planning to put it there at some point. That means we have a small window of opportunity.'

'And no thief would get anywhere by walking past an open window.'

'Jax said that.'

'I think we can agree he was occasionally right. And remember what Eliza told you, when we first taught you to pickpocket,' Nick said. 'A mouse can steal bait from a trap. It just needs care, speed and subtlety.'

'Carrying a big Reph off an island might be harder than lifting a watch off a mark.'

'We got him out of Camden, even if it drew attention. I'm just glad you've warned me this time.'

'I did say I would.'

Verča and Maria arrived at that moment, looking as tired as us. Soon we all had a drink and a meal.

'So tell us, Underqueen,' Maria said. 'Are we going to Naples?'

'Not yet. I've heard from Terebell,' I said. 'She wants to see me in Bologna tomorrow.'

'How did she get here?'

'No idea, but if she agrees with my theory that Warden might be on Capri, I'll go to Command and make a case for a rescue attempt. We'll need decent equipment – weapons, mine detectors, maybe diving gear. A way across, too.'

'I have a few old friends in Napoli,' Verča said. 'I'm confident they could find us a boat.'

'Any guards on the island would see a boat from a long way off,' Nick said.

Maria reached for the basket of bread in the middle of the table. 'Submarine?'

'You're not coming, however we get to it,' I told her. 'Not with that gammy arm.'

'Oh, come on, it's a flesh wound.'

'Maria,' Nick said. 'No.'

'Well, I'm coming to Naples. Verča, what is the voyant community like there?'

'Very old and tight knit,' Verča replied. 'The city has two main factions of voyants, as well as an underground market in the Catacombe di San Gennaro.'

'Will they be willing to help us?'

'Possibly, if I'm with you. I was on good terms with both factions when I lived there.'

'The Ranthen will want to be part of getting Arcturus back, and they'll be useful on the island,' I said. 'I need somewhere discreet for them to meet us.'

As Verča thought about it, she chased her salmon with a sip of pale wine.

'The Antro della Sibilla,' she concluded. 'It's a cave we used for séance parties, but it would make a good place for a secret meeting. It's said the Cumaean Sibyl used to live there.'

Nick looked curious. 'A sibyl?'

'Yes. Some Neapolitan voyants worship her,' Verča said. 'Legend says the god Apollo granted her long life, but when she refused to sleep with him, he elected not to preserve her youth. Her body shrivelled until it could fit inside a jar, and then only her voice was left. And whenever people asked what she wanted, the sibyl would say she wanted to die.'

'That could be the most dismal story I've ever heard,' Maria said. 'And I was in prison.'

'A cave sounds perfect,' I said. 'Where is it?'

'Pozzuoli, on the outskirts of the province of Naples,' Verča said. 'I'll mark it on a map for you.'

'Thanks. Once we're there, I can assess Capri from a distance,' I said. 'Since it was only cleared in the last few weeks, we think any defences will be minimal, but we need to do this as soon as possible, before Scion boosts security.'

'There's *something* there,' Nick said, 'or those investigation teams would still be with us. But I doubt the situation will improve with time.'

'Capri is a large island, Paige. To search it, you'll need locals, or you and the Ranthen will be wandering in the dark for hours,' Verča said. 'Many voyants in Naples prefer to speak Napoletano. I can intercede with them, so you have people on the ground to help.'

'I suppose I could always stand on the shore and set fire to a few spirits, in case you need a beacon.' Maria sighed. 'Thirty-six years without being stabbed. It really had to be this month.'

Verča patted her knee. I poured myself a little wine, telling myself there was reason to feel optimistic. Now I just had to hope that Terebell had something to confirm my suspicions.

And that we, unlike the others, would return from Capri.

---

Ducos had agreed to drive me to Bologna, a city about two hours from Venice, to meet with Terebell. With the knowledge that I might need all my strength to search Capri, I rested until Wednesday morning, when I rose early to eat breakfast and assemble a decent outfit.

Since the warmth showed no sign of easing, I dressed in a grey singlet, the wedge sandals, and black shorts that buttoned high on my waist. I propped on my sunglasses and scrutinised myself in the mirror. Terebell was going to think I looked like a tourist, but that had to be preferable to an overheated mess. I covered the sunburn with a shirt.

Before long, Ducos knocked for me, and Noemi took us to the car park. Soon we were driving away from Venice, the city that had forced me to live alongside water. Little by little, I was growing used to its constant sparkle, the sound of the waves swashing under my window.

The journey was a blur of fields. Even with the wind in my hair, the white aster towed me back to sleep. Ducos parked and shook me awake, and we made towards a high brick wall.

'This is the Certosa di Bologna, the municipal cemetery,' she said. 'I can see why your contact wanted to meet here. It's quiet at this time of day. No better place for a private conversation.'

'Very amaurotic remark,' I said. She eyed me. 'You think the spirits don't eavesdrop?'

'Oh, do shut up.'

Two sculptures flanked the entrance, mourning over jars. As we strode between them, my awareness of the æther climbed, as it always did in cemeteries. Ducos led me along a sun-baked path, lined with evergreens, cutting straight through a garden of bones. Most of the graves were pale mausoleums; some housed their own statues, posed in thought or lamentation. Though it wasn't yet midday, the air was thick and warm as fresh caramel. I was grateful for the shade when we entered a gallery, which overlooked one of the cloisters.

Ducos leaned against the balustrade. A few spirits came up to me, flirting with my aura. Most of them seemed content in this place, even if they had chosen not to move on.

*Meet the one you summoned at the Certosa di Bologna, two days hence, when the sun is highest.*

Terebell Sheratan appeared at midday on the dot. Despite the warmth, she wore a black coat over trousers, fastened almost to her chin, with matching gloves and boots.

'That's her?' Ducos said, watching her walk between the mausoleums. 'She's tall enough.'

'Yes,' I said. 'It's her.'

Seeing us, Terebell came up to the gallery. Her dark hair was as sleek and immaculate as ever, her sarx untouched by the intense heat. I had only ever seen Arcturus sweat when a Buzzer had wounded him, as if his body had been trying to push out the corruption.

'Hello, Terebell,' I said.

Terebell just looked at me, her silence deafening.

'I'm going to smoke.' Ducos took her cigarettes from her pocket. 'I'll give you half an hour.'

She left us alone. Scores of insects chirred nearby as we took the measure of each other.

'So you are alive,' Terebell said. 'You had no right to perform that manner of séance.'

'I'm sorry if it was presumptuous. Arcturus taught me to do it.'

'Arcturus has been languishing behind enemy lines for six months.' Her eyes blazed. 'Because of you.'

I deserved her resentment, but it was still hard to stop myself flinching.

'Nick told me you were looking for him,' I said, trying to keep my composure.

'Yes, because he is no traitor. If you thought for a moment that Arcturus Mesarthim would betray the Mime Order, after all he has done for the cause, you are unworthy of his trust.'

'Of course I didn't think he would betray us. I also didn't think he would ever raise a hand to me, but he did.'

'Did it never occur to you that he was being coerced?'

'Yes, but—'

'You could not have forced him to leave with you. I accept that,' Terebell said, 'but you could have tracked him down again. You could have used the golden cord and kept trying to save him. Instead, you vanished, forcing a subordinate to wear the Rose Crown. You left us to search with nowhere to start, all while you possessed a compass pointing straight to Arcturus.'

'I would appreciate it if you'd let me explain, Terebell.'

'Speak, then, and be quick about it,' she said coldly. 'I have no time to waste on your excuses.'

'A Domino agent snatched me from Paris after the airstrikes. She was giving me a lot of white aster. I was either brought to the free world against my will, or on false pretences.' I held my nerve. 'Look, you're right to be angry. I see now that none of it added up. I should never have believed Nashira, but I'm going to fix it. I'm going to find Arcturus.'

'I will find him. I no longer trust your judgement,' Terebell said. 'In any case, your long absence has demonstrated that the revolution is now capable of surviving without you.'

'Why do you hate me so much?'

The directness of it must have thrown her. Her eyes gave a flare, and she failed to reply.

'Why?' I asked her. 'What have I ever done to you?'

For once, Terebell didn't say anything. She seemed to be waiting for me to get this off my chest.

'I started a rebellion for you,' I said. 'I gave myself to Scion to be tortured. I deactivated Senshield. I united two syndicates against Scion. And you can't even call me by my name.' When she turned her back and strode to the balustrade, I sighed. 'Can you really not even afford me that, after everything, Terebell?'

She might as well have been one of the sculptures. It was then that I knew I had to take a risk.

'Is it because you're still in love with him?'

Terebell turned to face me, her gaze utterly devoid of humanity. 'What?'

This might get me thrown to my death, but playing nice had never got me anywhere with Terebell. She might respect me a little more if I gave as good as I got.

'I know you used to be his partner,' I said. 'And why you're not any more.'

Suddenly she was inches away. I stood my ground, but my aura shrank from hers.

'Did Arcturus tell you?'

She never laid a finger on me, but she was close enough that I would have seen myself in her pupils, had they reflected light. It took a few moments to get my tongue moving.

'No,' I said. 'I can reflect his gift, through the golden cord. I saw what happened by accident.'

Terebell stared into my eyes, seeking a lie.

'He traded his dignity for your life,' I said. 'He sacrificed himself to years of degradation and abuse to protect you, and you rejected him. I'd say we're about the same.'

Her gloved hand curled into a fist. At that point, I knew I was fortunate to be alive.

'My feelings towards you have nothing to do with my feelings for him,' she said. 'Past or present.'

It had been like chiselling blood from a sculpture, but I had cracked her. 'It's just us, Terebell,' I said. 'Nothing we say need ever go beyond this cemetery. Only the dead can hear.'

'Arcturus may not be the flesh-traitor Nashira claims he is,' Terebell said, 'but he does sympathise with mortals, despite your faults. And you – he cares for no human more than you. You do not deserve his depth of loyalty. Nothing in you is worthy of a Mesarthim.'

For the first time, her words smarted. I had never entertained the idea that the Ranthen would accept his relationship with me, but if I had, this would have been its death knell.

'I'm not asking you to like me, Terebell. Plenty of people don't like me,' I said. 'But with you, I can't lie – it hurts. You've led the Ranthen through a period of terrible indignity, and you're still going strong, fighting back. You inspire me to do the same as Underqueen.'

It was true. I had always respected her resilience. For once, Terebell looked as if she had no idea what to say. I supposed she hadn't banked on niceties.

'We both care about Arcturus. I can help you find him,' I said. 'He looked after me in Paris. If not for him, I don't think I would ever have been able to recover. Let me pay the debt.'

A long moment passed before she spoke: 'Have you sensed anything from the golden cord?'

It was a small victory, but I would take it.

'It's intact, but I haven't felt it move.' I watched her pace. 'Have you heard anything?'

'Yes,' she said. 'We searched Britain for months, but we could find no trace. Then a psychopomp came from France with a message from Arcturus, seeking my assistance to escape. From the timing, we believe he seized his chance to send word on the Day of the French Republic.'

That celebration took place at the end of July. He had survived for several months.

'He had told the psychopomp to return to him, so I could follow it to his position,' she said. 'The next day, we arrived in Calais. We tracked Arcturus to various rural strongholds in France, and finally, the fortified city of Carcassonne. There, we were intercepted by Sargas loyalists. Nashira had called many of her allies to her side.'

A breeze wafted through her hair. 'After our failure, Arcturus was moved to Toulon and placed on a ship.'

My heart thumped. 'When was this?'

'The last day of August.'

'And what sort of ship?'

'A *Dryden*-class patrol vessel. We lost his trail from there.'

For the first time in a while, the corners of my mouth twitched up. That was the exact sort of Scion ship that had been seen approaching Capri a few days later, in early September.

'I think I know how to pick it back up,' I said.

Terebell listened as I told her everything I had learned. When I was done, she seemed to withdraw into her own thoughts for a while, her gaze distant.

'Arcturus could be on either of the islands. Both have been evacuated,' I said, 'but my gut tells me it's Capri. Not only because that's where the ship went, but because of the code name.'

'Yes,' Terebell said. 'The name is clearly intended to taunt me.'

It could just as well be for her as for me, if Nashira had cottoned on to her search for Arcturus. Either way, I had to let her believe it.

'The voyants of Naples can help us search the island, and the Domino Programme might equip us,' I said. 'I'm willing to do anything to get Arcturus back, but two specialist teams have already disappeared on Capri. Before we take the risk, I'd like to confirm that he's there.'

'How would you confirm it?'

'He left a vial of his ectoplasm in my backpack in Oxford. When I drank it, it strengthened the golden cord. That's what let me trace him to Camden.'

'I have some of his ectoplasm,' Terebell said. 'I will give it to you in Naples.' I nodded. 'I will need time to bring some of the other Ranthen to Italy, to raise our chances of saving him.'

'How did you get here?'

'By a cold spot. We can use one to enter the Netherworld and another to leave, allowing us to circumvent great distances on Earth. The psychopomp led me to a cold spot in the Apennines. It is a dangerous way to travel, but faster than moving by terrestrial means.'

'I had no idea.'

'There are many possibilities that exist beyond the limits of the mortal imagination.'

'If you've been on the move for months, you haven't been in London. Is the Mime Order all right?'

'Yes. Pleione and Taygeta stayed behind,' Terebell said. 'I last heard from them in August. The interim Underqueen is surviving in her position, but she lacks your strength of character. The sooner we have Arcturus, the sooner we can all return to London, so you can relieve her.'

'Eliza doesn't lack strength of character. She's just too kind for her own good sometimes.' I reached into my pocket. 'Nick and I can't go back until January at the earliest.'

'Why not?'

'Because we still need to fulfil our obligations to the Domino Programme.'

'What of your obligations to me, and to your citadel?'

'Domino saved me from the Archon. They expect a return on their investment,' I said. 'More importantly, they've promised financial support for the Parisian syndicate, and possibly the Mime Order. Arcturus mentioned you'd lost access to your money since Alsafi ... passed on. Now his human ally in the Archon is dead, too. Unless she hid or moved the money, it will have been requisitioned by Scion. And unless you have other sources of income, I need payment. You're going to have to bolster Eliza up for a while longer.'

Terebell was silent for a while.

'I had assumed as much,' she said. 'We have some coin and assets, but if you can obtain more, so be it. We will steady London until your return.'

'Thank you.' I gave her a map. 'I'll see you at the Antro della Sibilla. My friend has marked the location.'

'I will be there at sunset in three days' time.' Terebell held my gaze. 'This was a pertinent place to meet, dreamwalker.'

'Why?'

'It reminds me that one day, it will be your bones in a garden like this one. Not mine.'

She walked away, leaving me to stand alone, surrounded by the dead.

After a while, Ducos returned to the gallery and raised her eyebrows. I folded my arms.

'Think you could help me persuade Command that Warden is worth saving from an island that's almost certainly a trap?'

Ducos looked at me for a long time, then stubbed out her cigarette on the balustrade.

'You are fortunate that I like you, Flora.'

# 11

# CAVE OF THE SIBYL

Naples sprawled across a bay in southern Italy, where summer clung with all its might. As Verča drove towards it, I kept an eye on Mount Vesuvius. No wonder this city attracted voyants – everyone here must accept the proximity of death, living in the shadow of the sleeping giant.

Command had taken some convincing, but I had a stronger voice in the network now. In the end, Pivot had agreed that Arcturus was worth a third and final attempt for a team to set foot on Capri. I had clinically explained his value. He had been a prisoner for half a year, and had still been able to communicate in July. He might have gained valuable information from the enemy. If anyone could help us crack Operation Ventriloquist, it was him.

The stakes were high. If Scion caught us on Capri, it would wreck the whole investigation into Operation Ventriloquist. It might even provoke Scion into attacking Italy. Ducos had wanted to join us, to ensure it went smoothly, but Nick had persuaded her that we could do it alone. I was getting the distinct impression that she trusted him to temper me.

I was glad she had relented. The fewer people who risked their necks, the better – because this wasn't really about intelligence, for me. That wasn't the reason I was putting my life on the line.

I was doing this for Arcturus.

*Be careful, Flora,* Pivot had told me. *We don't want to lose you again. At the first sign of danger, you must abort.*

Naples hit my senses like a fist smothered in paint, its knuckles raw and bare. Almost every building had some kind of art on it, from cramped scrawls to detailed murals. Overhead wires and laundry crisscrossed above its roaring streets and timeworn alleys, which rippled with heat. Those alleys were awash with spirits, mostly ghosts and shades. Verča had told us that Naples had thousands of years of history, and it looked it – somehow both decaying and defiantly alive, appealing to the part of me that thrived on chaos.

'I absolutely love this.' Maria leaned out of the window on her elbows. 'It looks you in the eye.'

'I agree.' Verča smiled. 'Napoli can be overwhelming, but it will reward your persistence.'

'Oh, I'm already planning a getaway.'

'President Sala has an official residence nearby,' Verča said, 'but she isn't there, according to Pivot.'

Nick pushed his sunglasses back up his nose. 'How long did you live in Naples, Verča?'

'About three years. It was the second place I moved after I graduated. I'd just broken up with my first girlfriend, and I needed to be … screamed awake, shaken back to myself. Napoli did that for me.' She turned the car on to a wide thoroughfare. 'This has always been a difficult city to govern. I wonder if that's why it was chosen. To bring it to heel.'

A moto chose that moment to cut in front of her. Verča slammed on the brakes and leaned out of the window.

'Neh, ma che cazzo stai facenno, strunze!'

Maria clutched her chest. 'Veronika Rachele Norlenghi. Did you swear at someone?'

'I fear I did.' Verča blew a tuft of hair from her eyes before driving again. 'My apologies, everyone.'

'No, no.' Maria chuckled. 'I like this side of you.'

'Drive like an idiot near me, and perhaps it will come back out, Maruška.'

Their loving conversations filled my chest with a dull ache. I looked away, resting my folded arms on the door, so the wind tore at my hair. Despite the heat, I wore my dissimulator. If our suspicions were correct, Scion would likely have spies in this city, monitoring and counting its voyants, making sure no one noticed the two islands had been annexed.

It had been a long drive from Venice. We had set out before dawn, stopping only to charge the car. I had spent most of the time asleep across the back seat, my head in Nick's lap.

Now Verča drove along the sweeping Bay of Naples, away from the heart of the city. She pulled up outside a small house on the seafront. This would be our local base of operations.

'Here we are,' she said. Nick got out. 'My contact works at the port. You should get some rest.'

'We can go with you,' I said.

'The group I need will close ranks around strangers, even an Underqueen,' she said. 'I might be a few hours.' She passed Maria a key. 'You should be able to see Capri from here.'

She drove away, while the others filed towards the building. All I wanted to do was sleep, but I needed to stretch my legs after spending the best part of a day in a car.

The others went in, leaving the door on the latch for me. I turned to face the Tyrrhenian Sea, the sun burning on my hair. Passing two palm trees, I went up to the railings that separated the street from the waves. I squinted past the haze of light and glimpsed it in the distance.

Capri.

The island had two distinct peaks. It was as if a pair of giants had reached into the sea for lost treasure, leaving their backs above the surface. I might be looking right at Arcturus.

I might also be looking at his tomb.

---

In the house, I changed into a sleeveless top and cargo trousers. For the rest of the day, I lay under a fan and tried to conserve my strength. Nick checked the equipment, which I hoped we wouldn't have to use. He had often dived in the Kattegat when he lived in Sweden.

It was almost five by the time Verča returned. 'Good news,' she announced. Maria sat up with a grimace, grasping her bandaged arm. 'I found my old friend, a voyant who commands great respect here. He's offered to help us reach Capri.'

I raised my eyebrows. 'Just like that?'

'I shared an apartment with him for the best part of my time here.' Verča cleared her throat. 'And he … may have been my fiancé. A hasty arrangement we broke a month later.'

'Wait.' Maria grinned. 'Is this your Neapolitan merman?'

'The very same. Federico Zitouni, the Sea King of Naples.'

'Do I have competition, my love?'

'Never, my love. Federico now swims in my past,' Verča said. 'But I am still fond of him as a friend.' She jangled the car keys. 'Come. He'll meet us at the Antro della Sibilla.'

As we all returned to the car, I tried not to look at Capri. All this might be for nothing. Arcturus might not be there.

I would soon know either way.

Verča drove back along the coast. I put my hair in an updo, keeping it off my nape.

'Tell me more about the factions,' I said.

'As I said, there are two large groups of voyants in Naples, the Figli di Partenope and the Vesuviani,' Verča replied, speaking over the blustering wind. 'The Figli are mostly hydromancers, and the Vesuviani are pyromancers. Naturally they are always fighting for territory, getting into scraps. Everyone else either chooses a side or tries to stay out of their way.'

'Which one is Federico?'

'The former. That's why we're able to visit the Antro della Sibilla, which the Figli de Partenope claimed for themselves a long time ago,' she said. 'The ruins are close to Lake Averno, a site revered by hydromancers. It used to be considered a gateway to the underworld.'

Maria cocked her head. 'Will I be welcome, as a pyromancer?'

'Federico will allow it.' Verča shot her a rueful look. 'I'm afraid he still harbours a flame for me.'

'Ah, we'll see whose flame is hotter.' Maria gave her lighter a playful flick. 'Won't we?'

'Verča, you should warn your contacts to leave Naples,' I said. 'They'll be in danger once Scion establishes Orcus IV. There could already be Scion operatives sniffing around the city.'

'Federico would sooner die than leave,' Verča said, 'but Napoli is a city of layers. Beneath its streets are many tunnels, dug through the volcanic rock – catacombs, quarries, secret passages. I will make sure the voyants here descend as soon as possible, preferably before we go to Capri. I hear that tactic has been working for the syndicates of London and Paris.'

'Very well,' Maria confirmed. 'Even if the Londoners had to crawl through sewage for the pleasure.'

'Don't remind me,' Nick said.

I shrugged on the shoulder holster from Domino, made for my preferred weapons, and fit my new revolver and knives into their places. For as long as Scion was nearby, I had to be ready for anything.

Half an hour later, Verča parked under an olive tree and led us on foot up a dusty path, alongside a hill of ruins. A hydromancer waited at the entrance to a cave, sleeves rolled up to show his lean forearms.

Federico was a sinewy man in his late forties, who I could well imagine sweeping Verča off her feet. Deep lines framed his mouth and scored his brown face. He wore his dark curls in a topknot and sported a trim beard, salted with grey.

'Federì.' Verča reached him. 'Grazie che c'hê fatto venì ccà.'

'Chesta è 'a casa toia, Verò.' Federico kissed her cheeks, then took off his sunglasses, showing large hazel eyes. The skin around them pleated as he smiled. 'Underqueen, I have heard of your deeds along the ley lines.' Before I knew it, he leaned in to kiss me as well. I let him lead, certain I would go for the wrong side of his face. 'Bemmenute. Welcome to Napule.'

'Thanks for having us,' I said.

'This is Nick, mollisher supreme,' Verča said. Federico bestowed his kisses on Nick. 'Federì, chesta è 'a guagliona mia, se chiamma Maria. Maruška, this is Federico.'

'Salve.' Maria smiled. 'Fire and water. I hear we're natural enemies in Naples.'

Federico took the measure of her. 'Mo t 'a faie cu na piromante, Verò?'

'Ué, 'a puo' fernì. Nun tene niente 'a spàrtere cu 'e Vesuviane,' Verča said, her tone sharp. 'Nun ce 'a faccio cchiù a stà mmiezo a sti ttarantelle inutile.'

'Vabbuò. Pe te fà piacere nun ce rico niente.' Federico kissed Maria. 'Welcome, Maria, and the rest of you. Welcome to the ruins of Cumae. Please, come into the cave.'

'I'll wait for the Ranthen,' I said to the others. They entered the cave, leaving me to roast.

I found a spot in the shade. The sun had toasted the grass, though bright wild flowers still grew strong. The sun and scents, the clement wind, the chirr of insects in the trees – it was all so different from anything I knew, I might as well have landed in the Netherworld.

When four Rephs approached from the north, I stood. Even though they might be older than the ruins, they could not have looked more out of place. Terebell gave me a curt nod.

'Underqueen,' Lucida said.

'Hi,' I said. 'It's been a while.'

Errai turned his nose up. Always a pleasure.

'Indeed,' Lucida said. 'Terebell told us where you have been. We are pleased that you escaped your captor, and that you have returned to the fight.'

I blinked. Either Lucida had softened since I had last seen her, or the Ranthen were learning to be diplomatic.

'Thank you,' I said. 'It's good to be back.' I looked up at the stranger. 'Sorry, I don't think I know you.'

'Lesath Mesarthim,' came the deep reply.

Most of the Mesarthim had perished in the civil war. I had only met two others. Lesath bore such a strong resemblance to Arcturus, it hurt to look at him.

'Paige,' I said. 'Where have you been living for the past two centuries?'

'Scotland, for the most part,' Lesath said. 'There was a small community of exiles in Knoydart, under the command of Cursa Sarin. We chose to reject the Sargas amnesty and eschew the safety of Oxford. Now we have moved to the Hálendið, the wilderness of Iceland.'

He spoke with a distinct Scottish burr, which surprised me. Every other Reph I knew had an Inquisitorial English accent.

'I have come here for the rightful Warden of the Mesarthim,' he went on. 'The sovereign-elect believes you can assist us. Given your victories against Scion, Cursa has confidence in you, Paige Mahoney. I choose to trust her judgement, and that of my Warden.'

'That's ... refreshing. Thanks, Lesath.' I cleared my throat. 'Let's get him back, shall we?'

The footprints led us to an artificial gallery, lined with green moss and lichen. Federico and his people had mounted lanterns on the walls. By their wavering light, we made our way down the gallery, following the others' voices. They had gathered in a chamber at the end.

'Ah, the Ranthen,' Maria called. 'Welcome, friends. Long time no see.'

'Maria,' Lucida said. 'We are pleased you are alive.'

She sounded like an automaton. Terebell must have told them all to be courteous for some reason.

'Of course you are,' Maria said. 'I'm fantastic.'

Federico peered at the newcomers, lips parting. We had agreed that we wouldn't tell him what the Ranthen were, even if he was curious. He would have to draw his own conclusions.

'Please sit down,' Verča said. 'Thank you for joining us.'

Errai glowered at her. 'Who are you?'

'I'm Verča, and this is Federico. He doesn't speak a great deal of English, so I will interpret,' Verča said. 'He and his voyants can help us reach Capri.'

She was keeping her cool well, but I could see she was intimidated, as was Federico. Errai folded his arms and remained standing, while Terebell sat on a stone bench and gave them both a level stare, eyes like heated iron. Federico stared back. He must sense her strange aura.

'Nun te preoccupà.' Verča spoke to him in a soft voice. 'Chiste stanne ccà pe' ce aiutà.'

Federico recovered. He clasped his veiny hands and spoke in Napoletano, which she translated.

'Neapolitans can tell that something is amiss with the evacuation of Capri and Ischia,' she said. 'Many of them have friends or family who lived there. They claim there were no warning signs, like earthquakes or landslides.' She paused to listen. 'The Figli de Partenope have noticed strangers in the city, watching its voyants. All speculation and gossip is being suppressed – even the media is silent – and the local authorities are refusing to say when their residents will be allowed to return.' She glanced at me. 'Your instinct was right, Paige.'

Federico nodded. Verča had been authorised to tell him why we were going to Capri, but he was under strict orders to keep this information to himself, even as he took steps to protect the voyants of Naples. If word got out, Scion would realise that somebody was on to them.

'Federico will take us to Capri under cover of darkness. Four of his voyants will join the search,' Verča said. 'They used to live on the island. All of us know it well.'

'A search in the dark will take longer,' Nick said.

'Yes, but it may keep us safe. Scion could have sent guards and drones, or requisitioned existing surveillance on Capri. Some of the villas have security cameras.'

'Scion would have got rid of those straight away,' I said. 'They didn't allow cameras in Oxford or Versailles.'

'That is a relief.' Verča chewed her lip. 'It will be impossible for us to search the island in one night. I doubt the funicular or the chairlift will be working. It may be sensible for us to hide at dawn, continue our search when the sun sets again, and repeat for a few days. If we are careful, we should be able to camp on the island for as long as necessary.'

'Will you ask Federico if there are any large buildings, anywhere a prisoner might be held?'

Verča did, and listened to his answer.

'A ruined Roman villa, an old charter house, several forts,' she said. 'Federico heard that dreamwalkers can sense the æther better than most. He asks if you will be able to keep us safe.'

'I can try,' I said.

'So will we,' Lucida said. 'We are with you, Underqueen.'

I raised an eyebrow. This was going beyond civility; now they were expressing solidarity.

That was when I realised that the Ranthen might actually have missed me.

———

The Figli de Partenope used the ruins as a retreat from the clamour of Naples. They slept in alcoves in the walls, lined with thin mattresses, which Federico encouraged us to use. As I lay in mine, my head cushioned by my oilskin, I thought of the sibyl who had once lived here, cursed by a god to wither to dust, her voice trapped in a jar.

*I'm almost there.* I closed my eyes. *Hold on.*

I must have slept. When I checked my watch again, it was seven in the morning. Federico and the Rephs were gone, but I sensed them all nearby.

I emerged from the cave with a churning stomach. It was cooler today, though the sky remained clear. I walked away from the ruins with my bag, heading for a beach Verča had mentioned.

When I reached it, I sat down and slid my legs into the sea. To reach Capri, I might need to swim for the first time since the flood in Paris. I had to get used to water I couldn't control.

Once the sun had warmed the shallows, I stripped down to my underwear, went in up to my waist, and let myself shiver. At last, I lunged into a breaststroke. I had learned to swim at Ancroft – of course the school had its own heated pool – but I hadn't been in the sea since I was five, when my grandparents had taken me to Cork for the weekend, and we had paddled in Clonakilty Bay. I still remembered the joy of it.

There was no joy in this. The waves shoved and sprayed me. I forced myself to duck my head under, trying to fight the strangling fear. When I surfaced, I coughed so hard it hurt, the salt water like sandpaper on my throat. Once more, and I was done. I waded back to shore.

I stayed on the beach to dry off, then donned a fresh set of clothes. By the time I got back to the ruins, Maria was sunning herself outside the cave.

'Morning, sweet,' she said. 'Did you swim?'

'Not well. Is your arm any better?'

'Yes, but Nick isn't relenting.' She nodded to higher ground. 'Federico is making breakfast up there. Once we've eaten, he'll drive us closer to Capri. Are you ready for this?'

'Not even a little.'

'You're going to find him, Paige. By tomorrow, he'll be with you.'

The thought lightened my breathing. I had to believe it, or I would never get up again.

Once the Ranthen had come back, we piled into two cars. Naturally I found myself wedged beside Errai, who gritted his teeth every time my arm brushed him, even with both of us wearing full sleeves. Terebell slid a small glass bottle from her coat and held it out to me.

'As requested.'

I took it. Inside was something like a marble, resembling smoked glass. 'This is his ectoplasm?'

'Yes,' she said. 'It has vitrified. Do not squander it.'

'Thank you.'

Rephaite blood lost its light and hardened once it had been outside their bodies for a while. I hoped my idea would still work.

Federico drove us through Naples and past Vesuvius, to the other side of the bay. After about two hours, we got out on a low cliff overlooking Capri, beside a crumbling outpost where four hydromancers waited. According to them, there had been no movement all night.

Terebell sent the other Ranthen off to scout, then turned to me. Capri was now close enough that I could see a spine of tall rocks near its southern coast, silhouetted against the blaze of sunlight. Keeping my gaze on it, I took out the gem of solid ectoplasm.

Though its glow had faded, touching it chilled my fingertips. I swallowed it with a sip of water.

I had been afraid that nothing would happen. The ectoplasm had gone dark, and this was a long shot.

Instead, the cord sang back to life. A flash of gold across the water. The needle of our shared compass, catching the sunlight at last, so I could see where it was pointing.

'Underqueen,' Terebell said. 'What do you sense?'

'Arcturus is there.' A weak laugh escaped me. 'He *is* there.'

'Good.' She followed my line of sight. 'Now we know we are not risking everyone for nought.'

The sensation was already waning, but I felt him. No emotion, no movement – just his presence, but heavier, like a weight on the end of a line, pulling me towards the island. I stared at those peaks in the sea.

*There are no coincidences*, Maria had said, and I believed it now. After six months apart, Arcturus and I had somehow both ended up in Italy. Nashira really had left him on that island.

Now to be the clever mouse that sprang the trap and lived.

———

Command had issued us each with a wristwatch, preloaded with a detailed map of Capri. I strapped it on and studied the map until my eyes were raw, while Federico called a friend, who brought his fishing boat, the *Ercole*.

The patrol ship had stopped next to the Grotta Azzurra. Federico refused to take us to the exact spot, since we knew Scion had been there. Instead, he would drop us off at a ruined fort on the western coast. From there, we could proceed to the small town of Anacapri, where any guards or soldiers were likely to be stationed. If we found them, we would leave someone there as a lookout while the rest of us searched the outskirts.

North of the town, an overgrown trail – part footpath, part stairway – threaded down to our destination, the Grotta Azzurra. Verča suspected that newcomers to the island would have missed it, or overlooked its potential, since there was an easier way up to

Anacapri. I would take this path with her and Nick and comb the area for any trace of Arcturus.

If we had failed to find him by dawn, we would take shelter for the day, then venture out for a second attempt, as Verča had recommended. Once we had ruled out one side of the island, we would make our way to the other, taking the narrow Phoenician Steps.

The longer we lingered, the greater the risk of detection, and I couldn't stomach the thought of Arcturus being a prisoner for any longer. I wanted to get this done overnight.

We sat beside the old tower and watched. Terebell and Errai paced along the rocks, talking in Gloss.

'Can you feel anyone?' Maria asked me. 'Any dreamscapes?'

'Too far to tell.'

Verča shielded her eyes from the sun. 'I don't see any patrols.'

'Yes, because this is definitely some kind of horrific trap,' Maria said. 'Like the protest in Edinburgh.' Her expression hardened. 'If Hildred Vance isn't behind this, I'll eat my boots.'

'Wells said she was in a frail condition,' I said.

'Vance could win a battle on her deathbed. I promise you, if that woman is breathing, she's a threat.'

Federico observed the island through a pair of binoculars. Even without them, I could see that there were no reconnaissance ships, no choppers. No obvious guard at all.

It felt too easy. Scion had only held this island for a few weeks, and had no idea that anyone but Sala and Rinaldi knew about the annexation; it made sense that it might remain undefended. Still, I had to keep my guard up, and not allow my previous successes to cloud my judgement. Every single victory had been won by the skin of my teeth; each had taken its own toll. There were only so many times a mortal could slip in and out of the underworld.

I would do it one last time, for him. One last reckless heist to remember – the most audacious theft of my career – before I finally retired the Pale Dreamer and became Black Moth.

At dusk, Federico deemed it safe to leave. As he and his friends readied the *Ercole*, I changed into a wetsuit and matching boots. If all went well, none of us would be diving, but we might have to swim to get to the island, if the boat took any damage.

Only Nick knew about my fear of water. I intended to keep it that way. Taking deep breaths, I fastened my diving vest and secured my equipment: combat knife, gun, waterproof torch, mask and oxygen tank.

'Call if you need help,' Maria said to us. 'And don't forget to pick me up on your way back.'

'Never,' Verča said.

Our team of twelve climbed into the boat. It churned away, leaving Maria watching from the shore.

## 12

# TRIAL BY WATER

As the *Ercole* approached Capri, night covered the Bay of Naples, speckling the sky with stars. There seemed to be no lights on the island. Once we were within a mile, Federico stopped the boat at my behest, so we floated in absolute darkness, save the single dim lamp on the deck. The Italian government hadn't banned fishing around Capri. That oversight would serve as our cover.

After a few minutes, no warning shots or announcements had come. Nick glanced at me.

'Do you sense anything?'

I closed my eyes, letting the æther take over. At once, goose-bumps stippled my forearms.

'Nothing human,' I said. 'And no other Rephs, as far as I can tell. But the æther doesn't feel right.'

'Should we keep going?'

Federico saw my nod and got the boat moving.

The *Ercole* drew closer and closer to Capri. By the time it skirted the towering southern cliffs of the island, the wind had turned cold, and our teeth were chattering.

'Naples was so warm,' Nick murmured. His breath came out in white puffs. 'What is this?'

'Cold spots.' Terebell watched the island. 'More than one.'

Verča was shivering in her coat. 'Cold spots?'

'This explains why there's no security. Why the other teams vanished,' I said softly. 'Capri is a death trap.' I checked my supplies. 'I'm going alone.'

Nick stared at me, his face white in the lamplight. 'No,' he said, realising I was serious. 'Absolutely not. We came to help you, Paige. We knew the risks when we signed up.'

'You knew there might be amaurotic defences, but if there are cold spots, there might also be Buzzers,' I told him. 'I'll risk my own life for Arcturus, but not yours, Nick. I've learned my lessons on that front.' I turned to Verča. 'Buzzers are creatures from the Netherworld. They come here through cold spots, and they feed on human flesh and spirits. Tell Federico and the others I'll be searching the island by myself.'

'Paige—'

'We Ranthen are coming,' Terebell said. 'All of us.'

'No,' I said. 'The Buzzers could turn you.'

Nick frowned, and I bit my tongue. None of the others knew the Buzzers were former Rephs.

'Arcturus was our ally long before he was yours,' Terebell said, her gaze steely. 'I have no plans to send one human to his rescue while I do nothing. In any case, if he is weak or injured – which seems likely – how do you intend to carry him alone, Underqueen?'

She had me there.

'Paige, without us you'll have no idea where you're going,' Verča said, grasping the side of the boat as it rocked. 'None of you know Capri. It will take too long to search by yourselves.'

'We are not leaving you after just having found you,' Nick bit out. 'Don't do this, Paige.'

'Nick, I hate to pull rank, but I'm still Underqueen. I'm ordering you not to come.' I faced the others. 'I can't order the rest of you, but I'm the only one whose gift might be useful on this island. Even fire and bullets won't work against its guards for long. Let me handle this.'

The hydromancers looked to Verča, who spoke to them in Napoletano, presumably skirting around the specific reasons I was stopping them from coming. None of them argued.

After a short exchange, Verča switched off the lamp on the deck, and Federico started the boat. When we reached the right place, he brought the *Ercole* in as close to the island as he could. Sheer untamed rock toothed the coastline, but I could see plenty of natural ways up.

Nick went into his medical bag and handed me a delicate silver earpiece. 'Domino gave us encrypted transceivers,' he said. I clipped it on. 'You take one, too, Terebell.' She hooked it over her ear with clear reluctance. 'Stay in touch. Call when you need us to come back.'

'All right.' I touched his elbow. 'I'm sorry. This is a risk I need to take alone.'

'You always think you need to take the risks alone.'

'Nick, this is personal.'

'No, it isn't,' he said under his breath. 'Domino backed this because Warden might have crucial intelligence. Respectfully, I am a Domino agent. I have more right to be on this than—'

'I'm not doing this for intelligence. I think it's more than likely Arcturus doesn't know a damn thing, because he would have been chained up in some dungeon for months. I'm doing this because I owe him, and because I want him back. And I can't let any of you die for that.'

He breathed out slowly.

'Please be careful, Paige,' Verča said. 'Maria will never forgive us if anything happens to you.'

'I'll be fine. Any hint of Scion, you get out of here,' I said. 'I'll hide with the Ranthen until you can get back to us.'

We had agreed not to use my torch until we left the coast behind, in case any patrol ships came. I switched on the small light in my watch, then climbed down to the sea. A deep tremor coursed through me as I let go of the ladder. Keeping my chin above the water where I could, I swam the short distance to the rocks, which the Ranthen had already reached. Lucida extended a gloved hand to help me out.

'Do you still feel Arcturus?' Terebell asked me. I nodded. 'Then let us move swiftly.'

'Hold on. Nick,' I called, 'we need the mine detector.'

He threw it. Terebell caught it with one hand, and we both watched the darkness swallow the boat.

'You know the sickness turns us into Emim,' she said. 'A secret we swore to protect.'

'Arcturus didn't break his oath. Someone else told me, and I confronted him about it,' I said. 'I wish you'd trusted me with the truth, Terebell.'

'You would not have been reasonable before you knew us well.'

'What should I do if a Buzzer attacks you?'

'If any of us are bitten or clawed, the sea will take care of our need for salt, allowing us to take aura again. We will have to use yours, Underqueen.'

'What am I supposed to do, drag you to the sea?'

'We have collected seawater.' She handed me a flask on a strap. 'You will not breathe a word to your allies about the sickness. Not even your mollishers. It would degrade us in their eyes. If you do not mind your tongue in future, I will cut it out. Is that understood?'

I answered her with a taut nod. She thrust the mine detector at me and strode ahead, her coat dripping.

We filed up the steps to a coastal path. I found the pole star and tried to keep it in front of me. For a while, the five of us made our way inland, undisturbed by anything.

After a time, we reached a wider path, which took us uphill again. I was already tired, but I couldn't let the Ranthen see even a flicker of weakness. This was a golden opportunity to win their respect, which I still hadn't quite secured. I was working against centuries of indoctrination. As soon as they weren't looking, I took the stimulant Ducos had given me, the same one used by spies in Scion. It was the only way I was going to make it through the night.

It was strange to be leading a team of immortals. Other than Arcturus, the Ranthen had remained in the background of the revolution, funding our efforts, but handling their own politics in private. Now four Rephs towered around me like bodyguards. Errai refused to take my shorter legs into account – he marched ahead without a backward glance – but the others kept to my pace, managing not to complain. Even with the stimulant, the aster weighed on me.

Capri had looked beautiful on Omnia, but at night, with all the streetlamps out, I couldn't see much – just the path underfoot, flowers and foliage to our right, trees on the other side. A few weeks ago, this place must have been thronged with tourists enjoying the end of summer. Now it truly had become the Lugentes Campi, the Fields of Mourning – quiet and forsaken, named for grief. I stopped to put on my gloves, protecting my hands from the cold, before I held out the mine detector again.

'Paige,' Lucida said, 'do you sense the Emim?'

'Not yet,' I said.

The stimulant was kicking in, making my heart beat faster. Despite the frigid chill, sweat trickled down my breastbone and lined my brow. There were no spirits around, which meant the Buzzers couldn't be too far away.

The path went on and on. At last, we came to Anacapri. Lucida and Errai went ahead to check for guards, while I stayed on the outskirts with Terebell and Lesath. From the looks of it, the residents had been allowed to evacuate in an orderly fashion, but mounds of fruit had been left to rot in a grocery, causing the whole street to reek. The transceiver in my ear crackled.

'*It's been over an hour,*' Nick said. '*Just checking in.*'

'We've reached Anacapri. It's deserted.' I kept my voice low. 'Not even the streetlamps are on. Scion must have cut electricity to the whole island. No cameras or alarms so far.'

'*As we thought, then. Federico has moored the boat near a lighthouse, south of where we dropped you off. If there's any sign of trouble, get to the coast and activate the beacon in your watch. We'll come as soon as we can.*'

'Okay.'

Most of the shops had been locked, but not emptied. I tried the door of a whitewashed house and glanced inside, finding it like a scene from a play, everything left untouched. The owners had believed they would be coming back in a few weeks. I closed the door behind me and went to Terebell and Lesath. Their eyes were the only light.

'What do you sense now?' Terebell asked.

'Arcturus is closer, but it's as if he's … below us. It feels like it did when he was in the Camden Catacombs.' I touched my earpiece. 'Vision, can you ask the others if there's anywhere you could hide a person underground on Capri?'

'*On it*,' Nick said. I heard voices around him. '*They can only think of the sea caves.*'

'Thanks.' I tapped out. 'Let's head for the Grotta Azzurra. That's where the patrol ship stopped.'

'Terebell told me about the golden cord,' Lesath said. 'How is it that you have this connection to our Warden?'

'No idea. It just happened.' I headed back to the path. 'What do you know about it?'

'A union of two spirits,' Lesath said. He and Terebell shadowed me. 'There was speculation on the possibility in the Netherworld, though I never knew any of us to have one. I was surprised to learn that a human could have formed such an intimate bond with a Rephaite.'

If any Rephs *had* shared a golden cord, he would have missed it. Even to sighted eyes, it was invisible.

'My own kin never spoke of it, in public or in private,' Lesath said. 'Most likely, the golden cord was among the sacred mysteries, known only to the Mothallath family. They were our divine leaders, our sovereigns. The secrets of the last light were theirs, and theirs alone.'

And the Sargas had wiped them out. I was starting to think our side might already have won this war if we had been able to consult the Mothallath.

'Well,' I said, 'good thing I do have the cord, or we couldn't be sure Arcturus was here.'

Lesath made no comment.

We picked up the pace, leaving the town behind, and headed for the trees on the northern outskirts, where the æther felt thick. Arcturus was so close, yet not quite here.

Errai and Lucida stood at the edge of a lemon grove, looking at something. I shone my torch on to a mangled animal, unrecognisable in death, lousy with flies.

'There is a cold spot here,' Lucida said. 'We should move on.'

Terebell looked over the low wall of the grove. I did the same. At once, I saw the perfect circle of ice, giving off a faint glow. I backed away, taking out my pistol.

'Yes.' My breath was paler. 'Terebell, let's go.'

*Come, dreamwalker.* Suddenly I felt the same overpowering temptation as I had when I saw my first cold spot, drifting like a siren song from the ice, luring me towards it. *Come into the beyond …*

The cold spot erupted.

The first Buzzer flew out like a breaching shark. I opened fire at it, just as a second Buzzer came through, screaming with many stolen voices. Terebell opened her coat, and the next thing I knew, she had an iridescent blade in her grasp. Lesath wielded an identical sword.

'Go,' Terebell barked at me. 'Get to the water and call the boat.'

'I can hold them off,' I protested. 'I can't just—'

'There are too many.' She shoved me away. 'Find the coastal path. We will follow.'

More Buzzers were breaking through the veil, constricting my aura. One of them locked its white gaze on me. I turned and broke into a sprint.

My torchlight was frantic, jerking each time my boots struck the ground. A shriek raised the hairs on my nape. Following the illuminated route on my watch, I hunted for the hidden path, risking a glance back to see those ghastly eyes, stark against the gloom. Their glow was a pale mockery of the golden fire that must have burned there.

*Who were you?*

Arcturus might be in the Netherworld. He could have turned into one of those Buzzers.

It was so dark that I almost missed the opening in the trees. Stopping myself just in time, I cleared the first set of cement steps and kept running. The Buzzer howled in my wake.

Thick greenery sliced at my face. This path must have been neglected for years. I hurdled a tree that had slumped over, then barrelled downhill, barely controlling my descent, my boots slewing on the rough ground. I almost lost my footing as the path turned into steps and back. As I whipped past a rusty construction fence, I glimpsed another cold spot in the foliage, and the gleam of a third, farther away. I had never seen them so close together.

The Buzzer dived at me. Just as I ducked under a branch, the ground vanished, and my stomach dropped. On instinct, I threw up my arms to shield my face.

The first impact crunched the breath from me. The next hit my ribs like a brick wall. I kept my arms wrapped over my head, unable to tell which way was up, waiting for a bone to snap or dislocate. By the time I slammed to a stop, I was bleeding from a gashed knee and elbow, my cheekbone was throbbing, and pain had exploded in my shoulder.

My torch clattered down beside me. Heaving for breath, I grabbed it and angled its beam up to see the Buzzer above me, ensnared by the branches I had missed. They overhung a final set of steps, steeper than any of the others. I was fortunate not to have broken my neck.

I seized my chance to get my bearings. Another wide road, smooth and tarmacked, stretched ahead of me. Fuelled by the stimulant, I sleeved blood off my chin and made a break for it.

Now I was closing on the Grotta Azzurra, the port of call where the patrol ship had been. Except now I was on my own, and if Scion had left guards there, I would be outnumbered.

I had no choice. If I stopped, the pain and shock of the fall would overwhelm me, and I couldn't let that happen. The golden cord felt stronger here than it had at the cold spot, and it was pulling me down, like an anchor. I hooked the torch on to my vest and kept running.

Behind me, the Buzzer tore free. I was caught in the open, with nowhere to hide. As it gave chase again, moving at twice my speed, I displaced my spirit and sent a wake of pressure through the æther, making the Buzzer release that awful sound, the screams of the people whose spirits it had consumed. I would only be able to keep this up for a moment longer …

And the path ahead had just run out.

I snapped to a halt, staring in fear. There was no way up or forward. Out of options, I unsheathed my dive knife and turned to face the Buzzer, right as it took a terrific swing at me.

My abrupt stop had thrown off its aim. Its arm collided with my side, hurling me not only off the path, but the edge of the cliff. The knife flew from my grasp, and then there was nothing but icy air in my ears, rushing past me. I fell and fell before I crashed into the sea.

For a moment, I thought the drop had killed me. I thought I might be in the æther – drifting, weightless, disembodied.

For a moment, that silence was peaceful.

Then my skin was smarting, and panic hit me with the cold. *Here we are again, Underqueen,* Suhail Chertan observed. His eyes floated up from the deep. *Look how much we have to drink.*

I kicked away from him. My head broke the surface, and my breath shot out in thick white smudges.

*Drink.*

The black sea rolled around me. As I trod water, I tried to focus on the crash of the waves and the taste of salt, to separate this moment from my torture, from the river, from the night I had almost drowned under Paris. Except for my own ragged breaths, I couldn't hear a thing over the din.

I shook my hair out of my eyes and blinked. My left side was in agony. Reaching for my torch, I shone it upward, revealing the cliffs. I had plummeted a long way, but the Buzzer had thrown me far enough that I had missed the rocks and plunged into deep water.

There had to be a way back up. My body ached, unaccustomed to swimming. As I fought with the sea, splashing back towards land, my torchlight hit the cliff face – and then disappeared. I swashed closer to see a small opening, barely discernible above the waves.

The golden cord was pointing me straight into that darkness.

This had to be the Grotta Azzurra, right where the Scion ship had been spotted. Metal stairs descended from the coastal path, just as Verča had described, ending in a flat platform.

Arcturus really was in the cave. The patrol ship had left him exactly where it had stopped.

I couldn't stand the thought of going into that pitch-black opening. As the waves shunted me towards it, I tried my best to stay calm. I had a tank of oxygen. I had conquered my fear before, to save my own life. I could do it again for Arcturus. He would do it for me.

All I had to do was swim.

Even with the gloves, my fingers were icy and stiff. I removed the mask from my diving vest, fastened it over my face, and switched on the built-in headlamp. Next, I returned my torch to my belt, leaving my hands free, and activated the tracking beacon in my watch.

'Terebell,' I shouted, trying to keep a finger on my earpiece, 'come to the Grotta Azzurra. There are steps. Nick, get Federico to bring the boat, quickly.'

If anyone replied, I couldn't make it out.

I made a grab for a rocky outcrop, stopping myself. There was a good chance I could drown in this cave. I pressed a button on the mask, causing statistics to scroll. I had plenty of oxygen.

The torchlight caught on a chain that led into the cave. I used it to drag my body along. My breaths were laboured. Thick seaweed threatened my grip, even with the gloves.

The sea gave a sudden roil, dashing me into the rock. At first, I thought the crack had come from my own skull. I illuminated the mask, just in time to see a teardrop seep in through a hairline break.

*Fuck.*

I steadied my breathing and forged on, keeping hold of the chain. When the space widened, I dialled up my headlamp, revealing the immensity of the cavern ahead of me. In the dead of the night, it was unfathomably black, like the basement of the Westminster Archon.

*Drink.*

Once more, I checked the golden cord. Still it was calling me deeper. As I faced the prospect of answering that call, the fear threatened to overwhelm me, but Arcturus was so close. I was right above him.

Dread tightened like a belt around my ribs. Drawing a long breath, I dived.

At first, my lamp revealed nothing. At once, water began to pool beneath my chin. I swam towards the bottom of the cavern, which I couldn't see. When I tasted salt, I turned back, nearly choking in panic.

*Do it for him.*

I emptied the mask before diving a second time, racked by memories of the flood in Paris, getting no farther than before. Teeth gritted, I tried again, pushing a little deeper into the abyss, but soon became disoriented. By the time I found the surface, I was close to passing out.

*Come on*, I told myself. *Don't you dare leave him again …*

With fresh resolve, I went under a fourth time. I focused on the golden cord, following it to one side of the cavern.

At last, I saw it. A limestone coffin, which had somehow been secured to the wall. Its sides were adorned with carvings of naked humans, writhing in ecstasy or torment. I swam to it, my chest straining, and read the words on its lid.

HERE LIES A FLESH-TRAITOR

My stomach turned. I dug my fingers under the lid and used my heel for purchase. Gathering all my strength, I pulled.

The seawater was about to blind me. I kicked off the coffin and back to the surface, where I wrenched the mask off. More of the sea rushed in from outside, almost crushing me. Shaking uncontrollably, I unclipped my vest, letting it float away with the oxygen, then adjusted the broken mask, sucked in a breath, and returned to the coffin, faster with less weight on me.

Once more, I planted my boot on the side. With every tug on the lid, my arms protested. Arcturus had always been strong for me, and here I was, too human and weak to free him.

A shiver in the æther. I spun to see Terebell, dark hair billowing around her face. Errai and Lucida appeared from the gloom, their eyes like headlamps. Never in my life had I been so relieved to see them. I pointed at the coffin. Terebell swam to one side, Errai to the other. Together, the two Rephs drew the lid off, letting it fall into the depths.

When I saw what was inside, I was sure this was my first night-mare, even though voyants never dreamed.

Arcturus was chained in the coffin.

The sight of him stopped the blood in my veins. He wore the same uniform as when I had last seen him.

Before the Ranthen could get near him, I grasped his lolling head between my hands. There was even a chain around his throat. Holding my breath as the mask filled, I shook him, fingers bunched in his doublet. I could feel his spirit in his dreamscape, but it was as motionless as the cord.

*No.*

Terebell broke my grip on him. She pushed me towards Lucida, who gave me a boost to the surface. I clung to the cavern wall with one hand, groping for the mask with the other. As soon as it was off, I hurled it aside, and an animal sound of denial tore out of me.

*If we cannot feed, we become delirious. We lose our gifts. Our ecto-plasm vitrifies, and finally, we cease to function.*

Arcturus was gone. His body was there, but it was no longer in touch with his spirit.

This was his underworld.

His tomb.

Terebell came up without breathing. 'Underqueen,' she said, over my sobs of rage and the sepulchral roar, 'calm yourself.' The water reflected the glow in her eyes. 'We are too late.'

'He was starved,' I forced out. Errai appeared beside her. 'She starved him, didn't she?'

'Yes.'

'Fuck.' I hit the wall. 'He—' My throat scalded. 'Help me get him out of here. Help me.'

'There is no point,' Errai snapped. 'He cannot wake from that state.'

'I don't care!'

'You demand that we drag a dead weight past the creatures, endangering our own lives?'

'His spirit is in there,' I shouted at him. 'He was your friend, your ally. You can at least give him some fucking dignity.' I looked between them, hair plastered to my face. 'She planted him on Capri to lure and taunt us, knowing those cold spots would open around him. She used him as bait. We can't let her keep him. I won't leave him in the dark again.'

'She put him here because we had no chance of saving him. We cannot wake his spirit now,' Terebell said, but I could tell she was caving. 'Arcturus is lost to us. He will only—'

'Behead him, then. But don't abandon him here.' My voice cracked. 'He deserves better than this.'

We drifted for a moment, lapped by the current. Terebell cast her gaze into the water.

'We will take him,' she said. 'To prevent Nashira from using him against us again.'

'Thank you.'

They went back under. I followed. When we reached the coffin, Lucida was still there, watching over Arcturus. Terebell swam past her and broke his chains with a twist of her hands – just iron this time, no red flower. Together, the four of us lifted him to the surface.

Nashira had no right to his body. She had no right to any part of him.

Between us, we pulled Arcturus out of the cave. I stayed close to his head, trying not to look at his face. I would break if I glimpsed it again.

Bloodthirsty screeches came from above. I sensed Lesath. Not just Lesath, but a swarm of Buzzers, at least twenty of them, their dreamscapes nauseating.

'Paige,' a voice roared.

I turned. The *Ercole* was approaching.

Terebell started towing Arcturus towards the boat. Keeping a tight hold of him, I helped as best I could, only to turn at the deafening sound of Buzzers. Lesath was hightailing it down the steps, pursued by a stampede, his arm oozing ectoplasm. Before they could overwhelm him, he dived into the sea. Now all he needed was aura.

'Paige, over here!'

Nick was reaching for me from the *Ercole*. I took his outstretched hand and let him pull me into the fishing boat, water streaming off my wetsuit as I stumbled up the ladder.

The first enormous Buzzer reached the bottom of the steps. It clawed the waves with an elongated arm, only to recoil, hissing. One by one, the creatures fell utterly silent, white eyes staring after us. Verča and the others were just as speechless, transfixed by the sight.

The Ranthen climbed aboard and set Arcturus down. Ignoring the others, I sank to my knees beside him and covered his gloved fingers with mine, desperately searching for any sign of awareness. Tears mingled with the sweat on my face, the blood trickling from my brow.

It couldn't be real.

He couldn't be gone.

My hearing was muffled. I whispered his name as a darkness stole in, and I slumped on to the deck beside him, my head on his shoulder, one hand wrapped around his arm like a vice.

The last thing I saw were the stars above Capri.

13

NIENTE

I opened my eyes to a plasterwork ceiling. At first, I thought I must be in Venice, but before long, I started to notice signs of decay in the room where I now found myself. By the faint light of a candle, I saw the cracked and flaking paint, the broken shutters on the windows.

My hair was damp and crisp. The ribs on my left side felt bruised, but all my cuts and grazes had been dressed. A leaden exhaustion clung to my bones.

It took a moment to remember. When I did, I closed my eyes, wishing I hadn't woken up.

I had danced with death for many years. My life had been a tightrope walk. Yet since I was a child, I had maintained an iron will to live. I'd vowed I would make Scion pay for murdering my cousin, and I'd always meant to survive long enough to make good on it. Each time I had risked my own life, it was because I had believed it might bring Scion down.

Now I felt indifferent to my own existence. I wanted to escape the grief before it could hit me in full. It would chip at every good part of my life, every happy memory, until nothing seemed worth the trouble of breathing.

Nashira had stopped Arcturus from taking aura. A voyant might survive a separation from the æther, but for Rephs, there was no coming back. They would be for ever locked into their bodies, unable to move or see.

*We call it latency.* I remembered our conversation in Paris. *How much we can perceive in that state, I do not know. What is known is that we become considerably more tempting to the Emim. They can sense latent Rephaim from great distances.*

He had foretold his own fate. I wondered if he had been proud to the end, or if he had been forced to his knees, made to beg for what he needed. The thought was more than I could stand.

As I lay there, my own question came back to me: *You can still become Buzzers, then?*

*To our knowledge, that is the only way a latent Rephaite can ever move again.* As I recalled those words, ice started to needle through the shell around me. *Our fellow Rephaim usually choose to remove the possibility by sequestering us.*

*That is, beheading you. Which can only be done with opaline.*

I snapped upright, a terrible chill rushing through me. Ignoring the pain, I pulled on the clothes that had been left for me. My wetsuit was nowhere to be seen.

Nick and Maria were in a derelict parlour, both looking gaunt and tired, a candle guttering on a table between them. When I appeared, they stood.

'Paige,' Maria said. 'How are you feeling?'

'Where is he?'

She hesitated, and they exchanged a defeated look.

'Terebell is watching over him,' Nick said. 'I'm so sorry, sweet-heart.'

The words sank in.

'We're about two hours northeast of Naples,' Maria said. 'Verča took a train back to Venice to update Command. The Ranthen said we needed to stay in an isolated area to … do what needs to be done.'

'Terebell says the Buzzers will come for him,' Nick said. 'That's why we took a detour here.'

'It's also why Nashira put him on the island. To … turn it into a trap. Like we thought.' My voice sounded distant to my own ears. 'Even if we survived, all we'd find there was his body.'

'It was a cruel trick. Scion never plays clean.' Maria sighed. 'The one Reph who was really on our side. I can't believe it.'

'We made Terebell wait for you.' Nick touched my shoulder. 'He's downstairs, sötnos.'

'Yes. You should go to him,' Maria said, pity shadowing her eyes. 'I doubt they'll let you have too long.'

---

The last memorial I attended had been when I was six. I had worn a black dress and a bow in my hair. We had all spoken in whispers, afraid the soldiers might find us; I remembered Aunt Sandra muffling her sobs. I had not spoken one word since the day of the Imbolc Massacre.

Sandra had got me out. Working at a hospital, she had been among the first to hear about the bloodshed. She had abandoned her post and driven straight for central Dublin, fearing that Finn had gone to the protest, even though she had warned him against it. By then, she knew Scion had come. She had slipped from her car and crawled through the streets, searching for her son and niece among the bodies, certain she would die if she was seen.

I had reached her first. Even with a nascent gift, I had been able to find my aunt. I had climbed out from under Molly Malone, soaked in blood, and stumbled towards her dreamscape. Sandra had carried me to the car, and we had fled to my grandparents in Tipperary, where we had mourned my cousin and the love of his life.

I had seen Kay die, but her body had been out of our reach. From what I heard later, most of the dead had been thrown into the river.

Finn had never been religious. So when I approached his grave with the others, I had thrown earth on the empty box, summoned all my silent rage, and prayed to Ireland itself.

I called upon the aos sí, the mountain hags and Crom Cruach; I bargained with the Fomhóraigh. I told the hungry grass to grow beneath the conquerors' boots, so they would eat our crops and drink our wine, but never once be full. I implored the mná sí to scream their deaths into their ears. I willed them grey and worm-eaten, their bones stripped for the dúlachán to spoke the wheels of his grim coach. I beseeched my island to defend itself.

To no avail.

I would not wear black to mourn Arcturus. Funerals had never been a part of voyant culture in London. We knew the spirit had departed; the body was just leftovers. Only syndicate rulers had their remains collected and preserved, so their bones could be used for readings.

It was different for Arcturus, whose body was now a sealed tomb for his spirit. It would never decay.

The Ranthen had put him in the wine cellar, which seemed appropriate. They could defend this room if the Buzzers came, long enough to decapitate him. It would stop him from coming back as a monster.

*Sequestration is not the same as mortal death.* My footsteps echoed on the steps. *Our bodies do not rot, and our dreamscapes remain intact, caging our spirits. As far as I know, there is no way to reverse this.*

Terebell stood guard outside. When she saw me, her stance changed, her chin lifting.

'You are awake.'

She had done away with her coat, showing the blade at her side.

'I hadn't realised you had one of those,' I said dully. 'Arcturus found one in Versailles.'

'All seven Wardens bore one under the Mothallath,' she said. 'Nashira confiscated mine when she removed my title, but Adhara Sarin offered hers in tribute when she joined the Ranthen.'

Adhara had done that only after learning that I had deactivated Senshield, proving that I was a competent leader. Terebell would not have that blade if not for me.

I had laid every paving stone to his end.

'I must sequester Arcturus before cold spots begin to form,' Terebell said. 'This will not be another Capri.'

'Oxford and Versailles,' I said. 'Did they attract the Buzzers because latent Rephs were kept there?'

'Yes,' she said. 'In Oxford, they were stored in a Norman crypt to the west of Magdalen, beneath the former St Edmund Hall. The Sargas laid their fallen there. That is why the Emim were attracted to that city, first and foremost. It is what sustained the myth of Oxford.'

My nod was small and wooden. The thought must have been forming unnoticed for a while, but seeing that island, turned into a death trap by one Reph, had finally given it shape.

'What will you do with Arcturus?'

'He is in a state we call latency, which he clearly explained to you,' Terebell said. 'There is no way to wake him, unless he were to turn Emite. To prevent that, I must sequester him. I will hide the head – and, by extension, his trapped spirit – in the Netherworld. As for the body, we must bury it deep, so the Sargas can never mistreat it again.'

Each word made me want to shrivel into nothing. For so long, I had thought of Arcturus as too strong to defeat. I had never imagined losing him to anything but my own death.

'I'd like the night,' I said. 'To say goodbye.'

'Arcturus may not be able to hear you.'

'I don't mind.'

Terebell considered me.

'I will give you until dawn,' she said. 'And then Arcturus will be lost to us, like Alsafi. Two of our best, for the sake of you. Let us hope that you will one day be deserving of that sacrifice, dreamwalker. That you might one day be enough to balance the weight of their loss.'

She strode up the steps. After a minute, I walked into the room beyond, my eyes stinging.

*You had better be worth all of this, Underqueen.*

Scarlett Burnish had said the same thing, in as many words. Now she was dead, too.

And I still didn't know if I was worth it.

A few candles flickered in the wine cellar. I closed the door behind me and stepped around a shelf.

Arcturus was lying on an old bed, head propped on a cushion, one hand resting on his chest. Terebell must have positioned him. She knew the way he slept, like I did. One of the Ranthen had poured salt around the bed, to hold the Buzzers back. Knowing Terebell, it was one of several lines of defence. I stepped over the salt to sit at his side.

'This is the last time I'll ever speak to you,' I said, 'and I don't even know if you can hear a word I'm saying.' I drew my knees to my chest. 'Isn't that just our luck?'

For a long time, I was quiet, gazing at the wall.

'I sometimes can't believe we only met last year, and now I can't imagine a world where you're not with me. Where you're not there at all,' I murmured. 'I don't know how to explain what you meant to me. I wish I could have found the words in my own time, but ... I can't let the last thing I said to you be that you were a monster. I thought you were, the first time I saw you. And then you spent nearly a year proving me wrong.'

Only silence answered me.

'It kills me that I'm never going to hear you call me *little dreamer* again,' I admitted. 'I'd have decked anyone else, but it made me feel like I could be smaller with you. Not in worth or importance, but ... like I didn't have to stretch myself so far, to be so much. I didn't have to be the Pale Dreamer or Black Moth or the Underqueen or Flora Blake. Every time you held me, you gathered all those people into one. With you, I could just be Paige.'

I remembered being in his arms. How much I had loved and craved that feeling of security.

'The other thing that kills me is that I'm never going to know if you were ever actually trying to be funny,' I said. 'Either way, you made me laugh. You made me feel safe and wanted and warm. You were patient and kind, and you never lost faith in me. I've no idea why you thought I was worth it, but in the short time we had, I was happy.'

At last, I worked up the courage to face him.

'You weren't perfect,' I said. 'But I think you might have been perfect for me.'

No reply. He looked the same as when I had last seen him, his sarx unmarked by weeks in the sea. If I hadn't known better, I might have thought he was asleep.

'I can't stand the thought of you trapped in that coffin. Or in your dreamscape,' I said, 'while I'm in the free world without you. You would have loved Prague. But you were in so much pain, for so long. Maybe you've earned your rest. I hope you can't feel the scars any more.'

Before I could stop myself, I stroked his cheek. His sarx had always been so warm. Now it was cold as brass.

This body had taken bullets for me, held me without fear or shame, and Nashira had thrown it away. Terebell would bury him out of sight and mind, like the evidence of a crime.

I brushed damp strands of hair off his forehead. They were stiff with salt, like his clothes.

'I'm sorry I believed the worst of you, even when you'd shown me every day how much you loved me. I'm sorry I was already so broken by the time we met,' I said. 'Whatever we've been to each other, you were my friend, first and foremost. I failed that friendship when I thought you were capable of betraying me.' My voice thickened. 'I think I did work it out, in the end. Cordier stopped me reaching you, but I need you to know that I would never have given up. I meant what I said in Paris. I wanted to be with you. I was ready.'

It felt selfish to cry, but a single tear fell. I had spent years tamping my feelings down, because my father had never known what to do with them, and Jaxon had resented their existence.

Arcturus had been nothing like them. Even though he revealed so few of his own emotions, he had never expected me to restrain mine. When I had broken down after my torture, he had afforded me the space to express my pain, letting me know he was there to listen. No matter how far I had plummeted, he had always been there, ready to break my fall.

'You wouldn't have wanted me to avenge you. I can't make any promises,' I said quietly. 'Either way, I will do everything we meant to do together. I'll bring Scion down, even if it takes me the rest of my life. I'll fight for Rephs and humans to share this world in peace.'

I was shivering all over now, and not because the cellar was so cold.

No one would ever love me the way Arcturus Mesarthim had.

'I wish I could have shown you the Golden Vale. I wish we could have gone back to Paris,' I said. 'Maybe we could have convinced Domino to give us that apartment, once all this was over. I don't need a lot to be happy. I just wanted you, and a place where we could be together. That was all I ever wanted.'

My voice cracked on that final word. I rested my head on his chest, so I could pretend I would wake up in Paris, with his arms around me and our whole lives ahead of us, knowing he would be there for as long as I drew breath.

———

I must have drifted off for a while. When I woke, I glanced up and found Arcturus in exactly the same position.

My watch glowed as I tilted it. It was still the middle of the night, but I needed to leave now, or Terebell would have to put me in the ground with him. I placed my hand over the one on his chest.

'You gave me an overture,' I whispered. 'You've left me to write the coda, and I'm no musician. But I'll try.' I touched my lips to his forehead, to press the exact feeling of his sarx into my memory. 'Codladh sámh, a chara, a chosantóir. Mo ghrá go daingean tú, go deo. Maith dom.'

As I stood, tears washed my face. I would never feel his gentle touch or hear his voice again. I had lost my home, lost my entire family to Scion, but this might be the pain that broke me. Step by step, I backed away, only to slide to the floor in a heap, my knees buckling.

I didn't know how to leave him.

Someone would have to drag me away.

And then, out of nowhere, I recalled the fifth card in the reading Liss had given me. *I know the world will change around you.* Her voice was clear as a bell. *Death itself will work in different ways.*

Death, inverted.

I paused, my gaze fixed on Arcturus. The fourth card had promised that we would be lovers, and not just for one night. *The card has weight,* Liss had told me. *This will be a pillar of your life.*

How could he be meant to leave me now, when there was so much left undone?

*Think.*

There was one thing I could try. It had never even crossed my mind, to enter a dreamscape that was also a tomb. There was no reason it should work; it felt like desecration, like trespassing. But all I had left were my instincts, and that morsel of hope that Liss had left me.

I returned to Arcturus and curled up at his side, so our faces were close together. Leaving a shadow of awareness behind, as he had taught me in London, I dreamwalked into him.

Like most of the tarot, the Death card wasn't always to be taken literally. It was the card most often seen in voyants' readings, that symbolised the æther itself. In my limited experience, it heralded a time of new beginnings, but in the inverted position, in this context, I wondered if I was meant to fight the change. To not give up on Arcturus.

He was hovering as close to death as Rephs could get. Perhaps that state could be reversed, regardless of what the Ranthen believed.

His dreamscape was as dark as that stone coffin must have been. Even my dream-form no longer glowed, as it usually did when I walked in his mind, but the golden cord held strong. I reached out a hand, finding one of the red drapes.

The cord was only just alight. I retraced the familiar steps around the drapes, putting my trust in our connection, which had, against all odds, survived his separation from the æther.

Even if this was false hope, I would follow it. I was voyant, and I would put my faith in the Death card, no matter its position.

I bumped into one of his spectres, a towering manifestation of memory. Under normal circumstances, it might have noticed an intruder in his dreamscape. Instead, it only listed, as if I had unbalanced it. As I backed away, I glimpsed my own terrified face in its eyes.

*Don't choose the side I'm not standing on*, it said in my voice. *I don't think I can bear to be your enemy.*

If the spectre touched me, that memory might leak, and I couldn't stand to go back to that night. I kept moving.

At last, I found Arcturus. I knelt beside him, like a mourner, and pressed my forehead against his, feeling his presence ring through my being. The essence of him, in direct contact with the essence of me.

It was as close as I had ever been to anyone.

'Come back. We still have more to do.' I touched his face. 'And I still want you with me.'

It was the longest of long shots. For several moments, nothing happened, and I faced the unbearable possibility that I had misinterpreted the card. That I was going to have to turn my back on him, to walk away a second time. To abandon him to his dark room for ever.

And then my fingertips sparked, and a tremor rolled to the outermost circle of his mind, breaking against its edge like a wave.

Whatever had just happened, I had caused it.

I listened and waited, not letting go. And then light seared in from above, so bright it was blinding. The brilliance shocked me back into my body, where I met a pair of golden eyes, dim as windblown candles.

'Arcturus?'

He stared at me, as if he had never seen me before. I stared back in wonder, my own eyes brimming.

And then I was flat on my back, and my wrists were pinned on either side of my head, held there by an iron grip.

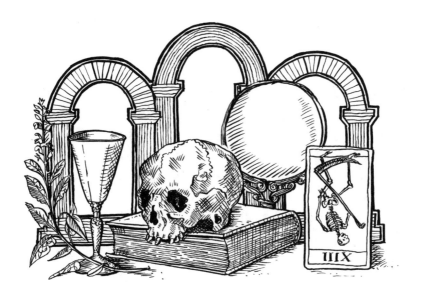

PART TWO

# OVER THE LETHE

**Beochaoineadh:** [Irish, noun] An elegy for the living;
a lament for someone who is still alive, but lost.

# 14

## THE FIFTH CARD

'I have done with your tricks, dreamwalker.'

Darkness laced my sight. Blinking, I tried to focus on his face, to keep me rooted to the present.

'Arcturus,' I said, my voice strained. 'It's me, it's Paige—'

'Enough.'

His massive hands might as well have been shackles. One moment I had been about to burst with elation, and the next, I was back in the torture chamber, at the mercy of a giant.

'Tell her,' Arcturus ground out, 'to sequester me.'

My vision blurred. 'What?'

Even though he wasn't near my throat, I couldn't breathe. He was asking to be executed.

His grip tightened, and that was it. The dark room slammed its doors around me. I needed to work out what could possibly be going through his head, but my body remembered this position, and fought like an alley cat to escape. I wrestled and kicked against Suhail – no, Arcturus, it was Arcturus – but he kept me where I was. My left wrist burned in his grasp.

I was drowning not just in my own fear, but his.

And I knew, looking into his eyes, that he had no idea who I was. He was somewhere far away.

'Arcturus, please, I can't—' I tried one last thing: 'Mothaigh an snáithe órga. Féach orm!'

He stilled. I hadn't finished teaching him, but he knew the sound of my first language.

Little by little, his right hand loosened. No change in his expression, but that small victory offered me a lifeline. Seizing it, I slipped my bad wrist free and reached up to cup his cheek, the way I just had in his dreamscape. Arcturus flinched, but let my hand rest there.

He had never flinched when I touched him before.

'See me,' I whispered. 'It's me.' As I brushed a thumb across his cheekbone, keeping the movement slow and light, the vice on my other wrist eased as well. 'Tá sé ceart go leor.'

If he really thought I was someone else, this would change his mind. Only I would speak to him in Irish.

Terebell must have sensed a disturbance. When she entered the wine cellar and saw Arcturus sitting up, they stared at each other in such disbelief that it might have been comical under different circumstances. Nick was down the stairs like a shot, shoving past Terebell.

'Warden.' His eyes widened. 'Arcturus, let go of Paige, now. Let go of her!'

Arcturus looked from him to me. His gaze sharpened in recognition, in shock.

At once, he released my other wrist, allowing me to scramble out from under him, so quickly I fell off the bed. Nick rushed towards me, but I scooted back until I hit the wall.

'Don't touch me,' I barked. My boots scuffed along the floor. 'Stay back. Do *not* touch me.'

'Okay.' Nick crouched a short distance away. 'No one is touching you, Paige. You're safe.'

I held myself tight and willed the memories down. (*Your wrists are bleeding, Underqueen. All you need do is answer my questions.*) I could feel the manacles again, the hungry presence in the dark.

Terebell marched to Arcturus and seized his shoulders, as if to restrain him. He couldn't take his eyes off me.

'Paige,' he rasped. 'Is it you?'

I had never thought I would hear him say my name again. Another tear ran down my cheek.

'Yes,' I said, heaving. 'It's me.'

Arcturus was awake. Not just awake, but fully aware. He remembered me. I felt him deep within – the sweet and comforting return of his presence, sunlight running through my blood. I wanted to go to him, but his grip had rattled me so badly I could hardly think.

Sometimes I forgot how strong Rephs were. How easy it would be for them to crush a human.

'Warden, stay put and get a hold of yourself,' Nick said hotly. 'What were you thinking?'

Arcturus looked at him. He looked at Terebell, who had been stricken into silence. He looked at his own scarred hands, at the salt on the floor, and at me, scrunched up in the corner. Before either of us could say a word, the other Ranthen reached the cellar, Maria in tow.

'What?' she said in astonishment. 'Warden!'

Errai just stood there, while Lucida went to Arcturus and framed his face, pressing their foreheads together, the way Rephs seemed to express deep affection. Lesath went to one knee and raised a fist to his chest. Arcturus took all of them in – his old friends, his allies.

'Where is this?' He sounded like he had lived through a severe drought. 'How long has passed?'

'It's October, and you're in Italy,' Maria said. 'Welcome to the free world.'

'Italy.'

His gaze returned to me, the needle of a compass settling on north. I tried to iron out my breathing.

'Your glow is looking faint, big man,' Maria said, her brow furrowed. 'Do you need aura?'

'Yes.' Terebell spoke at last. 'He does.'

Arcturus shook his head.

'It's all right. Have a hit of mine,' Maria said gently. 'I need to do something useful tonight.' She shot me a worried look. 'Nick, why don't you take Paige upstairs for some fresh air?'

Nick held out a hand. I convinced myself to take it. It was only Nick. I trusted Nick. As he guided me from the cellar, I glanced back at Arcturus. He watched me like I was a sunrise.

As soon as we were back under the stars, the terror and relief overwhelmed me. Nick held me close as sobs racked my frame. *Thank you, Liss.* I willed her to hear, wherever the æther had taken her. *Thank you.*

———

The abandoned house was overgrown, with an olive grove behind it. Nick had walked through that grove to check for cold spots, finding none. Now we sat in the parlour, far enough apart that I could breathe.

'How did you do it?' Nick said.

'I dreamwalked into him,' I said hoarsely. 'I touched his spirit.' My eyes felt raw. 'Liss did a reading for me. The fifth card was Death, inverted. If I hadn't remembered——'

I couldn't even say it.

'He's okay,' Nick said. 'He's okay, Paige.'

Liss Rymore was in the outer darkness, where no one could spool or bind or disturb her. I wished I could see her once more, to thank her for sharing her gift; for giving me the knowledge that had let me save Arcturus. Every one of her predictions had been right.

'I thought he was going to kill you,' Nick said. 'I don't think I could have stopped him.'

'He didn't know who I was.'

'Have you had this since the waterboard?' he asked me. 'This fear of being touched?'

I nodded. Nick hadn't been there for those early days, when I hadn't been able to bear my reflection, or the feel of my own human skin.

'It was a lot worse in Paris.' I traced the thin scar on my wrist, where the manacle had cut into me. 'I'm handling it better now, but I couldn't stand being held down like that.'

'Of course not.'

Maria came into the parlour. 'I'm absolutely fine,' she said, brushing off our concern before we could voice it. 'Nothing a nap and a stiff drink won't solve.'

'Thank you for doing that,' I said.

'I wasn't going to leave you to do it, not in your state. Nick already used his aura to heal Lesath,' Maria said. 'One of the Buzzers clawed him.'

That explained why Nick looked peaky.

'How is Warden?' I asked Maria.

'He's not saying much. I think he's in shock, poor thing. We need to get back to Venice before Scion realises he's gone. Federico brought us a people carrier.'

'It's three in the morning. Are you okay to drive?'

'For now.' She took a key from her pocket. 'Nick, I'll swap with you halfway.'

I collected my holdall and followed Maria to the people carrier. She opened the door to the front passenger seat for me, while Nick got in behind. Once she was in, Maria switched on the dashboard monitor and selected a radio station, so music played at a low volume.

'I'm not going to ask how you did it,' she said to me quietly. 'I assume you don't know.'

I shook my head.

After a while, the Ranthen emerged. Lucida and Errai took the two seats beside Nick, while Lesath and Terebell guided Arcturus into the back and sat on either side of him.

'It's been a long night, my friends,' Maria said. 'Is everyone coming to Venice?'

'Yes,' Terebell said. 'Arcturus needs somewhere to recover.'

'I don't think we should take you to Domino headquarters,' Nick said. 'There's been at least one security breach, and a few sinister parties are sniffing around for the big secret behind Scion.'

'Verča will find somewhere. I'll ask her now.' Maria took out her phone. 'We'll be driving for a while, everyone. Settle in.'

Once she had sent the message, she started the car. It jolted along a bumpy path. Behind us, night swallowed the abandoned house, which had almost been a place of execution.

Arcturus drowsed against Terebell, who kept her arms around him. Maria drove out of the countryside and joined the motorway that would take us to Venice. I had thought I was too wired to sleep, but the whole exhausting day soon caught up with me, and I passed out.

---

The drive took eight hours. I was out for most of the journey, the white aster demanding its due. Now and then, the Rephs spoke in Gloss, though I never heard Arcturus. The golden cord was still frozen.

*I suspect the sudden distance between us may have strained it,* Arcturus had told me after Oxford. *Now we are together, I trust it will strengthen again.*

Maria stopped at a service station. While she was paying, Nick got out to check on me. By then, pain was building in my shoulder, which had taken the brunt of my fall down the steps.

After that, Nick took the wheel, letting Maria get some rest. I was sound asleep by the time we reached Venice. One of the Rephs wrapped me in a coat and lifted me into the water taxi. From then on, there were only flashes of awareness – the grand foyer of the Palazzo della Notte, then Ducos and Verča, and one more glimpse of Nick before it all went dark.

---

I woke in my own bed in Venice, tucked under fresh sheets. My eyes were puffy, my shoulder hurt like hell, and I was stiff and sore all over. When I attempted to search the æther, my head started to throb, forcing me to stop. But I knew Arcturus was here. We had found him.

Nick had left a box of painkillers on the nightstand. I necked a couple and eased out of bed, stopping for a moment to listen. For the first time since Paris, I could hear rain.

In the bathroom, I inspected my injuries. I had too many scratches and grazes to count, an impressive bruise across my left hip, another on my knee, a third spanning my shoulder and collar-bone. When I touched the place where the purpling was deepest, I grimaced.

One day, I might go a few solid months without nearly getting myself killed. Until then, a few scrapes were a small price to pay for Arcturus.

I ran a bath, making the water as hot as I could stand it. It took a while to wash and untangle my hair. Every time I moved, it strained my overtaxed muscles. Inch by aching inch, I dried off, brushed my teeth, and put on a shirt and jersey, followed by dark trousers Nick had told me were called jeans, an American style that had never reached Scion.

He was in the bar, working on a data pad. When he saw me, he released his breath.

'You slept for two days,' he said. 'How are you feeling?'

I edged into the other chair, trying to find a way to sit without hurting my hip or tailbone.

'Like I fell down a set of cement steps, got thrown off a cliff, and had to swim through my worst fears, all to find Arcturus in a coffin,' I said. 'It's safe to say that was among the worst nights of my life.'

'It's over now. We got him.'

'So we did.' I raised a faint smile. 'A heist for the history books.'

'Possibly your finest work, Underqueen. Even if I hate that you insisted on going alone.'

'You all would have been killed.'

'*You* could have been killed,' Nick pointed out. 'Any of those Buzzers could have taken a chunk out of you. We should have gone back to Naples and reconsidered our approach.' I glanced away. 'You took precautions, but I worry you still think your life is expendable.'

'This wasn't a suicide mission like Senshield. I know everyone thinks I have a death wish, but it's not like that.'

'Tell me what it's like, then.'

I had to think about that for a while. Arcturus had broached this subject with me in Paris, but we had never plumbed the depths of it. I had been too defensive, too stuck in my ways.

'I survived the Imbolc Massacre,' I eventually said, 'when so many people didn't, Nick. Not just that, but Alsafi and Burnish both chose me over themselves when they saved me. I have to make my life count for something, the way you want to spend yours getting justice for Lina. Maybe that's why I push myself so hard – why I take so many risks – but trust me, I've no intention of dying before Scion falls.'

'Or after, I hope.' Nick pressed my hand. 'Alsafi and Burnish made that sacrifice for *you*, sötnos, not someone you still need to become. They thought you were already worth it. And you are.'

A lump filled my throat.

'I don't like the sound of those falls,' Nick said. 'Can I give you a check-up later?' My neck objected to my nod. 'I wanted to examine Warden, but Terebell wouldn't hear of it.'

'Don't take it personally. Nashira has always refused to let humans study their anatomy, to stop us making weapons that could hurt them. The Ranthen share her beliefs on some things.'

'Like the fact that Rephs shouldn't be with humans.'

'Yes.'

There was a brief silence, during which I poured a glass of orange juice and sipped.

'Warden did let me take a sample of his ectoplasm,' Nick said. 'He felt that since the Sargas have used theirs in machinery, our side should understand it, too.'

'You must be over the moon,' I said. 'Any deductions?'

'It's fascinating. I can already make a few observations, like the fact that Rephs don't seem to have any genetic material that I recognise. It's like something … carved them into being.'

'Is their blood acidic or alkaline?'

'It's neutral.' A smile lifted the corners of his mouth. 'I knew you were more interested in science than Evelyn Ancroft would admit.'

'It's hardly my fault that most of my teachers were anchorites,' I said. 'I heard that Rephs can't contract illnesses. Do you think it's true?'

'It must be. The human body isn't meant to be in water for too long. The skin breaks down, the organs fail. Weeks down there, and he just looked asleep.'

I tried not to remember.

'From what I can tell, his body would obliterate any pathogen that got into it. A virus wouldn't even know where to start,' Nick said. 'I can't see any way that Rephs could harbour or transmit illnesses.'

Except the one that turned them into Buzzers.

'That's nice for them.' I tucked my hair behind my ear. 'He's ... all right, then?'

'I couldn't see any obvious injuries, but his movements seem very stiff, and he's lethargic.'

'They severed him from the æther. That can be fatal for a voyant, let alone a Reph,' I said. 'They carry the æther inside them, so the shock is much worse. I don't think any of them have ever recovered from it before.' I paused. 'Did Verča find the Ranthen somewhere to stay?'

'Ducos did.' Nick sought my gaze. 'We all wanted you to be there when Warden told us what happened. He agreed to wait for you. Are you ready to see him?'

I dug my fingertips into my arm until it hurt.

'No,' I said. 'But let's get on with it.'

# 15

# FROM THE DEPTHS

Venice was a city steeped not just in water, but in shadow. There were many well-lit streets – tourist veins, lined with shops and restaurants – but behind that façade, there lay a dark maze of decaying backstreets, a step away from the souvenirs. A maze where shades and ghosts outnumbered the living, and there were doors that no longer existed, leaving only frames.

On paths like those, I felt as if I snapped out of existence between streetlamps. The streets were empty and silent, often deserted. In the maze, Venice went from a living city to a skeleton on the edge of the sea, the breath of life washed from its ribs. Nick and I would enter those intercostal spaces, only to emerge in a busy square, where sound and light returned. I had worked in the darkest layers of London, but Venice at night still unnerved me.

The rain had turned into a downpour, cold enough that I was grateful for my jacket as Nick led me back towards San Marco. All the while, I imagined what I would say to Arcturus.

Two hundred and thirteen days. Neither of us had experienced the whole separation – he had been in that coffin for some of it, while I had been wandering around with a broken memory – but somehow I still felt it.

Calle de la Verona was deserted. There was a lockbox to the right of the door. Nick used a code to open it and retrieve the key, then led me up to the apartment on the highest floor.

I took my time removing my jacket. Arcturus had seen me at my most vulnerable, in every way it was possible to be vulnerable. Now I was afraid to face him. I might yet see blame staring back.

Terebell sat alone in the parlour. The shutters were closed, leaving one lamp to light the room.

'Arcturus is asleep,' she said. 'I would prefer not to wake him.'

'We can wait.' I smoothed my jersey. 'Where are the others?'

'Lesath and Errai have gone to feed. Lucida wished to take the measure of the city. I will send them back to London tomorrow, to tell the others what happened.'

'We should be careful,' Nick said. 'The Mime Order isn't impenetrable. We can't risk Scion knowing we have Warden, or his intelligence will be worthless.'

'I agree,' I said. 'Eliza and the Ranthen should hear it. Maybe the high commanders. No one else.'

'For now,' Terebell said.

She watched as I sat down and checked my phone. Ducos had sent a message, informing me of when I was expected for debriefing. I switched it off.

Verča and Maria soon arrived, carrying bags of food.

'It seems that autumn has arrived in Venezia,' Verča said, pulling off her gumboots. 'This looks as if it could be a bad storm.' She switched on the lights in the kitchen. 'Paige, Nick, you really must try some homemade Italian food. I thought we could make dinner together.'

'Come on, sweet.' Maria steered me into the kitchen. 'Mama always said it was best to have difficult conversations on a full stomach.'

Verča tasked me with chopping and shredding. I recognised this for the distraction it was, but handled it without complaint, trying not to notice the golden cord, or where it led.

'Federico must have been terrified,' Nick said to Verča. 'Have you spoken to him?'

'Federico is honoured to have been able to help us steal from Scion, even if he is shaken. He's gone underground in case the *Ercole* was seen.' She was melting butter in a saucepan. 'I've told him to keep quiet about what he saw, for his own sake. I trust him. But we need to crack Operation Ventriloquist as soon as possible, to protect the voyants of Napoli.'

'I haven't seen anything on the news about us, but I don't speak much Italian.'

'There is nothing.'

'You'd think it was the handiwork of expert criminals.' Maria glanced at me as she uncorked a bottle of wine. 'Venice will be good for Warden. Plenty of wine and sea air to refresh him.'

I nodded, but didn't reply.

We ate at the kitchen table. I cleaned as much of my plate as I could, but my appetite had evaporated, along with my courage. Before I could think better of the idea, I drained a glass of wine.

By the time we all finished, Lesath and Errai had returned to the apartment and hung up their coats. Once we had cleared the table, we joined them in the parlour.

'Paige,' Terebell said, 'I do not know how you saved Arcturus, but you have my gratitude.'

'Yes,' Lesath said. 'On behalf of the Mesarthim, I extend our thanks to you for resurrecting our rightful Warden, Underqueen. Our family is small, but each of us is in your debt.'

Terebell had used my name. I thought it might be the first time.

'No debt,' I said. 'I'm glad it wasn't too late.'

'Such a thing should not have been possible,' Lesath said. 'How did you do it?'

'I used my gift.'

Errai looked even stiffer than usual. The thought of my spirit in his dreamscape must be disquieting.

'If we found other Ranthen who had been starved,' Terebell said, 'could you revive them?'

'I've no idea,' I said. 'I'd have to try it.'

'I mislike this, dreamwalker,' Errai said. His eyes were venomous green. 'You have downplayed and obscured the power of your gift. What other abilities are you hiding?'

'Why, Errai, are you scared of me?'

A tense silence gripped the room.

'Do not be absurd,' Errai spat.

'Simmer down, chrome dome.' Maria gave him a level stare. 'The Underqueen just saved your best warrior from a fate worse than death. Perhaps you could afford her a little courtesy.'

'I do not recall addressing you, augur.'

'I do not recall caring.'

'Let us try to stay calm, everyone,' Verča said. 'This is a small apartment.'

Maria pursed her lips, but desisted.

'Now we have Arcturus back, he will disclose what he learned behind enemy lines,' Terebell said. 'Nashira may have shared more than she ought with him, believing that her secrets would be safe once he was latent. We might soon know more of her plans than we have in decades.'

'We also need him to help Paige with her memories,' Nick said. 'To work out why she was captured.'

'If voyants survive spirit shock, they wake up amaurotic,' I said. 'Arcturus went through something like that – complete severance from the æther. Can he even use his gift any more?'

'His aura is exactly as it was,' Terebell said.

'Even still, we should give him time to recover. He might not want to—'

'Arcturus knows the importance of this war. He will give his report now,' Errai cut in. 'He is not some frail human, requiring months to recover from a splash of water.'

Maria stared at him with open disgust. I could only let out a huff of laughter.

'Errai,' Nick said, 'I would take that back, if I were you.'

'Do not imagine that you can threaten a Rephaite, oracle.' Errai looked at Terebell. 'I warned you it was dangerous to send Arcturus to mind her. Her weakness has enfeebled him.'

'Fuck you, Errai,' I said.

Before anyone could stop me, I left the room. Errai was someone whose company I could only take in tiny doses at the best of times, and now I was down to one strained nerve.

Nick gave me time to cool off before following. By that point, I was standing by a window, arms folded, watching rain seep down the glass.

'Paige.' He came to stand behind me. 'Don't give Errai the satisfaction. You're not weak.'

'It's not just him.' I tightened my arms. 'After I was tortured, I had time to mend in Paris. I'm afraid no one will give Arcturus that, because we all need him. Domino needs his intelligence on Scion. The Ranthen need him to keep fighting. And I need him to—'

A door opened to our right, and we turned. Arcturus stepped into the hallway.

'Warden.' Nick cleared his throat. 'Good to see you awake.'

Arcturus wore his usual black clothes. His brown hair was awry, the way it always was when he woke up. It was the only part of him that ever looked untidy.

'Nick,' he said. 'Paige.'

I was too aware of my breathing, the tender skin around my collarbone, the brush of a stray curl against my cheek. The light in his eyes had returned to gold, with a greener tinge than usual.

'Sorry if we disturbed you,' Nick said, saving me from having to speak. 'Everyone is waiting for you downstairs, but there's no hurry. We can always come back.'

'Time may not be in our favour,' Arcturus said. 'Sooner or later, my absence from Capri will be noted.'

'If you're sure.'

Arcturus nodded. His aura skirted mine as he passed, leaving me stippled with goosebumps.

Nick and I followed him to the parlour. Terebell beckoned him to sit beside her on the couch, speaking in low Gloss. Maria made a point of pouring wine for everyone but Errai.

'Warden, this is my girlfriend, Veronika Norlenghi.' She corked the bottle. 'She's a Domino recruiter.'

'Hello, Warden. I've heard so much about you.' Verča offered him a glass and a smile. 'I'm sorry for your poor welcome to Italy, but I hear you like wine, so you're in the right country.'

Arcturus took the glass. 'Thank you, Veronika.'

'Verča is fine.' She glanced at Maria. 'I'll leave you to it. See you back at Domino?'

'All right, love.'

Verča swung on her raincoat and left. I settled on the window seat beside Nick.

I still felt almost nothing from the golden cord. At first, I had thought it was overstretched to the point of shock. We had been so far apart, for so long.

Now I realised the obstruction stemmed from his end of the cord. He was making a concerted effort to conceal his emotions from me, in a way he never had before. I sensed his intent, and it punched me in the gut.

'Are you comfortable with us being here, Warden?' Nick used his bedside voice. 'If you'd prefer some of us to go, that's fine.'

'No,' Arcturus said. 'You should all hear, as members of the Mime Order. Ask what you wish.'

'Paige has already told us about the night you were captured, but we'd like to hear your side.'

'Take your time,' Maria said.

Arcturus nodded.

'The Vigiles came to the safe house when I was sleeping, armed with the windflower,' he said. 'After the confrontation in Versailles, I was weaker than my wont. Paige had left, so she was not taken.'

I looked away.

'To hide my position from her, I was dosed with alysoplasm and driven to the outskirts of Paris,' he said. 'Nashira arrived in due course. She reminded me that I had once sworn to serve her, and she meant to hold me to my oath. Of course, I could not return to being her consort, given her belief that I have been … intimate with Paige.'

Errai made a sound of disgust. I kept my face blank as memories came, unbidden.

'Nonetheless,' Arcturus said, 'Nashira has always tried to bring her enemies back into the fold. My crimes were grave, but if I endured my punishments and aided her in the conquest of Earth, she assured me that I would not be sequestered or starved. I could be forgiven.'

Nashira was famous for this. She went to great lengths to avoid executing her fellow Rephs, but that meant she had to twist and hammer them into a shape that suited her needs.

'For my first act of penance, I was to help her destroy the Mime Order,' Arcturus said. 'I had a visitor in my cell – a human I had once known as David Fitton. His true name is Cadoc Fitzours.' I stared at him. 'I had thought him an oracle, but I soon learned that he is a dreamwalker.' His eyes met mine. 'There is another, Paige. And he is strong.'

A terrible chill swept over my skin.

'Cade.' I finally spoke. 'Cade is a dreamwalker?'

Maria frowned. 'Who?'

'No. He sent me a vision in Oxford,' I said to Arcturus. 'He's an oracle.'

'Jaxon sees clairvoyance in fixed and distinct categories. We must not fall into that trap,' he said. 'It is possible that Fitzours can project visions like an oracle *and* possess like a dreamwalker. Since both abilities are exceptionally rare, he must have relied on ignorance to evade detection.'

Now I thought about it, it was more than possible. I had often been mistaken for an oracle myself.

*I hoped someone from my order would be a good ally.* My chest tightened as I remembered Cade saying those words in Oxford. *Birds of a feather, and so on.*

He had been screaming the truth in my face, but Jaxon had taught me I was the only dreamwalker, and I had been fool enough to believe it. I had missed what was right under my nose.

'Again,' Maria said, 'who are we talking about?'

'Cadoc Fitzours. He was in my Bone Season,' I said. 'I saw him in Paris.'

'Cadoc Fitzours.' She grimaced. 'Of all the self-important names, that one takes the cake.'

'Do continue, Warden,' Lesath said, dealing us a stern look.

We fell silent.

'The next evening, Nashira set the stage,' Arcturus said. 'I was positioned in a building on the Île de la Citadelle to await Paige. Nashira wanted me to convince her that I had been a Sargas spy since the start of our alliance. The intention was for her to panic and instruct the Mime Order to move, driving it from a refuge that had eluded Scion for several months.'

I had done exactly that.

That was why Nashira had let me leave that night. With perfect accuracy, she had anticipated my reaction and thrown me like a grenade at my own people.

'Fitzours would be in my dreamscape to guarantee my cooperation. He is adept in possession – I suspect he was trained from a young age – but even he could not keep indefinite hold of a Rephaite,' Arcturus said. 'I had to participate in the deception to ensure its success.'

'I can't imagine you doing that without a good incentive,' Nick said. 'Did they blackmail you?'

'If Paige did not believe the lie, she would be imprisoned, tortured and mutilated. Nashira intended to force the Mime Order out by holding its Underqueen to ransom,' Arcturus said. 'I had no intention of allowing Paige to return to their custody. I knew I had to make her leave, no matter the cost. They stopped giving me alysoplasm, to ensure that she would be able to find me.'

I stiffened, knowing what came next.

'The act began,' he said. 'I disrupted it only once, when Fitzours took drastic action to persuade Paige that I had betrayed her. He made to strike her, but I could tell that he had gravely misjudged my strength. The blow he aimed at her would have been fatal. I stopped him.'

*Even with gloves, I will not dirty my hand.*

'So Paige was allowed to leave,' Nick said, when Arcturus was silent, his gaze dull. 'To scatter us.'

'Yes. Nashira had a dreamwalker; she could afford to risk the other. Fitzours had offered his services in exchange for immunity from execution. She was also confident that Paige would return of her own accord – either to free me, if she realised the deception, or to punish my betrayal. She had no fear of losing Paige for good while she had me.'

She knew me well.

'Cade,' I said. 'Is he alive?'

'Yes,' Arcturus said.

'Nashira always meant to kill me, steal my gift. What entitles him to immunity?'

'Perhaps his loyalty. If he demonstrates that he is worth more to her alive than dead, she has no need to take his gift yet. For all intents and purposes, it is already hers to wield.'

'Why on Earth would he trust her not to execute him?' Maria said.

'Nashira does have a knack for convincing humans to do things,' I said quietly. 'She convinced Lord Palmerston to hand the whole of Britain over on a silver platter.'

'The motive hardly matters,' Lesath said. 'What matters is that our greatest tactical advantage – a dreamwalker – now has a disciplined rival. Our bodies are no longer our own.'

'It doesn't make *sense* for her to spare him,' I said, frustrated. 'Surely she could reactivate Senshield with his spirit, if nothing else.'

'I cannot yet explain her mercy on that front,' Arcturus said.

He refused to look in my direction, even as he answered me. I didn't know if I was grateful for it.

'Paige did order us to evacuate, but we guessed it was a ruse, thanks to Nadine. She spoke in your defence,' Nick said to him. 'We stayed put.'

My jaw set. I wanted to leave, but I willed myself to keep to my seat. I deserved to hear this.

'Good,' Arcturus said. 'Nashira had anticipated the airstrikes, thanks to her allies with precognitive gifts. She hoped the Mime Order, frightened from its hideout, would suffer heavy casualties in London. I am relieved to hear that you remained in the deep shelter.'

'The night of the airstrikes,' Maria said, seeing my face. 'Where were you by then, Warden?'

'In the crypts of the Île de la Citadelle. The next day, I was taken to a secure bunker. Although Nashira had foreseen the London bombing, her heir – Vindemiatrix – had not been able to ascertain who was behind it. She had also not known about the simultaneous attack on Paris.'

'You said Vindemiatrix worked in the free world,' I said. 'Is her network called Grapevine?'

Arcturus nodded. Even though he was clamping the cord, it had loosened enough for me to feel his exhaustion.

'Fitzours brought Nashira a hostage,' he said. 'Prior to the masquerade, he abducted Luce Ménard Frère to neutralise the rising threat of disobedience from Inquisitor Ménard. Now Ménard cannot move against Nashira without endangering his spouse and child.'

'So Cade was talking shite about wanting to help Ménard,' I said. 'He worked for Nashira.'

'So it seems,' Arcturus said. 'She must have indoctrinated him in Oxford.'

'He switched loyalties.'

Maria sighed. 'You really do meet the most deranged people, Paige.'

'The next thing I don't understand,' I said, 'is why Nashira wouldn't just kill Ménard on the spot.'

'Ménard is popular, and his tenure as Grand Inquisitor has kept France strong and stable. I imagine that she has left Tjäder in place for the same reason,' Arcturus said. 'If she executed two such prominent figures, especially after the loss of Burnish, the denizens of Scion would lose their sense of security. Nashira believes in the enduring power of appearances.'

'Frère must have given birth in captivity.'

'Yes. She was still a hostage when I was last conscious, kept in the cell beside mine. Fitzours took the infant, Victoire.'

Frère and I detested each other, but I had never doubted that she loved her children. Having her newborn wrenched away must have destroyed her. 'Is Cade the father, like he told me?'

'Frère insisted otherwise to me. She claimed the child was amaurotic, conceived with Ménard.'

It was surreal to imagine them talking about that sort of thing, not least because Frère despised Rephs. I could barely imagine her with a hair out of place, let alone in a prison cell.

'I saw the child,' Arcturus said. 'She is not voyant.'

'You can't usually tell until they're older,' Maria said. 'Can you?'

'Our eyes can see what yours cannot,' Terebell said. 'Even infant voyants have auras.'

'I suspect that Fitzours invented the affair to convince Paige that she would have power over him in the Hôtel Garuche,' Arcturus said, 'which, in turn, allowed him to lure her inside.'

Entering that place was the most reckless and short-sighted decision I had ever made, and that was quite the achievement. I had been exhausted, traumatised, and racked with pneumonia, but nothing excused that degree of stupidity. Cade had played me like a fiddle – though to what end, I had no idea. He had never hurt or crossed me in there.

'In Oxford,' I said, 'I questioned why he was trying to befriend me, and he made up a story to throw me off the scent. It didn't work, but he clearly thinks he's got the gift of the gab.'

'From observation,' Arcturus said, 'he attains a sense of superiority from manipulating those around him.'

'Oh, good. Another unscrupulous bastard,' Maria said. 'We needed more of those around here.'

'We have to find out where Frère and her child are, or Ménard is just a dangerous puppet,' Nick said. 'Paige worked hard to forge an alliance with him, even if it wasn't built to last.'

'Nashira moved several times during my captivity, but always kept to France, to oversee the Iberian Peninsula and keep watch on Ménard,' Arcturus said. 'She took strongholds in Léaz and the Jura Mountains. Frère may be in one of those locations.'

'Where did she keep you?'

'Carcassonne, where she could confer with her commanders in Spain. During this time, I was tortured for information about the Mime Order.'

He delivered this statement in a toneless voice. I had known – of course I had known – but the confirmation still broke something in me.

'My access to aura was restricted, to ensure I was too weak to escape,' he said. 'On the Day of the French Republic, I took advantage of the celebrations to invoke a psychopomp. One of my guards assisted me.'

Terebell spoke: 'Who?'

'Situla Mesarthim.'

That *was* a surprise. Situla had always seemed staunchly loyal to the Sargas, but now I thought about it, she had stopped just short of killing me in Versailles. I had thought it was because Nashira wanted to do it.

'Our cousin has made the right choice,' Lesath said.

'Nashira discovered her betrayal. She was sequestered for helping me.'

Lesath absorbed this.

'Another of us gone,' he said, 'but for a good cause.'

Arcturus was silent. I could only imagine how he was feeling. As rightful Warden of the Mesarthim, he was their guardian, and most of them had already been lost during the civil war.

'Nashira has always had a certain respect for you, Warden, despite your differing views,' Lesath said. 'It is why she fought so hard to break you over the centuries. She would not have bothered with a lesser adversary.' Arcturus glanced at him. 'Did you learn anything of use from her?'

It was refreshing to have a Ranthen-aligned Mesarthim in the group. Lesath looked at Arcturus with a clear, straightforward respect I had rarely seen other Rephs afford to him.

'It is true that Nashira has never quite let go of the idea that I could be moulded into a loyal consort. That she could make a true and lifelong ally of the Warden of the Mesarthim,' Arcturus said. 'That would be a far greater victory than merely claiming me as her trophy.'

*You will never be a war trophy to me.*

My own words echoed in my mind. I had meant them with every sinew of my being.

'After a time, I allowed her to believe she was convincing me, hoping she might share her plans. She told me she meant to conquer Italy,' Arcturus said. 'And she told me how.'

Nick leaned forward, his face intent. After all, this was the official reason we had rescued Arcturus.

'Cadoc Fitzours is her weapon,' Arcturus said. 'Using his gift, he can compel world leaders to do his bidding. With a dreamwalker on one hand and Grapevine on the other, Nashira can force countries not only to convert, but to appear willing, ensuring she does not violate any secret treaties or international laws. She can grow her army, but avoid open war.'

There was a long silence.

'Well,' Maria said, 'it seems you've cracked Operation Ventriloquist for us, Warden.'

I said nothing, sick to my stomach.

'I don't understand,' Nick said. 'Does he … possess them?'

'Fitzours begins with an outspoken politician. Someone with a history of opposing Scion,' Arcturus said. 'He commits a crime in their body in front of witnesses, or leaks evidence to law enforcement.'

'Helen Githmark.' Maria snapped her fingers. 'She was arrested for a hit and run.'

'Githmark was the first victim of Operation Ventriloquist. Once Fitzours has destroyed one politician, he threatens others with the same fate. He bypasses their security and demonstrates his abilities in private. With the knowledge that their bodies are no longer their own, they are vulnerable to coercion. In this way, Fitzours can break a government from within. He can also cause the politicians to ingest poison, or to otherwise injure themselves, if they do not comply.'

'Of course,' Maria breathed. 'If Scion invades a country, there's a risk that others will move to defend it. The airstrikes taught the anchor that. This way, the country seems to convert of its own accord. But he's the one pulling the strings.'

I had never been so ambitious with my gift. In three months, Cade had conquered Norway.

'He must have threatened Sala and Rinaldi,' I said. 'That's why they handed the islands over.'

'Yes,' Arcturus said. 'Beatrice Sala and Lorenzo Rinaldi were certainly targets of Operation Ventriloquist, and the islands were the first step in the conquest of Italy. They are a token of troth – a guarantee that Italy will convert, once Scion is ready to initiate the anchorisation and subdue any local resistance. It will be some time before the Second Inquisitorial Division can depart from the Iberian Peninsula.'

'We need to find President Sala now. More importantly, we need to get rid of Fitzours,' Nick said. 'A dreamwalker on their side is far too dangerous.'

I was starting to shiver, even with my jersey.

'Warden,' Maria said, 'after you heard all of this, how did you end up on Capri?'

Arcturus dropped his gaze.

'After the Ranthen raid on Carcassonne, Nashira deemed that the risk of keeping me outweighed the benefits,' he said. 'She decided I could be useful to her once more. I was chained in the coffin and starved. As I lost my grip on the æther, she told me that she meant to lay my body as a trap for my allies. I would be the death of anyone who came for me.'

'Ah.' Maria paused. 'Were you … still conscious when you went into the water?'

'Yes.'

Nashira was never wasteful. She used her foes to her advantage, even when they were defeated.

'Lugentes Campi was a trap, chiefly aimed at Terebell, while Orcus IV is another Rephaite haven,' Arcturus said. 'I also learned of three more prison cities. There is Tuonela III, which will be in the Swedish town of Visby, and two others, code name Erebus, in Scion East.'

'Tuonela III is dead in the water. I went to Visby,' Nick said. 'Tjäder has stalled the conversion.'

'That would fit with the current picture of events. Tjäder is still free to act, to some degree, while Ménard no longer is. During our time in Paris, Paige learned that she despises Rephaim.'

Every time he said my name, my skin tingled with fresh awareness of him.

'Nashira confided in you,' Terebell said. 'Did she tell you any other plans, aside from Operation Ventriloquist?'

'Not in full,' Arcturus said, 'but the last intelligence I gained is perhaps the most disquieting. Nashira has turned her attention back to ethereal technology.'

I closed my eyes.

'Don't tell us she's rebuilding Senshield,' Nick said.

'Senshield is still incapacitated, to my knowledge. This new technology is called Deathwatch,' Arcturus said. 'It will calculate and monitor the number of drifting spirits on Earth.'

'Why would she create something like that?'

'She did not tell me its purpose, but it means the Sargas are taking a greater interest in the veils between the planes of being, and in the ethereal threshold. It ought to concern us.'

Terebell narrowed her eyes. Nick and Maria exchanged blank looks, but I knew about the ethereal threshold.

*Ideally, we would have an advisory role in your world, to keep the number of spirits in check and establish a fair balance of power,* Arcturus had told me in London. *If we cannot do this, we fear there will be chaos.*

*What sort of chaos?*

*If the Netherworld can fall, so can Earth.*

# 16

## SIREN

Terebell asked us to leave after that. Arcturus had done his part. Regardless of what Errai and Lesath believed, she knew as well as I did that he needed rest. I walked out with Nick and Maria, but soon found myself striding into the downpour, my only thought to get back to my room.

Nick reached me first. He almost took hold of my arm, stopping himself when I tensed.

'Paige,' he said. 'Please, wait a moment.'

'Just leave it,' I said thickly. 'I need to be alone, Nick.'

'I respect that, but let us get you back to Domino first. I can't let you end up somewhere you don't want to be.' When I slowed down, he released his breath. 'Thank you.'

Rain was beading on my lashes, my nose. For once, I was too numb to feel it. While I stood unmoving, Nick opened his umbrella, right as Maria caught up. Seeing my face, hers softened.

'Oh, sweet.'

Nick laid a gentle hand between my shoulders. I let it rest there as I trembled. 'They did torture him.' I could barely get the words out. 'I knew it, I knew they would, but I hoped—'

My voice cracked away.

'I'll call Noemi,' Maria murmured to Nick. 'She can take us back.'

'No. I want to go for a walk,' I forced out. 'Please, both of you. I can handle myself.'

'You can handle yourself in Scion. I'm not leaving you in a city you don't know. Not like this,' Nick said. 'Paige, reverse our situations. Would you leave me in this state?'

I looked up. When I saw the concern on both their faces, I had to shake my head. Nick held me to his side, and Maria linked his other arm, so we could all fit under the umbrella.

They guided me back to Cannaregio. Before long, I was cold in my jacket, glad I had them at my side, and grateful that I hadn't run off on my own into the maze, even if I still wanted to be alone. When we reached the foyer of the Palazzo della Notte, Nick turned to me.

'We'll give you space now,' he said, 'but will you come and see me for that check-up tomorrow?'

'Yes.'

'All right. I'll be in the medical room until noon.'

'Sleep well,' Maria said, her forehead crinkling. 'Let us know if you want to talk.'

With a stiff nod, I went up the grand staircase. In my bathroom, I gripped the edges of the sink, tears running down my face again.

I went over every word Arcturus had said. Each time he had met or avoided my gaze. He hadn't ignored me, but he *was* tying off the cord. I didn't know what that meant, and I couldn't find out without talking to him.

Something had changed in him since Paris. Even from a brief reunion, I could see it. He had already been tortured in Oxford. I couldn't imagine returning to my dark room a second time.

When I thought of Cade, my grip tightened.

Another dreamwalker. Jaxon had always thought I was the only one.

I had been naïve to believe his flattery. Now a dangerous opponent had reared his head, and I was unprepared. Cade was stronger, he was ruthless, and he was on the other side.

He must have been laughing behind my back when my gift was discovered in Oxford. I had tried my best to conceal my abilities, but Nashira had baited them out of me, while Cade had maintained his self-control, passing both tests without revealing his skills in possession. Whoever he was and whatever he was doing, he knew how to play a very long game.

I had never fully trusted him – not in Oxford, nor in Paris. He had unnerved me enough that I had shut him out of our plans for the rebellion. Yet later, I had flung that caution to the wind, allowing myself to be hauled into the Hôtel Garuche on nothing but his word that he could get me out. Now I saw the madness of that choice, and why it had shaken Arcturus. I had put myself at the mercy of a stranger.

I thought back to the masquerade – my last memory, blurred at the edges. Cade had danced with me as if nothing was wrong, days after shattering my life with his deception.

Dreamwalking was a beautiful name for a brutal ability. It could render a person helpless in their own body. Cade had killed someone while inhabiting the Norwegian politician, Helen Githmark. Now she would be sentenced to life for a crime she would not remember committing. A crime he had committed in her skin.

If Cade had no limits, no moral compass, then he might be the single greatest threat the rebellion had ever faced, more dangerous than Ménard or Vance.

And I might be the only one in the world who could stop him.

I had the range to sense him and the means to be his match, in theory. To do that, I would have to fully inhabit Black Moth, who had killed a man by cutting his throat. The day Cade possessed Arcturus, he had tainted my gift; I was already stained by it. I could fight dirty to settle this score.

---

A heavy fog rolled into Venice from the Adriatic Sea. By six in the morning, I was sitting in an armchair by the window, watching the streetlamps glow through a silver veil. I had forgotten to put on an aster patch before I slept, and felt as if the mist had reached into my skull.

Arcturus might be waking up soon. I had never wanted so much to be with him, and never been so worried about seeing him again.

In Paris, we had come so close to overcoming all the barriers that had stopped us from committing to each other. The reserve, the mistrust, the uncertainty – all of it had faded there. He and I had made ourselves a bubble in that house, and it had burst, leaving us both vulnerable. His armour would be thicker now than it had ever been.

I went back to bed for a while longer. I had battled the exhaustion with the stimulant in Naples, and now the white aster was taking revenge. By the time I found the will to get up, it was almost ten.

The fog reminded me of Paris. I could dress more like myself in the cold, and that small comfort gave me fresh determination. I tucked a black turtleneck into belted woollen trousers.

Despite the red notice and the bounty, which must be there as a precaution, Nashira and Cade must really think I was dead. That meant I could get the jump on them. I would punish them for making a fool of me. I would make sure they never touched Arcturus again.

The grand fireplace in the bar had been lit, and a buffet had been set up for breakfast. If I was going to stand a chance against Cade, I had to keep my strength up. I piled my plate high before I took a seat at the table closest to the flames.

Maria came up with a plate of her own. 'Do you want to be alone, Paige?'

'You're grand,' I said.

'I won't ask how you're feeling.' She sat down. 'Did you sleep?'

'Not much.'

'I did some tossing and turning myself. Deathwatch,' she sighed. 'At least Senshield *sounded* reassuring.' She picked up a knife. 'Warden did well. I wouldn't have been that composed.'

'He's keeping a stiff upper lip for the Ranthen. You saw how they are.'

'Errai is a nasty piece of work, isn't he?'

'Ignore him. He's just uptight.' I pushed my breakfast around my plate. 'I should have realised Cade was a dreamwalker. There must have been signs.'

'Maybe you forgot them.' Maria dabbed chocolate spread on a pancake. 'How are you feeling about not being the only one?'

'I'm still digesting it.'

'Tell me a little more about your nemesis. I've always wanted a nemesis,' she added thoughtfully. 'I suppose it should be Hildred Vance.'

'Cade is from Brittany. He was in Oxford as a spy for Ménard,' I said. 'I didn't know that when I met him, but I did get the sense that he was up to something.' I shook my head. 'He knew Nashira wanted to kill me for my gift. He was in the audience when she tried.'

'Did he help you with the rebellion?'

'No, but he didn't hinder us, either. When he had a chance to betray us, he didn't take it.'

'And yet he does appear to be working for Nashira, despite knowing how badly she wants to be a dreamwalker.' Her brow knitted. 'A man with a dangerous ability and no apparent fear, willing to risk his own life to further her cause. This may be a problem, Paige.'

'I'm going to stop him.'

'You need your memories back first. Cordier could still be out there, and she's dangerous. I know you don't want to push Warden, but—'

'He isn't ready.'

'You haven't asked him.'

'I don't need to. I know.' I stirred my coffee. 'And what I'd be asking him isn't … a small thing. He'd need to create a shared dream, to see exactly what I saw. It's intimate.'

'But you want to be intimate with him again, don't you?'

I glanced over my shoulder, as if Terebell could be listening.

'Yes,' I said, 'but I believed in his betrayal. I didn't mount a second rescue attempt, even though I had the forces. I'd understand if he was hurt.'

'I don't know Warden especially well, but he doesn't strike me as the sort of man who sulks. Some light brooding over a glass of wine, perhaps, but I'm sure he won't hold any of it against you. You two just need to have a frank conversation, and not leave it too long.' She waved her knife at me. 'Now, eat your breakfast and stop overthinking, Underqueen.'

'Fine.'

I finished my fruit and yoghurt. Ducos appeared a minute later, a thick folder balanced on one hip.

'You know,' I said to her, 'I'm starting to suspect you've got a tracking unit in me, too.'

'I assumed you would be hungry. I'm here to remind you about your debriefing,' Ducos said. 'See you upstairs at half past two. We'll be in the Dogaressa Room.' She considered me. 'You were right about Capri, as you were about Versailles. Pivot is impressed.'

Before I could respond, she walked on.

'I can't work out if she likes you,' Maria remarked.

'She claims she does,' I said.

'You need to tell Command about the other dreamwalker. Now you're an agent again, you can use their supplies and connections to track him down.' She took a bite of pancake. 'Ducos knows the Ranthen are in Venice, by the way. Pivot might well ask you to arrange a meeting.'

'Why does everyone think I'm their secretary?'

'Because you're the resident expert in Rephs, sweet. You have a good idea of how to handle them.'

'If I could handle Terebell, she'd like me a lot more than she does.' I stood. 'I'd better let Nick have a look at these bruises. See you and Verča for dinner?'

'Verča has gone to see her family in Trieste, but I'll be there,' Maria said. 'In the meantime, I'd better keep resting the arm. I want to help you beat the stuffing out of Cadoc Fitzours.'

'I appreciate the enthusiasm.'

Leaving her to eat, I went to the coffee machine and filled two cups, which I carried to the medical room. Nick looked up from a screen.

'I thought I'd bring coffee,' I said.

'Thank you. I need it.' He took the cup I offered. 'How are you feeling today?'

236

'The same, with fewer tears.' I shook my head. 'I'm sure I never used to cry this much.'

'Paige, you've been through so much over the last year. It was going to get on top of you at some point. Besides, sometimes it's good to let it all out.' His face softened. 'You didn't get a chance to speak to Warden by yourself. Why don't you walk back and check on him?'

'I'll wait until tomorrow.'

'You're avoiding him.'

'No. I'm giving him space,' I said. 'He looked like he was ready to keel over yesterday.'

'I don't think I understood what he said about Deathwatch.'

I sat on the examination couch.

'You know the Rephs used to live in the Netherworld,' I said. 'The psychopomps would lead spirits there, so they could come to terms with their deaths and move on to the last light. But over time, humans treated each other so badly that Earth became overcrowded with spirits, and the psychopomps couldn't handle it. The Rephs call that point the ethereal threshold, and when it's reached, the veils between worlds begin to destabilise.'

'I remember this. You told me in London.'

'Well, here's what you don't know. The ruling family, the Mothallath, came to Earth to deal with the problem,' I said. 'They managed to lower the number of spirits – but something happened while they were here, which caused the decline of the Netherworld. Apparently, voyants also appeared around that time. All this started a civil war.'

'Okay,' Nick said, his brow furrowed.

'The veils eventually became so thin that the other Rephs were able to make the crossing to Earth,' I said. 'Now the Netherworld has fallen, and the Mothallath are gone. That means the number of restless spirits on Earth is only going to keep climbing, and we can't use the threnody to banish them all to the last light. There are too many.'

'And Nashira is keeping a sharp eye on this, but we don't know exactly what that could mean. That's what Warden was saying.'

'In a nutshell.'

'You need to ask him more.'

'I will. Just … let him have a couple of days, Nick. You'd give him that if he was human.'

'You're right. I'm sorry.' He turned back to his laptop. 'I know you've already sat through a lot of prodding and poking, but I need to reassure Command that you're fit to work after the last assignment. It's standard practice. Can you show me where you're hurt?'

I nodded and took off my jersey.

Nick examined the bruising and checked for breaks, asking before he touched me. When he was done, he sent me to the body scanner. I held still as a band of light passed over me.

'Go on,' I said. Nick studied the results. 'How bad is it?'

'Nothing is broken, and I can't see any spinal or cranial injuries. You were lucky,' he said. 'I'm more concerned about the old scaphoid fracture in your left wrist. I'll need to speak to a specialist, but I suspect the tissue in your bone is dying – avascular necrosis, to use the proper term. At this point, it probably needs surgery. How long since you fell on it?'

'Over a year.' I stepped away from the scanner. 'Will surgery fix it?'

'It might help with the pain, but you should have had a cast on it for months after the break.'

'Arcturus did his best.'

'But you could have told me how much it was hurting in London,' he said. I pressed the sore hollow at the base of my thumb. 'You have to start taking better care of yourself, Paige.'

'I haven't exactly had time for a spa retreat, Nick.'

'That isn't what I mean. You can't help that you've been under stress, but you can't run on coffee and nerve.'

'I've been trying to rest.'

'You've been sleeping more because the white aster hasn't given you much choice. I want you to do it of your own accord.' He closed the scan results. 'I need to think about how I'm going to report this to Command. If I give you a brace for your wrist, will you wear it?'

'I promise. By the way, do they have contraceptive injections out here?' I asked. 'My period came back in Paris. I don't want it to surprise me when I'm in the middle of something.'

'Yes. They have one that lasts for six months.'

Nick went to one of the cabinets and brought a syringe back. He gave me the dose in my upper arm.

'Thanks,' I said, reaching for my jersey.

'You're welcome.' He disposed of the syringe. 'Now, let's get you that brace.'

---

Once Nick was done with me, I found a workstation and accessed Protean. The splinted brace on my left arm kept the wrist straight, but allowed me to use my fingers as I searched for news on President Sala.

She had a long and detailed entry on Omnia. Her official picture showed a woman in her early sixties, thick black hair rippling down to her shoulders, a confident smile on her face.

> **Beatrice Sala** (born 27 March 1997) is an Italian politician and former archaeologist who assumed office as <u>President of Italy</u> in May 2041. She previously served as <u>Minister for Health</u> (2031–2034) and <u>Minister for Culture</u> (2034–2041). She is known for resuming the controversial reconstruction of the <u>Roman Forum</u> (see <u>Forum Project</u>), and for her strong opposition to the <u>Republic of Scion</u>.

A vocal critic of Scion, as Verča had described. I dug up a few articles. There was speculation on what sort of illness was keeping her from her public duties, but the media seemed far more interested in the Prime Minister, and Rinaldi appeared to be going about his business as usual.

The golden cord gave a sudden tremor. Arcturus had woken, then cut himself off again.

So be it. He was entitled to his privacy. I looked back at Omnia, but the cord had shaken my concentration. I returned to my room for a jacket before I left the building. Perhaps some fresh air would do me good.

For an hour, I explored the city on foot. The rain had stopped, and the fog was thicker in its wake. Venice was silvered and mysterised by it; I could barely see the tops of some buildings. I wondered if the Netherworld was anything like this – there and not there, adrift in itself. I found a public garden to the north, then went to see a landmark called the Bridge of Sighs. At last, I chose a bench on the Riva degli Schiavoni and watched boats passing by.

All the while, I thought of Arcturus. I could have gone anywhere in the city, but I had strayed to the district where he was staying. I wished I had the courage to go back to the apartment.

There had been fog like this on the day Scion took him. The day after our overture.

In Paris, I had accepted that I wanted to be with him. I had been ready to become his partner in all senses of the word; to commit to something more concrete than whatever had been flickering between us since Oxford. Paris had been the final step in a long realisation that we should fight to make it work, even if it always had to be a secret.

Arcturus was my counterbalance. We had made a formidable team in Paris. He had proven his loyalty time and again, and now he had been punished for it. *The card has weight,* Liss had told me, showing me the Lovers. *This will be a pillar of your life.*

There was no one else who fit the description. It was him.

It had always been him.

Another sprinkle of rain came down, dewing my hair. I headed back to the Palazzo del Domino.

At half past two on the dot, I knocked on a door marked STANZA DELLA DOGARESSA. Ducos let me in. It was smaller than the Blue Room, housing a round table and a few upholstered chairs. Pivot sat in one of them, wearing an elegant navy shirt over matching trousers.

'Flora. Welcome back,' she said. 'I'm told your assignment was a resounding success.'

'You could say that,' I said.

Beside her, a third amaurotic, sallow and stocky, scrutinised me from behind a pair of gold wire spectacles with a top bar. His suit was the same greyish brown as his receding hair.

'This is Spinner, one of my colleagues in Command,' Pivot said. Spinner gave me a curt nod. 'He would like to hear exactly what happened on Capri.'

'Have Nick and Verča already spoken to you?'

'Not yet.'

Spinner folded his arms, while Ducos stood by the door, her files gathered to her chest. Under their watchful gazes, I recounted almost everything that had happened in Naples and Capri, seeing no reason to spare any details, except for the fact that Arcturus had been dead (for all intents and purposes) when I found him. That would be hard to explain.

'These creatures you mentioned, the Buzzers,' Spinner said. 'What exactly are they?'

'Buzzers come from the same world as *Advena sapiens*,' I said. 'They eat flesh and spirits.'

'Right.' His mouth tightened. 'You say they came through a gateway. A cold spot, was it?'

'Scion can draw Buzzers towards certain places. In this case, they used them as a trap. That's the reason your investigation teams disappeared. The Buzzers would have overwhelmed and killed them.'

'So you're saying Scion planted a biological weapon on the island.'

'I ... suppose.'

'And now your associate is safely in Venice,' Pivot said. 'Was he privy to any useful intelligence?'

'Yes. He was able to identify the nature and aims of Operation Ventriloquist.'

They all looked at each other.

'Operation Ventriloquist is a covert attack on the free world,' I said. 'The Suzerain is using a dreamwalker – someone like me – to possess, threaten and blackmail politicians, forcing them to let Scion do what it wants. He's the weapon Wells mentioned. I'm convinced that's why Rinaldi and Sala allowed Scion to take the islands, and why Sala has vanished.'

Spinner pressed his lips together.

'I see.' Pivot drew her data pad towards her. 'Can you explain in more detail, Flora?'

Over the next hour, I told them as much as I could about Cade and his role in Operation Ventriloquist. I ran them through the mechanics of dreamwalking, and how I thought Cade had used his abilities to cow the Norwegian government into submitting to Scion.

'He might have intimidated an Italian politician before Sala and Rinaldi,' I said. 'To demonstrate his powers.'

'There is a possible Italian counterpart to Helen Githmark,' Ducos said. 'Umberto Bianchi, the Mayor of Turin. After the police received an anonymous tip-off, a large quantity of drugs were found in his family home. Bianchi claimed to have no idea how they had got there, but there was footage of him making the deal. He's awaiting trial as we speak. He was outspoken against Scion, advocating for Italy to help defend the Iberian Peninsula.'

'He's your man, then, and he's innocent. He did technically move the drugs, but he'd have had no memory or control of his actions.'

'What about Grapevine?' Pivot asked. 'Does your associate know anything more about the network?'

'He confirmed that it serves the Suzerain. The head of the organisation is a member of her family, and reports to her directly. She goes by the name Vindemiatrix Sargas.'

'Is she *Advena sapiens*, then?'

'Yes,' I said. 'That's all my associate could get.'

It wasn't quite true – there was the threat of Deathwatch – but these three were amaurotic. Trying to explain the intricacies of ethereal technology would be hard, especially when I didn't know a great deal about it myself.

'It's more than enough,' Pivot said. 'He has saved us a great deal of time and risk.' She consulted her data pad. 'So far, there is no evidence that Scion is aware of any of our operations on Capri. Your identification and extraction of a source was efficient, and reflects a more considered and mature approach to danger than you showed in Versailles. Well done.'

I nodded. Even if I was never going to be a model agent, I was glad I was keeping Domino sweet.

'All of this is well and good,' Spinner said, 'but we'd like to speak to this supposed non-human ourselves.' His accent was a nasal twang I had never heard before. 'When can he be here?'

Even if it was an accurate description, the way he said *non-human* got my back up.

'Warden is recovering from seven months of captivity and torture,' I said. 'He isn't in any state to be questioned.'

'I'm afraid I must insist, Agent Blake.'

'You've no right to insist. I work for Domino, but I'll thank you to remember that Warden doesn't owe you anything.'

'Flora, you have been straightforward with us. I will return the courtesy,' Pivot said, with a pointed glance at Spinner. 'While we have some limited knowledge of *Advena sapiens*, we have never received concrete evidence of their existence, other than what Widow reported from Paris. We need to confirm with our own eyes that we are not chasing shadows before we decide on what action to take.'

'It would be useful to establish a formal relationship,' Ducos said. 'And understand the role your allies play in the Mime Order.'

And the more they understood about the Mime Order, the more likely they were to fund it.

'Domino has been leaking like a sieve,' I said. 'Can you guarantee that Warden will be safe?'

'We would put stringent measures in place to ensure his privacy,' Pivot said. 'The Palazzo del Giorno will be off limits to all operatives for the night. It will only be the three of us who see him.'

'Do you want to see him specifically, or any Reph?'

'Wait.' Spinner leaned forward. 'You're saying there's more than one in Venice?'

'Yes,' I said. 'I know the leader of his faction.'

'Then by all means, bring them both.'

'It's not my decision,' I reminded him. 'They don't answer to me.'

'Of course not,' Pivot said, her tone placating. 'We only ask that you extend the invitation.'

Terebell would probably be willing, for the sake of gaining more support and money for the Mime Order. I was less sure about Arcturus, but I could pass the offer along.

'I can do that much,' I said.

'Thank you. We await their decision,' Pivot said. 'In the meantime, we must decide on your next assignment. As an ace, you have a say in your own deployment. You also know this dream-walker personally, along with his modus operandi. What does your instinct tell you?'

'I'd like to go to Rome and look for him. If he has the same range as me, he needs to be within a mile of someone to possess them, so he must have been in Italy when he framed Bianchi. After that, he would have found a way to Sala and Rinaldi. All signs point to him being there. I could try to see the Prime Minister, to offer him my support.'

Spinner shook his head. 'From what your associate and the whistle-blower said, Rinaldi could be under surveillance or communicating with Scion. My doublet will keep tabs on him, but direct contact could give the game away.'

'I agree,' Ducos said. 'We don't want to show our hand too early.'

'If you say so.' I looked between them. 'Have you had any luck finding President Sala?'

'Unfortunately not,' Pivot said, 'but Rome was the last place she was seen before her disappearance in September. Perhaps you will pick up her trail as you search for Mr Fitzours.'

'I'll do my best.'

'Make sure you prioritise the dreamwalker. If you believe you can neutralise this enemy asset and put an end to Operation Ventriloquist, we can arrange your transport and accommodation,' she said. 'I will need a day or two to agree your timeline and objectives with my colleagues. Widow will advise you on the next steps. In the meantime, your associate is invited to join us here tomorrow evening.'

'I'll speak to him in the morning.'

'Very good.'

'By the way,' I said, 'did you look into why the Grand Overseer might have a dissimulator?'

'Yes. As expected, he is not a known associate,' Pivot said. 'Sadly, I can only imagine that he obtained it from an imprisoned or executed agent.'

That did add up. Jaxon had no problem stealing from the dead.

'Thanks for checking,' I said. 'Sorry I couldn't kill him.'

'Not to worry,' Pivot said. 'There will be other chances to turn France against England.'

Ducos opened the door for me. We headed down the corridor, back towards the enclosed walkway.

'Well,' I said. 'Spinner is a charmer, isn't he?'

'He is sceptical of extrasensory perception, which is the most popular term for clairvoyance outside Scion.'

'He doesn't think clairvoyance is real?'

'No. He thinks Scion uses it as a convenient excuse for ridding itself of detractors and rebels, and that most of its victims are so indoctrinated that they come to believe it themselves.'

'I could prove it exists. Just let me at his dreamscape.'

'I do sympathise with him. There is no scientific evidence of clairvoyance. No explanation for why certain humans can perceive another layer of existence,' Ducos said. 'That's why Spinner is sceptical. It's also the reason he is so determined to see your associate. He believes Alice Taylan was deluded or mistaken about *Advena sapiens*.'

'But Warden would be proof enough?'

'Most likely.' She opened the door on the other side of the bridge. 'Spinner oversees our doublets, who pass valuable information on to our political contacts, the way Opseth did to Queen Ingelin. He will only inform them about *Advena sapiens* once he is certain they exist. Otherwise he fears our credibility might be called into question.'

I could understand that. If anyone had told me about the Rephs before I had ever set eyes on them, I would have assumed they were having me on. Eliza hadn't believed me after I came back from Oxford. Seeing them had cured her doubt.

'I will ask,' I said, 'but if Warden doesn't agree to this, Domino needs to respect that.'

'I'll make sure of it.'

Ducos made her way down the grand staircase. I followed, intending to go to my room.

A siren droned outside.

I stopped in my tracks, chills running all over my body. At once, my stomach was in free fall, my fingernails were biting into the banister, and for all I tried, I couldn't take another step.

Ducos stopped to listen as a long tone sounded. The note climbed once, then a second time.

'They raised the floodgates too late again.' She clocked my expression. 'What is it?'

I swallowed. 'Why is there a siren?'

'It's just the acqua alta. Were you not told about this?'

'No.'

'The Venetian Lagoon is vulnerable to high tides, which can flood some parts of the city. It happens every so often, especially in autumn and winter,' she said. 'People here are used to it.'

I almost laughed. Every time I escaped one body of water, another came rushing towards me.

'The lower floors will be sealed in a few minutes, to stop the water coming in. It will be over by morning,' Ducos said. 'Let me know by noon about the meeting. We'll be ready.'

She vanished down a corridor, leaving me rooted to the spot.

The tones continued. After a minute, I returned to my room, intending to lock the shutters and sleep until the flood had passed. Instead, I sat on the bed, so tense it hurt. I couldn't think straight. Even with my fear of water, I shouldn't be reacting this badly to a sound.

My breath came short. My palms turned clammy.

Before I knew it, I was grabbing my jacket.

---

I reached the door to the alley as a flood barrier was being lowered. Without stopping, I ducked under it and ran. So far, there was no water on the streets, though the Grand Canal had risen.

Around me, people were building catwalks or protecting the entrances to their shops. A few tourists stood ready with gumboots and cameras, some of them chatting with the locals. It was almost business as usual. Only I seemed to be stricken by fear.

It wasn't only the thought of a flooded city. Some other dread was driving me, one that I couldn't explain. It had to be something in my dreamscape. A memory I couldn't touch.

When I reached Calle de la Verona, I opened the lockbox, fumbling out the key. Once I had opened the door, I almost collapsed in the hallway, my ribs aching. No sooner had I got up to the parlour than I nearly slammed into Arcturus. I flinched back in the nick of time, avoiding his chest by an inch. He looked me up and down.

'Paige.'

'Arcturus,' I said.

He must have sensed me coming. Before I could speak, Terebell emerged from the parlour, dressed more informally than usual. I realised she could well have been asleep, given it was the middle of the day. She scrutinised my flushed cheeks, my wild hair.

'Did you run here?'

'No. I just—' I stopped to catch my breath. 'I just wanted to tell you about the siren.'

'Yes. We are capable of perceiving sound.'

'I mean that I wanted to tell you why it came on. It's flooding, apparently. But nothing to worry about.' My face was starting to burn. 'I didn't want you to think it was—'

Arcturus waited for me to continue, then finished my sentence: 'An airstrike.'

I met his gaze, realising.

That was why. Even if I had forgotten the civil defence sirens, I must have heard them in Paris.

'You ran here at full pelt to inform us that we are *not* under attack, and that nothing of note is happening,' Terebell said, clearly thinking I was off the cot. 'Will that be all, Underqueen?'

'Absolutely,' I said. 'I'll leave you to it.'

'Stay.'

I stilled. Arcturus had spoken so softly, I almost thought I had imagined it.

'Wait until the floodwater recedes,' he said. 'The tides are danger-ous these days.'

'Ducos said it could last until tomorrow.'

'Then sleep here,' Terebell said. 'There are matters to discuss, in any case.'

Even if I made it back to the Palazzo del Domino before the canals washed on to the streets, I would find myself shut out by the flood defences. The thought of having to wade through any amount of water, after that harrowing swim, was enough to shorten my breath.

Arcturus stood aside. I hid behind my hair as I passed him, following Terebell.

In the parlour, I hung my jacket up and sat. Two glasses and a bottle of red wine stood on the table. Clearly a classic night in for the Ranthen. Terebell took the opposite couch.

'Arcturus was intending to bathe,' she said, explaining his disappearance. 'He will join us.'

'Where are the others?'

'They have returned to Scion. Lucida is now our liaison to the Nouveau Régime.' She picked up a glass. 'As agreed, they will only tell our closest allies about Arcturus. He cannot defend himself in this state, and we must ensure that everything he learned retains its value.'

'Nick said he seemed lethargic,' I said. 'How is he?'

'When he lost the æther, the ectoplasm in his body vitrified. It quickened again when you revived him, but the ordeal has taken a physical toll. I do not know how long it will take him to heal, or if he will ever fully recover. There is no precedent.'

I tried not to imagine my blood turning to glass and back.

'Arcturus helped me after the waterboard,' I said quietly. 'You lived through a war together. You were both scarred in Oxford. What can I do to support him?'

'Do not concern yourself with his state of mind. That is something you, a mortal, cannot hope to understand. In any case, you will be preoccupied with your work for the Domino Programme,' Terebell said. 'Once he is able to travel, I intend to send him back to Scion.'

I kept my expression clear, but suddenly I felt as if I couldn't draw a deep breath if I tried.

'He's more likely to be detected in Scion,' I said. 'Is it a good idea to send him back this soon?'

'Scion is where our battle lies.'

'In the end, but he can't fight right now. While I work for Domino, I'm allowed to use their safe houses, like this one. He can stay here. Once my assignments are finished, we could go back to Scion together.'

Terebell assessed me. Her hand rested on the arm of the couch, snug in its tailored glove.

'I will consider your proposal,' she said. 'Do you now intend to hunt the other dreamwalker?'

'Yes,' I said. 'I made Domino understand the danger. My next assignment will be to ... neutralise him.'

'Where will you begin the search?'

'Rome.'

'You possessed Nashira for a matter of moments at the Bicentenary. From what I recall, it almost killed you. Fitzours seems far more accomplished. How do you intend to get the better of him?'

'Let's not overestimate his abilities. Cade had to blackmail Arcturus, or I doubt he would have been able to keep a foothold in his dreamscape for long,' I said. 'But I do need to strategise. If Cade was born into a dreamwalking family, he could have years of knowledge on me, especially if he's older. I wasn't even certain I was voyant until I was sixteen.'

'One of your kin must have been gifted. It does not spring from nowhere in humans.'

'My mother died when I was born. It was probably her,' I said. 'I'll do whatever it takes to stop Cade.'

'You must act with all haste. We cannot risk him serving Nashira for much longer. Either he will continue to win the free world for her, or she will kill him for his gift, as she intended to kill you,' she said. 'Given the severity of the threat, it may be prudent for all three of us to remain in the free world until he is dead. I am willing to assist you.'

'I really appreciate the offer, but Eliza needs you. You should go back to London, so the Mime Order has one of its leaders, at least,' I said. 'I'll take care of Cade.'

Once again, Terebell fell silent, her eyes burning.

'Very well. I will entrust this task to you,' she said. 'Do not make me regret it, Paige.' She picked up her coat and took four small vials from inside. 'Take some of our alysoplasm. It will allow you to catch him unawares.'

I hesitated. 'It will stop me from being able to sense him. Or to dreamwalk.'

'You will still have your criminal instincts. Arcturus told me how you tracked down the grands ducs in Paris. You possess the skills to locate Fitzours without relying on the æther,' she said. 'Once you have established where he is, you can restore your gift with fortified ectoplasm, which Arcturus will provide.'

Her sudden confidence in me was a surprise. I couldn't bring myself to remind her that I would be looking for Cade in a free-world city, which I lacked the experience to navigate.

'Okay.' I pocketed the vials. 'Speaking of gifts, I've realised I have no idea what yours is.'

'I am what you would describe as an augur.'

'Like your cousin.'

'Kornephoros claims to have skinned humans for sport. I use my talents to mend bone and sarx,' Terebell said, 'though I can only heal Rephaim, and not from the wounds caused by poltergeists. I call it *somatomancy*.' She tapped her fingers on the couch. 'Arcturus tells me you met Kornephoros in Paris.'

'I did. Big, isn't he?'

'Your observations are always illuminating, dreamwalker.'

'I see you got the hang of sarcasm.'

She closed her eyes. 'How Arcturus has not yet lost his patience with you, I cannot tell.'

'I'm sure he has, at one point or another.'

'No. He is precisely as tolerant of you as he appears.' Her eyes opened. 'From my perspective, you have begun to atone for your folly in Paris, but Arcturus may have some choice words for you, given your lack of faith in his loyalty. Since you are here, I will give him the opportunity to express them in private tonight.'

'He deserves that.'

We sat in patient silence after that. I dared not hope that I was making progress with her.

When Arcturus returned to the parlour, he sat beside Terebell. Nick had been right. There was a clear and unusual stiffness to his bearing.

'Paige,' he said, 'I understand you have aster poisoning and no memory of your captivity. I believe I can help you.'

Hearing his voice was still an indescribable relief. I wanted to wrap myself in that voice, sleep in it.

'I can't ask that of you,' I said. 'Not when you only just … came back.'

'You need not ask. I have offered,' Arcturus said. 'If not for your sound judgement and determination, I would still be imprisoned in my own dreamscape. I wish to repay that debt.'

'You got me out of the Hôtel Garuche. I owed you for that, if you want to keep count.'

'Paige.'

The way he said my name was so familiar, it stopped my reply in my throat.

'This must be done,' Terebell said. 'You will not succeed in routing Fitzours if your spirit cannot rest.' She rose. 'I will leave you for the evening, so you might begin. I intend to summon Pleione from London, to ask her more about him. She was his keeper in Oxford.'

'Before you go,' I said, 'I have a request from Domino. Command wants to talk to you. In person.'

'Why?'

'They've heard about the mysterious founders of Scion, but they have no evidence that you exist, which they'd appreciate. Their support could be useful.' I looked at Arcturus. 'You told me the Ranthen wanted an advisory role on Earth. That you wanted to establish a fair balance of power, and to maintain an open and cordial relationship with humans. Is that still true?'

'Yes,' he said.

'When do you want to start being open?'

He glanced at Terebell. They spoke a silent language I had yet to be able to interpret.

'Revealing ourselves to human authorities beyond Scion could work in our favour, or against us,' Arcturus said. 'So far, we have chosen to maintain our secrecy outside the Archon, to avoid the possibility of human scrutiny and mistrust. Nashira rightfully feared that.'

'Yes,' Terebell said. 'We are stronger than humans, but you outnumber us many times. As you pointed out yourself in London, the revelation of our presence would cause widespread consternation, if not worse. It could imperil every Rephaite.'

'You told me Nashira might reveal herself once she has Europe under her control,' I said. 'With a dreamwalker in her pocket and countries falling by the month, that may be sooner than we think, especially if Italy caves. I think you need to decide whether you want to beat Nashira to it. It *is* going to happen at some point. It's just a matter of who gets to shape the story.'

Terebell seemed to reflect on this. Arcturus let her think.

'It may be wise to undermine her plans by being the first to reveal ourselves, at least to your governments,' she eventually said. 'In a limited capacity.'

'Okay.' I looked between them. 'So you will speak to Command?'

Arcturus considered. 'Do you trust them, Paige?'

'I trust Ducos. She's been promoted to Command,' I said. 'I don't know the other two very well, but I've been assured they'll protect your privacy.'

'Ducos struck me as principled. I am willing, but I must defer to Terebell.'

'I will think on it.' Terebell swung on her coat. 'In the meantime, concentrate on fighting the white aster, Underqueen. You will need your strength in the days to come.'

The door closed in her wake.

# 17

## WHITE FLOWER

I had never expected to be left alone with Arcturus this soon. It gave me no time to armour myself. Before Italy, the last time we had seen each other had been when he was possessed. My skin warmed as if with a sudden fever. I felt my heart like a moth in my throat.

'I am glad to see you alive, Paige.'

He spoke with his usual soft courtesy.

'Same for you,' I said. 'You had us worried there.'

'So I heard.'

In the silence that followed, my nerve almost failed me. In Paris, we had grown as close as a bird to its wing, but so much had happened to us since then, and I didn't know how to start fixing it. His grip on the cord seemed firmer today, which only deepened my disquiet.

I hated feeling this way around him. He was my confidant, yet now he was back, I couldn't find the words.

'Lesath told me how I came to be here,' Arcturus said. 'It was you who realised where I was imprisoned. You who swam into the dark to find me. You who saved me from sequestration.'

'I wasn't alone,' I said. 'As for the last one, I really have no idea how I did it.'

'You should not be surprised by your strength. I never am.'

Those words gave me pause and lifted my gaze. His eyes burned on the lowest flame.

'I understand Eléonore Cordier took you to Wrocław,' he said, 'but you do not know why.' I shook my head. 'She was dosing you with white aster for six months.'

'I hit whiteout,' I said. 'Verča broke it with blue aster. I've been taking the odd dose, but it's only helping so much.'

'Your spirit is no longer at ease. It is no way to live,' he said. 'As I told you in Paris, I believe it is possible to undo the amnesia caused by white aster, but I have never attempted it. You may find it taxing. If you would like to eat or rest before we begin, I am happy to wait.'

'You don't have to do this, Arcturus. Not if you're not up to it.'

'I have the means to alleviate your discomfort. It behoves me to use it,' he said. 'Terebell is right. You will not be able to hunt Fitzours in this state. And it would be useful to know if my separation from the æther has affected my gift as much as it has affected my body.'

I didn't argue. We both knew I couldn't go on like this, and he was the only one who could end it.

'Lesath left a small amount of salvia.' He reached for a pouch on the table. 'I will prepare it.'

It took him a while to stand up. He was already in so much pain from the scars, and now this.

'Arcturus.' I started to rise. 'I can do it.'

'No need. Thank you.'

After a moment, I sank back into my seat, letting him go. He went into the kitchen and filled the kettle.

It had been months since he had last seen my memories. The last time had been in Edinburgh. Before that, he had ordered me to take salvia in Magdalen, so he could pry into my past.

Not his finest hour. He had needed to be sure that he could trust me to mount a rebellion. It had still been a violation, and I knew he regretted it.

I had come to understand his reasons. In the end, I had forgiven him. He and I were trespassers, with keys that no one should be

254

granted. My gift compromised the body, and his, the secret vaults of the mind. There was no hidden truth an oneiromancer could not bring to light.

'Paige,' he said, 'what do you last remember?'

'The masquerade to celebrate the conquest,' I said. 'I went to see Ménard. To discuss a truce.'

Arcturus stopped for a moment. He must have wondered if I would remember that night in my bedroom. No doubt he had been worried he might have to remind me.

'Your last clear memory.' He poured from the kettle. 'Had you left the masquerade?'

'No. I'm with Ménard,' I said. 'Cade is outside the door.'

'Is there a pallor in your dreamscape?'

'Yes. It's ... taken a new form, but I don't know if that's related to the amnesia.'

'Likely not.' He brought the steaming cup, placing it on the table beside me. 'Let it steep.'

He sat in the armchair beside me. I couldn't stand to be this close to him and feel so distant. It reminded me of our time in Oxford, every moment thick with caution and uncertainty.

'You never really explained how oneiromancy works,' I said, to lift some of the tension. 'You're not walking in my dreamscape, so how do you experience the memories with me?'

'While I am using my gift, my dreamscape reflects yours. Think of it as a mirror, and your memories as light. Salvia is like a polish on the mirror. It clarifies the memories for me.'

'You can ... see dreamscapes?'

'Not quite. Only a facet of what they protect,' Arcturus said. 'Perhaps a different metaphor is in order.'

'Go on.'

'Let us say that time is one great composition. I know the notes of each moment, the chords of the hours. When I play them, your spirit answers the vibrations by seeking the corresponding memories, which are conveyed, in turn, to me.'

'Like an echo,' I said. 'The note you play, bounced off me. The moment through my eyes.'

'Yes. It is a complex gift, like yours. A sort of puppetry.'

In all our months of talking, I couldn't believe I had never asked him to describe his gift in detail. Jaxon could have written a whole pamphlet, but for all his eloquence, I doubted he would have explained it so beautifully.

'No wonder you love music.' I shifted in my seat. 'Cordier was dosing me for a while. How do you even start combing through it all?'

'I will start with the first memory that remains untouched by the aster, and move towards the present day.'

'I assume we won't live the memories in real time, or we'll be here for six months.'

'I will have control over how quickly they unfold. I can slow them if you wish to linger, but otherwise, I will hasten their passage.' He held out the cup. 'The salvia is ready, if you are.'

I took it from him, knowing it might show me something I didn't want to see. After a moment, I drained the cup, grimacing at the bitter taste.

Arcturus waited for me to get comfortable. As the drink warmed my chest, I closed my eyes, feeling his influence steal over me.

'If you wish for me to slow a memory, pull on the cord,' he said. 'Other than that, you know how it goes. All you need do is dream.'

---

Before, I had dreamed my way through the past without any awareness of him. Now I knew how his gift worked, I did feel his presence.

I sensed the music of the spheres, calling out to me.

Before, I had echoed him unconsciously. Now I moved with purpose. I found a white poppy, with a single red petal, and took hold of its root.

And then I was a passenger in my own past, carried along a river of memory, to the night the Devil had been hunting on the streets of Paris.

The shared dream began exactly where I had pointed him. The Grande Salle took shape around me, candlelight and stone and shadow. I was leaving the masquerade, filching a coat. *Don't go, you idiot*, I willed myself, filled with sick foreboding. *Don't go without Léandre and Ignace.* That version of me was crossing the threshold. *Don't leave alone …*

Snow underfoot. I was walking with Cade on the riverbank, and I was seeing his dark lips, his fatigue. Terrible instinct reared in me – instinct that was finally rising in the memory, too. Just as I understood what he was, something hit me hard, and I fell into darkness.

So I had put the pieces together. I had seen, but too late.

Cade had used his gift on me. For the first time, I had known what it was like to be overcome by a dreamwalker. A taste of the same pain and fear I had inflicted on others.

He must have dragged me into a vehicle. Next I knew, I was stirring in the basement of the Hôtel Garuche, and Kornephoros Sheratan was unlocking my chains.

A blur to another room. Benoît Ménard slammed me to the ground, demanding to know where his spouse was. Now I was stumbling into the freezing cold, running through the streets of Paris, fire raining down. This was the airstrike I had survived. I wished I could forget again as I glimpsed chunks of bone and flesh, bloody confetti on the snow.

This was why I had run, when I heard the siren here, in Venice. I had run because part of me still remembered.

*Tell us, Arcturus.* Suddenly the memory wasn't mine. I saw a shaking human, someone whose face I couldn't see. *Tell us, or he suffers. And your dreamwalker will suffer far worse…*

Stained glass broke into nameless stars. His memory was wrenched away in a flurry of bloodstained snow and ashes. The next time I had woken, I had been a living corpse, staring at the ruins of the Sainte-Chapelle. Cordier had found me incoherent there, deranged by grief. I had been certain Arcturus was buried under all that stone.

Then Cordier had gripped my head and silenced me with the white flower. And I had breathed in.

I had breathed in, though I could have fought harder.

I had breathed in because I had wanted oblivion, because nothingness had been kinder than truth. The truth that I had sparked a war I could no longer control. That I had cut a man's throat and felt nothing.

That Arcturus was gone.

That was the first dose. That moment was where the amnesia started. And on the walls of my dreamscape, the first hairline crack appeared in the pallor. The dust was lifting from the ground, like snow called back into the sky.

The next memory was important. I pulled the cord, and it slowed, the voices refining.

*Where is this?*

*You're safe, Paige.* A soft French accent. *We're just outside of Paris.*

*Cordier.* My eyes flickered open. *I thought you'd been captured.*

*I nearly was. They came for me, but I escaped. I had to lie low.* Those red lips pressed together. *I tried to protect your safe house, but they took your auxiliary.*

*It was him. He betrayed me.*

*I know. I'm sorry.* Cordier leaned closer. *Paige, I don't want to scare you, but there was an attack, an explosion. You were badly concussed in the blast – I suspect you have post-traumatic amnesia.* I blinked to clear my swimming mind, my welling eyes. *What's the last thing you remember?*

*The masquerade ...*

I was starting to shake, both inside and outside the memory.

*It's all right. That's where it happened,* Cordier said. *Can you remember a specific time?*

*Not sure. About half nine, I think.*

*You're going to feel confused, with some emotional lability. Sometimes it will seem like time is muddled, or you're under threat. You'll feel angry and afraid. You have to stay calm.* She had been clever to manipulate the facts that way. All the while, she had looked so genuine, so caring. *Scion is on our trail. I'm going to get you to the free world, where I can protect you.*

*No. I have to go back to Paris,* I heard myself say in a faint voice. *I can't leave them now. I can't.*

*It's all right, Paige. We'll go back as soon as the danger has passed,* she said. My coughs filled the darkness in the vehicle. *We've still got to clear up that pneumonia, haven't we?*

There was how she had convinced me – compassion, and the white flower. I had forgotten the realisation that Cade was a dreamwalker. It didn't help that I really had been injured from the blast.

In the present, I released the cord. The memories poured again, carrying me with them. I trusted Cordier as we slipped under a weak point in the Fluke, as I left the Republic of Scion for the first time in twelve years. I had trusted her when we reached the relative safety of Switzerland.

Then I had started asking questions.

*What's happening?*

*You're safe, Paige. It's all right.* Cordier was stroking my hair, like a mother. *What's the last thing you remember?*

*The masquerade …*

*Good.* She released a long breath. *Paige, I don't want to scare you, but there was an attack, an explosion. I suspect you have post-traumatic amnesia.*

And on it went. She had trapped me in a time loop, giving me white aster each time I grew suspicious, so I never realised how many days had slipped through my fingers.

It had been easy, because she had the knowledge to work out my doses and marry them to sedatives, disguised as drinks or treatment for the lingering pneumonia – and because my subconscious had wanted to forget. Arcturus was gone, and the more aster Cordier gave me, the deeper that knowledge lay buried. So I welcomed oblivion, over and over.

A sudden change. *The next time you refuse to answer a question, your pet dies.* Thuban Sargas, his one remaining eye ablaze. *You have one more night to decide. Tell us where Eliza Renton and Laurence Adomako are hiding. Tell us where Terebell has gathered the remaining Ranthen. Tell us where Paige Mahoney fled. Do you miss her, concubine?*

I should not be seeing this. It was private. I knew it in the present, but I couldn't stop his memories flowing into me. This had happened in Edinburgh, too. I tried to close my eyes to it, and it must have helped him stem the bleed, because now I was rushing forward again.

*You need to take her off my hands.*

259

Arcturus hit the brakes on the memory. A hotel room, the curtains shut. Cordier was on the phone on a balcony, while I feigned sleep, listening.

*You're not the only one who wants her,* she was saying. I could just hear her through the door. *I can't keep them off my back for much longer.*

I slid up the hem of my oversized shirt. On my upper thigh, in faded marker, was a smudged message.

WHITE ASTER

DON'T EAT DON'T DRINK

DON'T TRUST CORDIER

I had seen it in the bathroom earlier that day. A desperate warning, left by my past self, in the precious moments before she had succumbed to the amnesia. It might be my only chance to escape.

*You say you care about her. Show it.* Her voice was calm and cold. *The package and the money, or I'll let my employer take her, and once she's gone, there's no going back.*

When she hung up and came back inside, I waited until she was in bed, then threw out my spirit, making her shout in pain. I was too drained and weak to keep hold of her dreamscape. Instead, I dived on her and pinned her to the bed, my arm pressed across her throat.

*You've been lying,* I hissed. *Who are you, and who the hell were you talking to?*

*Paige, I told you that you'd feel unsafe.* Her nose was bleeding. *Listen to me. It's your brain injury—*

*Only one of us is going to have a brain injury in a minute, and it's not me. I have had it up to here with people telling me I'm safe.* I spoke between set teeth. *I am going back to Paris. Stop me and we'll have a problem, Eléonore.*

*Fine. Go on,* she forced out. *See how far you get.*

Except I had no idea where I was. I slammed out of the room, running through corridors and past endless identical doors, taking the elevator to the ground floor, like I had in Wrocław. Two streets away from the hotel, a pair of muscular arms locked around me.

*Stop right there,* a voyant said against my ear. I kicked and clawed, but my strength was gone. Somehow it had vanished overnight. *You have nowhere to go, Paige. We can find you anywhere.* I tried to possess him, and realised, with dread, that he was unreadable. He could resist the only weapon I had left. *Now, take a nice deep breath of this. I'll make it all go away.*

*Get your hands off me.* He clamped the cloth over my face, smothering my scream. *No—*

---

I gasped awake, soaked in cold sweat, thrashing against the stranger. The cloth was plastered over my nose and mouth, and I could smell the cloying sweetness of the white aster inside. For a horrific moment, I was blind and screaming on the waterboard again.

'Paige.'

The voice brought me back to the present. When I remembered where I was, I sat up, hair tumbling around my face. Arcturus had moved away, almost to the other side of the room.

'That wasn't the end,' I said. 'Why did you stop?'

His palm was braced against the wall. It was so unlike him to look this weary. Before I could think better of it, I stood up shakily and stepped towards him.

'Stay back, Paige.'

I flinched to a stop. He spoke as softly as ever, but the order was firm.

*Get back, Paige, for pity's sake.* A different voice drifted from my past. *Why do you never give me room?*

'Okay,' I said, breaking a painful silence. Arcturus looked away. 'You pushed yourself too hard.'

'No.'

'You lie to me now, do you?'

He winched his gaze back to mine.

'You have been dreaming for hours,' he said. 'If we do not stop, you may begin to lose your ability to distinguish your past from your present.' He removed his hand from the wall. 'And I saw no need for you to relive someone touching you that way.'

He was still trying to protect me, even from the past.

'Sit down, at least,' I said.

It took him a fair while to move. He returned to the armchair and clasped his hands between his knees. I should never have approached him suddenly like that, knowing my own fear of touch after my torture.

I went to the window seat. It was too dark to see the water, but I could hear it. After the sea, it should have been nothing.

'We've learned some things about the night of the airstrikes,' I said, recovering my composure. 'Cade knocked me out with his spirit and took me to the Hôtel Garuche. He presumably freed Kornephoros, who then – for some reason – freed me. Why would he do that?'

'In Carcassonne, Kornephoros was tasked with forcing information from me,' Arcturus said, his face wooden. 'During one interrogation, he alluded to a favour he had done me, at significant risk to himself, to atone for his betrayal during the civil war. If he had not, Fitzours would have given you to Nashira.'

I thought all of this over.

'Cade must have captured me to prove his loyalty to Nashira,' I said. 'He meant to bring me *and* Frère to her. It would have shown his willingness to turn on his own kind.'

'Yes. He knew the fate Nashira had planned for the first dream-walker she met,' Arcturus said. 'To continue to lower his risk of being executed, he sought to offer her a worthy substitute.'

'Kornephoros threw a spanner in the works, then. Cade must be on thin ice now,' I said. 'He's at the helm of Operation Ventriloquist, flaunting a gift he knows Nashira wants. It's like putting your head in a noose and expecting it not to tighten at some point.'

Cade was turning into even more of a riddle than Jaxon, and that was saying something.

'So Kornephoros let me go,' I said, 'just as the airstrikes hit Paris.' If I kept talking, the awful silence couldn't return. 'I was close to the Sainte-Chapelle when it exploded, which knocked me out, and Cordier found me by the rubble.'

'I sensed you both,' Arcturus said. 'By then, I was inside the crypt. I believed Cordier had saved you.'

'She'd already put a tracking unit in me. And faked her own arrest to throw Ducos off the scent.'

'We can assume that she was the one who betrayed the safe house,' he said. I nodded. 'She waited for an opportunity to separate you from your bodyguard, then contacted Scion, ensuring I would not interfere with her plan. From her conversation, she was ordered to bring you to an unknown employer, but entered a negotiation with a third party.'

'Right. She was trying to exchange me for … a package. The other party is someone who claims to care about me, so I probably know them.'

*You're not the only one who wants her.* I went over those words again. *I can't keep them off my back for much longer.*

'Domino has a theory that Cordier was secretly working for an espionage network called the Atlantic Intelligence Bureau,' I said. 'A group of strangers tried to intercept me after I woke up. Chances are they're either the employer or the third party.'

'But you escaped.'

'I stabbed Cordier, but she'd already dosed me. When I came round, she wasn't there to tell me lies. She must have gone for help. I gave the suits the slip and found Maria.'

'And then you came here.'

'Yes. We've agreed I'll keep working for Domino until January.'

'It seems you are in more danger than ever. And that we underestimated Eléonore Cordier.'

'You warned me.' I gazed out of the window. 'When we played chess in Paris, you told me that I only had eyes for the king and queen. That I shouldn't overlook the other pieces.'

'I overlooked her, too.'

'Does that make us the pawns?'

'It means we made a sacrifice. In return, we gained intelligence we did not have before.'

'At what cost?'

He didn't answer.

'All the people who wanted me are still out there,' I said. 'So are Cade and Nashira.' My breath misted the window. 'I feel like all of this is suddenly spinning out of our control.'

'It was inevitable,' Arcturus said. 'You are right. We should reveal ourselves, before we are revealed.'

It was starting to rain, on top of the flooding. I turned away from the window.

'While I was gone,' I said, 'did you ever try the golden cord?'

'No,' he said. 'I hoped you would believe me gone, so you would not come looking for me.'

That explained why I had never felt the cord while I was with Cordier. It didn't explain why he was blocking it now. I risked a glance at him, meeting his eyes, trying to find the courage to ask.

*Just talk.* I wrestled with myself. *Tell him you're sorry, he's safe, you're here.*

'We should get some rest,' I said. 'No doubt you think I can't see how tired you are, but I didn't come down in the last shower, you know.'

'Hm.'

That sound warmed me to the core. I had missed it.

Arcturus started to get up, moving as if he was bearing the weight of the world on his shoulders.

'We must do this again,' he said. 'There are memories still buried.'

'I don't want you to push yourself too hard.'

'You overcame your limits to swim to me in that cave, in the dark. Let me do this for you, Paige.'

After a moment, I nodded, defeated. I couldn't refuse him.

Not when he said my name that way.

---

Arcturus went to bed after that, while I stayed in the parlour. His influence had cut through the white aster like a cloth through dust. I went into my dreamscape to see if it had changed. Clearing the remaining aster would take at least one more dream, but even after torture and severance from the æther, Arcturus had full control of his gift, mastered over centuries.

My flowers were growing over the floorboards. Some of them still had creamy petals, but others had flushed back to crimson, and now that there was less ash, a purer light shone on the bed. I wondered if the field would return, or if this was my haven now – this skeletal remnant of Paris, for ever mingled with the poppies of Arthyen.

I wondered if Arcturus feared me now, as he must have feared Cade, the architect behind his suffering.

At midnight, I returned to the couch and slept, deeper than I had in weeks. When I woke at four in the morning, a duvet had been tucked around me, keeping me warm. As I gathered it close, I tried to summon the memories Arcturus had brought to the surface. They had flown past so quickly, I would have to pinpoint each one and sift it for detail.

When I remembered, I sat up, heart pounding. The realisation hit me as hard as it had the first time.

*There is one way that you might see proof that I am on your side. Something that would betray me, if anyone but you could see.*

It had taken me so long to solve that puzzle. The red drapes in his dreamscape had been the answer all along. The safe place in his mind looked exactly like the trap room in the Guildhall, where he had kissed me like I had never been kissed, never dreamed of being kissed.

How many times had he told me the truth, even if he never said the words?

No amount of artifice could make a dreamscape lie. The place where I had first embraced him was the place he felt safest – so safe it had reshaped his inner sanctuary, gathering it wholly around that memory of us. Only a formative experience could do that. I didn't understand it – I couldn't believe it could mean what it did – but it had still been like that when I pulled him from the brink.

Did that mean he forgave me, or just that he had nowhere else to feel safe any more?

I had to ask him. He had experienced the memory with me; he knew as well as I did that I had worked it out that night. He knew that I had run across a burning citadel to find him.

I found a door ajar upstairs. Arcturus was asleep, lying the way he had in the wine cellar. I stopped, knowing I couldn't wake him. Not when he had overstretched himself for my sake.

Standing on the threshold, feeling more powerless than I ever had, I recalled an Irish word: *beochaoineadh*, a lament for the living. To weep for someone not yet dead, but out of reach, and missed.

# 18

## A WAKING DREAM

Terebell returned in the morning, confirming that she and Arcturus would speak to Command. By that time, the high water had come and gone. I walked through glistening streets and puddles, over the swollen canals, back to the Palazzo del Domino.

All the way, I couldn't stop thinking about Arcturus, or the fact that he had covered me with a duvet in the night. He cared enough to have made sure I didn't get cold as I slept.

He had looked after me for so long. It was my turn to be the strong one, and to stand behind him for as long as he needed. In Paris, he had let me open the door to my dark room in my own time. I would afford him the same patience. I would not fail our friendship again.

The walk should have drained me, but one dream had already lifted some of my fatigue, as if the aster had been a physical weight. I took a quick shower and chose an outfit, intending to find Ducos and give her the good news. I was drying my hair when I sensed Maria.

'Paige Mahoney,' she said when I opened the door. 'We had dinner plans. Did you stand me up?'

'Sorry,' I said. 'I went to see Arcturus.'

'Well done. How did it go?'

'He undid some of the amnesia. Other than that, I'm not sure yet.'

Maria chuckled. 'All right. Keep your secrets.'

'You're always going to be like this now, aren't you?'

'Possibly. Any word on your next assignment?'

'I've asked if I can go to Rome. I'm just waiting for confirmation.'

'I'll come with you, if they'll let me. If I have to sit around and wait for the arm to heal, I may as well do it where I can be useful.'

'I'd like that, if you're up to it. Are you?'

'At this point, I'm up for anything that doesn't involve resting. Verča and I are having a late breakfast, if you're hungry,' she said. 'We'll be in the bar at eleven. I'll ask Nick along.'

'I thought Verča went to Trieste?'

'She's back. It isn't far.'

'Okay.'

She set off down the corridor, cradling her sling. I shut the door and finished drying my hair.

Ducos lived on the second floor of the Palazzo del Giorno. I homed in on her dreamscape and found myself faced with an oak door. When I knocked, she opened it in moments.

'I was about to come looking for you,' she said. 'I never told you where my room was.'

'It's the mind radar.' I tapped my temple. 'Terebell and Warden have agreed to speak to you. I've told them to be here at dusk.'

'That was quick.'

'I know. I'm a brilliant agent,' I said. Ducos pursed her lips. 'No, I'm just as surprised, to be honest. I don't know how much they'll be willing to say, but they're coming.'

'We appreciate your intermediation. Is there anything we should know in advance?'

'Terebellum Sheratan is the leader of the Ranthen. She's prickly, and protective of her dignity,' I said. 'I'd advise you to treat her with the utmost respect. Maybe a tiny dash of deference. Oh, and she likes wine.' Ducos nodded. 'You already know Warden, but he was tortured after Scion captured him in Paris. It's … caused some lasting harm.'

'I'm sorry to hear that.'

'I want to confirm that he'll be safe here. He can't defend himself, Ducos.'

'I will take every reasonable precaution.'

'Okay. I was thinking of giving them both a phone,' I added. 'Any chance you could get me two burners?'

'I might be able to manage that,' she said. 'Pivot has approved you for a fact-finding assignment there. Your objective is to locate President Sala and Cadoc Fitzours, preferably in that order. It's unlikely that Sala is there, but you're aiming to pick up a trail, since the Palazzo del Quirinale was her last confirmed location. Knowing your heightened senses, you might have better luck than the people we've already sent to look for her.'

'How do I get there?'

'I'll drive you tomorrow. You'll receive a dossier with everything we have on President Sala, along with any other information Pivot deems useful. It might give you somewhere to start.' She crossed her arms. 'You must seek approval from Command before you move against the dreamwalker, or approach Sala. We believe her to be loyal, but given the nature of Operation Ventriloquist, we can't be sure. For now, this assignment is investigative only. I need you to confirm that you understand this, Flora. There is no room for you to go rogue this time.'

'I understand.' I turned to leave, then stopped. 'Does Venice have any bookshops you'd recommend?'

Ducos eyed me.

'Several,' she said. 'My favourite is near the Ponte Cavagnis.' She went back into her room and returned with a wallet, taking out a few Italian notes. 'An advance on your payment for the mission on Capri. You deserve compensation for interceding with the Ranthen.'

'Thank you.'

I pocketed the money as I crossed the alley. The others were in the firelit bar, all with breakfast in front of them. Maria waved me over with her good hand.

'Good morning.' Verča wore a belted skirt and a ribbed cream jersey. 'How is Warden?'

'As well as can be expected. Thanks for asking.' I took the seat beside her. 'Did you persuade your family to leave?'

'Yes. They're going to stay with my parents in Prague until December. Hopefully we will have stopped Operation Ventriloquist by then.'

'On that note, Command has agreed to my next assignment,' I said. 'I'm going to Rome, to see if I have better luck finding Cade and Sala.'

'Maria told us you'd applied for this,' Nick said. 'Do you have a plan?'

'I'd usually search the æther when I arrive, but if I can sense Cade, he can sense me,' I said. 'I'll have to switch off my sixth sense with alysoplasm and take any backdoor route I can. Someone in Rome must know where Sala is.'

'We know how to find people. We did it in London.'

'We're not in London,' Maria pointed out.

'I tracked down the Parisian syndicate in a day,' I said.

'I love the confidence, but this isn't Scion, sweet. You're going to need local help again.'

'Which is why I'd like to come with you,' Verča said. 'I know Rome. If you don't mind me joining another assignment, I will request permission from Pivot.'

'It's kind of you to offer,' I said, 'but does Radomír not want you back?'

'Operation Ventriloquist is more important than my usual work. I am many things the anchor hates: voyant, religious, a recruiter for an enemy network. It would mean a great deal to me to be able to help the Mime Order and defend Italy. Besides, I always hoped I could work against Scion on the ground.'

'You'd be a lot of help. Cade doesn't know you, so you can fly under his radar. And you speak Italian.'

'Maria and I would like to come, too,' Nick said. 'Now Harald is dead, I'm free to leave. Naples proved we can work as a team. Domino will let us do it again.'

After a moment, I nodded. If I meant to survive Cade, I would need backup.

'Assuming our requests are approved, we don't have long in Venice,' Verča said lightly. 'We should enjoy our last night here.' She topped up her coffee with milk. 'I've heard of a cocktail bar owned by voyants, the Apotèca dei Spiriti. Shall we try it after dinner?'

'I need to stay here tonight, but you go,' I said.

'I'll never refuse a good cocktail.' Maria nudged Nick. 'Can we convince you to join us, old man?'

'If I'm not mistaken,' Nick said, not looking up from his newspaper, 'you're eight years my senior.'

'Yes, but let's face it, I'm younger at heart. You're wearing a fleece.'

'Nothing wrong with a good warm fleece.' He turned a page. 'Since my patient is going, I'd better make sure she doesn't drink herself into oblivion. Unless you want company, Paige?'

'No. You have fun.' I reached for a slice of bread. 'I'll do some training while I wait.'

'In possession?' he said. 'Won't you need someone with you?'

'You know full well that none of you want to be target practice.'

I didn't mention that only Arcturus was strong enough to withstand my attacks, and that wasn't even a guarantee now. I couldn't risk inflicting any further pain.

In any case, I wasn't trying to possess Cade.

I was trying to kill him.

---

I had failed to kill people I should have before, namely Jaxon Hall. Much as I despised the man, I had a tie to him that I had failed to cut. Cade was a different kind of enemy. I owed him nothing. He wasn't even a friend. Just an acquaintance from the worst year of my life.

This time, I had to commit to my line of fire. Getting rid of Cade was the only way to stop him forcing the free world to its knees. No prison would hold a dreamwalker for long.

He had to die.

In my room, I warmed up my gift, easing back into dislocation. I pushed my spirit as far as I could without leaving my body, fighting a tight band of pain above my eyes.

So many other voyants had their gifts down to a fine art. Liss and Jaxon were two examples. All of us paid a toll for our abilities,

270

but mine seemed to resist me with such fury on some days. Cordier must not have let me practise during the months I had been with her.

At one, I headed back to the streets. I soon found the bookshop Ducos had recommended. Thick novels were piled into bathtubs and boats, protecting them from the high tides.

Arcturus loved to read. I could offer him that small comfort, if nothing else. Most of the books were in Italian, which was not one of his six human languages, but after some rummaging, I found an old French novel, *La Belle et la Bête*. From the cover and surreal illustrations, which showed a woman and a monster, it should have been destroyed in the biblioclasms.

A book that had escaped from France to Venice, like us. I paid and tucked it into my jacket.

Venice had been a tonic. Even with the water, I wished I could stay longer. I spent an hour sourcing a few supplies from its shops, including a windproof lighter and a rusty set of lockpicks.

In my room, I packed my clothes, then took out the last of the blue aster. I would use the rest of today to get some rest. I stuck on a patch and crawled into bed, drowsing until a knock came at the door. When I opened it, I found a package outside, containing two phones.

My own phone had gone off while I slept. The message was from Nick.

We've been approved to leave for Rome in a few days. All three of us will be there to help you.

Thank you, I wrote back. Chances are I'm going to need it.

---

Terebell and Arcturus arrived at dusk, as planned. By then, there was only one window illuminated in the Palazzo del Giorno, and I sensed that it was almost empty.

'Thanks for coming.' I showed them to the entrance. 'Did anyone follow you?'

'No.' Terebell wore a wide-brimmed hat. 'What have you already told these humans about us?'

'Most of what I know, apart from how to hurt you.'

'You are acting with a degree of prudence. An encouraging development, Underqueen.'

She removed her hat and smoothed her hair. Arcturus walked in silence at her side. Usually he would have been taking everything in, intrigued by the architecture or the paintings on the walls, but his gaze was flat and detached, as if he had no interest in his surroundings.

I stayed ahead of the Rephs, leading them to the Blue Room. Ducos had cleared the corridors, as promised. She waited for us with Pivot and Spinner. When I brought the two Ranthen into the room, Spinner gaped at them, his hand tightening on his glass of water.

Pivot, at least, maintained her composure.

'Flora,' she said. 'These must be your allies.'

'Yes,' I said. 'This is Terebellum, rightful Warden of the Sheratan, sovereign-elect of the Ranthen, and this is Arcturus, rightful Warden of the Mesarthim. Terebell and I share command of the Mime Order.'

'Welcome, both of you. I am Pivot, and this is Spinner. I hope you'll understand that we can't reveal our real names, for security reasons.'

Terebell inclined her head. Technically, Domino had no idea of her real name, either.

'We oversee the Domino Programme, an espionage network that aims to undermine the Republic of Scion.' Pivot motioned to two chairs. 'May I offer you refreshment?'

'Wine,' Terebell said.

'Red or white?'

'Red.'

Ducos went to get it. Terebell sat in one of the chairs, Arcturus following suit.

'You'll have to forgive our ignorance of your customs,' Pivot said. 'How do you prefer to be addressed?'

'Warden,' Terebell said. 'You may address us both by this title.'

'And you represent the faction known as the Ranthen.'

'I am its leader.'

'Then your visit is even more of an honour. We appreciate you agreeing to speak with us,' Pivot said. 'Our organisation calls your species *Advena sapiens*, but I understand the English named you Rephaim – a reference to the ancient giants, I presume. Now I see why.'

Terebell sat with impeccable posture, as always.

'*Advena sapiens*,' she said. 'What is the meaning of this binomen?'

'*Wise stranger*, or *wise newcomer*. We did think of classifying you as members of the *Homo* genus, given your resemblance to humans, but eventually chose to acknowledge your sentience instead.' Pivot looked at Arcturus. 'I understand you were the one who was held prisoner on Capri, and that you provided us with valuable intelligence. Thank you for your service.'

'Yes,' Spinner said, after not breathing for a solid few seconds. 'We have a great deal to discuss. That will be all for this evening, Agent Blake.'

I hesitated. My gut told me not to leave the Rephs, but I couldn't say it without implying that two capable warriors needed my protection. Terebell would not take that kindly.

'I'll be outside,' I said.

'We may be some time,' Pivot said.

'That's fine. I'll wait.'

Ducos touched my shoulder as I left, as if to reassure me. I heard the door lock in my wake.

The Palazzo del Giorno remained silent, as promised. For a while, I paced alongside the Gothic windows at the end of the corridor, too restless to sit.

Arranging this meeting could yet come back to bite me, but deciding whether or not to expose the greatest secret in history was probably above my paygrade. The Ranthen should be able to choose their own future, preferably with people who knew what they were doing – as opposed to me, a glorified thief with a track record of dangerous risks. I killed time by replying to messages from Maria, who was clearly getting drunk out of her skull.

It was nearly an hour before Ducos emerged. Seeing me, she escorted the Rephs back to my side.

'That was an invaluable discussion. Thank you again for attending,' she said to them. 'Command is made up of twelve individuals. Pivot and I would like to consult our colleagues, who may have additional questions. Is there any possibility you could be here on Sunday?'

'I must leave,' Terebell said, 'but Arcturus will remain in Venice for the time being.'

'I am willing,' Arcturus said.

'Thank you. You're welcome to stay here,' Ducos said. 'You would have to keep to a room for your own safety, but the concierge will provide you with anything you need.'

Arcturus glanced at me. I said nothing, unsure of what Ducos was doing.

'Very well,' he said.

'Good. I'll take you,' Ducos said. 'Flora, could you show the Warden out?'

When I nodded, she led Arcturus away, leaving me alone with Terebell.

'You say you have to leave,' I said to her. 'Are you going back to London right now?'

'Pleione sent a psychopomp,' she said. 'Apparently an urgent situation has arisen, and my presence is required. I will leave tonight for the cold spot in the Apennines.'

'You've no idea what this situation is?'

'No.' She started to walk. 'Arcturus is too weak to travel. I will return for him once Fitzours is gone. In the meantime, I expect you to ensure his safety, Underqueen. Do not lose him again.'

An urgent situation didn't sound good, but I pushed it out of my mind. I had to focus on the task at hand.

'I'm leaving for Rome tomorrow,' I said, 'but I'll check on him as much as I can. Ducos will keep an eye on him.' I managed to keep pace with Terebell. 'How was the meeting?'

'They asked many questions about our history and the reasons we came to Earth. They also asked about the Emim.' She looked straight ahead. 'I did not reveal our vulnerabilities. We cannot trust unfamiliar humans with knowledge that could be used against us.'

'Does that mean you trust me?'

'By necessity, not choice, Underqueen.'

'Thanks,' I said. 'I appreciate it.'

I opened the door to the alley. Before Terebell could leave, I took one of the phones from my pocket.

'This is for you.' I offered it to her. 'It will stop working in Scion, but I'd like you to call me as soon as you're back in Italy. I want to know what's happening with the Mime Order.'

'I cannot take that into the Netherworld.'

'Leave it near the cold spot, then. Hide it and pick it up on your way back.' I held it out. 'Look, with all due respect, you're the one who said you didn't want me doing séances. I put my number in there.'

Terebell accepted the phone. Giving it a look of distaste, she stowed it in her coat.

'I will tell your high commanders and the interim Underqueen of your survival. Use your time in Rome wisely,' she said. 'Fitzours poses as much of a threat as Senshield, if not more. Rid us of this enemy, Paige. Do this, and the Mime Order will survive to fight another day.'

Terebell vanished into the darkness. I wandered back inside, shivering at the chill of the night.

I debated leaving Arcturus to rest after the meeting, but the golden cord told me he was awake, and I might not have another chance to speak to him before I left. I didn't want to leave him here, miles away from me, but I had to protect him from Cade. He would be safer in Venice.

I collected the old novel from my room before I knocked for him. When he answered the door, he leaned against the frame at once.

'Good evening, Paige.'

'Sorry to disturb you,' I said. 'I wanted to make sure you were comfortable.'

'Yes. I did not expect Ducos to invite me to stay.'

'I suppose she has her reasons.' I shifted my weight. 'How did the meeting go?'

'Well enough. I trust our knowledge was of use to Domino.'

'I'm sure it was.'

This conversation was giving me whiplash. It seemed impossible that we could go from the complete trust and intimacy we had shared in Paris to this stiff excuse for an exchange.

Arcturus watched me, clearly waiting for me to continue. I took a moment to compose myself.

'I found this in a bookshop,' I said. 'I can take it back if it's not your sort of thing, but—' I held out the novel, clearing my throat. 'Well, I thought you might like something to read.'

He took it and surveyed the cover.

'Thank you,' he said. 'I know *La Belle et la Bête*, but I have never read the original. I feared they were all lost.' His gaze returned to mine, making my skin prickle. 'Terebell tells me you are going to Rome. She has ordered me to remain in the free world until you defeat Fitzours. If Scion were to detect me, it would alert them to a security risk and foil your plan.'

'I agree,' I said. 'Operation Ventriloquist has to be stopped before we chance you being seen.'

'You could not kill Jaxon. Can you kill Fitzours?'

'Different man, different situation. Anyway, I killed the Rag and Bone Man well enough.'

'You identified him after my arrest.'

'Yes. It was Alfred Rackham, a friend of Jaxon – the man who helped him publish *On the Merits of Unnaturalness*. He's also the one who edited *The Rephaite Revelation* behind my back, and I never once suspected the bastard.' I ground my jaw. 'Jaxon butchered him. I finished him off.'

'A mercy kill.'

'Not mercy. I could have used my spirit, but I didn't want to give him that dignity, after what he'd done. I used a sickle. He reaped us; I reaped him. He did like his poetic justice.'

His eyes darkened, tightening my stomach. I had let him down. He had chosen me for my compassion, and it turned out I was just as bloodthirsty as Jaxon.

'I see,' he said. 'When do you mean to return to Scion?'

'After my work for Domino ends. They're our best chance of getting over the Fluke, and the Alpine crossing would take us straight to France,' I said, 'so I can speak to our allies there before I go to London.' I paused. 'You could … join me, if you want. Le Vieux Orphelin needs to know where Frère is being held.'

'Lucida has taken that knowledge to him.' He studied my face. 'Terebell wants me to return to London as soon as you have defeated Fitzours, so I can assist with training new recruits to the Mime Order. I understand you will have to stay in the free world for a time.'

I nodded once. It had been naïve of me to think we could make the crossing together.

'Well,' I said, 'for now, you're safest in Venice. Are you going to be able to feed?'

'Yes. The others told me there are voyants enough in this city.'

The Ranthen were tight-lipped about how they fed, but I suspected they struck from the shadows, leaving the voyant with no idea what had happened. I only hoped Arcturus was strong enough.

'If we are to be separated again,' he went on, 'I ought to finish recovering your memories tonight. I am willing if you are.'

'I'm not sure I want to know any more.' I glanced away. 'It's hard to see myself in that state.'

'You must not let the fatigue linger.' His voice was soft. 'Our memories are stored in the ground of our dreamscapes. They are the bedrock of your being. Leaving the white aster where it is will suffocate your flowers' roots.'

'That might not be a bad thing,' I said. 'There are plenty of memories I wish I could erase.'

'That is beyond even my power. A memory can only ever be buried, killing the flower that grew from it.'

'Why would that matter?' I asked stiffly. 'What sort of flowers could grow from suffering?'

'Even if they die, those memories will always remain. Your spirit will feel a disturbance in the ground, but you will not understand why,' he told me. 'As an oneiromancer, I would counsel you to bring them into the light, where you can see them, even if they produce spectres. You deserve to live with your whole self in your keeping, Paige.'

I didn't deserve the unbearable gentleness in his voice, or the way he was looking at me.

I still couldn't bring myself to refuse him.

His room was similar to mine, with tawny bedding and a high ceiling. I locked the door while he approached the armchair. Finding nowhere else, I sat on the end of his bed.

'I have no more salvia. You may not see a great deal as you dream, but the memories will be clear when you wake,' Arcturus said. 'You will also be free of the aster fatigue.'

'Just the usual fatigue to deal with, then.' I took a deep breath. 'Okay. Let's get this done.'

He moved his chair towards me. It felt too intimate to lie on his bed, but there was nowhere else.

Without the salvia, I didn't quite sleep. The dream was more of a hallucination, like something I would see in the grip of a fever. He coaxed my buried poppies from under the floorboards and snow. The memories passed in a blur, the sounds muffled. I was locked in a room, screaming to be let out. I saw myself almost escape; saw myself succeed four times, unaware of the tracker under my skin, only to be hunted down by the cold-blooded unreadable.

Arcturus stayed at my side, refining the work he had done in the apartment. When it was done, I opened my eyes, blinking away the past. Nothing I had remembered was especially useful.

Other than a name.

'The Lepidopterist,' I murmured. 'That's what Cordier called the person who was trying to buy me.'

'That term refers to an individual who studies butterflies and moths.' Arcturus paused. 'Or collects them.'

A shiver trailed down my back.

'Thank you for doing this.' I sat up. 'I'll leave you to rest.'

'A waking dream can be disorienting.' He started to rise. 'I will escort you to your room.'

'It's all right,' I said quickly. 'My room isn't far. You really shouldn't be seen.'

'A wise thought.'

He sank back into his chair, his hand tight on its arm. I wet my lips.

'You seem like you're finding it hard to move,' I said. 'Are you in pain?'

Arcturus looked at his own gloved hand.

'In the coffin,' he said, 'my ectoplasm vitrified. Your intervention changed that, but it seems to recall its previous state. When I will my body to move, it obeys, but slower than its wont. I suspect it may take some time for my blood to flow with the ease it once did, if it ever does.'

When he drew his hand into a fist, his knuckles made a slight crackle, like the crunch of broken glass.

'Verča told me pink aster can strengthen the connection between the body and the spirit,' I said, relieved to have remembered something useful. 'Do you think that might help?'

'Perhaps.'

'Okay. I'll ask Nick if he can get you some,' I said. 'He's not joining me in Rome for a few days.' I could offer him quick fixes, if nothing else. 'I don't know if I'll see you before we're back in Scion.'

'You do not have to return there,' Arcturus said. 'I would choose no one else as Underqueen, but I know you found it difficult.' I looked away. 'Nashira gave you no choice but to enter this conflict. I believe I convinced her that you died in Paris, even if she took the precaution of keeping a price on your head in the free world. You could walk away from Scion, knowing the revolution will continue in your wake.'

'Maria already said this to me. I'm not hiding,' I said. 'I chose this path before I ever met Nashira Sargas. I chose it when Scion murdered my cousin and conquered my country. Besides, they need me in London.'

'Then I will await you there.'

A new flower bloomed. It was a flower of false hope, and I had to let it die, for both our sakes. Saying he would wait for me was not the same – not at all – as saying he still wanted me.

'I'll get you the aster,' I said. 'Is there anything more I can do?'

His gaze found mine once more. I tried not to shiver at the intensity of that look. At the same time, he tightened his grip on the cord, denying me any insight.

'No,' he said. 'You have done enough, Paige.'

I flinched inside.

'Yes,' I said quietly. 'I suppose I have.' I fished the other phone out of my pocket. 'I got this for you. All our numbers are in there. Nick will teach you how to use it.'

Arcturus took it.

'Thank you,' he said. 'This is goodbye, then. For now.'

I might not see him again for weeks or months. This was really happening, and it was the last chance to break this tension, to leave on good terms.

'Please call me if you're in trouble,' was all I could say. 'I understand why you don't want to use the cord, but … I'm here if you ever need me.'

'In turn, I am always at your command.' Arcturus held my gaze. 'Be safe, little dreamer.'

I managed a nod. Not trusting myself to speak again, I left.

———

I could sense the others at the cocktail bar, just across the Grand Canal, but I wouldn't be able to conceal how shoddy I felt. Instead, I crossed the alley to the Palazzo della Notte, my eyes prickling.

Arcturus hadn't denied that he was obstructing the cord. He had no wish to let me back in. That part of our lives was behind us. I understood. He had gone out of his way to atone for Oxford, to earn my trust, and I had still failed to believe in him. There was no point in pretending we had any chance of recovering from that.

He wouldn't say it outright. No matter how he felt about Paris, he would never want to burden or hurt me. Instead, he was trying to let me down gently, tell me in as many careful words that it was over. It was the bodyguard in him.

I knew why he had mentioned what I wanted to do next. He had chosen me to lead the Ranthen revolution, but he had never banked on caring for me, or having to watch me go through so much. Perhaps it would ease his conscience, to know I had taken my leave of it all. Or perhaps it would be a mercy for him if he never had to see me again, knowing I was just like Cade.

In my room, I locked the door and curled up in the dark, wondering if it would help to drink the minibar dry. I dried my face with my sleeve and tried to pull myself together, but every part of me was hurting.

Arcturus had seen all my faults, all my fears, and still wanted me. Liss had shown me the Lovers card; I had known it was all real. And in a single moment of doubt, I had let him slip away.

As I lay there, wondering if I would ever be able to get up again, my thoughts drifted to Cade. Planning how I would destroy him was the only way to quell the pain of losing Arcturus.

Cade had known me as a prisoner and insurgent, not the hardened criminal I had been in London. Even if Jaxon had never quite succeeded in wringing the morals from me, he had taught me how to be ruthless. In more than three years of working for him, I had been the weapon he used to ensure respect and control. I could take those lessons and turn them on Cade.

The others came back at one in the morning. Just after that, my phone went off.

Noemi will meet you in the foyer at 19:00, Ducos had written. A fresh dissimulator will be delivered in advance. Put it on before you leave your room. Wear a new outfit and cover your hair.

Even though I was drowsy, I reached for the æther. Ducos was still with Pivot. Before I could wonder what they were doing, or where Spinner had gone, I fell asleep.

———

I woke at seven on the dot. For the first time since Paris, I felt as if I had slept well.

In the bathroom, I checked the mirror. My dark circles had faded, and the deathly pallor was gone. At last, I had my whole self in my keeping. Or as much of myself as was left after Paris.

I took a last brisk walk around Venice, listening to its bells ring out. I would have run the slates right then, had I not been so bruised and sore from Capri. Instead, I crossed the Rialto Bridge and spent a while exploring the districts on the other side of the Grand Canal.

Verča was in the foyer when I got back, waiting for Noemi. 'I need to make a flying visit to Prague before I join you in Rome,' she explained. 'To speak to Radomír.'

'All right,' I said. 'See you soon, then?'

'Absolutely.'

By five, I was getting ready to leave. I read the message from Ducos, this time with a clear head. The instructions were odd, but I did as she ordered. I changed into an outfit I hadn't worn before, hid my hair in a woollen hat, and put on the dissimulator that had been delivered.

All the while, I tuned out the æther. It would only remind me that Arcturus was here, and soon I would be hundreds of miles away from him. All that mattered was that he was safe.

Nick was in the medical room, his fingers clasped against his lips. I put my head around the door.

'I'm off,' I said.

'Okay.' He stood. 'Be careful, Paige. If you catch wind of Sala or Fitzours, don't do anything until we get there. I'll keep an eye on Warden until I leave.'

'On that subject, can you do me a favour?'

'Of course.'

'He needs pink aster,' I said. His eyebrows snapped up, and I remembered its other use, my face warming. 'Not for *that*, you great plank. Verča says it strengthens the connection between the body and the spirit. That's why it *can* be used as an aphrodisiac, but it could help Arcturus feel more settled if he takes it in small doses. It's worth a shot.'

'I'll do my best, sötnos.'

'Thank you.' I hitched up my bag. 'See you soon.'

'Very soon.'

I met Noemi in the foyer. As her taxi forged towards the outskirts, my attention drifted to the æther. Arcturus was not where he should be. After a moment, I took out my phone, hoping he wasn't as opposed to human technology as the other Ranthen.

It's Flora. Are you all right?

His reply came quickly: Yes.

I need to be sure this is you. Tell me something only you would know.

The next message took longer. As I waited, I combed the æther, realising I was getting closer to him.

Your favourite plant is wild oat. I read it twice. You once asked me to sow it on your grave.

After a moment, I put my phone away. I had no idea why he would have left the Palazzo del Domino, but it would have to do.

It was dark by the time Noemi moored the taxi. She directed me to the meeting place, where Ducos waited in a black car. I opened the door to find Arcturus in the back seat.

'Get in, Flora,' Ducos said. 'I'll explain everything once we're clear of the city.' I climbed in beside her. 'Even our most protected haven is no longer safe.'

# 19

## CUCKOO

Ducos drove without speaking. I exchanged a glance with Arcturus, who was wrapped up in a heavy coat and gloves. 'Okay,' I said. 'We're out of Venice. Care to explain what's going on?'

'When Pivot first learned that Grapevine had turned one of our agents, she started to monitor all communications from headquarters. Even mine,' Ducos said. 'In the early hours of this morning, she called me to see her. Spinner had sent a message to persons unknown.'

She passed me her own phone, which showed me a screenshot.

### EXTRACT 2 – PRIORITY ULTRA – 23:00

'He wants to extract two people at eleven.' I looked at her. 'Is that what it means?'

'So it would appear.' She took the phone back. 'I suspect the targets are you and Warden.'

'Are you saying Spinner is an infiltrator?'

'I have my suspicions.' She changed lanes. 'The night you arrived, I had dinner with a woman named Rocío. She used to

284

be a member of Mannequin, but now works for Spinner. Over the last few weeks, she had observed a change in his demeanour. He was becoming short-tempered and cagey, which she found worrying, in light of recent events. At first, I didn't think anything of it. But the moment I saw that message, I had a gut feeling.'

'If Grapevine has a spy in Command, Domino is done. You're not coming back from that.'

'It may not be Grapevine.'

'Who, then?'

'Last night more than convinced Spinner that everything you told us is true,' Ducos said. 'He insisted our benefactors should know about *Advena sapiens* as soon as possible, arguing that we had an overriding moral duty to inform all countries opposed to Scion. Pivot and I were against this. We reminded him that we only serve the countries that fund our network; any decisions on disseminating the information farther would have to come from them. Spinner relented. Now I wonder if another party has been greasing his palm.'

'You think he's already told someone about the Rephs?'

'I think he's told Tinman.'

'Why?'

'I told you how they earned that name. Tinman is known for underhanded tactics and extreme self-interest, and we already know its agents want you. I can see them hatching this plan.'

'But Spinner knew I was leaving for Rome. Why didn't he grab me sooner?'

'I led him to believe that you were due to leave on Tuesday, not tonight. That's why I told you to disguise yourself when you left your room, so he wouldn't realise you were gone,' she said. 'We need him to believe that you and Warden are still in Venice.' She gave me a sidelong look. 'If Tinman gets hold of you, they'll want to turn you into their instrument by any means. If they get hold of Warden, I can almost guarantee he'll be locked in a military installation on some godforsaken black site and vivisected. You'll never see him again.'

Arcturus caught my gaze in the mirror.

Terebell had trusted me by agreeing to attend that meeting. I imagined Spinner calculating which of them would be easier to capture. Arcturus was the obvious choice, in his state.

'It was Spinner who suggested that we speak to Warden a second time,' Ducos said. 'It seemed reasonable, but when I saw that message, I acted.' She opened her window. 'Now you're both out, Pivot can secure the Palazzo del Domino. We'll catch Spinner in the act.'

'What about Maria and Nick?'

'They'll be fine. Pivot has it all under control.'

'I'm glad someone does,' I said tightly. 'Are you sure Spinner isn't aligned with Grapevine?'

'No. I'm not sure. But we'll know by tomorrow.'

'Wait.' I sat up straighter. 'Are you taking us both to Rome?'

'Yes. Why?'

'Cade knows Arcturus. That means he can detect him in the æther.'

'I have alysoplasm, Paige.' Arcturus spoke for the first time. 'I can use it to—'

'Not on my watch.' I rounded in my seat to glare at him. 'You think poisoning yourself for days is going to help you get better?'

If he was surprised by my outburst, he concealed it, meeting my gaze levelly. I flushed.

'I will not have to take it for long,' he said. 'When Terebell returns to Italy, I can leave with her.'

'I'm telling her right now.' I dug into my pocket. 'She might not have reached the cold spot in the Apennines. You need someone with you.'

'How do you mean to contact her?'

'I gave her a phone.'

'She would have discarded it. After Senshield, she swore never to use human technology.'

'Fucking hell,' I exploded. 'No wonder the Sargas are winning!'

'Calm down, Flora,' Ducos said firmly. 'I understand why you're angry, but Warden is conspicuous and unwell, and we can't just put him anywhere. I can get him to a sanctuary, but I'll need a few days.'

'Fine.' I sat back in my seat. 'Arcturus, if I haven't killed Cade within those few days, you need to leave. You know full well you can't be on alysoplasm for any longer.'

He looked out of the window. 'As you wish, Underqueen.'

'Ducos,' I said, 'what will happen to Spinner?'

'If he's been leaking information to Grapevine, he may be charged with treason in Australia, where he's from,' Ducos said, 'but Australia is closely allied with America, so if it's Tinman he's been serving, he may not be punished.' She took out her box of cigarettes. 'Turn your phone off. Spinner shouldn't notice your absence, but you ought to stay off the radar.'

'What if the others call?'

'You can't help anyone from here.' She reached under her seat and passed me a blanket. 'Take your mind off it and sleep. I'll wake you when we're getting close.'

I switched off my phone. Before I settled in to sleep, I glanced over my shoulder at Arcturus. Even if I was afraid for him, I was relieved he was still with me.

---

I woke to a gentle trill. Ducos hooked an earpiece on and gave it a tap, making her phone glow on the dashboard.

'Widow,' she said.

I blinked a few times. From the clock on the dashboard, we had been driving for over two hours.

'I have no idea,' Ducos said. 'Why, are you concerned?'

She listened for a while.

'That has to be a misunderstanding. I'm taking her on Tuesday,' she said. 'She might be with Noemi. She hasn't been outside Scion since she was a child. We don't want to keep her cooped up in the Palazzo.'

I could just hear a voice on the other end of the line.

'She was a career criminal. I'm sure she can handle herself in a city as safe as Venice at night.' She waited again. 'He was there when I left. I wouldn't disturb him. We'll have plenty of time to question him on Sunday.' Her eyes reflected the headlamps in the other lane. 'No, I'm heading for Matera to see Valentina Chen. I'll be back for the meeting.'

My heart thudded.

'Very good. See you then.' Ducos ended the call. 'That was Spinner. Pivot will cover your absence.'

Arcturus was asleep. I rested my head on the window, watching the other vehicles on the motorway.

'That black car,' I said, tensing. 'There's no dreamscape.'

'Remind me what that means.'

'It means the driver is concealing themselves.'

Ducos glanced at the rear-view mirror. 'Italy is the leading manufacturer of autonomous cars. That's one of them. There is no driver,' she said. 'It's probably just a test run.'

Another strange fact about the free world. I reclined my seat and tried to get back to sleep.

A bright nest of lights soon appeared in the dark, rousing me again. Ducos parked the car and hooked it up to a charging point.

'This will take a while,' she told me. 'I'm going inside for a coffee. Do you want to come?'

'I'm grand.'

She looked at me, then at Arcturus. 'I'll bring you something to eat.'

'Thanks.' I noticed the clock. 'It's past the time of the extraction.'

'Yes. Pivot hasn't called, but I suspect she has her hands full.' Ducos checked her phone. 'I'll touch base once we get to Rome.'

She strode into the service station. I resisted turning my phone on. Maria and Nick would have been able to defend themselves, if necessary.

Arcturus stirred in the back seat. He looked around the car before his gaze came to rest on me.

'Guess it wasn't goodbye after all,' I said.

'No. It seems that, as the saying goes, all roads lead to Rome.'

'I've never heard that.' I wound a curl around my fingers. 'I shouldn't have brought you to that meeting. I knew there had been leaks in Domino, but I trusted that Command was clean.'

'You are not at fault.'

His eyes were too dim for my comfort. In Paris, he had fed every two or three days.

'Arcturus,' I said, 'when did you last take aura?'

'The night you revived me. I will endure until we reach Rome.'

I doubted it.

'You could use mine,' I said, after a moment. 'It would be easier than trying to find a stranger.'

'I will not feed on you, Paige.'

'You're clearly in no state to look for random voyants in a city you don't know. Otherwise you'd have done it in Venice. You can't risk being seen in Rome.'

'I have never been seen.'

'Fine.' I undid my seatbelt. 'Stay here. I won't go far.'

Outside in the fog, I paced near the chargers, trying to stretch the ache from my back. Hours in one position had left me stiff, and my shoulder was killing me.

I was going to be alone with Arcturus for a few days. I had no idea how to handle that, or why it was irritating me that he refused to use my aura. As I blew into my hands, a black car turned off the motorway and drove towards the charging stations, just as several others had.

Except this one was different. This was the same car I had noticed earlier.

At once, I returned to my seat and reached across to lock the doors. The car approached ours.

'Paige,' Arcturus said. 'What is it?'

'Wait,' I said.

The car passed us without stopping. It had tinted windows, so dark I couldn't make out anything inside. It circled to the back of the service station and vanished from sight.

'Never mind.' I released my breath. 'I really am getting paranoid.'

'I doubt that.'

'No, I am. All the double-crossing is driving me insane.' I kneaded my forehead. 'I could deal with the concept of fighting Scion. That was simple. But now there are multiple factions in the mix, and they all seem to either want me dead or working for them.'

'Grapevine is the faction that ought to concern us most. Vindemiatrix Sargas is shrewd, and I suspect her knowledge of humans is second only to mine. Her agents stand ready to disseminate propaganda and buckle free-world nations from within. Fitzours may be able to force governments to convert, but the people will require further conditioning.'

'At least he can't possess everyone.' I slouched into my seat. 'I'm sorry I snapped at you earlier. Cade is stronger than me. If we lose the element of surprise, I've no advantage.'

'We do not yet know the extent of your abilities.'

'No, but he's clearly willing to go much further than I am. What he did to both of us in Paris – I wouldn't do something like that to my worst enemy. I don't think I have it in me.'

'If you did,' Arcturus said, 'what would distinguish their side from ours?'

I looked at him. He always knew exactly what to say.

Ducos chose that moment to return from the service station. 'You don't eat, do you?' she said to Arcturus. He shook his head. 'Coffee for you, Flora.'

'Thanks,' I said.

She passed it to me, along with a pot of chopped fruit and a sandwich, and took out a salad for herself. While we picked at our early breakfast, she kept an eye on her phone. When a light on the dashboard flashed, indicating a full charge, she started the car again.

'You had better take your … alysoplasm,' she said. 'We'll be in Rome in forty minutes.'

'I would be grateful for a syringe, if you have one,' Arcturus said to her. 'My dosage must be precise.'

'Why?'

'It makes him sick,' I said offhandedly. 'Sicker than it does me.'

Terebell would never forgive me if I let the truth slip. Even my closest friends had no idea that the Rephs could become Buzzers.

Ducos unzipped a medical kit and handed a syringe over. Arcturus used it to draw a tiny dose of diluted alysoplasm from a vial. I sipped from the one Terebell had given me, and the æther faded again.

'You both look as if you're about to die,' Ducos observed as she drove out of the station.

'Yeah, thanks.' I covered my mouth. 'I need to be quiet now, or I'll throw up.'

'Please don't. This is a work car.'

Ducos drove along a deserted stretch of motorway. Arcturus sat in rigid silence. I kept glancing at him, even as my skin turned clammy and my stomach cramped. Rephs could only tolerate one or two drops of pure alysoplasm when they were on good form. Even watered down, I couldn't stop worrying about the havoc it might be wreaking on his body.

I let myself doze off again, if only to escape the discomfort. I couldn't stand not being able to sense the æther. If I didn't find Cade quickly, I might have to endure it for days.

A sickening crash jolted me awake. I snapped forward before my seatbelt went taut. Ducos had barely spun the wheel before the car swung to the left, and suddenly we were careening off the road.

Ducos hit the brakes. The car slewed and tipped, and before I knew it, glass was exploding around us. Her phone escaped its holder and clipped my cheek. I kept my eyes shut and my heels on the floor until I was slammed back against my seat, pinned there by an inflated airbag.

There was no light. I could hear my own laboured breaths, then Arcturus: 'Paige, are you injured?'

'I don't think so,' I said, shaken. 'Are you?'

'No.'

'Ducos?'

'I'm alive,' she said, her voice straining.

'Fuck.' I tried to catch my breath. 'Did we roll over?'

'Yes. A car ran us off the motorway.' She pressed her gun into my hand. 'It's either bounty hunters, or Spinner got wind of us. Shoot to kill, if you must. I'll be right behind you.'

I only had one knife on me. Ducos had locked my other weapons in the boot. Once my seatbelt was off, I tumbled out of the car, using the door as a shield while I readied the gun. I was going to have to fight in the dark with only five of my senses.

The yellow lights of the motorway shone up ahead; so did a pair of headlamps. I ran, leading them away from Ducos and Arcturus. The car veered towards me and gave chase.

Had someone really come for that obscene reward?

Nick had trained me to have quick reflexes, but that had been with my clairvoyance. It was as much a part of me as my sight or my hearing, and the loss of it had unbalanced me. I fired at the windscreen, but the car still struck my thigh as it passed, knocking me down.

The car reversed with a wet screech. Teeth set, I pointed the gun, but even with all six of my senses, I had never been a crack shot. I landed a hit on one of the tyres, blowing it out just before the car reached me.

Someone got out of the passenger side. I raised my torch, aiming for the eyes. The beam revealed a massive bald man I recognised. Bohren, the unreadable who worked with Cordier. He grinned at the sight of me, turning my blood cold.

My gun went off.

The unreadable looked down at his chest. I froze as the grin slipped off his face, and a stain darkened his shirt. He collapsed to the ground, revealing a pale woman with short black hair. All the memories came pouring over me, roughening my skin with goosebumps.

'There you are.' Cordier levelled a small pistol at me. 'Get in the car, Paige.'

'I'd rather you shot me,' I said, my voice on the verge of cracking.

'If you insist, I'll aim for your knees.'

I had seen enough kneecapping to know I wouldn't recover from that sort of injury in a hurry.

'All right.' I threw away the gun. 'I'll come with you. Just leave the others alone.'

'You're in no position to make demands.' She marched towards me. 'You'd have used your trick by now, if you could.'

Arcturus suddenly came into the light of the headlamps. Seeing him, Cordier grabbed me and locked me against her, one arm across my throat, her gun jammed to my temple.

'Well, look at that,' she said, with a surprised laugh. 'You made it out.' Arcturus watched her back me towards the car. 'I will blow her jaw off if you come any closer, Warden.'

'I doubt that,' he said. My ears rang from the gunshot. 'Paige clearly has value to you, Dr Cordier.'

'Paige does,' she agreed. 'I can live without her teeth.'

'There is no cause for violence.'

'What, you're just going to let me take her, are you?' she asked. 'Because I do have to take her.'

'Then we are at a stalemate.'

His gaze seared into mine as he spoke. Through the dread, I understood that he was distracting her. I drove my elbow into her side, right where I had stabbed her in that final memory. She let go of me with a cry and dropped her pistol, which I kicked towards Arcturus.

'You vicious little—' She bent almost double, clutching her side. 'I should have left you in a hole to starve.'

'I remember it. All of it.' I grabbed her by the collar of her coat. 'You took me from Paris. Why?'

Her hand found my left wrist and pulled. Even with the brace, it was agony. As my sight went grey, she threw me aside, drew a revolver, and shot Arcturus. I had seen him absorb bullets without even flinching, but now that he was tired and poisoned, the rounds floored him.

The anger that rushed over me was uncontrollable, as if my body had been taken over by a poltergeist. Cordier turned the gun on me and wrenched me towards the car.

She hadn't expected me to know where she was wounded, or to lose her accomplice. With all the strength I could muster, I pinned her to the ground. My old self reared, the mollisher with a debt to collect, and before she could writhe away from me, I had a knife to her throat.

I was in the sewers of Paris again, a sickle in my grasp, the blade pressed against skin. A pair of dark wings seemed to cover my eyes. All I had to do was cut, and the Devil would bleed.

'Flora,' Ducos shouted. 'Don't. We need her alive.'

My hand tightened around the knife.

'Paige.'

Arcturus had managed to come to my side. I looked up at him through a stinging haze.

'She did this to us,' I whispered. 'She betrayed you to Scion.'

'If you kill her, we may never know why.' His voice was soft. 'Stay your hand, for both our sakes.'

Cordier looked between us, her face slick with sweat. I turned back towards her, just as she reached up to weakly grasp the blade, blood on her driving glove.

'I'll tell you,' she said. 'Paige. I'll tell you.'

After a pause, I shoved her down in disgust, resisting the urge to punch her. Arcturus passed me her pistol, which I trained on her as Ducos caught up, taking in her former colleague and the corpse.

'Eléonore.' With some difficulty, she picked up her gun. 'You have some explaining to do.'

---

Cordier had chosen the perfect spot on the motorway for an ambush. No one had come to investigate the collision. Now she was sitting on the grass, her wrists and ankles secured with cable ties. Despite her pallor and the blood leaking from her side, her gaze was defiant.

Ducos leaned on the hood of the car. From what she could tell, her seatbelt had broken a rib in the rollover. I had escaped with a bruised cheekbone and some cuts from the glass, while Arcturus had four bullets in his chest and a fifth in his shoulder. With the alysoplasm in him, I doubted his body would be able to force them out, as it usually could.

'You could have killed us,' Ducos said to Cordier. 'Then again, your morals seem to have evaporated. Albéric worked with us both for years, and you betrayed him to the Vigiles.'

Albéric had been another member of Mannequin. Cordier had sold him out to Scion, too.

'Don't talk to me about morals,' Cordier said hoarsely. 'I needed money. It wasn't personal.'

'That makes it fine, then,' I said.

'Give it a few years out here, Paige. You'll realise there's no bottom to the cesspit of humanity.'

'I doubt she'll need a few.' Ducos braced her ribs. 'How did you find us?'

'I could see Paige in the Alps before the tracker failed, and Harald Lauring had told me where Domino had its headquarters, so I … guessed that was where she was going,' Cordier said. 'Sooner or later, she had to come out. I told them I'd get her back.'

'Who?'

'Tinman.'

Ducos nodded. Her instinct had been right. 'When did you get involved with them?'

'I was never not involved.' Cordier took a shallow breath. 'I'll try to keep it short. After my parents' divorce, I stayed with my father in Roberval. My mother took my sister to Istanbul. I was fourteen at the time, and my sister was eight. Two years later, I was told that my sister and mother had been killed in a car accident. Their deaths led me to train as a paramedic.'

If she was hoping to tug my heartstrings, she was going to be here for a while.

'I joined an ambulance service in New York City. Four years later, I was approached by the Atlantic Intelligence Bureau,' she said. 'The recruiter said there was reason to believe my mother and sister were alive in the Republic of Scion, and promised me the means to find them if I worked for him. I quit my job and signed up without question.'

Now the link made sense.

'The recruiter wanted me to go undercover inside a European espionage network called the Domino Programme, so I could siphon their intelligence about Scion off to Tinman. We're called cuckoos,' Cordier said. 'You ever see what a cuckoo does with its eggs?'

'The cuckoo is a brood parasite,' Arcturus said in an undertone. 'It leaves its eggs in other birds' nests. The host bird may never realise that the chick it is rearing is an imposter.'

'Smart *and* handsome. Got yourself a real catch there, Paige,' Cordier said. I stiffened. 'Yes. I was a cuckoo among the warblers. There are others.'

Ducos clenched her jaw. 'How much have you told them, Eléonore?'

'I told them everything.'

'Do they know the secret behind Scion?'

'They know there is one. When I reported what I saw in Paris, they knew they were on to something good. A man … who didn't look human. A woman who could possess anyone. They couldn't let Domino keep two rare gems like that. America must always prevail.'

'That's why they came after Paige. They want to know what they're dealing with.' Ducos said it more to herself than to any of us. 'Go on. How did they manage to plant you in Domino?'

'A recruiter at Yerebatan is a cuckoo. He pretended to headhunt me, presenting me as a woman named Aysel Ekren, whose identity I stole.' Cordier looked at me. 'See, Paige – we're not so different. You voyants speak to the dead; we spies borrow their names.'

'Fuck you,' I said.

'You were sweeter when you had amnesia.'

It took all my restraint not to throttle her.

'I found documents pertaining to my sister at Yerebatan. Operation Stiletto – a successful first attempt to plant deep-cover agents in Scion,' she said. 'My mother and Alice were selected. Alice was always precocious – highly perceptive and intelligent, even when she was eight. Domino gave her a new identity and faked her death in Istanbul.'

'Alice.' I paused. 'Do you mean Scarlett Burnish?'

'Yes,' she said, sweat beading on her forehead again. 'Even if we'd been separated for years, Alice was my sister. I couldn't abandon her, knowing she never had a choice. She was a child when Domino put her in Scion. A fucking *child*, Isaure. You criticise Tinman for its tactics, but she was ten years old. Don't you dare mention morals again.'

'So this was about vengeance,' Ducos said coolly. 'All those extended assignments. You would disappear for weeks at a time.'

'Sometimes I was harvesting intelligence from other sub-networks. When I wasn't doing that, I was either at the Fluke, sharing it with my birdwatcher, or in London,' Cordier confirmed. 'I found my mother in Mayfair. She pretended she didn't know who I was, but I left her a means to contact me in Paris, in case she or Alice wanted to get out. I didn't hear a word for years.'

Claude Burnish kept a low profile, but I had glimpsed her in the *Descendant* every now and then. Now I wondered whether her Scion-born spouse had known the truth about her.

'In the Archon,' Cordier went on, 'Alice worked with a … sympathiser, code name Lepidopterist.'

Ducos narrowed her eyes. 'Another Domino agent?'

'No. An independent defector,' Cordier said. 'In December, Alice sent him to Paris to find me. To tell me she had accepted her duty, and that I should leave Scion. Leave her.' She closed her eyes. 'A week after Versailles, the Lepidopterist got in touch again. Alice had entrusted him with something of immense value, which he was meant to pass to me, but he wanted something in return – Paige. He knew I could get her. That's why I did it.'

'You're lying,' I said. 'You put the tracking unit in me before Versailles.'

'Yes, because Tinman had separately ordered me to extract you and Warden.'

'Why?'

'Why do you think?' Cordier wheezed a laugh. 'You're a miracle, Paige Mahoney. Don't you know how devastating a weapon you would be in the right hands, or the wrong ones?'

'I'm aware.'

'I really don't think you are,' she said. 'The Lepidopterist stipulated that I had to split you up from Warden. As soon as you left the safe house, I got him detained.'

So the Lepidopterist knew about Warden. That narrowed down the number of people it could be.

'You held me for six months,' I said. 'What were you waiting for?'

'He wanted you kept away. And he didn't want you anywhere near Warden.' Cordier took a deep breath. 'Tinman smelled a rat.

My birdwatcher had told me to bring you to Amsterdam, but I couldn't risk the loss of whatever my sister got out of the Archon, so I took you to Switzerland instead. From there, we had to go on the run.'

'Tell us how Harald Lauring got involved,' Ducos said.

'Harald had more experience with voyants than I did. He found a Domino associate who could keep Paige under control. His gift made him immune to hers.' Cordier glanced at the corpse. 'I hadn't realised Harald was Grapevine. When I realised he was going to try to take Paige, we gave him the slip. I bribed Lennart to come with me.'

'Harald found her,' Ducos said. 'He was on his way to Scion with her when our paths crossed.'

'Did you kill him?'

'Yes.'

'Shame. He was a good man, at one point.'

'Forgive me if I don't take your word for it,' I said. 'Not only did you hold me hostage for months, but you condemned Arcturus to a torture chamber.'

'I did try other ways. For what it's worth, I'm sorry,' Cordier said to Arcturus. 'I'm glad you made it out, handsome.'

'You just shot him,' I bit out.

'He can take it. Besides, there are worse things in store for him if you're not careful, Paige.'

'What the fuck does that mean?'

'Our world is about to change. The secret is bursting its bounds. Too many people know or suspect,' she said. 'It's only a matter of who gets to it first, and who is the one to reveal it. Tinman is grasping the extent of this. They'll do anything to get their hands on a specimen.'

'They'll have to come through me.'

'I'm sure they'd enjoy that opportunity. They have a tracker in me now, by the way,' she added to Ducos. 'You should move.'

'You're working for them again?'

'They caught up to us when Paige stabbed me. Thanks for that, by the way,' she said to me. 'I told them I could find her, but... they don't trust me on my own.'

'Tell me about Spinner,' Ducos said.

'Who?'

'John Prentice. He's a member of Command.'

'Oh, the Aussie.' Cordier took another breath. 'Tinman pays him for dirt on your benefactors. He was meant to facilitate a raid on headquarters last night, so they could take Paige and Warden. I was there as a safety net. I saw you leave.'

'And now here you are.' Ducos knelt in front of her. 'I'm taking you to Venice. If you give us concrete information on what Tinman has been doing in Europe, you'll be given a new identity.'

'They'd find me.' Her smile was thin. 'Alice was my reason for doing this. She's gone, isn't she?'

'Scion executed her. Do you know why?' Ducos said. 'Because she saved Paige. If you had sent Paige to any of these factions – none of whom can mean her well – you would have rendered your sister's death meaningless.'

I stayed quiet while Cordier absorbed this.

'Without Paige, I can't secure the intelligence that Alice collected. It was all for nothing,' she said. 'And when the cuckoo is found out, it either gets killed or abandoned.' She looked at her old friend. 'Tell me once more, Isaure. When does a spy know she needs to retire?'

Ducos answered, after a long pause: 'The day she becomes ensnared in her own web.'

'It was a good lesson, even for a cuckoo.' Cordier smiled again. 'Lennart back there mentioned a voyant custom, Paige. My name is Margaux Taylan. That's the name I still hold close.'

She tightened her jaw, and her throat shifted.

'No.' Ducos caught her as she slumped over. 'Margaux—'

Cordier shook her head and choked. Bloody foam escaped her lips.

'I told you not to keep it in your mouth,' Ducos ground out. 'I told you.'

All Domino agents were issued with a silver pill, allowing them to end their lives before Scion could get to them. Ducos had assured me that it caused a quick and painless death, but Cordier kept writhing and twitching for some time. Arcturus stayed beside me as I watched it happen, wondering if I should just relent and shoot her.

Ducos did it first.

Cordier lay on the grass. Even if I couldn't feel it, I knew her spirit had come untethered from her body. I glanced at Arcturus, who gave me a small nod.

'Margaux Taylan,' I said, 'be gone into the æther. All is settled. All debts are paid. You need not dwell among the living now.'

# 20

# SEVEN HILLS

We had to wait a while for a new car. Ducos called a second contact to get rid of the damaged ones, along with the bodies of Cordier and her accomplice, whose passport helped us identify him as a Swiss mercenary named Lennart Bohren, a former associate of the Domino Programme.

And just like that, it was over. I never had to worry about them coming back for me.

It seemed a hollow victory.

Rome wrapped us in the glow of its streetlamps. It was strange to not be able to feel the æther, which was the first thing I usually noticed in new places. Ducos stopped on a quiet street.

'Keep your weapons concealed, as you would in Scion. With President Sala out of contact, we might not be able to assist if you're arrested.' She offered me a thin metal card. 'You can use this to withdraw any money you require, whether for sustenance or bribes.'

I pocketed the card. I'd had a bank account in Scion, but it would have been closed when I was detained.

Ducos climbed out of the car with a grimace. I followed, taking my holdall and weapons from the boot. Once Arcturus was out, Ducos showed us into a Renaissance building. Beyond the entrance, a courtyard housed a few tables and a marble fountain. As far as I could tell without the æther, there was no one else around.

On the upper floor, a gallery overlooked the courtyard. Ducos led us to a pair of adjacent rooms, each with a lockbox mounted outside. She used different codes to open them and presented us each with a key.

'The Chiostro del Bramante,' she said. 'Domino personnel often meet here. It's essentially a private hotel.'

'Does Sala know about it?'

'Fortunately not. Before I leave, do you need any medical treatment, Warden?'

'No,' Arcturus said. 'Thank you.'

'You took five bullets from a revolver.'

'They are earthly metal.'

'I see.' She looked sceptical. 'You … get yourselves settled. I need to contact Pivot.'

I unlocked my door. In the bathroom, I rinsed the blood off my hands, watching the water turn rusty.

Lennart Bohren had enjoyed his work for Cordier. Each time I escaped, he had stalked me through the streets. He had let me believe I was getting away, only to crush my hopes with the white aster. I should not feel any remorse for shooting him, or any pity for Cordier.

My wrist throbbed. I flexed my fingers, knowing a tiny bone was dying inside me, and there was nothing I could do about it. I had ignored the pain for too long.

Ducos returned to the upper floor. By that time, I was leaning on the balustrade, gazing into nothing.

'Flora,' Ducos said. 'Are you all right?'

I nodded. 'Did you get hold of Pivot?'

'Yes. Spinner has been apprehended, as have multiple intruders from Tinman. Pivot has recalled the whole of Command to discuss our cuckoo problem. You and Warden are safe.'

'For now.' I rubbed my eyes. 'Are you leaving straight away?'

'Yes. I need to join my colleagues.'

'You can't drive all that way with a broken rib.'

'I'll take the first train back to Venice.' She handed me a thick file, bound with oilskin. 'This is our dossier on President Sala. It contains all information we have on her personal life, her public duties, her political career, and so on. If you haven't located either her or Fitzours after two weeks, we'll recall you to Venice and discuss a different approach. But I think you can find her, Flora. I think you will notice something none of us have.'

I was almost too surprised to reply. She had never expressed such confidence in me before.

'I'll do my best,' I said.

'Call if I can help from Venice. Remember to keep your dissimulator on,' she said. 'As soon as I've spoken to Pivot, I'll set about finding somewhere more secure for Warden.'

'Thank you.'

'All right.' She checked her watch. 'I'd better go to the station. Good luck.'

She left.

I switched my phone on. Nick and Maria had called several times. They were probably still awake and worried, but I sent my explanation as a message, too drained to talk.

A breeze went through the courtyard, unsettling my hair. I traced the white dots on the dossier.

Cordier had given me some closure. I was still left to face the stark reality of what she had done. It would almost have felt better if it had been personal, but I had just been a bartering chip, and Arcturus an obstacle. I was a queen on my own board, but a pawn on hers. Now I remembered the night of the airstrike, and the words of the medium who had grabbed me.

*The Devil has deceived you. Two horns, two wings, two cloven hooves.*

In the Major Arcana, the Devil was a symmetrical figure. It must always have represented two people, one to chain each of the Lovers – Cordier for me, and Cade for Arcturus.

*The way I see it, you must follow the path of the Lovers,* Elspeth Lin had said, building on the reading her niece had given me. *Stay close to the person you think the card might represent, and make sure you've identified that person correctly. If you stray from whoever it is, I suspect you'll be vulnerable to the Devil.*

Now I was living proof that voyants could be just as foolish as amaurotics. Even with all those warnings, I had walked into the jaws of the trap, away from Arcturus. One Devil was dead, but the other remained. I had to find and kill him, to put the card to rest at last.

As for the mysterious Lepidopterist, I might never know who had asked Cordier to abduct me, or why. With her death, my only lead was gone. And all I knew was that he was a Scion defector.

Arcturus opened his door and came to stand beside me at the balustrade. I glanced at him.

'How are you, Paige?'

'I'm grand,' I said.

'You know that does not work on me.'

Even Nick, my best friend, didn't know me as well as Arcturus did. I had missed being able to talk to him. I took half a step away, giving him space.

'Cordier took six months from us both,' I said. 'The whole time, we were just a means to an end.'

'It seems to me that Cordier was a victim of manipulation.'

'She can join the club.'

Arcturus waited. He had a way of knowing when I was finished, and when I needed more time to unpack a thought.

'I shot Bohren,' I said quietly. 'I didn't even do it consciously. I just shot him dead on instinct.'

'He took pleasure in hunting you.'

'But that's the reason all this happened, isn't it?' I murmured. 'Because humans kill like it's going out of fashion. We don't restrain ourselves.' I swallowed the sour taste in my throat. 'I didn't have to finish the Rag and Bone Man off like I did, either. Nashira isn't wrong to judge us.'

'You are not violent by nature, Paige. You have killed either by accident, in self-defence, or for others' protection,' Arcturus said. 'You took care to say the threnody for both Cordier and Bohren, even though they gave you no cause to show them any respect in death.'

'I could have been working on my gift for those six months, building alliances with other citadels in Scion. Instead, I was a prisoner again, and I've no one to blame for it but myself.' I shook my head. 'I couldn't train. I couldn't strategise. I lost all of that time for nothing.'

*I lost you for nothing.*

'What Cordier and Bohren did is indefensible,' Arcturus said, 'but it is possible to find a silver lining. Your absence gave the revolution an opportunity to overcome its growing pains. It has proven that you do not need to bear the entire burden of this war alone. You laid a strong foundation; now it is up to all of us, voyant and Ranthen, to build on it.'

I knew he would have touched me then, if things between us were the same as they had been in Paris. He would have taken my hand, or stroked my hair, to reassure me of his sincerity. As it stood, neither of us moved, because nothing was the same as it had been in Paris.

'I know,' I said. 'I just wish things had gone differently.'

'I told you once that all threads in the æther have their purpose.'

'What purpose was there in you being tortured?'

'Perhaps to remind me that I am no longer the warrior I was in the Netherworld,' Arcturus said. 'Protecting you with my body was the way I saw fit to help you in France, the way I served the Mothallath. Now my body is resisting me, I must reckon with my calling.'

'Arcturus, you're not some empty-headed bruiser. And you weren't always my bodyguard,' I said. 'You have so much more to offer the cause than your sword.'

'I fail to see what else I have to offer, in this state.'

'Don't say that.'

His gaze darted to mine.

'Look,' I said, 'if you want to help me with this assignment, I have something you can do from right here.' I slid the dossier towards him. 'How about some more reading material?'

Arcturus picked up the dossier and opened it. The first page showed the emblem of Italy.

'This is all about President Sala. I'm hoping it will give me somewhere to start looking for her,' I said. 'I told you I don't have the patience for reading. This needs someone who does. You're not just the brawn of this enterprise. You were always the brains, too.'

'Hm. And if I am the brains *and* the brawn, what are you?'

I flashed him a smile. 'The bravado?'

'You understate your intelligence.'

'You have a different sort,' I said. 'You read in more depth. You see details I don't, like when you worked out how to reach Versailles. Could you tell me if anything jumps out at you?'

Arcturus closed the dossier. 'I will read it by midday.'

'Thanks.' I paused. 'Are you sure you don't need any help with the bullets?'

'No. I will manage,' he said. 'Goodnight, Paige.'

'Goodnight.'

He went back to his room. When I heard the door lock, I rested my arms on the balustrade, heavy with all the words I couldn't say.

———

I slept deeply, though not for long. Around nine, I woke, my arm curled around a pillow. I lay in bed for another hour, dwelling on the two Devils.

The sixth card in my reading had been Eight of Swords. *You can't move in any direction with ease. You can stay in one place, trapped and stagnant, or feel the pain of the swords. All paths lead to anguish.*

At last, I got out of bed and threw a window open. I had been stagnant long enough. If there was more pain in store, let it come. Surely I knew how to carry it now.

Rome was a little warmer than Venice, the sun bright in a cloudless sky. For once, I didn't feel too exhausted to face it. I unfolded a long-sleeved blouse, a lightweight jersey, and a pair of black jeans. I braced my sore left wrist and put on my holster and weapons, covering them with my jacket.

I had drunk enough alysoplasm to conceal me through the night. Now I sipped a little more. Once I had scrubbed the foul taste off my teeth, I was ready for a day of hunting.

Arcturus had said he would be done by noon. Ducos had furnished me with a data pad, which I used to consult Omnia, giving me an overview of Rome.

It was known as the City of Seven Hills, or the Eternal City, which sounded like the perfect trophy for the Suzerain. Once the heart of an ancient and terrible empire, it held thousands of years of human civilisation, religion and culture. If Nashira did seize this place, it would be a symbolic victory, as well as a strategic one. I noted my own location on the watch. The district was Ponte, close to the River Tiber.

At midday, I went to the next room. Arcturus let me inside, his movements stiff again.

'Good day, Paige.'

'Hi,' I said. 'Any luck?'

'I believe so.'

He closed the door. I sat down in the chair by the window, where sunlight poured in.

'President Sala has a well-documented history of speaking out against Scion, and has expressed her personal support for voyants on several occasions. I am sure you already know that her official residence is the Palazzo del Quirinale,' Arcturus said. 'Most of the information in the dossier is public knowledge, and I doubt that it will serve you in your search. The only detail that caught my attention was an endeavour known as the Forum Project.'

'Go on,' I said.

'The Roman Forum was a plaza surrounded by ruins, which served as the administrative and judicial centre of Ancient Rome. An architect named Giosuè Barraco proposed rebuilding it. The Forum Project attracted protests from traditional conservators immediately, hampering its progress, but Barraco was determined and persuasive. Sala was his student at the Sapienza University of Rome, and later used her political influence as Minister for Culture to drive the project forward.'

'Just so I'm sure I understand this,' I said, 'they want to rebuild a ruin?'

'I gather conservation is the usual way in the free world, with ruins maintained to prevent deterioration. Sala and Barraco took a restorative and reconstructive approach. Their aim was to return the Roman Forum to its former glory, taking it from a ruin to a functional complex. There appears to be no precedent on this scale.'

'That does seem like an odd way to spend money. Any idea what gave her this passion?'

'Sala believed the Forum should be reintegrated into daily life, rather than left to crumble for tourists, but she agreed to use the same building techniques and materials as the ancient Romans, to make sure its original character was preserved, and to leave the neighbouring Forum of Caesar untouched. Only a portion of the project would be funded by the taxpayer, while Sala would raise the outstanding funds herself. Public access is restricted until August, but Sala visits the site frequently. Other than the expected team of architects, civil engineers, and so forth, a select few others have been allowed to enter. Domino has identified two of them,' Arcturus said. 'Rohan Mistry, a former diplomat, and Kafayat Ekundayo, a well-known barrister, who specialises in international law.' He showed me their photographs. 'They have no relevant expertise, which begs the question of why they are visiting so frequently.'

'You think I should try to see it, then?'

'Sala clearly has great passion for this project, despite the opposition she has faced. Unless you can find a more concrete lead, this seems a good place to direct your interest.'

'Okay. Any other lines of investigation?'

'Not in my opinion.' He shut the dossier and held it out. 'Sala has a presidential estate in Castelporziano, on the outskirts of Rome, but I imagine Domino has already looked there.'

'The Forum, then.' I accepted the dossier. 'Thank you. I knew you'd narrow down my options.'

'Will you leave at once?'

'I might talk to Verča first. She studied architecture in Italy. Maybe she worked on the Forum Project.' I sighed. 'I'm a mob boss. How and why am I suddenly investigating Roman ruins?'

'This war will be conducted in many arenas. I trust in your ability to adapt.'

'Thanks.' I took note of his eyes. 'Arcturus, you have to feed, and it's not safe for you to go out. If Scion gets wind that you're not on Capri—' I couldn't finish. 'Just use my aura. I know you're trying to be noble, but I'm offering.'

'Your connection to the æther will not sustain us both when you are taking alysoplasm.'

'You were already in a bad way, and now you're having to poison yourself. I don't know how you're expecting to hold out much longer,' I said. 'Have the bullets come out?'

'No. I suspect that I must take aura before my body will expel them.' Arcturus avoided my gaze. 'I will leave at dusk. I am more likely to move unseen once darkness has fallen.'

'Suit yourself.' I stood. 'Be careful.'

I left, closing his door behind me. As I returned to my own room, I took out my phone.

It's Paige, I wrote to Verča. Do you know anything about the Forum Project?

After a few minutes, she answered: A few of the top students from the University of Florence were invited to work on it, but I declined, as I wasn't especially interested in conservation architecture – my area of interest was interior design. I regret it now, as I've found its progress fascinating.

Sala is involved. I'm wondering if I can pick up her trail there.

It is her pet project. It won't open until next year, but I'm sure I still have the letter inviting me to attend the site. I can bring that and my diploma, and we'll try our luck.

When are you getting here?

I'll be on the earliest flight tomorrow. I can meet you in the Campidoglio at 11, if that works for you?

I sent back an affirmative. Given the amount of secrecy surrounding the Forum Project, I doubted I would get in there without my gift, but Verča might be able to talk us in.

For now, I would explore. I donned my dissimulator and left the Chiostro del Bramante. Under the afternoon sun, I walked across dark cobbles, past buildings built and painted in the pastel shades of dawn. Here and there, iron lanterns reached over the winding streets, lush green leaves cascaded down the walls, and people rode scooters and bikes.

Not being able to feel any spirits or dreamscapes was unsettling, but my other five senses were overwhelmed as it was. Though Rome was a touch calmer than Naples, it sprawled across more ground than Venice. I wove between flocks of people, finding shade under archways and awnings.

The first place I approached was the Palazzo Chigi, where the Prime Minister worked. The square was full of surveillance cameras and vehicles marked POLIZIA, and guards flanked the gates of the building. Cade could be living nearby, a constant lurking threat to Rinaldi. All of this security meant nothing to a dreamwalker.

I sat on the edge of a fountain and watched passers-by for a while. It was futile to think one might be Cade, but even in a city I didn't know, I could only rely on the sort of tactics I had used in London and Paris. If I did happen to see him, I had already decided that I would tail him to an isolated spot and knife him. He wouldn't sense me coming.

After a while, the guards noticed me. I left before they could question my interest in the building.

I walked to my next stop, passing a striking landmark called the Trevi Fountain. According to Omnia, the statue presiding over it was supposed to be Oceanus, an ancient god of fresh water. He had originated in Greece, where every trace of him would be long gone.

A young couple took a picture of themselves in front of his pool. As they grinned, a pickpocket relieved one of them of a wallet. At least some things never changed.

The Palazzo del Quirinale was up a shallow incline. I climbed a set of steps to reach it. Once again, I sat down and observed my surroundings for a while, but there was no sign of Cade.

Of course not. This wasn't Scion. Without my gift, I didn't know where to start looking for one man. I would give it another couple of days, to buy Ducos time to get Arcturus out, then let the alysoplasm wear off, so I could probe the æther. It would be a significant risk, but there might not be any other way to confirm whether or not Cade was here.

I returned to Ponte with nothing to show for my first excursion. Out of options, I checked Omnia.

The **Forum Project** (Italian: Progetto Foro) is an ongoing effort to reconstruct the <u>Roman Forum</u>. First proposed by <u>Giosuè Barraco</u> in 2020, and later galvanised by <u>Beatrice Sala</u>, the project aims to integrate the Forum back into public life. It has been partly funded by private donors and institutions. The project is scheduled for completion in the summer of 2061, thirty years after Barraco officially received permission to begin its restoration.

I read the whole entry, along with every article I could find on the Forum Project. There was a great deal of speculation, with an undercurrent of displeasure. Even if most Italians had accepted the Forum Project, the cost to the taxpayer was irritating a fair amount of people, including the Prime Minister. Some Italians felt that interfering with ruins was an act of outright vandalism. I skimmed the dossier myself, just in case Arcturus had missed anything, but he was thorough.

My stomach growled. I got up, wondering if meals were provided here, then shook my head. Venice really had given me notions.

I slotted my new card into a cash machine and used the money to buy a box of fresh pasta from a nearby restaurant. Once I was back in my room, I ate my supper, watching the Italian news on my data pad. All I could do now was wait until Verča landed in the morning.

My instincts told me to find Giosuè Barraco. He was an archaeologist and restoration architect, who had taught Sala at university. They had been close friends ever since, with Barraco stepping in when her father had died. She had no other living family. If she had entrusted her whereabouts to anyone, it had to be him.

Arcturus must have already left. I tried to stay awake until he returned, but by one in the morning, I hadn't heard him. Trying not to worry, I slept.

---

The next day was even warmer. I drank my alysoplasm. My body was getting used to the poison, but it still caused a bout of cramps and dizziness.

I knocked for Arcturus, but there was no answer. After a moment, I tried to open the door, afraid he might have gone out and been caught, but it was bolted from the inside. He must be asleep.

Verča would be at the meeting place in an hour. I left early so I could stop for breakfast. A waitron showed me to a table in the shade, where I took out my phone. I was sure I had rarely looked at my phone in Scion, but people seemed obsessed with them out here.

Did you feed?

It took Arcturus a while to reply. The waitron brought me an iced coffee, which I sipped as I read.

It was more difficult than I anticipated. I will try again tonight.

This was his sixth day without aura. I had never known a Reph to abstain for so long.

You can't wait any more, I wrote. My offer stands.

So does my answer.

I never thought you'd be this much of a fool.

I know how long it takes to succumb.

I couldn't argue. He had learned the hard way.

Once I had eaten and forced down a couple of glasses of water, I paid and kept walking. As I closed in on the Forum, the streets became longer, the buildings grander. The sun beat down on my shoulders. I went up a steep flight of steps and skirted a public square, keeping to the shade of a colonnade. As soon as I emerged, I stopped dead.

A bronze wolf stood at the top of a column.

Slowly, I approached the sculpture, which included two boys sheltering under the wolf, mouths open to drink her milk. I suddenly remembered the shadow on the wall, thrown by the casting Nuray had made. Verča was gazing up at it, her expression troubled.

'Verča,' I said.

She came back to herself.

'Paige,' she said, sounding relieved. 'Maria told me what happened with Cordier. Are you all right?'

'Fine. Just a few scrapes.'

'Tinman has a reputation, but this is worse than anything I've heard about their tactics. Pivot must be furious.' She glanced at the sculpture again. 'This is what I thought Nuray might have seen in her casting. It could be a coincidence, but it is strange that it's so close to the place you want to investigate.' She led me past it. 'Let me show you the Forum.'

The next street curved downhill. We stood by a railing and looked out at a wealth of pale stone.

A triumphal arch loomed ahead. It obscured most of the Forum, but I could make out a white plaza beyond it. To our right were three magnificent Roman buildings, boasting tall columns and sculptures, their roofs tiled in green and blue and lavender. Two had scaffolding on them. Beyond all this, I glimpsed trees on another hill.

'I take it you've read about the Forum Project,' Verča said.

'Yes. I'm curious to know why Sala has been so fixated on it,' I said. 'What do you think of it, as an architect?'

'I used to think it was an appalling waste of time and money, but I've come to see it as a remarkable achievement. I've been looking forward to visiting when it opens. But how do you think this will help us find Sala?'

'She wouldn't have left without giving someone a way to contact her. Giosuè Barraco might be that person. It's a long shot, but it's all I have.'

'You could be right. Barraco is like a father to Sala,' Verča said. 'He's often on-site, I hear. We can try.'

She led me down from the hill. We passed a sun-baked field of ruins, the ones Sala had agreed not to touch.

The entrance to the Forum was an enormous marble archway, covered in flowers. We both slowed at the sight of the three armed soldiers guarding it. That seemed like overkill.

'Excuse me, gentlemen,' Verča said. 'Can I ask a small favour?'

They eyed her in questioning silence. I couldn't tell if they were amaurotic or voyant.

'I know the Forum isn't open yet, but I was invited to work on the site when I studying at the University of Florence, and I've been curious ever since.' Verča sounded as calm as if she was talking to her best friends, not three large men with rifles. 'Is there any chance I could speak to the site administrator, to ask if my friend and I could have a look inside?'

The soldiers exchanged glances.

'Okay,' one of them finally said. 'Do you have proof of your invitation?'

'Yes.' Verča withdrew an envelope from her briefcase. 'It's signed by Signor Barraco.'

The soldier unfolded the letter. After reading it, he concluded, 'You may come in, but not her.'

He spoke as if I wasn't there. Verča looked at me, letting me decide what to do, and I gave her a subtle nod. She would have to take charge of this search.

'All right,' Verča said, turning back to the soldiers. 'Can my friend wait here?'

The nearest of the guards nodded. He led Verča under the archway, while the others stayed at their posts. I sat on a bench in the shade of an orange tree.

Verča was gone for a long time. I waited, growing more and more uncomfortable in the heavy warmth. At last, a dark-haired woman emerged from the Forum and came up to the bench.

'You speak Italian, or English?'

'English,' I said.

'Veronika sent me. She is still waiting for her meeting with the site administrator,' she said, 'so she may be a while longer. Would you prefer to wait here or leave?'

'I'll wait,' I said. 'I could use some water, though. Do you mind?'

'Of course. Do come through.'

'Non posso farla entrare,' the soldier reminded her.

'Vuole solo bere qualcosa,' she said. 'La porterò dentro solo per poco. Smettila di fare lo stronzo.'

'E va bene.' He shrugged. 'Se qualcuno chiede, è entrata di nascosto.'

He stood aside. I followed the woman under the archway, past a limestone wall, which formed one side of a building. She showed me to a drinking fountain.

'Thank you,' I said.

'No problem. It's hot today,' she said. 'Once you're done, just leave the way you came.'

She walked away. I was going to have to lap at the fountain like a cat, which wasn't ideal for someone with my debilitating fear of water, but I was parched enough to consider it.

'Paige,' a voice whispered. Verča was leaning around the corner of the building. 'They're letting me see the administrator. Come with me. Better to ask forgiveness than permission.'

'Couldn't agree more.' I went into the building with her. 'Have you seen much yet?'

'No. I was in the guardhouse,' Verča said under her breath, 'but I know this building was once the home of the Vestals, who kept the sacred fire alight. While that fire burned, Rome was said to be protected from its enemies, for the pax deorum – the peace of the gods – was assured.' She turned a corner, and I followed. 'The site administrator works in here.'

She led me into a colonnade lined with statues of women. It surrounded a tranquil courtyard, where sunset roses grew and two oblong pools reflected the sky. The walls were pale, while the roof had coral tiles. We headed up a flight of steps, to the second level of the colonnade.

At the end, a man stood outside a doorway, hands in the pockets of his suit jacket. He had smooth russet skin and dark eyes, and a silvered goatee framed his mouth. I hedged a guess that he was in his fifties. A moment later, I recognised him as Rohan Mistry, the former diplomat Arcturus had mentioned. When he saw me, his thick eyebrows furrowed, and he blocked our way.

'Aspetta un momento,' he said to me. 'Tu non puoi stare qui. Come sei entrata?'

'She's with me.' Verča linked my arm. 'We have an interest in the Forum Project, and—'

'What's the matter, Rohan?'

The voice came from beyond the doorway. I was sure that had been an Irish accent.

'Now you've done it.' Mistry heaved a sigh. 'In you come.'

He escorted us into a whitewashed room. I expected to see Giosuè Barraco, the architect behind the Forum Project, who I had assumed was the site administrator. Instead, two other people stood inside.

And I knew both of them.

One of them was Antoinette Carter, another fugitive from Scion. Like me, she had survived the Imbolc Massacre. I had seen her only once, the night I had been sent to detain her in London.

The other was Jaxon Hall.

# 21

## KASSANDRA

I gazed at my old mime-lord, my body turning cold. It took all my strength to restrain a frenzied laugh.

The last time I had clapped eyes on Jaxon Hall, I had left him to burn alive in Versailles, where he had been serving as Grand Overseer of the Republic of Scion, laundering voyants to sell to the Rephs.

And now he was somehow in Rome. Of course he was. Jaxon Hall, my own personal ghost, haunting me wherever I walked.

He looked at me with clear disdain, and without a shred of recognition. I was still wearing my dissimulator, and my aura was concealed. To him, I was just some upstart amaurotic.

'Do somebody get rid of the dullard,' he said. 'Why has she been allowed into the Forum?'

'This is my friend. She's a student architect,' Verča said defensively. 'We wanted to see the Forum, and to meet with Giosuè Barraco.'

I was silent, reeling from the shock. Jaxon ignored me in favour of scrutinising Verča.

*You may think me the pawn on this particular board, but I am playing on many others.* His voice drifted back to me from the past. *And mark my words, we are nowhere close to the endgame.*

Even though Jaxon had a way of turning up where I least expected him, he had never expressed a desire to leave the empire of his birth. He still dressed like a denizen.

He had made a failed attempt to meet Carter last year. They must have been able to arrange another rendezvous in the wake of Trafalgar Square.

*Every thread in the æther has its purpose*, Arcturus had told me. I was going to need a damned good explanation for this one.

'Giosuè is away,' Carter said, 'but we are very interested to meet you. Veronika, was it?'

'Yes.'

'And do you know what your gift is, Veronika?'

'No.' Verča hesitated. 'Why would you ask?'

'I can put an end to your wondering, dear sister.' Carter smiled. 'You are a sibyl, like me.'

Verča stared at her.

*On the Merits* had classified sibyls as a hypothetical type of fury, the sixth order. In later editions, Jaxon had expanded on the idea, claiming sibyls would be able to enter prophetic trances, like their namesakes in the ancient world. Carter had made accurate predictions on her show. She had also been able to defend herself against the Rephs.

For years, I had thought I would never meet a sibyl in the flesh. As it turned out, I already had, more than once. If Verča was a sibyl, so were Renelde and Danica.

'I had no idea.' Verča released a long breath. 'I was … starting to think I was alone.'

'No one is alone.' Carter took her by the hands. 'You already have five sisters here, Veronika. I am both sibyl and berserker,' she added, 'but my sibyl blood seems to run thicker.'

'Who are you?'

'Antoinette Carter. I'm a founding member of the Council of Kassandra, and head of the Sibylline House,' she said. 'We've been hoping the remaining sibyls will eventually find their way to the Roman Forum. Lo and behold, the æther has brought you to our doorstep.'

Verča continued to stare at her, then remembered me with a start.

'I would like to hear more,' she said, 'but I want my friend to stay.'

'Veronika, I'm sure this must be confusing, but there is a good reason we don't want amaurotics seeing the Forum just yet. I'd be happy to tell you, but I must do it in private.'

'My friend knows about voyants, even if she is amaurotic. I'm certain she won't—'

'Your new sibyl is a poor liar, Antoinette. Let us hope she tells more enlightening truths.' Jaxon stepped towards me. 'This woman is no amaurotic. She's taken alysoplasm.'

It was my turn to stare. Verča glanced at me, uncertainty leaping into her eyes.

'She is also wearing a dissimulator, indicating a link to the Domino Programme. Clearly this intruder is more than she appears.' Jaxon dealt me a cold smile. 'Come, my dear. Do unmask yourself.'

This was a dilemma. For all I knew, this entire Forum Project might be another grand attempt for Jaxon to trap and sell voyants. I didn't want to sacrifice my anonymity, but I couldn't leave Verča with him.

A surge of defiance went through me. I reached for my hairline and started to peel off my dissimulator. Carter recoiled from the sight of me shedding my face. Once it had detached, I raised my chin.

'Jaxon,' I said. 'It's been a while.'

His smile widened.

'Black Moth,' he said, dipping his head in mock deference. 'What an inconceivable pleasure to see you.'

'Paige Mahoney.' Carter raised her thin eyebrows. 'You're alive. And in Rome, of all places.'

'I've heard that all roads lead here,' I said.

'For voyants, we certainly hope so.' She grasped my shoulder. 'I've hoped to make your acquaintance for a long time, Paige. I'm glad to meet a fellow survivor of the Imbolc Massacre. Éire go brách.'

'Éire go brách.' I returned her respectful nod. 'How did you know I survived Dublin?'

'Jaxon told me.'

My attention flicked to him, then back to Carter. Despite her delicate build and papery hands, her grip was strong.

In London, her long hair had been crimson, worn loose as she fought off multiple Rephs. Now it was the brown of strong tea and arranged in a plaited crown, with a few wisps swirling down to frame her face, which had tanned and freckled since I had last seen her. She wore a pressed coral shirt and white linen trousers, belted with a length of braided leather. A small gold pendant shone between her prominent collarbones.

It was strange to be this close to someone who had shared the worst experience of my life. I had been six years old during the Imbolc Massacre, while Carter had been a celebrity in her early forties, but we had only been a few streets from each other when the soldiers opened fire.

'We feared you had died in the airstrikes on Paris,' Carter said, 'but held out hope, given the bounty on your head.' She let go of my shoulder. 'You can't possibly have known Jaxon and I were here. I presume you came to Rome for some other reason, Paige.'

'I'm here on behalf of the Domino Programme,' I said. 'I assume you know about it.'

'You're working for a network run by amaurotics?'

'For now. I'm trying to find President Sala,' I explained. 'I know why she's been hiding, and I wanted to offer my assistance. I hoped someone in the Forum would know how to contact her.'

Carter considered me. So did Rohan Mistry, who was observing from the doorway.

'Beatrice founded the Council of Kassandra,' she said. 'We were in regular contact before her disappearance in August, but not since. Her absence has baffled and worried us all.'

I tried not to feel too disheartened. This had been my best and only avenue of investigation.

'I'm sorry to interrupt,' Verča said, 'but what exactly is this Council of Kassandra?'

'Our answer to the tyranny of Scion and its makers, the Rephaim,' Carter said, a note of contempt in her voice. 'As you seem to have guessed, the Forum Project is something of a cover. Beatrice has framed it as a public space, but in fact, it is reserved for voyants' use.'

'The Council of Kassandra is a representative and legislative body for all voyants, founded in 2049. It is led by the Triumvirate – presently myself, Beatrice and Antoinette,' Mistry chimed in. 'The Forum is our headquarters, but we mean to send diplomatic missions across the globe, advancing voyants' rights and interests in defiance of Scion. Within a year, we also hope to offer knowledge of the æther to world leaders. For a price.'

Verča exchanged a speechless glance with me. I tried to digest what they were saying.

Over the last year, my aim had been to dismantle Scion. At some point in the future, I had meant to find a way for humans to live alongside the Rephs.

This vision went far beyond that, outstripping mine by decades.

'Offering knowledge to leaders,' Verča said. 'That sounds like the augurs of Ancient Rome – respected officials, consulted by emperors and generals.'

'Quite right,' Carter said. 'Scion was not the first to threaten our place in public life. Since the dawn of time, people with our gifts have been treated with both reverence and contempt. Over centuries, we've become the object of ridicule, sidelined by science and technology, or been persecuted as witches. Scion is only the most recent iteration of a deep-seated hatred – but we have been mistreated and exploited for too long. It is time for us to claim our rightful place as valued advisors in the modern world. Only with our foresight will humankind be able to resist the incursion of the Rephaim.'

Jaxon had been remarkably quiet throughout this speech. I turned my attention back to him.

'You're advocating for voyants' interests,' I said, 'but you're working with Jaxon Hall?'

He smirked, crinkling the corners of his eyes.

'My dear Paige,' he said. 'I have been advocating for our interests since before you were born.'

'There is a great deal for us to discuss,' Carter said. 'Paige, perhaps you'd be kind enough to share what you know about why President Sala has disappeared.'

'I can't do that. My assignment is confidential,' I said. 'All I can say is that I'm here to find her.'

'Well, until then, you are welcome in the Forum. We're happy to host you.' She turned back to Verča. 'Veronika, as a sibyl, you have a right to a permanent room here. Yours for no cost whatsoever, to be used whenever you wish.'

Verča hitched up a smile. 'Will I have to take a vow of eternal chastity, and keep a sacred fire burning?'

'We're not that old-fashioned. This is no longer the House of the Vestals, but the Sibylline House. It's somewhere for you to lay your head in Rome, and to confer with your sisters,' Carter said. 'We find sibyls' abilities are strongest together. A unique aspect of our gift.'

While they spoke, Jaxon and I locked eyes again.

'Paige, I imagine you would like a private word with Jaxon. Perhaps he can give you a tour of the Forum,' Carter said, 'but you should know that we do not permit any violence between voyants within its limits, as stated in the Kassandran Code. Is that understood?'

After a moment, I nodded. Verča gave me a hesitant look.

'I'll meet you later?'

I replied with another nod. She must be aching to question Carter, and I couldn't blame her.

'Very good. Now, let me show you the Sibylline House.' Carter extended an arm to Verča. 'You can meet its permanent residents, Caoimhe and Nasrin. They'll be so pleased you're here.'

While they walked along the colonnade of statues, Jaxon led me from the Sibylline House. As soon as we were out of sight and earshot, I slammed him against a wall.

'What the hell are you doing here, Jaxon?'

'I did tell you I had plans,' Jaxon said. 'I asked you to find me. Although I never expected you to do it in Rome.'

'Trust me, it wasn't intentional. I'd sooner be back on the water-board than anywhere near you.'

'Come, now. I ought to be the one who is vexed with you, given you left me to burn alive,' he said. 'Didn't I tell you that you hadn't seen the last of me?'

'Well, I don't know how you weaselled your way into *this* enterprise, but I imagine your new friends don't know all that much about your past,' I sneered. 'Did you tell Carter and Sala about the grey market, or how you betrayed hundreds of voyants to save your own skin?'

'I paid for a place on the Council of Kassandra. Where the money originated is irrelevant to Sala.'

'I'll wager you haven't tested the theory.' I drew a knife and pressed the point under his chin. 'Domino sent me to assassinate you. How did you get a dissimulator?'

'I was recruited as an associate. I assume my contact failed to inform their supervisors.'

'You're lying. No one would be stupid enough to trust the Grand Overseer.' I dug the knife in. 'You looted the box Colin left me. I want the contents.'

'All in good time.' His bony fingers closed around my arm. 'Carter will imprison you if you spill blood in here. The Council of Kassandra has its own rule of law, separate to the law conceived by amaurotics. Sala is the architect, but Carter holds the reins. Your shared history in Ireland will not protect you, should she ever see you as a threat.'

'What if I tell her the truth about you?'

'Paige, we are outside Scion now. Let us try to forgive and forget. We all did what was necessary to survive the anchor.' He levered the knife down. 'Why are you drinking alysoplasm?'

'None of your business,' I said. 'I'll see myself out. You can keep your damned tour.'

'Oh, but I insist. I want to show you the sum of my labours.'

'If you're going to show me anything, you can show me your back and walk away, Jax.'

'Come, my Pale Dreamer.' His voice was turning to honey, the way it always did when he wanted something from me. 'Surely you'd like to see where I was sending my share from the grey market. Why I was working you all so hard in London.'

'I'm not your Pale Dreamer any more. And no, Jax. I'd sooner not see where your dirty coin went.'

'I have always worked towards a better existence for voyants.'

'You sent voyants to their deaths. And there's no way you knew about the Forum Project when you were in Oxford.'

'I had my reasons for what I did in Oxford.' He leaned in close. 'There are fifty seats on the Council of Kassandra. Not all of them are occupied. Aren't you tempted, Paige?'

'I don't need a seat. I have a throne.'

'You *have* grown arrogant of late. I ought to blame myself, but it becomes you rather well. Just a short tour,' he cajoled. 'I promise you'll be impressed.'

As little as I wanted to be anywhere near him, I was burning with curiosity. I was also sure that Carter knew more than she was saying about Sala. She might even have a way to contact her, but I would have to earn her trust. If that meant controlling myself around Jaxon, I would do it.

'Fine,' I said.

Jaxon smiled.

'Welcome to the Forum,' he said as we stepped into the autumn sunlight. 'Each order of clairvoyance has its own dedicated building here.'

'You've convinced Sala and Carter that *On the Merits* is the correct way to classify us, then.'

'Sala accepts my theory that there are seven broad categories of clairvoyance, corresponding with our auras. All will stand on equal footing.' He pointed his cane. 'This is the Via Sacra, that most ancient of Roman roads. We hope that all the best voyants will have walked here in ten years' time.'

I followed him across the smooth old stones.

'Ten years,' I said. 'You think that's how long it will take to get this place up and running?'

'It will run from next summer, but we intend for the Forum to be the most beautiful of our embassies, as the cradle of the enterprise. Bringing it to completion will take a long time.' He walked past three fluted columns, chipped and severed. 'This was once the Temple of the Dioscuri. When it is resurrected, it will be our House of Perception.'

'What do you mean?'

'Let me show you.'

Jaxon led me along the Via Sacra. It was difficult to conceal my wonder, but I refused to let him see it. He gestured to the most restored of the buildings, which had arcades along its upper and lower floors, each arch housing a plinth.

'The erstwhile Basilica Julia, where the Romans conducted imperial business. Now it is our meeting chamber, the Basilica Arcana,' he informed me. 'Records of voyants' lives and predictions will be stored in the vaults below it. In the future, we intend for each embassy to be full of sculptures, paying homage to voyants from the region – but since this is our headquarters, this building will celebrate our predecessors from the world over. So far, we have plinths assigned for Allen Kardec, Bhrian Ruaidh, and the Oracle of Nusku.'

'How nice,' I said. 'And since when, exactly, did you care about the world beyond London?'

Jaxon chose not to answer this question.

'There were once seven honorary columns here,' he said. 'We hope to raise these once again, and adorn them with sculptures of voyants who lost their lives in pursuit of defeating Scion.'

I imagined a column for Liss. Jaxon probably wouldn't deem her worthy of remembrance.

'Three former temples,' Jaxon said, sweeping a hand towards the southern buildings, which I had seen from a higher viewpoint with Verča. 'This one to our left is the House of Divining. Here, we mean to provide wrought numa for soothsayers, and to commemorate the numa of history, from the *Yi Jing* to the Cup of Jamshid. Its neighbour is the House of Augury, or Auguraculum – a work in progress – where we intend to have a lush Garden of Fate, abounding with plants, fountains and eternal flames.'

Now I understood the painted roof tiles. They matched the corresponding orders' auras.

'I see,' I said. 'And will you provide for the vile augurs, Jax?'

'Of course. We have even obtained the Liver of Piacenza, to exalt the art of haruspicy.'

Somehow I doubted Jaxon was responsible for that.

'Here is the House of Possession, formerly known as the Temple of Concord. This one will open next year.' He led me towards the enormous arch I had seen earlier. 'All inscriptions have been removed from the triumphal arches, so we might celebrate modern heroes.'

'Modern heroes.' I huffed. 'Like you?'

'My contribution to this enterprise has been modest. You would make a much finer subject.'

Jaxon led me under the arch, giving me a few moments of relief from the relentless sun.

'The Old Tullianum.' He gestured to the building to our left. 'It will serve as our jail, and the Curia our courthouse, where the Kassandran Code – international voyant law – will be debated and upheld. Scion has proven that we cannot trust amaurotics to judge us.'

Stately letters above the door read IGNORANTIA JURIS NON EXCUSAT.

'I assume that's Latin,' I said. 'What does it mean?'

'*Ignorance of the law is not an excuse.* Few voyants know of the Kassandran Code, but all are expected to follow it by instinct. Anyone who flouts it must therefore be held accountable for their crimes.'

'I look forward to seeing you answer for yours.'

His only reply was another maddening smile. He strode past a lemon tree, into the shaded arcade of another building, almost a mirror image of the Basilica Arcana.

'This is destined to serve as our debate chamber,' he said. 'It also houses our treasury, the Bank of Charon.'

'How *has* the Council of Kassandra been able to afford all this?'

'A select number of generous patrons, as well as voyants like myself, who have donated money from both outside and inside Scion. Do you recall when I said we were low on coin in London?' he asked. I nodded once. 'That was because I was funnelling it here.'

'How noble. If only you hadn't done it by condemning *other* voyants to imprisonment and death.'

'All for the greater good.'

'It must have cost millions.'

'Oh, we're some way into the billions now, darling.'

'I can think of about a thousand better uses for that money,' I said frostily. 'Sala could have put the Council of Kassandra in any old building. Why all this showboating?'

'Do at least *try* to think it through, Paige. The Roman Forum is the ancient heart of this city. An undeniable symbol of power,' Jaxon said. 'In London, voyants are forced underground, stripped of heritage and standing, cast beneath amaurotics' boots. Sala will force them to meet us by daylight. In any case, we still have coin aplenty. There are voyants abroad who have used their gifts to gain influence, make sound investments, and rise beyond the constraints imposed on us by Scion. Sala has established connections with them.'

'You love Scion. You live and breathe London,' I said. 'Why are you here, Jax?'

'You took London,' he said. 'And perhaps I am tired of living under amaurotic rule.'

We stopped at the end of the arcade, and he steered me back on to the burning plaza. He indicated a temple with a tawny roof, covered in scaffolding.

'That will be the House of Guardians,' he said. 'Any furies that appear – other than the sibyls – will meet at the House of Change. And last but not least, the House of Dreaming, home of the seventh order.' He pointed out the building ahead, which loomed above the plaza. 'Let me show you inside. You will have a place of honour here, darling.'

My curiosity was rising. I followed him up the steps.

It was mercifully cool inside. While the building was pale marble, there were splashes of red, painted into alcoves and across the ceiling. A stone table stood in the middle of the chamber.

'The oracles will come together here, to discuss their visions.' Jaxon ran a hand along it. 'To represent dreamwalking, I have commissioned a painting of the benandanti, the Good Walkers.

They were Italian farmers who claimed to depart from their bodies at night, to do battle with evil forces, ensuring a good harvest. Our homage to your gift.'

I kept the table between us. 'Why?'

'No matter our differences, I will never stop believing yours to be the greatest form of clairvoyance. You could thrive as a member of the Council of Kassandra. After all, you are the only dreamwalker.'

He must not know about Cade. I hated the little stab of relief I felt, because the Pale Dreamer still wanted her mime-lord to think she was special.

'I don't have time,' I said. 'I've a citadel to run.'

'You've been away from London for months, and you still have the gall to call yourself Underqueen.'

'I am Underqueen.'

'I doubt it. An Underqueen who forsakes her own citadel is unworthy of the Rose Crown.'

'I won't hear one more word out of you about the Rose Crown, Jax. You are a trafficker and a traitor. I ran you out of London and Paris, so you had to beg for another throne.'

'Alas, the figurative throne belongs to Antoinette.' He turned back to the entrance. 'Allow me to show you one more thing, before I let you go.'

He went outside. I took a last glance at the interior before I trailed down the steps in his wake.

'The Column of Phocas.' Jaxon pointed out the free-standing pillar in the middle of the plaza. 'We intend to build an identical replica elsewhere in the Forum, honouring a local voyant: Spurinna, the Etruscan haruspex who warned Julius Caesar of his impending doom.'

'So now you plan to *honour* the vile augurs. Bit of a change of tune, isn't it, having turned other voyants against them?'

'At the time I wrote *On the Merits*, the voyants of London were falling apart. They needed a reason to pull together.' Jaxon walked up the steps at the base of the pillar, which was made of creamy marble. 'In order to better themselves, they needed somebody to despise.'

'That's absurd. Any civilisation that needs to subjugate part of itself to survive is not worth saving.'

Arcturus had told me that.

'A pretty quote. Not yours, I trust,' Jaxon said. 'Fear not. I have ended my vendetta against the vile augurs – the *àuguri domiciliari*, as President Sala has named them. She's an oculomancer.'

I stopped.

'Wait,' I said. 'Sala is voyant herself?'

'Obviously. Why else would she have done all this?'

I should have guessed sooner, but the possibility had never crossed my mind. No wonder Sala had taken such a vocal stance against Scion.

'A voyant at the head of a country,' I said at last. 'That's new.'

'It is beyond our wildest imaginings.'

'I'm surprised she let you in here, if she's a vile augur. Given what you did to them in London.'

'She did question me on the matter,' Jaxon said. 'I admitted that I could have chosen my words more judiciously in *On the Merits of Unnaturalness*, but that youth and bitterness had got the better of me, strengthened by my hatred of the osteomancers who tormented me when I was a child. I offered my sincere apologies.'

'Only because it benefits you now.'

'You wound me.' He nodded to the top of the column. 'Behold our tragic namesake, Kassandra.'

A young and barefoot woman stood above us, cast in bronze. She was pulling at her own dishevelled hair, eyes wide, snakes entwined around her arms.

'Kassandra was a mortal princess of Troy, loved by the god Apollo, who bestowed upon her the divine gift of foresight,' Jaxon said. 'But when his advances failed, Apollo cursed Kassandra. She would see the future, but no one would ever believe her predictions.'

Apollo was the same god who had pursued the Cumaean Sibyl. He needed to wind his neck in.

'Kassandra predicted the fall of her city – but, just as the curse promised, her warnings fell on deaf ears. Now she serves as a warning of what can happen when ordinary people do not heed those with godly insight.' He glanced at me. 'On that note, I have been working on a theory about the origins of clairvoyance. Would you be interested in hearing it, or are you too busy running errands for amaurotics?'

'Domino pays more than you.' I folded my arms. 'How the hell do you even know about them?'

'Beatrice told me, of course.' Jaxon turned away. 'If you do wish to continue your education, meet me tomorrow morning at the Maderno Fountain at half past nine. Good to see you again, darling.'

He left me standing by the plinths, alone with Kassandra.

---

Jaxon really was like a poltergeist – notoriously difficult to exorcise. I had driven him out of London, left him to die in Versailles, and the bastard still kept coming back.

After sending a message to Verča to tell her I was leaving, I walked back to the Chiostro del Bramante, digesting what I had learned. By the time I got there, dusk had fallen. I went up to my room, where I sat on my bed and opened Omnia.

**Antoinette Órlaith Carter** (born 1 May 2002) is an Irish author and former host of the talk show *Deepest Truths* (2038–2046). She was born in Roscommon to an Irish mother and a French father, who escaped from the Republic of Scion France. Carter studied at Trinity College, securing her first presenting role in 2025.

In February 2046, Carter joined a group of Irish celebrities, including her friend Fiadh Ní Rothláin (2007–2046) and ex-husband Barry Hourican (1998–2046), to protest an apparent diplomatic visit by Abberline Mayfield. She was among the few survivors of the alleged massacre that followed, and went on to become an outspoken participant in the Molly Riots, during which she distributed a pamphlet, *Stingy Jack* (2048–).

After fleeing the Republic of Scion Ireland in 2052, Carter was granted asylum in an undisclosed location. Her autobiography, *In the Shadow of the Anchor* (2054), was an instant #1 *New York Times* bestseller.

Carter must remember Dublin in excruciating detail. Even though she had survived, it had turned her from a popular and wealthy celebrity to a hunted rebel. I wondered if her archangel had protected her that morning, while everyone around her was murdered. Perhaps her book went into it.

I took another sip of alysoplasm before I lay on the bed. Even without the aster fatigue, my body was reprimanding me for running on so little sleep for so long.

By the time I opened my eyes again, it was almost nine in the evening. I couldn't get used to waking up with no sense of who was around me. I checked my phone, finding a new message from Nick: My replacement is on his way. M and I will get the first train to Rome on Thursday.

Jaxon is here, I replied. So is Antoinette Carter.

How are either of them in the free world?

Probably safer to explain in person, but apparently we aren't the only ones who've been thinking of impressive ways to fight Scion.

Any luck with the search?

I'm close, but I might have to refrain from killing Jax.

Be careful around him. You can't use your gift, and he still has every reason to hurt you, Paige.

I put my phone back down and stood. Before I slept any more, I needed to eat.

It was colder now the sun was down. I had intended to go back to the restaurant, but paused by the door next to mine, seeing a strip of light beneath it.

'It's me,' I said. 'Are you all right?'

'Yes.'

'Did you feed?'

There was a dead silence. I leaned against the wall beside his door.

'I found a way into the Forum,' I said. 'Jaxon is here.'

That got him to open the door. His eyes were dimmer than ever.

'Tell me,' he said, his voice soft.

I obliged. He listened without interrupting.

'I must inform Terebell,' he said, once I had described the whole earth-shattering afternoon. 'She will not be pleased to hear that Jaxon is alive.'

'I'm not exactly over the moon about it myself,' I said, 'but you and I did choose not to kill him, so this headache is our fault. You might want to omit that particular detail.'

'Hm. I will send a psychopomp.'

'You can do that while you're on alysoplasm?'

'With some patience. I still carry the æther in my veins,' he said. 'In the meantime, you should take the measure of this Council of Kassandra, to determine whether they are potential allies.'

'I'm not an especially good judge of character,' I said, 'but you did say the Ranthen wanted an advisory presence in the human world. If we can persuade the Council *and* Domino to work alongside you, this could well be how we manage after Scion.' I sighed. 'I can't get my head around the idea of voyants having any political sway, even out here. You should have seen the Forum. It's like a palace.'

'We should have built such a palace ourselves. Had the Sargas not won the war, we could have treated voyants as our friends and representatives, rather than condemn you. But since we needed you to survive, Nashira would not take any chances. She was bent on subjugation.'

'And here we are.' I folded my arms. 'I must sound like a broken record, but I can't help but notice that you still haven't fed. We're pushing a week. What exactly are you trying to prove?'

His eyes darkened even further.

'Fine. Ducos will find you somewhere else soon,' I said curtly. 'I can't stop you starving yourself, but at least I won't have to watch.'

I left without a backward glance, feeling his gaze on me all the way.

My heart pounded as I walked down the steps to the courtyard. No matter what I did, I was getting this all wrong. Arcturus was sinking, and I didn't know how to save him, because I wasn't gentle or patient, like he was.

In the courtyard, I sat by the fountain and sent a message to Ducos: Any updates on the place for Warden?

After a couple of minutes, my phone vibrated. I will collect him on Thursday evening and take him to our sanctuary in Orvieto, not far from Rome. He can stay there for as long as necessary.

'Paige?'

Verča touched my shoulder, distracting me. She took one look at my face and sighed. 'It's been a long day,' she said. 'Do you want to get dinner?'

'Please,' I said.

'All right. My niece recommended a place near the Colosseo,' she said. 'We'll get a cab.'

Arcturus was already back in his room. I knew my irritation stemmed from worry, but for once in his life, I wished he would be straightforward with me. The guesswork was driving me spare.

The restaurant was on a rooftop. Verča and I sat on upholstered red seats, overlooking a massive ruin near the Forum.

'The Colosseum,' Verča said, passing me the drinks menu. 'It was an amphitheatre in Ancient Rome, used for public entertainment. Most famously, it hosted fights to the death between enslaved warriors called gladiators. It was a cruel time. Then again, so is ours.'

'So I've learned,' I said.

Verča ordered our supper and cocktails in Italian. As soon as the waitron had gone, she released her breath.

'A sibyl,' she murmured. 'Apparently, I will be able to see my visions in more detail if I am with the others when they come. That's why Antoinette has been trying to gather us all in one place.'

'How did she use to make such good predictions on her show?' I asked. 'Did she know other sibyls even then?'

'I will have to ask her.' She swirled her drink. 'I'm not a fighter, like you or Maria. Perhaps this is the way I join the battle against Scion. Should I uproot my life and move to Rome?'

'Only if that's what you want. Just because you have a gift, it doesn't mean you need to use it, Verča.'

'What if it could help defeat Scion?'

'You'll have to square that with your own conscience, like I did. Scion forced my hand when they arrested me. I had no choice but to resist.'

'Yes. I will have to think.' Verča propped her cheekbone against her knuckles. 'My own gift aside, what this Council of Kassandra wants to achieve is quite something, isn't it?'

'It's certainly not what I expected to find here.'

'Now I see why Sala has put so much into the Forum Project. She wants voyants to be acknowledged, respected.'

'Do you think the Council might be willing to stand up to Scion?'

'They certainly have the funding and influence, though much of their money has clearly been spent on the Forum Project itself, which is frustrating. I'm sure you and your allies could have put it to much better use,' Verča said. 'Some of those who financed it are voyants whose precognitive abilities have allowed them to amass significant fortunes.'

I nodded. 'Jaxon told me.'

'Maria despises Jaxon. I was surprised to see him,' she said, her brow creasing. 'Did he not work for Scion?'

'Jaxon Hall has been involved in just about every dirty scheme you can imagine. I recommend you stay well away from him, for your own sake. He needs ... specialist handling.'

'All right.' She paused. 'Do you think Carter is lying about not being able to contact Sala?'

'I've a hunch, but even if the Council of Kassandra knows where she is, they have no particular reason to trust me. If I have to stick around and persuade them that I want to help, so be it. It's not as if we have any other leads,' I said. 'In the meantime, could I ask a favour?'

## 22

## GODS ON EARTH

The next morning dawned crisp, though the sun was just as bright. The last thing I wanted to do was start my day by seeing Jaxon Hall. He was clearly about to smooth-talk me, but I was wise to his ways now. And even though I despised him, he knew a lot about clairvoyance.

I wondered whether he knew about Deathwatch. If so, his knowledge could be useful – useful enough for me to make nice with the bastard, for now. I knew how to grit my teeth and bear him.

I'm going to see Jaxon, I wrote to Arcturus. If I'm not back by noon, assume he's done something heinous to me.

You ought not to be alone with him, Paige.

I'll keep to public spaces. Even Jaxon wouldn't murder someone in full view of the general public. I tucked my hair behind my ear. Are you able for a walk tonight?

I have no pressing engagements, to my knowledge.

It gave me hope to see that tiny flash of humour. I had been failing him for days, but if Verča came through with her favour, I might be able to do something.

It's a date, I wrote back, and tucked my phone away.

The Maderno Fountain turned out to be twenty minutes away, in a place called the Piazza di San Pietro. I took a bridge over the Tiber and walked north with grim resolve, slowing only when the plaza came into view. Shaped like a keyhole, it was lined by a colonnade topped with sculptures, and a column knifed up from the middle. A monumental building overlooked it all, a cross atop its pale dome.

Jaxon waited by the fountain, eyeing the mass of tourists with a sort of amused contempt. He was in his shirtsleeves, holding a cane I hadn't seen before.

'Good morning, my wayward mollisher.'

'Once again, Jaxon,' I said, 'I'm going to need you to get fucked.'

'Yes, you ought to be irritated by my choice of location. Vatican City, seat of the Catholic Church,' he said with disdain. 'Look at it. That wretched Pope is sitting on my hill.'

'Jax, it's not even ten in the morning, and you're already talking shite. What about the Pope?'

'Vatican, possibly derived from the Latin *vāticināri* – that is, to sing out prophecies. The men who rule this circus are not voyant. I checked,' Jaxon said darkly, tapping his cane. 'They perch on this hill in their absurd little hats, spewing archaic nonsense about—'

'Tell me why you asked me here, or I'm going. I don't even know why I came.'

'Because you enjoy my company, in spite of yourself.' Jaxon gave me his best look of remorse. 'I understand why you're upset with me – I have kept many secrets over the years – but you did take my crown and leave me to burn in Versailles. Would you not say we're even?'

'No. And I won't forget what you did to Arcturus.'

'Are you *still* whinging about a few scars on a useless Rephaite?'

'Don't make me punch you, Jax. Your teeth are one of the few redeeming features you have left.'

'I see I touched a nerve. Arcturus is here, isn't he?'

'No,' I said. 'We got separated in Paris.'

'How terribly sad for you both,' Jaxon said, sounding as if he was on the verge of physically rubbing his hands together in glee. 'A stroll will take your mind off it.' He walked back the way I had come, and I fell into reluctant step beside him. 'Still on alyso-plasm, are you?'

'Still not telling you why.'

Even though I walked at his side, I was ready for him to attack. I carried my revolver and all four knives.

'This stroll will be short,' Jaxon said. 'Will you give me as long as it takes us to reach the Castel Sant'Angelo?'

'If you tell me how you ended up here,' I said. 'That's the only reason I'm talking to you.'

'Carter invited me. She has been involved in the Forum since she was granted asylum in Italy, but she goes back to Scion at least once a year, to secure funding and search for suitable allies,' he said. 'Rackham represented her writing to Grub Street. She told him about the Forum, and he recommended me as a candidate for the Council of Kassandra.'

'I still can't believe the Rag and Bone Man was your damned agent.'

'Yes, his jocular face hid an admirably cold-blooded character,' Jaxon said. 'Alas, he could never compel me to meet my deadlines.' We passed a group of tourists, led by a woman with a flag. 'Alfred was my only friend when I returned from Oxford. He made a fine business partner until he tried to have you killed. I couldn't allow that to stand.'

'Well, congratulations for doing something yourself. Even if it *was* spilling your agent's intestines.'

'Only for you, O my lovely.'

In truth, Jaxon *had* saved me a lot of work by stopping Rackham. I might never have caught up to him.

'We have just crossed an invisible threshold. Having been in Vatican City, we are now back in Italy,' Jaxon said, running his cane along the ground. 'This is where I began to send a portion of our earnings, after I became convinced of the merits of the Forum Project. When Carter came to meet us in London, it was to collect money. She often did this through Rackham, but on that occasion, I wanted to introduce her to my remaining Seals.'

'Dani is a sibyl, isn't she?'

'Yes. Carter noticed at once. Sadly, you let her run off to Greece, but fear not. I will find her.'

'Carter must intrigue you.'

'A rare example of someone who inherited *both* gifts from her parents. Quite fascinating.'

We began to walk down the Via della Conciliazione. The leaves on the trees burned red and orange, fluttering loose to scatter on the cobblestones.

'I wanted to talk to you about our mutual friends, the Rephaim,' Jaxon said. 'Carter holds their entire species in contempt, after our violent encounter in Trafalgar Square. When I enlightened her as to what they were, she blamed them for the Imbolc Massacre. But as you know, I have worked alongside them. I see the potential for cooperation, as you do.'

'You worked with the Sargas. The conquerors,' I said. 'That's not the same thing at all.'

'Carter will see no difference. She would judge us both equally for our association with them. That is why it serves us both to resurrect our friendship.'

'We were never friends, Jaxon. You manipulated me into becoming your obedient little soldier.'

'And you loved it.'

The sad thing was that I couldn't deny it.

'Now, to business,' Jaxon said. 'In the years after I escaped Oxford, I lost myself in the stories of the ancients, trying to understand what I had seen. I devoured tales of angels and giants, demigods and demons, mortals touched by the divine. And so the first part of my theory was born. What if some of those stories – perhaps all – were inspired by the Rephaim?'

'You think they've been visiting Earth for that long?'

'A bold idea, I know.'

'If you do say so yourself.'

He let me think without comment.

'The Mothallath did come here before the civil war,' I said. 'There are Irish stories that remind me of the Rephs. Like the ones about Tír na nÓg, the Otherworld.'

'Many cultures have tales of at least one such place – an underworld or a heaven, populated by the dead, or by deities. Some of those deities are chthonic,' Jaxon remarked. 'Could they have stemmed from knowledge of the Netherworld?'

'Does it matter?'

'It might. When I was her tenant, Nashira told me about the ethereal threshold and the Mothallath family. I imagine Arcturus told you the same. The Mothallath committed some unspeakable transgression, rending the veils. What *was* that transgression, do we think?'

'Only they knew.'

'But it had consequences. And there may be more to come.' He turned to face me. 'In several of the stories I unearthed, there is a catastrophic event that ends life on Earth, sometimes destroying both humans and gods. What if those were glimpses of the future?'

'Another catastrophic event, you mean?'

'The circumstances appear ripe for it.'

*If the Netherworld can fall, so can Earth.*

'I think you might be seeing what you want to see,' I said. 'You're cherry-picking the stories that fit your theory.'

'The æther only ever sends us slivers of the truth. It is up to us to fit them together,' Jaxon said. 'The Mothallath are gone. If I am right, and the end is nigh, who will come to save us?'

'I imagine you've already put yourself forward,' I said. 'You always did have delusions of grandeur, Jax.'

'A little rich, coming from you.'

'I took the Rose Crown because you gave me no choice, as well you know.'

'All you had to do was wait, and you would have seen my plans to unite London and Rome.'

'Forgive me for not blindly trusting you.'

'You are forgiven.' He kept walking. 'We voyants share a connection with the Rephaim. It cannot be coincidence that we can touch the æther, as they can. When they declare their presence on Earth – or when their presence is revealed, against their will – it will be vital for us to ally with them, for protection and authority. Far more amaurotics will look unkindly on us then. The Ranthen are too few and weak to matter. So it must be the Suzerain.'

'I'm not working with Nashira.'

'Your fondness for Arcturus is your fatal flaw.'

'It's not about Arcturus. Nashira oversaw the conquest of Ireland, if you'd forgotten. She's a tyrant.'

'That was Gomeisa Sargas, to my knowledge. Perhaps Nashira would cease her tyranny if she felt she had nothing to fear from clairvoyants.'

'You really are off the cot if you think Nashira is a good bet. Stop licking her shiny boots and screw your head on straight, Jaxon. She's never going to see you as an equal.'

'And you believe the Ranthen do?'

'I believe we share a common purpose,' I said. 'Why don't you go back to Nashira now, if you love her so much?'

'Because she has sentenced me to death. But I do hope, one day, to bring her around.'

We soon reached the Castel Sant'Angelo, a reddish fort that crouched beside the Tiber. Jaxon led me to its gardens and stopped in front of a sculpture.

'Here is what I wanted to show you,' he said, hands clasped on his cane. 'This sculpture was saved from France during its anchorisation. It depicts one of the older race of Greek deities, a Titan named Prometheus. Like us, he was a thief. He pilfered fire from Zeus, and through it, gave the civilising arts to mortals – rather like Eve, the first woman, who defied the will of God by eating from the Tree of Knowledge. For his crime, Prometheus was bound to a mountain, where an eagle would eat his liver each day, only for it to grow back again.'

The sculpture was painfully detailed. Prometheus was contorted in agony, chained by his wrists to the crag, while the eagle feasted on his innards.

'You said that was the first part of your theory,' I said. 'What is the second?'

'I'll let you work that out. You know more about the gods on Earth than anyone,' Jaxon said. 'Dwell upon our friend, Prometheus. The realisation will dawn on you, just as it did on me.'

'I didn't come here for riddles, Jax.'

'No. You wanted knowledge, just like Eve.' He reached into his pocket and offered me a small velvet box. 'Your entry token for the Forum. Do visit again soon, Underqueen.'

'I'd rather not see you ever again if I can help it.'

'Paige, I was the one who taught you to lie. You can't turn my own tricks on me.' He gave me a flick under the chin, and I flinched back in annoyance. 'Do consider the idea of joining the Council of Kassandra. I would like an ally who appreciates the potential benefit of an alliance between voyants and Rephs. It can be your apology for leaving me to burn.'

'I could have made sure you were dead.'

Jaxon smiled.

'Indeed,' he said. 'Indeed you could.'

He left. I glanced once more at Prometheus before I crossed the bridge over the Tiber, watched by angels all the way.

––––––––––

The entry token was a square of gold leaf, inscribed with my name and order, which rolled small enough for me to carry in a matching case on the end of a chain. I zipped it into my jacket for safekeeping.

Even if I never took a place on the Council of Kassandra, I should use the opportunity to forge a relationship with them. If I played my cards right, they might be willing to help the Mime Order.

I spent the afternoon combing Omnia, diving into the myths and legends from around the world. No description perfectly matched the Rephs, but glints of them jumped out at me. In gods who had gold in their veins. In gods who looked human and lived among us.

In gods who gave humans their gifts.

I shook myself. Jaxon was sending me on a wild goose chase, and I refused to indulge him. I was about to put my phone away when a message appeared from Verča.

An anonymous member of the Council of Kassandra has just asked me for your number. Should I pass it on?

After a moment, I wrote back.

Yes.

I waited. My phone buzzed again, this time showing an unknown number.

We do know how to contact President Sala. Carter is trying to protect her – she doesn't know whether or not she can trust you – but when I informed Beatrice you were here, she agreed to speak with you in person. An ellipsis appeared on the screen as the next part of the message was composed. A black Cyrus Larunda will collect you on Via dei Cimatori at 11 P.M. tomorrow. I will send its registration number in due course. You must not speak to anyone about this.

Sala doesn't have to risk coming here, I wrote back. I can speak to her on the phone.

No. She wants to see you.

Who are you?

No reply. After a while, Verča reached out again: Was it anything useful?

I'll find out tomorrow, apparently.

That sounds promising. For tonight, I've done as you asked. The key is below the fountain.

Thank you.

I washed my face and steeled myself. Verča had done her part; now it was time to do mine.

Arcturus was silent in his room. When I knocked, he took a while to come to the door.

'Paige,' he said. 'How was your meeting with Jaxon?'

'A colossal waste of time, but at least he didn't try to kill me. And I did hear from someone else on the Council of Kassandra,' I said. 'I have a meeting with Sala tomorrow night.'

'Sala is in Italy, then?'

'Apparently,' I said. 'I suppose all I can do is try to convince her not to give in to Operation Ventriloquist. And that I can defeat Cade.'

'I believe you can,' Arcturus said. 'If President Sala is willing to risk meeting you in person, I imagine she will also be willing to hear you out. You have prevailed against greater odds.'

I held his gaze, my nape warming.

'I want to show you something. It's not far,' I said. 'Still up for that walk?'

He looked into my eyes, as hard to read as ever.

*Do not concern yourself with his state of mind. That is something you, a mortal, cannot hope to understand.*

'Yes,' he said.

I nodded. For days, I had been getting it wrong, but I thought I had a way to set it right. I would save Arcturus from himself, and then I would save Italy.

# 23

# IN THE GLOAMING

I fished an old key from under the fountain and led Arcturus on to the streets of Rome, past its golden streetlamps. Once I reached the door I needed, I unlocked it.

When I had asked Verča if she could locate a pipe organ in Ponte, she had risen to the challenge. With her general charm and fluency in Italian, she had soon found a place and talked someone into letting me use it for a couple of hours.

I went to the balcony above the door, where the organ stood ready. Arcturus stopped beside me and gazed up at it. Unless he chose to open up, this was all I could do. I owed him this much.

'The first time I heard you play the organ, it was like you were expressing all the things you couldn't say,' I murmured. 'It's all right if you don't want to talk about what happened in France, but I want you to be able to … let it out, somehow. I thought this might help.'

Arcturus considered the instrument. I waited.

'I had not thought I would be able to play again,' he said. 'Would you like to hear anything in particular?'

It took me a moment to realise he was inviting me to stay. To share the music with him.

'Just you,' I said.

Arcturus sat on the bench. I watched him get used to the instrument, familiarising himself with the pedals and stops and keys, making small adjustments. I kept my distance, feeling like an intruder. He tried out a few chords, then started to put the organ through its paces.

The music wrapped me like the warmth of a fire after days in the cold. I let myself bathe in it, as I no longer could with any ease in water. Sometimes it took my breath away, that someone who showed so little emotion on his face could weave so much of it into his music.

He played and played for what seemed like hours. When he stopped, the sound trailed away, and the chamber was silent.

'Thank you,' I said. 'It's a privilege to hear your music.' I turned to go. 'I'll leave you alone now.'

'You told me once that you like to sing,' Arcturus said, stopping me. 'Would you do me the honour of accompanying me, Paige?'

*Learning a duet entails time. And patience. Calls for us to move as one.* His voice came rushing back to me with the memory of his touch, hot against my skin. *I want you to show me where to touch you. I want to know how to make your body sing.*

'I don't know if I can sing alongside an organ,' I said.

'I can use the swell boxes to soften the sound.'

When I was a child, I had sung all the time. My grandfather had called me *éinín an cheoil*.

And then my teachers at Ancroft had got to me, making me afraid to speak, let alone sing. Even after I had left school and moved to Seven Dials, I hadn't often been able to practise. I had shared a wall with Jaxon, and he would have given me a clip on the ear for annoying him.

But I loved to sing, even if I rarely did. And I couldn't refuse this chance to be close to Arcturus.

'All right.' I approached, the temptation growing. 'Did you have a song in mind?'

'Anything you wish. I will adapt.'

I had to think about it. Now the possibility of singing was there, I hardly knew what to choose.

345

'You played a song on your gramophone in Magdalen,' I eventually said. 'It's just a short one, but I've always liked it. I heard it when I woke up after Gallows Wood.'

'I know it well.' Arcturus nodded to the bench. 'Do sit, if you wish.'

I perched on the end. This was the closest we had been since he rebuffed me in Venice. This time he let me stay there, my hip barely a handspan from him.

He eased one of the pedals down with his boot, closing the gilded shutters above us, before he glanced at me for approval. When I gave him a nod, he began. The music sounded quieter, with the swell boxes containing it, but it worked for the song.

Arcturus was such a gifted musician, I suddenly felt self-conscious at the thought of accompanying him. He had been honing his ability for two centuries. I tried to remember the techniques of singing – how to breathe, the correct posture – but I knew it was all about to fly out of my head. Before I could lose my nerve, Arcturus had finished the introduction, and I let the song pour out of me.

*In the gloaming, oh my darling, when the lights are dim and low*
*And the quiet shadows, falling, softly come and softly go*

The opening had been a little rusty, but Arcturus played with such power that I could only lift my voice to match him, my vocal cords warming at once. His variation of 'In the Gloaming' was slower than the one I was used to, but I soon worked out his cadence and settled into it.

I had unintentionally started with an English accent. Back at Ancroft, that was the only way I had ever been allowed to sing, or the Schoolmistress would rebuke me. Now I corrected my course, shaping the words as I pleased.

*When the winds are sobbing faintly with a gentle unknown woe*
*Will you think of me and love me, as you did once, long ago?*

Perhaps this had been a poor choice of song. I was already too aware of Arcturus. I kept going, swept along by his music and the exhilaration I found in singing again, after so long. The last time we sat together at an organ, wrapped in the candlelight of Magdalen, he had confessed to hearing me in my memories – murder ballads at the market, parting voyants from their coin – but this was the first time I had shown him my voice in the present.

*In the gloaming, oh my darling, think not bitterly of me*
*Though I passed away in silence, left you lonely, set you free*
*For my heart was crushed with longing, what had been could never be*

A knot was forming in my throat. I still managed to belt out the ending.

*It was best to leave you thus, dear, best for you and best for me*
*It was best to leave you thus, dear, best for you and best for me*

Arcturus brought the song to a close. The echoes of his music faded, leaving only the sound of my breath.

'You have a magnificent voice, Paige.'

I managed a smile. 'Don't lay it on too thick, now.'

'I would not pay you an insincere compliment.' He regarded me. 'Why are you so fond of this song?'

'It's about doing the right thing for someone you love,' I said. 'Even if hurts.'

'And yet we only hear one side of the story. One might ask how the other lover feels about their separation.'

He was so close to me, and still too far.

'Well,' I said quietly, 'maybe he wasn't being clear. So she had to guess what he needed.'

The tension was so heavy that I could almost reach out and grasp it. I looked up at his face, the face I had been sure I would never see again. Confronted with the strong cut of his jaw and his golden eyes, I couldn't deny how much I still wanted him.

And there was a deep ache between my legs that bordered on pain, an ache I recognised from Paris.

And my lips were no longer just my lips, but an invitation, a welcome. An offering.

Arcturus looked at our hands, and then back into my eyes, as if he was scrying for truth in their depths. The spreading chill had disturbed every fine hair on my body, all the way to my nape. I wanted to speak, but this silence felt sacred, rich and pregnant with possibility.

'Ducos has found you somewhere outside Rome,' I eventually said. 'You can stay there until Terebell comes back. Will you promise me you'll feed?'

'Will you be coming?'

'I wasn't—' I stopped. 'Do you want me to?'

He looked away, his eyes flickering.

'The alysoplasm you are taking is a poison,' he said. 'I do not know the long-term effects on humans. If you do not allow yourself a reprieve, it may damage your aura permanently.'

He still hadn't quite managed to say *yes*.

'I need to see Sala first,' I said. 'But I'll bear that in mind.' I stood. 'You can use the organ until midnight. Verča just asks that you lock up after.'

I held out the key. He took it.

'Thank you, Paige,' he said. 'For this, and for the book.'

All I could do was nod before I left him with the organ.

---

The next day, I could do nothing but rest. Arcturus filled my thoughts, distracting me from the task ahead. He clearly wanted me to join him in Orvieto, and I sensed it had been difficult for him to admit that one small thing.

A message arrived with the particulars of the meeting with President Sala. At quarter to eleven, I left the Chiostro del Bramante and waited in the right place, my hearing pricked.

When the car pulled up, I slid inside. The driver wore a suit and an earpiece and made no attempt to engage me in conversation, which suited me just fine.

The car drove through a pine forest. At first, I thought we must be approaching Castelporziano, the presidential estate that Arcturus had mentioned, but when the car stopped, it was outside a small and run-down farmhouse in the countryside. When the driver let me out, a man in body armour approached, with another guard not far behind him.

'Paige Mahoney,' he said. I nodded. 'Please follow me.'

He pointed me into the farmhouse. Inside, a woman awaited me, dressed in jeans and muddy boots and a chequered shirt.

Like someone who didn't want to be recognised as the President of Italy.

Beatrice Sala was a shadow of the bold woman I had seen in the news. She had lost weight since the last time she was photographed, and her face was gaunt.

'Paige Mahoney,' she said. 'It *is* you.'

'President Sala,' I said.

'I thought you were voyant. A dreamwalker.' The lines on her brow deepened. 'I see no aura.'

'I'm concealing it with a drug. I need to stay under the radar.'

'I have been trying to do the same,' she said. 'I understand Domino sent you to track me down.'

'Yes.' I stepped towards her. 'You're voyant.'

'A secret unknown to most of my staff,' Sala said, 'though I meant for them to know it soon, once we unveiled the Council of Kassandra. A dream that grows fainter with each passing day.' She slid her broad hands into her pockets. 'You requested my attention. I have risked a great deal by returning, so I hope you have something important to say.'

'I do,' I said. 'I know why you left, and I think I can help you.'

'I am listening.'

'Domino was informed of a Scion military plan called Operation Ventriloquist, which aims to bring countries down from the inside. It's the reason Norway fell,' I said. 'They believe Italy is the next target, and that's why you gave Capri and Ischia to Scion. Were you threatened by a man with a red aura – a man called David Fitton, or Cadoc Fitzours?'

'How do you know this?'

'I heard it from the prisoner Scion left on Capri.'

'You went there?'

'Yes, to free him. He told me more about Operation Ventriloquist.'

'You may have doomed us. Once I had evacuated those islands, no one was to set foot on them. Scion wanted to conduct its affairs there in secret.'

'I wasn't detected. The only way they'll find out is if they send people down to the Grotta Azzurra,' I said. 'Did Fitzours come to see you?'

'Yes,' Sala said. 'I was in a meeting with the Prime Minister when my aide, Valentina Chen, walked into the room. She spoke to us, but she was not herself. In the calmest manner, she told us she was Cadoc Fitzours, a dreamwalker. Through her, he explained what he had done to Umberto, and to Helen Githmark in Norway. Lorenzo didn't believe a word, so Fitzours made Valentina stab herself. I could not believe what I was seeing.'

I swallowed.

'He claimed he could do this to anyone. That none of us had free will any longer,' she said. 'He told us that he could enter our dreamscapes, see through our eyes, at any time. He ordered us to sign away the islands on the spot, under a new treaty between Italy and Scion, or he would leave Valentina to bleed out and frame us for her murder. The treaty promised that Italy would join Scion. It legitimises any future invasion.'

When Scion moved against Italy, nobody would come to punish it. Sala would appear to be fully complicit.

'Until then, the islands were a sign of our commitment, to lie untouched in the sea,' she said. 'Fitzours possessed Lorenzo and dropped the treaty from a window. Someone below took it away.'

Cade really had thought of everything.

'I had learned a little about dreamwalkers from Jaxon,' Sala said, 'so I knew Fitzours needed to be within a certain range of a person to possess them. I decided to go into hiding at once, so I could not be forced to act against my will again. Lorenzo agreed that he would remain behind, to uphold the impression of normality, but I fear for him.'

'Is Fitzours watching him?'

'I don't know,' she said. 'I haven't dared to speak to anyone. I've been trying to formulate a plan, but all I have been able to do is stay away. But there is only so long I can hide, and my powers are limited.' Her mouth thinned. 'The Roman Forum was to be our embassy, the first of many. If Rome falls, so do all of those decades of work for voyants. All of the time and money we have poured into the Forum Project will be for nothing. But what Fitzours can do – I have never seen the likes of it. How can anyone fight such a power?'

'Fitzours is just one person. He can't be everywhere at once.'

'And you know this because you are a dreamwalker.' Sala drew a deep breath. 'After what I saw from Fitzours, I was in two minds about meeting you, but you may understand the threat better than anyone. That's why I agreed to see you, against my better instincts.'

'I want to stop him,' I said. 'But I need to know where he is.'

'Probably abroad,' she said. 'He told us that if we behaved, we would be allowed to continue running the country until he decided to come back for us, to force us to announce the conversion. Thanks to this Operation Ventriloquist, we are already little more than a dummy government. Lorenzo is petrified. Fitzours told him he would force him to kill his family if he resisted. It is a power no one should have.'

I had once told a man I would kill his children, but it had been a bluff. Cade was clearly willing to make good on his threats. I could see why Sala might find my gift disturbing.

'Linda Groven was made into a Grand Inquisitor. I am unnatural, so I will be executed,' Sala said. 'I seem to have two choices. Either I flee into exile, or try to resist this attack on our country. But even as head of the armed forces, I do not know how to fight this man.'

I was already out of my depth. Despite my confidence, I had no business advising this woman.

'President Sala,' I finally said, 'I know this situation is terrifying, but I believe Fitzours is trying to intimidate you and the Prime Minister into giving up without a fight. Scion has its hands full with the Iberian Peninsula. They don't want to waste time and resources on more drawn-out invasions; not while the anchorisation is ongoing. That's why they're using this tactic to scoop up a few more countries in quick succession. They don't know who launched the airstrikes. They're nervous, so they're taking a short-cut. That has risks.'

'You are a young criminal with no military training,' Sala said. 'Why should I listen to you?'

'I'm not saying you should ask me for tips on how to win a battle,' I said, 'but I know about dreamwalking. I can make things difficult for Fitzours.'

'I did not stay away from Rome just to protect my own integrity. I also feared he could be in my head, like a silent observer. He told me so.' Her throat bobbed. 'I thought that if I spoke to Domino, or to the Council of Kassandra, he would be able to hear it.'

'No. Most people black out for the time they're possessed. You'd know if he was in your dreamscape.'

Sala absorbed this.

'If we stand firm,' she said, 'there is a possibility that Scion will use military force. You are right that the Second Inquisitorial Division is preoccupied, but even if they don't have the numbers for a ground invasion, they can launch missiles from France and Greece. If we resist, Scion could slaughter many Italians, but if I comply, I condemn all the voyants in this country – my fellow voyants – to death and misery. It is an impossible choice.'

So far, she hadn't mentioned the Rephs. I would do the same. If Carter was a strong influence on her, she could mistrust my association with the Ranthen.

'I can't make this decision for you,' I said, 'but I wanted you to know you have a dreamwalker on your side. If Cade invades your body, I can get him out. I can do the same for your ministers.'

'Are you offering to act as a bodyguard?'

'If necessary. Talk to whoever you need to consult,' I said. 'If you need me, I'll be here.'

'You are not planning to leave Italy?'

'Not while Cade is alive. I want a clear shot at him.'

Sala looked me over. I wondered if she could smell my lack of confidence.

'Fitzours said he would come back,' she said. 'He would not specify a date, presumably to stop us hatching any plans. But we could lure him.' I could see the gears of her mind turning. 'If we returned the residents of Capri and Ischia to their homes, it would send a message of defiance, and draw him back to Italy. But if you miss this shot, he could do untold damage.'

'Not quite as much as he pretends. Our gift is very rare. I think he's relying on ignorance to pull this off, trying to give the impression that he's more powerful than he is, but even dreamwalkers have limits. He can't possess multiple people at once. He can't hear your thoughts or see your memories. When he inhabits someone, his body is left in a vulnerable state. If we know he's got his claws in someone, I can dislodge him.'

'Can I keep him out of my head myself?'

'The only fail-safe way is to become unreadable. I doubt you want to do that,' I said. She grimaced. 'Even I'm not immune to his possessions. But I stand a better chance than most.'

Sala thought for a long time.

'I was losing hope,' she said. 'Now I feel a fool. I see that he was trying to terrify us with his best performance. But no voyant is without a weakness.'

'You didn't know what you were dealing with,' I said. 'Now you do.'

'Yes.' She lapsed back into silence. 'If I am to do this, it would be useful if I could return to Rome – to speak to the Minister of Defence, root out any incriminated politicians, and confer with the Council of Kassandra. But I fear that Fitzours could be waiting for me.'

'I can give you some protection.' I took a vial of alysoplasm from my jacket. 'This will suppress your gift and your sixth sense, but you'll be undetectable in the æther. A sip will last about a day. You should also get as much sleep as you can, to build up your defences. And remember, he can't see your memories. Or through your eyes, if you're still seeing.'

Sala slowly accepted the vial.

'Since you are confident he can't eavesdrop,' she said, 'I will reinstate contact with Domino tonight. It will take me a few days to steady the government as best I can, and to initiate the resettlement of Capri and Ischia.'

I nodded. By now, the cold spots on Capri should have closed.

'Should I decide to resist Operation Ventriloquist, I will let you know a time and date for us to plan our strategy,' Sala said. 'Until then, you should stay away, since you will be our best asset against Fitzours. The resistance will be riding on your shoulders, Underqueen.'

'I'm used to that.' I gave her a nod. 'Thank you for agreeing to see me, President Sala. From one voyant to another, I hope you make the right choice.'

Sala didn't reply, but she did slot the alysoplasm into her coat. I let her bodyguards escort me back to the car. As I left the President of Italy in the dark, I finally sent a reply to Ducos.

Assignment complete. And I'll go to Orvieto.

# PART THREE

# UNTO THE END

**Rúnsearc:** [Irish, noun] A secret love.

## 24

# MARTLET

When I told Arcturus I was coming with him to Orvieto, he answered with the smallest nod, but his eyes glowed. I hadn't seen them dance like that since our last morning in Paris.

Ducos picked us up from Rome the next day. Her rib was definitely broken, but she had received treatment in Venice to manage the pain. I supposed there was no one else Pivot trusted to drive us.

After the raid on the Palazzo del Domino, Pivot had contacted the head of Tinman, seeking an explanation for their meddling in European operations. A complex negotiation was underway. Sala had also been in touch with the Italian doublet, asking to re-establish contact with Domino.

'You did exceptionally well to find her in four days, when all previous attempts had failed,' Ducos said. 'I am starting to trust in your methods, chaotic as they first appear. Expect a bonus in your account.'

'Thanks, but I didn't do much. Warden was the one who pointed me to the Forum.'

'That's another interesting development. Let us hope that Sala will find her courage.'

'What if Fitzours comes back unexpectedly?'

'A Finnish politician was arrested for conspiracy to murder yesterday, so Fitzours is likely distracted by the thrills of a new playground for now. We have time to prepare Italy for his return.' She glanced at me. 'Are you absolutely sure you can kill him?'

'I'm sure,' I said.

She nodded.

'Until you hear from me, rest and prepare,' she said. 'You'll be safe in Orvieto.'

I glanced at Arcturus, who hadn't spoken. His eyes were now so dark, they almost looked human.

Orvieto soon appeared. The city stood on a steep hill, surrounded by the plains and vineyards of Umbria. This hill was abounding in caves and quarries, which led out to the countryside, allowing everyone to escape in the event of a siege. It had been an ideal place for Domino to establish a refuge in case Rome should ever fall to the anchor.

Ducos drove as far in as she could before leading us on foot to the sanctuary, past buildings made from golden brick. The city didn't just sit over a honeycomb of caves; it almost looked as if it was made of honeycomb, too.

Casa della Fermata had its own tunnel into the caves, which Ducos had forbidden us from using. I couldn't blame her for not trusting me around fragile structures. She unlocked a door and handed me the key.

'Make sure you keep your phone on at all times. You're on standby,' she said. 'Orvieto is a jewel of this region. Once again, please try not to damage any buildings while you are here.'

'Of course,' I said.

'Good.' She dug into her coat again. 'We searched Cordier, once we got her back to Venice. I thought I remembered you wearing this in Paris.'

She held up a familiar pendant. The one that deflected poltergeists.

'Thank you.' I took it, relieved. 'I wasn't sure I'd see this again.'

'All right. Leave Operation Ventriloquist to us for now,' she said, 'but be ready, Flora.'

She gave Arcturus a nod before leaving.

In the house, I put my bag down and shed my jacket. Even if I had to keep my phone on for the next few days, I would still use this opportunity to gather my strength before Cade arrived. Arcturus shut the door behind us.

'The pendant,' I said. 'Do you want it back?'

'No. It is yours, Paige.'

I fastened it at my nape without protest. It was a Mothallath heirloom, but the Ranthen had approved of me carrying it, and I felt braver when I did.

'We should probably sleep off the alysoplasm,' I said. 'Do you want to pick a room?'

'The choice is yours,' Arcturus said.

'If you're sure.'

The walls of the house were pale stone. On the upper floor, the main bedroom had a fireplace and a balcony. I left that for Arcturus. I would have liked a balcony after my imprisonment.

The other room was snug, with shutters on the windows and beams on the ceiling. As I started to unlace my boots, my phone chimed. Verča had sent a message.

Widow explained the situation. We can hold the fort.

Call if anything changes, I replied. I can get back quickly if needed.

I'll tell the others. Just at the station waiting for them. She kept writing. Orvieto is one of my favourite places. If you have time to look around, you should visit the Pozzo di San Patrizio, a medieval well named after the patron saint of Ireland. It's a very impressive feat of engineering.

Thanks. I'll try to see it.

I had missed another message. Maria had sent a picture of herself on the train with Nick.

The Mime Order is on its way!

I smiled and put my phone on charge.

It reassured me that Nick had almost reached Rome. He stood the best chance of controlling Jaxon, and I had enough on my plate without having to worry about what sort of tricks my old boss had up his sleeve. He might be acting prim and proper in front of Carter, but I knew Jaxon. There was only so long his ambition could be contained.

I really didn't know why he was on the Council of Kassandra. Whatever shite he spouted about wanting voyants to have a better standing in the world, he must be gaining something personally. I didn't trust his intentions, but I did trust Nick to defang him for a while.

Arcturus looked into the room. 'Do you prefer this one?'

'It's grand,' I said. 'You'll have more space in the other bed.'

He nodded. As he left, I thought of the nights I had slept beside him in Paris. How safe I had felt.

Even now, he was withholding his emotions, keeping a tight grip on the cord. I had no right to his feelings – neither of us had consented to this connection, and we still had no idea of its purpose – but it unbalanced me to have no idea if he could read mine. I certainly wasn't trying to stop him.

It was his choice. I would accept it. I put my washbag in the bathroom and faced the mirror, grimacing. My last dose of alysoplasm was still working its way through me, worsening my dark circles. It was time for a break. I closed the shutters and crawled into bed.

———

I slept for a day and most of the night. When I woke, it was two in the morning, and I had a crushing headache. I could also feel the æther. My body welcomed the return of my sixth sense, but my dreamscape was rebuking me for suppressing it for so long in the first place. I felt my way back to the parlour and took a box of painkillers from my holdall.

Arcturus was asleep. After days of absence, I could sense his dreamscape. I washed down the pills before I burrowed into bed again.

The next time my eyes opened, it was Saturday afternoon. Just over a month since I had woken in Wrocław.

Sometimes I wished my life would slow down.

At once, I rushed to the bathroom and purged the last of the alysoplasm. I had drunk too much in too little time. When it was all out, I slumped against the bath, drenched in sweat.

Arcturus had been right to tell me to come here. I needed to get this poison out of me. I felt like death warmed over, but I was hungry enough that I wasn't likely to get back to sleep.

Orvieto was colder than Rome. I bundled up in my fleece-lined jacket before I left the house. A thick mist had gathered in the valley below, but the city rose above it, alone in the sky. I wandered along its sun-drenched streets and lanes, stopping at shops to buy fresh bread and cheese and fruit. Lastly, I picked out a bottle of red wine. There were no tourists but me, and time moved like the first trickle of a spring.

Perhaps I could have woken up and lived every day as gently as this, if I had made different choices in life. I was under no illusion that it would last. Orvieto was a dream. A last intake of easy breath before I faced the Devil.

It had occurred to me that I might not survive the encounter with Cade. For all I knew, Orvieto could be the last time I ever knew peace.

When I got back to the house, I chopped the food and arranged it all on a wooden board. I sliced a pomegranate last.

Arcturus was still in his room, probably sleeping off his own overdose of alysoplasm. He must have gone out to feed at some point. I ate in the parlour, trying to get used to the feeling of not having to do anything in particular. It reminded me of our early days in Paris.

A stubborn little voice told me I should be using this respite to train. In my head, I went over the arsenal of techniques I had learned.

I didn't know exactly what I could do against Cade. I wasn't an unreadable, so my dreamscape could be breached. All I could do was try to drive his spirit out before he did the same to me.

Arcturus had been able to help me; now I had to step up to the plate and help myself. Except I didn't quite know how. If I was practising with a gun, I could use a dummy or a bullseye. For dreamwalking, I needed a living target. I couldn't subject Arcturus to it. After what Cade had done to him, I doubted he would ever want me in his mind again.

In that moment, something drew my attention to the æther. His dreamscape felt heavy – wrong, somehow. It took no time to realise it reminded me of Capri.

Not a minute later, I was in his room. The shutters were closed against the sun, but I could see him in the stripes of daylight, lying in the gloom.

'Arcturus,' I said. 'Have you still not fed?'

'Orvieto is too small for discretion.'

'Oh, catch yourself on. You've always managed.' I went to him. 'Enough with the excuses. Why are you doing this?'

'I am not swift enough any longer. I would be noticed.'

At least he had finally admitted it. When he turned away, I sat on the bed at his side.

'Then you have to use mine,' I said firmly. 'You have no choice now.'

'I am weary, Paige.' His voice was hardly there. 'I am weary of existing at others' expense.'

My stomach tightened.

'Don't talk like that,' I said. 'Arcturus, look at me.'

He didn't. At last, I threw caution to the wind and touched him for the first time since Capri.

For days, I had tried not to do this, even as my instincts told me to draw him close. Now I gripped his chin, forcing him to look at me. Only a hairline of light encircled his pupils.

'You said you were always at my command,' I said. 'I'm ordering you, as Underqueen.'

Terebell would never have let him sink this low. She had only left him with me for a few days, and I was on the brink of losing him a second time.

'Please,' I said, softer. 'I can feel you freezing. Don't make me see you like that again.'

Arcturus returned my gaze.

At any other time, I would have braced for the familiar discomfort of a Reph using me to bridge. Instead, I willed him to keep going. I willed it with everything I had. I had invited him to share my connection to the æther, and I wanted him to accept. Our auras were fusing.

His eyes blew into open flames. I almost tensed as I remembered the torture chamber, but I knew he would stop if I did, and I needed him to save himself. So I held on to him.

My skin prickled. An unexpected sense of calm descended on me. I felt drowsy, and my brow fell against his. His upper arm, which had been painfully tight, now slackened. I felt the warmth of his sarx through his sleeve. When I looked up, his eyes were bright red.

Our auras separated. The trance broke, and I let go of him, covered with goosebumps.

'You are a damned fool,' I said, 'for not doing that before we got to Rome. I was there. I offered.'

'Paige.'

'No, you listen to me, Arcturus Mesarthim. I risked this entire country to get you off Capri. The least you can do is keep fighting for your own life.' I turned away from him. 'I'm going for a walk.'

He made no attempt to stop me leaving. I was halfway down the street before I realised.

My eyes weren't bleeding.

And it hadn't hurt.

---

The Pozzo di San Patrizio was right on the other side of Orvieto. I strode through the cobbled and darkening streets, the yellow streetlights coming on around me as the sun went down.

Orvieto had spectacular outlooks. I stopped more than once, captivated by the sights of the valley. By the time I reached the right place, it was almost nightfall. The ticket office was closed, but I had never let a little thing like that stop me from going where I pleased.

The Pozzo di San Patrizio was near the edge of a cliff, covered by a brick entrance. I walked past it and rested my arms on the old city wall for a while.

Arcturus was putting up so many walls that he might as well be in that coffin again, and I still wasn't strong enough to break him free. I had been a fool to ever think I could help him recover.

Taking a deep breath, I sleeved my cheeks dry. Every other time a Reph had fed on me, I had felt dizzy and bled from the eyes, but these were ordinary tears, shed in frustration. He had known for days that he was too slow to feed, but had kept refusing to use my aura.

The door to the well had been locked for the night. I took out my new picks and made short work of it.

Inside, a set of steps wound into absolute darkness. I snapped my windproof lighter open, casting a soft glow. An arched opening appeared to my right, carved into the rock. I leaned through it and looked down, seeing a pool of glassy water far below, like a dark mirror.

As I descended, I came across more internal windows, each with a candleholder set into it. I lit the candles as I went, but my breath came short. This was already reminding me of the Archon.

Yet something told me to keep going.

I wished I could remember whether my family had ever discussed Saint Patrick. It had been too long since I left. All I had now were faint impressions, and even those were starting to blend together. Time was eroding my childhood memories of Ireland, as it eroded all things but Rephs. Arcturus would be able to resurrect those memories, but without him, they were lost to me. Another few years, and they might be gone for good.

There were more than two hundred steps. By the time I reached the bottom of the well, I had broken into a sweat. Now I was almost level with the water, which had a small bridge across it. The sight of it woke memories I tried and failed to force back into my dreamscape.

Still, I stepped on to the bridge, since I had come this far. I grasped the railing and stood there for a long time, gazing up the shaft. It had to be over a hundred feet deep. A clear dome covered it, letting the last faint glow of dusk spill down, along with the candlelight I had left in my wake. Tufts of greenery bloomed from the fine cracks on the walls.

'Did you come to make a wish?'

I looked down. Arcturus had appeared on the other side of the bridge.

'There was a spring near our farm. You'd dip a rag or ribbon in the water and tie it around the branch of a tree.' I reached into my pocket. 'I don't have a ribbon, so this will have to do.'

I dropped a coin into the water, right through my reflection.

*I wish he would see himself as I see him.*

'I have always found such traditions intriguing,' Arcturus said. 'Whether voyant or amaurotic, humans have long sought intervention from unseen forces. You make offerings. You pray. You call out to the other side, even if it does not answer. Scion has done away with such rituals, but they flourish beyond the empire. Even within, the old faiths endured in secret for a century.'

'Nashira wants you to be the only gods.'

'I believe that is her eventual intention. For all your stories to be sublimated into us.'

The coin glinted in the dim light of the candles.

'Jaxon thinks some of them were inspired by you in the first place,' I said. 'We'd be coming full circle.' I shot him a curious look. 'How did you get to that side of the bridge?'

'There are two intertwining staircases, with different entrances. It seems this bridge is the only place where they connect.' Pause. 'Do you wish to be alone?'

'Not especially.'

Arcturus came to stand beside me in the middle of the bridge. He looked up the candlelit shaft.

'Saint Patrick was said to know the way to purgatory. The liminal state between life and a final death,' he said. 'I see you have undertaken your own katabasis.' I raised an eyebrow. 'A descent into the underworld.'

'Verča told me about this place. I'm not sure why I came,' I said. 'Maybe to feel a bit closer to Ireland.' I clasped my hands. 'Do you feel any closer to the Netherworld down here?'

'The Netherworld lies beyond the veil. If you dug to the very core of this world, you would not find it there,' Arcturus said. 'Yet I do feel a sense of peace in the depths, just as I always have in darkness. Perhaps the concept of purgatory *was* inspired by the Netherworld.'

'Don't say that. I hate it when Jaxon is right.'

His gloves were on. I looked away.

'Nashira named all your cities after underworlds. She sees the connection,' I said. 'Do you think humans of the past could have learned about the Netherworld from the Mothallath?'

'Perhaps. We know little of what they did on Earth.'

'One of the sacred mysteries, is it?' When he looked at me, I said, 'Lesath mentioned them.'

'Hm.'

A deep silence descended on the well. I could talk to Arcturus for hours, but I had always treasured our silences, when the world seemed to grow still, and I could pretend that time had stopped moving; that it could hold me without leaving a trace, the way it did to him.

'There is a mythical bird called a martlet,' he said. 'It has no feet, and never lands. From the moment it comes into existence, it is always on the wing, even when it sleeps. A bird without a roost, only resting when it falls in death. I thought of that bird as I lay in Carcassonne. It reminded me of what you said in Paris – that if I made you my home, I would be destined to wander for ever. It seems we are both martlets, Paige.'

'Except you'll never fall.'

'I have come very close.'

Arcturus reached into his coat. He offered a coin of his own to the pool, shattering the faint vision of us.

His eyes should have terrified me in the dark. They should have reminded me of Suhail, who had fed whenever he pleased as he tortured me, leaving him with a red gaze. But seeing my aura burning in the eyes of Arcturus Mesarthim, I felt something quite different.

He caught me looking.

'Forgive me,' he said. 'I never wanted to feed on you.'

'That's not why I'm upset. How are you six foot nine and the point is still going over your head?'

Arcturus watched me, waiting.

'It didn't hurt,' I said. 'I didn't bleed. I don't … understand why.'

'If a voyant is willing, there is no blood or pain.'

'Why did you never tell me that?'

'I did not want you to feel obliged.'

'It would have been safer for both of us. In Paris, you kept having to go out to feed. If you'd just taken mine—' I released my breath. 'Look, I know it must be awful to have to use our auras to survive, but you've done it for two centuries. Why punish yourself now?'

He tightened his grip on the railing.

'Suhail made me hate my own nature. I was afraid to tell you what happened in the Archon, but you refused to let me live with any shame,' I said. 'You told me that a secret held within can be a poison. If you want to talk, I'm listening.'

Arcturus was silent for some time, gazing down at our reflections in that dark mirror of water.

'In Oxford, Nashira did not torture us for information. That pain was a punishment, not an interrogation. I can endure pain,' he said, 'but in Carcassonne, she wanted the Mime Order. She wanted you.'

The shaft magnified his voice, so the walls echoed it, even though he spoke as softly as he always did.

'At first, Nashira commanded the poltergeist to excruciate me for my crimes. She knows the myth of the golden cord, and suspects that our spirits are bound, after seeing how swiftly you found me in Paris. Perhaps she thought my suffering would draw you out again,' he said. 'When awakening my scars failed to achieve the desired outcome, she instructed Kornephoros Sheratan to use his gift against me.'

Kornephoros, the Reph that Ménard had kept in chains in his basement. He was a kind of osteomancer, capable of causing a sickening amount of pain through his touch, even with gloves. He and Arcturus had been lovers once, which must have made the torture crueller.

'Once it was clear that no amount of physical agony could sway me to betray my human allies,' he said, 'Nashira sent Fitzours to harrow my dreamscape. There was only so much he could inflict on a Rephaite, but he did what he could.'

'Like … what?'

It took Arcturus a while to reply.

'You of all people know the sanctity of the dreamscape. The necessity of it,' he said. 'It is the stronghold that shelters the spirit. Without its walls, we would be adrift in the æther, exposed and defenceless.' He never stopped looking at our reflections, as though they were safer than our reality. 'When you walk in my dreamscape, you are a welcome guest. Fitzours was an intruder. He stripped me of my shelter when I needed it the most. The longer I resisted interrogation, the more violent he became. He tore down the drapes. He attacked my spirit.'

Hearing this, I knew that I was capable of killing Cade.

When I saw him again, I was going to rip his spirit to shreds.

'Nashira eventually came to accept that I would not give in to any pain she could inflict, whether physical or spiritual,' Arcturus said. 'That was when she revealed that she had Michael.'

'What?'

Michael had been with us right from the beginning, in Magdalen. He had befriended Arcturus long before I arrived. In twenty years, I had never met anyone so gentle.

'After Michael was detained in London, he was sent to Versailles, as we saw in the ledger. When Nashira learned he was there, she had him brought to her side to serve her,' Arcturus said quietly. 'And when I would not answer her questions, Kornephoros tormented him.'

I let the tears run in silence, not wanting to distract him by blotting them.

'Situla freed Michael from his cell during the raid on Carcassonne,' Arcturus said, 'but he did not leave with the Ranthen. I do not know what became of him.' He lowered his face. 'I deserve none of your pity, Paige. I failed Michael, just as I failed Gail. Just as I failed you.'

'How did you fail me?'

'I was in Paris to protect you. I was unsuccessful.'

'Stop it. None of it was your fault.'

Before I could stop myself, I had touched his wrist, right where his glove met his sleeve.

'They want us to hate ourselves, even if we survive what they do to us,' I said. 'But remember what you told me in Paris. We don't let them win.'

He looked at my hand on his arm, and then into my eyes.

'I never thanked you for saving me,' he said. 'It is not the first time you have risked your life for my sake. I am grateful for this second chance, which no Rephaite has been granted before. I have been melancholy, these past few days, but I am glad to be here with you.'

'We've always saved each other. I can't keep flying without you.'

'I believe you could. I told you. You are a force of nature, Paige Mahoney.' He covered my hand. 'I have rid myself of my poison. Are you ready to ascend?'

I craned my neck to look up the shaft, to the sky above.

'That word you used. The descent into the underworld,' I said. 'What's the opposite?'

'An anabasis. The journey back to the surface, made by those who are not yet ready for death.' He nodded to the archway. 'You climb first, little dreamer. I will follow.'

With a nod, I went to the other steps. I walked in front of Arcturus, and trusted he was behind me, all the way.

———

By the time we got back, I was drained to the marrow. Now I knew what our enemies had done to him, and no amount of white aster would take his memories away. Learning that Michael was likely dead had only worsened the weight in my chest. Yet another person who I had met in Oxford, lost to the æther.

I secured the door behind us. Arcturus went to the table, where I had left the red wine and a glass.

'Thank you for this,' he said to me. 'Your acts of kindness have not gone unnoticed.'

'It's fine,' I said. 'I'll leave you to it.'

'Paige.'

I stopped.

'You are strong, even if Fitzours is well-trained,' Arcturus said, 'but I understand that it may be difficult for you to kill him. To our knowledge, he is the only person who shares your gift; the only person who might understand the burden you have always carried. Should you decide to stay your hand, as you did with Jaxon, I will not hold it against you.'

'I can't. He's twisted our gift into something terrible.'

'No.'

He joined me at the bottom of the stairs. With care, he brushed a trailing curl from my brow and tucked it behind my ear, lingering on the shell. His gaze darted over my face.

'Nothing in you is terrible,' he said. 'Goodnight, Paige.'

And then he left, and I was alone.

———————

The warmth of his touch should have faded in moments. Instead, it fanned across my skin, kindling the flames of memory.

To distract myself, I soaked in a hot bath, then took my time drying and scrunching my hair. I changed into a singlet and pulled it down over my hips, intending to forget about that fleeting touch and sleep. Instead, I lay awake, restless.

Arcturus had trusted me with the truth. He had taken my hand, told me that he was glad to be with me. For once, I had done something right.

But he was still blocking the cord.

Before I could stop myself, I got up and went back downstairs. I couldn't stand this any longer.

I found Arcturus sitting in the parlour with his wine. His eyes were already returning to gold, but they held on to some of my red, like embers.

'Paige?'

I stayed at the bottom of the stairs, wrestling with myself.

'I have tried not to ask you this,' I said. 'My feelings aren't your responsibility, and yours aren't mine to know. I have no claim on them. But for over a year, our spirits have been joined. And now there's … nothing. You're not there. I feel like half of me is numb.'

Arcturus broke my gaze.

'I respect your decision. Whatever it is, I won't blame you for it,' I said. 'I only want to understand why.'

'There are always reasons. I ask that you trust me in this, little dreamer.'

'But I didn't trust you. Not enough.' I took a step back. 'You *do* blame me.'

'For what?'

'All of it. I knew, but—'

'Paige, wait.' Arcturus stood. 'Do you believe I hold you responsible for my imprisonment?'

'You should. I left you,' I forced out. 'I left you with Nashira.'

His eyes gave a flicker. I couldn't always interpret their movements, but I saw the moment of realisation.

Now I knew for certain. In denying me his emotions, he had also shut out mine.

'I solved your puzzle, even if I was too late,' I said. 'The proof of your allegiance, which only I could see. The red drapes in your dreamscape, from the Guildhall. The place you first held me is where you feel safe.'

'Yes.'

His confirmation was as soft as it was shattering.

'It was the same night Oxford fell. That could have been the reason why,' I whispered. 'I wouldn't have assumed it was—' I shook my head. 'But I should have seen it sooner. I should never have believed that you would turn your back on me.'

'You tried all you could with the knowledge you had. What more could you have done, if you had seen?' Arcturus said. 'I would not have gone with you.'

'Then I should have stayed with you, so you didn't have to face it alone.'

'No. I wanted you to leave, so you would be safe. I wanted you to stay away, so she would never find you,' he said. 'If you seek absolution, I grant it, but you have not wronged me.'

My throat hurt.

'You're doing it again. Showing me who you are,' I said. 'You did that in Paris, and in London. You danced with me just to hear me laugh. You were so kind and sweet and respectful, every single day. And one pathetic charade was all it took to break my faith in you.'

'Because people have used you, Paige. I have used you.'

'I forgave you for Oxford. Even if I couldn't have stopped you being tortured, I betrayed our friendship.' My voice cracked. 'I don't deserve you, Arcturus. I could have come after you again. I could have kept trying, like Terebell did. I had the golden cord – I could have found you – but I thought you were gone, so I chose the white aster. I condemned us both.'

'You needed to forget, to survive. If you had come for me, Nashira would have killed you,' he said. 'You needed to forget. But I needed to remember. As I was tortured, it was your voice that kept me sane. Your face that filled my days and nights. I was in a dark room – but I had another, in my memories. The dark room that we shared in Paris. I could go there whenever I wanted. My torturers did what they pleased with my body, but I paid them no heed, with my gift to console me. In my dreams, I was still in your arms.'

I had given up on trying to stop the waterworks. My hair was clinging to my cheeks.

'But you don't want me any more,' I said.

'I have never stopped wanting you, Paige Mahoney.'

And just like that, he released the cord.

Before, there had been a tourniquet on it. Now his emotions came pouring out of him. The rush of them hit me like a weight, driving the breath from my chest.

He wanted me so much it was excruciating. I could feel his ache to hold me right the way through my body, as strong as my ache to be held. I didn't understand how he was standing there like a statue, keeping that much passion out of sight.

'Why didn't you tell me?'

'I had to be certain you wanted my touch,' Arcturus said quietly. 'Before I let you understand how much I wanted yours.'

'You would have known that if you'd let the cord breathe.' I stared at him. 'You pushed me away in Venice. I thought you didn't want to be touched – that or you were angry with me.'

'Never.'

'Then why?'

'Fitzours took your form in my dreamscape,' he said. I flinched. 'The first time, I believed he was you, in my exhaustion. I warned you to stay away, betraying the depth of my care for you. He tried to extract information, and when that failed, he preyed on the vulnerability I had revealed. It was a crueller torment than anything else that Nashira could inflict – to hear you taunting me, telling me that you despised me. He tortured me that way until the end, when I was sealed into the coffin.'

Cade had lived alongside me before. He must have observed me with care, allowing him to mimic me.

'When I saw your face again,' Arcturus said, 'I believed that you were Fitzours, returning to goad me. And then Nick was there, and I realised it truly was you I was holding, as if on a waterboard.'

'You didn't know.'

'I still hurt you. I sensed your fear of me for the first time since Oxford,' he said. 'I shielded you from my emotions at the cost of knowing yours. All I could do was interpret your actions. I saw you trying to ease my burden, but every time I came too close to you, you moved away. I had … thought that you no longer wished for the intimacy we shared in Paris.'

'I was trying to give you space. You didn't explain what you needed, so I had to guess. What was I supposed to think after you cut me off?'

'You have your own dark room to bear. How could I bring you into mine?' he said. 'How could I touch you again, knowing my touch had caused you pain?'

'A chroí,' I said, 'I'm not afraid of you.'

I took him by the hand and pressed it to my heart. As he looked at his own scarred fingers on my skin, I let him sit with my nearness, my pulse rising.

'It's easier to live with a dark room if you have company. You taught me that in Paris,' I said. 'And I've never stopped wanting you, either.'

For a long time, Arcturus just stood there, looking down at me. His other hand came to my waist, and at last, I let myself embrace him.

'We're both such fools,' I said thickly. 'Maybe we deserve each other.' I pressed my forehead to his chest. 'Your dreamscape. The red drapes. How could you have ever felt that safe with me in Oxford?'

Arcturus tipped up my chin, just as another tear seeped down my cheek.

'For two centuries, my existence was stagnant. I was a shade in Magdalen, following the same paths each night.' He brushed the tear away. 'And then you came, angel of vengeance.'

I clung to his shirt. He lifted me on to the counter, and I draped my arms around his neck.

'The night you left Oxford, I watched my prison burn,' he said softly, eyes locked on mine. 'You were in that fire – your wrath, your strength, your refusal to be tamed. And when it finally went out, the world lay absolutely still, just as it did before you came. For some, there is safety in stillness, in certainty. But you have ruined me for stillness, Paige Mahoney.'

An urgent chill was spreading in me, sharpening my senses. Our gazes held for a long moment, and then, all at once, our lips came together.

It was fragile at first, searching and cautious, even as my bolder instincts told me to drag him right on to the counter with me. My entire body revelled in his touch; it reverberated through every inch of my skin, and every part of me remembered. As the kiss deepened, his warm hands went under my singlet, baring the burning skin of my thighs.

'I want you.' I breathed the words against his mouth. 'I want all of you.'

'Good.' He looked me in the eyes. 'I owe you a duet.'

# 25

## D U E T

In Ireland, there is a story of the féar gortach, the hungry grass. It grows in all manner of places, sown by the wandering souls of the starved. If you step on that cursed ground, you will never be sated. No matter how much you eat, you will feel empty for the rest of your days.

I had wished that eternal pain on the soldiers. And yet I carried it myself, in so many ways, deep in my bones. A hunger for justice. A need to be seen. Most of all, a yearning for home.

But I was still far away from that land, and martlets could have no home but each other.

———

Arcturus had lit a fire in his room. In Paris, we had been in the dark, with only the waning moon to reveal us. This time, I wanted to see all of him.

I had rarely been able to dwell on his body. His face, yes – I must have spent hours trying to read it – but most of the time, he covered the rest of him, leaving me to imagine. Now I watched as he undressed.

The glow of the fire limned his powerful frame. By the time he stood naked before me, my skin was so hot, I thought I would burst into flame when he touched me. I drank in his defined muscles and the pure artistry of his chest and shoulders, too aware of my own shape, trying my utmost to keep my eyes above his waist. I wondered if all Rephs emerged with that much strength, or if he worked for it.

Arcturus sat on the end of the bed. I went to stand in front of him, meeting his fiery gaze.

'The night we met, I saw your face and knew that you could be the end of me. This night, I fear the same,' he said. 'Have mercy, Underqueen.'

His voice was dark and soft, sending a shiver over my skin. I answered by slipping off my underwear, leaving me in nothing but the singlet.

'You'll have to earn it,' I said, brushing strands of brown hair off his forehead.

'As you decree.'

When he offered me a hand, I accepted. By unspoken agreement, he lay with his back against the pillows, and I knelt across his waist, my calves lying on either side of his thighs.

'I thought I would never see you again,' I murmured. 'I still can't believe you're here.'

'So we both are, against the odds.' He kept hold of my hand. 'I know you are not inclined towards flattery, but I confess to being wonderstruck, to have you in my bed again.'

'Don't be too surprised. You seem to be the only person with a liking for chaotic Irish dreamwalkers.' I kissed the mount at the base of his thumb. 'But even if you weren't, I'm all yours.'

'Such is my honour.'

A hush fell as we both looked at our intertwined fingers. This would have been nerve-racking even at the start of our relationship, when both of us had been less scarred, inside and out.

'I know you might need to take it slow,' I said. 'Tell me if you need to stop.'

'If you will do the same.'

I nodded. When our lips met, I melted into his embrace, trying not to grip him too hard.

We took our time, even though I was burning for him. Two hundred and thirty-eight days was a long time to go without holding each other. He still touched me as if I really was a martlet, delicate from years of flight, but I had never felt stronger. When he edged my singlet up to my ribs, I stripped it off and threw it aside.

'Patience never was your virtue, Paige.'

'Don't even start with me.' I steered his willing hands to my waist. 'You've given me enough simmering looks, you infuriating tower of muscle.'

He countered me with the softest kiss, lingering on the bow of my lips. I knew when he was teasing me, but I had told him he could be slow, and he would surely hold me to it.

By now I was nearly as hot as the fire. He mapped the bruising on my shoulder, checking where to be gentlest, then skirted the underside of my breast. I clasped his whole hand to it. His self-control was exhilarating, but I wanted him to indulge himself. As the callused warmth of his palm enfolded me, I parted his lips, winning a resolute kiss that left my legs weak and my heart pounding. A thousand small chills blossomed where our bodies pressed together.

The cord guided me across his sarx. Now I knew he wanted my touch, I couldn't get enough of him under my hands. I ran them over his broad shoulders and chest, across his upper arms. I wanted to surround him with warmth, crushing all his memories of Carcassonne.

He couldn't forget, like I might, in the end. The years would not dull the teeth of his torture. But I could give him fresh memories, better ones.

As he devoted his attention to my breasts, I turned mine to the scars on his back. When I felt one I didn't remember, I slowed. It wasn't as cold as the others, but it stood out from the rest of his sarx. I followed its course, only to find more. There were scores of them, lying close to each other, layered over the older scars from the poltergeist.

'An opaline blade.' His voice was low. 'Do not be troubled. These ones will not always pain me.'

I tried not to imagine the blade carving his sarx. Before I could draw enough breath to answer, he tilted my chin up again and kissed the hollow of my throat.

'Show me,' he said. 'Write me the notes.'

Well, if he wanted a distraction, I would give him one. I moved his hand between my legs.

Arcturus leaned in close, eyes on fire. He propped his chin on my shoulder, and I placed a light kiss on his temple, my breath already coming short. The most sensitive part of me, unbearably soft against his fingertips. I felt utterly defenceless and fragile, like there was nothing left but him between me and the world.

My own fingertips pressed into his shoulders as he began to explore me. Now he was exactly where I wanted him, the empty ache only grew, becoming so vast and all-consuming that it erased my thoughts of anything but him.

Arcturus circled just inside. He skimmed a little higher, nudging that pinpoint of nerve endings, each touch a revelation. Not since Paris had I been so aware of one small part of my body, which now shaped every feeling as my senses centred on it.

He glided along the edges of me. I breathed his name like an invocation. The cord was taut between us, threatening to snap, but it held strong, like his restraint. He was as much a Reph as ever, only his eyes betraying his desire – but if I had wanted human, I wouldn't be here with him.

Out of nowhere, I remembered Suhail. Arcturus felt me tense and stopped.

'I'm all right.' I traced his jaw. 'Just keep me here.'

He obliged. As I tamped the memory down, he changed our positions, so my back was against his chest, before he quested past my ribs and stomach.

Once, he had always worn gloves around me. Now he was at my entrance, finding the evidence of my human arousal, and he wasn't turning away. He idled there until I coaxed him farther, into the warmth of me, and I could feel the scars he wore like rings around his fingers, the proof of his devotion to Terebell. I pictured him at the organ again, that masterful finesse that made the night resound with music.

It felt sacred, to be touched on the inside, like knowledge stolen from the branch of a tree. He never took his eyes off my face. I suddenly couldn't remember a time when I hadn't wanted to burn in those eyes.

My release came on as a feathering, wings unfurling to the tips before they swept all the way through me. Even after Paris, I still wasn't prepared for that loss of control, even as I recognised the first soft flutter of it. Arcturus pressed me close as I tightened around him.

'I have you.'

His voice in my ear sent me over the edge. A drumbeat overtook my body. Even as it arched my back and sang along my limbs, he spun out the cascade of sensation, as patient as he was resolved, until I was heavy and soft in his arms. When I sank against his chest, he withdrew in a slow glide that almost undid me all over again.

'What was that,' I said faintly, 'about mercy?'

'I trust that I granted it.' He caressed my collarbone. 'Are you satisfied, Underqueen?'

'Not even close.'

His eyes smouldered. In reverent silence, he eased my hips to the edge of the mattress and knelt in front of me. I watched in a haze, glazed with sweat, as he stroked the backs of my calves. A sudden flicker of nerves pressed my knees together, but one scorching look from him, and I let them fall apart again. I already knew he liked doing this.

Arcturus kissed my breastbone, hands encircling my hips. As I gripped the sheets in anticipation, he lifted my thighs on to his shoulders, laying me bare to his mouth. He followed the notes I had written in Paris, but he knew how to play by ear, and he improvised.

'Is ceol m'anama tú.' I trailed my fingers through his thick hair. 'Fan liom, a rúnseirce.'

I wasn't sure why it came out in Irish, but it emboldened me, knowing he had no idea what I was saying. When he glanced up at me, the light in his eyes dappled my lower stomach.

'Are you asking me for something, Paige?'

'I think I might be … praying.' My legs were trembling. 'Jaxon does … think you're gods.'

'Perhaps to some. But here, I am the supplicant.'

My head fell back as he tasted me, accepting my libation even as he knelt in worship. This time, he prolonged his mercy, keeping me on the cusp of release, caught in the crescendo.

And I began to understand what it was to be a Reph. It could have been moments or hours that were slipping away, and I would have been none the wiser. In this room, I was immortal.

After that short eternity, he lifted me to his chest again, so we faced each other. My breaths came quick and fast. I hadn't known that there were sweet and painless kinds of torture.

Arcturus stilled then, a question burning in his eyes. Without the dam on the golden cord, I knew what he was asking. I knew that he expected nothing, and that everything we had shared was enough.

In answer, I slid a hand down his front, savouring the silken finish of his sarx, until I reached a part of him that I had never touched. This was where things had gone wrong with the amaurotic, but I felt safe with Arcturus. He had composed a hymn to my body; now I wanted us to be one instrument.

He kissed along my jaw, letting me get used to him. Though I was no expert in this department, nothing came as a particular surprise. He was big, but that was hardly the shock of the century, given his general proportions.

As goosebumps spread across my skin, the unrelenting ache grew stronger. I drew Arcturus close. With the lightest touch under my chin, he stopped me.

'I do not believe we have any need of it,' he said, 'but I can use protection, if you wish.'

'You're grand,' I said. 'Like you say, I don't … see the point, in our case.' My face warmed a little, but I returned his gaze, and it steadied me. 'Are you sure you want to do this?'

'Quite sure. Are you?'

'Yes.' I kissed him. 'I'm very sure.'

Arcturus held me to his sarx. We had defied the doctrine of distance so many times. I refused to be afraid.

As I guided him, I felt my body starting to resist, like my gift so often did. A tight pressure mounted between my legs.

'Paige.'

'I'm all right.' I grasped his nape, trying to slow my breathing. 'Just stay there.'

'Be assured,' he said, 'that I am not going anywhere.'

'No, I imagine you're not.'

Over the course of a year, I had endured more than I would have once thought it possible for one person to survive. The needles, the aster, the knife, the betrayals – all those memories had sunk roots in every sinew, as well as in my dreamscape. Now my body was braced for another incursion. It was locking the doors, reminding me to defend the fort.

I willed it to accept that Arcturus posed me no threat. His touch was gentle on my face, brushing my curls back, gracing my lips and cheeks. I closed my eyes as he kissed me again, soft and tender.

And then I let my sixth sense overpower the others. I pressed our foreheads back together, so our spirits were as close as I could bring them without dreamwalking. I tuned into the tiny vibrations of the golden cord, reminding myself that this feeling was mutual.

'I have you,' Arcturus said quietly.

And finally, my guard dropped.

That first moment of his entry was like nothing I had ever felt, lacing my skin with chills and goosebumps. He searched my face every time he moved deeper, only continuing when I nodded, once my body had accepted his presence. I hardly breathed as he settled, eyes flaming.

We stayed like that for some time. I came to the distant realisation that I was shaking.

'Well,' I said, 'the world still hasn't ended.'

'Let it.' He cupped my cheek. 'Are you comfortable?'

'Yes.'

He waited for me to adjust to the feeling. His solid heat was more than physical, like I was holding a numen inside me. My dreamscape was ablaze, the cord pulling tight. Gathering my courage, I followed my instincts and made the first small move. I could only assume I had done something right, since my name escaped his throat.

'Paige.'

Hearing that loss of restraint bolstered my confidence. I rocked against him, finding a cadence I liked.

'I'm here.' I kissed him. 'I've got you.'

In answer, he cradled my hips, holding me like I was his deliverance.

We both tried to be slow at first. Arcturus was as attentive as ever, careful with my human frame, rising to meet the pace I set so we could move as one. The firelight played across our bodies. Every moment, I expected the pain that had struck me before, with the amaurotic, but it never came.

All the while, I watched for any sign of discomfort. I found only clear-eyed resolve. One of his hands was between my thighs, while the other returned to my cheek.

More than once, his body did stiffen. I framed his face when it happened, letting him know he could take his time. After a while, the tension eased under my touch.

At some point, I lost all sense of anything outside us. We had wanted each other for a long time, and my body was demanding as much of him as he would give. Soon our duet was a rhapsody, and both of us were on that cusp, barely holding on. Arcturus kept his brow on mine, his sarx as hot as my damp skin.

'Paige,' he said, soft as a prayer.

My spirit dislocated. I dug my fingers into his upper arms to ground myself, forcing it back into place with all my strength. He dabbed the blood from my nose.

'You can dreamwalk,' he said against my ear. I shivered. 'Move in me, as I move in you.'

I was tempted, when he put it like that. My spirit was reaching for him, wanting him the way my body did, but he couldn't want me in his dreamscape.

'Not yet. I want——' My head fell against his shoulder. 'I just want this. This is enough.'

With each surge of his body in mine, sweetness blossomed inside me, calming the headache. It faded as we reached the brink. He clasped my fingers to his chest, so I could feel his heart as well. I was soaring too close to the sun, but I trusted him to catch me as I fell.

In the end, we fell together.

----

I slept for a while, wrapped in his arms. When I opened my eyes, the fire had died out, but the shutters were open, letting in the lamplight from outside.

Arcturus lay beside me, stroking my dishevelled hair. I hadn't expected him to be awake. I nestled against his chest, so the heat of his sarx ran all the way along my skin.

He looked into my eyes. I lifted my hand, brushing his cheek with the backs of my fingers.

His palm grazed along my lower ribs. I already wanted him again. When I showed him as much, he tilted me towards him. My breath shallowed as our bodies locked together.

'You spoke to me in Irish.' His voice was a dark thrum in his throat. 'What did you say?'

It took me a moment to remember what he meant.

'Sounds like you need some more lessons,' I said, and kissed him again before he could ask.

I was so lost in us that I forgot a fundamental truth.

The world did not take kindly to mortals who thought themselves worthy of gods.

----

When I woke a second time, it was still dark, and Arcturus was gone. I sat up a little. Once I had sensed him nearby, I rested for a while longer.

In the bathroom, I attempted to tidy my hair. Knowing a lost cause when I saw one, I brushed my teeth and showered, finding I had more courage than usual. Once I was out, I drew on his discarded shirt, then caught my own gaze in the mirror and smiled.

When I reached for the golden cord, all I sensed was serenity. The same feeling that had warmed me all night, given and returned in kind.

I let myself accept it, as I never had before. At last, I released the weight of disquiet. I trusted that, in defiance of everything, Arcturus Mesarthim was in love with me.

And for once, I really did feel like the luckiest woman alive.

I found him on the balcony. When I stepped out to join him, he took me in, the sunrise forgotten.

'Thought you'd done a runner,' I said lightly.

'Forgive me. I was loath to wake you.'

'I'm teasing. You'd better get used to that.' I sat with him, circling my arms around his neck, and he ran both hands from my hips to my waist. 'You look deep in thought. No regrets?'

'Never. I was only reflecting.'

'On last night?'

'On every night since I first saw you.' He rested his forehead on mine. 'Would you care for some coffee?'

I kissed him. 'You always know what to say.'

He made the coffee on the stove downstairs, the way I had taught him in Paris. I accepted the mug and sat across his lap on the couch, my back against the armrest, my legs draped over his thighs.

'So,' I said, 'I think we've established that we play an outstanding duet.'

I kept my tone casual, but Arcturus took my hand, his gaze intent. His eyes were back to gold.

'In Paris,' he said, 'you asked if I knew what I wanted from this. I told you that I only knew I wanted you with me.'

'Yes.' I watched him. 'I thought we agreed to play it by ear.'

'It is the only way in war. Even with the foresight of clairvoyance, none of us can plan a future in a time like this. But as I lay in the coffin, I wished I had been more forthcoming.'

'Good thing you can fix that now.'

'Yes.' He held my hand to his chest. 'I have not had a partner since Terebell. I did not imagine taking another. But over this past year, I have wanted nothing more than to be yours. Even if our time in Paris had its trials, I was never so content as when I lived with you.'

I listened in silence. Even after last night, it was surreal to hear this sort of forthright expression from him.

'I told you this in Paris, but it bears repeating,' Arcturus said, keeping hold of my gaze. 'I have little to recommend me as a partner. Still less now I cannot raise a blade in your defence.'

'Not true.'

'Hm. But if you are willing to commit to me – if you grant me the privilege of your trust – then in return, I offer myself as your steadfast companion, who faces all things at your side. I will honour you in body and spirit. You will be my highest calling. Neither of us has a home, but as long as you want me, I will do all I can to be your harbour.'

My throat hurt. If I didn't get a grip, I was going to cry all over him again.

'Sounds nice.' I toyed with his collar. 'Are you asking me out?'

'That was my intention.'

'Took you long enough.'

'I am immortal. This has been a swift courtship, by Rephaite standards,' Arcturus said, 'but I would like our union to be a long one.' He touched me under the chin. 'If you feel the same.'

'I do.' I leaned into his embrace. 'I accept your offer, if you'll accept the same from me.'

'I do.'

We stayed that way for a long while. All those years of wandering, and I had found my safe place here.

'Paige,' Arcturus said, 'if your instinct is to dreamwalk in our bed, you should not hold back. I do not fear your gift.'

'I'm not saying I never will. I just think we should … build up to it.'

'Would you like to start now?'

I did happen to want him now. The cord must be giving me away.

'Not if you'd sooner rest,' I said, though I couldn't help but smile again. 'Are you not tired?'

'No. And I would not leave you wanting.'

He knelt before me again. Moving between my thighs, he traced the swell of one breast through my shirt and lowered his head to where the collar hung open, while his other hand glided under the dark cloth to brush my ribs, covering me in goosebumps. He unfastened the shirt and slipped it off my shoulders.

'I love it when you look at me that way,' I told him.

'I remind you that I can do far more than look at you.'

He folded back one of my legs, lifting my knee towards my ribs. I closed my eyes in anticipation, wondering how I was going to be around him in public, wanting him as much as I did.

Out of nowhere, I wondered how Ducos would react if she found out about this. I shook with laughter before I could stop myself. Arcturus glanced up, eyes aglow.

'Sorry. It's not you,' I said. 'I just had a ridiculous thought.'

'I would not mind if it had been me. I have not heard you laugh in far too long.' He raised himself up to me for a moment, so his gaze was level with mine. 'By all means, let your thoughts drift.'

'Stop it. This is serious.' I smiled into his kiss. 'We're committing a terrible flesh-crime.'

'Hm.'

My coffee soon went cold, but nothing else in that room did.

---

For a few precious days, we lived like there was no one else in the entire world. We spent most of that time in bed, but now and then, when it felt safe, we walked the streets of Orvieto. We had a sunset picnic on the city wall. We explored a small Etruscan ruin and stole into the ancient caves. I let myself forget that Cade might soon be coming.

One day, we got up at dawn and followed the trail that surrounded the city, to get him used to walking longer distances. It was slow going, but I could see him taking a real interest in his surroundings again, which reassured me. He noticed birds and plants I would have missed.

Months ago, Arcturus had warned me that this path would not be easy. That had never been more apparent. His recovery was only just beginning. I would stay the course for him, as he had done for me.

While he rested in the day, I trained as much as I could by myself, ensuring I could perform well-oiled jumps. I checked in with Nick, but there was no word from Sala.

You were overdue a rest, he said. Take it while you have the chance.

Arcturus slept for most of the next afternoon. I drowsed in bed with him, listening to the patter of rain on the roof.

Every so often, he stirred, though he remained lethargic. I remembered him being a deep sleeper, but now the smallest sounds or movements might disturb him. When he was in that halfway state, he murmured Gloss against my skin, leaving delicate chills in his wake.

My spirit understood him, even if the language eluded me. I hoped he felt the same way when I took refuge in Irish. I wanted him to learn – I knew he would – but I would still cherish this window of time, when I could bare my soul to him without a second thought.

The rain kept pouring. I laid my head on his middle and started to drift back to sleep.

And then Verča sent a message, rousing me.

The Prime Minister just made a public announcement, saying that the danger has passed, and the residents of Capri and Ischia can return to their homes. I assume President Sala has made her decision.

She sent a link to a video-sharing platform called Podium. The address was in Italian, so all I could do was study Lorenzo Rinaldi, a short and wiry man with a receding hairline. From the shadows under his eyes and the beads of sweat on his brow, his courage was barely afloat. President Sala must be keeping out of the way, not betraying her location. I could only assume Capri was safe, now there was no latent Reph drawing the Buzzers there.

I checked for any missed calls from Ducos. Finding none, I turned over and embraced Arcturus, my trepidation growing for the first time in days. His arm came around me, and I was soon asleep.

———

That evening found us on the balcony. Arcturus was reading the book I had bought him in Venice, his eyes casting a yellow glow on the pages, while I rested against his chest, gazing at the sky. After everything we had endured, the æther had reserved a pocket of time for us, but it could only ever be a short reprieve. I would savour it while it lasted.

President Sala had made her decision. She trusted me to protect her. To safeguard an entire country.

Now all I had to do was prove myself worthy of that trust.

A ribbon of pale light appeared between the stars. At first, I thought it was a cloud, and then I was sure I was hallucinating, but it soon brightened to the point that I sat up to look.

'Is that an aurora?'

Arcturus followed my line of sight.

'Yes,' he said. 'They appeared when we first came to Earth.' I sat up, entranced by the spectacle. 'We used to see them in the Netherworld, too. Your scientists believe they are caused by the winds of the sun, but the Rephaite belief is that they stem from the last light.'

'Nick said he used to chase them in Sweden. I didn't think they came this far—'

My phone vibrated.

We looked at each other. After the fourth ring, I answered it, my body turning cold by increments.

'Widow?'

'President Sala will address the Council of Kassandra at the Forum tomorrow night. Your presence is required,' Ducos said. 'Be ready to leave at any time.'

The line went dead.

'Sala wants me back tomorrow.' I lowered the phone. 'I might actually have got through to her.'

'I will accompany you,' Arcturus said. 'Terebell is on her way. She wishes to meet us in Rome.'

'When did you hear from her?'

'This afternoon, while you were sleeping.'

'You won't be able to use my aura. Terebell will have to help you go looking for voyants.' I took hold of his chin. 'Promise me you won't starve yourself ever again. Swear it on the æther.'

'On my oath.'

He never broke an oath by choice. I sank back into his embrace, watching the lights fade above us.

---

He joined me in the shower that night, so I could feel the water without fear, calmed by his presence. After, we curled up in bed, facing each other, and for once, he fell asleep before I did.

If Orvieto had taught me one thing, it was that I had to be more careful with my fragile life. I wanted to be able to share it with him after Scion. I wanted us both to see more of the world.

Sooner or later, something would have brought us crashing back to reality. Terebell was still going to take him back to Scion as soon as I got rid of Cade, while I had to stay out here in the free world. I would have to accept the separation, as I accepted many small hurts.

'Is tusa mo bhaile, mo dhídean.'

My voice was almost too soft to hear, but Arcturus opened his eyes a little. I pressed myself against his chest and listened to his steady heart.

If I had this, I might yet lose everything.

If I had this, I thought I could survive.

# 26

# TABLE TURNING

Orvieto was cold on the day we left. My breath came in clouds as I stood on the balcony, taking in the misted hills, as buttoned up as a Reph. I would probably never come here again, unless we succeeded in defeating Scion. I wanted one last sight of the place where I had taken what I wanted, and accepted being wanted in return.

When I sensed Ducos, I locked the balcony door and crossed our room. We had laundered the sheets and remade the beds, as if we had never been here. No one else would ever know.

Arcturus was downstairs, sitting on the couch with red eyes. Now he could use my aura without hurting me, I had insisted he do it again. When I gave him a nod, he stood, dressed to leave. I checked that I had everything, including my knives, which I slotted into my holster.

'You trained me for a good while,' I said. 'If it comes to single combat, do you think I can beat Cade?'

'Yes. Fitzours is disciplined, but I believe your potential is greater. You were strong even in your early days in Oxford, before I began to instruct you in earnest. You brought Suhail to the ground by instinct. If you can do that, you can overpower a fellow dreamwalker.'

'Why do you think my potential is greater?'

'Because you are driven by your emotions, while I suspect Fitzours is not. What *does* drive him, I cannot guess, but from what I observed, he suppresses all compassion for his targets.'

'You criticised my lack of restraint in Oxford.'

'I feared that your unvarnished anger might provoke the other Rephaim. But I have never judged you for embracing your rage or fear when you dreamwalk,' Arcturus said. 'You should trust your instincts, Paige.'

He had so much faith in my abilities. I hoped I could inspire Sala to have even a fraction of his confidence in me.

Ducos knocked on the door. I kissed Arcturus once more, a stolen indulgence. We took a final look at the room, and just like that, we left Orvieto.

It had only been a dream.

---

Ducos looked as if she hadn't slept in a week. She must be in pain from the broken rib, and it was cold enough that she needed to put the heating on.

'President Sala has agreed to update Domino after this meeting,' Ducos said. 'As a precaution, we're moving some personnel to our sanctuaries in Orvieto and Matera. If Scion has its customary reaction to defiance, we could be facing an invasion within a few days.'

'They're not ready for an invasion. If they threaten that, it's a bluff,' I said. 'Vance claimed that all resistance would be like fighting smoke. That's all Operation Ventriloquist is. Just smoke and mirrors.'

'I hope you're right.'

Arcturus sat in the back. I caught his gaze in the mirror, then looked away before Ducos could see. When we reached the outskirts of Rome, we took our alysoplasm.

The Eternal City soon reappeared. A thick mist had descended, straining the glow of sunset, and the temperature had dropped even more. Ducos parked outside the Chiostro del Bramante.

She waited in the car as I got out with Arcturus. 'I might be gone for a while,' I told him as we entered the building. 'Do you know when Terebell is arriving?'

'Very soon.' He offered me a vial. 'It is still possible that President Sala means to collude with Scion. Should you need your gift to defend yourself, drink all of this at once. It is ectoplasm mixed with hypertonic saline, and will counteract the alysoplasm in your blood.'

'Thank you.' I fastened it into my jacket. 'What did I ever do without you and your vials?'

'Hm.' His gaze darted over my face. 'Be safe, little dreamer.'

'I'll do my best.'

When he leaned down to kiss me, it swept me to the previous autumn, to London. I had been so hopeful about where our relationship was heading then, and I felt that same hope now, as I returned his kiss. A hope that we could outlast anything that lay in store. He pressed my hand and went to his room, while I got back into the car.

'His eyes were red,' Ducos said, a question in her tone.

'He's fine.' I fastened my seatbelt. 'Shall we go?'

---

Ducos drove the short way to the Roman Forum. As I started to get out, she caught a glimpse of my holster.

'Make sure you declare those weapons,' she said. 'Sala is a world leader. Her safety will be prioritised in there.' I nodded. 'Do you have an entry token?'

'Yes,' I said. 'Are you staying in Rome?'

'For the time being. I'll be at the Chiostro del Bramante with Match, another member of Command. We'll see you afterwards.'

She took off, leaving me alone at the entrance to the Forum. I approached the guards and showed them my gold pendant. As expected, they confiscated my weapons, including the knife I kept in my boot. Only then was I allowed to pass under the archway.

Candles and flaming torches lit the Forum. They must not have got the electricity going. I crossed the cobblestones, reminded of Oxford.

Nick and Maria waited outside the Basilica Arcana, wearing identical tokens to mine. They embraced me between them, Maria using her good arm.

'You look much better,' Nick said. 'How was Orvieto?'

'Good,' I said. 'Got some training in.'

Maria had a twinkle in her eye. 'And how is Warden?'

'Better for the rest, but I didn't want him to come here. I don't believe Jax isn't tipping Scion off.'

'It really is a sick joke that he's here. Sala and Carter don't seem to grasp the danger he poses.'

I looked at Nick. 'Did you talk to him?'

'Yes. He's giving the impression that the Council of Kassandra has been his only concern for years,' Nick said grimly. 'Carter seems to like him, and we have no solid proof of anything he's done to hurt voyants. You were the only person who saw him in the Archon.'

Verča came down the steps to join us, wrapped up in a warm coat, like the others. 'Welcome back, Paige,' she said, with a tired smile. 'Did you go to the Pozzo di San Patrizio?'

'I did, thanks. It was beautiful.'

'Good.' There were dark circles under her eyes. 'The atmosphere in there is very tense. Whatever Sala has decided, every voyant in this country will be under threat, and we all know it.'

'Paige will stop this,' Maria said.

'Let us hope. We should take our seats,' Verča said. 'The meeting is about to start.'

From the looks of the Basilica Arcana, it was the first part of the Forum to have been resurrected. The interior was a single vast chamber, about two hundred feet long. As my group walked between the columns of the inner arcade, a marble floor gleamed underfoot, lit by chandeliers, the candlelight dancing across a coffered wooden ceiling. A few people mingled in the upper arcade, their conversations echoing.

A table ran down the middle of the chamber, dwarfed by it. Sala sat at one end, with Rohan Mistry and Antoinette Carter on either side of her. From her drawn appearance, Sala was taking the alysoplasm I had left for her.

'Imagine the Mime Order having a place like this,' Maria said. 'Instead of having to hide in sewers.'

In truth, I found it all daunting. I must have lived in Scion for too long, to have grown so comfortable in hidden places. Still, the Basilica Arcana was breathtaking, and I could see why it could mean a lot to Sala, to conduct voyant business in such grand surroundings.

The floor was covered in detailed pictures from the tarot. The rays of a sun spread out around the table. Noticing us, Jaxon sauntered over, his face sharpened by the candlelight.

'How are we, my fellow runaways from Scion?'

'Always worse for seeing you, Binder,' Maria said icily. 'Have you brought us here to sell us?'

'Oh, Maria. We ruled our adjoining sections cordially for many years, despite our disagreements.' He folded both hands on his cane. 'Surely we can be friends in the free world.'

'Binder, you peddled voyants to the Suzerain. You did nothing while Paige was tortured.' She kept her voice too low for anyone to overhear. 'You might have tricked Sala into liking you, but we all know exactly what you are.'

'I doubt that.' His smile was frigid. 'Come along. We have grave matters to discuss.'

He went back to Carter.

'Stay calm around him,' Nick said quietly. 'He's up to something.'

I believed him. He knew Jaxon better than anyone.

The chairs had plaques in front of them, which told us where to sit. Opposite me was a slender woman whose plaque identified her as Kafayat Ekundayo, the barrister mentioned in the dossier. She wore an emerald head tie and tapped her matching nails on the table. Mistry gave me a polite nod, which I returned.

When everyone had arrived, President Sala stood. The chamber fell silent.

'Honoured guests and members of the Council of Kassandra,' Sala said. 'A few weeks ago, Italy became the target of a covert Scion military assault called Operation Ventriloquist. A dreamwalker named Cadoc Fitzours infiltrated the Quirinale and forced myself and the Prime Minister to surrender two Italian islands to the Republic of Scion. With one of our colleagues' lives at risk, we agreed that Italy would join the empire. This was the secret Treaty of Orcus.'

Every face was grim. Her expression flickered, but she maintained her composure.

'Scion has this treaty. There will be consequences for breaking it.' Sala lifted her chin. 'But I have called you all here to inform you that Italy will not give any ground to Operation Ventriloquist. From this point on, this country is at war with the Republic of Scion.'

A few worried murmurs followed. I released my breath.

'I understand your fear. We know how Scion treats our kind, and I have kicked the hornets' nest,' Sala said. 'But there will be no more appeasement. Scion does not take kindly to resistance, as some of you know from experience. If you wish to flee, I will do all I can to help.'

'As an Italian myself,' Verča said, 'I would prefer to know if you have a plan, President Sala.'

'I do.'

It didn't do much to ease the tension, but everyone was listening. This was not the Unnatural Assembly.

'Yesterday morning, the Prime Minister announced that the populations of Capri and Ischia would be allowed to return to their homes, breaking the conditions of the treaty,' she said. 'This news soon reached Scion. Fitzours contacted me and ordered me to meet him at the Quirinale in two days' time. What he does not know is that I have a shield. A dreamwalker who arrived in Italy just a few weeks ago, and is willing to help us fight.' She pointed me out, causing everyone to look. 'This is the Underqueen of the Scion Citadel of London.'

Ekundayo raised her eyebrows. 'You are Paige Mahoney?'

I nodded.

'My plan is as follows,' Sala said. 'The dreamwalker can possess anyone within a mile of his body. That is the radius we must establish around the Quirinale. We'll set up a perimeter to ensure he can't escape this zone. When he inhabits the host, Paige will dislodge him, driving him back to his own body, which we can then destroy, stripping Scion of its weapon. Whether or not Scion will retaliate, and how swiftly, we do not yet know. They may bluff; they may not. This could mean war. Either way, we must make a stand.'

'You want our support, yet gave none to Portugal,' a white-haired voyant said. 'President Gonçalves was amaurotic, but there are many voyants in my country. Where was Italy when we called?'

'I regret that we could not help Portugal,' Sala said, 'but my priority has been to keep Italy strong and stable, to ensure it can support this ambitious endeavour, financially and otherwise.'

'Spoken like a true politician.'

'I will not apologise for that, Osvaldo. This war will be fought on many fronts, potentially over many years. We need politicians, just as we need fighters and intelligence agents,' Sala said. 'Scion cannot be allowed to succeed in taking Italy, or the Rephaim will be virtually unopposed in Europe. They are the most urgent threat to our kind, as we have all agreed.'

That was not what I had expected her to say. A whole table of people who knew about the Rephs.

Cordier had been right. The secret *was* bursting its bounds.

'If Scion does strike, we have allies in the syndicates of anchorised Europe,' Sala said. 'There are other avenues of support.'

'Indeed,' Jaxon said, silken. 'Perhaps you'd like to tell everyone about your Rephaite allies, Underqueen.'

His words spread like frost over the table. There was an appalled silence, during which everyone stared at me.

'You are working *with* these creatures?' someone asked. 'You, the Underqueen of London?'

'There are two factions,' I said. 'The Sargas family founded Scion. I work alongside their enemies, the Ranthen, who lost the Rephaite civil war before they came to Earth. They don't want to subjugate humans. They've been providing the Mime Order with financial backing, and—'

'You've taken their money, made yourself dependent on them?'

'Our alliance with the Ranthen has been useful,' Nick said. 'When London was placed under martial law, we wouldn't have survived without—'

'They feed on our auras,' Carter cut in, her nostrils flaring. 'What help can they possibly give us?'

Nick gave her a cautious look. I could tell he was trying to fathom her out.

'Respectfully,' he said, 'what help have *you* given us?'

Carter turned to Sala. 'Did you know about this, Beatrice?'

'I did,' Sala said. 'Our instincts may oppose this alliance, but I believe we can lever it to our advantage. Jaxon claims these creatures' blood enhances our abilities when ingested. Is that true, Underqueen?'

'Yes,' I said, after a pause.

'Then we can use it to strengthen our forces against Scion. Perhaps it could even allow my amaurotic soldiers to tap into the æther.'

It was such an extraordinary idea that it rendered me speechless. Nick looked as disturbed as I felt.

'Beatrice.' Ekundayo looked stricken. 'You think we should give amaurotics the keys to the æther?'

'It may not be possible,' Sala said, 'but if so, it would only be a temporary measure, Kafayat. We will need every possible advantage over the Second Inquisitorial Division.'

'I'm not convinced it would give us one,' I said. 'Even if it worked, you would need … a lot of ectoplasm.'

'Perhaps the same amount the Suzerain provided to forge Senshield,' Jaxon said. 'During my time as a double agent in the Westminster Archon, I observed her providing her own ectoplasm to power the guns. Perhaps your Ranthen companions would do the same.'

A double agent. The brass neck on him. He must be framing his entire sojourn in Scion as the act of a rebel. Only a thin strand of self-control kept me from leaping across the table and shaking him until his teeth rattled.

'The Ranthen would never agree to give their ectoplasm to jack up thousands of soldiers, and I can't blame them,' I said coolly. 'I imagine they'd be insulted if I asked.'

'Then don't ask. They deserve no respect or quarter from us,' Carter said, losing her patience. 'You baffle me, Paige. It would be one thing if your alliance with the Ranthen was to glean information on these creatures, but the more I listen to you, the more I think you have sympathy for them. The Rephaim have taken everything from us. Even your Ranthen stood by and watched while Ireland fell. Why shouldn't we take from them in return?'

Her obvious displeasure stung.

'The Ranthen had no part in the Dublin Incursion,' I said firmly. 'I value my relationship with them, Antoinette. And if you think we can take anything from them by force, you are mistaken.'

A few glances were shared around the table. Jaxon smiled like a cat with the cream.

I didn't quite know why, and it chilled me.

'I understand your position, Underqueen,' Sala finally said. 'We do have other allies, including the Domino Programme. Its agents stand ready to sabotage the empire.'

Many looks of mistrust lingered on me. Even with my sixth sense buckled down, I had my primal instincts, and I was starting to feel scrutinised in a way I didn't like.

And I *really* didn't like the way Jaxon was smiling.

'While most of Domino is amaurotic, it employs many voyants as civilian personnel, including our new sibyl,' Sala said. Verča nodded. 'It has also given us a great boon. We recently learned of a data storage device that contains priceless intelligence from deep within Scion. The data was collected by a deceased Domino agent and brought here on her behalf by a courageous member of the Council of Kassandra. Once Domino has decrypted the data, we suspect it will expose numerous vulnerabilities within Scion, aiding our resistance. Thank you for your service, Jaxon.'

I looked slowly down the table.

'Of course,' Jaxon said. 'Anything for the cause, Beatrice.'

The pennies dropped, one by one, as if into that well. Each one sent cold ripples through my being.

Jaxon had spent at least a month in the Archon, working alongside Burnish. When Nashira had dispatched him to France, Burnish must have asked him to take the stolen data away from London.

398

Burnish had been living on borrowed time. She could only have been utterly desperate, to give the cache to a man like Jaxon. So she had told him how to contact Cordier, her sister, who knew where I was staying…

Now I was back in the flooding quarries of Paris, too weak to climb any farther, the water rising to devour me. A silver-haired man lifted me into his arms, saving my life.

*I know you*, I whispered, seeing his eyes in a strange face.

*No, darling. You never did.*

I saw it all then.

Scarlett Burnish was the one who had given him the dissimulator. She hadn't been able to get word out, so Command had still ordered me to assassinate him, not knowing he had been recruited. Not knowing he possessed an item of such value, he could exchange it for anything. Now my gaze was fixed on him, and he was looking back at me, his smile growing as the truth sank into my bones.

Jaxon Hall, the Lepidopterist.

He was the one who had coerced Cordier into abducting me, forcing her to betray Arcturus to Scion.

But I didn't know why.

I couldn't work it out.

Nick touched my elbow. 'Paige?'

I must have turned white. If my gift had been working, Jaxon would already be dead. Instead, my spirit was straining against the poison, only hurting me. A migraine bloomed, turning my stomach, and a thread of blood leaked from my nose. My lips parted, but I couldn't breathe, couldn't utter a word to explain the realisation I had just made.

Quick footsteps distracted us all. With a dull roar in my ears, I turned in my seat with the rest. A newcomer had walked into the grand chamber.

'Ah,' Jaxon said. 'There you are, my dear. Just in time.'

Nick stood up. I stared, at an utter loss.

Since I had last seen her, she had cut her golden hair, so it hung in waves to her shoulders. She wore a long skirt with a collared blouse and polished boots.

A slash ran from the right corner of her mouth to her temple, shot through with a railroad of stitches, and she had a black eye. A shallower wound crossed the other side of her face, from the left side of her nose to her cheekbone. She wore red tint on her lips, like she always did.

'Paige. Nick,' Eliza Renton said, her voice a rough whisper. 'You're alive?'

She rushed across the chamber, and before I knew it, she was embracing me and Nick, one arm around each of us. Nick clutched her at once, while I was stiff as a mannequin.

'I can't believe it. You're here.' Eliza crushed us to her, in tears. 'I missed you so much.'

'Eliza,' Nick breathed. 'What are you doing here?'

'You must be the interim Underqueen,' Sala said. 'There has been a development, as you can see.'

'A development?' Her gaze snapped to the table, landing on Jaxon. 'You said Paige was gone.'

'Apparently not. The Pale Dreamer cheats death yet again.' Jaxon rose. 'What a portentous reunion. Four of the Seven Seals, reunited in Italy. Are we not fated to be together?'

'You called me here. You told me—'

'Eliza.' I finally managed to speak. 'What do you mean, he called you here?'

She drew back, so I could see the fear dawning on her face.

'Paige, I'm so sorry. I thought—' Her throat bobbed. 'We thought you died in the airstrikes.'

'Eliza is here to formally offer me the position of Underlord, as agreed with the Council of Kassandra.' Jaxon paced towards us. 'After all, you were missing in action.'

Nick held me against him. 'Jax, what have you done?'

'Wait a minute.' Maria shot up. 'This is a coup. That's what you're doing, isn't it, Binder?'

Even as she said it, I understood, the last few coins hitting the bottom.

Jaxon had blackmailed Cordier into capturing me, all so he could usurp me. So he could not only defang me for good, but convince everyone I was dead. So he could take back the citadel I had stolen from him.

I don't remember exactly what happened in the moments that followed the realisation. All I knew is that I was suddenly on top of Jaxon, pounding him with both fists. The whole chamber erupted as Nick grasped my arms, trying to restrain me.

'You evil bastard,' I screamed at Jaxon. 'You ripped us apart. You, *you're* the Devil—'

Several pairs of hands were on me, pulling me away from him, but I fought back, spewing the worst abuse I could muster. Jaxon wiped his bloody lip, eyes glittering with triumph.

'Take her to the Tullianum,' Carter shouted.

That was the last thing I heard.

# 27

# CONSEQUENCES

ROME

21 October 2060

I woke in handcuffs. As I regained consciousness, my wrist seared, drawing a faint groan from me. It was swollen again, and every movement was excruciating. I didn't need Nick to know it was bad.

The memories washed back. My knuckles were bruised and bloody, and my head spun. I must have been sedated.

Jaxon Hall had always meant to reclaim the crown I had snatched from his fingertips. He had plotted my disappearance, seizing the chance Scarlett Burnish had given him, knowing it would create a power vacuum in London. A power vacuum only he could fill.

He was the one who had taught me to be an opportunist. The boy from the gutter, leaving no pocket unpicked, no open window left untouched, no grudge buried. I had to applaud his commitment to vengeance.

The alysoplasm was still going strong. I couldn't possess anyone to open the door, and my ankle was chained to the wall. For a long time, I lay on the floor, shivering. When the main door opened, a breeze ruffled my hair, and Jaxon was there, on the other side of the bars.

'Good evening.'

I sat up. From the looks of him, I had fractured one of those perfect cheekbones, as well as split his lip.

'You bastard,' I rasped. 'You're the Lepidopterist.'

'One of so many names,' he said. 'You really should have double-checked that I was dead.'

He sat on the flagstones, facing me in the dim torchlight.

'I *was* tempted to order Eléonore Cordier to kill you,' he said, 'but after you knifed me in the back for the whole syndicate to see, I'm delighted I didn't. A public humiliation is long overdue.' He took out a cigar and lighter. 'Call it a taste of your own medicine, Black Moth.'

'Did you tell her to betray Arcturus?'

'I told her to get him away from you. His influence on you was far too strong.'

'What would you have done if I hadn't given her the slip?'

'She would have brought you to me at my convenience,' Jaxon said, 'and you would have been at my mercy, just where you are now. Exactly where I want you.'

'Why?'

'I told you, Paige. Your gift is a marvel,' he said. 'If you die, it evaporates. Better to mould my enemies, as the Suzerain does.'

'How did you persuade Burnish to give you those files?' I asked. 'Alsafi was her ally, and he would never have let her trust you with them, after what you did in Oxford.'

'Alsafi was gone. Burnish had limited time to act, and I was leaving for Versailles. She gave me an address in Paris, promising her sister would find a way to repay me.'

I forced myself to listen, because I had to understand.

'As soon as Burnish gave me the files, I knew she was the one who had released you from the Archon,' Jaxon said. 'Before meeting Cordier, I observed her for a while, taking alysoplasm to ensure my anonymity. Though I never saw you, my suspicion grew that Cordier likely had. My suspicions were confirmed when I met her, and we struck a deal. In exchange for the information her sister had harvested, Cordier would remove you from Scion for seven months, creating a power vacuum in London, and then bring you to me.'

'And what then?'

'If you failed to cooperate, I could tip you over the edge, into oblivion. You soon would have forgotten about Arcturus Mesarthim. You would have been mine to remake,' he said. 'I might have taken inspiration from this other dreamwalker, and modelled you on him.'

His hold on me had been so powerful. Even now, I shrank from the idea that he could favour someone else; that he no longer thought I was special.

'Fitzours sounds like precisely the sort of person we need. The person you have always lacked the spine and stomach to become,' he went on. 'He has embraced the whole of his gift, while you remain fearful of yours. You still have the stain of your amaurotic father on you.'

'What, because I don't want to use my gift to torture people?'

'Because you are squeamish, Paige. Fitzours is using every advantage the æther granted him, and because of that commitment, he will always be the victor. And you wonder how I can believe Nashira will triumph.' He drew on the cigar, and the end flared. 'You two may be the keys to this conflict, but you refuse, as ever, to unlock the door.'

'That's my choice,' I said coldly. 'Tell me about Eliza.'

'Eliza cut me off after the scrimmage,' Jaxon said, 'but she never changed the phone she had been using. After Versailles, I escaped to London, using a dissimulator from Scarlett Burnish. I was in London during the airstrikes, after which I asked Eliza if she was alive.'

That must have tested her resolve. She had always been most vulnerable to his manipulation.

'She didn't reply until a fortnight later,' he said. 'No one had seen or heard from you since the airstrikes, which troubled her enough to agree to a meeting. As a Scion denizen, she had no way of knowing about the red notice. I told her I would always help if she had need of me. I told her I was leaving Scion – Nashira had conveniently placed a kill order on my head – and how I might be contacted in an emergency.'

I clenched my jaw.

'Eliza held out as interim Underqueen. My sweet Martyred Muse, wanting to prove that she could be strong,' he said. 'And then, on the third of October, some of your subjects tried to kill her, wanting to return to the old ways. They did not fear her gift, as they feared yours.'

'Who did it?' I asked. 'Your loyalists?'

'No idea,' Jaxon said. (I didn't believe it.) 'Eliza had slowly come to accept that you were never coming back. When Cordier informed me that Nick might be dead, his sub-network exposed by a spy, I made sure to pass on the bad news. The attack was the last straw, proving that even the Ranthen could not protect Eliza. To renounce her position, she had to choose either me or another scrimmage.'

'You or—' I stopped. 'The reservation clause.'

'Very good,' he said. 'During the scrimmage, you won the Spiritus Club over by knowing your syndicate law. I read *A Concise History of Clairvoyance* again myself, searching for any obscure way to snare the Rose Crown. Lo and behold, I found that clause.'

'If the leader of the syndicate dies or disappears, their mollisher supreme takes the Rose Crown,' I said quietly. 'But if they can't bear the burden of leadership, they can pass it to the last fighter standing in the Rose Ring, other than the victor. That fighter was you.'

'Yes.'

That clause was the only way to avoid a scrimmage, and a scrimmage would have been too dangerous for Eliza to contemplate. The Mime Order might have collapsed in one fell swoop.

'I had informed Eliza of the reservation clause,' Jaxon said. 'I had also told her how to reach and cross the Fluke, and left her with an Italian phone. The Glym Lord assisted her in leaving Scion, taking the route I had prepared.'

Glym had never liked Jaxon, but he wouldn't have wanted to risk another scrimmage, and he would have been worried about Eliza. She couldn't have visited a hospital in Scion.

That had to be why Terebell had suddenly been recalled to London. The other Ranthen could have dealt with the attack itself, but Eliza vanishing into thin air would have left the Mime Order without any of its leaders.

And Eliza would never have told them she was going to the man who had betrayed them.

'Two days ago, Eliza called me from the Alps, hurt and terrified,' he said. 'I persuaded Sala to bring her here, so she could offer me the Rose Crown.'

My heart pounded. With Eliza gone, no one in London had a right to the Rose Crown.

The entire underworld now hung in the balance.

'Your escape was annoying,' Jaxon admitted, 'but I had already set the stage for your return. During your absence, I was chipping away at the Council of Kassandra, trying to convince them to support my bid to take London back. I had seeded an idea of you as an inexperienced and unstable leader, a reckless little puppet of the Rephaim, whose disappearance was a blessing in disguise. And by attacking me just now ... you have made them wonder if I was right.'

My eyes closed. I should never have punched him, but I hadn't been able to see past my rage.

'So you've been dripping poison into their ears for months, all so I could be reshaped once you got me to Rome.' I huffed. 'It really would have been much easier to kill me.'

'But not half as much fun.' Jaxon blew out smoke. 'Don't judge Eliza too harshly. She truly believed there was no other way. In any case, she owes me far more than you understand.'

'Try me.'

'When you were in Oxford, you heard the rumours about me. The wicked traitor who betrayed the Ranthen to save his own skin ... but there was another survivor of that Bone Season.'

'The child?'

'Yes, little Zero,' he said. 'She was only three. I should have left her behind, but I took pity on her. I saw in that nameless girl a shadow of the orphan I had been, abandoned by the world. And so I carried her away with me, saving her from the bloodbath.'

'Eliza,' I whispered. 'Eliza was Zero?'

'A young woman had stopped taking the contraceptive pill, hoping a pregnancy would move Scion to release her,' he said. 'Unfortunately for her, she was mistaken. Still, Nashira spared the newborn, to rear her as a perfect soldier. The Suzerain is never wasteful.'

My ears rang.

'Eliza never knowingly lied to you,' Jaxon said. 'Once I had Seven Dials, I palmed her off to some courtiers in Soho, not caring to raise a child as my own. But I did keep her in my sights, in case she grew into someone worthwhile. When she was fifteen, she started using white and purple aster, trying to escape her distant memories of Oxford. I made sure a copy of *On the Merits* fell into her hands, and she asked me for a job.'

'Does she know now?'

'I told her in London,' he said. 'She was upset, of course. But you and Nick abandoned her; I never did. And Eliza fears nothing more than abandonment.'

Eliza had been in a terrible position. I had left her behind, and this was the consequence.

'If it helps, she never told me where the Mime Order was hiding. I still have no idea,' Jaxon said. 'Don't be too angry, Paige. Eliza loves you like a sister, as Nick does, but she is bound to me by more than blood. We survived the Bone Season together. We survived the Novembertide Rebellion. If not for me, Eliza Renton would be nothing but bones.'

'Which would *also* have been because of you,' I reminded him.

'If not for my actions, neither of us would ever have escaped. I believe the Ranthen would have failed that year, and I needed to leave Oxford.'

'Didn't we all?'

All he did was take another drag, making the end of his cigar glow like a dying ember.

The Devil had me on the end of his chain. Perhaps this night was proof that I had never been able to avoid the third card in my reading. I was always meant to end up here.

But the Devil had not been the last card. Whatever it meant, this cell was not the end of my journey.

'Sala needs me to defend her against Cade,' I said. 'So what happens now, Jax?'

'Wait and see. Even for me, it's a master stroke,' he said. 'Carter despises the Rephaim. Your weakness for the Ranthen is about to be your undoing.' He showed me a small packet. 'And look what I have to sweeten the deal. The precious files that Scarlett Burnish stole from the Archon. Entering the wrong access code will erase its contents.'

'And only you know the code.'

'Well done.' He fastened it back into his pocket. 'Even the amaurotics have their part to play.'

'Cordier wanted to do right by her sister. It was cruel of you to manipulate her,' I said. 'Then again, I would expect no less of you.'

'Whatever you think of me, I always work to protect you.'

'How is *this* protecting me?'

'Few places are safer than a prison.' He patted his pocket. 'I hold all the cards. And you have none.'

I swallowed past the drought in my throat, realising I hadn't drunk a drop for hours.

Jaxon had covered his own tracks with ashes. Almost everyone in the grey market was dead, and only I had ever seen him in the Archon.

'So you're going to let the Council of Kassandra control London,' I said. 'You're going to bow and scrape for them, like you did for Nashira, just so you can wear the Rose Crown.'

'Oh, darling, you should know by now. I don't think *anyone* is better than me.' His gaze bored into mine. 'I have wanted to rule London since I was a child. If I have to tell this sententious Council a few white lies to keep them out of my way, then so be it. Did you *really* think I would allow my own mollisher to sit on my throne for good, Pale Dreamer?'

'I am not your creature any more. Whatever happens to me next, it was all worth it, to be rid of your grip on me.' I looked him in the eye. 'You'll get yours, Jaxon Hall.'

'Not before you. Best of luck.'

He left me, and I was alone in the dark again, knowing very well that I had been outflanked.

———

I lay in silence in my cell. The golden cord felt thinner when I took alysoplasm, but I could feel its stifled movements. Arcturus was checking on me. *Stay away.* I pushed those words along it. *Don't come here.*

At some point, Maria was hurled into the next cell. I heard Verča protesting in furious Italian before the door slammed.

'Fuck.' Maria clutched her arm, panting. 'That sinister old skeleton. He's usurping you!'

'I noticed,' I said.

'Apparently this Council of Kassandra thinks it should have the final say on who rules our syndicates. They've been trying to meddle in Scion voyants' affairs for years,' she gritted out. 'Jaxon is even claiming he killed Hector *for* them. They want to plant their own approved puppets in our citadels, so they can take control once Scion is defeated. Now Carter says they need to question you, as if they have a lick of authority over an Underqueen.'

'Why have they put you in here?'

'Jaxon gave me one smirk too many. I tried to burn off his eyebrows, but they have three hydromancers. At least I ruined his waistcoat.' Maria gripped the bars. 'Does Warden know you're here?'

'Yes,' I said, 'but I don't want him to come. Not when the Council clearly hates Rephs. What time is it?'

'The middle of the night.'

'Sala doesn't have long before Cade arrives. She needs me, or she has no protection.'

'Jaxon is claiming *he* can protect her, saying his boundlings can expel any intruders in her dreamscape. You can tell that Sala is a politician, switching loyalties every few hours. Well, fuck Beatrice Sala, fuck Binder, and fuck the horses they rode in on. No matter how long you've been away, London is yours by right, and if they think they can take it—'

The door to the jailhouse opened. Rohan Mistry stepped into the corridor.

'Underqueen.' He was holding a set of keys. 'Sorry about the sedation. The Council of Kassandra has summoned you.'

'I'm going with her,' Maria said.

'Of course.' Mistry unlocked our cells. 'This is not a trial, and you are not under arrest.'

'Then why is the Underqueen in handcuffs?'

'For her own safety, and that of the Council.'

Three guards waited outside. I was escorted at gunpoint out of the Tullianum, back in to the Basilica Arcana. The cuffs were tight on my wrists, worsening the pain.

The Council of Kassandra had assembled again, or perhaps never left, but the table had been moved closer to the columns, leaving more of the floor clear. Jaxon was back in his seat with a glass of wine.

'Paige—'

Nick stood in the corner, held back by guards, while Verča hovered beside him, looking uneasy. One of the guards took Maria to them, while I found myself being steered on to the marble sun. Eliza was nowhere to be seen.

Eliza Renton, the child from the Bone Season.

'Underqueen,' Carter said, pursing her thin lips. 'I see you've calmed down.'

'Not much else to do in a cell,' I said.

She looked at me with a strange mix of pity and frustration. Her hair was in a sleek bun, her gold token hanging below her collar.

'Underqueen,' President Sala said, 'for months, I have heard conflicting opinions about you and your reign in London. I want your help against Fitzours, but given your conduct just now, I see no choice but to call an emergency hearing, so the charges against you can be considered.'

'What charges?'

'We'll come to that,' Rohan Mistry said. 'For now, I must inform you of the proceedings. The Council of Kassandra was founded as the first representative body for clairvoyants, but also as our first court of justice, where voyants may be judged by one another, not by amaurotics. We have claimed jurisdiction over all the clairvoy-ants of Europe.'

'Bold of you,' I said, 'considering most of us have never heard of the Council.'

'As part of our intended role as arbitrators of the voyant world,' he went on, undeterred by my retort, 'we mean to instal or support capable leaders in the syndicates of Scion, and remove those who fail to observe the Kassandran Code. After you became Underqueen, Jaxon had … concerns. He brought these concerns to us when he came here.'

'Jaxon believes you have colluded with the Rephaim,' Carter said. 'He has asked us to support his endeavour to remove you as Underqueen, so he can take your place as Underlord.'

I couldn't help but let out a hollow laugh, earning a few alarmed looks.

'And there was me thinking you hated panhandlers, Jax,' I said.

Jaxon only smiled in that cold way of his. He was going to let this play out without saying a word.

'We are reluctant to interfere with syndicate law,' Mistry said, 'but after your disappearance, we were prepared to support Jaxon. Now we find ourselves faced with two contenders for the Rose Crown. We have no choice but to decide which of you is the more capable.'

I should have known from the moment I saw Jaxon. The only reason he would ever come to the free world was for London.

'The Rose Crown is mine,' I said firmly. 'President Sala, I'm sorry for losing my temper just now, but I realised Jaxon was the one who arranged my abduction from Paris, to keep me from my throne. He manipulated a spy into holding me hostage for months, promising her the data from Burnish in return.'

Sala frowned. 'Do you have any evidence of this, Underqueen?'

'None but my word,' I said, 'but words are all that anyone seems to have against me.'

Jaxon sipped his wine, watching me with a smile in his eyes. He had his claws in all of them.

'Paige,' Sala said, 'I hoped Jaxon was mistaken about you, or that his claims were rooted in anger. I wanted you to help me set a trap for Fitzours. But before I can take any chances, I need to know that you will be able to comport yourself with dignity, and that you are a voyant whose actions and values correspond with the Kassandran Code.'

'None of us knew anything about your laws,' Maria burst out. 'This is preposterous.'

'No interruptions, please,' Mistry said.

'Oh, I do apologise. Are we Scion voyants too disorderly for you?'

'One more word,' Carter said sharply to her, 'and you will be removed from the Forum.'

Maria clamped her mouth shut, but looked furious.

'I remind you that this is only a hearing,' Mistry said. 'The Underqueen is not on trial.'

I wasn't sure I believed him. The voice of Pantaléon Waite came back to me from Paris, when I had accused him of trafficking. *What is this – a court of piepowders, to try us on the spur of the moment?*

I really was about to get a dose of my own medicine.

'While the finer points of the Kassandran Code are still being debated,' Mistry continued, adjusting his spectacles, 'we have set out four central tenets, which all trustworthy voyants are presumed to follow by instinct, even without knowledge of the Council. First, do not defy the æther. Do not seek the acceptance of amaurotics at your fellow voyants' expense. Do not assist Scion. And do not succour the Rephaim.'

'Well, I haven't done any of those things,' I said, 'so you've no cause to hold me here.'

In truth, I had done two of those things, but the Council didn't need to hear that from me.

'Paige,' Carter said, 'we were willing to give you the benefit of the doubt, but we have evidence that you've put their interests above those of your fellow voyants of your own free will.'

'What evidence?'

'I'll come to that.'

'We don't have time for this,' Nick said hotly. 'Fitzours could be here at any moment.'

'No,' Sala said. 'He needs to know where I am. He will come to the Quirinale at the agreed time.'

'I hope you're right. If you insist on this charade, Paige should have witnesses to speak in her favour.'

'If it comes to trial, she will,' Mistry said. 'Once again, this is only a hearing, Dr Nygård.'

'Paige Eva Mahoney,' Carter said in steely tones, 'you've taken a number of reckless actions that have resulted in serious casualties and setbacks for voyants in Scion. A few months ago, you met the Scuttling Queen of Manchester. Nerio Attard, her late father, had the full backing of the Council of Kassandra. His daughter succeeded him with our approval.'

'Wait,' Maria said. 'Roberta knew about you?'

'Yes,' Carter said. 'Paige Mahoney, thanks to your rash decision to release Catrin Attard from Spinningfields Prison, Roberta was killed, leaving Manchester in a state of chaos. You worked with Catrin to exploit her connection to the Vigiles.'

From the outside, I could see how bad this looked. In my desperation to destroy Senshield, I had cut a deal with a Vigile commandant and unleashed a violent mobster on Manchester.

'I regret what happened in Manchester,' I said. 'You're right to criticise my interference there. I was under a lot of pressure to deactivate Senshield, and I took a dangerous shortcut.'

'Deactivate it?' Carter said. 'We hear Senshield *improved* because of you. Is that true?'

'I didn't know that would happen,' I said. 'I don't even know *why* that happened—'

'And yet there is a pattern forming, Paige.'

'Are you accusing me of intentionally helping Scion?'

'No. I am accusing you of recklessness.'

'You have no right to judge the Underqueen,' Maria fumed.

'The Council of Kassandra is an arbitrator and enforcer of clairvoyant justice, as well as our rights. We choose our councillors and representatives through civilised and democratic means,' Carter said loudly. 'You voyants of London – the heart of Scion – have not been able to govern yourselves for many years. You've left us with no choice but to intervene.'

'I was trying to change the syndicate. I was succeeding,' I said. 'If you'd given me more than a few months—'

'We might have, had you not vanished off the face of the Earth. You abandoned the syndicate.'

'Jaxon had me captured,' I gritted out. 'Can you not *see* what he's doing?'

'This is all beginning to sound quite farfetched, Paige.'

'Then you don't know the White Binder.'

'No more of this,' Nick said, his voice hushed and dangerous. 'Take those handcuffs off Paige.'

Mistry rubbed the bridge of his nose. 'Once again, please maintain your silence in the court.'

'I see no court here. Paige doesn't even have a lawyer.'

'Oh, *now* we're all concerned about legal procedure,' Jaxon said. 'I don't recall Pantaléon Waite having a lawyer when the Underqueen turfed him out of Paris. In fact, I don't seem to recall having representation when I was accused of running a trafficking ring, either.'

'Again, this is not a trial, Dr Nygård,' Kafayat Ekundayo said from her place at the table. 'We would all prefer to avoid that. At hearings, we expect voyants to represent themselves. I assure you that if it does come to a trial, I will represent her myself, if necessary.'

'You've admitted to one charge,' Carter said to me, 'but there is an even more serious accusation – that you have aided the Rephaim, in direct contravention of the Kassandran Code. By your own admission, you exposed the entire London syndicate to the Ranthen, whose complicity in Scion we've all heard you excuse. These creatures not only misuse our auras, but have imprisoned our kind for two centuries, in Oxford and Versailles.'

'I know,' I said, incensed. 'I was *in* Oxford, and I was the one who burned down Versailles!'

It was crucial that I stayed calm, after I had beaten Jaxon, but this was more than I could take. After everything I had survived, I wouldn't stand for it.

'Not just that, but you've apparently had an affair with one of them,' Carter went on, her face tightening. 'The consort of the Suzerain, no less. You serve this creature, not your subjects.'

The entire chamber seemed to ice over.

'Do I, now?' I kept hold of my composure. 'And who told you this?'

'A witness.'

'Come out and say it to my face, Jax,' I growled. All he did was sip his wine. 'Carter, he's taking you for a fool. He's the one who serves a Reph. He serves the Suzerain.'

'Do you have evidence of that claim, Underqueen?'

'Not here, and he knows it, but it's true. Does he have evidence against me?'

'Yes, Paige. We have your phone.'

I almost reached for my pocket. My phone, containing exchanges between me and Arcturus. They had confiscated it.

*Fuck.*

'You've been advising your Rephaite allies to feed on voyants,' Carter said, heavy disapproval in her voice, while I groped for a reasonable explanation. 'I truly didn't believe it until I saw those messages for myself. Don't tell us you weren't communicating with one of them.'

I had always known Jaxon was clever, but this had to be his greatest work yet. A stroke of cold-blooded genius. He had taken every last thing I had done to hurt Scion and twisted it.

'The Ranthen do no lasting harm to voyants' auras,' I said. A few outraged protests went up. 'They have funded and protected us, and I will not apologise for my alliance with them.'

'Paige, we need you,' Sala said, while Carter shook her head. 'We want you as an ally of the Council of Kassandra.'

'But you *must* sever this relationship with the Ranthen,' Carter said, her eyes flashing. 'Paige, you must have survived Dublin by the skin of your teeth, and here you are, twenty years old, doing your best to help the founders of Scion. Do you not see how lost you are?'

'You dare accuse Paige Mahoney of siding with the enemy,' Maria said. 'Who among you has lived in Scion?'

'I have,' Carter shot back. 'And I've returned there many times, at significant risk to my own life.'

'All right. Anyone else?'

Nobody answered. Mistry pressed his lips together, tapping his pen against his notes.

'Paige has been forced to make some very difficult and painful decisions in the last few months,' Maria went on, her cheeks a little flushed. 'She is the reason that Senshield isn't already installed across Scion, because she gave herself *to* the enemy to destroy it. Nick and I will not allow you to sit in judgement – you, who have never assisted the oppressed voyants of Scion, but looked down your noses at us from afar.' Nick nodded. 'We all agreed to her alliance with the Ranthen, which won us coin and cover to weather martial law.'

A lump was coming up in my throat.

'If you accuse Paige Mahoney,' Maria said, 'you accuse us all.' She turned to Sala. 'Paige has offered to defend you from Fitzours, risking her own neck. If this is how you repay that gesture, we can leave you to rot. We'll return to Scion, where we belong.'

Once again, the chamber was silent.

'I am grateful that the Underqueen has offered to help,' Sala eventually said. 'Fortunately, we do have a quick and simple way for you to prove yourself, Paige.'

'Bring it on,' I said.

Sala nodded to a pair of guards, and they heaved the nearest doors open. When I saw the group of Italian soldiers, and what they were hauling behind them, I stiffened.

Two Rephs, bound with chains of iron, threaded with poppy anemones.

'We understand these are the Rephaim you've worked closely alongside,' Carter said, while the Rephs were shoved unceremoniously to the floor. 'Which is your paramour, Paige?'

'The taller one.' Jaxon interlocked his fingers beneath his chin. 'Good evening, Arcturus.'

Arcturus looked at him with burning eyes. He must have followed the cord as soon as I was sedated, only to run into a trap that Jaxon had prepared. Always two steps ahead of the game.

'President Sala, these two Ranthen are about the most important you could have chosen to insult,' I said, trying not to sound as shaken as I felt. 'I urge you to release them now.'

'If you want us to support your rule,' Sala said, 'then we must know where your loyalties lie, Underqueen. Choose one of these Rephaim to provide ectoplasm for my soldiers, and I will be assured of your allegiance to your own kind. You can defend me, as agreed.'

'You will pay for this,' Terebell said, addressing the chamber. 'I am the sovereign-elect of the Ranthen.'

'You are a parasite,' one of the voyants sneered. 'What are you without us?'

Terebell tensed. When she saw Jaxon, her eyes flared. 'Why are you here, arch-traitor?'

'How the mighty have fallen, Terebell,' Jaxon drawled. 'Did you know the windflower grows wild in Italy?'

'Listen to him, all of you. How do you think Jaxon knows how to restrain Rephs, or their names?' I demanded. 'Because he knows as much about Rephs as I do, if not more!'

'She just called him a traitor,' Mistry pointed out.

'Yes, because they're not the Sargas, as I'm trying to—'

'Time is short, Underqueen.' Jaxon rose from his seat. 'The leader of the Ranthen, or the Rephaite you love. Choose one of them to serve the Council of Kassandra. We'll destroy the other.'

'You are *obliterating* any chance of an alliance.'

'We don't need one with the Rephaim,' Carter said. 'We will use them, Paige. As they've used us.'

Jaxon pointed an air pistol at Arcturus. The guards blocked me, but somehow, even with the flowers, Terebell threw herself in front of him, taking the dart in her shoulder.

'Terebell—' I shoved towards her. 'Jax, was that pollen?'

'No.' Jaxon lowered the gun. 'Members of the Council, here is the proof of what I have told you all. The danger to which the Underqueen has exposed her subjects in London.'

Not pollen. The dart had been full of alysoplasm, and Arcturus was still weak. Terebell must have known his body might not be able to endure it.

She pulled out the dart, which rolled across the floor. Arcturus spoke to her in Gloss, his tone rough. Nick broke free of the guards. I did the same, and we met beside the Rephs.

'What does she need?'

'Salt and aura,' I said. 'But, Nick, it's not what you—'

'I know, Paige.' His voice was too low for anyone else to hear. 'They turn into Buzzers, don't they?'

I nodded. I should have guessed that he would see it before anyone else.

Nick had faced a Buzzer before. As Terebell started to seize up, he sliced the top of her sleeve with his penknife, revealing the puncture.

'I need my bag, now,' I barked at the Council. 'If you don't want to end up as a pool of blood on the floor, just do it.'

One of the voyants got up and ran for the doors. Terebell held on to Arcturus, who was still talking to her in Gloss, trying to keep her grounded.

'Hurry,' I shouted after the voyant.

He returned with my bag. Working around the handcuffs, I opened my flask of salt water and soaked the wound. Terebell drank the rest. The light waxed back into her eyes. When I gave her a nod of encouragement, she latched on to my aura. I leaned into the pull, rather than resisting.

When the link broke, Terebell sank against Arcturus, racked by shudders. He clasped her to his chest.

'So you knew,' Carter finally said, breaking the silence. 'Jaxon told us the Rephaim can become Buzzers – creatures that eat spirit and flesh. Once again, I had assumed that you were in the dark.' Her brow crinkled. 'This is very disappointing from an Irish woman, Paige.'

'I love Ireland as much as you do.' I stood, facing her. 'I have fought Scion tooth and nail for well over a year. My alliance with the Ranthen was to bring them down.'

It stung to be at odds with her like this. Two of the few survivors of the Imbolc Massacre, and we had already come to blows. But I had not taken a stand against Scion to hide who I was, or what I believed to be right.

'Well, Paige,' Carter said, 'you have shown your convictions. We must hold a vote as to whether this proceeds to a full trial. I did hope you would be an ally, to help us reclaim Ireland.'

'I can be, Antoinette.'

'That will be a collective decision. Erika, Rohan, please escort the Underqueen back to—'

'Stop,' Nick broke in. 'Jaxon just shot Terebell, knowing full well what would happen. He gambled with all your lives. I can't stop you judging Paige, but the White Binder is *not* fit to be Underlord.' Jaxon gave him a look so cold it would have put a Reph to shame. 'He colluded with the Rephaim that hunt us. And I can prove it. Paige can prove it.'

I met his gaze, realising.

In London, Arcturus had taught us how to share a memory with many voyants. The three of us – an oracle, an oneiromancer, and a dreamwalker – could dovetail our gifts, allowing Nick to share my recollections of the Westminster Archon. The ones only I had ever seen.

Arcturus slowly looked up at me. I returned his gaze, a knot in my throat.

Once, I had made him swear to me that he would never look at those memories. They were to remain untouched in my dreamscape. I hadn't wanted him to see my torture. I still didn't.

But I had been as vulnerable with him as it was possible to be. I trusted that he would keep loving me, even if I let him into that dark room. I gave him a tiny nod of permission.

'Arcturus is an oneiromancer. Paige can share her memories with him,' Nick said, 'and I can project them, so you can see.'

The Portuguese voyant spoke up: 'Is this permissible?'

'There is no precedent,' Ekundayo said, leaning forward with clasped hands. 'Show us, Dr Nygård.'

'I had no idea we allowed Rephaim to give evidence, Kafayat,' Jaxon said.

'The Underqueen has a right to defend herself,' Mistry said. 'If this is how she chooses to do it, so be it.'

I dug into my bag again, finding the vial of fortified ectoplasm. If the Council of Kassandra had decided to take me down, I would drag Jaxon Hall with me.

When I drank the ectoplasm, a few shocked murmurs broke out. The æther returned to me in a rush. At once, I sent my perception rippling outward, as far as it would go, making sure Cade was nowhere close. So far, I couldn't sense him. He hadn't arrived early.

Arcturus held out a hand. I looked down at him.

'I ask your forgiveness,' he said, too soft for anyone but me to hear. 'For what I must do.'

My jaw tightened. I reached back as best I could with the cuffs, and he gently took hold of my good wrist, knowing I would need the comfort.

The Basilica Arcana faded away, replaced by the terrible darkness of the Westminster Archon. Arcturus knew where to look, because he knew exactly when I had been tortured, and for how long.

I closed my eyes, breaking into a cold sweat. He skimmed over the memories of me on the waterboard, tormented by Suhail. My knees buckled as he found the right point in time, when Jaxon had invited me to speak to him. When Jaxon had confessed it all – the grey market, his treachery in Oxford, and his belief in Nashira Sargas.

*Only the Sargas can regulate our insanity.* I heard his voice as if through a thin wall. *I fell wildly in love with her mind – her deep understanding of the æther, her hunger to comprehend it entirely.* Arcturus tuned the memory, sharpening the words. *I betrayed the Ranthen in order to survive ...*

Nick caught me. Fuelled by the ectoplasm, I dreamwalked into him. My golden and silver cords tied all three of us together, and Nick projected the memories at the Council.

The whole chamber watched as Jaxon appeared before them, dressed in the clothes of a Scion official, detailing his treachery in his own words. Arcturus had no salvia – the memory was blurred, our voices muffled – but I had been angry when this happened. They could all hear it well enough.

*She wanted me to be her Grand Overseer, given my talent for spotting powerful voyants. I was allowed to leave Oxford, but only as a Scion employee ... I needed wealth to achieve my dream of taking Seven Dials ... I reported its mime-queen and her mollisher, who were detained within a day ...*

The whole conversation unfolded. I held on to Nick.

'Go forward,' I whispered to Arcturus, part of me still in the past. 'Go to ... half an hour ago.'

Arcturus didn't typically use his gift like this, but this was his chance to get even with Jaxon, and he knew it. The three of us went rocketing forward in time, stopping in the Tullianum.

*I had seeded an idea of you as an inexperienced and unstable leader, a reckless little puppet of the Rephaim, whose disappearance was a blessing in disguise. And by attacking me just now … you have made them wonder if I was right.* This recent memory was even clearer, sharp and fresh. *I have wanted to rule London since I was a child. If I have to tell this sententious Council a few white lies to keep them out of my way, then so be it …*

At last, the vision faded, and the Council of Kassandra blinked.

'Quite remarkable,' one of them said. 'The three of you can twine your gifts, as sibyls do.'

'He sees the past, not the future.' Mistry looked thoughtful. 'An unprecedented gift.'

Nick held me close. I was shivering.

'I hope you're satisfied,' he said bitterly. 'That's what Paige has done for London. What has Jaxon done?'

Mistry glanced towards the other two members of the Triumvirate. Carter and Sala both stood in grim silence.

'We must deliberate on this,' Mistry said. 'Underqueen, we'd like to keep you in the Tullianum until we've discussed the events of this hearing. Erika, please make sure the Underqueen is comfortable.' A sibyl nodded. 'Jaxon, for the time being, you may not leave the Forum.'

Jaxon scoffed. 'Do you really believe in these parlour tricks, Rohan?'

'The Council is duty-bound to investigate any potential complicity with the Rephaim. You must understand that.'

'Of course.' Jaxon sat back. 'After so many years of loyalty, I would hate for the Triumvirate to doubt my commitment now.'

'Cade will be here soon. You'll be grateful for a dreamwalker,' I warned as the guards led me away. 'You need my alliance with the Ranthen, President Sala. Don't waste it on the Grand Overseer.'

---

'So we're all fucked,' Maria concluded.

We did make a sorry picture. Terebell and Arcturus on one side of the jailhouse, me and Maria on the other, the bars dividing the humans from the Rephs. I had drunk some more alysoplasm, buying more time in the shadows, but removing my ability to escape.

'So the Buzzers *are* you. The plot thickens,' Maria said to the Rephs. 'How long have you known, Paige?'

'I found out in Paris,' I said.

'You would never have worked alongside us, had you learned the truth sooner,' Terebell said. 'Do you imagine it pleases us to carry this potential in our bodies?'

'No.' Maria lounged against the wall, one ankle crossed over the other. 'I do find it a little rich that you sneer at humans and wear those prim gloves of yours, all while you can rot from the inside.' She glanced at me. 'It was brave of you to show us those memories, Paige.'

'Thanks.'

My wrist was killing me. I grimaced, cradling it between my fingers.

'Paige,' Arcturus said. 'What happened to your wrist?'

'You know how Jaxon looked as if he'd run his face straight into a wall?'

'I see.' He considered. 'You should have used your stronger hand.'

Maria snorted.

'You're the one who specialises in hindsight.' I kneaded the hollow at the base of my thumb. 'Maria, where did Eliza go?'

'She's still weak from the ambush. I think the shock of seeing you and Nick alive was overwhelming, since Jaxon convinced her you'd died,' Maria said. 'Nick is looking after her.'

'Did she say who attacked her?'

'The Winter Queen, the last surviving member of the grey market,' Maria said. (The one I hadn't been able to find.) 'She assembled a group of voyants with a grudge against the Mime Order, including some of the disgraced Nightingales. Taygeta managed to get Eliza away.'

'She was the child from the Novembertide Rebellion,' I said. 'That's why she came for Jax.'

Arcturus narrowed his eyes. 'Are you certain, Paige?'

'No, but I believe Jaxon, on this occasion. I don't see why he'd lie about that. She was desperate enough to turn to him, but while we're all debating in Italy, London is vulnerable. No one there has a right to the Rose Crown. If we stay much longer, we lose the capital.'

'As soon as I am free of this cell, I will return,' Terebell said. 'Pleione and Errai will come for us. I summoned them.'

'Fine, but even then, *you* don't have a right to the Rose Crown. The only people who do are me, Nick and Eliza,' I said, 'and Jaxon, thanks to the reservation clause. And we're all here, hundreds of miles away.'

Just then, the door creaked open. A guard came in, and Maria was plucked from her cell, leaving me alone with the Rephs. Verča had probably convinced someone to let her out.

Arcturus caught my eye across the gap between our cells. I forced myself to meet and hold his gaze. He had skipped like a stone across the worst memories, but he must have glimpsed enough.

'Paige,' he said, 'if you wish, I will take white aster. I do not know if its amnesic qualities will work on an oneiromancer, but I can try.'

'No,' I said softly. 'I trust you with the memories.'

He nodded.

'Nashira told the truth about the two of you,' Terebell said. 'Did she not?'

When I realised what she meant, I turned cold. I waited for Arcturus to contradict her.

'You do not deny it,' Terebell observed, when neither of us spoke. 'I have suspected for some time. When we found Arcturus, I knew from the way you grieved, Underqueen.'

Arcturus watched her. Terebell looked at him, her expression as inscrutable as ever.

'It is not only the folly of it,' she said, 'but the fact that you lied to me, Arcturus. It was before our cycs, and you thought us

423

blind, insulting me as you desecrated your sarx. Errai and Pleione both shared my suspicions, but we had faith in your word. You are Ranthen.'

'He would have told you,' I said. 'He was trying to protect the Mime Order. And me.'

'I had reason to fear your wrath.' Arcturus spoke in a low voice. 'You know this, Terebell.'

I had no idea what he meant, but that was the least of my concerns. Terebell had been with Arcturus during the civil war. She was his closest friend, his sovereign, the person who understood him best. I didn't want to be the cause of any discord between them.

'You are very fortunate that I am in chains, dreamwalker,' Terebell said, her eyes blazing.

'Yes.' I slid into the far corner of my cell. 'I'm sure I am.'

'I should have you spurned,' she said to Arcturus, 'for endangering our return to power.' She must be using English for my sake, so I could grasp what a mess I had made. 'We are finally convincing our former allies to return to us, and you risk our standing for a mortal.'

'It is their doctrine, not ours,' Arcturus said. 'The Sargas do not rule us, Terebell. It is time we stepped away from their laws, as we did in Oxford. Regardless of my personal feelings for Paige, we are in open league with her. It ill behoves us to degrade our human allies.'

'So we lower ourselves to their level?'

'We raise them to ours,' he said. 'Paige is my equal. I see no reason not to take her as my partner.'

Terebell ignored him. Her face chilled me to the bone.

'Do not insult me further by cowering,' she said. 'I will not kill you. In any case, Arcturus is right. I have thrown in my lot with you, and you with me, for better or worse. If I were to reveal what is between you, I would look a fool. But the two of you must end this.'

'We already tried,' I said. 'It's not happening, Terebell.'

Terebell slashed her gaze between us.

'I will not pretend I understand it,' she said. 'I must inform some of the others. Pleione has never cared overmuch for doctrine, and Errai is too devoted to our cause to damage it. They will keep the secret. But if you cannot stop this, you *will* continue to conceal it. Your liking for their music is one thing, but this is too far, Arcturus. It is desecration.'

'Terebell, think for yourself,' I said, frustrated. 'We first touched a year ago, and nothing has changed.'

'The veils are thinning. How can you be certain your transgression is not the cause?'

'Oh, come on. I don't flatter myself by thinking that the entire *universe* hinges on my dating life.'

'None of us can be certain,' Arcturus said, giving me a look. 'But we cannot live in fear of all things.'

Terebell didn't reply. In fact, she acted as if he wasn't there.

He spoke to her in Gloss. Wanting to give them some privacy, I turned my back and curled up on the floor, wondering if I would be given a bed. Somehow I doubted it.

After a long time, Terebell answered Arcturus. Their conversation lulled me, despite what they must be talking about. Gloss was becoming a balm to my spirit.

I must have slept. The two Rephs were dead silent in the other cell.

And then I woke, my body cold, a vision filling my sight to the edges.

Nick usually sent me static pictures, easy to fashion and project – but ever since I had joined the gang, he had been working on crafting more complex ones. At some point, he must have got the hang of it. This wasn't a snapshot, but a living scene, unspooling as if it was taking place before my eyes. I was seeing exactly what Nick was seeing.

And what he was seeing was Cade.

28

# IRA DEORUM

Cadoc Fitzours, the other dreamwalker. He looked much the same as he had in Paris, except that he was dressed almost exactly like a Reph, down to his doublet and black leather gloves. His chin seemed a little sharper, his cheeks hollow, his lips almost as dark as mine.

They hadn't been like that in Paris. He must be taxing himself to the limit for Nashira.

A group of people had gathered in an ornate room, including Sala and Jaxon. This had to be the Palazzo del Quirinale. Two days had passed while I lay in the jailhouse, and Cade had arrived, ready to exact his vengeance. Sala had decided not to take me to the Quirinale.

Cade was flanked by two Rephs. One was unfamiliar, though clearly a Sargas, from his pallor and thick golden hair. The other, I recognised with a jolt as Kornephoros Sheratan.

'President Sala. I am Castor Sargas, blood-heir of the Rephaim,' the former said. 'I come on behalf of the Suzerain.'

Castor wore a livery collar set with amber, like the ones Nashira and Gomeisa had used to show their authority in Oxford. He was as daunting as his predecessor, Kraz Sargas. His face had been carved as if by a sculptor, his long hair drawn back from his cheekbones.

This Reph had once ruled the Residence of Balliol. From what Arcturus had told me, he had got his kicks out of tormenting the amaurotics.

'This is Kornephoros,' Castor went on. 'He is Warden of the Sheratan and blood-consort of the Rephaim, superseding the flesh-traitor, Arcturus Mesarthim.'

So Nashira had replaced both Arcturus and Kraz, the two Rephs I had taken from her.

Kornephoros smiled, something I fervently wished Rephs would never do. Their faces weren't made for that particular expression.

'Castor Sargas,' Sala said. 'What is it you want from me?'

'I think you know, President Sala. Why have you broken our treaty by allowing humans to return to Capri and Ischia?'

Nick was standing close to her. A few members of the Council of Kassandra had gathered on either side, along with some amaurotics, who I assumed were her ministers.

'Because the Prime Minister and I have no intention of letting you take Italy,' Sala said. 'A treaty I signed in fear of my own life, and that of my colleagues, is meaningless. You succeeded in claiming Norway, but Operation Ventriloquist goes no farther on these shores.'

'I suspected you might say that. After all, you are a unique case, President Sala. A clairvoyant at the head of a country,' Castor said, his eyes ablaze. 'Do you not fear our dreamwalker?'

'President Sala has a binder at her side.' Jaxon stepped from the ranks. 'As a member of the Sargas family, you are no doubt familiar with the art, Rephaite.'

'Indeed.' Castor considered him. 'The Suzerain taught you personally, as I understand it, Jaxon Hall. How disappointing, to see you on the losing side.'

'Come on, Jaxon.' Cade smiled. 'Do you really think a bound-ling is any match for me?'

He used his Breton accent now, not having any reason to hide it.

'Most boundlings would be fazed,' Jaxon conceded, 'but these ones are mine. And they have faced a dreamwalker before.'

The vision wavered. It must be taking Nick an extraordinary amount of strength to project it to me.

'Paige,' Cade said. 'You know where she is, then?'

'I do hope so,' Kornephoros said, his deep voice startling the humans. 'I owe that oathbreaker a death.'

*Shit.*

'Paige is already dead,' Nick said. 'She died in the airstrike on Paris.'

Cade gave him a look of intense scrutiny. For a sickening moment, I thought he could see me. Nick must be wearing his dissimulator, or the Rephs would know his face from the screens in Scion.

'No,' Cade said. 'You wouldn't be trying this unless you had backup. And I dreamed of her.'

Jaxon was clearly intrigued. 'You *dreamed* of her?'

'The æther has sent me visions all my life. I will face Paige Mahoney in the Colosseum,' Cade said. 'All of that aside, I can sense her. She's about two hundred feet away.'

*Fuck.*

'In the meantime, I'm glad to have found *you* here, White Binder,' he continued. 'The Suzerain has every intention of claiming your life for your betrayals, and for the loss of Versailles.'

Jaxon kept smiling in the face of the threat. Nashira really was out for his blood, then.

'You may have your own thin protection, President Sala,' Castor said, 'but if you wish to rise in opposition to Operation Ventriloquist, there will be grave consequences for your people. Those consequences will become apparent before the hour is up. I will give you one more chance to accept Rephaite rule of Italy. Join the Republic of Scion.'

Sala stood her ground as Castor took a step towards her. He dwarfed all of her bodyguards.

'In the days of Ancient Rome, humans would sacrifice to the gods to ensure the pax deorum. We only seek a return to those days,' he said. 'In Scion, tribute is paid through the Bone Seasons. Do as your ancestors did, and show respect to your gods, President Sala. All of the clairvoyants in Italy, in exchange for the lives of your amaurotic subjects.'

Beatrice Sala drew herself up. She was a small woman, but in that moment, she seemed tall as a Reph.

'I will not throw my own kind to the wolves,' she said. 'This is Rome. The wolves are on our side.'

'Then expect our wrath,' Castor said. 'Ira deorum, President Sala.'

---

The vision evaporated, leaving me shaking on the floor of my cell. My head pounded as I sat up.

'Paige,' Arcturus said. 'What did you see?'

'Nick sent me a vision. Cade is here,' I said. 'So are Castor Sargas and Kornephoros. They know I'm here. We have to—'

Before I could finish, the door crashed open, the bolt snapping in half. Lesath ducked inside, followed by Lucida, Errai and Pleione. They wore the blank masks they had sometimes used for anonymity in London, making them look even more daunting than usual.

'Wardens.' Lesath cocked his head. 'Did the humans imprison you?'

'The Council of Kassandra mislikes our alliance with Paige,' Arcturus said. 'It appears they see us all as enemies.'

'Of course.' Pleione planted a gloved hand on her hip. 'As ever, humans are intractable.'

'Underqueen.' Lucida had noticed me. 'Why are you in there?'

'Take a guess,' I said curtly.

Lesath wrenched the bars of our cells apart as if they were paper straws. He came to me first, making short work of the handcuffs.

'Sala has told Cade where to go,' I said, 'but Castor said there would be consequences.'

'That is quite apparent,' Pleione said. 'A number of cold spots have opened in Rome.'

'What?'

'One cold spot could be random,' Terebell said, 'but not several. There must be latent Rephaim nearby.'

'How could they have formed that quickly?' I said. 'What the fuck is going on?'

'The Sargas must have planned this in advance,' Pleione said. 'They anticipated defiance here.'

I strode into the other cell and removed the poppy anemones from Arcturus, allowing Lesath to break his chains. When I went to Terebell, our gazes met. If she was going to kill me for touching Arcturus, now was the perfect opportunity, while I was close enough to strangle. He wouldn't be able to stop her before my throat was in her grasp.

Hoping for the best, I snapped the stems of the flowers. Lesath came to deal with the chains. And still Terebell did nothing but look at me.

'Your blade, Terebell.'

Pleione offered an opaline sword. Terebell took it and rose, looking down at me in a way that reinforced my human frailty. I waited, expecting her to slice through my neck.

'You said there must be latent Rephs here,' I said. 'How could there be?'

Terebell did not reply.

'Grapevine may have a presence in Italy,' Arcturus said. 'Its agents could have assisted the Sargas in planting our fallen here, as Cathal Bell was a collaborator in the conquest of Ireland.'

The words hit on something. In that moment, I was torn between memories of Dublin and Paris.

*Compromise another of our fortified havens, and not only will we be more likely to become Emim, but those that already exist will no longer be drawn to a congregation of us,* Kornephoros had told me. *Our strongholds are a beacon. Without them, the Emim will scatter across your world.*

'Wait,' I said. 'I think I understand what's happening. It's an invasion from the inside. If the politicians refuse to play ball with Scion—' My mind was racing. 'They'll go for the heart, like they did in Dublin. Use the Buzzers to devastate the capital, weakening it enough that the Second Inquisitorial Division can breeze right in. There would still be a ground invasion, but they'd face a hell of a lot less military resistance if the Buzzers clear a path first. It will set an example for anyone else who wants to resist Operation Ventriloquist.'

'If you are right, it would be a significant deviation from the secrecy the Sargas have upheld for two centuries,' Lesath said. 'The whole of Rome is about to witness the might of the Netherworld. Why should they choose to reveal themselves?'

'I don't care about the motive right now. We have to stop this,' I said. 'Terebell, are you able for a fight?'

'Yes,' Terebell said.

'Good. I'm going after Cade,' I said. 'You deal with the cold spots.'

'We will need you in our party, Underqueen,' Pleione said. 'You may not be able to attack the Emim with your spirit without risking death, but the pressure from your dreamscape will keep them at bay. You can defend the rest of us.'

'Pleione is right,' Arcturus said. 'We stand a greater chance of success with you, Paige.'

'I can't miss this opportunity to kill Cade. If he escapes—' I thought back. 'He did say he knew I was here, and that he was going to face me. If he wants a fight, he won't leave yet.' I gave them all a weary look. 'Fine. I'll come. You really can't do anything without me, can you?'

Before they could answer, I left the jailhouse.

The mist had thickened while I was in there. To my surprise, President Sala was already in the plaza, marching towards me with about half of her entourage from the Quirinale, including Nick, Mistry, and a man I recognised as Gilberto Draghetti, the Minister for Defence. Maria and Verča came after them, emerging from one of the buildings.

'Paige.' Sala stopped in front of me. 'Fitzours escaped the perimeter.'

'No one could have seen that coming.' I folded my arms. 'What happened?'

'He arrived in person, with Rephaim. They murdered Lorenzo,' she said. That explained why there was blood on her face. 'None of my guards' bullets would stop them.' She gripped my shoulders. 'Can you find Fitzours again?'

'There may be a more pressing concern.'

Nick shook his head. 'More pressing than two Rephs murdering the Prime Minister of Italy?'

'Yes,' I said grimly. The six Ranthen came to stand behind me, unsettling the other humans. 'President Sala, I think there was a hidden layer to Operation Ventriloquist. A consequence to breaking the Treaty of Orcus.'

'Explain yourself, quickly,' Sala said, beckoning the Minister for Defence. 'What is it?'

'Look, you're not going to understand much of this, so I'll keep it simple. You can ask questions later,' I said, addressing the whole group. 'There are gateways to another world opening in Rome. They're going to spit out flesh-eating creatures called Emim, or Buzzers, which will kill every living thing in their path. You can't reason with them.'

'The Ranthen can assist in you in repelling the Emim, President Sala,' Arcturus said. 'First, we must sequester the latent Rephaim that have lured the Emim here. Once it is done, we can herd the remaining Emim back into the cold spots and seal them into the Netherworld.'

Sala stared at him. 'Underqueen?'

'Oh, *now* everyone needs my expertise,' I bit out. 'Okay. The Buzzers are coming for the bodies of unconscious Rephs. They're Rephs, by the way.' I jabbed a thumb over my shoulder at the Ranthen. 'We need to behead those bodies, and the only way to do that is with a certain kind of blade, of which we have two. Everybody with me so far?'

'What are you talking about?' one of the amaurotics demanded. 'Are you insane?'

'Mattia, please.' Sala took a deep breath. 'Never mind the specifics, Paige. What can I do?'

'First, everyone needs to get inside and stay there. Find a way to force people off the streets,' I said. 'Then you can help us reach the bodies. Can your soldiers keep the Buzzers off us?'

'Yes,' the Minister for Defence said, recovering. 'What sort of weapons should they use?'

'None of your weapons can destroy the Emim,' Arcturus said, 'but they do have a corporeal presence.' He had put on a mask of his own. 'Your soldiers can wound and slow them with concussive force, fire, acid and bullets. Do not be conservative with your ammunition.'

'So that's grenades and rockets, flamethrowers, sustained gunfire. Treat them like they're tanks,' I said. 'You can protect your soldiers with salt. Buzzers can't enter a salt circle.'

'We have gritting to clear ice from the streets,' the Minister for Defence said. 'Will that work?'

'Yes,' Arcturus said. 'Make sure the circles are unbroken.'

The Minister for Defence stepped aside with his phone, speaking in rapid Italian. Now I could hear the distant shouts of panic. It was starting.

'If you stop this,' Sala told me, 'you will have my vote of confidence as Underqueen.' She took a small black device from one of her bodyguards. 'My clairvoyance is not the sort that can be used in combat. I will evacuate the government to a secure location. Some of the Council will come with me, but anyone with a suitable gift will assist you.'

'President Sala,' one of the others said, 'we cannot mobilise based on the word of this one—'

'Credimi, Fatima. Sa di cosa sta parlando.' Sala clipped the device to my jacket. 'Keep this on. I'll be able to see and hear you, as well as track your movements.'

'My weapons,' I said. 'Where are they?'

Sala motioned to another bodyguard, who came forward with my holster and boot knife. They wouldn't do much good against the Buzzers, but having them gave me some courage.

'I'll take that nice rifle of yours, if you please,' Maria said. 'I'm sure you can find a spare.' The guard passed it to her without argument. 'You should leave now, President Sala. The Mime Order will handle this.'

'I will return as soon as I hear from you.' Sala looked me in the eye. 'Save this city, Underqueen.'

She let her bodyguards usher her away.

'Okay,' I said to the Ranthen. 'How do we find the latent Rephs?'

'We can go after the Emim. They will be drawn to the resting places,' Pleione said. 'I can also follow the nearby spirits' lamentations.'

'You're a whisperer?'

'As you would say.' Her eyes glowed. 'The songs flow in three directions.'

'And we only have two opaline blades,' Terebell said. 'We cannot split into more than two groups.'

'Here.' Lesath drew an opaline sword and presented it to Arcturus. 'Talitha Chertan offered this in tribute, Warden. We convinced her to join the Ranthen.'

Arcturus considered it. I remembered him using a blade like that in Versailles.

'You guard it for me, cousin,' he said. 'I am yet too weak to wield it.'

Lesath sheathed the sword without question. I felt another surge of appreciation towards him.

'Since only Pleione can act as a guide,' Terebell said, 'we must guess the locations, so we can spread our forces.'

I looked at Pleione. 'Can you not tell exactly where they are from here?'

'No,' Pleione said. 'I must allow the spirits to show me.'

'One of the sibyls' recent visions was of the Trevi Fountain, just north of here,' Verča volunteered. 'There is an old archaeological site underneath it, which might serve as a crypt. I know it well, if you need someone to lead you. I was a tour guide when I lived in Rome.'

'Of course you were.' Maria hefted the rifle, grimacing as she moved her left arm. 'Paige, do I get a commission for finding the most useful member of the Mime Order to date?'

'Accompany the sibyl,' Terebell said to Lucida and Lesath. 'If her instinct is wrong, follow the Emim. Arcturus, Errai and Paige, you come with me and Pleione.'

'I'll go with Verča,' Maria said.

'Good. Use your fire,' I said. 'Where are Eliza and Jaxon?'

'They went after Fitzours,' Nick said. 'I'm with you. Warden, will visions work against the Buzzers?'

'Possibly,' Arcturus said. 'They see as we do, to our knowledge.'

'We need a car,' I said.

'I have one,' a familiar voice said. I turned to see Rohan Mistry. 'I can't say I fully understood your instructions, Underqueen, but I'll do whatever I can to help.'

'I appreciate the offer, but you'd be wiser to lock yourself indoors and wait this out.'

'I can summon poltergeists,' he said. 'Will they help?'

'Yes,' Arcturus said. 'The Emim are vulnerable to apport.'

'It's settled, then.' Mistry took out a fob. 'My car will take five people. Where are we going?'

'Pleione will guide you. Maria, there's a guzzler parked over there,' I said. 'You could hotwire it.'

'Consider it done.'

She left with the other group. Somewhere on the streets, a siren began to whine, sending a frisson through my body.

'We should hurry.' Mistry headed for the entrance. 'Those are civil defence sirens, installed in case of any threat from Scion. The people know to find shelter when they sound.'

'You shouldn't fight,' I told Arcturus.

'I can seal the gateways while the rest of you hold off the Emim,' he said. 'You can use the pressure from your dreamscape to repel them – but do not overtax yourself, Paige. And do not abandon your body.'

I had made the mistake of dreamwalking into a Buzzer once before, and had only survived because Arcturus had used the golden cord to pull me out of its dreamscape. I never meant to do that again, but I could still play my part. This time, I would be his bodyguard.

Rome was already falling into chaos. A terrible cold filled its streets, rubbing my cheeks raw. It reminded me of the chill of Oxford, which had lingered all year, no matter the season. Mistry ran from the Forum and climbed into a sleek grey car. I got into the back seat.

'Mistry,' I said, 'why are you helping us?'

'Because you clearly know how to stop this, and I have no idea.'

'You were the person who put me in touch with President Sala, weren't you?'

'I knew she'd want to meet you.' He started the motor. 'Where am I driving?'

'Follow me,' Pleione said, appearing beside the car. Mistry jumped. 'I will lead you, summoner.'

Nick and Arcturus joined us. Shaking himself, Mistry peeled after the other three Rephs. 'Don't worry if you lose sight of them,' I told him. 'I can keep track of them in the æther.'

'Noted,' he said.

It was only now I truly realised how fast Rephs could move. Mistry sped up, shadowing Pleione. Errai and Terebell were hot on her heels. Around them, the streets were already overrun with confused people, all hearing a warning that no one had seen fit to clarify.

Above us, the sirens continued to drone. I tried to stop myself from sliding back to that last night in Paris, but my breath came short. Arcturus took my hand, and I held fast, letting him ground me.

In Dublin, Scion had planted soldiers among us, their guns concealed in bags and coats, showing no sign of their allegiance. I should have seen this coming. I had destroyed Oxford and Versailles, and now the Sargas would show us what happened when they didn't get their way.

An automated voice began to speak in Italian. 'A military threat to Rome is being announced,' Mistry told us. 'This is our established procedure in the event of attack. But these creatures you describe will be difficult to explain, should we survive this.'

Nick drew his jacket back, revealing a pair of pistols. 'Nashira must not care who sees the Buzzers.' He took out some ammo. 'Does that mean she's ready to reveal herself?'

'Perhaps,' Arcturus said. 'Or perhaps she means to teach the world to fear the Emim first. Then she will present herself as a saviour, as she once did to the government of England.'

'Not if I have anything to say about it,' I muttered.

Mistry stopped the car with a jolt as a woman ran across the street in front of us, followed by a crowd of panic-stricken people. His eyes widened when he saw what had scattered them.

A Buzzer was in front of us, in broad daylight, right in the middle of Rome.

The fog made it hard to see in full, but its white eyes locked on mine, glowing like full moons. It lunged at a man, catching him in its great scythes of claws, and ripped him in half.

'What—' Mistry had a fixed stare. 'What just happened?'

I gripped the back of his seat. 'Are you full-sighted?'

'Yes.'

The Buzzers' corrupted auras stopped the full-sighted from seeing them well. Mistry must have watched the man disappear into darkness, then come out in two pieces.

Nearby, a few vehicles smashed into each other in their haste to escape. Mistry sprang back to life. As he circled around the Buzzer, it swung for the car, its claws raking across the window, smearing blood in their wake. Mistry took a sharp left turn and drove along the bank of the Tiber. I could see Terebell, her blade glinting in the pale sunlight.

Just ahead were two more Buzzers, neither of them paying attention to the Rephs. They outpaced us with ease, their stretched limbs lengthening their strides. A third Buzzer leapt from a rooftop, colliding with a man on a moto.

Mistry stopped the car at the end of a bridge, the brakes squealing. There was another Buzzer ahead of us, blocking our way across the Tiber. Several bodies were scattered around it, and a lamppost had fallen across the pavement. A pair of voyants faced the beast, gathering spirits to spool. Mistry scrolled the window down, sweat beading on his face.

'Antoinette!'

'Rohan.' Carter came to the car, sporting a nosebleed. 'It's bedlam out here. Where are you headed?'

'Paige knows how to stop this. Her allies can—'

The Buzzer drowned him out with one of those appalling roars. The number of terrified voices tripled, coming from both the crowd and its throat. Carter jammed her fingers into her ears. Anyone who had frozen now ran for their lives. That was one good thing about humans – we knew how to adapt to danger. Nobody had a clue what the Buzzers were or why they were here, but it was clear they were bad news.

I was about to get out when Jaxon stepped into my eyeline, just as the rampaging Buzzer clamped its jaws around a man. He cast Weeping Sukie – one of his poltergeists – towards it, forcing it to drop its prey.

'Paige,' Arcturus said, 'Jaxon could be useful.'

As much as I hated to admit it, he was right. Jaxon was the most powerful binder I had ever met.

'Fucking hell, fine.' I leaned out of the window. 'Jaxon!'

He spotted me and strode over, Sukie racing after him. Herne the Hunter – a nasty piece of work, even for a poltergeist – was also at his side. The injured man crawled away from the Buzzer, leaving a trail of blood.

'Hello, darling.' He raked a strand of hair out of his eyes. 'I see you escaped your cell.'

'Shut up and get in, Jax,' I said over the din. 'We can use your 'geists to hold the Buzzers off.' To my surprise, Jaxon got in without a word of protest, taking the seat beside Mistry. 'Carter, Verča is heading for the Trevi Fountain. She could use your help.'

Carter acknowledged me with a nod. She turned with her archangel, which spread its apport wide, forming an invisible shield between her and the Buzzer. The creature swung for her, but the archangel deflected its claws, the clash radiating through the æther. Even now, after seeing it before, I was transfixed by the archangel – a spirit that had loved someone enough to protect their bloodline for as long as it could.

Mistry gripped the steering wheel. Once more, Carter wielded the angel, hurling the Buzzer clean off the bridge, and Mistry floored the accelerator, leaving her behind.

Jaxon glanced over his shoulder. 'Why in blazes are there Buzzers in Rome?'

'Scion was ready to punish Sala. They've dumped a bunch of starved Rephs here. They're like catnip to Buzzers in that state,' I said. 'Sukie and Herne could help us reach them. Do you have Jean, too?'

'I have them all.'

I clung to the back of the passenger seat as Mistry sped up again. 'You were a red-jacket in Oxford. Did you learn anything useful about fighting Buzzers?'

'I never faced them in Gallows Wood' – Jaxon stopped when Mistry drove over something that jolted the whole car – 'but I do recall that spools can be used to distract them. The spirits will try to get away, but force a spool close enough, and the Buzzer may give chase.'

I looked at Arcturus. 'Is he right?'

'Yes.'

'I'm always right,' Jaxon said. 'Rohan, where exactly are you driving us?'

'I'm following them,' Mistry said, his gaze pinned to the Ranthen.

'Jax,' I said, 'where's Eliza?'

'She is pursuing Fitzours,' Jaxon said. 'Her gift is not for battling Buzzers. Not like ours.'

'But you sent her after a dreamwalker?'

'She'll be fine. I left her with Jean.'

Jean the Skinner was ruthless. Eliza would still need to be careful, but she knew how to tail a target unnoticed.

The Buzzers were rampaging across Rome. In Oxford, they had attacked in pairs or alone, but now they seemed to be hunting in packs. So far I had counted thirty, but I sensed more of their dreamscapes, like black holes in the æther. Their very presence nauseated me.

Mistry was avoiding other cars by the skin of his teeth. He sped after the Rephs, through the winding streets, every corner jolting me between Nick and Arcturus. Somewhere nearby, an explosion sounded. Mistry hit the brakes, and half a building crashed down in front of us, sending up a cloud of dust. The rubble blocked the street.

'Draghetti must have got the message out,' Mistry said hoarsely. 'The city is fighting back.'

'Good,' I said.

Seeing our predicament, Pleione backtracked. Mistry reversed and drove after her, to a new street.

On this side of the Tiber, Mistry was proven right. Italian police and soldiers were blockading the main streets, slowing the Buzzers' onslaught. A few had clearly got the message about the salt, and were pouring it liberally, setting up artillery in the circles. In the distance, I could see a large group of them drilling a Buzzer with machine guns.

'There weren't nearly this many in Oxford,' I said.

'When cold spots first open, the Emim will flock to the new gateway,' Arcturus said. 'Oxford stood for a long time. They continued to be drawn to it, but not in such great numbers.'

'Fantastic. If we can—'

A crash deafened me before I could finish. A Buzzer had rammed one side of the car, almost rolling us over. Mistry slammed on the brakes again, but the force of the collision had sent the car spinning into a wall, shattering a window.

'Fuck.' I reached for the door. 'Come on, let's move!'

In unspoken agreement, we made a break for it. The Buzzer flung the empty car like it was nothing more than a toy, and it smashed down on top of a crowd of people. I blocked it out and followed the Rephs' dreamscapes, leading the others.

There were soldiers on the rooftops, armed with rocket launchers and rifles. Sala had got word out quickly. A few voyants were twitching on the ground, overcome by the coagulation in the æther.

I recognised this district. The same place I had walked with Jaxon. He ran alongside me, circled by Sukie and Herne, a sheen on his brow. He had never done legwork in the den, and I doubted he was enjoying it now. I wasn't faring much better.

Before Paris, I had been good at running. Now my chest was tight, my legs on fire. It took me far too long to realise it was fear, rather than a lack of training, that was making it so hard to breathe. I had expected to go to war against Scion, but not this soon.

Vatican City loomed ahead of us. It looked strange and unearthly in the mist, the sun a clear white circle above it. The Ranthen waited on the edge of the Piazza di San Pietro.

'The song leads just ahead,' Pleione told us. 'What is this building?'

'The Basilica di San Pietro.' Mistry gripped his knees, panting. 'The ... bodies are in there?'

'Apparently.' I drew my revolver. 'Sure you still want to help us, Mistry?'

He wiped his brow. 'Yes.'

A stampede of tourists had scattered all over the square, fleeing four enormous Buzzers. One of them hurled a woman into the Maderno Fountain. Two people tried to save her, only to be driven into the slosh of blood and frothing water, which stained the ground. A man in a striped uniform and old-fashioned armour went for the other Buzzer with a pole weapon I had never seen before, somewhere between axe and spear. He met the same fate.

Pleione headed into the square. Arcturus caught my elbow before I could follow, offering me another two vials. One was full of amaranth, while the other glowed with ectoplasm.

'To strengthen your gift,' he said.

'Thank you.'

I slotted the amaranth into my jacket, then drank some of the ectoplasm, pressing my eyes shut as my gift sharpened. A sickening headache bloomed as I combed the æther for Cade, but he was off my radar. Either he was on alysoplasm, or he was out of range.

I could deal with him later. This was more important.

Pleione led us through the slaughter in the square. One of the Buzzers charged towards her, but Terebell stepped between them, severing its head with her blade. I sensed the trapped spirits escaping its dreamscape, fleeing in all directions, as its body crumpled to the ground.

Arcturus brought up the rear of our group. He whirled a few spools together and sent them at the other Buzzers, diverting their attention as we made for the Basilica di San Pietro. So far, he was holding up, but falling well behind the other Ranthen. I waited for him, letting him pass me before I went on, so I could guard his back. I threw nearly all my knives as I ran, trying to distract the Buzzers from the people they were killing.

To my right, a Buzzer stood up on its hind legs, making it about twelve feet tall. I had never seen one of them do that before, and the sight of it froze me. It was like it was remembering its old life as a Reph.

'Paige,' Nick roared.

A rocket exploded against the Buzzer, and it fell back, wreathed in smoke. An Italian soldier lowered her launcher. Others rushed in with rifles, opening fire. I snapped out of it and sprinted up the steps after the others.

Mistry hurried between two broad columns, into the cool gloom of the Basilica de San Pietro. I had never set foot in such an immense building. Even the Westminster Archon paled in comparison to this palace of marble and gold. My boots squeaked on its gleaming floor as we ran beneath the arch of the ceiling, towards an ornate wooden canopy. The last few visitors hurried in the other direction, shepherded by guards and tour guides.

One person stood alone. An amaurotic, dressed in red and white. He waited by the canopy, in the weak daylight that came in from an opening in the dome above.

'Cardinal Rocha.' Mistry stopped in front of him. 'You should leave, Your Eminence.'

'No. This is where I remain, to welcome them back.' Rocha was gazing up at the dome, his liver-spotted hands clasped in front of him. 'God has sent his angels to us.'

'They're not angels,' I said.

'Don't waste your breath,' Jaxon said. 'One cannot reason with this sort of tomfoolery.'

'Your Eminence, you must get to safety,' Mistry urged. 'The Republic of Scion is here. It will not spare men of the cloth. The Holy Father ordered an evacuation.'

'Beatrice Sala told him to do it. They have all fled, for they are unbelievers. Daniela Gonçalves showed the same lack of faith. But I will stay to guard the house,' Cardinal Rocha said, calm as anything. 'God has chosen us to host the angels here in Roma, the Eternal City.'

Nick tightened his grip on his gun. 'Do you work for Grapevine?'

'I serve the Almighty.'

'Wait.' I pointed to the Ranthen. 'Are these your angels, Cardinal Rocha?'

Catching my intention, Pleione and Errai lifted their masks and drew themselves up to their full height. At once, Cardinal Rocha prostrated himself.

'*His body was like topaz, his face like lightning,*' he whispered to the floor. '*His eyes like flaming torches, his arms and legs like the gleam of burnished bronze, and his voice like the sound of a multitude.*'

'Our fellow angels told you to lay our fallen here,' Pleione said. 'Where are they, priest?'

'Castor brought them. I let him in, glorious ones. They lie below, in the Cripta dei Monarchi.' He looked at me through rheumy eyes, drunk on his devotion, a smile on his crinkled face. 'Do you see the divine fire in them, burning away the unnaturals?'

Mistry turned to me. 'The Cripta dei Monarchi is beneath the basilica. This way.'

'Wait. We don't want to wind up trapped with the Buzzers,' I said. 'Is there more than one way out of this Cripta dei Monarchi?'

'There is a second exit. We just need to—'

'Incoming,' Nick barked.

The Buzzers had followed us from outside. There were more of them now. Before I could run, Arcturus swung me on to his back. I held tight as he scaled the wall, climbing up to a ledge, followed by Terebell. Pleione scooped Mistry up, while Errai did the same for Nick. It took me a moment to realise they had all ignored Jaxon and Cardinal Rocha.

'Jax—'

His name escaped me before I could stop it. Arcturus glanced down, but the Buzzers were too close.

Jaxon dealt us an amused look, took a few steps back, and swept his poltergeists in front of him. The Buzzers avoided him and fell on Cardinal Rocha, who let out a cry before they devoured him. I turned away, grasping Arcturus. He kept an iron grip on both the ledge and me.

The Buzzers made a horrific cacophony as they feasted on Cardinal Rocha. Once they had stripped every last thread of flesh and sinew off his bones, they abandoned the skeleton, leaving a pool of blood in their wake, and disappeared through an opening I had missed.

'Terebell, you disappoint me.' Jaxon laughed. 'I expected you to give me a more specific death.'

'Your gift may be useful, arch-traitor,' Terebell said, 'but I will not assist you any more than I must.'

'I assure you that no assistance is needed.'

He was shrewd enough to know not to insult her. Not while she had that blade.

The Rephs returned to the floor. When Arcturus set me down, I tried not to look at the grisly remains of Cardinal Rocha, but Mistry retched. I grasped his shoulder.

'You don't have to go down there,' I said. 'There will be even more Buzzers around the cold spot.'

'No. You … need someone who knows the place.' He swallowed. 'Can you hold them off, Paige?'

'I can. Don't worry,' I said. 'I'll go first.'

Mistry nodded. Nick offered him a pistol, which he took. As I prepared to dislocate my spirit, Mistry muttered several names, drawing a few more poltergeists into the vicinity. A summoner couldn't exert the same ironclad control over the dead as a binder, but the spirits would usually lend them a figurative hand.

As we descended into the gloom, I tried to curb my nerves, memories of France rushing back to me. There was no water down here, but the æther was so heavy and thick, I might as well be suffocating. Soon it was like trying to breathe smoke instead of air.

'This is—' Mistry braced a hand against the wall. 'Why does the æther feel like this?'

'It's the Buzzers.' I blinked away dark blotches. 'Some of them do this.'

'The older ones,' Pleione said. 'They taint the æther more severely than the newly turned.'

Jaxon kept a watchful eye on Sukie and Herne. The poltergeists strained at the leash, ill at ease.

'Paige,' Arcturus said, 'use the ectoplasm. It will help you resist the corruption.' I took out the vial. 'Put it under your nose, and where the blood runs closest to your skin.'

Nick reloaded his gun. 'The pulse points, you mean?'

'Yes.'

With a nod, I opened the vial of molten light and dipped a fingertip. I dabbed it on to my skin like a perfume before offering it to the other humans, including Jaxon. The stronger he was, the higher our chances of getting out of here alive. By the time I tucked the vial back into my pocket, all four of us wore luminous war paint.

Arcturus was right. With his blood glowing on my skin, every deep breath clarified the æther, calming me. Mistry blinked several times, adjusting to the change in his sixth sense.

At the bottom of the steps, he showed us through an archway and down a corridor. 'The Cripta dei Monarchi is the newest wing of the Grotte Vaticani,' he said. 'It was built after Scion was founded in England, to honour the popes' long tradition of protecting devout monarchs. Let us hope the bodies *are* here, not in the Necropolis. That has a different entrance.'

Terebell moved in front of him, holding up her iridescent blade. I stayed close to her, ready to dislocate.

'They could have put Rephs in the coffins,' Nick said. 'Would any of them have been empty?'

'Yes, they prepare the tombs in advance. Queen Antonia of Spain was due to be laid here,' Mistry said. 'I've only visited once, on a private tour, but I'm certain I remember—'

A Buzzer appeared before he could finish. In this confined space, it looked even larger, a whirlwind of talons and teeth and unblinking white eyes. Terebell sidestepped out of its way and slashed, but it evaded the blow and dived towards Errai and Arcturus. They both avoided it, just as four more Buzzers stalked into the passage. Without hesitating, I threw out pressure. Mistry flinched away, his nose bleeding, while Nick grimaced. I tried to bend the force away from them, but it was difficult. It radiated from my dreamscape, surrounding me.

The sound of gunfire filled the crypt, followed by claws on a stone floor. Two Buzzers hurtled towards us. Without a word, Jaxon and I slid into the positions we had adopted during the last act of the scrimmage. Back to back, we brought our gifts to bear against the Buzzers – me using my own pressure, Jaxon wielding his poltergeists, creating a wall of powerful apport. When his Buzzer pushed closer, I spun and joined my strength to his, forcing the creature back.

The Buzzer opened its cavernous mouth. At once, Herne the Hunter was sucked towards the black hole in its head. I put three bullets in its throat, hoping to distract it, to no avail.

'Herne.' Jaxon clenched his fist, red seeping between his knuckles. 'Fall back, Richard Herne.'

'Arcturus, seal any cold spots,' Terebell ordered. 'The rest of you, fan out and search the tombs.'

Jaxon was starting to sweat again. No voyant was immune to this clotting in the æther.

'Caterina Sforza io ti invoco,' Mistry shouted. 'Ti invoco, Caterina Sforza!'

Another poltergeist was suddenly bouncing around the place like a pinball. My pendant deflected it, knocking it into the Buzzer, which let go of Herne.

'I'm going to help Arcturus,' I told Jaxon. 'Hold any others off at the stairs.'

The Buzzer yanked at Herne again. For once, Jaxon didn't answer me with some clever quip. He was laser-focused on the Buzzer, trying his level best to reel his poltergeist in. It had taken him a year to capture Herne in Windsor Forest, and he wasn't about to lose such a prize.

The Rephs spread out across the Cripta dei Monarchi. Mistry scrambled into an alcove, while Nick sent visions at the Buzzers, blinding them, making them clumsy. One of them charged at Terebell, but slammed into a wall. As I hurdled a stone coffin, she threw her sword towards another Buzzer, impaling it before it could bite me. I rounded a corner.

Arcturus had found a cold spot. It shone on the floor between three coffins, casting a strange light on the walls. As he spoke in Gloss, shrank, inch by painful inch.

'It will be hard to close it while the fallen lie here,' he told me. 'But I can stop more coming in.'

I nodded. Arcturus had one entrance covered, while Jaxon had the other.

A Buzzer had chased me from the main vault. Warding it away from Arcturus, I unleashed another torrent of pressure, blood trickling from my nose, my temples aching in protest. The creature let out a nightmarish scream and swung for me with a long arm, almost catching me. I scooted back, hammering it with everything I had. I had never fought them at such close quarters, and it was taking all my concentration, all my training, to stop this one from breaking in.

'Terebell, get over here!'

She appeared in moments. Just as she took off its head, the Buzzer ripped her coat.

'Shit.' I switched off the pressure. 'Did it get you?'

'No.' She inspected her sleeve. 'We found our fallen. Hold the creatures off while I sequester these last ones.'

Arcturus kept the cold spot shut. I had no idea how he was doing it, but I could feel him sewing the gap in the æther, apparently with nothing but willpower and Gloss.

Terebell opened a coffin, revealing a Reph with the dark hair and rosy sarx of her family. Unlike Arcturus, this one had not been chained in place, but lay in repose like a dead human, simply dressed, her gloved hands folded on her midriff. Errai caught up to Terebell.

'Hatysa,' he said, eyes burning. Terebell started to lift the Reph out. 'Wait. Wake her, dreamwalker.'

I looked up at him. 'What?'

'You resurrected Arcturus. Why not Hatysa?'

*Death itself will work in different ways.*

Terebell seemed to waver, cradling her cousin. Errai might have a point. If I could break other Rephs from latency, the Ranthen could replenish their forces.

Nick and Mistry appeared, followed by Jaxon. They gathered around the choke point of the entrance.

'Paige,' Nick said, 'more of them are coming.'

'Hold them off,' I said. 'Terebell, shut me into the coffin. It will protect me while you fight.'

She lifted me without protest. There was just enough room for me to squeeze in beside Hatysa. The lid rasped back into place. Before I could succumb to trepidation, I dreamwalked.

Now I was doubly entombed. In this mausoleum of a mind, all was dark and silent, and there was no golden cord to guide me. Struck blind, I stumbled forward, feeling my way around with no compass. I generally trusted my instincts, but panic was already taking hold, and Reph dreamscapes were cavernous. It was going to take too long to find her spirit.

My body kept on breathing. Through the dense stone of the coffin, I heard the Buzzers baying for my flesh. Every moment I had in here was a moment the others were buying me time.

Hatysa would be in the middle of her dreamscape. When I possessed a host, I always started at the very edge, facing inward. Fighting to stay calm, I ran in a straight line, on and on and on, until her dream-form tripped me. Her unresponsive spirit, left to lie for ever in her mind.

Arcturus and I had touched in his dreamscape. I didn't want to do the same to a complete stranger – Hatysa would likely hate to know that a human was in her safe place – but I had to try. Reaching down, I gripped her shoulders and willed her to wake, as I had with Arcturus.

'Hatysa,' I said. 'Come back.' I shook her. 'Hatysa Sheratan, can you hear me?'

No reply. This time, there was no flood of light, no spark at my fingertips. I was about to try again when my silver cord pulled me back to my own body. Arcturus had lifted the lid.

'Paige?'

'It's not working.' I grasped his arm and clambered out. 'I don't know why.'

'Try again.' Errai hauled me away from Arcturus, towards the next coffin. 'Pollux Chertan.'

'No,' Arcturus said. 'Paige must not overuse her gift, Errai.'

'I'll try,' I rasped, even though my head was in agony. 'Just keep … the Buzzers away.'

Errai nearly threw me into the second coffin. The Reph in this one had pale hair. Even though it was cut to his chin, he looked so much like Suhail that I forgot how to breathe. Before I could have second thoughts, Errai slammed the lid down.

Pollux was lifeless. He couldn't hurt me. I closed my eyes. Once again, I pushed out my spirit, overcoming the pain barrier, and my body fell limp in the coffin beside him, though my heart was still beating. I searched the darkness of his dreamscape, and I somehow found his spirit. Once again, no matter how hard I shook Pollux, he refused to wake.

'Come on,' I urged. 'Pollux Chertan, the Ranthen need you. Come back, now.' My temper frayed. 'Look, you've got a human in your dreamscape. Get up and throw me out!'

Pollux Chertan did not answer.

There was no more time for this. We needed to behead the bodies and get out of dodge. I turned on my heel and sprinted away, taking a running jump into the æther, then gasped back to myself. Arcturus spaded me out and set me on the floor, and I heaved for breath, leaning hard on the coffin. Errai looked inside it, then at me, his expression thunderous.

'He isn't waking up, either.' I clamped a hand over my thumping heart. 'I'm sorry, Errai.'

'Liar.' He pinned me to the coffin. 'Why could you only resurrect Arcturus?'

'I don't—'

'Are you favouring the Mesarthim?'

'Errai, peace.' Arcturus grasped his wrist, trying to break his grip on me. 'Paige has—'

'Whatever you're doing,' Jaxon snarled, 'do it quickly, you rabble of undying blockheads.' He was back in a tug of war with a Buzzer. Sukie floundered between them, her panic sending flickers through the æther. 'Or perhaps I should get you some *tea* while you hold a debate?'

Mistry was fighting to control his poltergeist, speaking to it in Italian, chanting its name between instructions. Caterina was none too happy, but her apport covered the entrance, a thin curtain of rancour that barely held the Buzzers back. It wouldn't be long before they overwhelmed us. Errai tightened his grip on my arms, hard enough to bruise.

'I will conceal your filthy secret,' he said to Arcturus, too low for anyone but us to hear, 'but not if you reserve the dreamwalker for your own use.'

'I'm not his to use,' I said hotly. 'Or yours.'

'Then save our warriors!'

'Enough,' Terebell said. 'She has made two attempts, Errai. No more.'

Pleione towed Hatysa out of the coffin, speaking a few words in Gloss before Terebell decapitated her cousin in one blow. The head dropped like a chunk of stone.

Errai released me, a cascade of anguished Gloss escaping him. Arcturus put himself between us, but Errai only cared about Hatysa now. Terebell sequestered Pollux.

When his skull hit the floor, it was as if a bell had tolled. The heavy force in the æther lifted. Three of the poltergeists huddled close to Jaxon, while Caterina Sforza took her leave, knocking a candlestick down as she went. The Buzzers slowed, their white eyes roaming.

'They are locating the next grave,' Terebell said. 'We do not have long.'

She took the opportunity to behead the distracted Buzzers. I watched her without flinching. Either I had developed a cast-iron stomach, or the sheer amount of carnage I had witnessed had numbed me in less than an hour.

'The exit is this way.' Mistry broke into a weary run. 'We can take the Passetto di Borgo, a corridor above street level. The College of Cardinals will have used it to leave the Vatican.'

'Right.' I swallowed a little blood, skirting around another headless Reph. 'Pleione, where next?'

'We must leave the vicinity,' Pleione said. 'Every Emite that came to this grave is about to move towards the next. We can follow them.'

Mistry led us out of the Cripta dei Monarchi and through the silent Papal Tombs, which lay undisturbed. I narrowed my eyes against the sudden flood of daylight, reaching for the amaranth in my pocket.

This still wasn't over.

# 29

## CALL OF THE VOID

In the time we had been underground, Rome had turned even colder, and the fog had thickened. We emerged into a chaos of sirens and screaming. Across the city, I could hear explosions and gunfire.

Mistry ran beneath the marble colonnade that surrounded the Piazza di San Pietro, which the Buzzers had strewn with limbs and heads. With unsteady hands, he unlocked a door and led us up a flight of steps, to an elevated path. My breath came in white puffs as I ran between its battlements, staying ahead of Pleione and Arcturus.

The Buzzers were no longer magnetically drawn to the basilica, but I could feel them nearby. If we were quick and quiet, the Passetto di Borgo would allow us to avoid their notice.

We stopped at the sound of planes overhead, impossible to make out through the fog. It took every ounce of my strength to keep moving.

'Mistry,' Nick said, 'any idea who our visitors are?'

'They're most likely Italian. Beatrice had planes at the ready,' Mistry said, 'but the French have an airbase and a missile launch facility on Corsica. They could be supporting the attack.' He stopped. 'Underqueen, give me that device on your lapel. I'll contact Beatrice.'

I passed it to him and looked between the battlements, clutching a stitch.

On the streets, the Buzzers were reorienting. Most of them stood upright, their heads turning. It was as if they were using an internal radar to find the latent Rephs. Even if we were one misstep away from being spotted, I had never been so relieved to be off the ground.

'There are so many of them,' I murmured.

Pleione came to my side. 'Another lamentation has ceased. Now there is but one.'

'I think I know where. Cade said he was going to face me at the Colosseum.'

We pressed on, trying not to draw attention. I stopped when gunfire came from below. Sensing a dreamscape I recognised, I looked back over the edge.

Eliza was down there, cornered by three Buzzers.

She handled a rifle with more assurance than I had anticipated. In the gang, she had generally avoided conflict, but more than nine months as interim Underqueen, living under martial law, had clearly hardened her. When one of the Buzzers stalked closer, a poltergeist drove it back.

'Ah, there's my Martyred Muse,' Jaxon observed unhelpfully.

'Eliza.' I grasped the balustrade. 'Pleione, can you bring her up?'

She vaulted between the battlements. As she landed, the spirits around her gave a hum that raised every hair on my arms. The Buzzers retreated, hissing. Pleione dumped Eliza over her shoulder and climbed back up to the passageway, pursued by Jean the Skinner, who returned to Jaxon.

'Eliza.' I helped her down. 'Are you all right?'

'Yes, but—'

'In the fullness of time, you will pay for your treachery,' Terebell told her. 'You broke my trust, interim Underqueen. Do not think I will forget it.'

She strode after Mistry again, leaving Eliza even more shaken. When she clutched her right arm, I saw that a Buzzer had slashed away most of her sleeve, leaving gashes.

'Paige,' she said, 'it clawed me.'

'You weren't bitten.' I ushered her in front of me. 'You'll be fine. Come on.'

Another plane flew past. To my right, part of a building exploded, spraying dust and masonry. I wondered if Sala might really be willing to fire on her own city to destroy the Buzzers.

The fog was so dense, I could barely see Eliza in front of me. The Passetto let us bypass the fighting around the Vatican, though we now had three hungry Buzzers on our tail. The Italian soldiers were fighting back with all their might, their guns drowning out the shouts of panic. Eliza faltered as the poison threw her balance off, making her sweat rivers. At my behest, Pleione picked her up and carried her under her arm like a rag doll.

Eliza Renton was the closest thing I had to a sister. No matter what she had done, I was not leaving her behind.

The corridor ended at the Castel Sant'Angelo. Mistry tried the door, but found it locked. Terebell smashed through it with ease, taking it right off its hinges.

'I could get used to having you around,' Mistry said, with a weak chuckle.

'We have been *around* for two centuries,' Pleione said. 'Expect us for a good deal longer.'

Castel Sant'Angelo was a blur. We slammed every door we could in our wake, stopping the Buzzers from following. I had avoided their claws, but their presence was still tarnishing the æther, even outside the Vatican. I resisted finishing the vial of fortified ectoplasm, wanting to save the last few drops to bolster me against Cade.

'You went after Fitzours,' I said to Eliza. 'Where did he go?'

'We lost him,' she answered. 'A bunch of Rephs got him away. They were too quick for us.'

Pleione went ahead once more, following the lamentation to the final grave. Once we had broken out of the building, we crossed the Tiber. Some of the angels' wings had been chipped, caught by shrapnel or bullets. When Pleione was tuned into the spirits' voices, her eyes brightened. She led us on with confidence, heading towards the Forum.

Arcturus had fallen to the back of the group again. When I turned, I saw him leaning on a balustrade, Terebell beside him. I rushed back to them.

'Nick,' I called, 'we need a car.'

'I'm on it.'

I reached Arcturus and looked into the eyeholes of his mask. 'Can you keep going?'

'Yes,' he said. 'I will be able to … seal the last cold spots, if they have appeared in the Colosseum.'

'Take my aura.'

He didn't put up a fight. Terebell watched as our auras twined, turning his eyes red again.

'You cannot sustain this for much longer,' she told him. 'Any more alysoplasm will turn you.'

'There's just one grave left. We can stop this,' I said. 'Scion wasn't expecting the Italians to know what hit them.' Nick got a truck going and beckoned us. 'We'll follow you again. Arcturus, you come with us.'

We climbed into the truck. Nick locked the doors and followed the Ranthen off the bridge.

'The others must have dealt with the Rephs under the Trevi Fountain,' he said. 'That's why Pleione stopped hearing the song, right?'

'Let's hope so,' I said.

'Is this what you've all been doing since you abandoned London, my company of intrepid heroes?' Jaxon asked, his tone almost pleasant. 'Putting your lives on the line to defend the amaurotics? Trying to save the world from Scion, all for hidebound fools like Cardinal Rocha?'

'Put a sock in it, Jax,' I growled.

Eliza had a hand pressed over her arm. It wasn't bleeding much, but she looked ill.

The Colosseum had stood for nearly two millennia. The ruin was thronged with old and new spirits, still drawn to a place of death. It was close to the Forum – close enough that you could almost throw a stone between them. If we defended it, we defended the Council of Kassandra. As much as I resented their meddling, I didn't want the Forum to fall.

I focused on the æther. Suddenly I could sense Cade, a light-house among the other dreamscapes.

He was right ahead of us, exactly where I had known he would be, waiting for his vision to come to pass. If the ruthless bastard wanted a fight, I was more than happy to give him one. It ended here.

As Nick drove after Pleione, a shadow fell across the street in front of us. He braked when two massive crates hit the ground, parachutes deflating around them.

'A supply drop.' Mistry got out. 'Beatrice has sent help.'

We ran to the armoured crates. Inside was almost everything we could possibly need, including medical supplies, sacks of gritting salt, several rifles, and a submachine gun. I helped myself to a couple of hand grenades, while Pleione and Errai took charge of the salt.

'Paige!'

Maria came towards us with Verča and the rest of the Ranthen. The Rephs were streaked with ectoplasm, Lesath bleeding from his chest. From his blue eyes, Maria had dealt with it.

'Verča was right.' She grasped my shoulder. 'We found the Rephs under the Trevi Fountain.'

'Well done, Verča,' I said. 'Are they sequestered?'

'Yes.' Lesath had the blade. 'All of them were Ranthen.'

The Buzzers were moving south. Abandoning the truck, we followed their trail of destruction. Lesath slowed to help Arcturus. I hung back to cover them, letting Pleione lead the others.

We turned at a rumble from above. The fog had thinned above the Tiber, and I saw a distant flash of wings. I hadn't known a thing about military vehicles when I was in the gang, but I had familiarised myself with the entire fleet of the Inquisitorial Air Force as Underqueen, wanting to know what sort of firepower the Mime Order was up against. From what I could make out, this resembled a strike aircraft, used for close air support.

It was heading straight towards us, its engines roaring. Hundreds of people ran to get out of its way. For a terrible instant, I thought it really was a Scion plane, coming to punish us for our defiance. Then I looked over my shoulder to see another swarm of Buzzers.

I covered my ears as the plane opened fire. A spray of bullets mowed down the street, followed by two missiles in quick succession, which collided with the swarm, exploding with enough force to shake the ground. The plane soared upward and vanished into the mist.

'Paige.'

Arcturus steadied me. I leaned into him, reminding myself that he was there, that I didn't have to find him.

Some of the Buzzers were still moving, their limbs reaching out of the smoking pile. As I gazed at the devastation, I began to understand the full implications of this day. This had been planned. Nashira had always been ready to show her cards when the right moment arose.

Scion must have realised that people were catching wind of the Rephs, and now, for the first time in two centuries, it was revealing the power of the Netherworld. It was showing us all that it possessed a weapon like no other, something that its enemies would never understand. If we had thought to steal a march on Scion, we had failed.

There was no coming back from this. Whatever the outcome, everything was about to change.

We kept running and skulking towards the Colosseum. Every last Buzzer would now be converging on this ruin, making it nearly impossible to sequester the latent Rephs.

Not all of us would get out of this alive.

More Buzzers raced ahead of us. Maria and Eliza took shots at them, as did every soldier in the vicinity. One of them hefted a flame-thrower, and a jet of flame roared towards the Buzzers. Crafting a spool, Maria sent it through the fire. One after the other, the spirits ignited, carrying her numen, and the spool burst apart in all directions, lighting up at least half of the monsters. The flame seemed to protect the spirits, allowing them to avoid being sucked into those terrible dreamscapes. Errai watched, his mask reflecting the glow.

'What sort of beings would create such weapons?'

'You'll be grateful for them in a minute.' I pulled the ring from a grenade. 'Stay back.'

I hurled the grenade at the Buzzers. The explosion shattered the pavement around them, setting off another round of unearthly screams. Another spool came spinning over my head and sent a Buzzer up in flames, right as a missile shot from the fog and clipped a nearby building. I coughed as dust covered us all.

We passed the Forum. Nick helped Eliza, who was short of breath and slowing.

'Eliza,' he said, 'go to the Council of Kassandra. You can't do anything against Fitzours.'

'No. I'm not letting you—'

'If all three of us die, Jaxon is the only one left with a right to the Rose Crown. We can't risk that,' I said, speaking over a barrage of gunfire. 'Please, Eliza. Stay here.'

'Are you going to fight the other dreamwalker?'

'I've not much choice.' I gave her a light push. 'Go on.'

She relented, running towards the Forum.

Ahead of us, the Colosseum loomed from the fog. The failing sunlight bestranged it, turning its many arches into lidless eyes. We stopped at the entrance, finding no guards to stop us.

'It was here?' Nick said. 'Why didn't we go here first?'

'I cannot always judge the distance,' Pleione said. 'But there are many latent Rephaim within these walls.' She turned her yellow gaze on me. 'Do you sense the other dreamwalker, Paige?'

'Yes, he's here. So are Castor and Kornephoros, and—' My blood iced over. 'Shit. It can't be.'

'Who is it?'

'Gomeisa.'

I had missed his dreamscape, with the contamination in the æther. The Reph who had personally overseen the conquest of Ireland. As a child, I had glimpsed him on the streets of Dublin. He and Hildred Vance had plotted the Imbolc Massacre together.

'The Rephs are probably beneath the Colosseum,' Verča said. Her face was smudged with dust. 'The hypogeum, the underground level. It's concealed by a modern floor.'

As she spoke, her voice shook a little. She must have seen Lesath behead all the bodies.

'Warden needs to go down there,' I said. 'Are you okay to lead him, Verča?'

'Yes.'

'Maria, you go with them. You can torch the Buzzers.'

'With pleasure,' Maria said.

Arcturus would need fire more than I would. Lesath joined him with the blade. As the four of them headed into the arches on the ground level, Arcturus stopped to look back at me, and I met his gaze, knowing it might well be for the last time. I nodded once and turned away.

'We need to keep Gomeisa and his lackeys busy. There might be more of them than I can sense,' I said. 'Will the Buzzers leave the city once it's done?'

'Not with this much flesh to feast on. They are in a feeding frenzy,' Terebell said. 'They will need to be driven from Rome by force.'

'I'll tell Beatrice,' Mistry said. 'The troops will be ready.'

'Good. I can handle Cade,' I said to the Ranthen. 'You deal with the Sargas loyalists.'

'Gomeisa can use apport to lift anyone he sees fit,' Terebell warned. 'You will sense his intent if he targets you, but you will only have moments to break his line of sight. If he succeeds in levitating you, move as much as possible. It will make you harder to hold.' She looked at me. 'The pendant will shield you from his power, Underqueen. Do not remove it.'

'Okay.' I checked my weapons. 'Let's do this.'

I entered the Colosseum.

Cadoc Fitzours was a tiny figure in the middle of the amphitheatre, standing in a circle of salt. I walked towards him across a wooden floor overlaid with sand.

I had expected Cade to appear in a stolen body, but it was becoming clear to me that he was too cocksure for his own good. Only someone with notions would presume they could survive among the Sargas. In any case, the jump had the most power when it stemmed from the dreamwalker, not a host. I had pinballed between dreamscapes before, losing momentum each time. No,

Cade wanted to defeat me himself, in his own body, to prove he was superior.

As I got closer, I noticed the bulletproof vest over his doublet. Maybe he did have a drop of sense left.

Gomeisa Sargas stood on an upper level, overseeing the scene, while Kornephoros and Castor guarded their dreamwalker. I stopped a good distance away, flanked by my own defenders. I had no armour, but I didn't expect anyone to shoot me. Nashira would still prefer to capture me alive.

Kornephoros sized up the Ranthen. They must not have realised there would be enemy Rephs here. All we had on our side was my gift, one sword, and the element of surprise.

'Paige,' Cade called. 'I knew you would come.'

'Cade.' I kept my voice as steady as I could. 'There was me thinking you were an oracle.'

'I can send and receive visions. It's what protected me in Oxford,' he said. 'Most voyants only receive one gift, but rarely, some of us get more.'

'Lucky you.'

Behind me, Jaxon had entered the arena, trailing his poltergeists. Mistry stayed back, a phone clamped to his ear.

Gomeisa kept watching. Always the spectator, keeping his distance. I had seen him so rarely, but whenever I had, it left a lasting impression. Like when he had murdered Liss Rymore.

'I'm curious.' Cade raised a smile. 'How did you escape the Hôtel Garuche?'

'Oh, your man there let me go.' I pointed. 'Did he not say?'

Cade glanced up at Kornephoros, whose eyes flamed. That ought to create some marital discord.

'I assume you were planning to give me to Nashira,' I said. 'I really can't work out why you'd join her, after seeing how she treated me in Oxford.'

'I made a bargain with her, like the Vigiles do. She can kill me after thirty years, if she doesn't get you first,' Cade said. 'It works for us both. She understands the dangers of our gift; how it pushes us to breaking point, even when we train our hardest. Why take the risk of absorbing my spirit, when she can have me at her side and reap the exact same rewards?'

'She could change her mind at any moment.'

'Any of us could die any day, Paige. We're mortal,' he said. 'Better to go for a good cause.'

'What could possibly be good about her cause?'

Nick poured salt around us. The Ranthen stepped out of the circle at once, approaching their enemies with just one useful blade between them. Castor sneered at Lucida.

This entire confrontation felt artificial in a way I didn't like, down to the stage. The Rephs were the audience, and Cade and I were the players.

'Nashira wants to make sure humans obey her rule,' Cade said. 'And we need that, Paige.'

I stood my ground. 'Why?'

'Because humans are broken. Even knowing the æther, we voyants fight and kill and torture each other for nothing. Scion has insulated you from reality, but Nashira showed me the depths. I've experienced it myself. I told you my family died in a house fire,' Cade said. 'Some bastard did it for—' He paused, face tight. 'He did it for fun, because humans are fucking insane. We are as monstrous as the Buzzers, and we'll never stop. Not without gods to control us. This place fell centuries ago, and humans are still just as brutal.'

'The Rephs use violence against innocents, too,' I said. 'I was only six when I saw that in Ireland.'

'Nashira uses our methods against us,' he said, 'so we'll see the folly of them. Don't you get it by now?'

*I have done nothing to you that you have not done to yourselves.*

While I kept Cade talking, I tracked the others. Verča and Maria had stopped – probably waiting in a safe place – while Lesath was pausing every so often. I imagined him and Arcturus hiding from the Buzzers, waiting for their moment to approach the latent Rephs.

Cade was noticing. His gaze drifted towards the floor.

'You talked about our names in Paris,' I said, regaining his attention. 'Are we related, Cade?'

'Maybe,' he said. 'Join us, and I'll tell you everything I know.' He held out a gloved hand. 'I can protect you from Nashira. I promise. Don't you want a family again, Paige?'

Once, an offer like that would have tempted me. Of course it would.

But over the last four years, I had learned that family was more than blood or names. It could be chosen.

'I can't do that.' I planted my boots. 'I know about Operation Ventriloquist. I have to stop you.'

'Stop me, and there will be more death, like there was in Dublin,' Cade said. 'Is that what you want?'

'There will be death either way. You know what Scion does to voyants. And to anyone who fights.'

Another swarm of Buzzers had reached the Colosseum. I could sense that most of them were making their way underground, but some crawled over the ruined walls. Gomeisa surrounded himself with a shield of apport, while the other Rephs prepared to fight.

'Once Nashira has the world, I promise you, she'll stop all that. She was only afraid that we wouldn't hear reason,' Cade said. 'She had to make the amaurotics fear us, to make sure they would never weaponise us against her. She had to cull our numbers so we couldn't pose a threat.' I huffed in disbelief. 'But when it's done, she'll raise us to power. She'll teach us to purge our human instincts, and then we'll rule over the amaurotics, as we always should have.'

'Cade, listen to yourself. You're deluded,' I said. 'None of what you're saying makes sense.'

'Not to you. You're in too deep with the Ranthen.' His mouth thinned. 'You really won't listen, will you?'

'I was never good at that.'

Kornephoros took a step forward, his gaze predatory. Terebell moved in front of me.

'Let the dreamwalkers do battle,' Gomeisa commanded his loyalists. 'Do not interfere.'

I raised my eyebrows. He really had lured me here for a demonstration.

'Defeat the dreamwalker.' Terebell only had eyes for her cousin. 'We will draw his protectors away.'

'Nick,' I said, 'when Cade jumps, his body is vulnerable. If I can't kill him, don't let him leave.'

He drew his pistol. The two hulking Rephs closed ranks around Cade, who widened his stance. I could sense the æther changing as his spirit prepared to dislocate.

'Sure you want to do this, Paige?'

'Yes,' I said. 'Shall we get on with it?'

He clenched his jaw. I schooled my expression, so he wouldn't suspect the depth of the anger I was hiding. Every instinct told me to rip his throat out for what he had done, but I couldn't reveal what I knew. Not without endangering Arcturus, alerting them to his escape.

What I could do – what I did – was pour all of that rage into the jump.

Our spirits clashed in the æther. I had never made direct impact with a spirit outside a dreamscape before, and the collision was seismic. It felt like I had hit a brick wall at breakneck speed. We shoved each other with all our might, then ricocheted into our own bodies.

Both of us had kept our balance. I fed the pain to my gift, my heart pounding at my breastbone.

Cade was as inexpressive as a Reph. Terebell charged towards Kornephoros, who swung a massive club against her sword. Errai and Pleione joined her, while Lucida fought her own cousin, Castor. Another five Sargas loyalists entered the fray, outnumbering the Ranthen.

The short distraction cost me. Cade beat me to the jump by a split second, driving his spirit against the barrier of my dreamscape. My eyes watered, and I clenched my teeth.

I had rested as much as I could in Orvieto. My barrier was keeping Cade out, but only just. My head throbbed from the blow. He swooped at me a third time, and I flew into the æther to meet him.

Once again, Cade deflected me before I could touch his dreamscape. When I returned to my body, my stomach pulled at the root, nauseating me. He took a few deep breaths.

On the other side of the arena, Terebell duelled Kornephoros. It shook me to see the size of him in comparison to her. Terebell was nearly as tall as Arcturus, but her cousin was a behemoth. Errai backed her up with spools. Kornephoros held them both off with ease.

His club was a thing of terrible beauty, made of opaline. Terebell parried with her sword. Neither of them were as fluid as Arcturus, but they fought with murderous precision, driven by an old grudge. Terebell was the rightful Warden of the Sheratan, acknowledged by the Ranthen. Kornephoros was fixated on her, his eyes burning a clean yellow.

Cade lashed out. I tasted iron, but took my turn. This time, I pushed close enough to make contact with the edge of his dreamscape, only for him to do the same to me, twice as hard.

My defences strained. We continued in this way, bouncing off each other with the force of two bullets, until I was clammy and heaving. Each time Cade landed a hit on me, my skull rang like a bell, blood leaked from my nose, and the æther shuddered around us.

Gomeisa Sargas never took his eyes off the fight. Even the other Rephs stopped to look.

If I kept this up, I was going to pass out. I had taken knocks to my dreamscape from many spirits over the years, but these attacks were strategic, as if Cade was feeling along my barrier for weak points.

'I expected more staying power,' he said. 'What *was* Arcturus doing with you in Oxford?'

'You're good. I'll give you that.' I spat blood on the sand. 'Who trained you?'

'My family.'

Cade had most likely been taught from childhood, then. It didn't surprise me. My attacks hadn't even made him break a sweat, while I was starting to feel as if I had run a marathon.

'I first walked in the æther when I was eleven,' he said. 'I've polished that skill for thirteen years.' He found a vulnerability again, driving into it with so much force it almost brought me to my knees. 'Even if a Reph taught you, you're still a novice, Paige. Arcturus Mesarthim was no dreamwalker. I'm sure he tried his best, but he didn't understand our power. The power to be anyone. The power to rip life away.'

I struck him again, and again, he repelled me. When I landed back in my body, I got straight up, my resolve stiffening.

Even if I had only been able to skim his dreamscape, it had boosted my confidence. His barrier was thin with exhaustion. No doubt it was hard to sleep, living in the belly of the beast. He might have trained for years longer than I had, but I had breached his dreamscape before. I knew that it was possible.

He still broke me first.

It was the vision that did it: Kornephoros and Castor, carving Arcturus with swords, over and over. This wasn't an imagined scene; it could only be this vivid because Cade had actually witnessed it. I saw the light of ectoplasm in the room. I saw Michael being hit by a Reph.

Cade was inside me before I could stop him.

All dreamscapes had defences, but mine had only dealt with this level of danger once before. Cade sprinted through my windflowers and vaulted into my secret room, my fortress, flowers trampled in his wake. Every footfall left a bruise. Before I could move, he made it to my sunlit zone. It paralysed me just to *see* another person in my dreamscape.

He seized my spirit. For the first time in my life, another human was touching the essence of me, the vulnerable quick at the core of my being. That touch might as well have stripped me naked, peeling layers of skin with it.

'Your dreamscape wasn't like this before,' he observed. 'There were only red flowers.'

His grip tightened, and it wasn't my body he was crushing. It was me.

'I'm going to make you kill Jaxon Hall,' he whispered, so close I would have felt his breath if this had been the outside world. Against my will, I trembled. 'And then you're going to kill Nick. And then you'll know how it feels to be me.'

'Over my bones,' I forced out.

He threw me out of my sunlit zone, into a darker circle of my consciousness. That careless act of violence – so easy for him – would have destroyed anyone but a dreamwalker. My silver cord stretched, as supple as ever, but the shock left me in a heap on the ground.

As Cade stepped into my rightful place, I had an overpowering urge to sleep, to relinquish control of my body. I would have welcomed it, in that moment. I felt as if his fingerprints were smeared all over me.

His dream-form grew still as he looked through my eyes. The sight of it jolted me back to my senses. I forced myself up and sprinted towards him. With all my strength, I dived at him, wrestling him for control of my body, trying to keep his attention on my dreamscape. I was no amaurotic – I could put up a good fight – but Cade had done this so many times, and I was battling the urge to let him take the wheel.

I could just see through my own eyes, though my vision faltered: Cade was pointing my revolver at Jaxon. With a supreme effort, I wrenched the gun to the left. Jaxon started as it went off, his eyebrows shooting up.

'Really, darling?'

'Paige.' Nick gripped my shoulders. 'Paige, is that you or him in there?'

'Me,' I ground out, but the ventriloquist had my chin on a hinge. 'It's … me, Nick.'

I had never experienced a horror like not having control of my own jaw and tongue. His words in my mouth.

My hand on the knife.

He worked a blade from my holster, every inch he gained sending a bolt of pain along my fingers. My body, fighting back against the puppeteer.

Nick was concentrating on my face. He wouldn't see the blade coming until it was too late. I looked into his eyes, hoping he could see my warning, sense the battle for control.

And then I had a sudden, desperate idea.

I only had one spectre in my dreamscape. One memory so harrowing that it had crawled free of the ground. It should have reacted to an intruder, but I went to great lengths, every hour of my life, to keep that memory from taking hold. I had pinned it in the hadal zone.

Now I focused on that memory with all my might. Arcturus had made it fresh, so it was easier to remember the tight grip of the manacles, the water filling my chest, the foul taste and the cold as it sliced down my throat. Suhail stood above me, his eyes turning red.

*Perhaps the Underqueen would care for a drink.*

The spectre moved. So did my hand, jolting closer to Nick. It shook as I resisted Cade.

*You are nothing.*

In my dreamscape, the spectre lifted Cade clean off the ground, distracting him from the physical world. He stared into its leaking eyes, and I knew that he was seeing my dark room, suffocating on my fear. His spirit went rigid, then limp. His silver cord gleamed once, and he vanished, leaving me to shudder.

The spectre retreated into the dark. I lurched back into my sunlit zone, and my eyes snapped open.

'Paige,' Nick said. His voice was muffled. 'Paige, is that you?'

'Get back. He almost—' I shoved his chest. 'Stay away from me, Nick. Help the Ranthen.'

'What happened?'

Cade had fallen to one knee. The pain in my head when I dreamwalked was bad enough, but the agony of his intrusion was so much worse. My eyes watered.

He couldn't have orders to kill me, or I would already be dead. That would be an unforgivable waste. He wanted me weak enough that the Rephs could collect me and carry me off.

For now, however, Cade was reeling. Jaxon scanned the battleground. Keeping my defences up, I followed his gaze.

Terebell executed a graceful spin and beheaded one of the Sargas loyalists, spraying ectoplasm. Considering the Ranthen were outnumbered, they were holding their own, all of them consummate fighters. More Buzzers were spidering in. A rumble filled the arena, and part of the Colosseum crumbled, causing an avalanche of stone. The rubble crashed and rolled down the stands and across the floor, scattering a few Buzzers, forcing the Rephs to divide to avoid it. Gomeisa raised a hand, and more came.

His gift was one of the most powerful I had encountered. At any moment, he could kill us all.

I could have sworn he heard the thought. His eyes flashed, and Nick was yanked off the ground.

In unison, Jaxon and I grabbed him. My mind went blank with fear as Nick fought the invisible force. With gritted teeth, Jaxon sent all of his poltergeists towards Gomeisa, breaking his grip. We collapsed to the ground, Nick pale in the face. His skin was icy, his lips dark.

That was the second time he had been singled out. The Sargas knew exactly who he was, and what he meant to me. I took off the pendant and fastened it around his neck, ignoring his weak protest.

'Fuck.' My gaze darted around the arena. 'Where the hell is Cade?'

'Underqueen,' Mistry called as I rose. 'Draghetti has been tracking the Buzzers. They're all here, in the hypogeum. He's giving us ten minutes before he detonates the Colosseum.'

'What?' Nick allowed me to bolster him up, panting. 'He's going to blow the whole place?'

'I need longer,' I told Mistry, glancing at my watch. 'You have to give the Ranthen a chance to stop this.'

'It's a bloodbath. Hundreds of people are dead,' Mistry shouted. 'We don't have time to—'

'Suzanna,' Jaxon barked.

I looked up, grasping Nick. Another hail of ancient stone was flying towards us. The poltergeist averted it, and it missed us by a foot, crashing along the floor instead. Sukie had died when some cruel boys threw rocks at her, and she definitely wasn't letting Jaxon go that way.

Jaxon doubled over. He was turning as white as his shirt, both sleeves damp with blood. Even at the scrimmage, I had never seen him use his gift so much. I jerked him back as a Buzzer began to stalk the edge of our protective circle, its elongated teeth on full display.

Cade was still nearby, no doubt trying to shake off the terror of the memory. I could sense him somewhere in the stands, but I was already too drained to send my spirit after him. I would need to track him down myself. When I started to run, Sukie came with me.

'Paige,' Nick bellowed. 'Don't leave the circle!'

467

I stopped when sand blew across my face. An Italian military chopper was hovering over the ruin. Gomeisa stared it down, as if he was daring this mechanical toy to move against him.

He made a gesture. As more of the Colosseum tumbled, he lifted a slab of broken stone and hurled it towards the helicopter. The pilot had no time to react, but Lucida Sargas thrust up her own hand. The slab came to a gradual stop, a foot away from the helicopter.

She had the same gift.

The chopper banked away from us. Lucida threw the rubble back at Gomeisa, who retaliated. Stone crashed on stone with a sound like a thunderclap, scattering chips across the ground.

Cade emerged from the dust, two more Rephs in his wake. He must have recovered his strength, and now he was back to finish me off. Seeing me, he charged, his expression livid. My spirit reared. I sprinted to meet him.

And then the floor split, right under my boot.

The ground became a chasm. I tried to back up, but it was too late. I was already falling.

A hand grabbed mine. I hung over the underground tunnels, where scores of Buzzers were loping through a labyrinth of walls and arches. The last of the daylight filled it, and the creatures saw me, their screams growing louder. In moments, I had lost count of them.

I looked up to see Jaxon, holding my weight.

A Buzzer snapped at my boots. I hadn't understood what was happening, but now I saw. The floor was retracting, exposing the warren of tunnels, and Jaxon Hall was all that stood between me and my doom. If he let go, the Buzzers would shred me. Our gazes locked, and I knew he was considering it, so nothing would stop him taking the Rose Crown.

Then he yanked me up to the floor. I crumpled into his arms, too shaken to speak.

'Watch your step, darling,' Jaxon said.

I had no time to question him. He pointed Jean towards another Buzzer, stopping it before it could reach us.

He carted me towards our circle as the floor slid farther back, taking us away from the battling Rephs. By the time it stopped, an insurmountable gap had opened between one side of the battleground and the other, revealing most of the hypogeum. All I could see down there were Buzzers. I couldn't feel anything but the great oily mass of their dreamscapes.

'I can't overpower Cade,' I said, breathing hard. 'He's too strong.'

Jaxon was the last person I wanted to ask for help, but I was desperate. His soft laugh chilled my spine.

'You are a queen of thieves and scoundrels,' he said, almost tenderly. 'Not a hero, Paige.'

A peal of Gloss drew our attention. Lucida was pinned under an immense slab of stone. Seeing her position, Terebell tossed her sword to Pleione and ran to their ally, hefting the stone aside. It must have weighed at least a tonne, but Terebell raised it enough to free Lucida. She turned over, her arm bent in an awkward position.

Kornephoros was stalking towards them. I stopped him with a surge of pressure, but the mental skirmish with Cade had drained so much of my strength. If I had any hope of protecting the Ranthen, I would have to get closer. Terebell laid both hands on Lucida, and the æther vibrated around them.

'Underqueen, we need to leave,' Mistry said. 'If we're going to have a chance of getting clear—'

'You go,' I cut in. 'Take the others with you. Jax, get out of here.'

'With pleasure,' Jaxon said. 'I recommend you do the same, Underqueen.'

He shadowed Mistry to the entrance, beckoning his poltergeists. Sukie circled me once more before she raced after her binder. As I regained my breath, I tried again to search the æther. Verča and Maria were now on ground level, but Lesath was below, likely with Arcturus.

'Paige.' Nick gripped my arm. 'Look.'

I looked. Cade was trapped on our side of the floor, without any Rephs to protect him, pouring another salt circle.

Our eyes met.

He tried to get the jump on me, cannoning his spirit out so hard the æther surged. Nick countered his attack with a vision, but Cade sent him crumpling to the ground. That sight was all I needed to spur me, even though the agony was hard to bear. I wrenched into the æther.

And I broke into Cade.

When I had seen his dreamscape in London, I hadn't had any time to look, and that remained the case. Still, I glimpsed the trunks of trees, red leaves scattered on the ground, before I made towards the light.

There was his dream-form, waiting for me, larger and more imposing than his physical self. It resembled a Reph, down to its eyes. I shunted it out of place, into the gloom beyond his sunlit zone. Before he could recover, I was in control of his body, fighting his resistance. I took one drunken step in his skin, walking him out of the salt circle. A Buzzer smelled fresh meat and came rushing towards him.

Cade kicked me out with frightening ease. Back in my own body, I watched him bowl a spool past the Buzzer, distracting it. As soon as it turned its back, I leapt up and ran at him.

The sheer madness of the sprint must have shocked him. I hurled a fistful of sand into his eyes, making him shout in pain, and then I was in his circle of salt, taking him to the ground. I drove my fist into his face, but I already knew I was no match for him. He must have been training in body as well, protecting the cradle of his gift.

As I knocked one of his back teeth loose, he rolled me over and trapped my arms above my head, the way they had been on the waterboard. My chest tightened.

Cade was too weak to dreamwalk now. In spite of all of his training, our fight had pushed him to the limit. I slammed a knee between his legs. As his grip slackened, I tried and failed to project my spirit one more time. Our tanks were both empty, but Cade was incensed. Before I could stop him, he let go of my right hand and tore the brace off the left one. I knew what he was going to do, and what I couldn't stop.

When he twisted my wrist, I knew I was finished.

A gut-wrenching scream escaped me. The pain was blinding, beyond anything I had ever felt. My left hand was in boiling oil. As tears streaked my cheeks, the golden cord rang.

'You know what this is, the feeling we have?' Cade asked, blood on his lips. Nick let out a groan and reached for me, nearly unconscious. 'That longing to join with the æther?'

That impossible *we*. I remembered the first time Jaxon had said it, inviting me to belong among voyants.

'It's the call of the void,' Cade ground out. 'Some amaurotics claim to feel it. That urge to jump from a high place. The belief that you can soar, even though you have no wings.' I inched my hand towards my boot, trying to ignore the agony that seared along every bone, every finger. 'But that isn't the call we hear. You and I have known the void, and we are part of it.' I sensed his spirit dislocating again. 'I wish I didn't have to do this. I don't want to be alone in the world. But the void is calling, and it's time for you to answer, Paige.'

He used both hands to grip my throat. That was when I drove my boot knife into his neck, using the wrist he had thought was too weak, the fractured bone that had already died.

'Not just yet,' I hissed.

Cade hadn't been expecting that. It took him a long moment to understand that I had stabbed him. That I had used such an amaurotic ploy in the midst of the spiritual conflict he wanted.

'I'm not just a dreamwalker,' I said, my voice straining. 'I'm a professional fucking lowlife.'

I twisted the knife deeper, wringing a choked gargle from Cade. His spirit might be powerful, but his mortal body could still betray him. Before I could pass out from the pain, I wrenched the blade from his neck and brought it up to finish the job. I could not flinch this time.

An unseen force knocked the knife from my grip. I looked up to see Gomeisa, his gaze set on us.

Cade was yanked towards the pit. I lunged after him, but he levitated over the edge, pulled by the same apport that had disarmed me. He drifted over the battleground, blood dripping in his wake, whipping the Buzzers into a frenzy. I drew my revolver and fired, missing twice before I heard a hollow click. Not even these dire straits could turn me into a sharpshooter. A Reph caught him and carried him away.

I threw away the gun and shoved the knife into my boot. Even if I hadn't killed Cade outright, I had aimed for the jugular. He would die.

And then I would be alone in the world.

Across the Colosseum, the Rephs were at war, clashing with blades and spools alike. Terebell ducked a blow from Castor, who wielded some kind of spear. Kornephoros was still circling them. None of them had a clue that Gilberto Draghetti was about to blow us all into the æther.

I checked my watch. Five minutes left. If I didn't leave now, I wouldn't make it.

'Terebell,' I shouted. 'Terebell, we have to go!'

She was too far away, unable to hear.

Nick was now out cold. Without a Reph to help, I wasn't likely to be able to get him away in time. I towed him into our circle before I returned to where the floor ended.

As I watched, two figures emerged from the subterranean maze. Arcturus and Lesath were climbing one of the arches, the latter with the blade on his back, both of them slashed all over. My heart leapt into my throat.

Kornephoros was battling Pleione, who sailed around him, weaving spools. Gomeisa clenched a fist, shaking the column that Arcturus and Lesath were scaling.

Lucida sprang into action. She stretched a hand towards the arch, calming it, allowing Lesath to crane himself higher – but Gomeisa kept pushing, and both Rephs slid back down. Terebell called to the other Ranthen. Pleione and Errai made for the stands, pursued by the Sargas loyalists. Lesath clambered over the top of the wall, even as it quaked.

'Lesath.' I beckoned him. 'Can you take Nick?'

Arcturus spoke to him in Gloss, voice stifled by his mask. Lesath threw his sword to Terebell and came to my side.

'Sala is going to bomb this place,' I told him as he lifted Nick. 'Unless Rephs can survive an explosion, everyone needs to leave.'

'I will take Nicklas and return for the others,' Lesath said. 'Warn them, Underqueen.'

I had expected Arcturus to come straight after him, but when there was no sign, I looked back down. Arcturus was no longer moving. Some part of his body must have seized up, so all he could do was hang on to the wall. I started forward, preparing to climb to him.

Terebell had seen as well. With her blade in hand, she took a running jump off her side of the arena, on to the ruins. That was when my whole body prickled.

Gomeisa's gaze was fixed on me, and there was nowhere left to hide.

A moment passed. My skin turned numb. The æther pulled taut between us, seeming to resist his will. Then he lifted a hand again, as if to physically wrench me towards him, breaking whatever force had protected me.

All at once, I was airborne, soaring over the hypogeum. Even as the Buzzers roared up at me from the pit, I fought his influence with everything I had, knowing he would condemn me to death. When I broke free and hit the floor, the landing slammed the breath from me.

My right arm shook as I pushed myself up. I was cold and stiff, as if a poltergeist had touched me. Now I understood how the Sargas family had dominated the other Rephs for so long.

Some way above, Pleione reached Gomeisa, distracting him from the rest of the battleground. Lucida was doing her best to steady the column so Arcturus could get higher.

And Kornephoros Sheratan was closing in on me.

My breath came in white gusts. The levitation had shaken me to the core, turning my limbs to stone. As Kornephoros approached, I pointed my bloody knife in defiance.

'You never give up,' he observed. 'I will enjoy breaking you, fleshworm.'

'You saved me,' I rasped. 'You let me go.'

'For Arcturus, not for you.' His grip on the club tightened. 'And now the debt is paid.'

He raised the weapon. The thing was almost as long as me, and the top of it was spiked, like quartz.

A blade sliced above me, stopping it. Terebell was back for her cousin, spirits rushing to her aid. I looked across the pit to see Arcturus, still on the lower ruins.

She had chosen me over him.

As Terebell fought Kornephoros, she stayed in front of me, not letting him close. I crawled away from them with no idea where I was going, trying to get out of the way. When a frisson passed through the æther, I turned, just in time to see the blade go flying towards Gomeisa. He seemed to draw strength from a bottomless well.

Kornephoros spoke in Gloss. I might not understand the language, but I knew a taunt when I heard it. Terebell was now empty-handed, and Pleione had the second blade.

The club slammed into Terebell, sending her to the floor. I made towards her, only to buckle to my knees, my legs too weak to hold me. Still, I kept fighting, knowing only I was left to hold Kornephoros at bay. Every spool I made bounced off his ironclad dreamscape.

'Get up, Terebell,' I urged. 'Come on!'

She planted a hand on the ground. Her side was misshapen, the ribs staved in. In desperation, I tried to leap into the æther, but my broken wrist was excruciating, the pain chaining me to my body. Even if I had succeeded, Kornephoros was a Reph, and I was exhausted.

'Terebell.' My voice trembled. 'Please, Terebell. We have to leave—'

'I will hold the line,' she said. 'Get away.'

'No. Witness the price of a shattered oath,' Kornephoros said. 'I cannot kill you. That pleasure is reserved for the Suzerain. But what happens next is on your head, Underqueen.'

His shadow fell across us both. Terebell threw me out of his reach, almost off the edge of the floor. I turned around in time to see the club arc down.

I heard the crunch of Rephaite bone, which should have been unbreakable.

My blood roared in my ears; my vision blurred. I was rooted to the spot, unable to look away, or to breathe, as Kornephoros laid into Terebell. The club rose and came down, over and over.

*No.*

Now Lucida charged into the fray. She tried to wrest the club from Kornephoros, but she was outflanked and poorly armed, as the Ranthen always were. Kornephoros seized her arm, and she let out a high-pitched keen as his power entered her bones, flooding her with agony.

Terebell somehow lifted her face. Tears stung my eyes as our gazes met.

'Get up,' I whispered.

She was a healer. Surely she could mend her own bones. At least, that was what I believed, in that final moment of denial, when I thought Terebell Sheratan would find her strength and rise.

'Go,' she said to me, her voice barely there. 'End this for me, Paige.'

Her gaze strayed towards Arcturus, right as Kornephoros brought the club down on her skull.

My entire body was numb.

Kornephoros threw her broken form into the hypogeum. His club dripped with her ectoplasm. I pushed myself backwards, face soaked, chest heaving. The telltale cold stole over my skin as Gomeisa prepared to lift me again. He would take me away to be executed.

*You will only have moments to break his line of sight.*

There was nothing for it. I turned and jumped into the pit.

A lifetime seemed to pass before I hit the ground. My old instincts kicked in, and I rolled to soften the landing. Even then, pain flared in my heels, sharp on the right. A fall from that height could have broken my legs, but even if they shook as I got up again, they held.

I had eluded Gomeisa, but now I was among the hungry Buzzers. The hypogeum rang with their screams. I limped along its main passage, following a trail of ectoplasm. Terebell was being pulled far away, out of the ruins, preoccupying the Buzzers. That was the only reason I wasn't dead.

Down here, I might as well have been wading through deep water. Even if I hadn't been injured, I would have been slower than usual, and the Buzzers were already on to me. More than one of them was on fire, making unearthly sounds. A scythe raked across my back, then another, but I hardly felt it, even when the cold hit my wounds, because Arcturus was suddenly there, scooping me up with one arm.

He had come for me.

'Arcturus,' I gasped out, 'she's gone. The Buzzers—'

'Did they hurt you?'

I nodded, light-headed from the pain, the exhaustion. We backed away from the creatures, but their presence was overpowering.

'I will hold them off while you climb,' Arcturus said. 'You must go quickly, before the wounds incapacitate you.'

'No.'

'Paige—'

'I am *not* going without you.' My throat burned. 'I'd rather die right here.'

Now the Buzzers were surrounding us. I pushed them back with a surge of pressure. Before I knew it, the swarm was too thick for us to penetrate, blocking our way to the walls. I looked at the darkening sky, which seemed impossibly far away, down here in the pit. I was sure I could see those strange lights again, forming a crown over the Colosseum.

Arcturus took the Buzzers in. I stared up at him, hoping against hope that he might have a plan.

'I will not leave you,' he said, his voice soft. 'Forgive me, little dreamer.'

The Buzzers were howling, held off by the last of my willpower. Soon I would be ripped apart. Arcturus might even be the one to devour me, once he turned. Perhaps we could hold out just long enough for the explosion. It would be clean and quick that way. I hoped that it would take him; that he wouldn't be left with pieces of me.

'I'm still glad we met.' I shut my eyes. 'And I would do it all again.'

Arcturus gathered me to his chest, shielding as much of me as he could. I pressed the last of my knives into his grasp.

'You have to do it,' I whispered. He gripped the back of my head. 'Don't let them eat me alive.'

He said nothing, but kept hold of the blade.

The Buzzers pushed closer, fighting the invisible resistance from my dreamscape. The small circle of space I had carved out for us was closing.

I remembered this feeling of hope being lost, the night I thought Arcturus had betrayed me. A fear that I was abandoned. As I risked a glance at the Buzzers, I felt it once more, stronger than ever.

And then an echo of it. As if something had seen and understood my pain.

*Help us.*

Arcturus looked down at me. The golden cord was moving like it never had before. It encircled the two of us, binding us even closer together, before it suddenly went taut. His eyes burst into flame. My spirit ignited with them, lighting up my entire dreamscape.

An exquisite agony gripped my skull. My hair crackled. I drew a deep breath. The walls of my dreamscape seemed to break down, and as I screamed through my teeth, power erupted – power beyond my control, a pressure so impossibly strong it seemed to swallow my whole being before it burst its banks. It slammed into the Buzzers with the torrenting force of the whole Tiber. Arcturus was still holding me, but if he said a word, I couldn't hear. I couldn't even hear the Buzzers any longer. I was thousands of years away from myself.

I could not say exactly what happened next. I know I tasted blood again, and then the world just disappeared.

# 30

## NO HARD FEELINGS

I woke to the sound of a heart monitor. My body felt so heavy, I doubted I would ever move again, but I managed to crack my eyes open.

'Paige.'

I blinked, my lashes thick with sleep. Nick was at my side.

'Arcturus,' I rasped. 'Where is he?'

'He's okay, sötnos.'

A sound of relief escaped me, turning into a groan when a deep cold seared across my back.

'Cade attacked you,' I said.

'I won't pretend it didn't hurt, but he only glanced off my dreamscape.' He kept his voice slow and clear. 'Paige, you're at the presidential estate of Castelporziano. You've been out for three days. A Buzzer clawed your back, one of your heel bones is bruised, and I've put your left arm in a sling, to help prevent any further damage to your wrist.'

That explained about half the pain. I tried to recall what had happened, through the migraine that clotted my temples, the sludge of sedatives.

'Terebell,' I said, after a pause.

'She's gone.' There were dark circles under his eyes. 'The Buzzers took her to the Netherworld.'

I let it sink in, a bitter taste in my mouth.

Terebell had been a fixture of my journey. From the night she had first protected me in Oxford, she had always been there, even if we had never been friends. And now she was gone, senselessly murdered, just as I had thought we might be reaching a place of mutual respect.

'The Ranthen have no leader.' I closed my eyes. 'That's it. The Mime Order is finished.'

'No. The rest of the Ranthen survived,' Nick said. 'They'll honour her wishes.' The heart monitor was going haywire. 'Paige. Listen to me. Operation Ventriloquist has failed in Italy.'

I took a few unsteady breaths, helped by a cannula under my nose. It might not have been a military incursion, but for the first time in history, Scion had failed to claim a prize. Vance and Gomeisa had gambled and lost.

'The Buzzers weren't leaving,' I murmured. 'Sala was going to destroy the Colosseum.'

'She didn't need to. Something … happened down there, in the hypogeum,' Nick said. 'We don't know exactly what, but the Buzzers were all killed at once. Mistry convinced Draghetti to stop the bombing.' He held out the pendant. 'This is yours.'

If I had kept it with me, Terebell might not be gone, but it had shielded him. He lowered it back over my head, so the wings rested between my collarbones.

'I'm giving you some more painkillers. Just rest.' His voice faded as a chill streaked down my arm, stemming from the back of my hand. 'I'll tell Warden and Pleione you woke up.'

A tear ran down my cheek. I wished for the white aster, the drug that would let me forget.

My sleep was restless. When I stirred again, Arcturus was sitting on the edge of the bed, his eyes dim. Seeing me wake, he touched my cheek.

'Paige.'

I reached for him with my good hand.

'I'm sorry,' I whispered. 'I'm so sorry.'

He closed his fingers around mine.

'She was devoted to the cause,' he said quietly. 'We will ensure her courage is honoured. And find her.'

It took me a moment to understand what he meant. The Buzzers had taken Terebell, which meant that she was certainly one of them by now.

'She saved me,' I said. 'I was … so tired. Kornephoros and Gomeisa would have taken me.'

'You are the beating heart of this rebellion. She knew it.'

'None of this was worth us losing her.'

'If Scion had succeeded in taking Italy, the violence and loss would have been far greater, and far harder to end. I believe Terebell would sooner have secured this victory than seen Scion take the whole of Europe.'

'Kornephoros said he did it because I broke my oath.'

'He would have said that only to torment you. Do not let him.'

I swallowed.

'She knew you for longer than I can even imagine,' I said softly. 'I can only ever touch a small part of your existence, in comparison.'

'Terebell and I had both lost hope in Oxford. She was first to see how you awakened mine once more. If she had not accepted my decision to be with you, she would have killed you in the Tullianum.' He stroked my hair. 'You heard us speaking Gloss after she learned the truth. One day, I will show you that memory, so you may know what she told me, and what she thought of you. Were you a Rephaite, I believe she would always have approved.'

A lump filled my throat.

'Whatever part of my existence you have touched,' Arcturus said, 'is the best of me, Paige Mahoney.' He leaned down to kiss my forehead. 'Rest, Underqueen. You are still needed.'

───────

It took me a while to get out of bed. My skull felt brittle, I couldn't put much weight on my heel, and the wounds on my back were slow to heal, leaving me unable to dreamwalk. That was probably for the best. I had pushed my gift so hard that I needed to give it a rest for a while.

Cade might yet return. He would have access to the best treatment in Scion, if they had been able to get him there fast enough. Nashira might kill him, or she might work to keep him strong.

I could only watch and wait.

Nick kept me updated while I rested under his vigilant eye, and that of Sala's personal doctor. For now, Pleione was staying in the free world, while Lucida had returned to France. Errai and Lesath had left for London, to inform the Ranthen there that their beloved leader was gone.

As for the people of Italy, they were trying to understand what had unfolded in their capital. The day after the attack, Sala had announced the death of the Prime Minister and claimed that a city-wide incident was being investigated. Once she had all the facts, she would make a detailed statement. The social network Gazebo was flooded with speculation, tributes to the dead, and blurred pictures of the Buzzers.

Castelporziano was nestled in a forest. Arcturus helped me take a few walks. My muscles were tense from the slashes – a stiffness that mimicked that of a corpse. I needed to keep my body moving.

Arcturus had always been reserved, but now he was barely saying a word, even to me. I let him grieve, knowing he would open up in his own time. My only small comfort was that Terebell had known about us. Otherwise they would have parted with a lie between them.

One afternoon, we sat under an oak, listening to the birds. My left arm was snug in a sling.

'Arcturus.' I looked up at him. 'How did we escape?'

He was silent for some time.

'I do not understand what happened,' he said. 'The Colosseum was to be destroyed. The Emim surrounded us. And then the golden cord appeared to change, and so did you. A force came from your dreamscape – akin to the pressure you release when you dislocate your spirit, but far more powerful, charged with ethereal light. Many voyants in the vicinity sensed it. Maria compared it to

481

a shockwave in the æther. When I woke, the Emim were piled up around us, hollowed out, stripped of their spirits. Only their physical shells remained.'

I stared at him.

'Mistry heard them all fall silent. That was how he persuaded Draghetti to revoke the order to destroy the Colosseum. The Sargas loyalists fled,' Arcturus said. 'None of us had ever felt a force of that magnitude. It came from you, Paige.'

I tried to remember the way it had felt.

'I think it was us,' I said. 'Not just me.'

'You would not let go of me for hours, even though you were unconscious,' he said. 'We must ascertain what happened. I will consult the other Ranthen once the dust has settled.'

'Once you have a new leader?'

'Yes.'

I rested my head on his shoulder, and his arm tightened around my waist. We sat that way until the sun went down.

———

After another day of convalescence, my stubborn headache faded. A few hours after Nick conveyed this to Mistry, the Council of Kassandra summoned us both to a meeting. A black car took us back to Rome, where the Prime Minister of Italy was lying in a nearby morgue, along with over three hundred others, including Cardinal Alexandre Rocha. Most people had gone inside when the sirens went off, but many others had been caught on the streets.

The Council had assembled in the Basilica Arcana. Maria waited by the door for me. She had a few cuts and bruises, but had otherwise escaped the fight unscathed.

'We have matching slings. On the same arm,' she observed. 'It's like showing up in identical outfits. I don't know if it's adorable or mortifying.'

'Mortifying, I think,' I said. 'How are you?'

'In one piece, thanks to you and your party trick. I expect an explanation later.'

'I'm not sure I can give you one.'

'Another mystery to solve. We're going to have a long few years.' She nodded me in. 'The Council has requested that you stand beside Jaxon. My deepest condolences.'

Inside the Basilica Arcana, Rohan Mistry greeted us with a nod. I was still thoroughly impressed by his nerve. Beside him, Carter sat with folded arms. The archangel was nearby, watching over proceedings.

Jaxon was on the marble sun, fingers clasped on top of his cane. I went to his side, neither of us speaking. I detested him, but he had chosen not to let me fall to my death.

'Good afternoon,' President Sala said. 'I cannot express my relief that you all survived the attempted conquest of Rome. We mourn our friend, Erika Sato, who died while defending a group of civilians. May the æther embrace and carry her.'

The sentiment was echoed in murmurs. From the way Carter looked, Sato had been one of the sibyls.

'Despite this appalling loss,' Sala went on, 'we have a great deal to celebrate. For the first time in history, an incursion by the Republic of Scion has been stopped. And by voyants.'

A loud round of applause followed.

'Scion will return,' Sala said, her eyes like dark stone, 'but we have time to prepare. Since their attempt to crush us failed, they must wait until the Second Inquisitorial Division has anchorised Spain and Portugal. This victory would not have been possible without the Underqueen and her Ranthen allies. We mourn for Terebellum, Warden of the Sheratan.'

Terebell had been weaker than usual when she fought Kornephoros. If not for the Council of Kassandra binding her with poppy anemone and exposing her to pure alysoplasm, she would have stood a better chance of beating her cousin. She might still be here.

'I have brought us all together here to discuss the outstanding matter of London,' Sala said, before I could decide whether or not to hold my tongue. 'Now more than ever, we must work together against the anchor. The Mime Order is the most important of the European syndicates, the largest organised group of voyants within the Republic of Scion, and is holding strong in the heart of the empire. We have unanimously agreed with our sponsors that this organisation deserves our financial support, but only with the right leadership.'

I lifted my chin.

'Under the tyranny of Haymarket Hector, the London syndicate almost crumbled,' she said. 'Jaxon Hall prevented that by removing him. Rohan also informs me that Jaxon was a valuable member of the team who put a stop to the conquest.'

Jaxon inclined his head. 'My boundlings should take the credit, Beatrice. But thank you.'

'Yes, Jaxon, you showed courage. Nonetheless, we believe the evidence offered by Dr Nygård – the memories of the Underqueen, as delivered by Arcturus Mesarthim – to be authentic. While oneiromancy is an unprecedented gift, you personally acknowledged its existence in the third edition of your pamphlet, *On the Merits of Unnaturalness.*'

'As a possibility,' Jaxon said, his tone icy. 'A theory.'

'We have every faith in your instincts, Jaxon,' Mistry said, offering him a smile.

I decided, in that moment, that I liked Rohan Mistry very much.

'Jaxon, you have aided Scion. We understand you did this to gain knowledge for your fellow voyants,' Sala said, 'but the memories Paige provided call some of your methods into question. You have also expressed contempt for the Council of Kassandra. Now, it is true that Paige has also made some questionable choices. Nonetheless, her alliance with the Ranthen has proven essential. Half of us now favour her as Underqueen, while the other half favour you. The Triumvirate is divided on this issue. Antoinette has cast her vote for Jaxon, while I have cast mine for Paige. The tiebreaker is Rohan.'

Carter gave Jaxon a nod, not sparing me a glance. I felt a twinge of exasperation.

'Both of you have won a scrimmage, earning the right to rule London,' Mistry said. 'If possible, I would prefer that the Council of Kassandra did not interfere with the established laws of the syndicate, as upheld by the Spiritus Club. I therefore recommend – and firmly believe – that you should rule the syndicate together, as Underlord and Underqueen.'

Jaxon and I looked at each other, then at the Council of Kassandra.

'Absolutely not,' I said. 'You've accepted that he worked for Scion. He sold his own kind.'

'As a means of earning their trust, to—'

'Where is the proof of that?'

'Paige, if you refuse this, you rule without our blessing.'

And without their funds.

The money I needed to honour Terebell, and ensure our alliance could weather the storm.

'Most of the Council of Kassandra prefers Jaxon as the older and more experienced candidate, who controlled a successful part of London for years, and has provided money to our enterprise,' Mistry said. 'But you saved Rome, and it may be that we need the Ranthen. You are also the voyant with whom Le Vieux Orphelin has a firm alliance.'

'Each of you comes with your advantages,' Sala said. 'Why squander them?'

She really was a fine politician.

'Ignace won't accept Jaxon as Underlord,' I said. 'He was in the prison Jaxon oversaw.'

'Le Vieux Orphelin will accept you. He already has,' Sala said. 'And you will still be Underqueen.'

There was a long and tense silence. Jaxon drew himself up, his grip on his cane tightening.

'Shall we discuss this in private, Paige?'

'Yes,' I said. 'I think we must.'

---

The guards opened the doors for us, letting in a flood of sunlight. We walked out of the Basilica Arcana and up a dusty path to Palatine Hill, finding an open-air terrace that afforded us a dazzling view of the Forum.

'Well done, Jax,' I said coolly. 'You came very close to pulling off your little coup.'

'No hard feelings, darling,' he said. 'But is this not your coup as well?' I looked away. 'I had the whole Council in my pocket. In a matter of days, you plucked half back out. It bodes well for our reign.'

I would have folded my arms at that moment, had one of them not been stuck in a sling.

'As little as I enjoy the thought of sharing my throne with the person who stole it, it might be fun,' Jaxon mused. I ground my jaw. 'I always meant to rule the syndicate with you beside me. Between us, we have secured an impressive amount of coin for the Mime Order. Your work for Domino, the Ranthen assets, my savings from various schemes – together we could escalate this humble rebellion into a splendid revolution. A revolution with panache.'

'You do not want revolution,' I said. 'And I do not trust you with the Mime Order.'

'I will never betray the syndicate, no matter what name or form it takes.'

'You can't expect me to believe that. Not when you sold out everyone in Oxford, all for—'

'Oh, the Inquisitor take you, you little hypocrite. Do you really suppose that I expected Nashira to slaughter the entire city?'

His tone was suddenly cold. My entire body tensed, trained to react to his anger.

'I imagined that she might punish the humans,' he said, 'but not that she would let the Emim kill them all. In fact, I expected her rage to fall squarely upon Arcturus and his Rephaite accomplices, and I had no reason to care about them. For all I knew, Arcturus was as heartless as the rest, and his so-called rebellion was a ruse, designed to root out the disloyal. I was, and remain, astonished that Nashira chose that option.'

Jaxon was a consummate liar. I shouldn't buy into this.

Except that I had seen his dreamscape. It looked like Nunhead Cemetery, where he had unlocked his gift, allowing him to make his way to the highest circles of power in London. But now I remembered one fine detail, staining his safe place, as difficult to clean as blood.

Every one of those graves bore a number. A number for each human killed in the Novembertide Rebellion.

Even a dreamscape could be tainted.

'Do not stand in judgement of me, Underqueen. I have stomached that for too long,' Jaxon said curtly. 'If someone had offered *you* a chance to sow discord between the Rephaim, ensuring your escape, you know you would have taken it. Look me in the eye and tell me you would have been any nobler, were it not for Arcturus. That you would have put a Rephaite above yourself. That you would have wasted an opportunity to reclaim your old life.'

He was right. More than once in Oxford, I had considered betraying Arcturus. I had outright threatened him with it. And part of me knew I had meant every word.

'I didn't think so.' Jaxon looked out at the city. 'As for what happened with Cordier, I told her to separate you from Arcturus, and to keep you safe. Nothing more or less.'

'You believe we can negotiate with Nashira. That endangers the Mime Order,' I said. 'How are we going to rule together when my entire campaign is based on overthrowing her?'

'I'm not an idiot, darling. An idealist, but not an idiot,' Jaxon said. 'At present, Nashira would crush the syndicate at the first hint of its whereabouts. I believe we should remain open to negotiating with her, at some point in the future, but that would be a joint decision. If you insist that the Mime Order continues to work with the Ranthen—'

'I do insist.'

'—then I will let go of my hopes for peace with their enemy, and hope they prove capable of protecting us. Trust that I am willing to join your revolution, if only so that voyants will no longer be forced to live at the mercy of amaurotics.' His face softened. 'Do you know the story of Persephone and Hades?'

'No,' I said, 'but I'm sure you're about to regale me with it.'

'Hades was the ruler of the underworld in Ancient Greece. He took a fancy to Persephone, the goddess of spring,' he said. 'When Persephone was picking a narcissus flower, Hades opened a chasm in the earth, which swallowed her up, into the realm of shadows beneath.'

Those gods really were terrible.

'Persephone was the daughter of Demeter, who oversaw the harvest,' he continued. 'Realising her child was gone, she let the earth wither. The harvests failed; the flowers died. The gods intervened, and it was agreed that Persephone would be allowed to leave the underworld. But Hades had tricked her into eating a handful of pomegranate seeds, binding her to the domain of the dead. And so, for all eternity, Persephone was queen of the underworld. For half the year, she lived with Hades. For the other half, she lived above.'

The temptation of it was an ache, as sudden as it was intense. The sunlight and the dark.

I might have both, if I took this plunge.

'You'll never admit it, but I know you. I have seen the side of you that thrives in conditions of chaos. You don't just want to sit on a throne. Not with a gift – and a spirit – like yours. You belong in the vanguard of this war,' Jaxon said. 'You are restless and wild, yearning for a chance to spread your wings. The Ranthen trusted you to rule, but they don't know what it's like to be twenty and mortal, because they never were.'

I dared not meet his eye, because I knew he would convince me.

'You were away for a summer. Take a few months longer,' Jaxon said gently. 'You can be Persephone, the queen who comes and goes with the seasons – just as you leave your body, both dead and alive. I will be Hades, bound to the underworld, ruling for us both. Do we have a deal?'

My jaw tightened.

Jaxon Hall had manipulated me since I was sixteen years old. He was a cold-blooded narcissist whose charm was as dangerous as his gift, and who loved nothing but London.

He wasn't a good man. I doubted he would ever become one. But good men did not make good Underlords, and I knew Jaxon would. He was born to delegate. If he was surrounded by people I trusted, like Nick and Maria, they could temper his crueller instincts.

'Even if I agree to this,' I said, 'I do not forgive you for what you did to me and Arcturus this year. I never will, as long as I live.'

'I don't seek forgiveness, darling. Unlike the late Cardinal Rocha, I do not believe in sin.' He tapped his cane. 'Speak with the Ranthen, if you must. I will await your answer.'

I started to leave, then stopped.

'Jaxon,' I said. 'What was in the box Colin left me?'

'Something that I do not understand. If you consent to our partnership, I will send it to your French allies. Then you can inspect it upon your return to Scion.'

'No. Give it to Arcturus,' I said. 'If I agree to any of this.'

'Of course.'

I walked down the hill, leaving him to gaze at the city.

Isaure Ducos waited beside the entrance to the Forum. Her car was parked nearby.

'The Colosseum appears to have suffered extensive damage. They think it will take a decade to repair,' she said. 'But I also hear you're the reason it wasn't destroyed altogether, so perhaps we can call that personal growth.' She gave me a nod. 'Good to see you alive. May we speak?'

---

The Chiostro del Bramante was full of Domino associates, called to Rome to help evaluate the situation. Cardinal Rocha had already been identified as a member of Grapevine, along with an archaeologist named Giovanna Amato. Both had aided the Sargas in concealing the Rephs' bodies around the city, and both had been killed by the Buzzers.

The Pope had survived. No comment, apparently.

Ducos showed me inside. A tall man in a tailored navy suit awaited us. He was about the same age as Spinner, with dark brown skin and eyes, and hair shaved almost to his scalp.

'Flora.' He extended a manicured hand, which I shook. 'Match. I'm a member of Command. We understand Italy owes you a debt. Have you recovered?'

'Mostly,' I said. 'How can I help you, Match?'

'First, I thought you might like to know that Jaxon Hall has given us the Stiletto Files, as we've dubbed the information harvested by Alice Taylan. For a price,' he added, pursing his lips.

Of course. If Jaxon couldn't have me in a cell, he was going to fill his pockets to the brim.

'Veronika Norlenghi has volunteered to transport the files to the Yerebatan Institute for urgent analysis,' Match went on. 'Whatever Alice was able to discover in the Westminster Archon, we'll know it soon.'

'That's good to know,' I said. 'I'm glad you got something out of it all.'

I said it with wholehearted honesty. Burnish had not died in vain.

'We have a proposal for you. It relates to your outstanding contract with Domino.' He motioned to the courtyard. 'Will you hear it?'

'Sure.'

'Thank you.'

There were quite a few people in the courtyard. One of them sat with Ducos, drinking coffee. When he saw me, he stood.

'Hello.' I raised an eyebrow. 'Steve Mun, wasn't it?'

'Yes.' He looked embarrassed. 'Good afternoon, Paige.' I sat down beside Ducos, and he did the same. 'I'd like to start by offering my sincere apologies for what happened in Wrocław. We clearly made a bad impression, but we really did only mean to speak with you.'

'Right. Except your man Spinner tried to forcibly extract me and my associate from Venice.'

'The Bureau has been driven to desperate measures. We don't have enough information about what we're facing here,' Mun said. 'If it helps, I don't work exclusively for Tinman. I'm a liaison from one of its sister networks in Asia, which specialises in counterintelligence against Scion. We'd still like to speak to your associate, if you'd—'

'No.'

There was absolutely no way I was letting them near Arcturus.

'Domino has already spoken to him,' I went on. 'If you'd like any information, you can ask Command for it. But I'd be interested to know what you want from *me* first, Steve.'

'Of course.' Mun reached for his briefcase. 'We've been tracking a hostile network called Grapevine, affiliated with the Republic of Scion. Over the last few years, we've identified several individuals who we believe are involved, and who pose a significant danger, given their positions of influence, but we haven't been able to prove their complicity.'

'How do you think I can help with that?'

'Margaux Taylan told us what you were doing in Paris. You spied on the Grand Inquisitor of France by possessing his spouse, Luce Ménard Frère,' he said. 'Is that true, Paige?'

I said nothing.

'If it is,' he said, 'you're exactly the sort of person we need. We're looking for concrete evidence of collaboration with Scion. If you were in their skin, I bet you could find it.'

'You believe in extrasensory perception, then.'

'I do.'

'What would I get in exchange for my services?'

'You'll be paid. We'll provide you with any training you need, and cover the cost of surgery on your wrist. We can drop supplies and weapons to your rebels in Scion.'

'Where would I be sent?'

'Your base would be with an associate in Canada.' He took out a laptop. 'She recorded a message for you. I understand you know each other.'

He turned his laptop towards me. When I saw the associate, I sat forward, my lips parting.

I listened to everything she said.

'I'm going to need specifics about my pay,' I said to Mun. 'And a lot more information about the kind of support you can offer the Mime Order.'

'We can negotiate on your behalf, Flora,' Ducos said. 'You don't have to decide now. Steve is here for the next week.'

'Yes,' Mun said. 'I am sorry again about Wrocław. I do hope we can work together, Paige.'

When Ducos gave him a nod, he left, taking his briefcase with him. She looked at me.

'What do you think?'

'I can't believe you're even putting this to me,' I said. 'Why would I touch Tinman with a bargepole?'

'Because we have the upper hand. Tinman need to make nice, and they're willing to share their intelligence, which would allow us to learn more about what Scion is doing in the free world. A joint enterprise like this may pave the way towards a working relationship,' Ducos said. 'You would officially be on loan from the Domino Programme. As a condition of this loan, their current Director of Operations will be fired. You will have our protection, funding, and additional support for the Mime Order. Sala is also behind you.'

'Sala just said she wanted me to be Underqueen,' I said. 'Now she thinks I should go abroad?'

'We understood that you would have a co-ruler in London, who has agreed to hold the fort in your absence.'

It seemed like everyone already thought I would agree to this arrangement.

'If Fitzours survived your fight, he is likely to go farther afield,' Ducos said. 'If he does, Tinman has agreed that you can pursue him as a matter of urgency. If you help neutralise the threat of Grapevine, you might stop this madness from spreading any farther than Europe.'

'Can you guarantee they won't harm me?'

'They'd have no reason to do that if you're working for them. I'll make welfare checks at regular intervals, so Tinman knows we're keeping a sharp eye on you.'

I drummed my fingers on the table.

'Warden is in a bad way,' I finally said. 'I don't know if I can leave him.'

'Sala informed me that Terebell was killed. I was sorry to hear it,' Ducos said. 'With her influence, I hoped we might find a way to peace with the Rephaim.'

'Me, too.' I released my breath. 'Can I get back to you?'

'By all means, but Scion knows where you are, so we'd like to get you both to Venice.'

I nodded, wanting to be gone. This place held too much grief.

---

None of us said much on the journey. I dozed against Arcturus in the back, with Verča on his other side. The others had joined us for the ride, craving the peace and quiet of Venice.

Verča had been the one to activate the retracting floor of the Colosseum. Once she had shown the Rephs into the hypogeum, she had realised they might need a second way out, broken into the control room, and waited for a chance to isolate Cade. She had mistimed the trap by a second, resulting in my fall – days later, she was still apologising – but I was glad she had done it. Maria was right. She had proven invaluable to the team.

At some point, Ducos turned on the radio. Verča leaned in to listen.

'Sala is saying that she intends to make a presidential address on the fifth of November.'

I shook my head. 'What the hell is she planning to say?'

'I really don't know.'

'Neither do we,' Ducos said. 'Let us hope she's found a middle ground between telling the truth and sounding relatively sane.' She lit a cigarette. 'There is irrefutable proof, at least.'

Maria frowned. 'What sort of proof?'

'The remains of the Buzzers.'

We all exchanged glances.

'Yes,' Maria said. 'That sounds like proof enough.'

---

Venice was swathed in fog again, and cold rain flecked our faces as Noemi took us along the Grand Canal. It was almost dusk by the time we disembarked at the Palazzo del Domino.

Nick went up for his debriefing, the first of several Pivot would hold. Maria and Verča headed into the warmth of the bar, wanting to enjoy their last few days together. Ducos led Eliza to the concierge, while I took Arcturus to my room, which had been left untouched.

'I am glad to be here again,' Arcturus said. 'I hoped to see more of this city.'

'I can show you around, if you have time.' I shut the door. 'What will the Ranthen do now?'

'We must elect a new sovereign. It may take several weeks, if not longer.'

'You should put yourself forward. Terebell would have wanted you to be her successor.'

'I cannot lead the Ranthen.'

'Why not?'

'If I did, I would always have to be with them. I would never be able to see you, Paige.'

That sent me into a long silence. I wished I was unselfish enough to tell him it didn't matter, that he should sacrifice me for the cause. But we had played that game before.

'It has to be someone who cares about humans,' I eventually said. 'Does anyone spring to mind?'

'Personally, I would favour Adhara Sarin or Marsic Sheratan.' He sat on the bed. 'I will return to Scion to confer with the others. Do you plan to remain in the free world?'

'I need to talk to you about that.' I joined him. 'I got two offers yesterday. One was from the Atlantic Intelligence Bureau. They want me to help investigate a circle of suspected Grapevine agents. The pay will be handsome, and they'll cover surgery on my wrist.'

'Do you mean to accept?'

'I was going to tell them where to shove it, but then I found out Nadine would be my associate. She did some big interview after she got back to Canada, and Tinman employed her. I owe her for standing up for you in London. For keeping the Mime Order in place.'

'Would Nick take over as interim Underlord?'

'That's … the other thing.' I took a deep breath. 'Will you promise to hear this out?'

'Yes.'

'The Council of Kassandra wants me to rule with Jaxon, as Underlord and Underqueen. It's never been done, but I think it's legal, provided both participants consent to a joint rule.'

Arcturus searched my face.

'Yeah.' I looked away. 'I know.'

'Jaxon orchestrated our separation,' he said. 'You have suffered a great deal because of him, Paige.'

'So have you. I feel sick to my stomach even contemplating it, especially given what Terebell thought of him. But ... there are reasons I'm considering the idea.'

He waited.

'Nick is my mollisher,' I said, 'but he won't want to be Underlord. He likes to be the fixer, not the head that wears the crown. He also needs to work out here until January. As we've seen, my other mollisher is even less interested in ruling. Neither of them asked for this.'

'Jaxon mistreated you for years,' Arcturus said, his voice low. 'He collaborated with Nashira.'

'He *is* clinging on to some absurd notion that Nashira will change her mind about voyants, but the syndicate is his purpose. I don't believe he would intentionally endanger it. He's wanted the Rose Crown since he was a child, and part of me thinks I should just let him wear it. That way, he won't be a thorn in my side for the rest of my life. I don't want to be looking over my shoulder for ever, expecting him to usurp me, because one day, he will succeed. We already know I can't kill him, so I have to live with his existence.'

'You do not have to give him the Rose Crown.'

'I'm not. I would still be Underqueen,' I said, 'but Jaxon would rule with me. He would bring coin to the table, and the full endorsement of the Council of Kassandra, which includes President Sala. I don't think we have the luxury of turning down that kind of support.'

'They wish for him to be Underlord, even after the memories you showed them?'

'Yes, because Jaxon Hall knows how to keep people eating out of the palm of his hand, even if it's poison. But Terebell is gone because we were outgunned and outnumbered,' I said quietly. 'In the end, beggars can't be choosers, and we are the underdogs of this war.'

Arcturus seemed to consider.

'Could you rule beside him?' he finally asked.

'With support. I was his right hand before,' I reminded him. 'Could *you* stand to work with Jaxon?'

'If you wished for this alliance, then I would do all I could to facilitate it, for your sake. We could introduce checks on his power to satisfy the Ranthen. But if this is the wrong choice, it may cost us a great deal, Paige.'

'I don't see another way that secures us enough money to make our side a real threat.'

We were silent for a while. I rested my head against his arm, suddenly exhausted.

'I don't want to go to Canada,' I said. 'I don't belong out here.'

'You do. You were born in the world beyond Scion.' He laid a hand on my knee. 'You took the Rose Crown to spur the syndicate into action, but it is not in your nature to wait in the wings. We must stop Vindemiatrix before her network grows too powerful. Killing the root will take a long time, so we must cut off the stems, wherever they grow.'

'Then you think I should go?'

'Only you can decide.'

'Not helpful.' I sighed. 'I'll talk to the others tomorrow.'

'As you wish. For now, you ought to sleep,' he said. 'No decision can be made without rest, Underqueen.'

---

He stayed with me while I ruminated, thinking my head sore. Even when he fell asleep, I lay awake at his side for a long time. I pictured the sixth card in my reading, Eight of Swords. A woman surrounded by blades, unable to move in any direction without slicing herself.

There was no right and easy choice to be made here.

By morning, I had still not come to a decision. Leaving Arcturus to rest, I went for a walk around the city, my breath clouding in the crisp autumn chill.

If I went back to Scion right away, I would never come back out to see Nadine. I was making one return journey into the free world. If I was going to hit Grapevine, it had to be now.

But I would be so far away from Arcturus.

He had lost Terebell. He had been tortured for months. I wanted to be there for him, as he had been for me. But he was right about the importance of stopping Vindemiatrix Sargas in her tracks, and no matter what happened, no matter the cost, our revolution still came first.

Nick and Eliza were coming to see me at noon. By then, the fog had lifted, and sunlight bathed the city. I waited on my preferred bench on the waterfront.

'Can I sit with you?'

Eliza had arrived early. I gave her a nod, and she joined me on the bench.

'Do you hate me, Paige?'

'No,' I said. 'You're the one who has every right to hate me.'

'You didn't leave by choice.' She sighed. 'I can't believe Jax had you abducted.'

'Can't you?'

'Okay. Maybe I can.'

A seagull landed near my boots and picked at some dropped food.

'I would never have considered giving him the Rose Crown,' Eliza said, 'but then I saw him on the screens. The Vigiles had orders to shoot him on sight. I couldn't imagine why Nashira would issue a kill order if he was still working for her.' She glanced at me. 'I heard the Council wants you to rule together. What do you think we should do?'

'I don't know.' I watched the seagull. 'Did you tell him where the Mime Order was hiding?'

'No,' she said, 'but he knows, Paige.' My heart dropped about a foot. 'After the airstrikes, he told me that he'd worked it out. That we could only be in the Beneath.'

Jaxon had known for weeks, but hadn't given the game away. He hadn't told Nashira.

'I don't like it out here,' Eliza said. 'It's ... not the same, is it?'

I shook my head. When I leaned into her, she wrapped my hand in hers and squeezed.

After a while, Nick joined us on the bench. He passed us both coffees.

497

'Thanks,' I said. 'How was Pivot?'

'She told us about the offer from Tinman and agreed to cut my contract short so I can go with Jax,' Nick said. 'We'll lose my share of the money, but I think it could be worth it, in my case.' He sighed. 'I can't offer to rule with you, sötnos. My migraines have been getting worse. I can be your fixer. I can keep Jax under control. But I can't be Underlord.'

Eliza linked his arm. His face was pinched.

Nick had always respected his limits. I needed to do the same, or he would buckle.

'I can't fucking believe we're considering Jax,' I muttered. 'Just as we all managed to escape him.'

'He will be watched around the clock. He will rule by your values,' Nick said quietly. 'Once you're back, we can judge what he's done. And we can decide what to do with him.'

'And if he goes to Scion?'

'I'd kill him with my bare hands before I allowed that to happen, Paige. So would the Ranthen.'

'If they even let him live long enough to take the throne. They might break the alliance, for all I know,' I said. 'It depends who they vote in as the next leader.'

'It should be Warden,' Eliza said.

'He doesn't want to do it.' I looked at Nick, who gave me a nod of encouragement. 'Because we're together, and he has to keep that a secret. For both our sakes.'

'You and—' Eliza stared at me. 'You and Warden?'

'Yes.'

She managed not to crumble under the weight of this revelation, but she did look as if she might fall off the bench. Nick and I watched her go back over it all.

'You don't have to say anything.' I patted her hand. 'I know it might take a while to digest.'

'I'll say.' Eliza snorted. 'You really are a woman of extremes, Paige. Not one date in our whole time in London, and now you've gone and scored a Reph.'

I cracked my first smile in a few days. It felt good to have the secret off my shoulders.

'I keep wondering if I ever saw Warden in Oxford.' She used her coffee to warm her hands. 'I used to have flashbacks, when I was younger. It's why I started taking the aster.'

'How did you forgive Jax for leaving you with those dealers?'

'I didn't, Paige. I just see how much worse he could have been,' she said. 'It's a low bar, but when you're raised among criminals, it's how you end up judging people.'

'They mourned you in Oxford. The performers left you little trinkets.'

'Then I need to amount to something, for them.'

'You already have.' I breathed out a flurry of fog. 'If I accept this job offer, I can bring money back. A lot of it.'

'We need it. We've made plans, but we have to be able to afford food and weapons. With your coin from Tinman and support from President Sala, we have a proper shot at scaring Scion.'

'Jax won't win everyone over.' I tightened my fist. 'Wynn and Vern will probably leave the syndicate, along with the other vile augurs. They'll need safe passage out of London. Ivy will never forgive me. I doubt Le Vieux Orphelin will be too happy with me, either.'

'I'll go to Paris to explain.' She hesitated. 'Is Warden coming with us, or going with you?'

'I need him to represent me in France for a while. He also has to be involved in electing a new leader. He'll try to get some of the Ranthen to stay with you in London, if they can stand to be around Jaxon.'

The three of us sat together for a long time.

'This might be the hardest choice I've ever made,' I said. 'And I've made some tough ones.' I lowered my gaze. 'I'll be so far away from you all. And Warden—'

I couldn't finish the sentence.

'We'll look after him,' Nick said. 'I promise.'

'All of this could take a while,' Eliza said gently. 'We need to get our fighters up to scratch, get ourselves properly armed, and keep making alliances. We can't rush this fight against Scion. You can afford to stay in the free world for a bit longer, Paige. And to help Nadine.'

'You put all these pieces in place, sötnos. Look at how far you've already come.' Nick grasped my hand. 'Let us carry the weight for a while. Go out there, and then come back to us.'

A tiny nod was my only reply.

'We'll let you think.' He stood. 'Whatever you decide, we'll support you.'

They both left me alone. The queen of the underworld, who had gone away for a whole summer.

I was already Persephone.

## 31

# PERSEPHONE

My flight was booked the next morning. Sala secured me a new identity and a diplomatic passport, the best protection she could offer, and told me to return as soon as I could.

That afternoon, I recorded a message for the Mime Order, which Nick would take to London. There would be no scrimmage. I had reconciled with the White Binder, whose values now aligned with mine. I was needed in the free world, but I would send coin and support.

I hoped that they would understand. My army of criminals, bound to the underworld.

---

I spent my last night in Italy with Arcturus. Ducos set us up behind a screen in the bar, so he could try Italian wine. After that, we listened to a troupe of violinists playing on the street.

As night fell, we found a secluded set of steps and sat on them for a while, watching boats on the Grand Canal. Arcturus drew me into the warmth of his overcoat, so I was snug against his side, only my face catching the chill. Even though I still tensed when the water sloshed too close, I forced myself to sit there and stomach it, breathing through the nerves.

Arcturus stroked my windswept hair. His face was pensive, eyes burning low. He had avoided taking aura for a few days, to keep them dim enough for him to pass as human. His height attracted looks, but it was nothing we hadn't been able to shake by slipping into the maze of backstreets. This city embraced those who needed to vanish.

I closed my eyes, nestling against him. He kissed the top of my head.

'Are you all right?'

I nodded. 'I'm just going to miss you.'

He clasped my hand, which had been resting on his thigh. Both of us wore gloves tonight, given the sudden cold.

At midnight, we returned to the apartment in San Marco. We hadn't slept together since Orvieto, and I didn't want to broach the subject, unsure if he would feel like it. But as soon as I had locked the door behind us, I sensed his need through the cord and kissed him.

The sling made me a little clumsy, but we took it slow, both of us craving intimacy. Later, we lay in a sliver of lamplight, the same gold as his eyes.

'After my torture, I needed you with me,' I said softly. 'Now you've lost the most important person in your life, on top of what happened in Carcassonne. The last thing I want to do is leave you.' I brushed his cheekbone. 'If you want me to stay with you, I will go back to Scion with you. We can forget about Domino and Tinman.'

Arcturus turned his face into my palm.

'I always want you with me,' he said. 'But remember what I told you in the chandlery.'

I thought back. 'Our lifelines will meet when the æther sees fit?'

'Yes.' He interlinked our fingers. 'Domino needs time to scrutinise the Stiletto Files. Jaxon needs time to establish your joint rule in London. And you need time, Paige. Time to heal, and to prepare for the crescendo of this conflict. It may drag on for many years.'

'Eliza said the same. I need to stop taking shortcuts, whether that's in war or with my own body,' I said. 'You helped me unlock my gift in Oxford, but I stumbled into all this as a criminal. Domino will give me specialist combat training between assignments for Tinman.'

'You must find a way to practise dreamwalking.'

'I've thought of one.'

'Oh?'

'It might not work.' I gave him a tiny smile. 'I'll tell you when I get back.'

'I look forward to it.'

I traced his features. Every time I confronted the thought of leaving him, my chest ached.

'We have the cord,' he said, reading me. 'I am always with you.' He clasped me to his chest, and I nested my head under his chin. 'The æther bound our spirits. I trust that it will always find a way to reunite us.'

———

The next day, we returned to the Palazzo del Domino to find the others waiting, except for Eliza, who had already gone to collect Jaxon. They needed to start the journey towards the Fluke.

'We thought we'd see you off,' Nick told me. 'We're all leaving tomorrow.'

'Yes. I will be going to Istanbul,' Verča said. 'I'll let you know once the Stiletto Files have been analysed.'

'Verča,' I said, 'thank you for everything. I have no idea how we would have done all this without you.'

'I am the one who should be thanking you, for stopping the fall of Italy.' She kissed my cheeks. 'If there's ever anything I can do to help, don't hesitate to call.'

'I will. And consider yourself a member of the Mime Order.'

'It's my honour. Truly.'

She walked into the bar to give the rest of us some time.

'This feels familiar.' Maria hitched up a smile. 'We still haven't decided if we're criminals or spies, have we?'

'I think we've proven we can be both,' Nick said. 'I can't believe we're about to send you off on your own, Paige. It was hard enough when you went to Paris.'

'I'll be fine,' I said.

'I know you will. Send our love to Nadine.'

'I almost envy you,' Maria said. 'Part of me wants to stay out here, but Jaxon needs a few handlers, and I couldn't be more delighted to volunteer. We can be your voice while you're away.'

'Thanks.' I embraced her. 'Don't have too much fun without me, will you?'

'I can't promise that.' She held me close, mindful of my injured arm and back. 'We'll make sure Warden doesn't sink. Leave it to us, sweet.'

'Don't make me cry. I've done more crying out here than I ever did in Scion.'

She ruffled my hair and went after Verča. Nick hugged me.

'Be safe,' he said. 'We'll be waiting.'

He walked away as well, leaving me with Arcturus, who escorted me towards the water taxi.

'Vindemiatrix will be ready for you,' he said. 'Do not let your guard down, even far beyond Scion.' When we reached the jetty, he turned to face me, placing a tender hand on my waist. 'Have no fear, Paige. I will do all I can to advocate for your beliefs in your absence.'

'I appreciate that,' I said, 'but if you decide Jax isn't worth it, just throw the bastard off a mountain on your way to France. Then the Council of Kassandra won't be able to complain.'

'I will consider it.'

I smiled, but it soon faded.

'Sala is going to have to explain what happened,' I said. 'If she plans to tell the truth, it will mean exposing all of this. All of you.' I breathed out. 'I'm afraid of what happens next.'

'Sooner or later, our two worlds must come together. They can never do that if one lies under the shadow of secrecy.' Arcturus touched my cheek. 'It has been two centuries. It is time.'

I nodded.

'You have a phone. If you leave Scion, call me,' I said. 'I'll come back as soon as I can.' Arcturus wrapped me into a tight embrace, and I clutched him. 'Please don't get yourself hurt or captured again while I'm away.' My voice was muffled by his coat. 'You hear me?'

'I hear. Would you extend me the same courtesy?'

'I'll try.'

We had fought so hard to be together. It didn't seem fair that I had to leave him now, right as he most needed me. But we had always known that we were taking the hard road.

'Fly, little dreamer.' He pressed a kiss to the crown of my head. 'I will see you in Scion.'

---

It had been almost thirteen years since I had last been in an airport. The sights and sounds turned my palms clammy. Ducos walked me to the right desk, and I handed over my new passport.

'Your flight is on time,' Ducos said as we proceeded to the security line. 'Best of luck, Paige.'

'Oh, it's Paige, now, is it?' I said. 'Do I get to use *your* real name?'

'I'll tell you when the war is over.'

'That might not be in either of our lifetimes.'

'Then you'll never know.' She slid her hands into her pockets. 'Steve Mun has accepted personal responsibility for your welfare. His job is on the line. I'll give you a few days to settle in, then come to check on you.'

'Okay. See you soon.'

She watched me go through.

Domino had put me in business class, whatever that meant. Soon enough, I was on the plane with my seatbelt fastened.

'Good afternoon,' a flight attendant said. 'Would you like some champagne?'

I raised an eyebrow. 'Some what?'

'Champagne.' He hesitated. 'We also have water?'

'I'm fine, thanks.'

He moved on, and I was left to wonder what *champagne* was, other than a region in France. Clearly this was going to be a long few weeks.

When the plane took off, I gripped the arms of the seat, remembering the fear of the first time. The white screen in front of me, showing the anchor. My father beside me, trying not to meet my eye, knowing his decision might have doomed us both. But that feeling of flight was a pleasure as well – a pull in my stomach, like a kite against its line. I only wished Arcturus could have come with me.

If we were going to defeat Nashira, we all needed to play to our strengths. I would do this for all of us.

And then I would go back to Scion, knowing I was ready to bring an empire crashing down.

---

I would have liked to sleep, but all I could do was watch the flight map on the screen in front of me, expecting the cord to snap from the strain. Arcturus and I had never been this far apart since we first met, but no matter how far I flew, it held strong. Eight hours later, when the plane landed, I took my holdall from the overhead compartment.

If the Canadian authorities were bewildered by me – a woman with an Irish accent, an Italian diplomatic passport, and the face of a Scion fugitive – they were good enough not to say anything. Steve Mun waited in Arrivals. I shouldered my holdall and walked up to him.

'Paige. Welcome to Canada,' Mun said. 'We're grateful you decided to come. On behalf of Denise Benally, our new Director of Operations, thank you.'

'It's fine,' I said. 'Is Nadine here?'

'Right this way.'

He took me around a corner, to a busier part of the airport. When Nadine spotted me beside Mun, she grinned. She wore stonewashed jeans and a top that slouched off her shoulders.

To my surprise, Zeke stood beside her, looking much the same as he had in Scion, except for his beard and earring. They rushed towards me and enfolded me in their arms.

'Wow,' I said, laughing. 'Look at you both. I hardly recognised you!'

'I'd say the same for you, but you still dress exactly like you did in Scion,' Nadine said. 'Zeke wasn't sure if you would come, but I knew you wouldn't be able to resist a challenge.'

'Yes. Thank you, Paige,' Zeke said. 'We know this must be keeping you from London.'

'It's all right. I came to an … arrangement with Jaxon.'

Nadine frowned. 'Really?'

'I'll explain later.'

'Okay.' She glanced around. 'I was expecting Warden to be with you.' I dredged up a tired smile and shook my head. 'I guess he would have had a hard time scrunching into a plane seat.'

'We should get Paige to the car,' Mun said. 'She's on Incrida.'

'All right. Let's get this show on the road.'

Nadine and Zeke draped their arms over my shoulders. I walked between them, out of the airport, towards the next stage of my reign.

---

Mun drove us through a snowy night, on the wrong side of the road. It took me a while to stop bracing for a head-on collision. Seeing that I was tired, Nadine and Zeke let me sit in silence, for the most part.

'Paige,' Nadine said. I looked at her. 'You should know that your friend is alive. Julian.'

It took a moment to sink in. 'Julian Amesbury?'

'Yeah. He's in New York with a couple of other Bone Season survivors.'

'How did they get here?'

'A Reph helped them, apparently. Rigel, I think?' Nadine said. 'Julian was left behind, but he made it in the end. He'd really love to see you.'

Some good news, for once. I had started to lose hope.

When Mun stopped the car, it was right by the glowing windows of a house. Nadine led me inside and up a flight of stairs, to a tidy bedroom.

'This is yours. Let's catch up tomorrow,' she said. 'There's a heated pool outside. I left a bathing suit and a towel in the hallway. You can swim whenever you like.'

'Thank you,' I said.

'You're welcome. Just watch out for bears.'

She closed the door before I could work out if she was joking.

Even after sleeping on the plane, I was exhausted. I unpacked my holdall, and was about to go to bed when I looked out of the window. The swimming pool was right below.

*You must find a way to practise dreamwalking.*

No time like the present.

Downstairs, I opened a sliding door and walked to the edge of the pool. The sky was so clear, I could see tiny stars reflected in the water.

Arcturus had shown me how to embrace my gift, but while the Atlantic Ocean stood between us, I had to learn to train alone, without a living target. And I thought I had a way. As I had sunk into the waters around Capri, I had felt weightless, as I did in the æther.

And I was finally beginning to realise why Scion had tortured me with water.

Why they used water for all the dissenters.

An anchor stood against the sea. The wild sea, full of things that people found impossible to understand.

This was how I would train.

How I would go back to Scion with my whole self in my keeping.

I stepped into the pool, sinking in up to my waist. I looked down at my own reflection, circled by the stars. The dark mirror that was the key to my recovery.

Soon, Beatrice Sala would make her broadcast to the world, and everything would change.

Until then, I could only swim.

**ROME**—*Beatrice Sala has announced that a 'catastrophic incident' in Rome, which left more than three hundred people dead, was orchestrated by the Republic of Scion. In a national broadcast, the President of Italy claimed that Scion had used biological weapons of 'historic significance' against the capital, representing 'an unprecedented threat to humankind' that Italy and its allies would counter by 'any and all' means.*

*Witness reports continue to perplex the public, as do images of unidentified four-limbed creatures wreaking havoc across the Italian capital. Scion fugitive Paige Mahoney was seen in Rome during the incident, accompanied by a number of masked figures. The same day saw vivid aurorae across Italy, adding to the mystery and speculation around the event that has been dubbed the Ora di Follia, or Hour of Madness.*

*A statement from Frank Weaver, the Grand Inquisitor of the Republic of Scion England, is expected imminently.*

**LONDON**—*Frank Weaver, Grand Inquisitor of the Republic of Scion England, has announced that a high-ranking Scion official, known only as the Suzerain, will make a broadcast on Monday. No further information has been provided.*

*Please stand by for real-time updates as the situation unfolds.*

# People of Interest

† – For humans, the dagger indicates that the character is dead by the beginning of *The Dark Mirror*. For Rephaim, it indicates that they have been sequestered.

## CLAIRVOYANTS

*Humans with the ability to commune with the æther. They are identifiable by an aura, the colour of which is related to their specific means of connecting with the spirit world.*

**Paige Mahoney**

**Order**: Jumper
**Type**: Dreamwalker
**Also known as**: The Pale Dreamer, Black Moth, XX-59-40

Born in early 2040, Paige lived a quiet life on Feirm na mBeach Meala – her grandparents' dairy farm in County Tipperary, Ireland. Her mother, Cora Spencer, died of placental abruption not long after giving birth.

At the age of six, Paige narrowly survived the Imbolc Massacre, the first stage of the Dublin Incursion. Two years later, as guerrilla war raged between Scion and Ireland, Paige was forced to move to the Scion Citadel of London when Scion conscripted her father,

Cóilín, who legally anglicised both of their names to protect them from rising hibernophobia. Her first significant encounter with the spirit world was in a poppy field near the Cornish village of Arthyen, where a poltergeist made physical contact with her, leaving a scar on her left palm. It was here that she met Nick Nygård, who treated her wounds.

At sixteen, Paige reunited with Nick in London, and he invited her to join the clairvoyant underworld as a member of the Seven Seals, a gang founded by Jaxon Hall. Prizing her rare form of clairvoyance – dreamwalking – Jaxon made Paige his mollisher.

In 2059, Paige was detained and transported to the prison city of Oxford, where she learned of the existence of the Rephaim. Arcturus Mesarthim was assigned as her keeper. The two eventually put aside their differences and, with help from some of the other humans and Rephaim in Oxford, organised a rebellion against Sargas rule. Paige returned to London and resolved to become Underqueen in order to expose the Rephaite threat. During this period, she came into conflict with the Rag and Bone Man and uncovered his trafficking network, the so-called grey market. In the fourth scrimmage in London history, she betrayed and defeated Jaxon, who was not inclined towards rebellion against Scion, to win the Rose Crown.

As Underqueen, her main legacy was the neutralisation of RDT Senshield. After a rigorous search across Manchester and Edinburgh for a way to destroy it, Paige surrendered herself to Scion to reach its power source in the Westminster Archon. She endured twenty-three days of imprisonment and torture before banishing the spirit inside Senshield's core by unknown means, deactivating all the scanners. Alsafi Sualocin and Scarlett Burnish organised her escape from Inquisitorial custody. Burnish sent her to Paris to work for the Domino Programme.

Paige's first assignment for Domino was to identify the source of tension between the Scion Republics of England and France. To this end, she infiltrated the Hôtel Garuche, home of Inquisitor Ménard, and discovered his disdain for the Rephaim. During this time, she reunited with David Fitton, real name Cadoc Fitzours, who offered her support. She also convinced Kornephoros Sheratan, an imprisoned Reph, to give her the location of the second Rephaite city – Versailles – and worked alongside the perdues, loyalists of Le Vieux Orphelin, to infiltrate and destroy it. Domino tasked her with assassinating Jaxon, the Grand Overseer, but Paige failed to do this.

After returning from Versailles, Paige committed to a relationship with Arcturus, only for him to be detained by Scion. When Paige attempted to rescue him, Arcturus claimed to have been a double agent, spying on her for Nashira. A heartbroken Paige threw her focus into hunting down the Rag and Bone Man and striking a truce with Ménard, preventing him from executing voyants. Paige was then taken prisoner by Cadoc Fitzours. Kornephoros Sheratan released her. Paige came to the realisation that Arcturus had not betrayed her, and attempted to find him. After surviving the ensuing free-world airstrike on Paris, she was found by Domino medic Eléonore Cordier, who subdued with a dose of white aster, an amnesic drug.

## Antoinette Carter

**Order**: Fury
**Type**: Unknown

A member of the Triumvirate, the trio of leaders of the Council of Kassandra. Before Scion invaded Ireland, Carter was the host of the talk show *Deepest Truths*, during which she would often make accurate predictions about her guests and the news. During the Molly Riots, she became an outspoken insurgent and established an illegal pamphlet, *Stingy Jack*.

In 2059, Carter visited London to meet Jaxon Hall and his gang. Against her will, Paige was among the team sent by Nashira Sargas to detain her. With the help of her archangel, Carter fended off several Rephaim and escaped by jumping into the River Thames. Paige has not seen her since.

## Beatrice Sala

**Order**: Augur
**Type**: Oculomancer

President of Italy, a member of the Triumvirate, and a key proponent of the Forum Project. She has not been seen for several weeks.

### Cadoc 'Cade' Fitzours

**Order**: Jumper
**Type**: Oracle
**Also known as**: David Fitton, XX-59-12

As a spy for Georges Benoît Ménard and Luce Ménard Frère, Cade engineered his own arrest and transportation to Oxford under the name David Fitton in early 2059. He quickly rose through the ranks to become a red-jacket. His immediate fate after the rebellion was unknown to Paige, but she met him again in Paris, where he claimed to be helping Ménard resist the influence of the Sargas family. Later, he turned on Page and imprisoned her in the Hôtel Garuche. His motives and whereabouts are unknown.

### Danica Panić

**Order**: Fury
**Type**: Unknown
**Also known as**: The Chained Fury

The former gunsmith and inventor of the Seven Seals, who also worked for Scion as an engineer. Danica helped rescue Paige from Oxford and ostensibly sided with her after the fourth scrimmage, but secretly applied for a transfer to the Scion Citadel of Athens, disinclined to participate in the revolution. Her status is unknown.

### Divya 'Ivy' Jacob

**Order**: Augur
**Type**: Chiromancer
**Also known as**: The Jacobite, XX-59–24

A Bone Season survivor and former mollisher to the Rag and Bone Man, who was an unwitting accomplice of the grey market. She is now a close ally of Paige and works for Le Vieux Orphelin in Paris, whom she helped rescue from Versailles. Ivy is training to destroy Thuban Sargas, her former Rephaite keeper, who tortured her in Oxford.

### Eliza Renton

**Order**: Medium
**Type**: Automatiste
**Also known as**: The Martyred Muse

The former breadwinner of the Seven Seals, now interim Underqueen of the Mime Order. Eliza sided with Paige after the fourth scrimmage, despite her previous loyalty to their shared employer, Jaxon Hall.

### Ezekiel 'Zeke' Sáenz

**Order**: Fury
**Type**: Unreadable
**Also known as**: The Black Diamond

A former member of the Seven Seals, who participated in rescuing Paige from Oxford. After the fourth scrimmage, he and his sister, Nadine, sided with Jaxon Hall. This forced Zeke to separate from his boyfriend, Nick Nygård, who chose to pledge his loyalty to Paige.

Jaxon proceeded to imprison the siblings in Versailles. Paige later rescued them and gave them enough money to buy passage to the free world.

### Federico Zitouni

**Order**: Augur
**Type**: Hydromancer

A high-ranking member of the Figli de Partenope, a gang of Neapolitan hydromancers. He was briefly the fiancé of Veronika Norlenghi.

### Giosuè Barraco

**Order**: Augur
**Type**: Lithomancer

The architect behind the Forum Project. He taught Beatrice Sala at the Sapienza University of Rome.

## The Glym Lord

**Order**: Medium
**Type**: Physical medium
**Also known as**: Laurence Adomako, Glym

Known to the clairvoyant syndicate as Glym, Laurence is a high commander of the Mime Order, who ruled as its interim leader while Paige was preoccupied in Manchester, Edinburgh and Paris. He has since ceded the role to Eliza Renton, but is still closely involved in the management of the organisation.

## Hector Grinslathe †

**Order**: Soothsayer
**Type**: Macharomancer
**Also known as**: Haymarket Hector

The former Underlord of the Scion Citadel of London, Hector was notorious for his greed, cruelty, and sloth. In retribution for his decision to sell Paige on the grey market, Jaxon arranged for Hector and his gang to be assassinated by the Abbess, a fellow marketeer, who was possessed by the spirit of Jack the Ripper. Along with almost all of his gang, the Underbodies, Hector was murdered in his own den.

## Jaxon Hall

**Order**: Guardian
**Type**: Binder
**Also known as**: The White Binder, the Grand Overseer, An Obscure Writer, XVII-39–7

Orphaned at the age of four, Jaxon Hall was an impoverished gutterling until 2031, when he shot to underworld fame as the author of *On the Merits of Unnaturalness*, a pamphlet that divided clairvoyants into seven orders and caused an outbreak of gang warfare in

London. His writing saw him arrested by Scion and transported to the prison city of Oxford for Bone Season VIII.

Upon discovering a nascent rebellion against the Sargas family, he betrayed it in exchange for his own freedom. This resulted in the massacre of almost every human in Oxford and the disfigurement of the Rephaite conspirators, including Arcturus Mesarthim. Although it was initially agreed that Jaxon would remain under Scion surveillance for the rest of his life, he slipped the net, returned to the underworld, and built a new life as mime-lord of I-4, founding a gang named the Seven Seals and calling himself the White Binder. Meanwhile, unbeknownst to his gang (including his mollisher, Paige Mahoney), he maintained contact with Nashira Sargas – never meeting her in person – and began selling her rare clairvoyants for the Bone Seasons, accruing significant wealth in the process. Several syndicate members joined this enterprise, including the Rag and Bone Man, the Abbess, and even the Underlord, Hector, forming a trafficking ring known as the grey market.

Jaxon attempted to become Underlord in 2059 and came close to winning the Rose Crown, but Paige betrayed him and used her gift to force him to yield. With the grey market exposed and the crown no longer in his grasp, Jaxon revealed himself to Nashira and apparently defected to Scion. He was granted the title of Grand Overseer and given authority over the second Rephaite city, Versailles.

When Paige arrived in Versailles, tasked by Domino with assassinating him, Jaxon faced Arcturus (unapologetically) for the first time in twenty years. Unable to shoot Jaxon in cold blood, Paige struck him with her spirit, set fire to the building, and left him to the mercy of the flames. However, Jaxon recovered quickly enough to join her group, wearing a dissimulator to disguise himself, as they escaped through the underground Passage des Voleurs. He saved Paige from the flood in the tunnel before leaving by train for London. His motives for his actions remain unclear.

## Julian Amesbury

**Order**: Unknown
**Type**: Unknown
**Also known as**: XX-59-26

One of Paige Mahoney's closest friends during her time in Oxford. Julian worked with Paige to plan and execute the rebellion of 2059, and was responsible for setting fires on the evening of the Bicentenary, which prevented the Rephaim from sending an assistance call to London. He never reached the escape train. Paige initially assumed he had died in Oxford, but Scion is still looking for him, suggesting that no body has been found.

## Kafayat Ekundayo

**Order**: Medium
**Type**: Automatiste

A barrister associated with the Forum Project, specialising in international human rights.

## Lennart Bohren

**Order**: Fury
**Type**: Unreadable

An associate of the Domino Programme.

## Liss Rymore †

**Order**: Soothsayer
**Type**: Cartomancer
**Also known as**: XIX-49-1

A talented cartomancer, Liss was another of Paige's closest friends in Oxford, where she was imprisoned for a decade, having been captured during Bone Season XIX. Gomeisa Sargas was once her keeper, but he expelled her to the Rookery, where she became a performer, specialising in aerial silks.

Frightened by stories of the failed rebellion of Bone Season VIII, Liss was initially reluctant to resist the Sargas – but after Arcturus Mesarthim saved her from spirit shock, she joined Paige and Julian in planning the rebellion. Before she could leave with Paige on the train, Gomeisa murdered her by causing her to fall from the silks.

### Michael Wren

**Order**: Fury
**Type**: Unreadable

A Bone Season survivor who was stationed at the Residence of Magdalen. Nashira Sargas gave Michael to Arcturus Mesarthim, who taught him Scion Sign Language. Michael grew to trust Arcturus and later assisted him in planning the rebellion of 2059 with Paige. After leaving Oxford on a hijacked train, he and Paige were separated while fleeing the Tower of London. Michael was then captured by the Rag and Bone Man and imprisoned in Versailles, but was taken away from the city before Paige could liberate it. His whereabouts are unknown.

### Nadine Arnett

**Order**: Sensor
**Type**: Whisperer
**Also known as**: The Silent Bell

A former member of the Seven Seals, who participated in rescuing Paige from Oxford. After the fourth scrimmage, she and her brother Zeke sided with Jaxon Hall, who proceeded to imprison them both in Versailles. Paige later rescued the siblings and gave them enough money to buy passage to the free world.

### Nicklas 'Nick' Nygård

**Order**: Jumper
**Type**: Oracle
**Also known as**: The Red Vision

Born in the Scion Republic of Sweden, Nick – a child prodigy – was training as a doctor when his younger sister, Karolina, was murdered by soldiers under the command of Birgitta Tjäder. This incident led Nick to the path of rebellion, and he resolved to move to England, the heart of Scion, to fight the anchor from within. He first met Paige Mahoney in Arthyen.

During a visit to London, Nick met Jaxon Hall and became the first member of his gang, the Seven Seals. After meeting Paige again, Nick brought her into the gang. He has been her closest friend and confidant ever since, and served alongside Eliza Renton as mollisher supreme. He sided with Paige after the scrimmage, forcing him to part from his boyfriend, Zeke Sáenz, who chose to support Jaxon.

Nick was drafted into the Domino Programme at the same time as Paige and sent back to Sweden to stir up anti-Scion sentiment there.

## Noemi Morpurgo

**Order**: Medium
**Type**: Unknown

A gondoliera working for the Domino Programme.

## Nuray Erçetin

**Order**: Soothsayer
**Type**: Molybdomancer

Born in Antalya, Nuray moved to Sofia with her mother and aunt at the age of twelve. After joining the failed defence of the city during the Balkan Incursion, she was imprisoned in the Chakalnya – a mountain fortress – and sentenced to death for unnaturalness. To avoid execution, Nuray chose a decade of hard labour, followed by enrolment into the Night Vigilance Division, as her sentence for rebelling.

In early 2060, Nuray was serving as a night Vigile when her old friend Yoana Hazurova, also known as Ognena Maria, found her. She gladly joined the Domino Programme as a member of sub-network Plashilo (Scarecrow), with the aim of breaking into the Chakalnya and liberating a Greek agent known as Kostas. After being identified during the raid, she was swiftly extracted from the Scion Republic of Bulgaria and given refuge in Prague.

## Ognena Maria

**Order**: Augur
**Type**: Pyromancer
**Also known as**: Yoana Hazurova, Nina Aprilova

Born to Ekaterina Hazurova and Petar Hazurov in 2025, Yoana Hazurova was among the many Bulgarians who resisted the Republic of Scion during the Balkan Incursion. After the fall of Sofia in the autumn of 2040, she was imprisoned in the Chakalnya and sentenced to a decade of hard labour in the new Scion Republic of Bulgaria, to be followed by enrolment in the Night Vigilance Division.

When Yoana was nineteen, she escaped across the Black Sea and travelled west through Europe, seeking a large community of fellow clairvoyants. She found sanctuary in London, where she eventually became mime-queen of I-5 under the alias Ognena Maria, the name by which she is now most commonly known.

When Paige Mahoney won the fourth scrimmage and was crowned Underqueen, Maria became one of her six high commanders and travelled with her to find the core of Senshield. After its deactivation, the Domino Programme sent her back to Bulgaria to rekindle the resistance there.

## The Rag and Bone Man †

**Order**: Soothsayer
**Type**: Bibliomancer
**Also known as**: L'Homme au Masque de Fer

The former mime-lord of II-4, leader of the Rag Dolls, and a key member of the grey market. After the rebellion in Oxford, Paige came into conflict with him when she found Arcturus Mesarthim imprisoned in his lair.

As Paige grew closer to discovering the grey market, the Rag and Bone Man organised an unsuccessful attempt on her life. Finally, after the end of the fourth scrimmage, Ivy Jacob – his former mollisher – told the truth about the market, and the Rag and Bone Man fled London.

In Paris, the Rag and Bone Man cut a deal with the grands ducs, offering handsome sums of money in exchange for voyants they considered troublesome. These voyants would then be sent to Versailles. Paige and Le Vieux Orphelin finally tracked him to Montmartre, only to discover that Jaxon had already mortally wounded him, apparently in retribution for the Rag and Bone Man's attempt on her life. Upon unmasking him, Paige saw that the Rag and Bone Man was Alfred Rackham, Jaxon's former agent. She cut his throat and left his body in a derelict sewer.

### Renelde Du Linceul

**Order**: Fury
**Type**: Unknown
**Also known as**: Renée Gilson

A member of the perdues – the followers of Le Vieux Orphelin – and a high-ranking member of the Nouveau Régime, the clairvoyant syndicate of the Scion Citadel of Paris. Renelde was part of the team who infiltrated the Rephaite city of Versailles and liberated its prisoners.

### Roberta Attard †

**Order**: Soothsayer
**Type**: Capnomancer
**Also known as**: The Scuttling Queen

The elder daughter of the late Nerio Attard, a former Scuttling King of Manchester. Roberta was murdered by her sister, Catrin Attard, who Paige Mahoney had released from prison as part of an attempt to find the core of Senshield.

## Rohan Mistry

**Order**: Guardian
**Type**: Summoner

A member of the Triumvirate, the trio of leaders of the Council of Kassandra. He is a retired diplomat.

## Veronika 'Verča' Norlenghi

**Order**: Fury
**Type**: Unknown
**Also known as**: Veronika Zhangová

A civilian recruiter and administrator for the Domino Programme. Verča grew up in Czechia with her parents, Lia Norlenghi and Daniel Zhang, and her older sister, Debora. From an early age, she had a love of languages and a passion for the arts. During a year of travel, Verča and Debora were caught up in the Balkan Incursion, during which they met Yoana Hazurova in Sofia. Yoana saved their lives by bribing a station guard in exchange for their safe passage to Belgrade.

Verča went on to study interior design and embark on a diverse career in Italy. At thirty-six, she returned to Prague, where she was employed by the Libuše Institute. She is now their most successful recruiter, reporting to Radomír Doleček. In 2060, Verča finally reunited with Yoana – now known as Ognena Maria  and started a relationship with her.

## Le Vieux Orphelin

**Order**: Jumper
**Type**: Oracle
**Also known as**: Ignace Fall

The incumbent leader of the Nouveau Régime. Originally one of three grands ducs who ruled over the syndicate, he was betrayed by Le Latronpuche and La Reine des Thunes, who sold him on the grey market. Paige was part of the team that freed him from Versailles. Upon their return to Paris, the pair forged an alliance between their syndicates and ousted the corrupt Le Latronpuche, while La Reine des Thunes pledged her loyalty – and her valuable jewellery – to the revolution.

# AMAUROTICS

*Humans who are not clairvoyant, sometimes known as rotties. They have no connection to the spirit world and are unable to sense it.*

## Albéric †

A field agent working for the Domino Programme, responsible for the safe houses of sub-networks Mannequin and Figurine in the Scion Citadel of Paris. He was detained and executed by Scion.

## Aparna Wells

A defector from the Scion Republic of England, now assisting the Domino Programme. She was a classmate of Scarlett Burnish at the Ancroft School in Bloomsbury, where Paige was later a student.

## Birgitta Tjäder

**Also known as**: The Magpie

The Chief of Vigilance in Stockholm and commander of the Second Inquisitorial Division of ScionIDE. Rumour holds that she controls the weak-willed Ingrid Lindberg, the Grand Inquisitor of Sweden. Known as the Magpie by her enemies, Tjäder is a merciless Scion fanatic with a zero-tolerance approach to all degrees of lawbreaking.

In early 2060, Paige discovered that Tjäder was nursing a grudge against the Rephaim, seeing them as just as unnatural as voyants, and had been working with Inquisitor Ménard of France to undermine the Sargas family. Tjäder is currently overseeing the anchorisation of Spain and Portugal, following the success of Operation Madrigal.

## Eléonore Cordier

A field agent working for the Domino Programme. She was the medical officer for sub-network Mannequin before her apparent detainment by Scion in February 2060. Her name is an alias.

## Frank Weaver

Grand Inquisitor of the Scion Republic of England. He succeeded Abberline Mayfield, who ruled Scion when it conquered Ireland. Prior to Operation Madrigal, Weaver had no military victories to his name.

## Georges Benoît Ménard

**Also known as:** The Butcher of Strasbourg

The Grand Inquisitor of Scion Republic of France, usually known as Benoît Ménard. He is spouse to Luce Ménard Frère, with whom he has four children.

In 2060, Paige came to blows with Ménard when she possessed Frère and infiltrated their family home, the Hôtel Garuche, in an attempt to gain information. She discovered that Ménard had turned against the Rephaim and intended to overthrow Nashira Sargas. Paige escaped with the intelligence she needed, but later arranged another meeting with Ménard to propose a truce. In exchange for the Mime Order focusing its efforts on the Rephaite-supporting England, Ménard agreed not to execute any voyants for two years. Following the airstrike on Paris, it is unknown whether this arrangement stands.

## Gilberto Draghetti

Minister of Defence in Italy.

## Harald Lauring

A courier for the Domino Programme, previously a field agent in Sweden.

## Helen Githmark

A former Norwegian politician, strongly opposed to the Republic of Scion. She was publicly disgraced and stripped of her government position after being arrested for a hit and run in Oslo.

## Hildred Vance

Grand Commander of the Scion Republic of England and authority maximum of ScionIDE. She has been hospitalised since Paige destroyed the core of Senshield while they were both inside Victoria Tower. Patricia Okonma, the Deputy Grand Commander, is currently acting in Vance's stead.

## Isaure Ducos

A member of the Domino Programme, formerly a field agent, now based in Venice as a member of Command. She was previously the supervisor of sub-network Mannequin, of which Paige was a member. Her name is an alias.

## Johan Ospeth

A former doublet for the Domino Programme, who worked in the court of Queen Ingelin of Norway. He left Oslo with Queen Ingelin and her entourage shortly after ScionIDE entered the country.

## Linda Groven

The former Prime Minister of Norway, now Grand Inquisitor of the new Scion Republic of Norway.

## Lorenzo Rinaldi

Prime Minister of Italy.

## Luce Ménard Frère

**Also known as**: Madelle Guillotine

Spouse and official representative of Georges Benoît Ménard, the Grand Inquisitor of France. Paige first saw Frère in person during her imprisonment in the Westminster Archon and later possessed Frère in Paris, on the orders of the Domino Programme, to obtain intelligence on the tension between France and England. During this time, Frère was pregnant with her fourth child, Victoire. She disappeared just before the airstrike on Paris, and her current whereabouts are unknown.

## Pivot

A member of Command. She is head of the Palazzo del Domino, the paramount headquarters of the Domino Programme.

## Radomír Doleček

A member of the Domino Programme, who heads the Libuše Institute of Prague. His name is an alias.

## Sandra McCarthy

**Also known as**: Alastríona Ní Mhathúna

Paige's paternal aunt and mother of Finn Mac Cárthaigh. She rescued Paige from Dublin after the Imbolc Massacre.

## Scarlett Burnish †

The former Grand Raconteur of the Scion Republic of England, known as the Voice of Scion, and the host of its only news station, ScionEye. In January 2060, Burnish unexpectedly helped Paige escape the Westminster Archon and revealed that she was a deep-cover agent in the employ of the Domino Programme and an ally of Alsafi Sualocin. After her disloyalty was discovered, she was executed in secret.

### Spinner

A member of Command. He is responsible for instructing and liaising with the doublets, the representatives stationed in countries that support the Domino Programme.

### Umberto Bianchi

The Mayor of Turin, recently arrested for drug possession, which he denies.

### Yelyzaveta Covali

A member of the Domino Programme. She specialises in training recruits to enter Scion East, where her mother was born.

### Yousry El-Khatib

A courier for the Domino Programme, specialising in high-risk assignments.

# REPHAIM

*Immortal humanoids of the Netherworld, a decayed and uninhabitable dimension that once served as an intermediary realm between the æther and the corporeal world. Rephaim exhibit similar abilities to clairvoyant humans.*

THE RANTHEN

### Arcturus Mesarthim

**Type**: Oneiromancer
**Also known as**: Warden of the Mesarthim, the concubine, the blood-consort

The former Warden of the Mesarthim – the guardian and ruler of his family – Arcturus was among the most devoted to the Mothallath family, whom the Mesarthim were sworn to protect.

Despite repeated accusations that the Mothallath were responsible for the Netherworld's deterioration, he remained loyal and fought on their side during the Waning of the Veils. When the war was all but lost, Nashira Sargas blackmailed Arcturus into a betrothal to signal the surrender of the Mesarthim family, forcing him to part from his existing partner, Terebellum Sheratan. Arcturus was given the title of blood-consort.

On Earth, Arcturus spent most of his time confined to the prison city of Oxford, where he and several other members of the Ranthen hatched the ill-fated Novembertide Rebellion of 2039. After a young Jaxon Hall betrayed the plot, Nashira slaughtered almost the entire human population of Oxford and punished the Rephaite participants by using a violent poltergeist to mutilate their backs. Following the betrayal, Arcturus developed an intense distrust of humans, though he tried to protect them by fighting the Emim in secret, limiting injury to the red-jackets. In March 2059, Arcturus reluctantly took Paige Mahoney – a dreamwalker – as his 'tenant' in the Residence of Magdalen. With the approval of the Ranthen (and the vocal disapproval of Paige), he helped her to hone her skills, hoping she would be able to defeat Nashira at the Bicentenary. Nashira, meanwhile, wanted Paige trained so she could absorb the gift of dreamwalking at its fullest. After six months, Arcturus and Paige sparked a mass breakout with help from some of the other humans and Rephaim in Oxford.

After being captured by the Rag and Bone Man in London, Arcturus reunited with Paige, who rescued him from the Camden Catacombs, and became one of the high commanders of the Mime Order following her coronation as Underqueen. He and Paige had a brief and illicit relationship before she ended it, afraid it would become a distraction – or that his fellow Ranthen would discover it, leading to the dissolution of the alliance. After the destruction of Senshield, Arcturus volunteered to accompany Paige to Paris, where he supported her in her work for the Domino Programme.

After their successful attack on Versailles, Arcturus and Paige decided to rekindle their relationship, but their happiness was short-lived, as Arcturus was detained by Scion. Paige attempted to rescue him from the Sainte-Chapelle, only for him to tell her that he had been a Sargas spy from the beginning. Paige fled the scene, leaving Arcturus with Nashira. His fate is unknown.

Arcturus is an oneiromancer, able to make others 'dream' their memories, and to experience them alongside the subject. In Oxford, he used this gift to judge whether or not Paige could be trusted.

### Adhara Sarin

**Type**: Unknown

The original Warden of the Sarin, who still uses that title, despite being stripped of it by the Sargas. She joined the Ranthen after Paige deactivated Senshield.

### Alsafi Sualocin †

**Type**: Unknown

Alsafi was a Ranthen double agent throughout the Waning of the Veils and continued in that role on Earth. Masquerading as a Sargas loyalist, he remained with Nashira after the rebellion in Oxford and fed valuable information to his fellow Ranthen. He colluded in hiding most of the clairvoyant syndicate of London in the Beneath, having already created a network of human contacts within Scion, which allowed him to send Paige Mahoney, Ognena Maria, Tom the Rhymer, and Eliza Renton north to Manchester and Edinburgh to find the core of Senshield.

After Paige disabled the core in London, Alsafi carried her from the ruined Victoria Tower and duelled with Nashira to give Paige time to escape. Nashira beheaded him. Scarlett Burnish, his ally, subsequently got Paige out of the building.

### Errai Sarin

**Type**: Unknown

A member of the Ranthen. Despite his disdain for the Sargas family, he strongly dislikes humans and has immense respect for the doctrine of distance.

**Lesath Mesarthim**

**Type**: Unknown

A member of the Ranthen and former servant of the Mothallath. Rather than accepting the Sargas armistice after the civil war, he followed Cursa Sarin to Scotland, where they formed a community of exiles. Lesath is staunchly loyal to Arcturus, the original and rightful Warden of the Mesarthim.

**Lucida Sargas**

**Type**: Apportist

A member of the Ranthen who rejected her family and departed from Oxford before the Novembertide Rebellion.

**Pleione Sualocin**

**Type**: Audient

A member of the Ranthen who served as a keeper in Oxford, stationed at the Residence of Merton. Her human 'tenants' included David Fitton (also known as Cadoc Fitzours). She avoided detection during the Novembertide Rebellion, but revealed her true allegiance during the uprising of 2059.

**Situla Mesarthim †**

**Type**: Unknown

A mercenary who fought for both sides during the Rephaite civil war, but grew loyal to the victorious Sargas family. She was stationed as a guard in Oxford and Versailles. Her devotion to the Sargas finally wavered in Carcassonne, when she witnessed Arcturus Mesarthim – her former Warden – being tortured by Kornephoros Sheratan, who mocked all of the Mesarthim. Situla made a vain attempt to help Arcturus escape, resulting in her sequestration.

### Terebellum 'Terebell' Sheratan

**Type**: Somatomancer
**Also known as**: Warden of the Sheratan, the sovereign-elect

The incumbent sovereign-elect of the Ranthen. Terebell was Warden of the Sheratan before the civil war and still uses the title. Throughout the Waning of the Veils, she was a ferocious supporter of the Mothallath family and fought for them alongside her partner, Arcturus Mesarthim. When the war was lost and Nashira took Arcturus as her betrothed, Terebell fought Nashira in single combat and lost. After relocating to Earth in 1859, she was stationed at the Residence of Oriel and often volunteered as a keeper in the Bone Seasons.

In 2039, Terebell, Arcturus, and a number of their old allies resolved to stage a coup against the Sargas with the help of the humans in Oxford. Terebell was named sovereign-elect of the new and clandestine Ranthen. She was among those who were scarred in punishment after the failed rebellion of 2039, and assisted with the successful rebellion of 2059, after which she escaped Oxford and went to London. Terebell is currently co-ruler of the Mime Order.

THE SARGAS AND THEIR LOYALISTS

### Nashira Sargas

**Type**: Binder
**Also known as**: The Suzerain, the blood-sovereign

Blood-sovereign of the Rephaim and creator of the Republic of Scion, Nashira is the highest power in the empire, but uses the Grand Inquisitors of England as her puppets and mouthpieces. She shares her authority with Gomeisa Sargas, her fellow blood-sovereign.

Formerly a scholar, Nashira spearheaded the war against the ruling Mothallath family during the Waning of the Veils, which resulted in their complete destruction. After her victory, she blackmailed Arcturus Mesarthim into becoming her blood-consort to demonstrate the surrender of the Mesarthim family. She then led all of the Rephaim across the veil to Earth, where she established Scion, with herself as its supreme authority. She spent the next two centuries presiding over the prison city of Oxford while Gomeisa largely remained in London.

After Jaxon Hall informed her about the imminent rebellion of 2039, Nashira allowed the Emim to kill almost every human in Oxford and used the spirit of Jack the Ripper to torture the Rephaite instigators, including her own blood-consort. When Paige Mahoney arrived in Oxford in 2059, Nashira tasked Arcturus with training her, partly as a test of his loyalty. Her plan backfired when Paige and Arcturus struck a tentative alliance and organised a second, successful rebellion. Nashira is the only person to have witnessed their first embrace at the Bicentenary.

Nashira is a 'super-binder' who can not only bind spirits, but use the gifts they had in life. This necessitates her killing her victims in a specific manner. The enraged spirit of Jack the Ripper is among her entourage of so-called fallen angels, and she can use it to cause the scarred members of the Ranthen excruciating pain on a whim. She is responsible for the doctrine of distance, which prohibits physical contact between humans and Rephaim.

## Gomeisa Sargas

**Type:** Apportist

Warden of the Sargas and male blood-sovereign of the Rephaim. He was present in Oxford for the Bicentenary, where he murdered Liss Rymore. He is also thought to be the mastermind behind the conquest of Ireland, which he accomplished through his most powerful puppets, Hildred Vance and Abberline Mayfield. Gomeisa can harness apport, the energy of breachers – a rare and highly dangerous gift.

## Kornephoros Sheratan

**Type:** Skeletomancer

The new blood-consort of the Rephaim. Kornephoros initially fought on the Ranthen side in the Waning of the Veils, but betrayed the star-sovereigns at the eleventh hour, resulting in the fall of the Mothallath family. Nashira rewarded him with the title of Warden of the Sheratan – a title formerly held by his cousin, Terebellum – and he now serves as her emissary. Arcturus Mesarthim is one of his former partners.

Kornephoros is able to connect with the æther using bones, and his touch can cause excruciating pain. In the past, during his brief stays in Oxford, he used his talent for the bones to read the future for Kraz Sargas.

### Kraz Sargas †

**Type**: Unknown

The former male blood-heir of the Rephaim. When he caught Paige stealing supplies in Oxford, she used the pollen of the poppy anemone and a bullet to incapacitate him. He is presumed to have been sequestered.

### Suhail Chertan

**Type**: Unknown

A low-ranking Rephaite. In Oxford, he was charged with keeping the peace in the Rookery, the slum that housed the performers. He was assigned to torture Paige after her capture in November 2059, with the aim of forcing her to disclose the whereabouts of the syndicate. Despite subjecting her to physical and mental torment, he was unsuccessful.

### Thuban Sargas

**Type**: None
**Also known as**: Le Basilic

One of the few Rephaim who lost their gifts during the Waning of the Veils, leaving him with a rudimentary connection to the æther. Thuban was a keeper in Oxford, stationed at the Residence of Corpus. Notorious for his cruelty, he subjected Ivy Jacob to six months of torture before her escape in September 2059.

In Versailles, he was known as Le Basilic, after the basilisk, a creature with a fatal gaze. He lost an eye during a confrontation with Arcturus Mesarthim.

**Vindemiatrix Sargas**

**Type**: Unknown

The female blood-heir of the Rephaim. She has spent most of her time on Earth creating and supervising Grapevine, a network of spies and sleeper agents, who predominantly operate in the free world.

# Glossary

**Ace**: [noun] The advanced rank for an agent of the Domino Programme.

**Æther**: [noun] The spirit realm, which exists alongside the physical or corporeal world, Earth. Among humans, only *clairvoyants* can sense the æther.

**Alysoplasm**: [noun] The blood of the *Emim*. It can be used to conceal the nature of voyants' gifts, or to hide their dreamscapes in the æther, making them undetectable to a *dreamwalker*. However, it also prevents them from being able to use their clairvoyance for a time. Rephaim can tolerate a small amount of alysoplasm, but any more transforms them into Emim.

**Amaranth**: [noun] An iridescent flower that grows in the Netherworld. Its nectar can heal or calm any wound inflicted by a spirit; it can also fortify the *dreamscape*. Warden and Terebell take amaranth to ease the pain of the scars on their backs, inflicted by one of Nashira's *fallen angels*.

**Amaurotic**: [noun *or* adjective] A human who is not clairvoyant. This state is known as amaurosis, from an Ancient Greek word referring to a dimming or dulling, especially of the senses. Among voyants, they are known colloquially as *rotties*.

**Anchor:** [noun] The symbol of the Republic of Scion, often used as a metonym for it, e.g. countries are described as being 'in the shadow of the anchor' when they come under threat from Scion.

**Anchorisation:** [noun] The process of converting a conquered or amenable country into a territory of the Republic of Scion. This includes the dismantling of democracy, the suppression of religion, the mass arrest of clairvoyants and dissenters, and the destruction of anything deemed unnatural, e.g. art that acknowledges the existence of spirits, deities, or the afterlife.

**Anchorite:** [noun *or* adjective] A disparaging term for people who work directly for Scion, or are especially committed to its message. It can also be used as a descriptor, e.g. *anchorite propaganda*.

**Angel:** [noun] A category of *drifter*. There are several known sub-types of angels:
  – A *guardian angel* is the spirit of a person who died to protect someone else, and now remains with the living person they saved
  – An *archangel* protects a single bloodline for several generations
  – A *fallen angel* is a spirit compelled to remain with their murderer
  All sub-types of angels can be *breachers*

**Apport:** [noun] The movement of physical objects by *ethereal* means, derived from Latin apportō ('I bring, I carry'). Among spirits, this ability is unique to *breachers*. Rarely, clairvoyants or Rephaim may be able to use apport.

**Aster:** [noun] A genus of flower. Certain kinds of aster have *ethereal* properties:
  – **Blue** strengthens the link between the spirit and the dreamscape. It can sharpen recent memories and produce a feeling of wellbeing

- **Pink** strengthens the link between the spirit and the body; consequently, it is often used by voyants as an aphrodisiac
- **Purple**, highly addictive, is a deliriant that distorts the dreamscape
- **White** causes amnesia. Prolonged overuse of white aster can lead to narcolepsy, followed by *whiteout*

**Augurs**: [noun] The second order of clairvoyance according to *On the Merits of Unnaturalness*. Like the *soothsayers*, they are reliant on *numa*. They often have blue auras. The so-called vile augurs, who use the substance of the human body to connect with the æther, were persecuted by the syndicate for many years.

**Aura**: [noun] A manifestation of the link between a clairvoyant and the æther, visible only with the *sight*. Since the Netherworld began to deteriorate, *Rephaim* have required human auras to sustain their own connections to the æther.

**Bicentenary, the**: [noun] A key event in recent Scion history, the Bicentenary was the celebration of two hundred years of Rephaite rule, held in Oxford in September 2059. The *Great Territorial Act* was to be signed on this night, and Nashira intended to kill Paige in front of the assembled guests.

**Binder**: [noun] A type of clairvoyant who can compel and tether spirits. A spirit that serves a binder is called a *boundling*.

**Blood-consort**: [noun] The consort of a *blood-sovereign* of the Rephaim. Following the Rephaite civil war, Nashira Sargas forced Arcturus Mesarthim to be her blood-consort for two centuries, treating him as a war trophy.

**Blood-sovereign**: [noun] The leader of the Rephaim. There are always two – a male and a female. Nashira and Gomeisa Sargas are the incumbent blood-sovereigns.

**Bone Season**: [noun] A harvest of clairvoyant (and some amaurotic) humans, organised by Scion to appease the *Rephaim*, to compensate them for protecting humankind from the *Emim*. For two centuries, clairvoyants were detained over the course of each decade and sent together to the prison city of Oxford. Paige was drafted into Bone Season XX.

**Boundling**: [noun] Any spirit controlled by a *binder*.

**Breacher**: [noun] A category of spirit that can affect the corporeal world, e.g. by moving objects or injuring the living. The ability to breach is usually related to the manner of a spirit's death – a violent death is more likely to produce a breacher. The most common types of breacher are *angels* and *poltergeists*. When breachers touch either a human or a Rephaite, they can leave cold scars and a profound chill.

**Buzzers**: [noun] See *Emim*.

**Clairvoyant**: [noun] A human who can sense and interact with the spirit world, the *æther*. They are identifiable by their *aura*.

**Cold spot**: [noun] A portal between Earth and the Netherworld, which manifests as a perfect circle of ice. Humans cannot pass through a cold spot, but *Rephaim* and *Emim* can.

**Denizen**: [noun] A resident of the Republic of Scion.

**Deuce**: [noun] The starting rank for an agent of the Domino Programme.

**Dissimulator**: [noun] A form of free-world technology, apparently unknown to Scion, that changes the wearer's face. The Domino Programme issues them to many of their field agents.

**Doctrine of distance**: [noun] A Rephaite law preventing all physical contact between humans and *Rephaim*, based on a superstition that the *Netherworld* fell due to unsanctioned intimacy between the inhabitants of the two worlds. While the law originated from the Sargas family, the vast majority of the *Ranthen* also adhere to it.

**Doublet**: [noun] An envoy for the Domino Programme in a benefactor country.

**Dream-form**: [noun] The form a spirit takes within the confines of a dreamscape. It may or may not reflect how an individual looks physically; rather, it is a self-image. Once a spirit leaves a dreamscape and enters the æther, it no longer has a clear form.

**Dreamscape**: [noun] The house or seat of the *spirit*, where memory is stored. The term is often used interchangeably with *mind* by clairvoyants.
  The dreamscape is thought to be how the brain manifests in the *æther*, and often resembles a place where an individual feels safe. Clairvoyants can access their dreamscapes at will, while amaurotics may catch glimpses in their sleep. The dreamscape is split into five zones or rings:
  – **Sunlit zone**, the centre of the dreamscape, where the spirit is supposed to dwell. The *silver cord* fastens it in place
  – **Twilight zone**, a darker ring that surrounds the sunlit zone. The spirit may stray here in times of mental distress. Only *dreamwalkers* can go beyond this zone without injuring themselves
  – **Midnight** and **abyssal**, the next two zones
  – **Hadal zone**, the outermost and darkest ring of the dreamscape. Beyond this point is the *æther*. There may be *spectres* – manifestations of memory – in this zone

**Dreamwalker**: [noun] A contraction of *dreamscape walker*, referring to an exceptionally rare and complex form of *clairvoyance*. Comparable to the esoteric concept of astral projection, dreamwalking involves the dislocation and projection of the *spirit* from the *dreamscape*. Dreamwalkers have an unusually flexible *silver cord*, allowing them to not only walk anywhere in their own dreamscape, but to possess other people.

**Drifters**: [noun] Spirits that have not gone to the *outer darkness* or the *last light*, instead remaining within reach of the living. They are broadly divided into two categories: *breachers* and *common drifters*. Within these categories are numerous sub-types of spirit, including *angels* and *ghosts*.

**Ectoplasm**: [noun] The Rephaite equivalent of blood. It is luminous and slightly gelatinous, and considered to be molten *æther*. As such, it heightens *clairvoyant* abilities.

**Emim**: [noun] Large and violent creatures that have infested the *Netherworld* and are now venturing to Earth. They are known colloquially as *Buzzers*, due to a distinctive sound that voyants hear when they appear. The Emim feed on human flesh to sustain their earthly forms, and are also believed to devour spirits, trapping them in their dreamscapes. Despite their immense power, they cannot enter a circle of salt. During her time in Paris, Paige learned that the Emim are former Rephaim.

**Ethereal**: [adjective] Pertaining to the *æther*.

**Extrasensory perception**: [noun] The most common name for clairvoyance outside the Republic of Scion.

**Free world**: [noun] A catch-all term for countries outside the Republics of Scion.

**Furies**: [noun] The sixth order of clairvoyance according to *On the Merits of Unnaturalness.* They often have coral auras.

**Ghost**: [noun] A spirit that prefers to dwell in one place – often their place of birth or death. Moving a ghost from its *haunt* will upset it.

**Glossolalia**: [noun] The language of spirits and Rephaim, distinguished from the fell tongue. Usually shortened to *Gloss*. It is impossible to acquire Gloss; one can only be born with it. Among humans, only polyglots are capable of speaking it.

**Golden cord**: [noun] A connection between two spirits. It creates a seventh sense, allowing the linked individuals to track one another and convey their emotions. Arcturus Mesarthim and Paige Mahoney share a golden cord.

**Grand Inquisitor**: [noun] Leader of a Scion country. Each has its own Grand Inquisitor, but they all submit to the authority of the Grand Inquisitor of England, currently Frank Weaver.

**Grey market**: [noun] A trafficking ring founded by Jaxon Hall after he broke the terms of his release from Oxford. In London, the grey market specialised in procuring clairvoyants of interest and selling them to Scion and the Rephaim. While Nashira Sargas did accept clairvoyants from the market, she forced Jaxon to shut it down when he pledged himself to her service in late 2059.

**Guardians**: [noun] The fifth order of clairvoyance according to *On the Merits of Unnaturalness*. They often have orange auras and exhibit a particularly high degree of control over spirits. A *binder* is a type of guardian.

**Inquisitorial**: [adjective] Referring to the authority of a Grand Inquisitor, e.g. Inquisitorial law.

**Invocation**: [noun] See *séance*.

**Jumpers**: [noun] The seventh and rarest order of clairvoyance according to *On the Merits of Unnaturalness*, made up of *dream-walkers* and *oracles*. They often have red auras.

**Last light**: [noun] The end or heart of the *æther*, the place from which spirits can never return. What lies beyond it is unknown.

**Latency**: [noun] A state that *Rephaim* enter if they are unable to access voyants' *auras*, causing them to lose their own connections to the æther. Their *ectoplasm* vitrifies, rendering them unable to move. After a period of delusion, their spirits become unresponsive in their *dreamscapes*, locking them in the spiritual equivalent of a coma. There is no known way to reverse the process, but latent Rephaim can still be transformed into *Emim*, and they are a particular temptation to the creatures in that state.

The pollen of the *poppy anemone* can push Rephaim to the brink of latency, even if they have recently fed.

**Mecks**: [noun] A non-alcoholic drink. Comes in white, rose and blood (red) to imitate wine.

**Mediums**: [noun] The third order of clairvoyance according to *On the Merits of Unnaturalness*. They are vulnerable to possession by spirits.

**Mime-lord** *or* **Mime-queen**: [noun] A high-ranking member of the clairvoyant syndicate of London. Together, they form the Unnatural Assembly. Under Paige Mahoney's rule, they have become commanders of small cells of voyants.

**Mollisher**: [noun] The heir and second-in-command of a mime-lord or mime-queen. The Underqueen or Underlord's mollisher is known as the *mollisher supreme*.

**Mothallath family**: [noun] The former rulers of the Rephaim, who claimed to have been sent from the *last light* to reign over the Netherworld. Originally, they were the only Rephaim who could cross the veil to walk among humans. During one of their crossings, an unknown event caused the Netherworld to begin to decay. The Sargas family blamed the Mothallath and declared war on them, finally usurping them. The Mesarthim family, which was duty-bound to defend the Mothallath, supported them to the last.

**Netherworld**: [noun] The home world of the *Rephaim*, which once functioned as an intermediary realm between the æther and Earth. At some point, the Netherworld was overrun by the *Emim* and began to fall into decay, forcing the Rephaim to relocate to Earth.

**Numa:** [noun] [singular: numen] Objects used by soothsayers and augurs to connect with the æther, e.g. mirrors, tarot cards and bones. The term originates from the seventeenth century and refers to a divine presence or will.

**Off the cot:** [adjective] A slang term for *mad*.

**Opaline:** [noun] An iridescent and translucent Netherworld material, believed to be the only substance that can sever Rephaite bone.

**Oracle:** [noun] One of the two categories of *jumper*. Oracles receive sporadic visions of the future from the æther, often experiencing intense migraines at the same time. They can also learn to make and project their own visions.

**Performer:** [noun] In Oxford, this term referred to humans who had either been evicted from the residences or received the *yellow streak*. Performers specialised in various arts to entertain the red-jackets, and were under the command of the Overseer.

**Poltergeist:** [noun] A class of *breacher*, most often created by a violent death, a belligerent personality, or an especially intense and negative emotion at the time of death. They are considered by voyants to be the most difficult spirits to control, but a skilled *binder* can bring them to heel.

**Poppy anemone:** [noun] A red flower, also known as the wind-flower. In Greek myth, it grew from the blood of the hunter Adonis, a lover of Aphrodite. Though named for its short-lived fragility, its pollen can inflict serious damage on *Rephaim*.

**Psychopomp:** [noun] A spirit that once led the spirits of the dead to the Netherworld, before the Waning of the Veils. Many psychopomps now carry messages for the *Ranthen*.

**Querent:** [noun] A person who seeks knowledge of the æther. They may ask questions or offer part of themselves, e.g. their palm, for a reading.

**Ranthen**: [noun] A group of Rephaim who supported the doomed *Mothallath family* during the Rephaite civil war. The surviving Ranthen see the Sargas family as usurpers and do not wish to subjugate humans. They are currently in a tenuous alliance with Paige Mahoney and the Mime Order.

**Red-jacket**: [noun] The highest rank for humans in Oxford. Red-jackets were primarily responsible for patrolling Gallows Wood to protect the city from the *Emim*. After the fall of Oxford, most of the surviving red-jackets became Punishers, a class of *Vigile*.

**Rephaim**: [noun] [singular: Rephaite] Humanoid beings of the Netherworld. Among humans, they are known colloquially as *Rephs*. Since their world fell into decay, the Rephaim have been forced to use human *aura* to sustain themselves.

If Rephaim exposed to a large enough dose of *alysoplasm*, or their sarx is broken by an *Emite*, they can become Emim themselves. This process can only be stopped by using salt water and aura.

**Sarx**: [noun] A name given to the skin and substance of Netherworld beings. Rephaite sarx is slightly metallic and more durable than human skin, showing no signs of age. While Earth-made weapons may pierce it, it will heal quickly, while *breachers* and Netherworld metals cause significantly more damage.

**Scimorphine**: [noun] The most effective painkiller in Scion.

**Scionet**: [noun] The intranet of the Republic of Scion.

**Séance**: [noun] An event where voyants seek to invoke and communicate with a spirit. Most séances are performed in groups, but they may also be conducted alone, in which case they are usually described as an *invocation*. The *Ranthen* most often use séances to converse with their messengers, the psychopomps.

**Sensors**: [noun] The fourth order of clairvoyance according to *On the Merits of Unnaturalness*. Most sensors can perceive and interact with the æther through smell (sniffers), sound (whisperers) or taste (gustants), while the polyglots can speak and understand *Glossolalia*. They often have yellow auras.

**Seven Orders of Clairvoyance**: [noun] A system for categorising clairvoyants, first proposed by Jaxon Hall in his pamphlet *On the Merits of Unnaturalness*. Despite its controversial implication of higher and lower sorts of clairvoyance, the system was adopted as the official method of categorisation in the London underworld, resulting in a spate of gang wars and the persecution of the so-called vile augurs.

**Shade**: [noun] A type of *drifter*, older than a *wisp*.

**Silver cord**: [noun] The link between the body and the spirit. The silver cord wears down over the years and eventually snaps, resulting in death.

**Soothsayers**: [noun] The first order of clairvoyance according to *On the Merits of Unnaturalness*. They use wrought *numa* to connect with the æther and often have purple auras.

**Sovereign-elect**: [noun] The leader of the *Ranthen*, currently Terebellum 'Terebell' Sheratan.

**Spirit shock**: [noun] A state that voyants can enter if their connection to the æther is severely weakened or shaken. Soothsayers are particularly vulnerable to spirit shock, as it can be induced by destroying their favoured numen (see *numa*). It differs from the process of becoming *unreadable*.

**Spirit sight**: [noun] Sometimes referred to as the *third eye* or simply as the *sight*. The ability to perceive the æther visually, indicated by one or both pupils being shaped like a keyhole. Most voyants are sighted, but some are not. Half-sighted voyants can choose when to see the æther, while full-sighted voyants must see it all the time.

**Spool**: [1] [noun] A group of spirits; [2] [verb] to draw spirits together. All *clairvoyants* are capable of spooling.

**Summoner**: [noun] A clairvoyant who can call spirits across great distances. Jaxon classifies summoners as part of his own order, the *guardians*.

**Threnody**: [noun] A series of words used to banish spirits to the outer darkness, a part of the æther where they can no longer be contacted. There are many threnodies, developed by clairvoyant communities across the world.

**Underlord** *or* **Underqueen**: [noun] The head of the Unnatural Assembly and mob boss of the clairvoyant syndicate of London, whose authority is symbolised by the Rose Crown. The incumbent Underqueen is technically Paige Mahoney, but since her disappearance, Eliza Renton – one of her two *mollishers* – has stepped up to fill the position.

**Unnatural**: [noun *or* adjective] The formal name for clairvoyants under Inquisitorial law.

**Unreadable**: [noun *or* adjective] A type of clairvoyant whose dreamscape has collapsed, often as a result of trauma, and regrown with thick armour, rendering them immune to all spiritual interference.

**Veil**: [noun] A word used to describe the boundaries between the three known planes of being – the corporeal world, the æther, and the Netherworld.

**Vigile**: [noun] A member of the police forces of Scion. Day Vigiles are amaurotic and work for the Sunlight Vigilance Division (SVD), while night Vigiles are clairvoyant and work for the Night Vigilance Division (NVD). Night Vigiles agree to be euthanised after thirty years of service.

**Voyant**: [noun *or* adjective] See *clairvoyant*.

**Waitron**: [noun] A gender-neutral term for anyone in the service industry of the Republic of Scion.

**Whiteout**: [noun] A state caused by prolonged overuse of white *aster*, where the user succumbs to narcosis. This is followed by a complete loss of identity, or, in rarer cases, death.

**Windflower**: [noun] See *poppy anemone*.

# Acknowledgements

First, my deep thanks to long-term readers of this series, many of whom have waited for *The Dark Mirror* since January 2021. I left you on a sickening cliffhanger, and I truly hope this book was worth the wait. I'll do my best to get the sixth one out in better time, so you can see where Paige and Arcturus go next. Don't worry – they won't be on separate continents for long.

To my dynamic duo of agents, David and Sebastian Godwin, and to Aparna Kumar, Philippa Sitters, and Rachel Taylor at DGA. To the team at Andrew Nurnberg Associates, and to Sylvie Rabineau and Olivia Burgher at WME.

To the global Bloomsbury team, including: Áine Feeney, Alexis Kirschbaum, Amanda Shipp, Amrita Paul, Ben Chisnall, Ben McCluskey, Beth Maher, Callie Garnett, David Smith, Donna Gauthier, Elisabeth Denison, Ellen Chen, Emilie Chambering, Emma Allden, Faye Robinson, Genevieve Nelsson, Grace McNamee, Grace Nzita-Kiki, Hattie Castelberg, Ian Hudson, Inez Maria, Jillian Ramirez, Joanna Vallance, Joe Roche, Kathleen Farrar, Katie Vaughn, Katy Follain, Kenli Manning, Laura Meyer, Laura Phillips, Lauren Dooley, Lauren Molyneux, Lauren Moseley, Lauren Ollerhead, Lauren Whybrow, Lucie Moody, Maisie McCormick, Mariafrancesca Ierace, Marie Coolman, Nancy Miller, Nicola Hill, Nigel Newton, Paul Baggaley, Phoebe Dyer, Rachel Wilkie, Rayna Luo, Rosie Barr, Sarah McLean, Scarlett Kaplan, Suzanne Keller, Trâm-Anh Doan, Valentina Rice, Valerie Esposito, and Vicky Leech Mateos.

To my publishers, distributors and translators around the world, who allow my stories to travel across oceans and continents. Special thanks to Mpumi Mgidlana, who kept me company on my recent tour of South Africa, and to Benjamin Kuntzer, my extraordinary French translator, who has been working incredibly hard to get *The Dark Mirror* out alongside the revisions.

To Carmen R. Balit, David Mann, Emily Faccini, and Ivan Belikov for their artistic talent and imagination. I am so grateful to you for making the Bone Season series so beautiful, and for capturing both the darkness and the magic I've tried to bring to *The Dark Mirror*. My further thanks to Erica Chan, the artist behind the pre-order campaign.

To Alana Kerr Collins, the voice of Paige, for her dedication to narrating the audiobooks with versatility, energy and heart.

To Sharona Selby and Lin Vasey for finding the spanners in the works.

To Ciarán Collins, Lenka Kapsová, Manuela D'Alessandro, Marco Corsi, and Professor Nicola de Blasi for their help with the translations, and to the many followers on Instagram who were generous enough to respond to my call for help with some linguistic details. I am so grateful to all of you for your time and generosity.

To the friends who kept me company in the trenches, including: Alwyn Hamilton, Cherae Clark, Hannah Kaner, Holly Bourne, Kat Dunn, Kate Dylan, Katherine Webber Tsang, Nina Douglas, Rebecca Kuang, Saara El-Arifi, Tasha Suri, and Taylor Vandick.

To every reader, bookseller and librarian who has ever championed this series.

And finally, to my beloved family – Mum, Dad and Alfie – who never fail to remind me, when I inform them that I'm on deadline again, that I've been cheerfully on deadline for over a decade. Thank you for supporting me as I keep following my dream.

# A Note on the Author

**Samantha Shannon** is the *New York Times* and *Sunday Times* Number One bestselling author of the Bone Season series and the Roots of Chaos series. Her work has been translated into twenty-eight languages. She lives in London.
samanthashannon.co.uk / @say_shannon

# A Note on the Type

The text of this book is set Adobe Garamond. It is one of several versions of Garamond based on the designs of Claude Garamond. It is thought that Garamond based his font on Bembo, cut in 1495 by Francesco Griffo in collaboration with the Italian printer Aldus Manutius. Garamond types were first used in books printed in Paris around 1532. Many of the present-day versions of this type are based on the *Typi Academiae* of Jean Jannon cut in Sedan in 1615.

Claude Garamond was born in Paris in 1480. He learned how to cut type from his father and by the age of fifteen he was able to fashion steel punches the size of a pica with great precision. At the age of sixty he was commissioned by King Francis I to design a Greek alphabet, and for this he was given the honourable title of royal type founder. He died in 1561.